Prize of Gor

Prize of Gor

John Norman

AN [e-*reads*] BOOK
New York, NY

An E-Reads Edition
www.e-reads.com
Print ISBN 0-7592-4580-0

The Gor books available from E-Reads:

01 - TARNSMAN OF GOR
02 - OUTLAW OF GOR
03 - PRIEST-KINGS OF GOR
04 - NOMADS OF GOR
05 - ASSISSIN OF GOR
06 - RAIDERS OF GOR
07 - CAPTIVE OF GOR
08 - HUNTERS OF GOR
09 - MARAUDERS OF GOR
10 - TRIBESMEN OF GOR
11 - SLAVE GIRL OF GOR
12 - BEASTS OF GOR
13 - EXPLORERS OF GOR
14 - FIGHTING SLAVE OF GOR
15 - ROGUE OF GOR
16 - GUARDSMAN OF GOR
17 - SAVAGES OF GOR
18 - BLOOD BROTHERS OF GOR
19 - KAJIRA OF GOR
20 - PLAYERS OF GOR
21 - MERCENARIES OF GOR
22 - DANCER OF GOR
23 - RENEGADES OF GOR
24 - VAGABONDS OF GOR
25 - MAGICIANS OF GOR
26 - WITNESS OF GOR
27 - PRIZE OF GOR

Table of Contents

Chapter 1

She Ponders How to Tell Her Story, and Attempts to Provide Some Understanding or Guidance for a Possible Reader

I do not know how exactly to express these thoughts.

Yet I have been commanded to ruthless honesty. And I fear that if I did not comply, somehow they would know, as always it seems they do, perhaps from some small cue, perhaps some slight movement, or cast of feature, or shading of complexion, or tremor, or reluctance, unbeknownst even to myself. We are so helpless, so vulnerable. They seem to know so much. I seem to be transparent to them. I am not permitted to hide, even within myself. I do not know if you understand how terrifying that is, to have one's most intimate emotions, feelings and thoughts, one's soul, one's innermost being, so to speak, bared, exposed, even to a casual, even indifferent, scrutiny. How trivial, how inconsequential, compared to this is the mere baring of the body. Only they have known how to make me naked to myself, truly, and to them, sometimes to their amusement, and to my consternation and amazement, my shame, and my misery, as well.

I must decide how to tell this story. They have permitted me that much. It is my story, a very personal story, and so, it seems, one might most naturally use first-person discourse, and say, for example, "I did this," and "I saw that," and so on, and yet I am reluctant, afflicted with a certain timidity, to affect this voice. Perhaps I could speak more straightforwardly, more candidly, if I saw myself as another might see me, and yet, at the same time, saw myself, as well, from within, candidly, openly, hiding nothing, as one within, as I myself, might know me. So then I might say "She did this," and "She saw that," knowing that the "she" is myself, my own sentient, so much, sometimes so painfully so, self-aware self. How shall one speak? Perhaps I shall shift my modality of discourse, as seems appropriate, given what I must say, what I must tell. I do not know. How foolish to hesitate before such a small matter you might suppose, but to me it does not seem so small at all. It might seem a simple thing, how to tell a story, but it is not so easy for me. You might, of course, I do not know you, find no difficulty in this. But had you had my experiences, and were you I, were you faced with yourself, and frightened, or disconcerted, or shamed, you might, too, seek to distance yourself from that most sensitive, usually most zealously concealed, of subject matters, yourself. So I thought that I might begin, at least, by speaking in the third person, by considering myself, by seeing myself, from within and without, rather as an object, a particular object. Too, this is, I conjecture, in my current reality, not altogether unfitting; indeed, it is altogether appropriate, for you see that is what I now am, categorically, explicitly, an object, and not merely in the eyes of the law, but such irremediably, incontrovertibly, in the very reality of this world. So perhaps then I should write of myself as an object, for that is what I now am, as a simple matter of fact, an object, no longer a person, that no longer, if I were once that, but an object, to be sure, a very particular object, but one of countless hundreds, perhaps thousands of such, I do not know, in many cities, and towns, and camps and villages, like me, a vital, sentient, so much alive, so vulnerable, essentially helpless, beautiful I am told, *object*.

Perhaps the next problem that she must solve is how to speak frankly, honestly, of her age. In one world, in one reality, she was in her fifties. It does not make much difference, of course. She might have been in her forties, or in her sixties, or seventies, or such. Such matters, recorded in the routes of a world about a star, calculated in the increments of calendars and clocks, constitute no more in themselves than the memoranda of convenience, taking their true significance only in their application to changes which might be noted with interest, the germination of the seed, the blind struggle from the earth, the response to the lure of light, the birth of the anxious bud, the bursting into beauty of the flower, the glory of the unfolding, exultant petals, and then the loss, the drying, and casting away, of the petals. We count these things in hours, in days, in seasons, in years and years of years. But the clock is indifferent to what it counts; it considers with equanimity the antics of the foolish, the ecstasies of saints, the sweet, lovely nonsense of dreamers, the delusions of realists, the comings and goings of nations and empires, the passing of immortal faiths and eternal truths, life, and death, and suffering, the contumely of armed, belligerent error, the division of cells and the birth of stars. But if these things should begin again time would take no notice. It makes nothing happen; it only watches. You see, the calendar does not determine the flower; it only watches; and it will see what the flower does, and will not, indeed cannot, interfere. I suppose that these things are mysterious, or, perhaps, rather, so simple that it is difficult to speak of them. Obviously time counts the rock and the flower, the atom and the molecule, similarly, and yet the rock may witness the passing of several calendars, and the atom may in itself remain much the same as it was long ago, in the fiery midst of some distant, exploding star. Too, one would suppose that the theorems of geometry have not aged. They are doubtless as young, as fresh, as lovely, as new today, as they once were in a study in Alexandria. And should any beings anywhere, of whatever appearance, or shape, or chemistry, or origin, even after the dissolutions and births of countless worlds, devise such a system, the same, with its definitions and postulates, these theorems will await them, as pristine, as irresistible as ever in their austere, apodictic beauty. They do not hear the tickings of clocks. Too, if things, if processes, were to begin again, or go back, and begin again, or remain much as they were, save for small differences, the clock of time, so to speak, would simply observe, perhaps bemused, but would not interfere. What is being suggested here, or better, I think, noted, is that time does not dictate reality, or life or death, or change, but measures it, and that it is indifferent to what it measures, that it is independent of what it measures. Time imposes no inevitabilities. It guarantees nothing. This may be hard to understand but only, one supposes, because of a habit of mind, in virtue of which, because of natural associations, common experiences, general expectations, and such, one tends to link the thought of process and time together. Even if the clock does not presuppose time as the object it measures; even if one were to think that the clock somehow created time, inventing it *ab ovo*, on the spot, still that clock would determine only itself, nothing else. She, she of whom I speak, is led into this disquisition, this tiny, uncertain, timid, troubling venture into metaphysics, for a particular reason. What is it, for example, to be of a given age? If one measures years, for example, by the peregrinations of a planetary body about its primary, then the year would obviously differ from body to body. To be sure, these diverse years might be transformed into equivalencies, for example, the year of planetary body A being understood as being twice the year of planetary body B, and so on, but that is not really to the point one would wish to make. Let us suppose, rather, as a matter of speculation, if nothing more, that a given physical process normally, or customarily, takes a given amount of time, say, that it normally proceeds in a given amount of time through phases A, B and C, and so on. Then, let us suppose, as all physical processes are theoretically reversible, that this process is altered in such a way that it moves from phase C back to phase B, where it appears to be stabilized. The question, then, is what is the age of the process, or, better, one supposes, what is the age of that which exhibits the process? Obviously, in one sense, the entity exhibiting the process continues to age according to the calendar, or any clock, just as, in a sense, the theorems of Euclid continue to age, or, better, just as the ebb and flow of tides, the many cycles of nature, the recurrent orbits of planetary bodies, and such, continue to age. In another sense, of course, the entity in question is stabilized in phase B, or something indistinguishable from, and identical to, phase B. In one sense, then, it is *x* years of age, and, in a more revealing, practical sense, setting aside calendars, which are now for all practical purposes pointless, and simply irrelevant to the facts of the case, it is B years of age, so to speak. Perhaps more simply put, though perhaps too abstractly, it is stabilized in its B phase, or something identical to its B phase, or, perhaps, in a renewed, or different, B or B-like phase.

So it is difficult for her to speak simply and clearly of her age, not because of any personal embarrassment or vanity, which she might once have felt, and would not now be permitted, but because the matter put in one way would be extremely misleading and put in another way might appear at least initially surprising. Her age now then, one supposes, would be least misleadingly, and most informatively, understood as that which it seems to be, and that which, in a very real sense, it actually is. Her age, then, is that which you would suppose, were you to look upon her, were you to see her as she is now. Perhaps, better, it is that which it is, in actuality, biologically and physiologically, in all respects. It is that which it would be determined to be, after a thorough and careful examination by a qualified physician, of any world, even the terribly thorough physicians of this world.

That is the age she is, for better or for worse, on this world.

But it was not so, on another world.

Now let her note that this document is composed with a certain guarded anonymity. The name she bore is, of course, unimportant, and certainly so now, on this world, and it might have been any name, perhaps yours or another's. So we will not give her a name, not until later, when one was given to her. Too, in accordance with the admonitions to which she has been subjected, she will attempt to conceal the names of institutions, and references to streets, and localities, museums, theaters, parks, shops and boulevards, and such things, which might serve to identify or reveal, even tentatively or remotely, the *venue* of this story's beginning. The purpose of this injunction is not altogether clear to her, as it seems to her that they have the power to come and go, and do, much as they please. Who could stop them? But certainly she will honor it in detail. Doubtless they have their reasons. Perhaps they do not wish you to be on your guard. She does not know. What difference would it make, if you were on your guard? What difference would it have made, had she been on her guard? Would anything, truly, have been different? Perhaps they do not wish you to know the areas, or locales, in which they work. But it is her impression that their doings, their functions or operations, if you prefer, are not limited to a particular city or town, or even nation, or hemisphere, or season, or year. There seem many reasons for supposing that. But she knows, actually, very little of these things. She, and those like her, are commonly little informed, commonly kept much in ignorance. Such things are not their concerns. Their concerns are otherwise, and are commonly supposed, they are told, to be more than ample to occupy their time and attention. Still, of course, they wonder, not that it makes any difference in their own cases. That is the sort of entities, or objects, that they are. So she will speak with care, concealing details which, in the fullness of the case, may not much matter anyway. Too, she dares not be disobedient. She has learned the cost of disobedience, and she shall obey, as she must, instantly, in all things, and with perfection. Yet she would suppose, from her narration, that some will understand more than she has dared to write. She would surmise that the city involved, and such, may be sufficiently obvious, even concealed beneath the cloak of an imposed discretion.

But that, of course, is left to the reader, if there eventually should be such.

She adds that this manuscript is written in English. She was literate, quite so, on her first world. On this world, however, she is illiterate. She cannot read, or write, any of its languages. She can, however, speak what seems to be this world's major language, or, in any event, that spoken almost exclusively in her environment, and she can, of course, understand it. These things are needful for her.

Lastly she might call the reader's attention to what has seemed to her an oddity, or anomaly. On her first world she understood, or knew, little or nothing of this world. She was familiar with, at best, allusions to this world, seldom taken seriously, and most often, it seems incredible to her now, lightly dismissed. She has now wondered if various authorities on her old world did not know something of this world, at least a little something. It seems some of them must have. How could they not know of it? But perhaps they did not. She does not know.

The oddity, or anomaly, has to do in its way with law.

The state, or a source of law, it seems, can decide whether one has a certain status or not, say, whether one is a citizen or not a citizen, licensed or not licensed, an outlaw or not an outlaw, and such. It can simply make these things come about, it seems, by pronouncing them, and then they are simply true, and that, then, is what the person is. It has nothing to do, absolutely nothing to do, with the person's awareness or consent, and yet it is true of the person, categorically and absolutely, in all the majesty of the law. It makes the person something, whether the person understands it, or knows it, or not. The person might be made something or other, you see, and be totally unaware of it. Yet that is what that person, then, would be. It is clear to her now that she must have been watched, and considered, and assessed, perhaps for months, utterly unbeknownst to her. She had no idea. She suspected nothing, absolutely nothing. But her status, her condition, had changed. It seems that decisions were made, and papers signed, and certified, all doubtless with impeccable legality. And then, by law, she, totally unaware, became something she had not been before, or not in explicit legality. And she continued to go about her business, knowing nothing of this, ignorantly, naively, all unsuspecting. But she had become something different from what she had been before. She was no longer the same, but was now different, very different. Her status, her condition, had undergone a remarkable transformation, one of which she was totally unaware. She did not know what, in the laws of another world, one capable of enforcing its decrees and sanctions, one within whose jurisdiction she lay, she had become. That she finds interesting, curious, frightening, in its way, an oddity, and anomalous. She did not know what she had become. She wonders if some of you, too, perhaps even one reading this manuscript, if there should be such, may have become already, too, even now, unbeknownst to yourself, what she had then become. Perhaps you are as ignorant of it as was she. But this reality was later made clear to her, by incontrovertible laws, and deeds, which did not so much confirm the hypothetical strictures of a perhaps hitherto rather speculative law, one extending to a distant world, as replace or supersede them, in an incontrovertible manner, with immediate, undeniable, unmistakable realities, realities not only independently legal, and fully sufficient in their own right, but realities acknowledged, recognized and celebrated, realities understood, and enforced, with all the power, unquestioned commitment and venerated tradition of an entire world, that on which she had found herself.

That world did not long leave her in doubt as to what she was.

Chapter 2

She Begins Her Story

She was not a particularly bad person, nor, one supposes, a particularly good person. She was perhaps rather like you, though perhaps not so good. Have we not all been upon occasion petulant, selfish, careless, arrogant, sometimes cruel? Have we not all upon occasion behaved disgracefully, unworthily? Have we not ignored others? Have we not, in lesser or larger ways, injured them, and enjoyed, if only briefly, the smug gratifications of doing so? What happened to her might happen to anyone, one supposes, to those gentler, kinder and deeper than she, and to those more shallow, more petty, nastier than she. It is true however that such as she, and her sisters, so to speak, under discipline, are quickly brought into line, the gentlest and the sweetest, and those who hitherto, perhaps in their unhappiness and lack of fulfillment, in their vanities and impatience, and haughtiness, were not only permitted but encouraged by an androgynous society to abuse their liberties. We are brought into line. Our lives are changed, profoundly. We are taught many things, all of us, including ourselves.

We do not know, in full, what their criteria are, for such as she, and others, not at all why such as she, and others, are selected.

It does seem clear that their criteria include high intelligence. If one's intelligence is high, they seem to find that arousing, literally arousing, perhaps unaccountably to one accustomed to the criteria prized on my first world. It seems to considerably increase our value. In virtue of it they seem to relish us all the more, and then dominate us all the more imperiously and ruthlessly, making us all the more helpless and at their mercy. Perhaps, too, they are pleased to know that we understand clearly, and in the depths of our very being, more than might some others, what is being done to us, what we have been made, what we now are, helplessly, fully, incontrovertibly. Our intelligence then, like certain other properties, is sought; it is a desideratum. It gives them pleasure, and, of course, in virtue of it, as perhaps a not negligible pragmatic consequence, we train more swiftly and surely. They tend to be demanding and impatient. Little time is wasted on us. Too, if we are selected, or often are, at least in part, on the basis of our intelligence, one supposes that we would be more likely to be more alert, more sensitive, more inventive, more attentive than might otherwise be the case; we would be likely to be better, for example, one supposes, at reading the subtlest of expressions, the brief, shadowed flicker of a mood, perhaps a sign of danger. One quickly learns to apply one's intelligence, *per force*, to new ends, in new spheres. No choice is given us. Their intelligence, incidentally, seems to us to be dimensions beyond ours. Intelligent as we are, our intelligence does not begin to compare with theirs. I do not know why this is. Perhaps it is a matter of genetic selections, or a simple result of an honest, freer, less debilitating acculturation. I do not know. Forgive this lapse into personal discourse.

It came as a great shock to her, after the performance, following the curtain calls, the lofting of roses, of bouquets, of so many flowers to the stage, to see the male in the audience.

The house lights were on now.

Others about her were discussing the performance.

He looked the same, absolutely the same. But surely thirty, or better, years had passed.

She rose from her seat; she stood still, almost unable to move, her eyes on him. Others desired to press past her. "Please," someone said, not pleasantly. She moved, not steadily, trembling, toward the aisle, unable to keep her eyes from him. He was chatting, it seemed, with a companion, a charming, but, she thought, a surely stupid looking female. She felt, unaccountably, a wave of anger. Surely he could do better for a woman. And he was so young. "Please," said someone, irritably. She moved into the aisle, unable to take her eyes from him. She backed up the aisle. Others, impatiently, moved about her. She then stopped, and, in a moment, stepped back into an empty row, the next closer to the exit, still not taking her eyes from him.

He looked the same. But it could not be he, of course. The resemblance was remarkable, the build, so large, so muscular, the carriage of the head, insolently, as she recalled it, the shock of carelessly unmanaged hair.

It was like seeing again something she had seen long before, and had not forgotten. Many of those memories remained as fresh today in her mind as they had in that time before, so many years ago.

She was then again, it seemed, in the aisle, near the exit, at the edge of the empty row. Somehow she was again in the aisle.

"Excuse me," said someone.

Why was she in the aisle? Why had she left the empty row? Why had she not exited the auditorium?

Was she putting herself before him?

Did she want him to see her?

Surely not.

If so, why?

How strange is memory!

She was tempted to approach him. Surely he must be a relation, perhaps even the son, of he whom she had known, so many years before.

It could not be a simple, merely uncanny coincidence, surely not.

There must be some relationship with the other, he from long ago, a cousin, a son, a brother's son, something.

To be sure, her relationship to him, that of his teacher, she then in her late twenties, in a graduate seminar on gender studies, in which he was one of the few males in the class, had been a strained one. He had failed to conform. He had not seemed to understand the nature of the class, which was to selectively and unilaterally propagandize a view, or, better, to raise the consciousness of such as he. She had failed him, of course, for his consciousness had not been raised. That could be told from a number of perspectives. He had not accepted her pronouncements without question, though they were, for the most part, merely being relayed by her, almost verbatim, from the *dicta* of various scholar activists in the movement, women who had devoted their lives to the promulgation of a political agenda. He had pointed out the weaknesses and failures of a number of studies she had favorably cited, and had, worse, brought to the attention of the class a considerable number of other studies of which she would have preferred to have had the class remain in ignorance. Too, she herself had been unfamiliar with many of these other studies, not having encountered them in approved gender literature, which, also, it seemed, had ignored them. The tenor of these various studies, or of most of them, clearly inveighed against the simplicities and dogmatisms of the propositions to which the students were expected to subscribe. His questions, too, were unacceptable, inviting her to explain the universal manifestation in all cultures of embarrassing constants, such as patriarchy, male status attainment and male dominance in male/female relationships. When she tried to cite cultures in which these properties were allegedly absent, he would inquire into the original source materials, the original ethnological accounts, and show how the constants were indeed acknowledged, even insisted upon, in the primary sources, though that might not have been clear from a sentence here and a sentence there, a paragraph here, and a paragraph there, judiciously excised from its context. The semester was a nightmare. Even militant young women eager to hear men criticized and denounced, who had taken the course to be confirmed in their ideological commitments, who had anticipated having a ritualistic quasi-religious experience, were confused. What they had enrolled to hear, and wanted to hear, and demanded to hear, was not what they heard. Some of them blamed her for not replying adequately. They had been angry. It had been humiliating. She had little with which to respond to simple, clear points having to do with fetal endocrinological hormonalization studies, hormonal inoculation studies, animal studies, and such, let alone the overwhelming cultural evidence with which she was confronted. She insisted, of course, on the irrelevance of biology, the insignificance of human nature, if it might, in some trivial sense, exist, the importance of ignoring millions of years of evolutionary history, the meaninglessness of genes, of inherited behavioral templates, and such. But the semester, by then, was muchly lost. How she hated a student who thought, who criticized, who challenged! Did he not know he was there not to question but to learn, or subscribe? He could have had at least the courtesy of pretending a hypocritical conversion to the prescribed doctrine. Others did, surely. One supposes he could have done as much, but he had not. Politeness, if not prudence, would have seemed to recommend such a course. She insisted on the importance of social artifacts, for example that men and women were not natural beings, but mere social artifacts, the manufactured products of culture and conditioning, that that was all. He had then asked for an explanation, or speculation, as to why all cultures, without exception, had designed their social artifacts in exactly such a way as to produce the various constants at issue. Since the most obvious, simplest, uniform, universal explanation for this fact would seem to be congruence with biological predispositions, with human biogenetic templates, she had dismissed the question as naive and pointless. She had declined to clarify why the question had been naive or pointless. Lastly, she had insisted, in anger and confusion, on fashionable postmodernistic analyses, on the alleged social aspect of, and role of, "truth," as a weapon of ideological warfare, on the right of the scholar activist to alter, conceal, suppress, invent and falsify in order to comply with political requirements, that "truth" must be politicized, that propaganda must have priority, that one must practice the pragmatics of intimidation, that reality, objectivity, truth, and such, were only deplorable inventions, manufactured by men to oppress women, and such. He then asked her, if this were her view, if her earlier assertions, and such, had surrendered any possible claim to objective truth, and might be dismissed as mere propaganda. She refused to respond to the question. He then asked her if her general views on truth itself, its alleged subservience to political ends, its relativity, subjectivity, or such, were themselves true, or not. Did she claim that her theory of truth, that there was no objective truth, was itself objectively true, or not? Again she ignored the question. She looked away from him, dismissing him, and his questions, and addressed herself to others in the class, inquiring into their views of an assigned reading. After the class she detained him, to speak with him alone. "Why have you taken this class?" she asked. He had shrugged, looking down upon her. Now, it seemed, it was his turn not to answer her question. How she then hated men, and him! He was so large, she felt so small, almost insignificant, almost intimidated, before him. She was older than he, of course. She, at that time, was in her late twenties. He may have been in his early twenties. This difference in age, as well as her status as the instructor, should have given her dominance in this encounter.

That she knew. But, oddly, it did not seem to do so. He seemed muchly different from other students. Suddenly, unaccountably, before him, she felt strange, unusual sensations, which seemed to swell upward through her body, permeating, suffusing it. She had never felt exactly this way before. She felt suddenly weak, delicious and helpless. She put her head down, and she knew that her face and under her chin, and the very upper part of her throat, and her hands, and the exposed parts of her body, all of it not covered by the tight, severe, mannish, professional garb she affected for teaching, the dark suit, and the severely cut white blouse, buttoned rather high, closely, about her neck, had suddenly turned crimson. Heat, and confusion, welled within her. She drew herself up, angrily. "You may leave," she informed him. He turned away, and left. He had not taken the midterm examination, and he did not, of course, take the final examination. With a clear conscience, and with not a small sense of pleasure, she filled in the grade report at the end of the semester with a failing grade for him. She was pleased that he had taken no examinations. She did not think that he had been afraid to do so. Perhaps, she wondered, from time to time, to her irritation, if he had not regarded her as competent to examine him. There were certainly many facts indicating that he deserved to fail the course, his questions and recalcitrance, for example. Too, clearly, he had failed to meet the most important requirement of the course, the adoption of its ideological viewpoint. Certainly his consciousness had not been "raised." That could be told from, if nothing else, how he had looked at her in class. How uneasy he had made her feel, though his face was almost expressionless. She suspected that that was why he had registered for the class, why he had taken the course. It was not because of the subject matter, which he doubtless found less than congenial, and with which he had little brief, but because of her. He had come to see her, *she*. That had been most clear, though suspected constantly throughout the semester, that day she had called him forward to the desk after class, the last day he attended class. No, his consciousness had not been "raised." That could be told from the way he had looked at her. She had never been looked at like that before.

It was with great satisfaction, and with no small bit of pleasure, that she had assigned him his failing grade.

So many years ago!

It could not be he, of course, seemingly so young, after all these years. But the coincidence was unsettling. The resemblance was remarkable.

It had been a performance of Richard Strauss's *Salomé*, based on a short story by Oscar Wilde. The lead role had been sung by a famous Italian soprano, a visiting artist. The performance had been by the older, and most famous, of the two major opera companies in the city. Both are fine companies, and either, in her view, would have been capable of mounting splendid productions of the work performed. She wonders if the preceding few sentences will be excised from the manuscript, as perhaps too revealing, or if they, perhaps in their amusement, will permit them to remain, perhaps as an intriguing, almost insolent detail. She does not know.

She was alone, as she often was, not that she did not have friends, colleagues, professional associates, and such. She was invited to parties, occasionally, her academic post assured that, and was the recipient of various academic courtesies, received reprints, invitations to participate in colloquia, and such. She had never married, and had never had a serious relationship with a male. Her background, training and scholarship had not been conducive to such relationships. She was regarded as severe, inhibited, cool, intellectual, professional. She no longer found herself attractive. The beauty she had once professed to scorn, and had upon occasion demeaned, was faded, if not gone, and was missed. She was idolized by young feminists, and regarded by some in the "movement" as an ideal, as presenting a superlative role model for young women. She feared men, for no reason she clearly understood, and distanced herself from them. When younger she had repelled the occasional advances of men, partly by habit, partly by disposition, sometimes because of a sense of the inferiority of the sort of men, professed male feminists, for example, who were most likely to approach her, plaintively assuring her of their profound sense of guilt for their maleness and their wholehearted support for her ideological commitments. And she was terrified by virile men, but few of them had seemed to find her of any interest; some such, who might have found her of interest, she had fled from in a sense, discouraging them, treating them with contempt, trying to chill and demean them. She had sensed, you see, that their intentions might have been physical, at least in part, and thus to be resisted and deplored. It was rather as though, if they were interested in her as a woman, their intentions could not be honorable, and she rejected, and feared, them; and if they were such that she had little doubt of the honorableness of their intentions, she had found them inferior, despicable, repulsive, hypocritical and boring. She had, through the years, thus, dutifully preserved the independence and integrity of her personness. As her body grew older, and began to dry, and wither, and tire, and began to regard her ever more reproachfully, and sadly, in the mirror, and she went through her change of life, which had been a terrible and troubling time for her, in her loneliness, and in her lack of love and children, she remained aloof, severe, unsexual, professional, virginal. She realized she was growing old, and was alone. She was disappointed with her life. And she saw nothing much before her to look forward to. She insisted to herself, naturally, that she was happy, content, and had no regrets. She insisted on that, angrily in her privacy drying gainsaying tears. What else could she dare to say to herself? What else could such as she tell themselves, in private, grievous, insistent moments? One could scarcely acknowledge an emptiness, a whole frightening, oppressive, looming reproach on a misspent life; it was not well to look into the emptiness, the threatening abyss, the void, and, too, she assured herself, such things, the void, and such, being nothing, could not even exist. And yet few things existed more obdurately, more outspokenly, more terribly, deeply within her, than that silent, vocal, unrepudiable, proclamatory, denunciatory nothingness. It seems clear that she, despite what she would tell herself, despite the lies, the carefully constructed, defensive fabrications with which she sought to delude herself, had many regrets, a great many sources of sadness, that there was in her much that was only half articulated, or scarcely sensed, much that was hidden, much concealed and put aside as too painful to be recognized, so much that she refused to face, and yet which, upon occasion, would visit her in the loneliness of her night, as her head lay thrust against its pillow, whispering in her ear that what might have been could now no longer be, or, upon occasion, it would reveal itself to her, in her mirror, as she looked upon the image of a weeping, aging woman. But she did not suppose, really, that she, in such respects, was much different from many others. What was there, truly, for she, and others, such as she, to look forward to? Another honor, another paper published, another conference attended, another point made, another small dinner, prepared by herself, another lonely evening in the apartment?

He was getting up now, and assisting his companion with her wrap. How she hated that young woman for some reason, the blond-haired, simple, surely stupid-looking one, how could he be interested in her, and yet there was a certain something about her, in the fullness of her lush, painted lips, how frightful, she used make-up, the sweet width but suggested softness of her shoulders, the roundedness of her bared forearms, something animal-like there, and, in her way of carrying herself, even sensual, primitive. Doubtless she granted him sexual favors, the whore, the slut! And he so naive and undisciplined as to accept them, to permit her to be such, not to call her to her higher self, had she one, and reform her, if it were possible with such as she! She had no right to be with one such as he! She was not an intellectual! Surely she knew nothing! Yet there was a vitality, and sensuousness, about her, and consider that vital, well-curved figure, even buxom, so animal-like, one of the sort which might attract lower men, or perhaps even excite unwary, better men in moments of weakness, men were so weak, and note that movement of the shoulders, just then, and, there, now, that way of looking about, over her shoulder, that cunning motion which might deter them from noting the absence of cultivated, worthy personness.

How she hated the woman!

When the woman turned about, she seemed for a moment surprised to find herself the object of such a regard, one so disapproving, so severe. Then the lips of the younger woman curled and her eyes flickered for an instant with amusement. Perhaps she had met such gazes before from such as the older woman, gazes, and stares, and such, perhaps of envy, hatred, and hostility, the cold, fixed gazes and stares of women whose youth and beauty were behind them, and who seemed to wish to do little now but resent and castigate, and scorn, the possessors of the treasures now forever lost to themselves, the pleasures, fruits and ecstasies of which they, in their own time, had been denied, or had denied themselves; perhaps they had been the unwitting victims of politically motivated secular asceticisms; perhaps they had been tricked out of their own birthright, having been led to accept a voluntary unrealized incarceration, taught to make themselves miserable, grieving, self-congratulating prisoners, required to pretend to contentment within the bars, within the cold walls, of an inhibitory value system; perhaps they were merely the unhappy, cruelly shaped, psychologically deformed products of an engineered apparatus, one designed to take natural organisms, bred for open fields, and grass and sunlight, and force them into the prepared, procrustean niches of a pervasive, self-perpetuating, invisible social mechanism, into a titanic, neuteristic architecture of human deprivation, and social expediency.

The younger woman was then coming up the aisle, toward the exit.

How their eyes had locked together for that moment, the eyes of the older woman bright with hatred, and cold hostility, the eyes of the younger woman sparkling with a secure, insouciant amusement.

The older woman had seen in that moment that the eyes of the younger, those of the charming, stupid-looking slut, as she saw her, were blue. Her hair then might be naturally blond, not that that mattered in the least. She was a low sort. Her hair was long, rich, and silky, the sort in which a man's hands might idly play. It was probably dyed, false, dyed! She had no right to be with such a man!

The young man had followed his companion into the aisle.

Their eyes met, and the older woman shrank back. She trembled. She almost fell. She turned and seized the top of a seat, with both hands, to steady herself. It seemed the same! He was so close! The resemblance was uncanny, shocking, indescribable.

He looked at her with no sign of recognition.

"Excuse me," he said, and moved about her.

The voice, she thought. It is the same! The same! But it could not be the same, of course. Yet it seemed so much the same!

He was moving away.

Unaccountably, unable to restrain herself, she hurried after him, and pathetically seized at his sleeve.

He turned about, seeming puzzled.

She stammered. "Did you enjoy the performance? I thought I once knew someone like you. Long ago!"

"Do I know you?" he asked.

"Do you, do you?" she begged.

"Are you well?" he asked.

"Yes, yes," she stammered. "I just wondered if you enjoyed the performance."

"Why?" he asked.

"I thought I knew you," she whispered, "I mean, someone like you, once, long ago."

"It was adequate," he remarked. "I must be going now. My friend will be waiting."

"I thought the performance was powerful," she whispered.

He shrugged, the same shrug, it seemed!

"Do you attend the opera often?" she asked, pressingly.

"Sometimes," he said. "Next Saturday we may see the new staging of *La Bohème*."

A husband and wife, interestingly, were to sing Rodolfo and Mimi in that production.

"Good-day," he said, and turned away, moving toward the exit.

She felt herself a fool, and how annoyed he must have been, though his demeanor was the image of forbearance and courtesy itself. Perhaps, she thought, she should run after him, to apologize, she, in her fifties, and despite her status as an academician, one not unknown in her field, surely one with suitable publications, one with, too, impeccable credentials. But that would not do, of course. She should not run after him.

It was only an oddity, a coincidence, something to be forgotten by tomorrow.

But she did hurry after him, not to approach him, of course.

That would not have done, at all. But, somehow, she did not want to lose sight of him. She did not understand the importance of this to her, or fully, but doubtless it had to do with the oddity of the resemblance, so remarkable, to the student, from so many years ago, he who was never forgotten, he who was recollected with ever fresh humiliation and anger, but, too, invariably, with fascination. This was at least, she told herself, a small mystery, whose denouement, however predictable and disappointing, might prove to be of interest.

In the outer lobby she was momentarily disconcerted, even frightened, that he was gone. But then she saw him to one side, waiting to buy an opera book, an account of the history and staging of the piece. His companion was waiting some yards away, looking toward the exit.

She approached the younger woman. It did not seem courageous to do so, but, somehow, necessary. She would have been terrified to approach the young man again, after their first interlude, for beneath the facade of his politeness there had seemed a subtle severity and power in him, but the other was merely a woman, and she did not much care what transpired between them. It was as though the blond woman did not really matter in these things, save in so far as she might prove useful.

She would later revise her view on these matters.

"Excuse me," said the older woman, approaching the blond, younger woman, she holding her wrap about her. How well she stood, how well-figured she was, thought the older woman, with a touch of envy. That was doubtless the sort of body that men might seek. She herself, the older woman, in her youth, had not been so large, so buxom. She had been small, and delicate, and exquisitely, but not amply, figured. She had been sometimes thought of as "dainty," but she hated that word, which seemed so demeaning, so minimizing. It had suggested that she might be no more than a biological, sexual confection of sorts, a bit of fluff, of interest perhaps, but unimportant, negligible in a way, as a human being. She had once thought of ballet, when she was quite young, before being brought in her young majority into the higher, sterner duties and understandings of the movement. But, too, she had been, in her way, interestingly, though not buxom, or obtrusively so, a bit too excitingly figured for that. Small as she was, and slim as she had been, there had been no doubt about, in its lovely proportions, the loveliness of her bosom, the narrowness of her waist, the delightful, flaring width of her hips, the sweetness of her thighs. She was, as thousands, and millions of others, though perhaps a bit short, and a little slim, a normal human female, of a sort greedily selected for in countless generations of matings and prizings. So, it seems, she was neither excessively buxom, nor, neither, tall, linear, flat-chested and boyish, a variety often praised and recommended for imitation in cultures which encourage the denial or blurring of sexual differences. Rather, she was much like most women, the normal human female, though perhaps a little shorter, and a tiny bit slimmer, that of course on the brink of her early womanhood and beauty.

The fact that she might have bit a little shorter, and a little lighter, a little slimmer, than many women had given her from a very early age a deep, internal understanding, more than that of many other women, of the size and power of men. To be sure, this can be brought home to all women, and with perfection.

The blond woman turned about, surprised.

"I am very sorry to disturb you," said the older woman. "I didn't mean to stare in the theater. Please forgive me. But I am sure I have seen your friend before, or, rather, I mean I am sure that I have seen someone very much like him, long ago. There must be, there might be, it seems possible there might be, a relationship. Perhaps he is a son of my former friend, of many years ago, or such. I am sorry to trouble you about this, but I am very curious about this matter."

The blonde regarded her, coldly.

"I'm sorry," said the older woman, "but I wonder if I might trouble you for his name?"

"I do not know you," said the blonde, and turned away.

"I'm sorry," said the older woman, "very sorry."

The older woman backed away, chagrined, embarrassed, and mingled in the crowd, trying to be unobtrusive, mixing in with milling patrons, with those dallying in the lobby, with those waiting for friends, or perhaps for arranged transportation.

The young man returned to his companion, and she must have said something to him, doubtless annoyed, for he looked in the direction of the older woman, who instantly looked away, pretending to busy herself with nearby posters, that their eyes not meet.

The couple then made their way through the exit to the sidewalk outside.

As they left, the older woman watched them, shaken. Then she noticed that, about the left ankle of the blonde, there was a bandage, wrapped tightly there, in several layers. Doubtless she had sustained an ankle injury, though her gait did not seem affected. Oddly, it seemed that something like a ring, or ridge, might lie beneath the bandage. That was suggested by the closeness of the bandage to the ankle at the top and bottom and its widening out, or bulging a little, in the center. The ring, or ridge, seemed to encircle the ankle, and, whatever it was, it was fully concealed by the bandage. Doubtless it was a medical device of some sort, designed to strengthen, to lend support to, the injured ankle.

The older woman followed the couple from the theater discretely, hovering near them, hoping to hear an informative remark, or an address given to the driver of a cab. But the couple stepped into a limousine, a long, dark limousine with darkened windows, which drew near with their appearance outside the theater, its door then opened by a deferential, uniformed chauffeur. The young woman ascended into the dark recesses of the limousine. She did so with a subtle, natural elegance. The older woman saw again the bandage on her ankle, it in odd contrast with the class and quality of her couture. The young man followed her into the vehicle. He must be rich, she thought. Suddenly she feared that they might be married. But there had been no ring on her finger. But then perhaps, in accord, with her own ideology, and such, the blond woman might have scorned to accommodate herself to such demeaning, restrictive and obsolescent conventions. Then she wondered if she might be rich, and not he. But that could not be. She had seen him, and how he looked upon her, and, in his way, gently, but with an undercurrent of iron, had sheltered, commanded and guided her. There was no doubt that he was dominant in the relationship, totally dominant, powerfully so, unquestioningly so, even frighteningly so.

The driver politely closed the door, took his place in the vehicle, and they drove away.

She looked after them, and then hurried to the ticket window, to buy a ticket, as near as possible to the same seat as she had had today, for the performance of *La Bohème* next Saturday.

Chapter 3

How She Awakened in a Strange Room; She Finds That She Has Been Ankleted

She stirred, uneasily.

She kept her eyes closed, fearing that if she opened them the room might turn slowly, surely, patiently, mockingly, about her. She lay there, under the covers, for the moment, half conscious, not feeling well, utterly disoriented, groggy, lethargic, affected as though with some indefinable, eccentric, disconcerting malaise. This was doubtless an aftereffect of the chemical which had been taken into her system, though that was not clear to her at the time. She twisted about, a little, softly moaning, a tiny whimper, protestingly. Surely she was in her own bed. But it seemed oddly deep, somehow too soft, for her simple bed. Her head ached, dully; she still felt tired; she was weary; she was unwilling to awaken. She lay there for a time, trying not to move, wanting to again lose consciousness, she felt so miserable. She desired to return to the favoring, understanding, redemptive kindness, the supposed security, of sleep. But, after a bit, despite what would have been her choice, her deeper subjectivity, anxiously, frightened, seemingly more informed than she herself, calling out, began to make itself heard; it seems then that her consciousness, patiently, insistently, responding, began little by little to overcome her resistance, the misery and weariness of her fifty-eight-year-old body, and reassert itself, groping ever nearer the doors of awareness.

She opened her eyes and cried out, suddenly, in consternation.

Clearly she was not in her own bedroom, in her apartment.

She sat up, abruptly, gasping, in the deep, soft, luxurious, strange bed, and put her hands swiftly to her own body. She wore what must be, or was similar to, a hospital gown, such as that with which patients are familiar, or those awaiting examinations in the offices of their physicians. It was all she wore, save for one unimportant, negligible exception of which she, in her consternation, in her immediate concerns, was unaware at the time.

From the bed, sitting upright upon it, half under the covers, she looked about, wildly, for her clothing. There was no sign of it.

The room itself seemed elegant, almost rococo, with a high ceiling. There were carved moldings, a marble floor, a sparkling chandelier, lit. There were no windows. There was one door, paneled, flanked by pilasters. There was a chair in the room, surely an antique, or similar to such, delicate, elegant, richly upholstered. There was a mirror to one side, in which she saw herself, beside herself with consternation, in the simple, severe, white, starched garment. She put her hand to her head swiftly. Her hair had been loosened and, it seemed, trimmed, and shortened. She had been thinking of having it trimmed, but not shortened to that extent, but had not had it attended to. She had tended to be a bit careless, and a little dilatory, in matters pertaining to her appearance. But later that would not be permitted to her. Commonly she wore her hair up, tightly bound in a bun at the back. That had suited her professional image, and had been a part of her strategy to proclaim and make manifest her independence, and personness, and to distance herself from males, to chill them, and warn them away, to show them that she did not need them and despised them, those insensitive, boorish, lustful others, her enemies. She had not worn her hair in this fashion, that short, rather at her nape, since she was a girl. Against the wall there were a highboy, and two chests. She considered the bed in which she seemed so improbable an occupant. It was large, deep and luxurious, the sort of bed on which a sovereign might have sported with concubines, or a virile king with his pet courtesans. It had four sturdy, massive posts. The first thought which flared into her mind, though she forced it away immediately, in terror, was that it was a bed on which might be spread-eagled a woman, wrists and ankles bound to their respective posts. To be sure, they could not, for the size of the bed, have had fair limbs fastened directly against the dark wood of the posts themselves. The ropes, fastened to the posts, would have to lead to, say, a yard away in each case, the wrists and ankles of their captive.

She hurried in horror from the surface of that great bed, from the whispering of its softness, the intimations of its posts, from its decadent suggestions of ecstatic, unbelievable pleasures imposed mercilessly, perhaps even curiously, or indifferently, on helpless, writhing victims.

She felt the shock of the cool marble floor on her feet, and realized that she was, of course, barefooted. She looked about for slippers, or footwear of some sort, but detected none.

She moaned, angrily.

Then, suddenly, she cried out in dismay, and backed toward the bed, until she felt its obdurate, solid frame against the back of her thighs, beneath the gown, which could be opened from the back. She sat back, disbelievingly, on the bed, on the discarded, unruly covers.

She looked down at her ankle, her left ankle.

On it there was a narrow, but sturdy band, or ring. Swiftly she drew her feet up on the bed, and sat there, at its edge. She reached to the object, to unclasp it from her ankle. To her amazement she could not open it. She turned it, as she could, a little, on her ankle, searching for the simple catch, or spring, which, at a touch, would release it. There was clearly a hinge, and a catch, but, too, there was a locking area, with an aperture, for a tiny key. She jerked at the device, trying to remove it from her ankle. She could not do so. She realized, with anger, and a sinking feeling, that its removal was not in her power, that the device had been closed, and locked. It was locked on her.

Irrationally she thrust down at it, trying to force it from her ankle. She wept. Her ankle was bruised. The grasp of the device was close, obdurate and perfect. She realized that such a device had not been designed to be removed by its wearer. The wearer of such a device has no choice in these matters. The wearer must await in such matters the pleasure of another.

There seemed to be some marks on the band, or ring, tiny marks, marks intentionally inscribed, clearly, but they were in no script with which she was familiar.

She saw herself in the mirror, her image reflected from across the room, she sitting on the bed, with her knees drawn up, her left ankle toward the mirror, the gown up about her knees.

Hurriedly she drew down the gown, though not so much as to cover the ring on her ankle, which she continued to regard in the mirror, and herself.

In the instant before she had drawn the gown down she had seen her calves in the mirror, and, to her surprise, to her fear, and with perhaps an unwilling, sudden moment of apprehensive pleasure, she realized that there was still there in her body, even now, a turn of roundedness, and softness, about them. They were still, even now, even in her present age, obviously the calves of a female, and perhaps those of one once not altogether unpleasant to look upon, even in the deplorable physical sense, and she did not think them unattractive.

She sat there, then, for a moment, regarding herself, the gown now modestly drawn downward, but the steel still visible in the mirror.

Then she drew the gown upward a tiny bit, the better to see the device, she told herself.

Then, hurriedly, she drew it down again.

She regarded herself in the great mirror.

She saw herself.

She did not understand where she was, or what had been done to her. She did know that she was in a strange bed, in a strange room, and in a strange garment.

She regarded herself in the mirror.

She was ankleted.

Chapter 4

How Certain Things Were Explained to Her, But Much Remained Still Unclear

"I thought you were awake," he said, looking up from the desk. "I thought I heard you cry out, a bit ago, from within."

She stood in the threshold of the bedroom, having emerged from it, now facing the room outside.

"Where am I?" she cried. "What am I doing here? What is the meaning of this? Where are my clothes? Why am I dressed like this?"

"Did you enjoy the performance of *La Bohème*?" he asked.

She looked about the room, frightened, tears burning in her eyes. The room seemed rather officelike, and there were shelves of books about the walls, and certain curios here and there, and occasional meaningless bric-a-brac, or so one supposes, and some filing cabinets, some office machinery, diverse paraphernalia, some chairs.

There was no window in the room, but it was well lit, indirectly.

"I want my clothes!" she said.

"You may inquire later about your clothing, but not now," he said.

The blond-haired, blue-eyed woman, to whom the older woman had taken such an instant dislike, whom she had scorned as so simple, so unworthy of the male, the one who had accompanied him to the performances, and had been his companion in the limousine, she who seemed so vital, so alive, so sensuous, who was so insolently, so excitingly figured, who was so primitive, so sensual that she seemed little more than a luscious, beautiful, well-curved animal designed by nature to stimulate and satisfy with perfection the lowest, the most basic and the most physical needs of powerful, inconsiderate men, was also in the room. Oddly, in spite of the fact that there were chairs in the room, she was kneeling, beside the desk. She wore a brief, silken, scarlet, diaphanous gown. It left little to conjecture of, concerning her beauty. The older woman enjoyed looking down upon her, seeing her there on her knees, so garbed. Hostility, like cold wire, was taut between the women.

The young man rose from behind the desk, and drew a chair toward the desk, placing it before the desk.

"Please seat yourself," he invited the older woman.

"You will let her sit?" cried the woman kneeling beside the desk.

He turned a sharp glance upon the speaker, and, suddenly, her entire demeanor changed, and she trembled, shrinking down, making herself small, and holding her head down.

"Tutina, it seems, forgot herself," said the young man. "I apologize. Do not fear. She will be disciplined."

So 'Tutina', then, thought the older woman, is the name of that stupid tart! It seemed an odd name, an unfamiliar sort of name, but it did not seem inappropriate for one such as she, one who was so elementally, so simplistically, so reductively female. The older woman did not understand the meaning of the reference to "discipline," but something in that word, seemingly in its very sound, terrified her. Did it suggest that the woman's femininity, the very principle of her femininity, was somehow uncompromisingly subjected to his masculinity, to the very principle of his masculinity?

The young man then turned again, affably, toward the older woman, indicating the chair.

Clearly the blonde was frightened.

The older woman, too, was frightened, for she had seen his glance. She looked about, wildly.

"There is no telephone in the room," he said.

"I shall scream," whispered the older woman, knowing she would not do so.

"It would do you no good," the young man said. "We are in an isolated dwelling, on a remote estate."

There was another door in the room, other than that which led in from the bedroom. Suddenly, awkwardly, she fled toward it, and flung it open. Outside two men, large, unpleasant looking men, one of them the chauffeur, rose suddenly from chairs, blocking her way.

She shrank back.

"Do you want her stripped and bound, and thrown to your feet?" inquired the chauffeur.

"No," said the young man, agreeably.

"She wears the anklet," said the chauffeur.

"That will be all," said the young man to the chauffeur, and then the chauffeur and his companion drew back, chastened, deferentially closing the door behind them. "Please," said the young man to the older woman, gently, indicating the chair he had placed before the desk.

She stood before the chair.

"I searched in the all the drawers, and the chests, in the bedroom," she cried, "and my clothes were not there! Then I came out."

"Dressed as you are," said the young man.

"Yes," she whispered.

"I had thought you might have wrapped yourself in a sheet, or comforter, or such," he smiled.

"I shall go back and do so," she said.

"You have chosen to present yourself as you are, and you will remain clad as you are," he said.

The blond woman looked up from her knees, a tiny smile on her lips.

"I want my clothing," said the older woman.

"I told you that you might inquire later about your clothing, not now," said the young man, evenly.

"This is all I have on!" protested the older woman, indicating the starched, white, stiff gown, so simple, so antiseptic, in its appearance. It was substantially open in the back, save for two ties, one at the back of the neck and another at the small of the back.

"Not all, actually," said the young man.

She looked down at her left ankle. "Remove this horrid thing from my ankle!" she demanded.

"It is certainly not horrid," he said. "It is actually quite attractive. It sets your ankle off very nicely. Indeed your ankle looks as though it might have been made to be encircled by such a ring. Do not concern yourself with it. The steel, circling closely about the flesh, is indisputably lovely, as well as, independently, of course, quite meaningful."

Tears sprang to her eyes.

"You are not alone," he said. He turned to Tutina, who was now, as he stood, to his left. "Anklet!" he snapped.

Instantly she turned about, sinuously, and, half lying, half kneeling, extended her left leg, gracefully, toward the older woman, her knee slightly bent, her toes pointed, extending the line of her well-curved calf. There, on her ankle, there was a similar ring.

The older woman gasped, in misery. Did this mean that she, somehow, now shared some status, or condition, with that other woman, that trivial, simple, stupid, hated, beautiful Tutina? Surely not! Too, she now understood the meaning of the bandage which had been worn by Tutina to both performances. It was to conceal the device on her ankle, which had not been removed. It seemed that Tutina might be no more capable than she of removing the device, and, too, that she might be kept within it much as a matter of course. Too, the older woman was alarmed, and troubled, by the sudden, prompt, immediate, graceful response of Tutina to the utterance "Anklet!" It was as though she had been trained to present the device for easy view, and immediately, gracefully, beautifully, upon the utterance of that word, which, it seemed, constituted an understood, familiar command. Lastly the older woman sensed, from the sharpness with which the command had been issued, that the young man was not pleased with Tutina. That doubtless went back to Tutina's protest when the young man had invited her to seat herself. The older woman suspected that the young man might recall this lapse, if lapse it was, to Tutina when they were alone. Certainly, after the incident, Tutina had appeared to be uneasy, and perhaps apprehensive.

The older woman recalled that the young man had made a casual reference to "discipline." She had not understand the reference, but, somehow, it had frightened her. She recalled that the reference had been made easily, almost in passing, treating it as though it might be something unimportant, something trivial, a mere matter of course, something to be simply taken for granted.

But the blonde, Tutina, had not taken the matter so lightly. She had been clearly frightened. Even now she was clearly frightened.

The young man snapped his fingers, and Tutina swirled back to her original position, and kept her head down.

"There is some sort of marking on the thing," said the older woman, looking down, to her own ankle.

"Do not concern yourself with it," he said. "It is a reference number, yours, in our records."

"Who undressed me? Who put me in this gown?" asked the older woman, frightened.

"Tutina," said the young man.

She glanced at the blond woman, who then, lifting her head, smiled up at her, knowingly, scornfully. No longer then, at that moment, did Tutina seem timid. To be sure, she was then relating to the older woman, not to the young man.

The older woman flushed, and then, in embarrassment, closed her eyes briefly, and then opened them, looking down, angrily, toward the rug. Vaguely she recognized that it seemed to be an oriental rug, and might, she speculated, be of considerable value.

How amused must the blond woman, Tutina, have been, she thought, when she removed her clothing and would then compare her own abundant, vital, provocative riches with the worn, slack, tired, withered, pathetic, impoverished form which, helpless and unconscious, lay before her. She would then presumably, turning the old form about, have proceeded to see that it was once again concealed, though now perhaps, to her amusement, in such a reductive, simple, thin, single, embarrassing, uniform, meaningless, dehumanizing cover.

"I want my clothing," said the older woman. She touched the gown. "I do not want to wear this," she said.

"You would not think twice about it, if you were in the office of an examining physician," said the young man.

"I do not want to wear it!" she said.

"You may remove it," said the young man.

"No!" she said, frightened.

The young man smiled.

"I have no money, no wealth, I have no family, no loved ones, nothing, you can get no ransom for me! I mean nothing to anyone! I am a mature, middle-aged, woman. You can have no interest in me. It is not as though I were young and lovely! What can you want of me? There is nothing I can do for you!"

Again he smiled.

"I do not understand!" she said.

He did not respond to her.

"Monster!" she wept.

"Perhaps, perhaps more than you know," he mused.

"Release me!" she begged.

"Please be seated," he said.

"Release me!" she said, imperiously, coldly, drawing her small frame up to its full height, summoning all the rigor, all the severity, of which she was capable.

How she would have terrified weak men, administrators, colleagues, and such, by the presentation of such a fierce mien, suggesting implacable resolution, and full readiness to have instant and embarrassing recourse to various devices, procedures, pressures, laws and institutions engineered to impose the will of such as she, with the full force of the coercive apparatus of a captured state, upon the community at large.

"Do not try my patience," said the young man. "Sit there."

"No!" she said.

"You will sit there, clothed," he said, "or you will kneel here," he indicating at the same time a place to the side, on the rug, "naked, before me."

"I have a Ph.D.," she quavered. "In gender studies!"

"You are a stupid bitch," he said. "The choice is yours."

She sat down, quickly, and turned a bit to the side, keeping her legs closely together, moving the gown down, as she could, to protect herself.

"I am not stupid," she said weakly.

"No, I suppose not," he said, irritably. "Indeed, in some respects, you are extremely intelligent. If you were not, you would not be of interest to us. But, in other respects, it seems you are incredibly stupid.

"But I suppose," he said, "you will prove capable of learning." He glanced down at Tutina, kneeling to his left. "What do you think, Tutina?" he asked.

"I am sure she will learn quickly," said Tutina, her head down.

The young man returned his attention to the older woman. "Interesting, how you sit," he said.

She looked at him, puzzled.

"I thought that subscribers to your ideology methodologically affected bellicose facades of what they mistakenly believe to be masculine body language, for example, leaning back, and throwing the legs apart, indicating, supposedly, their masculinity, and openness, their lack of inhibitions, and such, their repudiation of femininity, for feminists seem to seek to be the least feminine of all their gender. And yet you sit there in a manner undisguisedly, and, I suspect, naturally feminine."

She held her knees the more tightly together, and trembled. She felt so open, and vulnerable. She did not care what he thought! Perhaps it was because the gown was all she had to shield her body from his gaze. Too, it was muchly open in the back. Or, perhaps, it was because she now had a different, frightened sense of herself. She now wore an anklet.

"How did you enjoy *La Bohème*?" he asked, rather as he had, earlier.

"I thought it was beautiful," she whispered.

"I, too," he said. "Beautiful!"

She regarded him, helplessly, pathetically.

"There are other forms of song dramas, elsewhere," he said. "They, too, are very beautiful. Perhaps, suitably disguised, or unobtrusively positioned, in order not to produce offense, you might be able to see one, or another, of them."

"What do you want of me?" she begged. "Why am I here? What are you going to do with me?"

"I shall explain a small number of things to you," he said, "a portion of what I think you are, at present, capable of understanding. Later, of course, you will learn a great deal more. Some of what I say may seem surprising to you, even incredible, so I would encourage you, despite your possible impulses to do otherwise, not to interrupt me frequently or inopportunely. If necessary, I will have Tutina tie your hands behind your back and tape your mouth shut. Do you understand?"

"Yes," she whispered.

"First," he said, "you have been unconscious, for better than forty-eight hours."

She regarded him, startled.

"That is partly a function of your age," he said. "Younger individuals recover considerably more quickly."

Then there are other individuals, she thought.

She remembered the performance of *La Bohème*. As she had planned she had arranged to have a seat for that performance as close as possible to the seat she had occupied for the earlier performance, that of Richard Strauss's *Salomé*. To her delight, the couple, the young man and his companion, too, had had seats comparable to those of the first performance. Though she had scarcely managed to take her eyes from the couple during the performance, and had sat there, breathing quickly, heart beating rapidly, tense, nervous, excited the whole time, she had had no intention of approaching them again. She recalled, smartly, her rebuff, earlier, at the hands of the blonde and the civil tolerance, no more than that required by simple courtesy, surely, of the young man. But, interestingly, to her delight, and alarm, the couple, after the performance, seeming to see her for the first time, had smiled at her, rather as if acknowledging that they had met her before, and pleasantly. Thus encouraged, feeling almost like a young girl, timid, shy, bashful, almost stammering, she had dared to approach them, ostensibly to chat, inconsequentially, about the performance. They had permitted her to apologize for her forward actions of some days ago, not that such actions really required any such apology, and had expressed interest in her small observations, and speculations, particularly the young man. The blonde, though attentive and pleasant, had tended to be somewhat reserved, and, on the whole, had lingered in the background. That had suited the older woman very well, who did not care in the least for the young man's companion, whom she viewed as obviously far beneath him, profoundly unworthy of him. Did he not know that? The older woman, then pleased with the reticence and, for most practical purposes, the disappearance of the blonde, addressed herself delightedly to the young man, realizing that she was now somehow the center of his attention. She felt a wondrous warmth, and a strange animation in his presence. Seldom, it seemed, had she been so voluble, and witty. Her various allusions, and subtle references, to various matters, performers, and composers, demonstrating how well informed, and how well read, she was, seemed to be instantly understood, and appreciated, by the young man. His smiles, his expressions of understandings, his tiny sounds, of amusement, and such, at exactly the right moments, encouraged, and thrilled, her. She found herself basking in his approval, and she wanted, more than anything, it seemed, to please him. She was elated to be before him, being found pleasing. How she wanted to win his smile, to impress him! She hoped that no one who knew her, particularly ideological colleagues, would see her thus, before this large, powerful male, trying to please him. It was true; she desperately wanted to please him, to be found pleasing by him, despite the fact that he was a mere male, a mere insensitive, boorish, rude male, an enemy. It was almost, she had felt, as though she were preening herself before him, turning about, showing her feathers, impressing him, and delighting herself in doing so. It was almost as though she were slyly courting him, and even, though the thought should surely be abhorrent, and offensive, to her, attempting to show herself before him as an attractive member of the opposite sex. How abhorrent, at her age, at her age, and he a man, the enemy! And she remembered vaguely, scarcely with full consciousness, and fighting, even in her animation and delight, to keep the insistent glimmerings from rising forcefully and undeniably before her, how, many years ago, she, then in her late twenties, had been the teacher of such a young man, one whom this young man so remarkably resembled. She recalled, unwillingly, yet with an odd delight, how that young man had troubled her, and how he had watched her, and how she had, she sensed it now, moved before him, and presented herself before him. She had prepared herself for the classes, eagerly, looking forward to being before him, wanting to impress him, wanting to perform for him. She had attended to her prim appearance, to her polished, severe mien, to her coiffure. She had even considered applying lipstick on the days of the class, but had, of course, thought the better of it. Lipstick was so daringly sensual, worthy of only unworthy women. But once, daringly, she had worn two light, narrow, golden bracelets on her left wrist, that might sometimes strike together, making a tiny, provocative sound. He made her terribly uneasy, and yet she was thrilled, undeniably, with the way he watched her, almost without expression. Many times, as though inadvertently, with no intent, of course, she had turned in such a way as to display the slim, provocative delights of her figure before him. Once, after such a display, she had seen him smile, knowingly, and he so young! How furious she had been! He had misunderstood! It was inexcusable! Were there only two in the class? She sensed now how she had been before him, how she, as a female, had tried to attract him, though, of course, not admitting this in any obvious way to herself, and, indeed, on a fully conscious level, she supposed she might have denied it, doubtless vehemently, except perhaps, in quiet, private moments, when she was alone, when she might perhaps, tears in her eyes, softly kiss her pillow. She had tried to resist these things, and scorn him, and, upon occasion, demean and defeat him, and humiliate him before the class, utilizing the full authority of her position to do so. But she had had little success in such endeavors. Indeed, in exchanges with him, she had often found herself confused, and reeling, almost as though from physical blows. It was almost as though he had seized her, and thrown her to her belly at his feet, and bound her hand and foot, and then stepped away from her, to look down upon her, she helpless at his feet, no more than a female captive, his to do with as he might please. She had dreamed, more than once, that he had torn away her prim garmenture and put her on her back on the desk and raped her, while the class looked on, bemused. Finished, he had thrust her from the desk to the floor, where she had then knelt naked before him, her head down, kissing his feet in gratitude.

"Perhaps you would like to have a drink with us?" he asked.

"Oh, that would be lovely," she said. "But perhaps your friend would mind?" She had supposed that the blonde would indeed mind, of course, but that she would have no choice but, in the situation, to acquiesce with the pretense of graciousness. This gave the older woman no little pleasure.

"You don't mind, do you?" asked the young man of his companion.

"Certainly not," she assured them.

She had not seemed as dismayed as the older woman had hoped she would be.

Outside the theater the young man, not entering the waiting limousine, spoke briefly with the waiting chauffeur, and it drew quietly away from the curb.

In a secluded, upholstered booth, rather toward the back of a nearby, small restaurant, convenient to the theater, the young man ordered. He ordered a Manhattan, a sweet Manhattan, for the older woman and a Scotch for himself. "You will have water," he told his companion. She looked down, toward the table. The older woman assumed that she might have some medical condition, or perhaps an allergy to alcohol. In any event she was to be given water. The older woman was surprised, too, when the young man had simply ordered for her, too, without asking her what she might prefer. But she did not question him. It was he, after all, who was the host. She might have preferred a tiny glass of white wine, as she scarcely ever drank, but she did not object to his choice. She found that she desperately wanted to please him. Too, she sensed in him a kind of power, and will, which might brook no question or test. Although he seemed to be gentle, thoughtful, and courteous, she was not sure that this was truly he. She wondered if such things were natural to him. She wondered if he might not, perhaps in the interest of some cause, be merely concerned to project a semblance of solicitude. There seemed something frightening about him, something powerful and uncompromising about him. She could imagine herself naked before him, frightened, on her belly, he with a whip in his hand. In retrospect she had supposed that he had ordered the dark, sweet drink for her in order that the traces of any unusual ingredient it might contain would be concealed. But that now seems unlikely to her. Tassa powder, which was presumably used, as it commonly is in such situations, though doubtless most frequently with younger women, is tasteless, and, dissolved in liquid, colorless. She now believes that he ordered that drink for her for different reasons, first, to simply impose his will upon her, and that she might, on some level, understand that it was so imposed, and, secondly, that he might, in his amusement, cause her senses to swirl, thus producing a calculated, intended effect within her, and putting her thusly more in his power. He knew many things about her, many things, she now realizes, and among them he doubtless knew that she drank seldom, if ever, and thus his joke of having her, of her own will, imbibe, to please him, for he knew she desired to please him, for nothing could have been more obvious, a drink much too strong for her.

"Are you well?" he had inquired.

"Yes, yes," she had smiled.

"I have been thinking," he said, "about your interest in, your question concerning, my supposed resemblance to someone you once knew."

"Yes?" she said. She smiled. She felt unsteady.

"I may be able to shed some light on that matter," he said. "Indeed, perhaps I can introduce you to the individual you have in mind."

"I knew—knew— it!" she said. "You must be the son, or a cousin, some nephew, something, some relative!"

"Are you all right?" he asked.

"Yes," she said.

"I think I can introduce you to him," he said.

"Oh, I would not want to meet him," she said. "I was only curious. I was just asking."

"Are you afraid of him?" he asked.

"No," she said. "Of course not!"

"Perhaps you should be," he said.

"What?" she asked.

"Nothing," he said.

"I will introduce you to him," he said.

"No, no," she smiled. Then she felt him lift her to her feet, and draw her from behind the table, and away from the booth. She had no intention of resisting and, in any event, it seemed she could not do so. She recalled the waiter asking after her. "She is all right," said the young man. "We have the car waiting." She recalled seeing a bill, of large denomination, several times the amount of the bill, left on the table. Then she was aware of being helped outside, and, a bit later, she felt herself being placed gently, solicitously, into a long, dark car, the limousine, which had apparently been waiting in the vicinity. She remembered little more after that, until she awakened, considerably later it seemed, in a strange bed, clad in what seemed to be a hospital or examination gown, and wearing, on her left ankle, a locked steel ring.

* * * *

"Do you feel well enough for me to continue?" asked the young man.

"Yes," she said.

"Perhaps a little to eat, and some strong coffee?" said the young man. "You must be very hungry."

She held her legs closely together, turned a bit away from him. She drew the gown more closely about her. She was pathetic, frightened.

"Tutina!" said the young man.

Swiftly Tutina rose to her feet and hurried from the room.

"Doubtless, as an informed, intelligent person," said the young man, "you are aware of the existence of many worlds, and the overwhelming statistical probability that many of these, indeed, given the numbers involved, millions of them, are suitable for life as we know it, and that, further, given the nature of chemical evolution, and organic evolution, and natural selections, and such, that there is an overwhelming statistical probability that not only life, but rational life, would exist on many of these worlds, indeed, once again, given the numbers involved, on millions of them."

She nodded.

"I ask you to believe nothing now," he said. "But consider the possibility of alien life forms and exotic, alternative technologies, life forms of incredible intelligence, say, far beyond that of the human, with, at their disposal, enormous powers, the power even to influence, and manipulate, gravity. With this power, they could, for example, move their planet from star to star, as it seemed appropriate to them, and, when they wished, if they wished, they might conceal its presence gravitationally, by affecting certain fields involved. Do you understand this, at least as a logical possibility?"

"Yes," she said.

"Suppose then that human beings might exist, too, on such a planet, perhaps originally brought there for scientific purposes, say, as specimens, or perhaps as curiosities, or perhaps merely in the interests of aesthetics, much as one might plant a garden, putting one flower here and another there, or perhaps as one might stock an aquarium, such things. Do you understand?"

"Yes," she said.

"But this seems quite fantastic to you?" he asked.

"Yes," she said.

"On such a planet," he said, "presumably the dominant life forms would supervise, to some extent, the technology of human beings."

"I suppose so," she said.

"They would not wish, for example, to allow human beings to develop a weaponry which might threaten them, or to develop in such a way as to impair the viability of the planet for organic life, such things."

"I suppose not," she whispered.

At this point Tutina, carrying a tray, in her brief silk, and anklet, followed by one of the two men who had been outside, entered the room. The man behind her carried a small table, which he put down, before the older woman. Tutina, then, placed the tray on the table. On the tray, tastefully arranged, with napkins, was a plate of small pastries, a saucer and cup, some sugars and creams, some spoons, and a small pot of coffee.

The man who had brought the table withdrew.

Tutina regarded the older woman with hatred, unseen by the young man, as her back was to him.

The older woman returned her stare, coldly.

Tutina, of course, must await the consent, the signal, of the older woman.

The older woman made her wait, for several seconds. Then she said, sweetly, "Yes, please."

Tutina then poured the coffee, carefully, and then replaced the small container on the tray.

Then Tutina waited.

"Thank you," said the older woman, politely dismissing her.

Tutina then backed away, gracefully, her head down, humbly. She knew that she was under the eye of the young man. The older woman smiled inwardly. She suspected that that serving, and humble withdrawal, had cost Tutina much. Tutina then knelt again, as she had before, at the side of the desk. The older woman did not neglect to look down at Tutina where she knelt, and smile upon her, sweetly.

"One does not know the full nature or extent of the technology at the disposal of the alien life forms on such a world," said the young man, "but it is doubtless not only powerful but sophisticated and widely ranging. For example, they may have, we might suppose, unusual, though it seems not perfect, surveillance capabilities. Should they detect a breach of one of their ordinances, say, one forbidding certain varieties of weapons to humans, it seems they are capable of imposing swift, unmistakable and effective sanctions."

"I do not understand any of this," said the older woman.

"You understand it on some level, surely," said the young man.

"Yes," she admitted.

"On such a world what do you conjecture would be the nature of human culture?" he inquired.

"I do not know," she whispered.

"Please eat something," he said.

She looked at the plate before her. Her lower lip trembled.

"It is perfectly all right," he said. "It is not poisoned. It is not drugged. When we wish to drug you in the future, it will usually be done with your full awareness. A syringe will be used."

"Let me go," she begged.

"We did not bring you here to release you," he said. "Too, you are now ours, literally ours, in a sense far fuller, far deeper, and far more perfect, than you can even begin at present to comprehend."

Her dismay was obvious.

"Please," he said.

Under his gaze she obediently lifted one of the small pastries to her mouth, and began to eat. Then she sipped the coffee. Then, in a moment, so hungry, she began to eat voraciously. Angrily she noted Tutina regarding her, and smiling. To be sure, the desperation, the eagerness, with which she ate seemed scarcely compatible with the dignity of a Ph.D., particularly in one with a degree in gender studies.

"On such a world," continued the young man, "being subjected to externally imposed limitations, those of the alien life forms, for example, various limitations on weaponry, transportation and communication, human cultures would exist, and develop, and express themselves rather differently, at least in some respects, than they have on this world, the one with which you are familiar. For example, on such a world, on this supposed other world, instead of adjudicating differences with, say, bombs and bullets, or thermonuclear weaponry, destroying life indiscriminately, irradiating soil, poisoning atmospheres, and such, points at issue might be adjudicated rather with the fire of torches, the bronze of spearheads, the steel of unsheathed swords."

"It would be so primitive," said the older woman.

"In some respects, yes, in others, not," said the young man.

She continued to eat greedily. She now realizes that much of her earlier malaise, her headache, and such, if not associated with the alcohol she had imbibed, which seems unlikely, was presumably associated with her lack of nourishment. To be sure, her age might have had something to do with her condition. Tassa powder, which she later learned was used on her, allegedly has few, if any, lingering aftereffects, or at least, she was assured, on younger women. And it is on such women, of course, considerably younger women, that it is most often used.

"With respect to understanding the cultures of such a world," he said, "it is helpful to keep various considerations in mind. First, human beings were apparently brought to such a world from many different areas and over a period of many hundreds, indeed, presumably even thousands, of years. Accordingly they would have brought with them certain native customs and cultures. Thus it is natural to suppose that on such a world many cultures would bear obvious signs of their origins. The languages of this world, too, would be expected to exhibit similar traces of their antecedents. Secondly, it is useful to keep in mind that the cultures of this supposed world have not been affected by the development of certain vast, far-reaching, centralizing, reductive, dehumanizing, mechanistic technologies; they have not been affected by, for example, global industrialization, socially engineered mass conditioning programs, and gigantic nation states, removing freedoms and powers, one by one, bit by bit, from their victims, hastening to disarm their populaces lest they resist, retaining for themselves alone the means, and tools, of coercion and violence, reducing their supposed citizenries to implicit serfdom. Accordingly, in many respects, not being afflicted by these processes, the human beings of our supposed world, that on which I am inviting you to conjecture, might tend in many ways to be healthier and happier, and to find their lives more rewarding and meaningful, more worth living, than many of their numerous, aimless, confused, unhappy, reduced counterparts on the world with which you are most familiar. The supposed world is then, one supposes, given the evolutionary heritage of the human animal, likely, on the whole, at least, to be much more congenial to human nature, and its fulfillment, than the world with which you are most familiar."

She wiped her lips with a napkin.

"Would you like more?" he asked. "I can have Tutina fetch you more, or something else."

The older woman enjoyed seeing Tutina, as she knelt, stiffen slightly, in anger. Was that almost a slight hint of resistance? But when the young man turned to Tutina, her manner underwent an instant transformation, and she shrank down a little, making herself smaller, and, trembling, averted her eyes, not daring to meet his. It pleased the older woman to see the sensuous, hated, beautiful blonde so much in his power.

"No," said the older woman.

"Thirdly," said the young man, "consider the following. Incidentally, these are only some simple general things, out of thousands, which I might tell you about this supposed world. I have selected only three, thinking that these might be most helpful to you at this moment."

The older woman nodded.

"Thirdly," said the young man," I would like to call your attention to certain medical, or biological, advances, or, at any rate, capabilities, which exist on this supposed world."

"I thought your supposed world was primitive," said the older woman.

"In certain respects, so, in others, not," said the young man. "The particular advance, or capability, I have in mind may be of some interest to you. Let me begin, first of all, by reminding you that certain areas of technology, of investigation, and such, were denied to humans on our supposed world. The energies then which might have been plied into certain channels, those of weapons, electronic communication, mass transportation, large-scale industrial machinery, and such, were diverted into other channels, for example, into the medical, or biological, sciences. In short, the supposed world, whose existence I should like you to entertain for the moment as a possibility, is, in some respects, far advanced over that with which you are most familiar. For example, on the supposed world aging was understood over a thousand years ago not as an inevitability but, in effect, as a disease and, accordingly, it was investigated as such. Clearly it is a physical process and, like other physical processes, it would be subject to various conditions, conditions susceptible to manipulation, or alteration, in various ways."

"I do not understand what you are saying," whispered the older woman, frightened.

"I did not mean to upset you," said the man. "Forgive me. Let us briefly change the subject. Doubtless you have seen old examples of the film-makers' art, silent films, for example. Or perhaps even talkies, but dating back perhaps fifty or sixty years?"

"Of course," she said.

"In the silent films might be seen many women of incredible loveliness and femininity, films made in a time in which these precious, marvelous attributes were celebrated, rather than castigated and belittled by an envious potato-bodied self-proclaimed elite of the plain and politically motivated. Too, even in old talkies, how beautiful, how feminine, were so many of the actresses! How poignant then to realize that these luscious, marvelous creatures would, by now, have so sadly changed, would by now have been mercilessly humiliated, ravaged, eroded into almost unrecognizable caricatures of their once fair, wondrous selves. It is sad. Too, there were women in those days, true women, and two sexes, real sexes, not one blurred, androgynous pseudo-sex, and they were harmoniously interrelated, fitted closely and beautifully to one another as male and female, each inordinately unique and precious, not set at odds by the disappointed, the greedy and rancorous. In those days the pathological virago would not have been a role model but a poor joke, as she is in actuality today, though a joke it is unwise to recognize. Then the forty-nine natural women would not have been belittled, twisted, and commanded to behave like the unnatural "fiftieth woman," the authentic, disturbed malcontent, consumed with envy, intent on working her vengeance and will on an entire community. If one is to be sacrificed, why not the fiftieth, she alone, why the forty-nine?"

"Let each be as she wishes," said the older woman.

"But it does not work in that fashion, does it?" he asked.

"No," she whispered. Then she said, angrily, "We know our values! Let the forty-nine be sacrificed!"

"Perhaps men will not permit it," he said.

She drew back in the chair, behind the small table, frightened, and put her legs more closely together, and gathered the white gown more closely about her slender body. It had never occurred to her before, perhaps oddly, that men might not permit the transmogrification of her gender. That had never occurred to her, that men might take a hand in such things. Men had always been so stupid, so simple, so weak, so easily confused, so easily influenced, so easily controlled and manipulated. Those, of course, were the men of Earth.

"I have upon occasion," he said, "seen photographs of older women, sometimes very old women, taken when they were much younger, in the bloom of their youth and beauty. One realizes then, suddenly, that once they were young, and so beautiful. How hard it seems to believe that sometimes, knowing them as they are now. But if one had known them then! Ah, if one had known them then! Then would one not have found them terribly attractive? Would one not have wanted then to know them, to approach them, to touch them?"

"Everyone grows old," said the older woman.

"I promised you that I would introduce you to the individual whom you remembered from long ago," he said.

"Is he in the house?" she asked, suddenly.

"Yes," said the young man.

"Please be merciful!" she begged. "If I am to see him, give me clothing to wear! Do not let me appear before him like this!"

"Was he a lover?" asked the young man.

"No!" she cried. "Of course not!"

"I shall introduce you to him now," he said.

"Please, no," she begged. "Not while I am like this!"

"But you have already appeared before him, so clad," he said.

She looked at him wildly, in confusion.

"I am he," he smiled.

"No," she said. "You are too young, too young!"

"I am he," he repeated.

She shook her head, disbelievingly.

"It will all become clearer later," he said. "Let us now simply inform you, and you may believe this or not, it makes no difference at this point, that our "supposed world," as we spoke of it, does exist, in actuality. It lies within our very solar system. I have been there. I have seen that world. I have adopted it, and its hardy, uncompromising, fulfilling ways, as my own. I will not recognize the pathologies of this world any longer. I repudiate them. The world is called, after one of its cultural artifacts, "Home Stone." In the language most commonly spoken on that world the word is "Gor." Perhaps you have heard of Gor?"

"You are mad!" she wept.

"Have you heard of it?" he asked.

"Of course," she said. "But it does not exist!"

"Later you will be in a better position to make a judgment on that," he said.

The older woman looked to the kneeling blonde, if only to corroborate her own consternation, her own disbelief, but Tutina stared ahead, not meeting her eyes.

"Tutina," said the young man, "is from Earth, like you, but she was taken, let us say, as a guest, to Gor. I bought her there."

"Bought her?" asked the older woman.

"I, on the other hand," said the young man, "was, in a way, recruited."

"You are not the young man I knew," said the older woman.

"I am," he said. "Let us return briefly to those medical advances I mentioned earlier, those developed on Gor, or, as it is sometimes spoken of, the *Antichthon*, the Counter-Earth. Among these advances, or capabilities, if you prefer, are the Stabilization Serums. These ensure pattern stability, the stability of organic patterns, without degradation, despite the constant transformation of cells in the body. As you probably know, every seven years or so, every cell in your body, with the exception of the neural cells, is replaced. The continuity of neural cells guarantees the viability of memory, extending back, beyond various seven-year periods. The Stabilization Serums, in effect, arrest aging, and, thus, preserve youth. Further, the Stabilization Serums also freshen and rejuvenate neural tissue. In this way, one avoids the embarrassment of a declining brain incongruously ensconced in a youthful body. That feature represents an improvement over the original serums and dates from something like five hundred years ago."

"You said you *bought* Tutina?" she asked.

"Yes," he said. "Can you think of any simple way in which I might convince you that I am who I claim to be? I probably remember some of our exchanges in class, some of my fellow students, some of the reading assignments, such things. Would anything like that help?"

"You might have researched such things," she said.

"True," he admitted. "What if I described your clothing, or manner, or such?"

"Such things were muchly the same," she said. "I know!"

"What?" he asked.

"Once, and only once," she said, "I wore jewelry to class. You could not know what it was. You would have no way of knowing what it was. Your data, your records, the roster, the familiarities of my garb and demeanor, could not give you that information."

"You wore two narrow bracelets, golden bracelets, on your left wrist," he said.

The older woman was aghast, stunned. The bracelets were precisely as he had stated. She had never forgotten that class. She had only dared once to wear them, to that class and none other. And she remembered how she had sometimes moved her wrist, as though in the most natural and apt of gestures, in such a way that they would make that tiny, provocative sound.

"They contrasted nicely with your prim couture," he said. "They reminded me of slave bangles. They made small sounds, sometimes, as you moved your wrist. I suppose you know you did that on purpose, to present yourself before me, as a female slave."

"No!" she cried.

"I recall thinking that it would be pleasant to have you remove those severe garments, slowly and gracefully, and then kneel naked before me, except for the two bracelets on your left wrist."

The older woman cried out in misery, and hid her face in her hands.

"There has been a new development in the Stabilization Serums, or, better, I suppose, serums rather analogous to the Stabilization Serums, a development which has occurred in my own lifetime, indeed, within the last few years," he said. "In this development, though there are dangers associated with it, and it is not always effective, it is often possible to reverse the typical aging process, to an earlier point, and then stabilize it at that point."

"You are mad," she said.

"I had never forgotten you," he said, "and so, naturally, when I learned of this possibility, I thought of you, and, indeed, several others, in this regard.

"You may now ask about your clothing," he said.

"Where is it?" she said.

"It was destroyed," he said. "You will not be needing it anymore. You are going to be taken to Gor."

"You are mad," she whispered.

"Not at all," he said.

"You never forgot me?" she said.

"Do not mistake our intentions here," he said. "This is a business venture. We are interested in profit. There is a rich harvest to be had now, with this new development, only recently available to us for commercial exploitation. There is now, suddenly, an entirely new, rich, untapped area which is ripe for our endeavors, an area which we may now use to supplement our routine work."

"You remembered me," she whispered. "You were *interested* in me."

"A nice word," he said.

"You found me of *interest*—?"

"Certainly."

She was in sudden consternation.

Interested?

Surely she had misspoke herself. Surely she had gone too far!

Was she feminine?

She must not be feminine!

Surely it would be wrong for her to be such, to be so female, so simply, so radically, so vulnerably female!

Was such not a mere social artifact?

But what if it were not a mere social artifact?

What if it were something very different, what if it were something very real, something natural, precious, important, and beautiful, something utterly independent of her wishes and indoctrinations, something which, whether she or others approved or not, or wanted it to be or not, she was?

And could it be wrong to be what one was?

And what might be the consequences of becoming what one was, truly?

Could it be so terrible?

Or might it not be the most welcome and glorious of liberations?

She looked at the wall, to her left, at a picture, a landscape. It seemed a strange landscape, in its way, with gentle yellow trees nestled in a valley, and, in the distance, a range of scarlet mountains. One could almost smell the breeze, the freshness of the air.

A strange picture!

Surely there was no such place.

But what if there were?

What would it be to be in such a place?

Would not things be different?

Perhaps very different?

She looked away from the picture.

"But how could that be?" she asked, lightly. "In what possible way?"

"You are not stupid," he said. "Do not pretend to be stupid. In precisely the sense you had in mind when you used the word 'interesting'."

"—*As a female*?" she said.

"Of course," he said.

"How horrid!" she said.

"You are actually quite pleased," he said.

"I decry the very thought," she said. "I reject it as insulting and repulsive!"

"No, you do not," he said. "You are very pleased. And I assure you that you will come to hope, and soon, with all your heart, and every fiber of your little body, that men will find you interesting *as a female*—for your very life may depend on this."

"I do not understand," she said.

"In a few days, perhaps weeks," he said, "you will understand."

"I think you are mad," she said.

"Perhaps," he smiled.

She drew the pristine, starched white of the hospital or examination gown more closely about her.

"How lovely you were," he said, "and how lovely you will be again, when you are what you should have been, from the very beginning."

"I do not understand," she said.

He laughed, and she felt frightened.

She trembled in the small, starched gown. It was too short! On her left ankle was a puzzling, inexplicable ring of metal; it was a stout, sturdy little ring, and it closely encircled her ankle; it was closed and locked in place; she could not remove it; it was fastened on her, snugly, effectively, inescapably; it was warmed now from her body.

She had never worn such a device.

She did not understand such a device.

What could it mean?

There was writing on it.

He had spoken of records.

Such a device, she thought, in its obduracy and beauty, is inappropriate for me. It is the sort of thing which should be on the body of a young woman, a coveted, desirable female, one who must wait fearfully to learn its significance, a significance already half suspected, and in what plans she might figure.

"I do not understand," she thought to herself. "I do not understand!"

"Yes," he said, "I was interested in you. Certainly I was interested in you. But you must clearly understand that I was interested in you in only one way, in one way alone. I thought of you with only one purpose in mind, the only purpose in terms of which you could possibly be of any value. And you must understand, too, that that is the only way in which you are of any interest or ever will be of any interest whatsoever. That is the only interest, and the only meaning, you will have, ever, for any man."

"I do not understand," she whispered.

"In what other way might one be interested in one such as you?" he asked.

She looked at him, wildly.

He smiled.

"No," she said, "no, no!"

"I wonder what color cords would look well on you," he said. "White, yellow, red?"

"I do not understand," she cried. "I do not understand!"

"Doubtless any," he said. "They are all nice. I think you will be very pretty, later, of course, not now, later, when you are luscious, helplessly bound in them."

"Luscious, I?" she said. "Cords? Bound?"

He then drew from the center drawer of his desk a small, rectangular leather case, from which he withdrew a syringe, and a vial. "You are going to be given an injection," he said, "which will, in a few moments, produce a lapse of consciousness. I would rather that you did not resist. If you choose to do so, I will have Tutina, who is considerably younger and larger, and stronger, than you, hold you."

The older woman said nothing, but wept.

Meanwhile, Tutina had, from a cabinet to the side, to the right of the desk, as one would face it, taken what appeared to be a bottle of alcohol, and, from a small white sack which had been beside the bottle, what seemed to be a cotton swab.

"Lie down there," said Tutina, "on the rug, before his desk, on your right side, with your knees drawn up."

Awkwardly, and with unsteadiness, and some pain, the older woman, tears in her eyes, humiliated, went to her hands and knees, and then to the position to which she had been directed.

"Hereafter," said Tutina, "when you hear the command 'Injection position', in whatever language, you will instantly, and unquestioningly, assume this position."

The older woman whimpered.

"Be quiet," said Tutina.

The older woman cried out, softly, in sudden protest, as the gown was thrust up, rudely, above her waist. She felt the cool touch of alcohol, applied from the swab, at her waist, on the left side, above the hip, a swabbed area of some two square inches. Then, a moment later, as Tutina withdrew, taking with her the alcohol and swab, she sensed the young man crouching beside her. Then she felt the entry into her body of the syringe, sharply and precisely penetrating the alcohol-cooled area, and there was a small, growing, painful, swollen fullness in her side, as the liquid was forced under the skin.

Chapter 5

The Young Man Visits Her, Prior to the First Phase of Her Transformation

"Do you find your quarters pleasant?" he asked.

The room, or what one might even think of as an apartment, was large, comfortable, attractive, and well-appointed. There was furniture not too much unlike furniture with which she was familiar from her first world, an attractive rug, two easy chairs, a small table, a chest at the side, for clothing and small articles, such things. She might have preferred that there had been a separate bedroom, as she did not much care for her bed to be visible when the room was entered, but that, as it was, was not the case. There were no pictures on the wall, or tapestries, or representations of any sort, which might inform her more accurately as to the nature of her larger surroundings, those beyond the room. There was a large mirror, in which she could see, not that she much cared to, her small, frail, wrinkled, flattened, aged, tired body. The furniture, including the bed, was fastened in place. She could not change its position. It was thus impossible, for example, to try to barricade the door, to protect her privacy, or move it to the wall and attempt to use it to obtain a glimpse outside, through the small window, high there in the wall, well over her head. She could see the sky, and occasional clouds, and, at night, the darkness and some stars, through the window, which views, though reassuring, were not particularly informative. More informative, perhaps, was the fact that the window was barred. That detail seemed somewhat incongruous, given the pleasant, genial, comfortable nature of the room, but it does, she believes, warrant mention. It was barred. There was one door. It was a heavy door, of some dark wood. Oddly, it lacked a handle on her side. When it was opened, as it frequently was, usually to admit respectful young ladies, who seemed incredibly beautiful to her, who wore long, sedate gowns, who brought her food and drink, she could see the hallway outside, which, contrasting with the pleasures of the room, seemed quite dismal. It was walled and floored with heavy stone; it might even be damp; it was surely dark and forbidding. There was a man outside sometimes, a doorman, or guard, who attended to the admittance, and egress, on a signal, of the young ladies. She did not see much of him, but he apparently wore some sort of short robe, and bootlike sandals. His mien frightened her. Something about it made her feel unusually vulnerable, and feminine. The young ladies would not speak directly to her of this world in any detail but she had gathered something of it from the lengthy, intensive language lessons, hours in length, which they administered to her, lessons in a language whose name she did not even know. There were five young ladies. Two of them, happily, spoke English, one with a French accent, the other with a German accent. The other three, she suspected, did not know English. She did not know what might be their native language. She suspected that they were native to this new world. The language apparently contained no words for hundreds of the most common objects on her former world, such as automobiles and radios. On the other hand, it contained many words for implements; artifacts, items of apparel, botanical forms, comestibles, and such, with which she was unfamiliar. In such a way she had begun to suspect something of the nature of the world which must lie beyond the enforcements of her current horizon, a horizon limited by four walls, a patch of sky detected through an inaccessible window and an occasional glimpse into a forbidding corridor. To be sure, her most widely ranging, and far-flung, and ambitious speculations and conjectures, of necessity under the circumstances, must fail to prepare her for the reality without. They could not even begin to scratch at the foot of a high, majestic wall, beyond which there lay a world. The realities of such a world, at the moment, understandably, were simply beyond her ken. The young ladies were barefoot, and their sedate gowns, while long, were sleeveless. She was dressed better than they, which perhaps suited her age. Her own ankle-length gown was of finer material, came high, modestly, about the neck, and had long sleeves. Too, unlike her fair visitors, she wore soft, attractive, embroidered slippers. She did have at least one thing in common with them. Each, they and she, on her left ankle, wore a closely fitting, closed ring. All, she and her visitors, were apparently ankleted. She wore the same anklet the discovery of which on her body had so disconcerted her on her first world. The encirclements of the ankles of her fair visitors were various in nature and appearance, but all were sturdy, and, she conjectured, locked. Although her garmenture was lovely, and modest, one detail troubled her. She had been given nothing in the way of panties, or pantyhose. Curious, after the first few days, and apprehensive concerning this presumed oversight in the inventory of her issued garmenture, she had tried, delicately, to inquire whether her visitors had been permitted the trivial modesty which she, apparently, doubtless due to some oversight, had been denied. When the two young ladies who spoke English had finally discerned the nature of her inquiry, they had laughed merrily, and translated it delightedly for their companions, who, too, then, looking from one to the other, two clapping their hands with pleasure, burst into laughter, the older woman having apparently made some fine joke.

"The room is lovely," she responded to the young man. They sat in the two easy chairs, facing one another.

"You have been indoors," he said, "but perhaps you can tell the difference in the air."

She nodded. Perhaps it was more highly oxygenated than the air of her first world. Or perhaps, more likely, it was simply not as contaminated, not as fouled and poisoned as the air of her first world. How alive it made her feel. When the world was young, she had thought, it must have been like this; the air must have been like this.

"The food is acceptable?" he inquired.

"Yes," she said. It was plain, but delicious. It was fresh, not shipped or stored, she supposed, for days or weeks, and frozen and such. For all she knew it had been picked or gathered that morning. Sometimes it was almost as though the dew was still upon it. Too, she doubted that it had been saturated with preservatives, or coated with poisons, to discourage the predations of insects. It did not have the stale, antiseptic reek of alien chemicals. The bread might have been an hour from the oven. She had been given only water to drink, but it had seemed to her water such as might have gushed forth from secret woodland springs in classic groves or might in remote days have been dipped by kilted herdsmen from rushing mountain streams.

"Are you still aware of the difference in the gravity?" he asked.

"No longer," she said. "I was aware of it at first. Now I am no longer aware of it."

"Good," he said, rising from the chair.

"When am I to be returned to Earth?" she asked.

"What were the first words you were taught to say on this world?" he asked.

"'La kajira'," she said. "But I was not told what they meant."

"Say them, clearly," he said.

"La kajira," she said. "What do they mean?"

"This is the last time I will visit you in these quarters," he said. "Your treatment will begin within the hour. Hereafter, as your treatment progresses, it is you who will be brought before me."

"That seems rather arrogant," she said.

"Not arrogant," he said, "—fitting."

"What is the nature of this treatment?" she inquired.

"You will learn," he said.

"What is its purpose?" she asked.

"You will learn," he said.

"How long does the treatment take?" she asked.

"It varies," he said. "But it will take several days. Such things take time. Indeed, much of the time, while the changes take place, you will be unconscious. It is best that way. I have decided, in your case, incidentally, that we will think of the treatment as consisting of four major phases, and each will be clearly demarcated for you, for your edification and my amusement. To be sure, the division is somewhat arbitrary."

"I think you are mad!" she said.

"Let us hope the treatment goes well," he said. "Sometimes it does not."

She shuddered.

"Look into the mirror, deeply, and well," he said.

She regarded her image in the mirror.

"It may be the last time you see yourself," he said.

"I do not understand," she said.

"It is not necessary that you do," he said.

"Please stay! Do not leave!" she begged.

She watched him in the mirror.

He went to the door, and called to the man outside. The door opened. When he took his leave, another man entered, one she had not seen before, who wore a green robe. He carried a small case, as of implements.

She turned to face him, frightened.

"Injection position," he said.

Chapter 6

She Is Presented Before the Young Man, Following the First Phase of Her Transformation

"The female," said the man, indicating that she should stand within the yellow circle, on the marble floor, in the lofty room, before the curule chair.

Light fell upon her, from a high window.

The young man, in a robe, she had never seen him before in such garb, leaned forward in the curule chair.

Then he leaned back, continuing to regard her.

She was angry.

The curule chair was the only furniture in the room, and it was on a dais. There was no place for her to sit.

He had not, as he had warned her earlier, come to see her, but, rather, it was she who was brought to him.

She had recalled awakening, some days ago, slowly, groggily, on some hard, narrow, tablelike surface. But she had scarcely had time to orient herself, to understand where she was, to understand the white walls, the shelves of instruments and vials, before a dark, heavy, efficient leather hood was thrust over her head, pulled down, fully, and buckled shut, beneath her chin. She then, within the hood, was in utter discomfiting, confusing, helpless darkness. She was then drawn from the tablelike platform, apparently by two men, placed on her feet, and, between them, taken from the room, each grasping an arm. She surmised she was being hurried down a corridor. Abruptly the men halted her, and turned her, rudely, to her right. The hood was then unbuckled, and, as it was jerked away, she was thrust stumbling forward. Behind her, as she sought to keep her balance, hands outstretched, she heard a sound, as of the closing of a gate. She whirled about, and rushed forward, only in an instant to find herself to her dismay grasping heavy, narrowly set bars. She was in a cell.

"I have not been treated well," she told the young man before whom she stood.

"How do your lessons proceed?" he asked.

"Twice," she said, "I was denied my evening meal!"

"On the whole," said he, "I gather that you have been doing well with your lessons."

"I am not a child!" she said.

"But you must try to do better," he told her.

When she had assured herself that she was indeed in a cell, and that it was locked, a cell abutting on a dismal, stone-flagged, dark corridor, much like the one she had glimpsed from her room, or apartment, perhaps even the same, she discovered that she was clad differently from what she had been before. Instead of the long, long-sleeved, ankle-length, white gown of fine material, coming high, modestly, about the neck, she now wore a simpler white gown, of less fine material, with half sleeves, and its hem came midway upon her calves. The garment had a rounded neck, which permitted her throat to be seen, in its entirety. Her slippers were gone and she wore instead sandals. She cried out, angrily, and shook the bars, and demanded to be returned to her former quarters, and her earlier finery. The material of the gown she wore was from the wool of the bounding hurt, which is distinguished from the common hurt not only by its gazellelike movements, particularly when startled, but by the quality of its wool. It is raised on this world for its wool. The cell was not really uncomfortable. It was large, and its floor was covered, for the most part, with a woven fiber mat. In it there was a cot, and a stool.

There was also a mirror in the cell, to her right, on the wall, as she would face the cell door.

It was not, however, the sort of mirror with which she was familiar, for it was rather more in the nature of a polished metal surface, set well within the wall. There was no way it could be removed from the wall, at least without tools, or shattered, perhaps to produce fragments of glass.

Since her image was not so instantly and clearly available to her as it would have been in a more familiar sort of mirror, she approached it more closely, puzzled, and peered into it.

She then gave a soft cry of surprise, for she did not immediately recognize her image in the surface.

To be sure, it was she, but she as she had not been for perhaps ten years. The woman who regarded her, wonderingly, from the metal surface might have been in her late forties, not her late fifties.

She put her hand gently to her face. Certain blemishes to which she had reconciled herself were gone. There seemed fewer lines in her face. Her throat seemed smoother to her. Her entire body felt differently. It seemed somewhat more supple. Certainly the occasional stiffness in the joints was not now afflicting her, not that it always did. It was not so much that her body did not ache, or that she was not in pain, as that she had the odd sense that something might now be different about her, that her body might not now be so likely to hurt her, in that way, as it had in the past. To be sure, that conjecture, that intimation, that timid hope, might, she supposed, prove illusory.

She was not long left to ponder her surprising situation before her lessons began again. This time there were only three young women, and they were not the same as before. Too, whereas they treated her with respect, they did not seem as deferential, or concerned to please, as had been their predecessors. She did not seem to have the same easy familiarity with them as with the others; they did not, for example, seem to see her in the role of a dignified older woman, one entitled to respect in virtue of her years, and weakness. Clearly they did not regard her as obviously superior to them. These new instructrices were less patient with her, too, than had been the others. They were garbed rather like her, in plain white gowns, of similar material and length, except that their gowns were sleeveless. The necks of their gowns were rounded like hers. Given the mid-calf length of their gowns there was not the least difficulty in instantly detecting that their left ankles, too, like hers, were closely encircled with steel rings. Two of them spoke English.

She now began to be instructed in what is known as the First Knowledge, which is that level of understanding common to most individuals on this world, a knowledge of myths, stories, and popular lore. Too, they spoke to her of animals and plants, and their properties, and values and dangers. Pictures, and samples, were often adduced. In the case of certain of the animals she dismissed the accounts and pictures as a portion of the mythical background of the world to which she had earlier been exposed. Such beasts, she was confident, could not exist in reality, serpents nearly a hundred feet in length, six-legged, sinuous, nocturnal predators, gigantic hawklike birds, and such. They also gave her some understanding of the social arrangements common in what were called the "high cities," in particular, the caste system, and the existence of codes of honor, and such, apparently taken seriously on this world. They did not, incidentally, explain to her one aspect of the social structure, or perhaps better, of the culture, in which she would have been almost certain to have taken a great interest, that condition, or status, which was irremediably hers on this world, that category, so to speak, to which she herself belonged. Perhaps this was because they had received instructions in this matter, or perhaps it was because they thought that she, an obviously intelligent woman, was already aware of such things, her status and condition, and such, or, more simply, what she was, what she, simply, absolutely and categorically, was. But, in fact, at that time, she was not aware of what she was.

"How many words is she learning a day?" the young man asked the attendant, he who had conducted her into his presence.

"One hundred," said the man.

"Let it be two hundred and fifty," said the young man.

She gasped, lifting her hand in futile protest.

"Too," said the young man, "let her grammar be sharpened, for it is allegedly in need of much improvement, and see to it that her phrasings become more felicitous, certainly better than they reportedly are. One does not object to a certain amount of ignorance and fitful illiteracy in such as she, an occasional misuse of words, and such, which can be charming, even amusing, but it is important that she attain a considerably high level of fluency, in order that she may understand, instantly and perfectly, all that is required of her."

"Do you want her accent improved?" asked the attendant.

"That will come in time," said the young man. "At the moment her accent is useful. It will instantly serve to mark her out to native speakers."

She determined to work zealously on her accent. She sensed that it might be in her best interests, for some reason, to conceal her origins. Perhaps there was something about her origins which might make her special on this world, at least to some, and special in a sense in which she might not care to be special. What she did not understand was that there were traces in her own body which would continue to betray her origin, in particular, fillings in the teeth, and an inoculation scar on her upper left arm. Too, of course, there were things which a native of this world would know, which she would not. Shrewdly questioned, her ignorance would soon be apparent. Too, though such things tend to be of no real consequence on this world, there would be, at least in this city, papers on her.

"There is no chair here for me to sit on," she said to the young man in the curule chair. She said it coldly, in order that he might be shamed, and thus recalled to the simple amenities of courtesy.

"In four days," he said, to the attendant, "let her treatment be resumed."

She regarded the young man with fury.

He waved his hand, dismissing her.

The attendant indicated that she should precede him from the room.

Angrily she turned on her heel and strode away. In a few moments the door of her cell again closed behind her. She turned about, and, angrily, grasped, and shook, the bars of her cell.

"The arrogance of him! The arrogance of him!" she thought. Then she went and sat down, determinedly, on the stool.

When the attendant with the cart of food, for there were other cells, too, it seemed, in the corridor, passed her cell he did not stop.

"Feed me!" she had called.

But he had gone his way.

Grasping the bars then she realized that she did not have control over her own food. What she was fed, and, indeed, if she were fed, was no longer up to her, but to others. She had complained about the loss of two meals, as a punishment, presumably, for not doing well in her "lessons." Now the attendant had simply passed her by.

She went to bed, on the hard, narrow cot, hungry that night.

The next morning the cart did not stop, either.

"Please!" she begged.

She was extremely attentive in her lessons that day. And she was extremely cooperative with, and pleasant to, and deferential to, even desperately deferential to, her lovely ankleted instructrices. It was almost as though they were the adults and she a timid, frightened, disciplined child, trying desperately to please them, to win from them even the tiniest of smiles.

She was miserable with hunger that night.

The attendant, in passing her cell, threw a roll into the cell, which she ran to, seized up and, on her knees, devoured in haste.

Tears rolled down her cheeks.

Some days later her treatment was resumed.

Chapter 7

She Is Presented Before the Young Man, Following the Second Phase of Her Transformation

"The female," said the man, announcing her presence.

She took her place within the yellow circle, in that lofty room, before the dais, on which reposed the curule chair.

The light, as before, from a high window, fell upon her.

"Ah!" said the young man, he robed, leaning forward.

She then stood a little taller, a little more gracefully. Stirrings in her, subtly sensed, informed her that she was before a male, causing her some uneasiness. In her lifetime, of course, she had been before thousands of males, in the sense of standing within their vicinity, and such, but this seemed muchly different. Here she was rather alone, in a special situation, being looked upon, in a particular way. In this way she could not recall having ever been before a male before, in this particular way, the way that she now sensed she was.

When she had stood before him some days ago, she supposed it had been some days ago, perhaps as long as two weeks ago, it had not been the same. She had been before him, so to speak, but not in this way before him.

"Do you enjoy your present accommodations?" he asked.

"They are doubtless as you have decided they will be," she said.

She felt stronger now than she had before. She suspected that she could now better withstand, and resist, the lack of food, at least for a longer time. She did not think that he could now so easily bring her to helpless futility before him. She was stronger now. She did not care, of course, to put the matter to a test. She accepted that he could change her diet, or limit her intake of food, or deny it to her altogether, as he might please. That lesson had been learned. She understood that, sooner or later, he could bring her to her knees, or belly, whimpering, begging, groveling for a crust. But, still, she was stronger now.

This time, too, she had been hooded, and dragged from a narrow table, but she had been placed in a different cell.

Her new cell was quite different from the former cell. It was much smaller, some seven feet by seven feet. There was no mat of woven fiber on the floor; the floor was bare, and hard, consisting of heavy blocks of fitted stone, such as those in the corridor. There was no furniture in the cell, no cot, no stool. There was a flat mat, on which she might sit, or sleep. She had a blanket.

"Your curves have now reappeared," he said, casually, idly.

She stiffened.

He had not seen her, as far as she knew, since their last interview in this room.

"You bled, as I understand it," he said.

"Yes," she said.

When this had happened she had cried out, and had been alarmed, not understanding what had occurred, it had been so long, and so unexpected. But the women who were now her teachers, three of them, different from before, only one of whom spoke English, and that a broken English, had laughed at her, thinking she must be very stupid. But they had found her water and cloths, that she might clean her leg, and a rag which she might insert into her body. They made her clean the floor of the cell. After all, it was she who had soiled it. Perhaps, surprisingly, the flow had not been negligible, at all, as one might have expected, it beginning again, but had been abundant. She wondered if, while she had been unconscious, it, or things associated with it, had begun again, only she would not then have been aware of such changes in her body.

"While we are on such matters," he said, "I would suppose that it was explained to you that you will later be given a particular drink, the name of which is unimportant now, which will temporarily, but indefinitely, preclude any possibility of biological conception on your part?"

"Yes," she said. "But I fail to understand the need for such a drink. I myself can manage such things. I am the mistress of my own body."

He smiled.

"Was it also explained to you that there is another drink, one which one might think of as a releaser of sorts, which will not only restore your possibility of conception, but ready you for it, indeed, prime you for it, so to speak?"

"Yes," she said, embarrassed.

"And thus make you available, if one wishes, for utilization."

"I do not understand," she said. "No, no one said anything about "utilization.""

"I see," he said.

"What do you mean by that?" She regarded him, apprehensively. "What do you mean by "utilization"?"

"Forgive me," he said. "I have been unnecessarily obscure. You are, of course, available for a large number of diverse utilizations, in theory, I suppose, for an infinite number of utilizations. The utilization I had in mind was "stock utilization.""

"Stock utilization!" she said.

"Yes," he said.

"I do not understand," she said.

"As in "livestock,"" he said.

"I do not understand," she said.

"Some men cannot be blamed for wishing to increase their holdings," he said.

"Holdings!"

Again, he smiled.

"Please!" she said.

"Your ankle looks well in its ring," he said.

She looked down at the steel cuff on her ankle. It was on her as fixedly as ever, as efficiently, as perfectly, as it had been on her former world, in the house where she had worn the white hospital or examination gown, in the house where she had been given the first injection, while lying on her right side before his desk.

She regarded him. "I see you do not choose to clarify these matters," she said.

"Your perception is correct," he said.

"You cannot mean!" she whispered.

"Such things will be decided not by you, but by others," he said.

She turned white.

"Yes," he smiled.

It was perhaps at that moment that she began to suspect what she might be, and what might be done to her.

She recalled a remark he had made of the hated Tutina, whom she had not yet seen on this world, that he had "bought her."

"No," she cried. "This cannot be!"

"What?" he inquired.

"What am I?" she asked. "What is my status here?"

"Can you not guess?" he asked.

"There is still no chair for me here," she said.

"You are being permitted to stand," he pointed out.

"Please!" she begged, her momentary pretense to strength and resolution gone. She felt confused and weak.

"You have seen yourself in your cell mirror, of course," he said.

"Yes," she said. There was a mirror in the new cell, rather like that in her former cell, on the right, of polished metal, as one faced the gate.

"How old would you say you were?" he asked.

"I do not know," she whispered.

"If I were to see you on the planet Earth," he said, "I would conjecture that you were somewhere in your late thirties, say, thirty-seven or thirty-eight. I would say thirty-eight. When you were acquired, you were fifty-eight."

"Fifty-five," she said.

"Fifty-eight," he said.

She put down her head. It was true.

"I see that you retain something of what must once have been considerable beauty," he observed. "Certainly many men would find you of great interest even now."

She blushed, brightly and hotly, all of her body, that exposed, bursting into uncontrollable, involuntary flames of outrage, resentment, embarrassment, and pleasure. She was not dismayed to learn that she might be, once again, after so many years, found attractive.

"Do like your new garmenture?" he inquired.

"It is that in which you have seen fit to put me," she said.

Her new garment was relatively modest as such garments go. Certainly a younger woman would have been likely to have been put in less. It was a tunic, but rather reserved for such. It was simple, plain and white, its material again, as that of her former garment, of the wool of the bounding hurt. Its hemline now came a bit above her knees. It had a rounded neckline, rather like that of her former garment, but it was, scooped somewhat more deeply, perhaps a bit less reluctant to hint at concealed delights. Interestingly, it was the first garment she had been given which was sleeveless. The baring of a woman's arms, on the world on which she now was, was normally regarded as revealing and sensuous. Indeed, women of a status, or station, above her own commonly veiled themselves when appearing in public, particularly those of the high castes. She did not know this at the time, of course. Men on this world, it seems, tended to find the short, rounded, lovely arms of women attractive. It might be mentioned that in her new quarters, she was no longer permitted sandals. They had been taken from her. She now went, as had her various instructrices, in her various quarters, barefoot. Bared feet on women, on this world, are also regarded as sensuous, and provocative.

He regarded her.

She was attractive in the tunic.

It was all she wore, except, of course, the anklet. That device now, due to the absence of footwear and the shorter nature of her new garment, appeared even more striking, more meaningful and lovely, on her ankle. Aesthetics were surely involved here, but, too, other matters, matters having to do with deeper things, meanings and such. In any event, there was the softness of her small foot and then, above it, close about her slim ankle, the encircling, locked steel, and then the beginning of the delightful curve of a bared calf. It all went together, he thought, beautifully, and meaningfully. He did not find this surprising, of course.

"How are your lessons progressing?" he asked.

She shrugged, angrily. "Doubtless you have your reports," she said.

She was not much pleased with the turn that her lessons had taken, save for her continuing instruction in the language. She was now being taught to do things, many things, rather than, primarily, to learn things, to apprehend and understand facts, lore, and such. Her education, of late, did not seem fitting for an intellectual.

"I am a not a wife," she said, angrily.

"No," he granted her.

Taken from her cell and instructed in special rooms, she had been given lessons in cooking, in cleaning, sewing, laundering, and such, domestic labors, labors such as were vehemently denounced and eschewed by scions of her ideology as demeaning, degrading, boring, repetitive and meaningless, who then hired other women, either directly or indirectly, to perform them for them. With respect to cooking she had prided herself on "knowing only the basics," but it seems that here, on this world, her skills did not extend even so far. Most of the cooking seemed to be done in small ovens and over open flames, attentively, almost a serving at a time. Cooking, here, involved cooking, actually, and not, for example, the simple heating of tasteless materials extracted from colorful packages. She discovered that cooking was an art, and required mastery, as any other art. She had never thought of it in that fashion before. Similarly, she learned that the skills of needlework of various sorts were indeed skills, and not at all easy to acquire. How often her instructrices despaired of her, as being ignorant, stupid and hopelessly inept. Finally, in misery, in tears, she had denounced them as low, vulgar, stupid women, far beneath her, women who, unlike herself, might aspire to labors no higher than the menial and servile, labors unfit for such as she, an educated, highly intelligent woman, a woman important on her own world. "Ignorant, pretentious barbarian!" cried one of the instructrices, angrily. Then to her consternation she was seized by her other two instructrices and dragged to the side of the room, where she was thrown down, on her back. There was a low, horizontal wooden bar there, raised some six inches above the floor, by means of metal mounts at each end. She had not understood its meaning. She would now find out. Her ankles were placed on the bar, and lashed to it. Her hands were held on each side of her, and she could not rise. "No!" she cried. The first instructrix had fetched a supple, springy, flat stick, about a yard long, some two inches in width, and about a quarter of an inch thick. "No, no!" she cried. Then she squirmed, and writhed in misery, bound and held, crying out, weeping, begging for mercy, while the first instructrix, again and again, angrily, struck the bare soles of her exposed, fastened feet, stinging them until they burned like fire.

When the first instructrix had finished she put the stick away in a nearby cabinet but then fetched forth from the same cabinet three long, supple, leather switches, giving one to each of her fellow instructrices, and retaining one for herself.

Lying on her back, no longer held but her ankles still bound to the wooden bar, unable to rise, she looked up, apprehensively, at the switches.

"We have been forgiving, and tolerant, of you," said the first instructrix, "because of your ignorance, and stupidity, but that is now at an end. No longer do you deserve our patience, and lenience."

She looked up from her back, tears in her eyes, questioningly, her ankles still bound to the bar.

"Yes," said one of the instructrices, "in this phase of your training the bastinado, the switch, is authorized."

"*Training*?" she asked.

"Yes, training, little fool," said the third instructrix, not pleasantly.

"In the next phase, and thereafter," said the chief instructrix, "the whip, close chains, torture, anything."

"Will you now attempt to be pleasing?" asked the second instructrix.

"Yes," she said.

"Say it," snapped the second instructrix.

"I will attempt to be pleasing," she wept.

"Fully?" she was asked.

"Yes, yes!" she wept.

"Release her," said the first instructrix.

She drew her legs, painfully, from the bar, the straps untied. "I cannot walk," she moaned.

"Crawl," said the second instructrix.

"Be pleased we are not men," said the third instructrix, "or you would not only walk, but you would dance, dance, frenziedly, and to switches!"

She crawled back to her lessons.

Later in the day she could rise to her feet and walk, awkwardly, painfully.

When it came time to return her to her cell she was muchly returned to normal, and the pain, though still there, as a burning when she put the soles of her feet down, was not excruciating.

"Cross your wrists, before your body," she was told. Her wrists were then tied together, in the center of some fiber, and the two ends of the fiber were then taken behind her, and knotted behind her back, so that her wrists were held pinioned before her, at her waist.

"Now, proud, noble barbarian woman, woman so important on your own world," said the first instructrix, "return to your cell."

No sooner had she turned about, to make her way to the cell, than she cried out in pain for the first instructrix had struck her a sudden, sharp stinging blow across the back of the right calf. Then, laughing, pursuing her, running behind her, taking turns, striking one calf and then the other, the other two joined in the sport, and she fled weeping before them, on burning feet, crying out in misery, in shame, frequently and muchly stung. She ran stumbling, weeping, into her cell, through the opened gate, and even pressed herself desperately, piteously against the opposite wall. They desisted then, untied her, and left, closing the gate behind them, it automatically locking with its closure.

She rubbed her wrists, and hobbled to the metal mirror at the right side of the cell. She regarded the image in the mirror. It revealed less the image of a dignified, mature woman than that of a frightened captive. She put her face closer to the polished surface. Her hair now, she noted, was mostly dark. She stepped back and regarded the figure in the rude mirror. It wore a tunic. How outrageous! Yet she did not think it unattractive. Suddenly she trembled, though not altogether in fear. Doubtless there were dangers on a world such as this. She had considered many possibilities of such, as her instruction had progressed. But now, for the first time, she realized that there might be special dangers on such a world for such as she, for lovely, vulnerable, perhaps even beautiful, creatures such as she saw reflected in the mirror. Might they not, she feared, stand in some special jeopardy. What if, say, they were desired by powerful, mighty men, and she had little doubt there were such men on this world. What might then be their fate on such a world?

Her lessons became somewhat more troubling later. For example, she was taught, in theory at least, how to bathe a man, the oils, the strigil, the sponges, the deferences, the touchings, the beggings, the handling of the towels, the words to be spoken at different times, the final grateful prostration of herself following the honor of having been permitted to bathe him, and such. A block of wood served as a surrogate for the male figure. But, even so, she felt herself frightened, and aroused, tenderly and gently ministering to it, following the instructions of her instructrices.

"You will be better at bathing a man than cooking for him," observed one of the instructrices, wryly.

She also learned how to brush clothing, and clean, soften and polish leather.

The duties she was taught were common to most women of her sort, of whatever variety, but tended to be especially associated with such as served in the towers, in the high cities, in the cylinder cities.

Needless to say there were many other sorts of duties, too, in which women such as she were expected to be proficient, duties, and services, in which, indeed, they were expected to excel. Indeed, these other duties, at least for such as she, were duties commonly regarded as far more interesting and important than less exotic, homelier labors, such as cooking and laundering.

At this point, however, she knew nothing of that further aspect of her instruction, or training.

Her teachers, incidentally, were changed with each phase of her education, so to speak. Some may have had diverse aspects of expertise. Certainly not all of them could speak English. But, she suspects, they were more likely frequently changed in order to preclude the formation of closer associations with her, associations which might lead to friendship, and, consequently, a possible diminution of the professionalism, the rigor, of the instruction.

One might also mention that, from her new, smaller cell, she was occasionally able to see other women, often in custody, sometimes even hooded, in the corridor. Some, with those she could tell, she thought might be in their forties, others, as she had been, in their fifties. She saw at least one woman who must have been in her sixties, and one who seemed pathetically older, frail, unconscious, being gently carried past in the arms of an attendant. She also saw, but turned away immediately, in horror, several younger women in the corridor, perhaps in their teens or twenties, not instructrices. Their hands were tied together behind their backs. They were incredibly beautiful. They were naked. They did not wear anklets. Rather there were narrow metal collars on their necks. One group of such were literally chained together by the neck, and their hands, behind their backs, were not tied, but held in metal cuffs.

"What manner of place is this?" she asked. "Why am I being taught what I am being taught? What are you going to do with me?"

"You have many questions," he said.

"Please!" she begged.

"I have planned two more phases in your treatment," he said.

"Two?" she asked.

"Yes," he said. "Two."

He then lifted his hand, indicating that she was to be removed from his presence. The attendant took her by the left arm, which was bared, as you may remember, and pulled her beside him, from the room. He had never handled her in this way before. She whimpered in protest, but was hurried along.

He soon put her in her cell, and closed its gate.

She turned about, to see him standing there, outside the bars, looking at her. He had not stood there before, and looked at her like that. She backed away, until she was stopped by the back wall of the cell.

On Earth there might have been many ways to respond to such attentions, a sneer, a chilling stare, a look of contempt, a scornful dismissal, a demeaning question, a nasty, caustic word, a haughty, supercilious shrug and a turning away, many ways to respond, and to all of these she had had recourse at one time or another, but here, somehow, she sensed that the entire force of society and an armed state might not stand visibly, menacingly, behind her otherwise meaningless little stare or word. So she stood against the back wall of the cell, frightened, and said nothing to him. After a time he left. She looked at the image in the metal mirror to her right.

She supposed that, perhaps, on this world, women, or at least women such as she, women such as she who was revealed in that mirror, in the tunic, she so interestingly curved, might be looked upon in that way, and with impunity. Perhaps it was acceptable to do so; perhaps it was done without thought, as a matter of course. What of the young, naked women, those whom she had seen sometimes in the corridor, those who had been bound, or cuffed, or chained by the neck, those women, she asked herself, those women, their necks in collars? How could a man not look upon them, she wondered, without feeling interest or desire?

Later a man in green robes entered the cell.

"Injection position," he said.

Immediately she lay down on her right side, drawing her knees up.

Chapter 8

She Is Presented Before Her Master, Following the Third Phase of Her Transformation

"A slave girl," announced the attendant.

She knelt within the yellow circle, on the marble floor, before the curule chair on which he, robed, reclined. Her back was straight, but her head was down. The palms of her hands were on her thighs.

This time there were several individuals in the room other than she, the attendant, and he. There were several men there, in robes and tunics of various cuts and hues, and some women, in a variety of tunics or gowns. The women were all ankleted or collared.

She had heard exclamations of pleasure from the men as she had entered, and knelt. Too, there had been some soft cries, it seemed of admiration, and surprise, from some of the women. She dared not look, but wondered if some of her instructrices might not have been there. She wondered if they were pleased with her, with their work, how she had turned out. She hoped so, fervently. She had learned the importance of pleasing them, her ankleted superiors.

"Lift your head," he said.

She did so, and looked into the eyes of her master.

She wore a tiny slave tunic. It was light, white, and silken. It came high on her thighs. At the left shoulder, where it would be convenient to a right-handed man, there was a disrobing loop. She was, of course, barefoot. The anklet was still on her, as it had been, even since her first world.

He suddenly clapped his hands with pleasure. "Yes!" he said. "She is the same, the same! That is how she was, and now that is how she is!"

She doubted that she had ever been before as what she was now, a barefooted, half-naked slave on an alien world.

Still she did not doubt that she looked now much as she had when she first knew him, he then merely a student, among others, not her master.

"Splendid!" he said.

She wondered if he had, even then, as a student, she feared he had, while she taught, sitting at her desk, behind its modesty screen, or moving before the class, she was sure of it, speculated upon her, stripping her in his mind, considering what she might look like as a female slave, his.

And she now knelt before his chair, on the cold marble, a slave girl, his.

"That is exactly," he said to the assembled throng, "how she was when I first knew her!" He turned to some men in the room who wore green robes. "You have done well with her," he said, "as you have with the others."

They bowed courteously.

He descended from the curule chair, for the first time in their encounters in this room, and walked about her, scrutinizing her, perhaps appraising her. She kept her head up, her back straight, maintaining position. One can be punished terribly for breaking position without permission.

He then, again before her, crouched down before her. "You are twenty-eight again," he whispered to her. "You are the same, the same, again!"

She was silent.

She remembered back, so long ago.

Her hair had been dark and glossy. She had worn it high on her head, in a severe bun. She recalled studying her figure, critically, approvingly, in her apartment, standing before the mirror in brassiere and panties. It was so long ago.

"You are the same," he whispered.

Her hair was now loose, as women such as she must commonly wear it.

She had known that she would be brought before him today.

No longer was she kept in a cell but was housed now in a slave kennel, on the sixth level of an entire wall of such kennels, reached by steel steps and grilled walkways. Her kennel was the same as the others, uniformly so. It was something like four feet by four feet, with a depth of some ten feet. To the right of its small gate, rather as in the cells, there was a mirror of polished metal, a large mirror for the size of the kennel. It occupied a part of the wall to the right, as one faced the gate, extending from the floor of the kennel to its ceiling. It had that location, near the gate, presumably that the light might better reach it.

The kennel was furnished, for amenities, with some loose straw and a small, short, torn, thin, threadbare blanket. It was enough for slaves such as she. Such are seldom spoiled.

After having made certain, as she could, that the attendants were not on the grilled walkways giving access to the tiered kennels, she had removed her tunic and knelt before the polished metal surface at the side.

Her figure now, she was sure, was superior even to what it had been so long ago. In a way this pleased her, but, too, it frightened her because she realized that it made her more desirable, considerably so, and on a world where female desirability was, it seemed, approved and prized. She remembered the young women in the corridor, naked and bound, some chained. She was sure that her figure was superior now even to what it had been so long ago. Perhaps, she thought, this might be due to some subtle, benign, ameliorative effect of her treatment. But, more likely perhaps, it had to do with her diet, that diet imposed upon her, and, presumably, the variety of exercises she had recently been taught, and in the zealous, stressful performance of which she was closely supervised. She heard a step on the steel ladder outside, some yards below her kennel. Quickly she slipped into the tunic again. She lay down, her legs drawn up, very closely together, pretending to sleep. Through half-closed eyes, she saw the attendant pass. When he had gone, she rose up again to her knees. She then regarded herself again, now in the tunic. She straightened her body, and shrugged. She was not displeased with the slave she saw. One who knew women, she thought, as these men seem to, would have little difficulty, she in such a tunic, in conjecturing her most intimate and delicate lineaments.

Then she had lain down to sleep.

Tomorrow she knew she was to be presented before her master.

* * * *

"Yes," he whispered. "You are now the same, the same."

She did not break position.

He then stood up and, approvingly regarding her, stepped backward a pace, and then turned and ascended the dais, and resumed his place in the curule chair.

It seemed he could scarcely bear to take his eyes from her.

Could he like me, she wondered suddenly, frightened.

He turned to one of the men near him, a tall fellow in white robes trimmed with gold, the dress robes, she had learned, of the Merchants. "What do you think of her?" he asked.

"A pretty little piece of collar-meat," he said. "A standard property-girl. Typical flesh-loot. There are thousands like her in the markets. She is meaningless."

"I remember her from long ago," said the young man.

"Perhaps she is special then in some way to you," said his interlocutor.

"No," said the young man, "except insofar as her flanks are of some interest."

She understood little of their exchange. Some of the expressions seemed clear enough, but she did not, truly, register them in their full import, as they applied to her. It was rather as though she heard them, but would not understand them.

In particular she was puzzled by, and vaguely alarmed by, the reference to markets.

So I am of no concern to him, she thought, except insofar as my flanks might be of some interest! But then, suddenly, she feared it was true. Indeed, of what other interest could she, or such as she, on this world, be to any man? Again she remembered the bound, naked beauties in the corridor. Here, on this world, she feared that men were the masters and would simply, as they wished, have their way with women, doing as they pleased with them, as is the wont of masters; she feared that everything would be on their terms, on the terms of the men, on the terms of the masters, fully, precisely.

Surely, she thought, there must be some way to trick them out of their power! But she feared that these men were not so stupid.

No, in no particle, manner or facet, in no way, would they give up their power.

They were not stupid.

She dared not break position.

"How do your lessons proceed?" he inquired.

"Well, I hope," she said, adding softly, "—Master."

He smiled. She saw that he was pleased to hear that word on her lips, addressed to him. Never before had she used this form of address to him, save, of course, in her dreams and thoughts. She felt warm, beautiful, stirred, helpless, so much more aware then of the reality of her enslavement. How weak he is, she suddenly thought, angrily, that he would wish to be so addressed! Is he so pathetic, she thought. Does he really need that, she thought. Is he so weak? But then she realized that these were merely the automatistic, defensive, frightened, programmed responses, the mindless, inculcated reflexes, of her culture's conditioning program, with its reductive, leveling, negativistic agenda, the outcome of centuries of resentment, denial, hatred, sacrifice, and fear. It was only weak men, she now understood, who would fear to accept, wield, and relish the mastery, the birthright of an ancient biological heritage. How she would hate and despise men who were too weak for the mastery, who would fearfully seek to avoid its privileges, powers and responsibilities! No, he, and others like him, were far from weak! They were strong, much stronger than the timid, boring weaklings so endemic, like bacteria, on her former world. He, as others on this world, was strong enough, mighty enough, to expect, require, and enforce the deference due them, to require and enforce the submission of the principle of femininity, in all its wondrous softness, desirability and beauty, to a more severe, more dangerous principle, that of their masculinity.

On this world men were the masters, at least of women such as she. That was the simplicity, and the terror, of it.

"Does that word cost you much?" he asked.

"No, Master," she whispered.

"Slave," he sneered.

"Yes, Master," she whispered, putting her head down. She felt that this was true, but that there was nothing wrong with it, that this was nothing to be ashamed of, certainly not if that was what one truly was, if one were a slave, truly.

Some people undoubtedly were, she thought, and she had learned, in the last few days, that she was one of them.

She was thrilled to address this word to him, and, too, to other males.

She had learned, incidentally, that she must address all free men as 'Master' and all free women, though she had not yet encountered one on this world, as 'Mistress'.

She was uneasy at the thought of free women. How would they regard her, she only a slave?

Her training, in this last period, that in which she had come to understand that she was most perfectly and naturally a female slave, had been quite different, on the whole, from her former lessons, save of course, for the continuing instruction in the language. She had been taught how to kneel, and move, and lie down, and remove her clothing, and present herself for binding, and enter and leave rooms, and greet masters, many such things. She had also learned various forms of deference and obeisance. She could now dress and undress a man. She could do it with her teeth, with her hands tied behind her. She had been taught uses for various aspects of her body, for example, her tongue and hair. She had learned how to move on all fours, and fetch a whip in her teeth. She had learned how to beg to be beaten, but she trusted earnestly that she would be spared that for which she was trained to beg. She could now lick and kiss a whip in such a way that it would drive a man wild. She had learned how to put chains on herself from which, once closed, she could not free herself. She had learned how, kneeling before a man, to take food from his hand. She had learned how to eat from pans on the floor, forbidden to use her hands. She was taught how to lie provocatively on furs, on the floor, at the foot of a master's couch, chained there by the neck to the slave ring. She was taught how to beg prettily to be permitted to ascend the couch itself, to serve. She was taught, even, how to bring sandals to a man, head down, on all fours, carrying them in her teeth. She had learned which sandal was to be placed first on which foot, and in what order they were to be tied, and the kisses, expressing her gratitude that she was permitted to perform this service.

"What is your name?" he asked.

She looked up, startled. It was a test, of course.

"Whatever Master pleases," she said. "I have not yet been named. I am now only a nameless slave."

He leaned back.

She caught her breath a little. She wondered if she had had a name since the time, on her former world, when she had been ankleted. From one point of view, of course, though she must be forgiven for not understanding this at the time, she had lacked a name for months before she had even seen the young man again, after a hiatus of so many years, at the opera. It had been taken from her when a certain document, in its turn, among others, had been signed, and rudely stamped. From that time forth then, from at least one point of view, she had been a nameless slave, though naturally, at the time, quite unaware of this.

She wonders now, as she writes this, if you, reading this, if you are there, reading this, if you might unwittingly be now as she was then. Perhaps you, similarly unbeknownst to yourself, have been scouted, and selected. Perhaps you were noted at work, say, in an office, or shopping in a supermarket, or on the street, or driving. Perhaps you should not have worn those shorts, or bared your midriff, or worn your hair in that fashion, or worn that svelte, mannish suit, or moved in such a brusque manner, or spoken sharply to the cab driver. Perhaps it was a small thing. Perhaps in the cocktail lounge, in your short, lovely outfit, with the chiffon, you should not have been so animated, so charming, should not have worn those three strands of pearls about your neck, so closely, so much like a slave collar. Perhaps it was merely your appearance, suddenly striking someone with a telling import, nothing you could have anticipated, or prevented, or how you moved, or how you spoke a given word, or phrase. Who knows what is meaningful to them? Perhaps you were noted with interest, and jottings made. Perhaps you were filmed, perhaps more than once, say, at different times of day, in different lights and such, and the films reviewed in secret screening rooms. And so, perhaps, unbeknownst to yourself, you are now as I was then, one designated for harvesting, and for transportation, to an alien world. Perhaps you are now, as I was then, now, at this very moment, no more than a nameless slave.

She wondered if she were now to be named. The name, of course, like an anklet, or a collar, would simply be put on her. It would be merely a slave name, hers by the decision of the master, a name subject to whim or caprice, subject to change at any time. Yet it would be her name. It would be her name as much as any such name, for example, one put on a pig or dog.

But he did not name her.

She remained, for the time, a nameless slave.

She wondered why there were so many people in the room.

He spoke to the assembled throng. He spoke in the language she had been learning and he did so fluently. Kneeling, she struggled to follow him. She was sure that she figured somehow in what he was saying. Sometimes, as he spoke, one or another of the men, or women, looked at her and laughed. This made her uneasy. He had a slight accent in the language. She thought that she would, even if she had not known him, have been able to conjecture with plausibility that his native tongue might be English. To be sure, there were many different accents in the house, and even, as far as she could tell, among those who natively spoke the language she had been learning. Doubtless they came from different areas, or walks of life, or such.

His remarks, to her uneasiness, had been greeted with much amusement.

When he finished, all eyes turned upon her. She was now the focus of attention. She felt very vulnerable, in the tiny garment, all she wore, save for the anklet, kneeling on the marble floor, before the dais. She trembled. Surely it was more common, she thought, for slaves to be simply kneeling to one side, inconspicuously, unobtrusively, waiting to serve.

"Did you follow what I said?" he asked her, in English.

"A little," she said, in her new language.

"I told them," he said, "of the pathological world from which you derive. I told them how you were once a teacher. I could not explain to them very clearly how you had, when I first knew you, been a proud, young, new Ph.D., with a degree in gender studies. That is not an easy concept to convey in Gorean."

Gorean, she thought, of course! That is the name of the language. But there are other languages, as well, doubtless, spoken on this world.

"I am afraid their concept of gender studies is not yours. Their concept of gender studies would have more to do with the care, feeding and training of slave girls, how one puts them through their paces, and such, but I did give them some idea of the matter, of your certification, its ridiculously pretended importance, the eccentric, warped, and politically laden subject matter, such things. And now, you are going to perform for us." He clapped his hands, sharply. "Tutina!" he called.

She looked up, wildly. *Perform*? Tutina? She, here, on this world? Yet it was only that she had not seen her here. She had no reason for supposing that she was not on this world, and, indeed, many reasons for supposing that she would be here. Surely she was too desirable to have been left behind. And, after all, had her own master not once "bought her"?

She was suddenly dismayed. Then her master must have at least two women!

She heard sharp commands in a female voice, coming from behind her and to her left. They were in the language she had now learned was called Gorean. For an instant they seemed just inarticulate, angry noises to her. Why could they not have been uttered in English? Then, suddenly, after a moment's delay, she understood them.

"Here, slave girl, here, to me, hurry!"

Swiftly she leaped to her feet, turned, and ran to Tutina, who stood near the entrance to the room. Even had she not been trained she might have fallen to her knees before that stern, looming figure.

It was indeed Tutina! But it was a Tutina far more formidable, and terrifying, than the one she had scorned on Earth. Her figure was even more striking than on Earth. Doubtless she, too, perhaps after some unavoidable leniencies or lapses on Earth, had, on this world, been subjected to the discipline of a prescribed diet and a regimen of exercises. Tutina was more fully clad than she, but rather as she herself had been in her former presentation before the young man whom she had recently learned owned her, in a sleeveless tunic which came just above the knees. Tutina, as she, was ankleted. Tutina's blond hair was bound back with a woolen ribbon, or fillet, which went completely about the head, across the brow, and was knotted behind the back of the head, two ends then dangling downward, each about six inches in length. It was a talmit, indicating some authority among slaves, rather as "first girl." In her right hand she carried a long switch. The young Ph.D. in gender studies feared that implement. She had felt it frequently enough from impatient instructrices. Tutina's eyes flashed like blue flame. With a gesture she indicated the opened door, and her terrified charge quickly rose to her feet and went through the door, which Tutina closed behind them.

Chapter 9

She Performs Before Her Master, And Concludes the Performance Suitably

There were cries of interest, and pleasure, when she reappeared in the marbled audience chamber. She stood just within the doorway, timidly, uncertainly.

"How oddly she is garbed," whispered one of the women.

She was prodded forward by Tutina's switch, until she stood within the yellow circle. It did not seem appropriate, somehow, to kneel, as she was dressed.

How strange she felt, to be dressed in this manner, in this place.

She felt that, dressed as she was, it might be permissible to speak, but she did not dare to do so.

"You are going to perform," said her master.

"How?" she whispered.

"To be sure," he said, "you cannot play the kalika, nor do you know the dances of the yearning, begging slave girl."

She began to suspect how, on this world, slaves might perform for men, how men might use them for their entertainment.

"That is how," said the young man to those gathered about him, "she appeared in her classroom, when I was a student, and she a teacher."

"So strangely garbed?" inquired a man.

"The garb is not so strange for her world," said the young man, "but the intent of her particular garb is to act as the banner of a disposition. It is proclamatory; it speaks a message. Its intent is to present a formal, tidy, cool, businesslike, professional, rather severe image, not simply one demanded by a conformist, socially prescribed ideology, one in accord with politically recommended proprieties, but, beyond that, one she felt it important, interestingly, to impose upon herself. The garb bespeaks her pretensions, of course, certain delusions, and such. But, too, in a way it bespeaks her fear. It is a defensive facade, just like the ideology she adopts for a similar purpose."

"Her fear?" inquired a fellow in blue and yellow robes. At that time she did not know the significance of blue and yellow robes.

"Her fear of her own sexuality, which she is terrified to recognize, and insists on hiding."

"Yet the excitement of her body is not altogether concealed," said the fellow in blue and yellow robes, appraisingly.

"She is at war with herself," said the young man. "She has deeply ambivalent feelings about her own body, its beauty and needs, her own emotions, the true meaning of her sex."

"That war can be ended here," smiled a man in yellow robes, those of the Builders.

She felt herself again the center of attention, as she stood in the circle.

When Tutina had closed the door behind them she had ordered her to her knees before her, near three packages on the floor. Her kneeling young charge, to her amazement, noted that these packages, sealed with tape, bore names and slogans with which she was familiar on Earth. She herself was familiar with these stores, and had shopped in them several times. She remembered the aisles, the counters, the crowds. Attentive to the injunctions placed upon her in connection with this narrative the names of these stores are omitted. Certainly they would be immediately recognized, at least by many familiar with a certain city.

The young charge looked up at Tutina, questioningly.

Tutina raised her switch menacingly, and the young charge put down her head, quickly, and cringed, but Tutina did not strike her.

"With moneys given to me by the master," said Tutina, "I made these purchases, according to his instructions."

Her young charge put out her hands and, with the tips of her fingers, touched the crinkling paper of one of the packages.

Then the young charge felt Tutina's switch beneath her chin, lifting it. She looked into Tutina's blue eyes.

"You are not now sitting on a chair, are you?" asked Tutina.

"No, Mistress," said her charge. She addressed Tutina as "Mistress" because Tutina, obviously, was in authority over her. She had learned, in the last few days, to address her instructrices similarly.

Rank, distance and hierarchy are ingredient in Gorean social arrangements. The intricate stratification of society tends to produce social stability. The myth that all are equal when obviously they are not tends to ferment unrest. Each desires to climb the invisible ladder he claims does not exist. In Gorean society, with its emphasis on locality and neighborhood, with its diverse Home Stones, each with its own history and traditions, with its many castes and subcastes, each with its acknowledged privileges and rights, and obligations, respected by all, political upheavals, social disruptions, are not only rare, but to most Goreans almost incomprehensible. There is little cause for such things, little interest in them, little place for them. They just do not fit. In Gorean society there is no nameless, faceless, anonymous, ponderous, swarming many ruled by a secret few. Too richly formed, too proud, too self-respecting, too intricately structured, too much like nature herself, is Gorean society for that. Too, there are the codes, and honor.

"It was because of you," said Tutina, "that I was beaten."

Her charge remembered her outburst, on a far world, it seemed long ago now, objecting to the fact, it seemed so strange at the time, that a frightened woman in a white gown had been permitted to sit on a chair.

"I was beaten!" hissed Tutina.

"I am sorry, Mistress," whispered her charge.

She did not doubt but what Tutina, for that lapse, had been put under discipline. She did not doubt but what the young man was fully capable of taking a whip to a woman who did not please him.

"And how I was forced to serve you, and you acting so superior to me," exclaimed Tutina angrily, "you treating me with such contempt, and you then only an ignorant, nameless slave!"

"Forgive me!" begged the frightened, kneeling charge. "I did not know, Mistress!"

"I now wear the talmit," said Tutina, indicating the fillet on her brow, binding back her long, luxurious blond hair. "So fear, stupid little slut. Know, ankleted little slave bitch, that upon the least provocation you will feel my switch, richly!"

"Yes, Mistress," wept her charge, cringing, putting her head down. Like any low girl, she feared the wearer of the talmit.

"Now," said Tutina, seemingly somewhat mollified, "remove your tunic. Open the packages. Dress."

* * * *

And so she stood now in the circle, before the curule chair.

The garments she wore were really muchly as they had been, so many years ago.

She wore a black, jacketed, skirted suit, with a cool, front-buttoned, rather severe, rather mannish white blouse, buttoned high about her neck. Her hair was drawn back severely, bound tight, and bunned, at the back of her head. She wore black, figured stockings, rather decorative, and shiny, black pumps, with a narrow two-inch heel.

"One thing is missing," said the young man in the curule chair. He motioned her forward.

Into her hand he placed two small, plain, lovely golden loops, bracelets.

"Put them on," he told her.

She slipped them on her left wrist. He knew, of course, that that was where they went. She did not wish to be beaten.

"Return to the circle," he said, "and, hands at your sides, turn slowly for us."

She did as she was commanded, and then again faced him, and the others.

She knew herself displayed.

She wondered if a nude slave girl on an auction block could feel more acutely conscious of her exhibition.

She did not know these people, even these sorts of people. How different they were from what she knew, in their naturalness, in their laughter and assurances, in their colorful robes and miens, all this so different from the tepidities, apathies, lethargies, and gray conformities of her old world! She had not known such people could exist. To her they were alien, not only linguistically but, more importantly, more frighteningly, culturally. This is what human beings can be, she thought, so different from those of Earth! She was not on her own world. And she was in a very different culture, one with different laws, customs, and values. Things were so unfamiliar. What could she, given no choice, brought helplessly here, be to these people?

What could one such as she be on this world?

She feared she knew.

How strange it is, she thought, to be fully clothed, according to one's culture, so decorously, even primly, and yet, here, in a different culture, in an identical garmenture, being presented, being put on view, to feel so exposed, to feel oneself an eccentric object of curiosity.

She would have preferred her tunic, however brief. Then she would at least have better fitted in with her surroundings; she would then have felt less anomalous, less conspicuous, more congruent with her lovely milieu. There were others of her status in the room, and surely they, at least, were appropriately garmented, were accorded the simple, natural garmentures, so brief, so clinging, so revealing, which seemed to be culturally prescribed for those of their station, which station she had no doubt was hers, as well. They were attractively, and suitably, garbed, at least for what they were.

So why not she?

Why not she?

Too, she knew, and this did not displease her, at all, that she was quite attractive, perhaps even extremely so, in the tunic. That had been evident from the appraisals of guards.

In their eyes she was clearly a female.

She had no doubt about that.

And one of great interest.

That, too, had been clear.

Sometimes the guards had bound her, with colorful cords, sometimes in exotic fashions, and had then ordered her to free herself, but she had been unable to do so. But how their eyes had glinted upon her, as she had twisted, and reared up, and fell back, and squirmed and writhed, in her unsuccessful attempts to elude her constraints! To see her so before them, bound so helplessly, so predictably and absurdly futile in her commanded struggles, had given them much pleasure. Once she had intended to defy them, to remain quite still, but she was then switched, and so, again, she had addressed herself, now stung and weeping, desperately to efforts she now realized were foredoomed.

She recalled the words of the young man, on Earth, now her master on Gor, that he had thought she would be very pretty in such cords, later, when she would be luscious, helplessly bound in them.

Certainly she had been helpless in them, in those so simple, so soft, so attractive, so colorful bonds.

Am I, she asked herself, "luscious"?

She well remembered the eyes of the guards.

Perhaps, she thought.

And she was not displeased.

What female, and particularly one such as she, on this world, would not wish to be attractive, even luscious?

She shuddered.

She recalled that the young man on Earth, now her master, had suggested to her that her very life might depend on such things.

How often in history, she thought, it had been only a woman's beauty which stood between herself and the sword. How grateful she might be then when she felt her hands roped behind her and a leash put on her neck!

The other girls in the room, those such as she, were in their tunics!

Why was she not then in her tunic?

Long ago she had ceased to feel such a garmenture was inexcusable and insufferably improper, that it was scandalously outrageous. To be sure, she supposed in some sense it was still all these things, and by intent, but now, too, it seemed appropriate, delicious, provocative, maddeningly exciting, sexually stimulating to the wearer and doubtless, too, to the bold and appraising onlooker beneath whose gaze its lovely occupant found herself without recourse. But even on Earth she had, she was now aware, viewed such garmentures rather ambivalently, perhaps even hypocritically, viewing them, or pretending to view them, on the one hand with the prescribed indignation and rage, and, on the other, wondering curiously, and excitedly, what she herself might look like, so clad. And she wondered, too, if some of the cumbersomely clad free women in the room, several even veiled, might not envy the others, their sisters, the freedom of their simple garmentures. And, too, what woman, in her heart, does not desire for her beauty to be displayed, does not desire to be seen, and understood, and openly relished, as the special and exquisite treasure she is? Are we not all forgivably vain? In any event, it was such as men would have for them. They were dressed as men would have them dressed, such as they, if they were to be permitted clothing. But why then not she? Most were kneeling, some not. They did not wear anklets. About their throats, rather, closely fitting, locked, were flat, slender metal bands, slave collars.

She envied them their collars. Not all animals, you see, are collared. The collar is for special animals. It was a visible statement that they were worth something. They had been found of interest; they had been found worthy of being purchased and owned. The collar, thus, in its way, is a visible acknowledgment of value. A terrible insult, on this world, to a free woman, is to tell her she is not worth a collar. To be sure, how would one know that, if one had not seen her? But she herself had only an anklet, the role of which, it seems, was more notational than anything else, little more than a way of keeping track of her in this house, whatever sort of house it might be.

Why did they not let her, too, kneel, or stand, inconspicuously aside, scarcely noticed, deferent, ready to be summoned, at so little as a snapping of the fingers of the free?

"Girl!" snapped her master.

She looked up, frightened.

"Now," he said, "you will perform. How is your Gorean?"

"Not good enough, Master!" she said.

"You will use it," he said. "There are very few present who can understand English."

"What am I to do?" she asked.

"We are your students, we are your class," he informed her. "You will lecture to us. Tell us all about men and women, and social artifacts, and roles, and such things, how conventional everything is, and political and capricious, and how the human species, alone of all the other species, has no nature, and how genetics is meaningless, and biology false, and endocrinology irrelevant, and so on, and how anything can be anything, and everything is nothing, and nothing is everything, and how the true is false, and the false, true, and such. Raise our consciousnesses, indoctrinate us, convert us."

She was silent, in consternation.

He had spoken to her in English, of course.

"Those garments," said the fellow in the blue and yellow robes, "do not really conceal her figure. Surely her loveliness is detectable within them."

"As I am sure she knew," said the young man.

"The things on her feet are pretty," said a fellow.

"How can she keep her hair up like that?" asked another.

"She has a very pretty face," said another.

"She has a small, trim, excellent figure," said another.

The young man lifted his hand for silence. These brief remarks just preceding had all been in Gorean, of course. They had been spoken casually, with no particular intent in mind that she should understand them. But, of course, by now her Gorean was sufficient to follow them. She heard them with mixed feelings, and apprehensions. It is a strange thing to hear oneself referred to in such a fashion, so objectively, so casually. Did they not know she was a person? Did they think that she was an object, an animal on display?

"Begin," said the young man.

Hesitantly, frightened, she began.

"As I told you," warned the young man in English.

She moaned. He would have nothing less than that she attempt to honestly and forthrightly make clear to those in the room what she had taught for many years, what her colleagues in the movement expected of her, what she had been commended for, the views on which her standing, reputation and prestige had been founded, the sorts of things she had abundantly published, in journals created specifically to accommodate and broadcast such views, the ideology to which she had, in effect, given her life.

Occasionally he helped her with a word in Gorean; occasionally he prompted her, reminding her of this or that, for clearly he wanted her to express her position as forcibly and plausibly as the subject matter might admit.

He asked her upon occasion to move about. She did so, now acutely conscious of her figure within her clothing. Never on Earth had she been so much aware of the movements of her body within her garments, or how they rested upon it, or clung about it. But here she was much aware of such things. How frighteningly, how vulnerably soft and beautiful it was, shielded within her garments, she sensed. Twice he asked her to gesture, in such a way that he might hear the tiny sound of the two bracelets striking against one another, as though so accidentally. That sound was very meaningful to her, particularly under the circumstances, and she did not doubt but what it was similarly meaningful to him.

"Thank you for the lecture, slave girl," he said, when she was done. "Now remove your garments."

She first removed the jacket, and put it on the floor beside her. She then removed her pumps, and put them side by side, beside the jacket.

She then regarded him.

At a small gesture, she continued.

She unbuttoned the blouse, beginning with the high collar, and then slipped it from her shoulders.

More than one of the men present struck their left shoulders with the flat of their right hand.

She looked at the young man.

"They are expressing approval," he informed her, in English.

She wore a white brassiere, which hooked in the back, and had two narrow shoulder straps.

She then unfastened the black skirt, and dropped it about her ankles, then stepped away from it, and lifted it to the side.

Interest was expressed in the garter belt. She freed the stockings from it, unfastened it, put it to the side, and then, sitting on the marbled floor, rolled the stockings down, and removed them.

As she removed the stockings, there could be no mistaking the loveliness of her thighs, the sweet bend of her legs at the knees, the turn of her calves, these lovelinesses each, slowly, in turn, being bared.

She then, again, stood. She was clad now in only brassiere and panties, except, of course, for two bracelets, and a locked ring, on her left ankle.

"Loosen your hair," he said.

She did so, and shook it loose. It was very beautiful, dark brown, and glossy. She swept it back behind her with two hands, with a lovely gesture.

There were expressions of pleasure, of admiration, from several of those in the room.

She was clearly a lovely slave.

She went to slip the two golden loops from her left wrist, but the young man shook his head, almost imperceptibly, negatively.

She stiffened, but obeyed.

Those it seemed would be left her, at least for the time.

She slipped the shoulder straps of the brassiere over her arms, where they hung for a moment, and then she pulled the brassiere down.

"Excellent," said the fellow in the blue and yellow robes.

She blushed.

Even had she not known the word, she would have understood him, from his tone, and expression, only too well.

Some of the men struck their left shoulders. Some of the women present uttered small sounds of admiration.

She realized suddenly that that of which they approved, her body, was not hers, that her body, and, indeed, she herself, was another's property.

She turned the brassiere about, until the hooks were before her, at her belly.

She then unhooked it and dropped it with her other garments.

Suddenly tears sprang to her eyes and she looked piteously to the young man in the curule chair, that he might leave her some sop to her modesty, that he would not be merciless with her, not publicly, not before this throng.

But his eyes were stern.

Then she stood bared before him, a naked slave, save for two loops of gold on her left wrist, and an anklet of steel.

"Now," said he to her, "my lovely young instructor with your Ph.D. in gender studies, you may crawl to me, naked, on your belly."

She went to all fours, and then lowered herself to her belly. Then, inch by inch, she approached the dais, ascended the steps, and was then before him.

"More closely," he said, "and spread your hair over my feet."

She brought her hair forward, and put her head at his sandals, her hair about his feet.

"This, now," he said, "is truly you. This is how I wanted you, and how you wanted to be, even then, so long ago, at my feet, a slave."

She looked up at him tears in her eyes.

He removed the two golden loops from her wrist. She now wore only the steel anklet.

"Lick and kiss my feet, slave," he said.

"Yes, Master," she said.

"And thus," said he, "you are the living refutation of your own ideology."

"Yes," she whispered, "—Master."

After a time, to her consternation, he pulled his feet away from her soft tongue and lips, her tears and her hair.

"Guard," said he, "take this slave away, and see that the last phase of her treatment is concluded."

"Surely there is no more, Master!" she cried.

"Oh yes," he said, menacingly, "I have something very special in store for you, slave girl."

She was dragged naked from the room.

Outside the door she, still held, was permitted to bend down and seize up her tiny tunic, that which she had left in this place, when she had donned the other garments. The paper wrappings, the tape, the cardboard boxes, were still there, where she had left them.

She was then drawn naked, rudely, through the corridors, her upper left arm, hurting her, in the powerful grip of the hurrying guard. She clutched her tiny tunic in her right hand, but could not put it on. She was taken through the corridors much as she had seen other naked beauties, save that she was not bound or chained.

Faces, some of them frightened, of young women, peered at her from behind bars.

In a short time she was in her kennel area and was urged up the steel ladder until she reached her tier, at which point she was forced to crawl painfully on all fours over the steel grille work until she reached her kennel.

In a moment she was locked within.

She tried, hysterically, to thrust the anklet from her, but could not do so.

She began to weep.

She turned about, kneeling, and clutched the bars, crying.

After a time she drew on her tiny tunic, and moved some straw about in the kennel. She then lay down, wrapping herself, as she could, in the short, thin blanket.

She wept.

He had had the fullness of his vengeance on her, surely. It seemed that she could not have been more thoroughly reduced and humiliated.

And yet she knew that she had been thrilled to be at his feet, a helpless, subdued, submitting, dominated slave.

It was what she was, she realized, and what she most profoundly wanted to be, and had always wanted to be, a slave.

What did he have in mind for her?

She did not know.

All she knew was that he would do what he wished with her, and that she was his slave.

Chapter 10

She Is Presented Before Her Master, Following the Fourth and Final Phase of Her Transformation

She wept, trying to hold the guard's wrist, where it was fastened so deeply, so cruelly, in her hair, she bent over, her head at his hip, hurried forth, into the room, in a common Gorean leading position.

She was then thrown to her belly within the yellow circle, before the curule chair. Hastily, fearfully, she struggled to her knees, lifted her arms, tried to smooth and straighten her hair, and brushed it back, behind her shoulders, and knelt, before her master.

Though he was the same, clearly to her, now, he seemed older, more mature, certainly now older than she, more frightening to her.

"Are you in a suitable position, for what you have been told you are?" he inquired.

She knelt in the beautiful position that had been taught her, back on her heels, back straight, head up, palms of the hands on her thighs.

He continued to regard her.

Tears sprang to her eyes.

She widened her knees. It was the last, small adjustment that had been taught to her, and that most recently. It was a position appropriate for her type of slave, the Gorean pleasure slave.

He continued to regard her.

Sobbing, she widened her knees still further before him. She wore the same tiny tunic she had been given before, except that now it had been slit at the sides, from the hem on both sides, to both the left and right hip, so that a flash of hip might be bared as she moved, and so that, when she knelt, it might fall between her thighs, as it now did. And so she knelt before her master, in the one of the common positions of the Gorean pleasure slave, her knees spread widely, she vulnerably opened then, save for the tiny veil of cloth, before him. The same position, of course, is commonly used by naked slaves.

She looked up at him, tears burning in her eyes.

"Has Tutina been nice to you?" he asked.

She shuddered. It was a test. "She has treated me precisely as I have deserved, Master," she said.

He smiled. His smile told her how clever he understood her to be. Could she conceal nothing from him?

No love was lost between herself and Tutina. She had hated Tutina from the first, even from the moment she had first seen her at the opera, so long ago, probably because she had seemed simple, stupid and so beautiful, but, more likely, as she was, in fact, neither simple nor stupid, because she was beautiful and was with the young man. Too, Tutina now held authority over her. Tutina wore the talmit, and was to her and, indeed, to several others, it seemed, "first girl." And that authority was exercised over her charges, and particularly over her, it seemed, with a malicious pleasure. She, as the others, had learned to fear her switch.

Tutina, who derived from Earth, and, indeed, had once a been a native of her own nation, and city, was abundantly, natively, fluent in English. But Tutina would speak only Gorean to her. In this way Tutina, who was fluent in that language, put her, at this time, at a considerable disadvantage. Her young charge must then tensely strain to understand, struggling to apprehend the subtleties of an unfamiliar tongue, trying desperately not to miss a word. How uncertain, frightened, and ignorant her young charge so often felt. How cleverly Tutina had her then at her mercy.

But, as Tutina perhaps had not realized, she was thereby rapidly improving her charge's Gorean.

The young charge was jealous of Tutina, of her power, her beauty, and her standing closer to the master. The young charge would have preferred to be her master's only slave, lying contentedly, curled, licking, at his feet. But he had at least two slaves, and perhaps more. She did not know. So she knew why she feared, and resented, and hated Tutina. What she did not understand was why Tutina should seem to hate her so. After all, what had the beauteous Tutina to fear from her? What had Tutina to fear from such as she, a low slave?

Then his gaze became harder.

"Have you seen yourself, as you are now," he asked, "in the large mirrors in the training room?"

"Yes," she said.

Those mirrors were as fine as any she had known on Earth.

"Naked?"

"Yes," she said, putting her head down. She had been forced to look, stunned, taken aback, by the incredible, youthful, vulnerable loveliness she had seen there.

"How old are you, or would you say," he asked, "looking upon yourself as you are now?"

"I do not know," she whispered.

"I would say," he said, "that you are something like eighteen or nineteen years of age."

She nodded. She could remember photographs of herself at that age, or near that age, and what she had seen in the mirror was the same, or much the same, save, of course, for the nudity, and, she suspected, some present superiority of figure, that from the serums, or perhaps the diet and exercise. The background reflected in the mirror had been quite different, of course, that of a training room on an alien world, with its painted lines on the floor, its rings, and whips and bars, and such, from the background of the photographs.

"Have you had your slave wine?" he asked.

"Yes," she said. She shuddered. She had been knelt and held, her head forced back, and cruelly held so by the hair, and her mouth forced open, and the spike of the wooden funnel forced between her teeth. Then the wretched, foul stuff was poured into mouth, her nostrils at the same time being pinched tightly shut. When she had to breathe she must imbibe the slave wine. Afterwards her hands were tied behind her, that she might not induce its vulgar emission.

"You cannot now conceive," he told her. "If a releaser, as one speaks of it, is later administered, which is a quite sweet, flavorful drink I am told, you will again be able to conceive. Conception in slaves, of course, is closely supervised. They are crossed, mated, and bred only as, and precisely as, masters desire."

She nodded.

Masters must be careful of their stock.

"Sometimes, in rural areas," he said, "there is a breeding festival, and slaves from miles about, hooded and bound, carefully selected, of course, on leashes behind wagons, in crates, and so on, are brought to the breeding grounds.

He could *breed* me, she thought.

"It is a time of much feasting and merriment," he said, "much like a fair."

He could literally *breed* me, she thought. I wonder if he will *breed* me.

She looked at him. Before he had been as he was now, much as he had been as a student, at least physically, but she had been, say, in her late twenties. She knew now, of course, given their last encounter, that he could own, dominate and master her, even were he as he was now, and she older, she in her late twenties. The principle of her femininity had been helpless before, and overwhelmed by, the principle of his masculinity. She would have obediently writhed at his feet and obeyed him in all things. He would, even then, have been the total and categorical owner of, and master of, her womanhood. She had sensed that even in the classroom, so long ago. She knew how she would have been, on any terms he might have set, helplessly his. But now she was only, say, eighteen or nineteen, and he, surely, somewhere in his early twenties. Now he was older, and even more mature, than she. She was now no more than a girl before him.

Could he like me, she wondered.

Has he plans to keep me for himself?

I love him, she thought.

"How do your lessons proceed?" he asked.

"I trust, well," she said. "But there is something I do not understand."

"What is that?" he asked.

"I sense that there are many things I do not know, that there are many things that I am not being taught."

"That is true," he said.

"I am still very naive, very ignorant," she said.

"True," he said.

"Would I not be more valuable if I knew them?" she asked.

"Certainly," he said.

"Why am I not taught them then?" she asked, puzzled.

"Think," he said.

"In order that I remain naive and ignorant, in order that I remain negligible, in order that I remain meaningless, that I remain nothing, that I not be more valuable?" she asked.

"Do you like your present accommodations?" he inquired.

"Doubtless they are in accord with the directions of Master," she said.

"Certainly," he said.

"Master is cruel to his slave," she said.

"You could have been put in close chains, or in a slave box, or a slave pit," he said.

Her new accommodations were a tiny slave cage. It was some four feet, by four feet by four feet, formed of closely set metal bars, a half inch or so in thickness, except for the floor, which was of metal. She could not stretch out her body fully within it. The bars were somewhat narrow, one supposes, with that half inch or so in thickness, but they were fully and perfectly adequate for holding a female. It was not unlike the sort used by many hunters in the field, in their base camp, for the temporary confinement of their catches. There was no straw in the cage, but she had been permitted to retain her blanket.

"Each time," she said, "you have treated me more cruelly, granted me fewer privileges, been harsher with me!"

"The better to accustom you to your bondage," said he, "slave girl."

"Do you not like me, Master?" she asked.

She looked at him, trying to read in his visage some glimmering of emotion, some small sign of his feelings.

He had brought her to this world, he had remembered her, he had made her his slave.

Surely then he must have some feeling for her.

I am his, I love him, she thought.

How could he have known that I wanted to be owned, and ravished, and mastered? Why else would he have ankleted me, and imposed his will upon me? She realized, as many professedly sharing her ideology, how foolishly naive it was, how little account it took of the biotruths of human existence. Men, if they were not crippled, were ambitious, jealous and possessive. She knew that her sex, by nature, belonged to them. They did not wish to relate to their women as contractual associates, but as masters. They wanted to own them. Men truly loved only that which they owned, that which was fully theirs. They treasured their possessions, their dogs, their tools, their books, their homes, their cars, their women. How can what does not belong to a man wholly be treasured by him? When his heat is upon him does he wish to fence and banter with a contractual associate? Nay, he wishes in covetous, exultant lust to bind and master a slave! She wondered in how many marriages, in the secrecy of their homes, wives were the slaves of their husbands. But here on Gor, she thought, slavery is explicit, acknowledged, sanctified in tradition and law, and here men are the masters, at least of women such as she. And the women, she thought, how many there must be, as she, who longed to be owned, who longed to obey and serve, who would give all, all their beauty and devotion, all their helpless, surrendering love, to the man they longed to meet, who would put them at his feet, and make them his, their master.

She looked up at him.

He looked much as he had before, robed, and such, save that now, as he reclined in the curule chair, across his knees there lay a whip.

She spread her knees a bit more widely, as she feared that she had, inadvertently, let them close a bit.

She was deeply stirred, so kneeling before him, so clad, with no nether shielding, with her knees so spread.

She needed no one to tell her that bondage was sexually arousing to a woman. Frigidity she knew was not acceptable in a female slave. Inertness was forbidden to them. Passivity was not tolerated. Inhibitions were not permitted. If necessary, such culturally inculcated impediments to the flames of love could be lashed from their bodies. They would be given no choice but to become their natural, hot, animal, yielding female selves. They would have absolutely no choice. They must become what they were, the female to the male, the slave to the master.

"May I speak?" she asked.

"Yes," he said.

It is not uncommon for a slave girl to ask permission to speak. She is, after all, a slave. To be sure, there is a great deal of variation in such matters, among masters and slaves. Delicate considerations are sometimes involved, and much depends on a given context, the occasion, the location, who is present and such. The slave, particularly after a cuffing or two, tends to develop a great sensitivity to such things. Some slaves are permitted a liberty of speech by their masters which is not obviously inferior to that enjoyed by a free woman, until a stern look puts them to their knees, reminding them of what they are. And it is a rare slave who has not, upon occasion, her master's patience at an end, been put upon her knees, facing a wall, gagged, her hands tied behind her back, or perhaps, bound hand and foot, her mouth taped shut, thrown naked on a bed. Too, the Master may gag his slave "by his will," and then she must serve in silence.

"I do not understand fully what has been done to me," she said.

"In what way?" he asked.

"Am I—immortal?" she asked.

"Certainly not," he said. "You are quite mortal. I might, if I wished, for example, feed you to sleen, or cast you to leech plants."

She did not believe that the animals called "sleen" existed, thinking them part of the mythology of the world, and she had not heard of "leech plants," but the tenor of his remarks was sufficiently clear.

"You have been returned to a former condition of your body, and have been stabilized at that point," he said. "That is what has been done to you."

"Will I stay like this?" she asked.

"Yes," he said, "unless your nose and ears are cut off, or such," he said.

She looked at him with horror.

"You will try to be a good little slave, won't you?" he asked.

"Yes, Master!" she said. "Master," she said.

"Yes?" he said.

"Why did you make me this age?"

She was surely, as one would think, were one to look upon her, something like eighteen years of age, perhaps nineteen, at most.

"Why do you think?" he asked.

She resolved to speak boldly before him.

Her belly flamed before him. He was her master.

"I think, Master," she said, "that you cared for me, that you remembered me, that you had never forgotten me, that you came for me, that you carried me away by force, that you made me your slave because you wanted me, because you desired me, and loved me. And that you have made me this age in order that you would now be more mature than I, that I might now be no more than a girl to your man, a most fitting object for your chains."

"No," he said. "I brought you here because I hate you, because I despise you, because I scorn you, because I hold you in utter contempt. That is why I have brought you here and made you a slave."

"No!" she cried.

"But you said that you found my flanks of interest!" she said.

"That is the only thing about you which could be of the least interest," said he, "slave."

She buried her face in her hands, weeping.

"Knees," he said.

Quickly she spread her knees again.

"But there are two reasons I have had you made the age you are," he said. "First, I was curious to know what you would have looked like at this age. Now I know, and I acknowledge that you are a pretty little slave, a well-curved, youthful, little slave. The second reason I have had you made the age you are is because you will now be, though you are admittedly pretty, a meaningless, negligible little slave to almost anyone. You will not bring a high price in markets. You will be poor goods. You will be purchased, presumably, by low, ignorant fellows, for small coins, who will put you to repetitive servile labors. Most slave girls are as in their twenties. Even they will look down upon you, as no more than a pretty girl, one who need not be taken seriously, one unimportant and largely worthless."

She sobbed, holding her face in her hands, not looking at him.

"This, too, is the reason that I have not had you taught more, the reason I have not had you more thoroughly trained. I want you to be largely ignorant and valueless. And thus I will cast you into the terrors and realities of a world which will seem utterly strange to you."

"You hate me?" she asked.

"Stand," said he. "Disrobe."

She stood, her eyes burning, tears streaming down her face. She reached to the disrobing loop at the left shoulder and tugged it, dropping the garment about her ankles. She stepped from it, it lying then beside her, a small atoll of cloth on a calm marble sea. She stood before him, weeping, but erect, gracefully, as she had been taught. She knew how to stand before a man.

He took the whip, which had lain across his knees, and cast it the floor before her.

She looked down at it.

He then stood, rising from the curule chair. He put aside his ornate robes, as of state or office. He stood then above her on the dais, in a simple, belted brown tunic.

She had not realized how large he was, or exactly in this way, as he was now revealed before her, or how formidable he was, how fine, how supple and muscular he was, how sturdy were his legs, how long and powerful his arms. He had large hands. She had realized before, of course, that he was large and strong, but now she gasped, looking upon him. She had not seen him like this before, revealed in this way, in a tunic. It was a simple garment, but how revealingly, how casually, how splendidly it displayed the mighty frame it housed. She was terribly uneasy then, stirred profoundly, these thoughts disturbing her deeply, by the sturdy legs, the width of the shoulders, the strength of the arms. He was disturbingly physical and she, to her horror, found herself thrilled to the quick by the very sight of his body. How wonderful to wear the chains of such a man, she thought. How wonderful it would be to lie embonded in his arms, will-less, ravished, yielding helplessly. She looked at him, and trembled. She had not seen him this way before. She saw him now as Gorean, a scion of this world, and herself as what only such as she could be on such a world, a slave.

"Fetch the whip," he said.

She went to her hands and knees, and, putting down her head, picked the whip up, delicately, in her teeth.

She looked up at him, the whip between her teeth.

He motioned that she should bring it to him.

Slowly, head down, she crawled to him, and then, after crawling up the steps of the dais, she lifted her head to him.

He took the whip from her and held it before her. Obediently, delicately, she began to lick and kiss the whip. There were the gentle kisses, some prolonged, some as light and quick as the shiftings of sunlight and shadow among stirring leaves, some as bright and unexpected as the pattering of momentary, shimmering drops of rain, some as tender as the falling of the petal of a flower, and the other kisses, the swirling, begging, meaningful kisses, the kisses almost beside themselves, uncontrollable, and the petitionary kisses, reluctant to draw away from the shaft; and there were the movements of the tongue, the tiny dartings, the teasings, the supplications, the tastings, the long, and the short, and the circular caresses, the placatory caresses, the caresses of yearning, and begging and total submission; and she moved her hair about the whip, and thrust the side of her face lovingly against it, rubbing against it, and then looked up, tears in her eyes, at her master.

Angrily he pulled the whip away from her.

"Position!" said he.

She backed down the steps of the dais, crawling, and then went, crawling backward, to where her garment lay on the floor and then knelt beside it, in position, looking at him.

Is he afraid, she asked herself.

He has nothing to fear from me. I am only a slave, his, and I love him with all my heart.

"You do well with the whip," he snarled.

"Thank you, Master," she said.

Some have suggested that there is more to the kissing of the whip, and many such things on this world, than may be readily visible on the surface, that such things, in their way, are meaningful, that they, in their way, have symbolic dimensions, that they, in their way, express truths, relationships, acknowledgments, and such. I leave such speculations to the reader.

Her belly flamed before him.

How grateful she was to him, that he had permitted her to kiss his whip.

Without symbols, she wondered, would it not be difficult to live on more than the surface of our being.

He walked about her, whip in hand. She had no doubt that she was being appraised for her value as a naked slave.

She held position, beautifully.

"Common position of obeisance," he said.

Immediately, kneeling, she put her head to the floor, the palms of her hands on the floor, beside her head. In this position the knees are closed. It is a position commonly assumed by a slave when a man enters a room. To be sure, this varies from city to city. In some cities all that is required is the common kneeling position, instantly assumed. In other cities, a complete bellying, instantly assumed, is required. Such things may differ, of course, from master to master. The girl is, after all, his.

"You look well in a position of obeisance," he said.

She was silent.

She was frightened.

She felt the coils of the whip lightly touch her left side, at the waist, and move lightly on her back.

Is he going to have me, she wondered. Oh, please, not like this! Surely not like this! Do not take my virginity from me in this fashion!

She remained in the position of obeisance. He stepped away from her, a little. She sensed he was standing before her.

"I think I will beat you," he said. She sensed that the blade of the whip was shaken free.

"Please do not beat me, Master," she begged.

She sensed now that he was behind her.

"Please, Master," she said. "Please do not beat me, Master!"

"I think I will name you," he said. "I have thought of names, 'Filth', 'Feces', 'Fecal Matter', such names."

She moaned.

"But I think I will call you 'Ellen'," he said. "That is a pretty name for a pretty slave."

"That is a beautiful name, Master!" she breathed, her head down, touching the floor.

"You are Ellen," he said.

"Have I been named?" she asked, frightened.

"Yes," he said. "What is your name?"

"'Ellen'," she said.

And so that is the name by which we may now refer to her, for it is her name. The other name, that which she bore long ago, has been concealed for the purposes of this narrative. And such things would matter little anyway. Such things are now gone, meaningless; they are irrelevant to, and far from, her current reality, that of a slave, that of the slave girl, Ellen.

"Thank you for giving me such a beautiful name, Master," she said, not raising her head.

"It might improve your price a little," he said.

"Surely Master has no intention of selling his slave," she said. Surely not after having given her such a beautiful name, she thought. He must like me, she thought. He has given me such a beautiful name!

"I had thought, as long ago as the class room," he said, "that 'Ellen' would make a lovely name for a slave, and, as I watched you, moving before the class, I thought of you as a slave, for that is what you are, and were, you know, and I thought of you, too, as one who might well be named 'Ellen'. Indeed, I decided then that if I were one day to own you, be your master, that that is what your name would be, 'Ellen'. What is your name?"

"'Ellen', Master," she whispered.

"To be sure," he said, "aside from the fact that 'Ellen' is a suitable name for a meaningless, pretty little slave like yourself, that name, as many similar names, has other connotations, connotations and suggestions of which I am aware but you in all likelihood are not. And I welcome those other connotations and suggestions. They fit in nicely with my plans for you."

"Master?" she asked.

"Do you enjoy participating in a conversation while you are in a position of obeisance?" he asked.

"It is as Master has decided," she said.

"'Ellen', you see," he said, "is an Earth-girl name. An Earth-girl name. And such names are regarded here, on this world, as slave names, and names fit for the lowliest and most worthless slaves. Goreans who know of Earth, and many now do, hold it in great contempt, and enjoy having its women as their slaves. Sometimes an Earth-girl name is given to a Gorean girl to reduce, demean and punish her. An Earth-girl's bondage on Gor is often a particularly uncompromising and harsh one."

"Why?" she asked.

"I am not sure," he said. "Perhaps it is because they are regarded as being pretentious. Perhaps it is because they are blamed for having collaborated in the reduction and degradation of the males of Earth."

He was still behind her, with the whip.

"Yet," he said, "interestingly, they are often prized and sought in the slave markets. Do you know why that is?"

"No, Master."

"Because they make superb slaves," he said. "In their world they have been denied their womanhood. They have been kept in a sexual desert. They have been starved for sex. On Gor, in a collar, and under the whip, meeting true men, many for the first time, they find themselves taken in hand, and taught their womanhood, at the feet of a master. They yield themselves up in joy, choicelessly. They become the helpless, obedient, zealous, flaming slaves of their masters."

"'Tutina' is not an Earth-girl name, is it?" she asked.

"No," he said, "it is Gorean. If she displeases me sometime, however, I might give her an Earth-girl name. That would terrify her. Can you imagine her fear, bearing such a name on this world?"

Still the slave kneeling head down in the position of obeisance was not displeased, even so, to have been given the name 'Ellen'.

Besides, what had she to fear from Gorean males? Did she not know who had brought her to this world, doubtless to have her here, as his slave?

I love him, she thought. I love him so.

It had begun, of course, with anger and dismay, irritation, consternation, fascination, and then fear, when he had cuffed her about intellectually in the classroom, when he had indifferently and decisively refuted her again and again, when he had had her reeling from blows of logic and fact, until she had wanted to kneel before him and acknowledge him as her master. Many times she had dreamed that he had put her to his pleasure, mercilessly, publicly. And her fear, and fascination, had gradually turned to love and the desire to submit herself selflessly to his will. He had proved to her that he was her master. She loved him. She suspected she had always loved him. And now she was his slave, truly, on an alien world! It must be clearly understood, of course, that the relationship of master and slave, in its legal aspects, is totally indifferent to, and completely independent of, matters such as affection, caring, or love. Many masters, for example, never see the slaves they own, who may be employed in distant shops or fields, and, of course, the slaves may never see the masters who own them. So emotional relationships, of any sort, are inessential to, and immaterial to, the institution in question. What concern had the law, in all its power and majesty, with such matters? Whether he loved her or he did not, whether she loved him or she did not, did not matter. Their institutional standing was clear. They stood related as master and slave. He owned her, and she was owned. He could do with her as he wished. And so, too, of course, could any master into whose possession she might come, whose property she might find herself.

"I think I will beat you," he said.

"Please, no!" she said.

The thought suddenly came to her, however, taking her off guard, to her surprise, perhaps to her horror, that she wanted to be whipped.

She wanted that attention, the meaningfulness of that pain. Would that not show that she was of some interest or importance to her master, that he would put the whip to her? Would that not be reassuring, that he correct her behavior, that he teach her the limits that she must not exceed, that he might take a moment now and then, whether she required it or not, to remind her, with some strokes of the leather, that she was a slave, that she was owned.

As a slave she knew she was subject to such things. They could be done to her.

Too, I deserve to be whipped, she thought. I have richly deserved many times to be whipped. Doubtless thousands of times. But no man has whipped me. There are so many things for which I should have been punished, but never was. On Earth, she thought, a woman is never punished, no matter what she has done, no matter how cruel and nasty, how vicious and petty, she has been, no matter how much hurt she has brought about, no matter how much injury she has inflicted, no matter how much misery and pain she has caused, no matter how many lives she may have ruined or destroyed. But here, on this world, she suspected, it might be different, at least for women such as I. Here, I have learned, she thought, I might be whipped for dropping a plate, or not having responded instantly to a command. For such tiny things I could be put as a slave under the leather.

I am your slave, she thought. Prove to me that you are my master. Whip me. The slave may be beaten by her master. Let me learn that I am a slave. Beat me, that I may truly know I am a slave!

He stood behind her, not speaking.

"Master?" she asked.

"To your belly," he said.

She was then prone, before him.

"I had thought, often," he said, "of having you before me as you are, a naked slave at my feet.

"The war is over, for you," he said.

"War?" she asked.

"Do not those of your ideology dare to use that sacred, holy, terrible word, that word for nature's last and fiercest arbiter, that maker and unmaker of states, that creator and destroyer of cultures, singing songs of armies, and blood and steel, that ultimate and terrifying tribunal, with all the marches, the charges and rides, and the sacrifices, all the horror, all the triumph, all the glory and the shame, the tenderness and cruelty, the best and the worst, the highest and the lowest, the grandest and the most despicable, the most loved and most hated, that moment when beasts and gods look into mirrors and each sees the other, do not those of your ideology dare to use that word, that name for the most fearsome and terrible of all institutions, for its trivial, pretentious, absolutely safe, risk-free, puerile machinations, for your petty political threats, your jockeyings and maneuverings, for your sneakings about, and trickery, and burrowings from within to deprive an entire sex of its birthright?

"Well," said he, "if it is a war, it is one that is over for you. You have lost. You have been conquered. You have been taken and in an ancient, time-honored tradition of true war you have become the slave of the victor. You are spoils, pretty girl, understand that, and to the victor belong the spoils!

"Fear, feminist," said he.

"I am not a feminist!" she cried. "Such things are behind me!"

"They are more behind you than you can possibly now understand," he said. "Where are you?"

"I am on the planet Gor!" she cried.

"Know then that you are on the planet Gor, slave girl," said he.

Then the whip began to rain blows upon her.

She screamed and scratched at the marble, and turned from her stomach to her side, and back, and tried to fend the blows, weeping.

"So," said he, pausing, "the little feminist beneath the whip."

"No!" she cried. "I am not a feminist. I am a slave, your slave. Please do not strike me further, Master! Please be merciful to your slave!"

Then, again, as she screamed, and cried, and writhed before him, he put the leather upon her.

"Know yourself owned," he snarled.

"Yes, Master, yes, Master!" she wept.

She was now a beaten slave. She had no doubts now that she was owned. She had been beaten by her master.

He threw the whip to one side.

"The beating was nothing," he said, angrily. "It was not the five-bladed Gorean slave lash. You were not even tied at a ring."

She looked up at him in horror, from her side, bright stripes upon her body.

"Were you given permission to break position?" he asked.

Instantly she went again to her belly, being then as she had been before.

"Do you think you will soon beg to give pleasures to a man?" he inquired.

She put her cheek down to the marble, sobbing.

"I have made you the age you are," he snarled, "so that you will be no more than a bit of fluff in the markets."

He looked down upon her.

The anklet was on her.

"To be sure," he said, "a bit of pretty fluff."

"Guard!" he called.

The guard came forward, from near the door, where he had kept his post.

The young man, he in the brown tunic, he who had wielded the whip, the girl's master, indicated the slave at his feet. "This is Ellen," he said. "Her anklet may now be removed. But first, of course, see that she is branded and collared."

The guard reached down and then lifted the youthful slave to her feet. She seemed dazed, and in disbelief. He permitted her to bend down and retrieve her small tunic, but not to put it on. Then he indicated she should precede him from the room, and she did so, uncertainly, stumbling sometimes, sobbing, returning to her cage.

Chapter 11

A Supper Is Served, In an Unusual Apartment; She Is Spoken With by Her Master

"What a pretty little thing she is!" laughed the woman. "Is she to serve us?"

"Yes," said Mirus.

"What monsters you men are!" laughed the woman.

Ellen, crouching down, set forth the plates of *hors d'oeuvres* and the tiny glasses of sherry on the coffee table before her master, Mirus, and his guests, a man and a woman. Tutina sat nearby, in an arm chair, with purple upholstery.

It had been explained to Ellen how she was to serve, how to speak, if spoken to, and how to conduct herself throughout the evening. In the adjoining room there were two guards, with their own supper. That room gave access, as well, through a short corridor, to the kitchen. A serving cart was used to bring the food from the kitchen, through the corridor and adjoining room, into the apartment.

Ellen had been quite startled to see the apartment, entering it for the first time, for it might well have been one on Earth, in the house or mansion of some leisured, comfortable, wealthy individual. Surely it was tastefully and elegantly appointed, and the quality of the rug, the furnishings, and such, was, without being obtrusive, obvious. The oddity of it was that it was on Gor. She had been reminded, entering it for the first time, of pictures in large, glossy magazines, the sort claimedly and pretentiously devoted to the arts of gracious living, those magazines intended to supply apparently desperately desired and much-needed instruction to the ignorant affluent, informing them in what ways they might most appropriately expend their abundant resources, what should be the nature and location of their residences, how they were to be landscaped and furnished, what automobiles they should buy, the type of music and artwork which should be in evidence, what books and how many, how their pantries were to be stocked, the arrangements of tennis courts and pools, many such things. Doubtless, she supposed, serving, there must be some reason this room has been designed as it has. She wondered if it were some subtle joke, some irony. But, if it was, it had apparently been lost on the woman in the room whom she did not know. Perhaps that woman was used to such surroundings, and took them for granted, not really seeing them any longer. Generally one does not see, really see, one's familiar surroundings. One takes them so much for granted. Perhaps, on the whole, that is just as well. But sometimes she supposed that even husbands and wives, on her old world, did not really see one another any longer, either, but simply took one another for granted, much like the walls, the furniture. Such things would be muchly different, of course, she supposed, if their relationship were to be changed, radically, for example, if the husband were to make his wife, at least in the secrecy of his own home, an obvious, explicit slave. Is that not what many vociferous proclaimers of her former ideology maintained that wives were, anyway, slaves? How silly that was, what infantile semantic slight of hand! Is there no better way to abolish the family and surrender children to the centrally designed, and centrally directed, conditioning programs of the state, the state they expected to put to their own purposes, using it, with its legal monopoly on violence and coercion, to promote their own self-serving agendas? So saying, they seemed to believe that they had manufactured an argument against marriage, refuted matrimony with a lie. But, she wondered, suppose men believed that lie. It did not follow from that, that if they should take it seriously, that they would immediately forgo their genetically conditioned proprietary inclinations, selected for in millions of years of primate evolution, and promptly terminate long-term, intimate relationships with desirable women and abolish families. Rather, might they not choose to accept that view of the matter, the feminist view, so to speak, and rearrange the institutions of society accordingly?

Mirus, her master, indicated that she might withdraw, and so she stood to one side. For some reason she was not to kneel.

The woman at the coffee table bantered lightly with the two men, her companion and Mirus. Tutina sat to one side, smiling. Ellen made certain she did not meet the eyes of Tutina. She stood to one side, keeping her head down. If she were to be summoned, a word would suffice.

But suppose the husband did make the wife, within their marriage, his slave, explicitly. Then, surely, their relationship would have changed, considerably. No longer might they not really see one another. No longer could they overlook one another, so to speak. No longer could they take one another for granted. The slave cannot take the master for granted because he owns her, and she must be diligent in his service, and be desperate to please him. And the master does not take the slave for granted for he now owns her; she has now become to him a source of delight and pleasure. And if she prove momentarily troublesome she may be disciplined as the slave she is. Let her beg naked to enter his bed and serve his pleasure. And if he does seem to take her for granted, it is only that she may zealously, piteously increase her efforts to be even more pleasing.

She supposed, serving, that such an arrangement would not merely freshen a stale marriage, not simply renew a flagging relationship, but that it would alter it utterly, transform it beyond recognition, catapult it into hitherto unsuspected, astonishing dimensions, replacing the wearying familiarities and tepid placidities of accustomed rounds and routines with a new, moving, exciting, dramatic, startling reality, replacing them with an altogether new life, one incontrovertibly meaningful, as the participants suddenly found themselves the inhabitants of a newer, deeper, more natural world, one of intense emotion and unbelievable feelings, one of perfectly clear identities and relationships, one of abject obedience and strict command, one of absolute submissiveness and uncompromising mastery.

She wondered what might be the reactions of her former feminist colleagues if society were to take seriously their effusive, tiresome, repetitive, propagandistic allegations pertaining to matrimony as slavery, and the general position of women in society as one of being held in bondage, and decide to make them true. What would they think if they were to suddenly find it necessary to be licensed to men, or simply owned outright, as women?

Mirus, her master, suggested that the group rise and go to table.

The table, long, with sparkling linen, polished silver, candles and flowers, was in the same room.

Mirus indicated that Ellen might ready herself to pour wine at the table.

'Mirus' is an extremely common male name on Gor. It is doubtless the name of thousands of individuals. Indeed, that consideration might have figured in its selection. It was the Gorean name, so to speak, of her master. His Earth name is not to be included in this narrative, no more than that name which had once been Ellen's on Earth. The 'us' ending is the most common ending for a male name on Gor. The most common ending for a Gorean female name is 'a'. There are, of course, numerous exceptions.

Ellen poured the wine, beginning with the woman, and then Tutina, and then the man she did not know, and then her master. The order had been prescribed. The woman, surely, did not know Tutina's status. The woman had speculated that the bandage on Tutina's left ankle must be the result of some earlier injury, and Tutina, smiling, did not disabuse her of this plausible surmise.

The new woman, whom Ellen did not know, had glanced at her at various times during the evening, curious, interested, but Ellen had kept her head down, serving silently, deferentially.

After a time Mirus indicated that Ellen might serve the soup, which, she began to do, ladling it from a large tureen on a serving cart, filling the bowls one by one, and placing them on the table, in the order prescribed.

Once, on her former world, in an officelike room, Ellen had relished being served by the hated Tutina, coffee and pastries, and had, in her manner, subtly and abundantly exploited the situation in such a way as to make abundantly clear to Tutina the servile nature of the task, and her own implicit superiority to her.

Now, of course, Ellen must suffer before Tutina, whom she must struggle to please with her serving.

And Tutina was not easily pleased.

Ellen was in misery, but she had no alternative but to serve with all the perfection of which she was capable. She was in the presence of her master. Too, later she knew, she might have to face the switch of Tutina. She feared that even a drop might be spilled upon the tablecloth. The subtleties between Ellen and Tutina doubtless escaped the attention of the guests, though, one supposes, from his amused expression, not that of their master.

Masters are often amused by such things, the small rivalries, altercations, frictions and tensenesses among their properties.

As the meal continued Ellen continued to serve the various courses, bringing them to the table.

At one point her master indicated the coffee table, and said, "You may clear, Ellen."

"Yes, Sir," she said, and went to clear the glasses, the plates and such, left earlier from the *hors d'oeuvres* and the sherry, from the coffee table. She referred to him as 'Sir', as she had been told.

She supposed that the room might have been arranged, as it was, in order that the new woman would be pleased, and feel more comfortable, more at home. It was certainly not Gorean in style, appointments, furnishings, and such. Gorean decor varies from latitude to latitude, from city to city, and home to home, but, in general, it tends to simplicity and openness, this presumably a heritage deriving from some remote tradition.

Ellen, quietly, deferentially, soon returned to the larger table, with its sparkling linen and elegant appointments, and, as appropriate, resumed her duties there, continuing to attend unobtrusively to the various courses. It was a lovely supper, surely, in its stateliness, gentility and sophistication, and might have been pleasantly, congenially served in almost any affluent, elegant home on her former world.

When spoken to she would quietly and respectfully respond with titles she had been told were to be used, 'Sir' and 'Ma'am'. She used 'Ma'am' also to Tutina.

She had now come to the fourth meat course.

It might be mentioned that the diners' clothing was elegantly congruent with their surroundings. The two men wore tuxedos. The two women wore evening gowns. It was apparently a celebration of some sort, perhaps one at the conclusion of some piece of business brought to a successful conclusion, or some piece of work that was now finished, and with which they might be well satisfied.

In all the appointments and furnishings, in all the garmentures of the diners, and such, in all that seemed so elegant, so nicely arranged, so well fitted together, there was only one oddity, or anomaly, in the room.

"You men are monsters," laughed the new woman, she unknown to Ellen.

"How is that" smiled her benign companion.

"Come now!" she laughed. "I have been silent long enough!"

Ellen's master indicated that she should continue serving.

"No, no," said the woman. "Your name is 'Ellen'?"

"Yes, Ma'am," said Ellen.

"Stop what you are doing," said the woman, "and come here, and stand beside me."

Ellen looked to her master, who indicated she should comply, and so, in a moment she had come about the table, and was standing beside the chair of the new woman, she unknown to her.

The one oddity, or anomaly, in the room was Ellen, for she was naked. She wore only a narrow band on her neck, a slave collar.

"You're very pretty, Ellen," said the woman.

"Thank you, Ma'am," said Ellen.

"Why have you not been given clothing?" she asked.

"I am to serve as I am, Ma'am," said Ellen, head down. She fought to hold back tears. Why, indeed, wondered Ellen, had her master had her serve in this fashion, naked, before strangers, before his guests, one of them a woman? Surely this could not be a common thing. Then she feared that it might be a common thing, or that it would be a common thing, at least *for her.* Can he hate me so much, she asked herself. Does it please him, she wondered, to treat me so ignominiously, to so unmitigatedly subjugate me, to so completely and absolutely humiliate me in this fashion, forcing me to serve as a naked slave? Then the thought came to her that of course it pleased him, and richly pleased him. He would derive from it much pleasure. She remembered their past. Yes, he would indeed enjoy having her serve guests as his naked slave! And then she had a sense of the powers and pleasures of the master.

But then she wondered, and this frightened her even more. Perhaps her master had had her serve so for no particular reason that had to do with her personally. At least in the one case, she would have some importance to him. At least in that case, she would have his attention, and interest. But perhaps he had merely had her serve naked in order to show her off, to display her, much as any lovely object one owns might be displayed. And if that were the case there was nothing particularly personal in his decision. Perhaps she was in no way special to him, but was now only another of perhaps several properties.

But then she thought, no, he wanted me here, me, exactly. He is doing this to me, personally. He wants me to feel the power and might of his will, and what he can have of me, what he can, if he wishes, make me do.

How he must hate me, she thought.

But I would rather have him hate me than ignore me, she thought. I love him. I love him!

"At least you have been given a piece of jewelry," said the woman. "It sets you off nicely. It is extremely attractive. It is a collar of some sort, is it not?"

"Yes, Ma'am," said Ellen.

"Bend down, here, near me," said the woman, "so that I may have a closer look."

Ellen complied, and the woman, then turned about in her chair, began to examine the flat, close-fitting, narrow band on her neck.

"Lower," said the woman.

"Yes, Ma'am," said Ellen.

Ellen felt her hair, at the back of her neck, brushed aside.

"There is a lock here," said the woman, surprised.

"Yes," said Mirus.

"Can you remove the collar, Ellen?" asked the woman.

"She cannot remove it," said Mirus. "To be sure, it may be removed by means of the key, or by means of appropriate tools."

The woman indicated that Ellen might straighten up, but did not dismiss her. Accordingly, Ellen must remain where she was, beside her.

"Shame on you, Mirus," smiled the woman, "for not giving this pretty little thing clothing, for making her serve us naked."

"Do not concern yourself," said Mirus.

"And for putting her in a locked collar!"

"It is a slave collar," said Mirus.

"A slave collar?" asked the woman.

"Yes," said Mirus. "She is a slave girl."

"You have female slavery on Gor?" said the woman.

"And male slavery," said her companion, lifting his wine glass to her, as though toasting her.

"At least you are consistent!" she laughed.

"Male slaves," said Mirus, "are less in evidence. It is not unusual for them to be kept chained, and put to heavy labors, in the fields, the quarries, the galleys, such places."

"Female slaves, on the other hand, like our pretty little Ellen here," said her companion, "are usually set to less arduous labors, though perhaps to tasks commonly more repetitive and servile. They are useful for domestic labors. Too, of course, they can be used with great frequency for purposes which comport with their beauty."

"You can't be serious," said the woman.

"They are slave girls," said her companion.

"They must do as they are told?" she asked.

"Yes," said her companion, "absolutely, and instantly."

"Are you a female slave, Ellen?" asked the woman.

"Yes, Ma'am," said Ellen.

"Then you must obey in all things, absolutely and instantly?"

"Yes, Ma'am," said Ellen.

"I thought that slaves were branded," said the woman to Mirus.

"Not all," said Mirus, "though it is recommended by Merchant Law. Turn your left thigh to our guest, Ellen. Look high, just under the hip.

"She is branded!" said the woman.

"Yes," said Mirus.

"What a beautiful mark!" said the woman.

"It is the most common brand for a female slave on Gor," said Mirus. "It is the cursive kef. 'Kef' is the first letter in the Gorean expression 'kajira', which means 'slave girl'."

"How beautifully it sets her off," said the woman.

"It is recognized throughout Gor," said Mirus. "It instantly, anywhere on this world, identifies its wearer as a female slave."

So, thought Ellen, I have been given a common brand, that appropriate for any low girl! So that is how he thinks of me! That is how he rates me! But it is beautiful! And it is doubtless, if it is indeed the most common brand, worn by thousands, at least, of girls on this world. A common brand! But, of course, she thought, that is exactly the brand he would see to it that I would have!

He is that sort of master!

Ellen recalled that the first words she had been taught on Gor were 'La kajira'—'I am a slave girl.' She had not understood at the time what they meant. How she had cried out with terror and misery when she had learned! It had occurred in the lesson where she was learning to bring a switch to a man in her teeth. She had had, of course, little doubt as to her nature and condition before that, but it had never been made so simply, so explicitly, clear to her. Perhaps it had been best left unsaid? Perhaps she was only being trained to be some sort of intimate servant? But surely that seemed unlikely, that the young man would have accorded her so exalted a status as "servant." Not as his eyes had feasted upon her! Perhaps it was all a joke, or a dream? But then she heard the word, explicitly, and realized that *slave* was what she was, that that was now her absolute and incontrovertible identity, and that this identity, mercilessly imposed upon her, had behind it the full force of law.

It was interesting, she thought, that these words had been required of her so early, so soon after her arrival on Gor. Even then, it seemed, despite her reputation, her professionalism, her credentials, her achievements, her years, even then, it seemed, they had thought of her as no more than a slave girl.

So, thought Ellen, not all slaves are branded. But she supposed that most were, doubtless the overwhelming majority of them. Certainly in her case, it was easy to note, indeed, one had but to look in the mirror, that her master had not seen fit to exempt her from that apparently optional mercantile and social convenience, from bearing, it burned nicely into her thigh, that lovely, small, simple token of her condition. To be sure, it has its effects on the slave, as well. It impresses upon her that she *is a slave,* no more than a marked property, and this understanding profoundly affects her concept of herself, that she is only, *but exactly,* slave, giving it, perhaps to her terror and misery, structure, identity, depth, substance and meaning. She is no longer something vague, uncertain, confused, free-floating, unanchored, intangible, a nothing, a troubled, unhappy cipher, humanly meaningless, something without purpose, without definition, without direction. She is now something, and very precisely so. It informs her sense of her own body, its richness, vulnerability and beauty; it affects her thoughts, her feelings, her needs, her emotions, her entire existence. She now knows herself, in the very depths of her heart, something—*slave.*

How routinely she had been branded and collared!

To be sure, he had waited until he had had his fill of amusement, or vengeance, exploiting her, humiliating her, commanding her, exhibiting her before his guests, having her perform before them.

Then she had been routinely branded and collared.

Is it so obvious, she had asked herself, that I am a slave, that I should be a slave?

But on a world such as this what could a woman such as I be but a slave?

Is that not the purpose for which women such as I are brought to this world, to be the helpless, rightless slaves of absolute and sovereign masters?

But had he not, apart from such things, aside from all such considerations, such general things, simply looked upon me long ago, personally, individually, uniquely, and seen that I was a slave, and should be a slave?

Had he conjectured me then, I wonder, stripped, perhaps bound helplessly, hand and foot, lying before him, at his feet, his?

Certainly there had been little ceremony about it. It was rather as though it were to be expected, as though it were something to be taken for granted, something obvious, something to be accomplished in the normal course of things, at least with one such as she. She had been taken to a room, where she had been stripped and had had her hands braceleted behind her; she had then been placed in the rack, in which her left leg had been held immobile. The marking itself took only a few moments. While she was gasping, and sobbing, and crying, shuddering, trying to comprehend the enormity of what had been done to her, the collar had been put on her neck, and locked. The anklet was then removed. It was apparently no longer needed. Her tunic had then been put in her mouth and she had been returned, bent over, in leading position, a guard's hand in her hair, to her cage. In the hall a girl laughed and said, "You are now no different from us!" Another said, "See the one who was the pretentious little Ubara, now only another marked slut!" "Are you humbled now, Collar Meat?" inquired another. "Put the little Ubara up for sale!" said another. "She is well ready!" "Beat her and throw her to a master," called another. "Mind them not," called another. "You are exquisite!" "The sleek little beast has been well marked," said another. "It is high time," laughed another." "Why did they wait?" asked another. "Who knows?" "Do not question masters," said another. "They do as they wish!" "You have a lovely brand!" called another. "Do I, Master?" begged Ellen. "Yes," he said. "You are now no different from us," cried another. "See the collar! See the collar!" laughed another. "More collar meat!" cried another. "For the masters!" added another. "See the collar!" "How nicely it fits!" "Slip it, slut!" "Oh, you cannot, can you?" moaned another in mock sympathy. "Poor kajira!" "It looks well on you, little Ubara!" "It looks nice on you!" "Get used to collars, Earth slut! You will doubtless wear dozens!" "Your collar is pretty," said another, "but not so pretty as mine!" "Master?" asked Ellen. "No," said the guard. "Yours is quite as pretty, perhaps more so." Ellen could not even feel the collar on her neck, but she turned her head, and moved it, as she could, the hand so tight in her hair, to feel it. It was there. Her thigh still stung, but that would pass in a day or two. "How beautiful she is," said a girl, from within a cell. "She should bring a high price," commented another. "No," said a third, "she is too young!" "And she is too stupid and ignorant," said another. "She is from Earth, no more than a little barbarian!" "But she is pretty!" said another. "A very pretty girl!" "Men will prefer a woman," said another. "She is a woman," said another, "and men will find her delicious." "She will writhe well beneath their whips," said another. "See yourself, see yourself!" called another. "See yourself as you are now, pretentious little Earth slut!" "Kajira! Kajira!" called another. "May I see, Master? May I see, Master?" she had begged. "No," he had said. So she must wait. The bracelets would not be removed until the next morning. At her first opportunity, the next day, she hurried to her training room, to take advantage of the mirrors there. And she beheld in one of the great mirrors—as she gasped, as she stood there, stunned, even disbelievingly—a startlingly beautiful young female slave. The Gorean culture, with its penchant for naturalness and beauty, and with skills doubtless honed in slave houses over generations, had learned well how to dress and adorn its lovely chattels, so natural, and essential, and beautiful a part of its rich and complex world. There would be no mistake about such things. She regarded herself in the mirror, taken aback, almost in awe. Could it be she? It was she, she realized, it was! It could be no other! It was she! How the collar enhanced her beauty, in a thousand ways, aesthetically and psychologically, and how delicately, unmistakably, and beautifully, too, was her status, condition, and nature made clear, fixedly and absolutely, by the tiny, tasteful mark placed in her body, in her thigh, just beneath the hip, a site recommended by Merchant Law, a mark proclaiming her the most exciting and beautiful of women, *kajira*.

And so Ellen was now in attendance at table, waiting on her master and his guests in an unusual room. The linens, crystal and tableware, the tasteful appointments and gracious furnishings, the general decor, were all very much, as we have noted, as though of Earth. Surely as far as she could tell, they were indistinguishable in quality and nature from the finest which her former world might have offered. It would not have been surprising to have found such a room in the suburban mansion of a man of wealth and position. She wondered if it might not be a reconstruction of such a room. Perhaps its furnishings, and such, had been brought from Earth? Everything was much as it might have been on Earth. There was one anomaly, of course, as we recall, she, herself. Ellen, amongst fully clothed, elegantly attired guests, serving, was naked, and branded and collared.

This was doubtless as he wanted her, as it amused him to have her, as it pleased him to have her.

To be sure, men are fond of looking upon their properties, their houses, their works of art, their collections, their lands, their gardens, their forests, their dogs and horses, their women.

Too, men, the vain beasts, enjoy showing off their possessions.

Oh, she had little doubt that her master enjoyed showing her off, but his pleasure, she was sure, extended well beyond the simple pleasures and vanities of displaying a possession. It involved, as well, she was sure, a sense of exultant triumph, that had much to do with their biographies. It was not then simply a matter of display, but of triumph, of the sweet taste of total victory, as well. She was being paraded, if only the two of them understood that, rather as a subjugated antagonist, a conquered foe, a former fair opponent now vanquished and helplessly enslaved. Conceive, if you will, the analogy of a once-haughty, once-vain princess, her armies now scattered and crushed, chained naked to the chariot of a general, being led in triumph through jubilant crowds. How soon she would hope that this noise, this pressing and raucous clamor, might end and that she then, a lowly, unimportant slave, might be permitted to simply lose herself amongst other slaves, and become what she, in her chains, has now discovered herself to be, a female, and the rightful property of a man.

She wondered if he had sometimes, in the classroom, so long ago, pondered what she might look like, nude, so marked, so collared. Perhaps he had imagined her, long ago, in the classroom, as she moved about before the class, as being so, as being naked, and branded and collared. She no longer wore the anklet. But it had not been removed until she had been branded and collared. Thus, there had remained, at all times, some token of bondage on her body.

"Then, Ellen," laughed the woman, "you are nothing but livestock, nothing but a pretty little piece of livestock, nothing but a domestic animal, nothing but a pretty little branded domestic animal!"

Tears sprang to Ellen's eyes. But she must stand in her collar where she was. She flung a piteous, begging look at her master.

"Answer our guest, Ellen," he said, kindly.

"Yes, Ma'am," Ellen sobbed.

"Please forgive Ellen," said Mirus, her master. "She has not been so long in the collar. Much is new to her. She may not yet fully understand the meaning of the band on her neck, the mark on her thigh."

"But is it not unusual that you would have her serve naked?" asked the woman.

"Gorean feasts are often served by naked slaves," said Mirus.

"Why?" demanded the woman, angrily.

"It improves the appetite," said Mirus, smiling.

"Of course!" she said, angrily.

Her formally dressed companion, who had been muchly silent, but muchly, too, intent upon her, laughed.

"Do not encourage him," she chided.

"If you were a man," he said, "you would understand how it is very pleasant to be served by a naked slave."

"I do not doubt it," she said, coldly.

"It can be very pleasant for the slave, as well," said Mirus. "It can give her many warm and delicious feelings, the honor of being permitted to approach and serve masters, the understanding that she is wanted, and desired, and owned, the gratification of being enabled to display herself, in the order of nature, as an acknowledged and total female before strong men, and so on."

"Undoubtedly," said the woman, angrily.

Ellen noted that the woman was very beautiful. She wore an off-the-shoulder evening dress, and her shoulders were sweetly wide and soft, perhaps alluringly so. The charms of her bosom were amply but subtly, not vulgarly, suggested. She was doubtless a woman of high intelligence and exquisite taste. Her companion seemed unable to take his eyes from her. About her throat there was a tasteful, close-fitting, single strand of pearls.

Ellen thought to herself, somewhat reluctantly, that she had perhaps not minded so serving as much as she might have supposed. To be sure, there had been an intense sting of humiliation as she understood what she was to do, and that she must obey unquestioningly, and that her helpless service and abject obedience would amuse and gratify her master, but, after her initial confusion, shame and blushings, and stumbling once, and almost dropping a plate, she was aware, bit by bit, that she did not mind, so much, what she was doing. She had begun to feel warm sensations, and a sense of her place in these things, and her specialness. She was pleased, too, to be naked before her master, and she did not doubt that he "found her flanks of interest," and the gaze of the other man had certainly been, at the least, warmly approbatory. After their eyes had met once, fully, she had not dared to look at him again, not so openly or directly. But several times during the evening, when his attentions were not completely absorbed by his charming companion, she had sensed his eyes, those of a powerful male, on her youthful, well-turned, stripped body. So she did have some sense of what it might be to serve masters thusly, and she found herself, in her way, appreciated and prized. And so she served shyly, sometimes fighting strange sensations in her body. She could not deny that serving men as a naked slave called up from deep within her strange, surprising, unfamiliar feelings. It disturbed her in some very unsettling, but warm and pleasant, and deliciously troubling, way. It made her feel terribly feminine, helplessly and beautifully feminine. She wondered if this might be an erotic experience for her. What a strange thing, she thought, and so surprisingly beautiful, to begin to feel the warmth and wonder of one's own sex. How few women, she feared, felt their femininity. It had been denied to them for centuries by one sort of fanatics and now it was again being denied to them, on her own world, by a new form of fanatics, building on the insanities, cruelties and envy of their predecessors, utilizing the poisons of the past in the interests of unnatural, self-serving political objectives. What are these strange feelings, she wondered, which I am beginning to feel, these enticing, delightfully tormenting feelings? Will I be able to resist them? Will they take me over, will they conquer me, will they put a rope on my neck and drag me zealously, helplessly, eagerly, panting after them? Am I to become their captive, their victim and prisoner? Am I to wear their leash, their bonds, as a helpless slave? Am I to become one of those low girls who whimper and scratch at the sides of their kennels? She was beginning, she feared, to feel sensations sometimes referred to vulgarly in Gorean as the burning, or the fires, in the slave belly. If she had been alone with her master, so serving, she would have begged for his least caress. Even had he impatiently cuffed her to the side, she felt that she might, in gratitude, have crawled back, begging to lick and kiss the hand that had administered the blow.

She loved him. He was her master. She was his slave.

"Surely you are aware," said Mirus, her master, to the woman whom she did not know, she in the lovely off-the-shoulder gown, "that in the history of Earth, for thousands of years, slavery was an accepted, approved, and prized institution."

"No longer," she said.

"In certain parts of the world it still is," he said, "but, more to the point, the intelligence of the ancients and medievals, and such, was not inferior to our own, and, in many respects, most would grant, many of them, perhaps the majority, were morally superior to large numbers of our lying, cheating, thieving, greedy, envious contemporary representatives of manufactured "mass man." Most of them had no objection to slavery, and, indeed, saw its values. Certainly you can understand how it might alleviate many social problems, one among many being that of expanding, uncontrolled populations intent on transforming a once verdant, lovely planet into arid, sterile ecological garbage. To be sure, there are many ways of solving social problems, and Earth is clearly moving to imperialistic centralization, to statism, collectivism and authoritarianism, in which, to control matters, human beings will become in fact, if not in name, slaves of the state. An alternative to both a lying world in which it is claimed that all are free, when they are not, a world hastening to disaster, and a world in which all are slaves, would be a world in which masters are masters and slaves are slaves."

"Such things are not possible on Earth," she said.

"They were," he said, "and may be again. Propaganda mills, as you know, may be quickly adjusted. Reality occasionally intrudes. Houses of cards do not well withstand the winds of a changing world. Obvious historical imperatives may dictate policy, at least to those capable of understanding them, and with the power to act upon them. The media will run like dogs to the whistles of their masters, whether it be their audiences, their advertisers or the state. What is seen as necessary will be adopted. Falsity and absurdity can be defended, so why not truth and practicality? If certain words are offensive, those particular words need not be used; I prefer them because I like to speak plainly; I prefer 'master' and 'slave' to 'servant of the people' and 'citizen'."

"You have never spoken to me like this before," she said.

"This is a memorable night," he said lifting his wine glass to her. "I do not think you will ever forget it."

"For me?" she asked.

"For all of us," said her companion, he, too, lifting his glass to her in a pleasant salute.

"Putting aside deeper matters," said Mirus, "you expressed interest in Ellen and in the fact that she must serve naked."

The woman looked at him. She, too, had lifted her glass of wine, though, to be sure, merely to take from it a tiny, dainty sip.

"We are all familiar with war," he said. "In war, it is a familiar practice for the victors to despoil the conquered. They take from them what they desire, whatever seems of value. For example, in this fashion, it has been a familiar practice of victors to take the women of conquered men from them and make them their slaves. Surely you are aware of this."

"Of course," said the woman.

Ellen wondered if the woman was aware of her companion's gaze, of how his eyes seemed to glitter upon her.

Would she not have screamed in terror, and fled?

"You are perhaps also aware that at the victory feasts of conquerors not unoften the women of the enemy, the women of the conquered, and, ideally, those formerly of the highest station, the most aristocratic of the enemy's women, those of the richest and most exalted blood, the noblest and the proudest, the most envied, as well as the most beautiful, all now embonded, must serve their new masters."

"I knew something of this, vaguely," she said.

"But did you know," he asked, "that they must serve their new masters naked?"

"Yes," she said, reddening, "I knew something of that."

"Well," said Mirus. "That is much what is the case with our little Ellen here."

"You have taken her from conquered men?" she asked.

"In a sense, I suppose so," he said. "For the men of her world have for the most part been conquered by their women. Thus they are conquered men, or many of them. And all I have done is to take one of those "conquering women" and bring her here, to return her, for my amusement, to her place in the order of nature. I thought I might let her see what it is like to be among true men."

Ellen trembled.

She was a slave—utterly—*and on Gor.*

"Ellen, of course," said he, "is not of the upper classes, or such, such as yourself, though we occasionally take in such, but she makes an excellent example of a type. She was a feminist, and was accordingly, in a sense, engaged in a war with men. To be sure, not an open war, not an honest, war. That war, however, for her, is over. And so she is for me a prize of war. She lost. To the victor belong the spoils. I have made her mine, as a slave. Thusly, compatible with historical precedent, I have her serve at my feast, my victory feast, naked."

"Bravo!" said the other man.

"Have we not business to attend to?" asked the woman.

"But supper is not yet over," said her companion. "Surely you would not deprive us of further courses, nor of our dessert?"

"No," she laughed. "Of course not!"

"Ellen," said Mirus.

"Sir?" said Ellen.

"You will continue to serve," he said. "After dessert, we will have the coffee and liqueurs at the coffee table."

"Yes, Sir," said Ellen.

* * * *

"It is beautiful," said the woman, she in the off-the-shoulder white gown, admiring the twenty weighty double ingots of gold.

They had been carried in, ingot by ingot, and stacked on the rug, near the coffee table, by two guards.

"These, too," said the woman's companion, "were, as I recall, a part of our arrangement." He produced a small leather pouch and, loosening its draw strings, opened it. Into the palm of his hand he poured a small shower of scintillating diamonds.

"Lovely!" she exclaimed.

He returned them, carefully, to the pouch, and handed them to her. She put them into her small, white, matching dress purse.

"Thusly are you paid," said her companion.

"Even were you not heretofore a rich woman," said Mirus, "you would be now."

"You are surely generous," laughed the woman.

Tutina stood nearby, smiling.

Ellen was to one side, standing. She had not yet been given permission to clear. She had struggled, during the evening, to understand the conversation. It was in English and so there was no difficulty in her following the words, only the meanings. It was not as though they took care to speak guardedly in her presence, for she was only a slave. It was rather that they understood so much among themselves, and took so much for granted, that to the uninitiated, to the outsider, such as the slave, Ellen, it very little made sense. Too much was implicit. Ellen did gather that clandestine business arrangements of considerable scope were afoot. The concerns, or tentacles, of whatever combine or conglomerate, or organization, was involved seemed to have far-reaching ramifications, ramifications affecting worlds. Surely it had its representatives, or outposts, or offices, on her former world as well as on this, her new world. Many highly placed individuals on both worlds, it seemed, for example, on Earth, in government and business, were not only apprised of, but implicated in, these matters. They extended far beyond the trivia of harvesting lovely women for vending in Gorean markets. The business of capturing, transporting and selling well-curved, helpless living flesh might, she suspected, be little more than a byproduct of more serious enterprises. To be sure, it doubtless had its at least minimally significant place in the economy of their schemes. There was doubtless money to be made in such matters. Her collar, for example, was quite real. She accepted that she was property, and could be sold. There was no gainsaying that. On the other hand, she was confident that her master would not sell her. Surely he had not brought her here to sell her, not after their relationship of long ago. She suspected that he must somehow love her, though perhaps in his own hard, severe, uncompromising, possessive way. Surely she loved him, and, doubtless, even from the first, though such things had not been so clear to her then, as a vulnerable, submissive slave. I think he loves me, she thought, though this may now be unbeknownst to himself. And even if he did not love her, she had little doubt that he "found her flanks of interest." And this did not dismay her. Rather she welcomed it. She, his slave, wanted to be an object of commanding, unabashed lust to him, wanted to be to him an object of powerful, violent sexual desire. On this world she had become so aware of the stirrings in her own blood, confronted with his physicality, that she, in her own complementary, soft, vulnerable, beautiful physicality, longed to be taken in his arms, longed to yield to him as the property he owned, longed to be put ecstatically, in rapture, to the ruthless pleasures of her beloved master.

"But as you know," laughed the young woman in the white, off-the-shoulder gown, "I never joined you as a mercenary. I am not the sort of person who would work for mere pay. On Earth, I am quite amply provided for, independently. Your riches, marvelous as they may be, were not the lure that brought me to your endeavors."

"We understand," said her companion, "that it was not mere gain, worthless pelf, which brought you into our service."

"Into your endeavors," she smiled. "No," she said, "it was for the adventure of the thing. Life was so boring for me. I had everything, and so it held so little. But here I found excitement, intrigue. I require stimulation. I thrive on danger."

"Oh?" said her companion.

"Yes," she said. "It was to escape boredom that I joined your cause, that I became a secret, unsuspected agent in your cause."

"Your contacts were useful," said her companion. "They were of great value to us."

"I also appreciated your attention to some small details," she said.

"The women, the debutantes, certain women who had dared to be critical of your life and behavior, certain gossips, certain rivals you disapproved of, those you called to our attention?"

"Yes," she said. "You did not hurt them, I trust."

"They would not be hurt by *us*," he said.

"Not by *you*?" she asked.

"At least in no way that was not in their new long-term interest."

"What did you do with them?" she asked.

"Guess," he suggested.

She then caught sight of Ellen, standing to the side, unobtrusively awaiting the command to clear. Ellen looked down, immediately. Something in her belly, which she did not entirely understand, made her apprehensive in the presence of a free woman. A free woman, in her status, in her loftiness and power, in her glory and might, was another form of being altogether, quite different from herself.

"No!" exclaimed the woman, delightedly.

"Yes," smiled her companion, "we made them slaves. Some changes had to be made in some of them, as you would suppose, recourse had to certain serums, and such, to make them acceptable for the markets, but it was all taken care of, in good order."

"What of Annette?" she asked.

"She wears her collar on the island of Cos."

"Annette in a collar!" she said. "How delightful!"

"She is fetching in it, as other desirable slaves."

"And Marjorie?"

"Sold south to Schendi, where she now serves a black master."

"Allison?"

"To the Barrens, for two hides."

"Michelle?"

"To Torvaldsland, as a bondmaid, for a keg of salted parsit fish."

"And Gillian?"

"The columnist?"

"Yes."

"The serums worked well for her. She became quite comely."

"Do you know her disposition?"

"She was sold south to Turia, but the caravan was ambushed by Tuchuks, a fierce nomadic people. I would not worry about her. She will doubtless show up, eventually, in one of the southern markets."

"Perhaps one of Turia's markets itself," said Mirus.

"I would not doubt it," said the woman's companion. "And have no fear but what the others were judiciously distributed, as well."

"Did you let them know my role in this, that it was I who designated them for their fates?"

"Certainly," he said, "and you may well conjecture their dismay, their wild cries, and tears, their helpless rage, how they pulled at their chains, trying to rise, or seized and shook, in futile fury, the bars of their tiny cages."

"Wonderful! Wonderful!" said the woman. "Jeffrey, you are such a dear!" She then gave him a quick, affectionate kiss on the left cheek. "You are a darling!" she said.

This was the first time Ellen had heard the name of her companion.

"I will arrange to have the gold delivered to your chamber," said Mirus, "where you will spend the night."

"I must thank you for your hospitality," she said to Mirus, warmly. "It was a lovely supper. It is a beautiful room. I am so pleased to make your acquaintance." She turned to Tutina. "You have been terribly quiet all evening, my dear," she said. "I feel so terribly guilty. But the men and I had so much to talk about. You understand. But still you should not have allowed us to monopolize the conversation."

Tutina smiled.

"I hope your ankle improves quickly," said the woman.

"Thank you," said Tutina.

"You may clear, Ellen," said Mirus.

"Yes, Sir. Thank you, Sir," she said. She set about clearing the table, putting the various utensils, vessels and plates on the serving cart. She would later clear the coffee table.

"Good-bye, Ellen," called the woman in the off-the-shoulder gown, sweetly.

"Good-bye, Ma'am. Thank you, Ma'am," said Ellen.

Happily, the woman's pleasant, dismissive tone of voice had been absolutely clear. Else Ellen might have been terribly frightened. But the utterance had clearly involved no suggested recognition of Ellen as a person, suggesting that she might be a human being in her own right, instead of the animal she was, for that would have been improper, and would have frightened Ellen, particularly as she was in the presence of her master. But, happily, the utterance had been no more than a casually generous, almost thoughtless, unbegrudged gift from a superior to an inferior. And surely it was. For Ellen knew herself as her absolute inferior, as the woman was free, and she, Ellen, was bond. Ellen cast a quick, frightened glance at her master but his gaze reassured her that her response had been apt. Indeed, she saw, with mixed feelings, that he regarded her as a quick, bright slave. She feared that that might put him more on his guard against her. But surely he must understand that the intelligence of a woman did not disappear in the searing moment her flesh took the iron, or the instant that her small neck felt clasped upon it a steel band.

Ellen, head down, continued to clear. She made as little noise as possible.

"It has all been so exciting," said the woman. "I have been so stimulated. I used to be so bored, but now I am not bored, at all!"

"Excellent," said her companion.

"I have enjoyed the intrigue, being a secret agent!" she laughed.

"And you have done well," said her companion. "Because of you the politics of two worlds are now subtly different from before. The Kurii are grateful to you. In their wars with Priest-Kings you have served them well."

"Served?" she smiled.

"Let us say then that you have proved yourself a useful, valuable agent."

"That is better," said the woman.

This puzzled Ellen.

She had heard of Priest-Kings, but did not believe they existed. Supposedly they were strange men of some sort, and lived in a remote area called the Sardar Mountains. She understood them to be a part of the mythology of this strange world, nonexistent, like sleen, tarns, and such. Kurii she had never heard of, at all. Perhaps they were another sort of strange men, who lived somewhere else. Since they were mentioned in connection with Priest-Kings, she thought that perhaps they did not exist either. Such expressions, she surmised, might be code names for competitive organizations or factions. That hypothesis pleased her, though she was not clear why free persons should have recourse to code names before a mere slave.

"Alas, now," smiled the woman, "I fear I must return to my daily, boring round of parties, and such."

"Surely there must be uses to which you could still be put," said her companion.

"I hope so," she said, warmly.

"I am sure of it," he said.

"I do crave excitement," she said. "I want stimulation. I hate being bored."

"I suspect," said her companion, "that there is more excitement in store for you, and I doubt that you will, in the future, lack for stimulation. And whatever your problems might prove to be in the future, I doubt that boredom will rank high amongst them."

"You are such a dear, Jeffrey," she smiled.

"Surely I can be rewarded with another kiss," said her companion, as though plaintively.

"Naughty boy!" she chided.

"Please," he wheedled.

"Very well," she said. Again she touched him briefly on the left cheek, a flick of a kiss, a tiny peck. "There!" she said.

How beautiful and white her shoulders, thought Ellen. How she must excite a man. I wish I were so beautiful. I wonder what a man would pay for her, a great deal I would suppose.

"I fear it is late," said her companion, the man called Jeffrey.

"Yes," she agreed.

The woman then bid good-night to Mirus and Tutina.

"The gold will be delivered to your chamber, where you will be spending the night," said Mirus.

"Thank you," she said.

Various leave-taking pleasantries were exchanged. Ellen, in this leave taking, to her relief, was ignored.

"On the way to your chamber," said her companion, "there is another chamber, too, which I would like to show you."

"Very well," she said.

A moment later, Tutina, too, with a glance at Mirus, left.

Then Ellen and her master were alone.

He went to the long table, and took the chair at the head of the table, which he had occupied during dinner, and pulled it a bit away from the table. He then sat within it, seemingly lost in thought.

Ellen supposed that he had drawn the chair away from the table, before reposing in it, to enable her the more easily to clear the table. It only became clear to her later that he had wanted the chair more in the center of the room, for a different reason, that there might then be a cleared space before it, on the rug.

When the guests had departed the two guards returned and, ingot by ingot, picked up the gold, and, slowly, carefully, carried it into the next room. A broad, flat wagon was there, too large to fit flat through the smaller door, that leading from the room to the corridor and kitchen. There was another portal, one wider and more auspicious, in the room, a double door of some dark wood, that through which the guests and Mirus had originally entered. Ellen had, of course, used the smaller door in her serving, that giving eventual access to the kitchen. Interestingly, the woman's companion, conducting her, had exited with her through the smaller door. That led to the corridor, and thence to the kitchen, and various other corridors, and to several areas more in the back of the house.

Ellen worked to clear the table.

She did not rush to do this.

At times, at least, she was sure that her master's eyes were upon her.

Whereas a slave may be forced to humiliating haste, perhaps crawling in terror before the strokes of a whip, unseemly hurryings, the industrial frenzies, so to speak, of technological cultures, are generally alien to the Gorean consciousness. Theirs is not a clock-ridden culture; on Gor life tends to be genially paced, regulated more by the season of the year and the position of the sun; it is not conceived of in terms of metaphors drawn from factories, in material terms, in terms of input and output, in terms of units of product processed over units of time. Its rhythms are less the periodic turbulences of rush hours, the blinkings of colored, regulatory lights, carefully timed, the staccato clickings and hammerings, the stops and starts, of the assembly line, than those of tides, and winds, and clouds and rain, the appearance and disappearance of stars, the comings and goings of light and darkness, the cycles of hunger, the cycles of desire, those of the beating of the heart and the circulation of the blood.

Ellen did not hasten in her work but took care, rather, to do it well. To be sure, she knew that clumsiness was not tolerated in a female slave. If she should drop a plate or break a glass, or spill a beverage, or even move awkwardly, she knew she might expect to be tied to a ring and beaten.

Above all, though this may seems strange to some, the female slave is not permitted to move with the abruptness, the clumsiness, the awkwardness, the gross, unconscionable, offensive, mannish motions permitted to a free woman. As a female slave she is expected to be muchly aware of her very different, very lovely, very special body, so exciting and wondrous, and to carry it, and present it, beautifully. She is not a free woman. She is a female, and must move as such. The female slave is a female, and thus femininity is required of her. She is trained to be aware of her body and to move well. Sometimes men do not know why they are so exciting, but sense, somehow, that each movement, each nuance of expression, bespeaks subtly their profound, released femininity.

And so Ellen worked, muchly aware that she was a slave, muchly aware that she was in the presence of her master.

She had never felt so beautiful and feminine as she had on Gor.

Never before had she even begun to sense the depths of her sex. There had been nothing of this, surely, in the courses she had taught, in the texts she had read.

Strange, she thought, how those who on her world made so much of women were oblivious, as far as she could tell, of these things, to these sensations, and feelings. Perhaps they had never met a true man, she thought.

She wondered if women of her own world, or many of them, realized that they might be graceful and beautiful, and feminine. Did they understand that even small labors, like clearing a table, might be performed beautifully, gracefully? Did they understand that anytime, at their various activities, even, say, during their day, at their various forms of work, or play, or whatever, they might be beautiful, and graceful, and women?

Or did they fear the scorn, the ridicule, the cruelty, of the female haters of their own sex?

She hoped that her sisters on a far world might one day become conscious of themselves, truly, despite what might be the consequences attendant upon such an awakening.

"You move well, slut," snarled Mirus.

She had not doubted that he was watching her.

"Is master aroused?" she asked.

"You will rue that," he said.

"You have had me trained," she said, "at least to some extent. I find that I move unconsciously now in certain ways. I do not even think of it any longer. Given my training, how could I help but move as I do now? Surely you do not object. And did I not move in this way now, did I not now move in a way natural for my body, would I not be beaten?"

"Continue your work," he said.

"I shall be finished shortly," she said.

She did not know this at the time but many Goreans can tell the difference between free women and female slaves, even when the latter are clothed in the garments of the former, so internalized, so ingredient, so manifest is femininity in the female slave. Sometimes fleeing female slaves, runaways, attempting to escape hated masters in the clothing of free women are simply stopped, unceremoniously, and stripped, their brands and collars then revealed. They are then returned to the dreaded mercies of their masters. The garmenture of free women and slaves, of course, differs considerably, that of the slave tending to be far briefer and more revealing. Incidentally, a slave can be slain for putting on the garment of a free woman. It is permissible, though frowned upon, for a free woman to put on the garb of a slave. Also, it is quite dangerous to do so. Many free women, so garmenting themselves, as an adventure, thinking to have the run of the city, to go into areas forbidden to free women, to see the insides of paga taverns, and such, have, to their horror, found themselves, gagged and blindfolded, struggling futilely in the tight ropes of slavers.

A slave may also be slain for touching a weapon.

She did not doubt but what her master found her of interest.

No longer, of course, did she feel it incumbent upon her to pretend to indignation or dismay, such hypocrisies and dishonesties, when she sensed a man's interest in her. She now, as a slave, was well aware that she might be found of interest. Indeed, given her beauty, and her current status and condition, she took it as a matter of course that she would be found of interest. Who would not find a slave of interest, particularly one such as she? How boldly and with what pleasure men now looked upon her! Too, she now expected to be so viewed and hoped that she would be so viewed. Indeed, she might fear that she might not be so viewed, that she might not be found of interest. Her very life, as she now knew, might depend on such things.

Perhaps long ago," she said, "you imagined what I might look like, as a naked slave, yours, obeying, doing your bidding, as I am now, knowing that I had no choice, too, but to move as a female slave before you."

"You have not yet finished your work," he said.

"To be sure," she said, "Master could not have known what I would have looked like at the age of eighteen."

"It seems the slave is garrulous," he said.

"I trust that Master is not disappointed with the body of an eighteen-year-old slave," she said.

"You are a pretty eighteen-year-old slave, Ellen," he said.

She finished the table, putting the last plates on the serving cart. How strange, she thought, that I should have this eighteen-year-old body. And yet it is mine, or, better, I suppose, it is now what I am. To be sure, its neck is in a slave collar. Or, better, I, I myself, am in a slave collar. I myself, what I now am, am in a slave collar. She dared not tell him that she loved to be in a slave collar, to be a slave. She dared not tell him that she had now come to recognize herself as a natural slave, who should, in all propriety, and in view of all rights whatsoever, wear a collar. She loved her new condition, and her collar. How could she tell him that? How could he respect her, if he knew that? She wanted his respect. Thus, surely she must pretend to be a lamenting free woman inappropriately subjected, however categorically, to an unfortunate fate.

"It is customary for a slave to thank a free person for a compliment," he said. "You may thank me," he said. His remarks were not really critical; rather, they seemed instructional, their intent seeming to be merely to help an ignorant girl to better understand her collar.

"I should thank you for making me an eighteen-year-old slave?" she asked.

"For pointing out that you are a pretty eighteen-year-old slave," he said.

"Thank you, Master," she said. She had blushed, totally, suffused with warmth and pleasure, when he had commended her. She hoped that it had not been obvious, in the subdued light of the room. Then she had pretended, of course, to be reluctant to acknowledge the compliment.

She must keep from him what she was in her heart, a natural slave, a rightful slave.

She would later learn to live for such things, a kind word, an approving glance, a crust cast to the floor before her, a caress.

She had now moved the cart about the long table, and to the front of the coffee table. There, bending down, crouching gracefully, under her master's eye, she cleared the smaller table.

He enjoys seeing me do this sort of work, she thought. He enjoys seeing me perform such small, trivial domestic labors. I was once his teacher. Now I must clear his tables, and such. He is having an erotic experience, watching me do this, she thought. Surely she, herself, was having an erotic experience, so serving. She understood then something of the subtle, radiating, profound, pervasive eroticism of female bondage. It was an ambiance, a condition, in its way, of her life.

"You have now reverted, I note," said he, "to the normal modalities of discourse, the use of 'Master' to the master, and such."

"Yes, Master," she said.

"You are a bright slave, Ellen," he said.

"Thank you, Master," she said.

It had seemed to her that 'Sir', and such expressions, for whatever reasons they were used during the supper, would not now be appropriate, and might even be offensive, if not inexcusable. It was her sense that she should return to the normal, appropriate modalities of discourse, those normal and appropriate for such as she. That she did so without explicit permission she trusted would not be an occasion for the imposition of discipline. To have asked would have seemed to her, in the circumstances, stupid, and she did not wish to appear a stupid slave before her master. There are many delicacies, many subtleties, in the relationship in which she found herself, that of abject slave to total master, and slaves, as you may suppose, come very quickly to appreciate them. Commonly the slave will ask permission to speak, but not always; she may behave in one way before her master if a free woman is present, in another way if only another man is present, and in yet another way if she and the master are alone; sometimes she knows her master delights to hear her speak eloquently and lyrically before him, even for Ahn at a time, and is eager to attend to, share and relish, the smallest of her thoughts and feelings; at other times she knows that so little as a raised head may bring her a stroke of the lash; at times the master will wish to be alone; at other times she knows it will be acceptable for her to crawl to him and whimper, beggingly, of her needs. She soon learns, or suffers for the failure to do so, to read the whims and moods of the master. This is common, of course, in a variety of other domestic animals, as well.

"You have finished with the clearing," he said. "Take the cart back to the kitchen."

"Yes, Master," she said. "When I have done so, should I report back to my cage?"

"You want the leather, don't you?" he asked.

"No, Master!" she said.

"You will return here, and kneel before me."

He indicated the place on the rug before his chair.

"Yes, Master!" she said. Then she put down her head, quickly, that he might not see how elated she was.

In a moment she had wheeled the cart to the smaller of the two doors, and worked it through, and was soon in the hall outside.

There were two guards outside.

She knelt and put her head to the stones of the floor. "I am expected to return, Masters," she said. When she looked up she saw the expressions of the guards. Had she not expected to return?

Quickly she leaped up and sped the cart down the corridor. Then she slowed her pace, as she heard the guards laugh. She was embarrassed to show herself an eager slave, hurrying to return to the master's presence. But as soon as she rounded a bend in the corridor, she once again began to hurry. Are you an eager slave, Ellen, she asked herself, for she was now Ellen, and thought of herself as such. Of course not, she told herself! I would not run to him like a common, amorous slave, a helpless, panting bitch beside herself with heat! But she did not slow her pace. It would not do to keep the master waiting, she told herself. Indeed, it might not be wise to do so. If I dally in my return, he might give me the leather! This thought, that she might be beaten if she were late, thrilled her. It was not that she wished to feel the leather, certainly not now, but rather that she was thrilled to be such, a slave, that she must fear it. He is so strong, so commanding. I must obey him, she thought. Over me he is totally dominant. Before him I can be only what I am, a helpless, submissive slave! I wonder, she thought. I wonder if I am in heat? Could I, given what I was on Earth, that lofty, respectable, cool, remote, formal, inert, frigid thing, now be in heat, be simply in heat? Could I now be only another low girl, another common, amorous slave, another bitch beside herself with heat! Not I, surely. But perhaps I am in heat! In any event it will be wise for me to return to my master soon. It charmed her that she thought of him so simply, so directly, as her master. But then she shuddered, for she knew that in truth, in reality, he was her master. He owned her.

* * * *

She knelt naked before him, on the rug before his chair.

She knelt before him, in her collar, in the basic position of the Gorean pleasure slave, back on her heels, her back straight, her head up, the palms of her hands on her thighs, her knees spread, widely.

A rather different sort of slave, familiar in the "high cities," in the "cylinder cities," one more domestically oriented, is the "tower slave." She is permitted to kneel with her knees closed. On the other hand, when her master, perhaps one evening, orders her to spread her knees, she understands that the scope of her duties has been enlarged. Ellen was under no delusion as to the sort of slave she was. Her duties would doubtless include those of the tower slave, but would, given the sort of slave she was, a spread-knees slave, so to speak, extend well beyond them. Even before Ellen had been told that she was a pleasure slave, it had not been difficult to gather from the nature of her training the sort of slave she was intended to be. It is hard for a girl to kneel with her knees spread widely before a man and be in the least doubt as to this point. Too, she recalled the young man from class, so long ago, and how he had looked at her. She had little doubt as to the nature of the slavery he would have from her.

And now he owned her.

Now she knelt before him, in basic position.

"How did you like serving, as you did this evening," he asked, "naked, in such a room, the men in tuxedos, the women in evening gowns."

"May I speak with some freedom, Master?" she asked.

"Yes," he said, "at least for the moment."

"You truly own me, don't you?" she asked.

"Yes," he said. "Certainly."

"I was humiliated," she said.

"You must learn to serve naked," he said. "You are a slave."

"Did you enjoy having me so serve?" she asked.

"Certainly," he said.

"You enjoyed making me do that?" she asked.

"Yes," he said. "Seeing you serve naked gave me a great deal of pleasure. There are many satisfactions connected with the mastery. Such things, my dear former teacher, are amongst them."

"You are hateful!" she exclaimed, tears welling into her eyes. She wanted to cover her eyes with her hands and weep, but was afraid to break position.

"Is my pretty little slave upset?" he asked.

"Yes!" she cried. "Your pretty little slave is upset!" She moved her head wildly, lifting it, seeing the ceiling, throwing it back and forth, but dared not lower it.

"I see you are under some stress, pretty Ellen," he said. "Accordingly I permit you some latitude in position."

Immediately, uncontrollably, she put her head down and buried her face in her hands, weeping.

"Knees," he cautioned, gently.

With a cry of misery she widened her knees.

"I gather," he said, "that you found your service humiliating, but did you find that it had other aspects, as well?"

She looked at him, through her hands, as though she would cry out some hysterical denial, but did not do so.

"I see that you found your service welcome, warming, elating, reassuring, fitting, even delicious," he said.

"Master!" she protested.

"You enjoyed serving as a naked slave," he said. "You enjoyed, so subtly, so deferentially, so seemingly involuntarily, so seemingly helplessly, exhibiting your beauty."

She sobbed.

"You are very beautiful," he said. "You know that, don't you?"

"Perhaps," she whispered.

"So it is very natural that you would wish to show your beauty," he said. "It is natural that it would give you great pleasure to do so. Surely, too, you must rejoice in the happiness, and pleasure, that the sight of it brings to others."

"But it could also bring me into great peril, could it not, Master?" she asked.

"Yes," he said, "particularly on this world. It makes you an object of enormous interest, of almost uncontrollable desire. This is particularly dangerous for you, inasmuch as you are only a slave. It is not as though you were a free person, and had a Home Stone."

"A Home Stone, Master?"

"Commonality of Home Stone extends beyond concepts with which you are familiar, such as shared citizenship, for example. It is more like brotherhood, but not so much in the attenuated, cheap, abstract sense in which those of Earth commonly speak glibly, so loosely, of brotherhood. It is more analogous to brotherhood in the sense of jealously guarded membership in a proud, ancient family, one that has endured through centuries, a family bound together by fidelity, honor, history and tradition."

"I see," she whispered.

"So do not concern yourself with Home Stones," he said. "They are beyond your ken. You are only a slave."

"Yes, Master," she said.

"Surely," said he, "you are not only aware of your beauty, but you must be excited by it, happy with it, and proud of it, and love it."

She thought it well not to respond to his words.

She put her head down.

"And you must, too, begin to suspect what power it might give you over men."

"I have little power," she said.

"More than you know," he said. "But remember this, slave. Ultimately all power is with the master. It is he who holds the whip."

"Yes, Master," she said.

This, incidentally, is exactly and perfectly true on this world, as I have learned, forgive me, as *she* has learned.

"And, too," he said, "you are growing intrigued by, and pleased with, your sexiness."

"My *sexiness*, Master?" she asked.

"Do not play your silly Earth games with me," he said, angrily. "Do not pretend to be stupid. On this world there are two sexes. Here one need not pretend to celebrate androgyny or make it a point to flourish pompous, hypocritical puritanical platitudes. Let those who are now as you once were mouth bromides in their classes and ignore realities under their very noses. The pretense to blindness must ultimately fail in a world where sight persists. To be sure, most people will see what they are told to see. So many people blindfold themselves with words; so few look upon the world as it is, radiant and real, with its own nature. The sight of a woman like you, and thousands like you, will enflame a man. Let those of Earth denounce and castigate straw for burning when it is set afire. Goreans do not. They would find that incomprehensibly stupid. You are very well aware, slave, of your sexiness. Do not feign ignorance. You are well aware that you are beautiful and desirable, that you are, whether this pleases you or not, but I do not doubt but what it pleases you, and well pleases you, excruciatingly sexually stimulatory, that men will see you and want you, that your neck calls for the collar, your flank for the brand, your wrists for slave bracelets, your ankles for the shackles of masters!"

She cried out in terror, and misery, and, shrinking down, covered her breasts with her arms, crossed before her body.

"Palms on thighs," he said.

Then she was again in position.

As her treatments had progressed she had become aware that she had become of considerable sexual interest to men. She did not think it made much difference, really, whether she had been stabilized at thirty-eight years of age, or twenty-eight, or eighteen. In each of these ages, she knew, she was lovely, and of considerable interest. In each of these ages, she had little doubt that men, thousands of men, would have enjoyed having her before them, rendering slave obeisance. She thought that many men might have preferred her at twenty-eight, the age when she had first met her master, he then a student in one of her courses. On the other hand, most Gorean slave girls, she had gathered, were as though in their early twenties. Most of the older women, she gathered, had been returned to that point and stabilized there. On the other hand, there was also doubtless something to be said for a virginal, dewy, youthful eighteen, not so much perhaps from the point of view of the slave herself, as she would tend to be looked down upon, and be regarded as relatively inconsequential, even by her sister slaves, but from the point of view of masters, who tend to be less exacting, less demanding, in such matters, generously not tending to hold her youthfulness against her, provided, of course, it is lovely and helplessly responsive to their touch, as should be the body of any slave. In any event, it was where her master had chosen to have her stabilized, and so that is exactly where she was stabilized. Perhaps he wished her so, as he had suggested, as a part of his vengeance upon her, that in virtue of her youth she might be rendered negligible, inconsequential, and thus demeaned. In any event, whatever may be the truth in these matters, she found herself by his will made a young slave, one who could be no more than a girl to his man.

"Cease your hysteria, your silliness, you narcissistic little bitch," he said.

She regarded him, from position, tears in her eyes.

"Women are narcissistic," he said. "Even on Earth, consider their obsessive concern with their appearance, with their ever-present desire to present themselves attractively before men, their concern with the right make-up, the right jewelry, the right earrings, the correct, fashionable clothing, their concern with their hosiery, their shoes, their concern even with the nature and lovely delicacy of their undergarments. And there is nothing critical affected in this. They should be narcissistic. They are beautiful. They are women. They wish to allure, to be attractive prey to men, the predator sex. The true woman should be pleased with her beauty, proud of it, and desirous of showing it off. My criticism of you, little slave, is not that you are narcissistic, for that, as a female, you should be, but that you are a little bitch."

"I am sorry, Master," she whispered.

"Surely you were aware this evening," he said, "that our guest, Jeffrey, admired you."

"He had eyes mostly, I thought," she said, "for his friend."

Mirus laughed, and she did not understand his laugh.

"But you must have noticed, sometime," he said, "that he was looking at you."

"It seemed so, Master," she said.

Indeed, who could have doubted it?

"He was regarding you with desire, *sexual* desire, if you can understand that, you stupid little bitch," he said.

I am not a stupid little bitch, she thought. Have I not seen desire in the eyes of the guards? Does he think I do not know I am a slave, and how slaves are seen by men? Does he think, truly, I am a stupid little bitch? I fear so. But I am not a stupid little bitch. Must I admit everything? Must I be so open? I am from Earth! What does he want? The collar has not been long on my neck!

"Bitch?" said he.

"Yes, Master," she said.

"Do you think you are sexually desirable?" he asked.

"It is not for a slave to say," she said.

"Do you know you are in a collar?"

"Yes, Master!"

"Speak," he said.

"It is a slave's hope that she will be found pleasing to masters," she said.

"Excellent," he said.

"Thank you, Master."

"You are intelligent," he said, "actually quite intelligent."

"Thank you, Master."

Gorean men, she had learned, prize high intelligence in a woman, and seek it in their slaves. The intelligent woman, taken in hand, overwhelmed, subdued and mastered, taught her womanhood, wholly submitted, understanding now what she is, fully, makes an excellent slave. Certainly they sell for more.

Had she claimed she was sexually desirable, she might have been reprimanded for conceit; had she denied it she might as easily have been punished for lying.

"But in many respects," he said, "you are quite stupid."

"Yes, Master," she said.

"Do you think you are sexually desirable?"

"I do not know, Master!" she sobbed.

"You are," he said.

"Thank you, Master."

"As any slave," he said.

"Yes, Master," she whispered.

"Had his friend not been present, he might have seized your ankle and dragged you under the table."

"So simply?"

"It was a Gorean feast," he said. "Surely you do not think that those women of whom we spoke earlier, serving their conquerors naked, simply returned that evening with impunity to their kennels and cells.

She lowered her head.

"They would be seized, ravished, and enjoyed," he said. "They would be seized by the hair, knelt, wine poured down their throats, spilling over their breasts and bodies, forced to dance drunkenly, put to their bellies, their lips to the feet of men, and ordered to beg for use. Then, huddled together, kept in place with the lash, they might be gambled for. And the evening might then end pleasantly as they, the winnings of men, caressed into supplicatory beasts, thrashed on the carpets and rushes. And then, toward morning, when the fires had burned low, and the room was gray, damp and cold, when those who had won them would be asleep, sated with the repast of pleasures derived from their winnings, their hands tied behind their bodies, their necks roped to the left ankles of their new masters, they might rest. Later, bent over, held in leading position, by groggy, stumbling masters, they would be conducted to their new dispositions. They are the women of a conquered foe. Thus, as prizes, they belong to the victors."

"Yes, Master," whispered the slave.

"In a sense," he said, "as I suggested earlier, it is similar with you."

"Master?"

"I am the victor here, am I not?" he asked.

"Master?"

"And you were a woman of the enemy?"

"The enemy?"

"Of Earth," he said, "but in a sense larger than you know."

"Master?"

"Surely you remember my earlier remarks," he said, "when I was explaining the lack of attire in a charming waitress."

"Yes, Master," she whispered.

"Your lies, your ideology, your manipulations, your slynesses, your schemings, your trickeries, your agendas, your subversions."

"Yes, Master," she whispered, tears in her eyes.

She wondered if the indoctrinated, servile men of Earth were even worthy to be accounted enemies.

They were so manipulable, and weak.

It was embarrassing for her to think of herself as a woman of them.

But would most not wish weak foes? Only Goreans, she supposed, desired strong foes, perhaps that they might be the better tested, that an ensuing victory might be the more worth winning.

She thought of so many of the men of Earth, such mindlessly herded dupes, taught to deny their blood, hastening sellers of birthrights, so whiningly eager to win a smile from those who despised them for the very weakness they sought to promote in them.

She wondered if it might not be better for such a subverted, betrayed world to perish.

No, she thought. Wait. Mayhap one day it will awaken, rise up, shout, and be reborn. Let it be reborn, she thought. Let it be reborn!

"Have you, woman of the enemy, been defeated?"

"Yes, Master," she said. The answer to that was obvious, as obvious as the gleaming, snug, obdurate band encircling her throat. What she did not tell him was that she had wished, in her deepest heart, to be defeated.

"So," said he, "should I have you slain, or kept as a slave?"

"It is my hope," she said, "to be kept as a slave."

He looked her over, carefully.

She reddened.

"Perhaps," he said. "You are well-curved."

She was silent.

"Those are slave curves," he said.

"It is my hope," she said, "that Master will find me pleasing."

He laughed. "Long ago, on Earth," he said, "in your classes, in the corridors, in the cafeteria, in your office, on the streets, on the avenues and boulevards, in the library, I suspect you did not anticipate that one day you would kneel before a man and express such a wish."

"No, Master," she said. She had not anticipated that. She had, however, longed for it.

He laughed, again, and leaned back in the chair.

"How did you feel, to know that you were the object of Jeffrey's interest, *in that way*?"

"Please, Master, have mercy on a new slave!" she begged.

"Speak," he said.

"It pleased me!" she wept.

"Of course it did," he snarled, "for you are a slave!"

"Is it true?" she asked. "Did Master Jeffrey desire me?"

"Yes," he said, angrily.

She looked down.

It pleased her that he was angry. Could he be jealous of another man's interest in her? Surely she hoped so.

"And you might be sent to him," he added.

She lifted her head, to regard him with fear.

"Yes," he said.

She knew more then, in that moment, of what it could be, to be a slave.

It could be done to her.

She was slave.

"May I speak?" she asked.

"Yes," he said.

"Might Master Mirus desire me, as well?" she whispered.

"What?" he asked, disbelievingly.

"Nothing, Master," she said, quickly.

"You, me?" he asked.

"Forgive me, Master! It is well known, the contempt in which Master holds his slave!"

"Are you now begging, you, with all that you were, now begging as an amorous slave to be used?" he asked.

"No, Master," she said, quickly.

She resolved that she must not let him know the depth of the slave she was.

How could he then respect her?

But how absurd was such a concern!

Dignity, respect, and such, were not for slaves. Did she not know that? One did not respect slaves; one commanded them, worked them, ravished them, perhaps loved them.

She might demand respect from weaklings of Earth; before Gorean men she would kneel, and hope to be found pleasing.

She was in torment.

She must remember she was of Earth!

Did she truly desire the tepidities and formalities of respect, she wondered. Perhaps, rather, she wished something else, say, a radical fullness of life, wished rather fulfillment, wished, rather, to be coveted, prized, and relished, owned.

No, she must insist on respect!

"I think, Ellen," he said, "that you have not been lashed enough."

"Forgive me, Master," she said.

"Perhaps you think that you may be a saucy slave," he said.

"Forgive me, Master," she said.

"Sometimes," said he, "a slave girl needs the whip."

"Yes, Master," she said.

"It is good for their behavior, and their comprehensions."

"Yes, Master," she said.

"You are a virgin, are you not?" he asked.

"Yes, Master," she said. Surely that was clear from her papers.

"But," said he, "of the many things that may be done to a female slave, whipping is only one."

"Oh?" she said.

"You tread a thin line, slave girl," he said.

"Oh?" she asked.

"You are a bright, pretty little slave," he said.

The monster, she thought. I was his teacher. To be sure, what am I now, with my eighteen-year-old body, but a bright, pretty, little slave? It is true, true! That is what he has made me!

"Thank you, Master," she said.

"Are you prepared to beg to please a man, any man?" he asked.

"I am a slave," she said. "Surely Master can force me. He can bend me to his will. A mere snapping of the fingers will suffice. I must obey, with all the perfection with which I am capable, and instantly."

"I am awaiting a response to my question," he said.

"Is the man my master?" she asked.

"You have heard the question," he said.

I am of Earth, she thought. I am of Earth!

She decided that this would be the moment to convince him of her value, of her nobility, of her loftiness, of her worthiness, the moment to earn his respect. She must lead him to believe that she was essentially a free woman who unfortunately, inexplicably, astonishingly, found herself in a collar. That way he would doubtless respect her. She now wanted his respect, desperately. She must never let him know that there knelt before him on the rug a woman who in her deepest heart of hearts was a helpless, vulnerable, submissive, craving, begging slave girl.

"Master may of course order me to beg," she said. "Then I must beg, as I am a slave."

"Then you would not choose to beg?" he asked.

"Certainly not," she said, tossing her head.

She was frightened by the sternness of his gaze.

"I may, of course, be subjected to slave rape," she said, quickly. Indeed, she hoped that he would simply take her and work his will upon her, a will she longed to satisfy. She desired desperately to be taken in hand and put to his purposes, to be ravished by him, uncompromisingly, thoroughly, ruthlessly, as befitted her slaveness, by him, her master.

I love him, she thought.

He brought me here. He must want me. Perhaps he loves me. No, that could not be. But he must like me a little. Oh, I hope that he likes me, if only just a little! Please, Master, like me, if only a little!

Take me, she thought. Take me! I am your slave! You are my Master! We are your slaves, oh Masters. Do you not use us as you wish, ravishing us whenever, and however, it might please you to do so?

Oh, take me, beloved Master, she thought. I am yours! I am ready! Be merciless! Be ruthless! Take me! Take me!

"Perhaps you were curious," he said, "as to the modalities of discourse required of you at supper this evening," he said.

"Master?" she said.

Inwardly she reeled, in shock.

She had expected, at any moment, to be thrown back, to feel the rug's harsh nap on her back, to feel her ankles seized and her legs, he laughing with exultation, spread cruelly, widely.

Why had he not, at least, issued the "Sula!" command? That was one of several commands she had been trained to respond to instantly. Upon hearing this command, the slave immediately assumes a supine position, her hands at her sides, palms up, her legs open.

"You understood very little of what transpired this evening, I would suppose," he said.

"Yes, Master, very little," she said.

"These are matters of war," he said. "Involved are the fates of two planets, Earth and Gor."

"Master?" she asked.

"You are a slave," he said. "It is no concern of yours."

"Yes, Master," she said.

"No matter how things turn out you will still be in a collar."

"Yes, Master."

"You are of no more account in these things than a pig or a horse."

"Yes, Master."

"Perhaps you are curious as to why the room is as it is, and why you were required to use certain forms of address to myself, and our guests, and Tutina, this evening."

"Certainly, Master," she said, eagerly.

"Curiosity is not becoming in a slave girl," he said.

"Please, Master!" she begged.

"You silken little beast," he said.

"Please, Master!"

"You are all the same," he said. "The room was to reassure, and comfort, our fair guest, whose name is to be 'Evelyn'."

"Whose name is *to be* 'Evelyn'?" she asked.

"Too, in a way, it is to put her off guard, psychologically, of course, for there is no way she could guard herself now, at this point, in any practical fashion."

"I do not understand," she said.

"In its way, too, it is a joke on Jeffrey's part, for he has had to put up with her for several months, rather on her terms. His role, I fear, has been rather an embarrassing, frustrating one, much like that in which many Earth males spend their lives, but he is patient, and knew that his patience would be eventually rewarded."

"I understand nothing of this, Master," she said.

"Surely you noticed that she was strikingly beautiful?"

"Yes, Master." There was no gainsaying that.

"And quite bright?"

The slave nodded.

"But perhaps a bit bitchy," he said.

"Master?" she asked.

"The whip can take that out of a woman," he said.

"The whip?"

"The Kurii, in whose service I labor," he said, "tend to be quite tolerant of the interests and dispositions of their human agents."

"The Kurii are not human?" she asked.

"I gather not," he said, thoughtfully. "To be sure, I am not clear on the matter. I have never met one in person. At least to this time. That may change in the future. I do not know." He then returned his attention lightly to Ellen, who knelt before him, his stripped chattel. "In any event, they allow their human agents a considerable amount of latitude in their work, at least in matters in which they feel it unimportant to involve themselves.

As a result we, and those akin to us, tend to seek out, and recruit, as female agents women who are on the whole unusually beautiful and desirable. It pleases us to work with such. To be sure, with the developments in the serums over the last few years, our options have been multiplied. For example, if, through photographs, or such, we can determine that a woman was once beautiful and desirable, she may still be of considerable interest to us, for we may always return her to her former youth and beauty. One might add, as well, that while beauty is of great importance, desirability is not always linked with beauty. For example, some women, for no reason that is fully clear to us, are not beautiful, but are extremely desirable. Just to look at them is to want them naked at your slave ring. And desirability is surely most important. On the other hand, if one can conjoin such desirability with remarkable beauty, then that is so much the better for the markets."

"For the markets?"

"Yes."

"Are you not speaking strangely of Mistress Evelyn, Master?" she asked.

"The female agents, who are commonly egotistical, petty, vain, self-seeking and mercenary, need not be informed of their eventual disposition. They will discover it in good time."

"Master?"

"The female agents, thus, do not really consume our resources, so much as, in the end, add to them. You seem frightened. You seem dismayed. She whom you referred to judiciously as Mistress Evelyn, you must understand, has served her purpose. No longer do we need her. She was exceedingly helpful, particularly because of her connections, her many affiliations, in the worlds of society, business and finance. But we have now absorbed, and profited from, and will continue to profit from, those connections and affiliations. She is no longer needed. Too, Jeffrey wanted her."

"You are betraying her?"

"Not really," he said. "It is merely that the entire arrangement was never fully explained to her."

"But the gold, the diamonds!" she said.

"We kept our word," he said. "She was paid for her work."

"She will soon with her treasures then be returned to Earth?"

"Sometimes I think that you are very stupid, Ellen."

"Forgive me, Master."

"The gold and diamonds were hers," he said. "That is true. That was our part of the bargain."

"I understand so little of this," said Ellen.

"Surely you recall that he whom you judiciously refer to as Master Jeffrey, you see, you are learning, Ellen, informed our fair guest that, on the way to her chamber, that in which she would spend the night, there was another chamber which he would like to show her."

"Yes," she said, uncertainly.

"And she will indeed be shown that chamber."

"And what manner of chamber might that be, Master?"

"It is, of course, a slaving chamber," he said. "There our fair guest will be stripped, fingerprinted and toeprinted, measured with care, and papers prepared on her. She will then be branded and collared, following which the final certifications will be placed on the papers. She will then be taken in chains to the chamber where she will spend the night, a cell. The gold will be waiting in the cell, all the twenty double-weight ingots of it, carefully stacked. Too, after she has been chained to the wall, she may notice that, dangling from the ceiling, before her, just out of her reach, is the sack of diamonds We do not want her to be able to reach them lest she should attempt something foolish, such as trying to hide some of them in her body. It will be soon enough tomorrow for her to learn that she belongs to Jeffrey."

"How could you do this to her?" she asked.

"I do not understand the difficulty," he said.

"Master!" protested the slave.

"It is appropriate for her," he said. "She is a female. All females should be slaves."

"Yes Master," moaned the slave.

"It is right for them."

"Yes, Master," said the slave.

She shuddered, kneeling naked before him, in his collar. She knew that she was a slave, in the deepest heart and belly of her. But could what was so obviously right for her, so obviously true of her, she wondered, be right, or true, for all women? Already, in her heart, she had begun to fear free women. They must be so proud, so wondrous, so lofty and formidable, she thought. But then she wondered if they could, truly, be so different from she. Did they not bear in every cell in their bodies, those billions of cells, the same genetic heritage, going back to thongs and caves? She suspected that perhaps they were not so different from her, really. Would they be so different from me, she wondered, if they were, too, as I, on their knees, naked and collared, owned, before an uncompromising, powerful, virile master.

"Did you see how pleased she was to learn that certain selected female rivals, enemies, and such, women she had listed, had been abducted, brought to this world and embonded?"

"Yes, Master," she said.

"Now she is simply following them in her turn."

"Yes, Master," said Ellen. She could well imagine the horror, the dismay, the consternation, which might be felt by the fair guest when her disposition, what men had decided for her, was made clear to her. How her misery would mingle with the viselike grasp of the opened, then closed, spun shut, tightened, then locked-closed branding rack on her thigh, the meticulous, brief, carefully controlled, searing fury of the marking iron, the futile pulling at the light, attractive bracelets that held her hands confined so perfectly behind her, and the sudden awareness of the clasp of a metal band snapped shut, locked, about her neck!

"But you promised her the gold, the diamonds," said the slave.

"And, for a time," said he, "she possessed them. To be sure, now, she does not, for a slave owns nothing. Rather it is she, herself, who is owned. She does not even own her collar, or the pans on the floor from which, tomorrow, we will have her eat and drink."

The slave nodded.

"Certainly you see that she would make a beautiful and desirable slave," he said.

"Yes, Master," she said. There was no doubt about that. The fair guest would make a most beautiful and desirable slave, a luscious bit of collar-meat, a veritable prize of flesh-loot. She would doubtless attract much attention in a public cage.

"So all is in order," he said.

"Yes, Master," she said.

"Who knows?" said he. "Perhaps, in time, Evelyn, for that is the name Jeffrey has selected for her, and she will learn her name tomorrow, that will be soon enough, may eventually serve naked in this room, as you did this evening."

"Yes, Master," whispered the slave.

"And now, Ellen," said he, "do you beg to serve the pleasure of a man, any man?"

She determined to convince him of her worthiness, that he would respect her, that she was worthy of attention, of consideration, perhaps even of love, that there was a great deal more to her than he might be aware of, that she was not merely a small, well-curved, owned, despised little animal which must squirm helplessly in rapture, writhing within the chains of a master.

"What do you think I am?" she asked.

"I know what you are," he said. "What is your response to my question?"

"Certainly not," she said.

"Very well," he said. "Return to your cage."

"Master?" she cried, in dismay.

But with a small gesture he dismissed her.

She leaped up and, in consternation, hurried to her cage.

Chapter 12

She Decides to Beg

She feared her hands and arms might be ruined forever, from the heat, the suds and water. How reddened, how rough, how wrinkled, they seemed to be. How could a master care for them? She and the other girls, you see, in this terrible place, were not permitted lotions. How hard and rough were her hands. How hard and rough they might be on his body, not soft, silken, as should be the hands of a slave. Would a master not recoil from contact with such hands? Surely we should have at least lotions, she thought. That is not so much. Are we not slaves? Surely the touch of a slave should be as soft as the timid pressing of her lips on the master's chest or thigh, as gentle, as stimulating, as caressing as the flow of scented slave silk drawn across his belly, as piteously sweet as a tender whisper in the night, at his feet, from the slave ring, begging for his touch.

Suddenly she cried out in pain, for the whip had struck her back.

She wept, and plunged her arms down again, to the elbows, into the hot water. Though she was still within the house the laundering went clearly beyond what might be the needs of the guards, trainers, servants and slaves. She had little doubt, as the gigantic bundles, bulging with tunics, blankets, himations, veils, shawls, robes and scarves, were brought in that most of the work had its origins on the outside.

Most of the slaves at the tubs were naked, save for their collars. She, too, was naked, except for one device, other than her collar, which had been locked upon her.

She knelt on her mat, beside her tub.

She was a slave laundress.

She could not leave her mat without permission. Too, at the command "Mat!" she and the others must scurry to their mats and kneel upon them. Failure to do this promptly was cause for discipline. She had seen two of the girls tied to rings and lashed. She herself had always gone quickly, obediently, to her mat.

She lifted the garment she was washing, dripping and hot, from the suds. It was a garment doubtless of a free woman. The material was of high quality, and so the woman must be of reasonable station, if not of high caste. She herself did not even know how to put on such a garment, how to drape it, and such. Such women, she supposed, were above menial chores. They would not, for example, do their own laundry. High-caste women, in general, or those of the Merchants, she supposed, would not do their own laundry either, but they might have a slave, or slaves, in their own domiciles to attend to such work. Perhaps this woman had fallen on hard times and had had to sell a slave, and must now send her robes and veils to a commercial laundry. But perhaps she lived alone and thus chose to have the work sent out. Certainly the work came back well-aired, clean-smelling, bright with sunlight, pressed and folded. Ellen, sweating, almost fainting with the heat, the hot, dripping garment in her hands, knelt back for a moment, and, in the hot, moist, close, steaming atmosphere of the low-ceilinged room, gasped for breath. The cost of the laundry work, she conjectured, would be minimal, even negligible, to the laundry's patrons, particularly given its volume. Certainly on such as she the laundry lost little money. She, like the others, was fed on slave gruel and, on all fours, must drink from a pan on the floor.

"Do you dally in your work, little Ellen?" asked a voice.

"No, Master! No, Master!" she cried, and returned the garment to the tub, frenziedly rubbing its folds together.

She had seen the shadow of the legs of Gart, the work-master, on the side of her tub, and the shadow of his whip.

He was a short, gross, blocklike man with a massive bared chest and heavy legs. He wore a half tunic, and bootlike sandals. He had often had her kiss his feet.

She put the back of her hand to her forehead. She gasped, and moaned. She was afraid she might pass out, from the heat, the steam. Her body was soaked with sweat. She could not see it, for there were no mirrors in the laundry, but she supposed that her face, as that of many of the other girls, particularly the fair-complexioned ones, such as she, was red, blotched with red, grossly mottled with red patches, irregular patches painfully, roaringly scarlet, from the heat, from the closeness of the laundry, the oppressive, tropical atmosphere of the cemented, low-ceilinged room.

I do not want to faint, she thought.

I must not faint.

I might be beaten.

A girl who had fainted at her tub was commonly lashed back to consciousness, recalled by the impatient, implacable leather to her labors.

She lifted the garment a bit again from the water.

It was the garment of a free woman. How different it was from the small tunics, the camisks, common and Turian, the scandalous ta-teeras, or slave rags, the slave strips, little more than a shred of cloth and a string, so frequently allotted to slaves, assuming that they were permitted clothing.

She herself did not even know how to wear the garment of a free woman.

One of the girls had, two weeks ago, stood and held such a garment before her, posing, in play. "See!" she had called. "Look here! I am a free woman!" We had laughed in relief, at the delight and farcicality of this, but, unfortunately, Gart, unbeknownst to us, had returned. "We shall see if you are free!" he had roared. "No, no, Master, please, no, Master!" she had cried. "Mat!" had cried Gart, and we all fled to our mats. He then took the slave by the hair and drew her sobbing, and crying out, beneath the high ring. In a moment she was on her tip toes, extended painfully, her wrists crossed and bound, tied to the ring. "It was a joke, Master!" she cried. "Have mercy! Have mercy!" "It is not for *kajirae* to make sport of free women!" he told her. "Never forget that they are a thousand times, an infinite amount of times, your superiors! Now we will see how the joke turns out." "Mercy, Master!" she pleaded. "Beg the whip to forgive you," he suggested. "Perhaps the whip will be merciful." "Oh, dear whip!" she cried. "Please forgive me, dear whip! It was a joke! Be merciful, dear whip! Please forgive me, dear whip!" "What a stupid girl you are," said Gart. "Do you not know that a whip cannot hear you, that it has no ears?" And he then put the leather to her, and not pleasantly. She spun in her bonds, weeping, lashed. When he had finished he released her and she fell to his feet. "You may now thank me for your beating," he informed her. She licked and kissed his feet. "Thank you for beating me, Master," she said.

Gart had then had her crawl back to her tub.

Ellen did not want to be beaten.

She feared that if she fainted she might be beaten.

Surreptitiously Ellen viewed the garment of the free woman. She hoped she had not been too rough with it, in her fear of Gart. It must, above all, not be rent. Even a tiny tear at a seam, she knew, could earn her a beating, but a real beating, not just the two or three strokes that might awaken a girl from a faint.

She heard a girl crying out, a few tubs from her, and, looking over, she saw blond, blue-eyed Nelsa flung on her belly over the water, she gripping the sides of the tub, desperately, to keep from falling into the water. Behind her, Gart had lifted and spread her legs. Ellen shuddered, and looked away.

Ellen was thankful for the device she wore, though sometimes she felt like crying out in misery, because of discomfort, its weight and heat.

She had seen her master only once since the evening in the special room, that so like a room on Earth, in which she had suitably, properly served a lovely supper, stripped.

It had been the morning following that supper, when he had come to her cage, released her, and had her stand, bent forward, gripping the roof of the cage, her back to him, her legs widely spread.

He had been carrying an object whose nature was not immediately clear to her.

Facing away from him, her legs widely spread, she had become aware of him reaching in front of her, and then of two circular, hinged, straplike bands being put about her waist, and then being brought together, front to back, behind her. Another piece of the apparatus dangled before her, but it was, in a moment, on its hinge, drawn up between her legs. She felt the object being jerked about, and, with two hands, being adjusted on her. These three parts of the apparatus were then fitted together, the two side straps over a staple welded to the central portion of the device which had been lifted up between her legs and was now at the small of her back. She then felt the bolt of a heavy padlock thrust through the staple and snapped shut, this holding the pieces of the apparatus together, at the small of her back. When she moved she was conscious of the padlock, its weight, and how it moved, against the three parts it secured in place. Again the object was moved about, and adjusted, with two hands, on her body.

"A good fit," said a guard.

"Yes," had said her master.

"Master?" she had asked.

"You have not been given permission to speak," he said.

"Forgive me, Master," she had said.

Because of the narrowness of her waist, and the natural flare of her hips, she could not hope to elude the device.

She wore the iron belt.

"Send her to the laundry," had said her master.

* * * *

When she had been presented to Gart, and performed obeisance before him, had kissed his feet and had begged to be permitted to serve in the laundry, he had growled in rage, regarding her. He had thrown her to her side and examined, in detail, the device she wore.

"What is this?" he had snarled.

The guard had merely shrugged.

Ellen, lying frightened on her side, locked in the device, at his feet, had no delusions with respect to the work-master's displeasure.

A glance at the room, as soon as she had entered, she almost suddenly overcome, almost suddenly fainting, from the heat and the steam, had shown her, almost as through a hot fog, that there were several girls in the room, that they were naked, that many were apparently lovely, and that all were kneeling, sweating, their hair streaming down, limp, working at tubs.

Ellen had been struck with horror at this environment. Then she had knelt down, performing obeisance.

"How am I to tub this one?" asked the work-master.

"Tub the others," suggested the guard.

"A virgin?" asked the work-master, incredulously.

"I think so," said the guard. "As you can see, she is quite young, little more than a girl."

"Kneel up," ordered the work-master.

Ellen assumed position.

"I do not like virgins," the work-master informed her.

Then Ellen cried out, cuffed, struck to the side. She could not maintain her balance, but fell to her right side. She could taste blood in her mouth, from her lip.

"To my feet," said the work-master. "Beg my forgiveness for being a virgin."

Ellen went to her belly before him, her lips over his feet. "Forgive me for being a virgin, Master," she said. "Please forgive me for being a virgin!" Then, fearfully, terrified before this man, she kissed his feet.

He stepped back then, angry, but mollified.

"We will get her a mat and put her to a tub," he said.

* * * *

Ellen drew back, suddenly, crying out, for a stream of hot water, poured from a ewer, streamed into her tub, almost scalding her.

"Please, Mistress!" protested Ellen. She was the least in the laundry, because of the youth of her body, and that she was newest at the tubs. Accordingly, she must address her sister laundresses with such respect, though they, too, were but slaves.

"Why did you look when Gart put me to his pleasure?" demanded Nelsa.

"I looked away, Mistress!" cried Ellen.

"Not soon enough!" said Nelsa. "Do you think I like being put to the pleasure of such a brute?"

"Perhaps, Mistress," said Ellen. "Surely I have seen you wriggle well, lifted at the tub, his arms about your legs." Nelsa was certainly one of Gart's favorites.

"I hate him!" said Nelsa.

"Is that why you whimper, moan and cry out as you do?" asked Ellen.

"I cannot help it if he masters me," said Nelsa, angrily.

"Then you must be a slave," said Ellen. "No!" cried Ellen.

Nelsa had lifted the ewer of boiling water.

"Stay on your mat!" said Nelsa.

"Please, no, Mistress!" cried Ellen.

"You will not be so pretty when you are a mass of scar tissue!" snarled Nelsa. "Stay on your mat!"

"Please, no, Mistress!" cried Ellen.

"Do not be stupid, Nelsa," said a shapely redhead, kneeling at a nearby tub. "Let the child alone!"

"Do your work," snapped Nelsa.

"If you damage her you will be boiled alive," said the redhead.

"Look," said Nelsa. "She has moved part way from her mat. Gart must hear of this!"

Ellen scrambled back, that she might be on her mat, fully. For once she wished that Gart was in the room. She looked upward, apprehensively, at the poised ewer.

Then Nelsa lowered the ewer.

"You think you are so special, little she-urt," said Nelsa to Ellen, "because you are belted! Well, there are many ways in which a slave can give pleasure to a man. And you are not in lock-gag!"

Ellen did not know what an urt was.

There are several varieties of lock-gags. One common variety consists of a short, leather-sheathed metal chain which, at its center, passes through a heavy ball-like packing. The packing is thrust back in the slave's mouth, over the tongue, filling the oral orifice, making it impossible for her to do more than moan or whimper. The two ends of the short chain are then drawn back, tightly, back between the teeth, this holding the packing in place. The ends of the chain are then taken back about the sides of the neck and brought together behind the back of the neck where they are fastened together with a small padlock. The gag's dislodgment must then, since it is locked on the slave, await the master's pleasure. Another common variety of lock-gag involves a pair of narrow, rounded, curved, hinged rods, the hinge embedded in a heavy, leather, ball-like packing. This packing, as before, is inserted into the slave's mouth and thrust back, over the tongue, denying her any capacity to speak. The rods, which are back, between the teeth, holding the packing in place, curve back about the sides of the face and meet behind the back of the neck, where the ends may lock together, or, if a padlock is used, be locked together. An advantage of a lock-gag is, of course, that the slave, while totally unable to speak, may yet attend to whatever other duties her master may set her. To be sure, a simple tie gag, which the slave is forbidden to remove, has the same effect. Too, of course, her mouth may be simply taped shut. Similarly, more mercifully, and at greater convenience to the master, she may be "gagged by the master's will." In that case she is simply forbidden to speak, save perhaps for moans and whimpers. She may, of course, speak later, once she has received permission to do so. If the slave is in lock-gag, one understands, there are certain pleasures she is unable to give the master. Doubtless it was with respect to these pleasures that the remark of Nelsa had reference.

"I do not think that master would approve," whispered Ellen, frightened.

She would have loved to have pleased her master in this intimate fashion, and had dreamed of begging to do so, but Gart, or another, would surely be a different matter.

Giving the master such pleasures, and many others, is fitting for a slave.

"So you think I wriggle well?" said Nelsa.

"It seemed so to me, Mistress," said Ellen.

"And how do you wriggle, little belted pudding?"

"I have never wriggled, Mistress," said Ellen.

"Men can teach you to wriggle," said Nelsa.

Ellen put down her head.

"So you think I am a slave?" asked Nelsa.

"Yes, Mistress," said Ellen, shyly.

"Do you think I can help how I now am?" asked Nelsa.

"I am sure I do not know, Mistress," said Ellen.

"Do you not understand, you stupid little virgin, how men can enflame a woman, can make her helpless, can make her crave their least touch?"

"Perhaps if she is a slave," said Ellen.

Nelsa's hands tightened on the handle of the ewer.

"Do not hurt her," said the redhead.

"She was off her mat," said Nelsa. "I will tell!"

"You, too, have been off your mat when Gart was not in the room," said the redhead. "And if you tell, we, too, can tell!"

There was assent to this from several of the slaves at the tubs.

One was an auburn-haired beauty who claimed to have once served the pleasure of Chenbar of Kasra, Chenbar the Sea-Sleen, Ubar of Tyros. More likely, some said, she had served in a prison on Tyros, and had been periodically cast to the prisoners, and handed about, amongst them, to reduce their unruliness. Ellen supposed both stories might be true. Perhaps the woman, who was very beautiful, had once served in the pleasure gardens of Chenbar, but had then in some small way displeased him, or perhaps he had merely tired of her. Later, as others might replace her in her prison duties, she might be sold on the mainland, and thence south. Another was a lovely slave of mixed blood, whose eyes bore the epicanthic fold. Another was a black woman with a chain collar and disk. It was said she had already been spoken for by a black merchant. Two others were sisters from a city called Venna, taken when returning from a pilgrimage to the Sardar Mountains. They would presumably be separated in the markets.

"You, too, will learn to beg and scratch, little tasta," said Nelsa to Ellen.

Ellen did not know what a tasta was. Later she learned that it was a confection, a small, soft candy mounted on a stick.

Ellen pulled back, suddenly, softly crying out, shielding her face as

Nelsa, in a sudden, plunging stream, too close to her, water splashing and hissing, emptied the ewer into the tub.

"Get to work, slave," sneered Nelsa.

"Yes, Mistress," said Ellen. Then she cried out with pain. "It is too hot, Mistress," she said. "I can not put my hands in the water!"

Nelsa had turned away.

Another slave, an exotic, bred for stripes, put more laundry beside her.

Ellen looked up in misery. There was so much!

She shrank down beside her tub, on her mat. She wished it was night so that she might be alone in her bin, with her blanket.

She supposed that women of low caste must do their own laundry.

Why had her master put her here, in this terrible place, she wondered. Perhaps she was being punished, but for what? Had she been put here for instructional purposes, that she might better understand her bondage? Why did he hate her so? Or did he hate her? Or could there be another reason? I must be special to him, somehow, she thought, that he has done this to me. Then she thought, fearfully, but perhaps I am not special to him, at all. Perhaps he does not even think of me. Perhaps I am here because I am not special at all. Perhaps I am to him only another meaningless slave. No, she said, I am here because it amuses him to put me here, his former teacher, one he perhaps found, to his irritation, troublesomely, even disturbingly attractive, to put me here in this terrible place, here in the laundry, miserable, sweating, no more than a naked work-slave, set to the meanest and lowest of duties. But he brought me to this world, she thought. He remembered me. I think he wants me! Yes she thought, *wants*, as a man *wants* a woman, or rather, she thought, thrilled, as a master wants *a slave*. Oh, I hope so, I hope so! I love him so! He is my master! She lay on her side, on the mat, beside the tub. She felt the heavy device locked on her body. She lightly traced with her finger the narrow curved plate between her legs, with its curved, long, slender, saw-toothed opening. The saw-toothed edges were sharp. Twice, in cleaning herself, she had cut herself. Then she had learned to go above and behind the edges, pulling the belt down and away a little. This can be managed by pulling it down an inch or so at the waist, but then, of course, it can go only so far, being stopped by the width of the hips, which she had, more than once, abraded. He put the belt on me, she thought, happily. Oh, I hate it, for its weight, its clumsiness, its bulkiness, its embarrassment, its inconvenience, but does it not show that I am special to him? Is he not keeping my virginity for himself? Or, to use the vulgar Gorean expression, at least as applied to slaves, does he not wish to be the first to open me?

At this point she pauses briefly in the narrative.

The saying is given more fully, commonly, as "open *for the uses of men*." She adds this, it occurring to her that some who read this might feel that she was overly delicate, or insufficiently explicit or informative, at this point. She fears she might be chided for a lack of candor, and perhaps with the leather.

She was glad Gart was not in the room.

There was much laundry beside her tub, but he would have no way of knowing, upon his return, that it had not been just placed there.

Surely Kiri, the exotic, would not volunteer this information. If explicitly questioned, of course, she must, kneeling, head to the floor, tell the truth.

She wished that it was night and that she was in her cement bin. It was so much cooler there. The blanket gave her some protection from the cement. The bins had no gates or ceilings. Their walls were about four feet high, but one could not see over them once one had been chained by the neck to the ring at the back. The chain was about two feet in length. One could do little more than rise to one's knees, perform obeisance, and such things. The girls were forbidden to speak to one another when in their bins. This rule tended to be scrupulously kept, for it was difficult to tell, chained low as one was, when a guard might be in the vicinity, behind the bins. One would dread, looking up and back, seeing the sight of his upper body and angry frown suddenly appearing, looming, over the back wall of one's bin. Soon he would appear in front of the bins, with his whip, and the errant slaves, to their dismay, their pleas for mercy unheeded, would be appropriately admonished. In the laundry Gart was more tolerant, though he did not encourage frivolous discourse. When he was absent, of course, the frenzy of work slowed and the buds of conversation, warily, timidly, began to open.

She thought again of the garments of the free woman. She did not even know how to arrange such garments on her body. Too, she had no footwear. Too, there was no place to hide such garments, the tubs being turned and emptied at night. Too, such garments were counted, and would be soon missed.

Although Ellen had never been outside the house she understood that there was no escape for the Gorean slave girl, even outside. There was the brand, the collar, the garmenture. More importantly, there was no place to go, no place to hide, no place to run. The legal rights of the masters were everywhere acknowledged, respected and enforced. At their back was the full power of custom, tradition and law. The most that a girl might hope for would be a change of masters. If she managed to elude one master, and were not, when captured, returned to him, perhaps for mutilation and hamstringing, she would soon find herself in the power of another, and doubtless one far less likely than the first to treat her with trust and lenience, to mistakenly indulge her with abusable privileges. It is not pleasant to wear close shackles or a double-padlocked six-inch chain joining one's ankles. The Gorean slave girl has no way to free herself or earn her freedom. She is simply and categorically slave. Her freedom, if she is to be accorded freedom, is always in the hands of another. Too, there is a Gorean saying that only a fool frees a slave girl.

Ellen thought, again, of the garment of the free woman.

She shuddered.

Even to put on such a garment, she knew, could be a capital offense for such as she.

No, Ellen did not think of freedom, for she knew that on this world that was not possible for her.

But more significantly she knew herself slave.

It was what she was, and wanted to be. It was right for her.

Too, for many years she had been free. Certainly she knew, and understood, and had enjoyed all that that condition could possibly bestow upon anyone. There was nothing in that condition which was unknown to her, or unfamiliar to her. Freedom, in itself, while undeniably precious, and doubtless a value, and doubtless appropriate for males, whom she now understood, having met true men, were the natural masters of women, tended, in itself, to be an abstraction, a possibility, an emptiness, in its way. It might be no more than a rootless boredom, in itself an invitation to nothing. Certainly those on her former world who most shamelessly exploited the rhetoric of freedom did not lack freedom, but rather wanted to use such rhetorics, and allied pressures and subterfuges, in order to have goods, unfair advantages, special privileges, and such, given to them, such as economic resources, prestige, and power. Their test for freedom was the receipt of ever-greater amounts of politically engineered unearned benefits. She had been free, and had not been fulfilled, or happy. Now, as a female slave, she suspected that her true fulfillment, her true happiness, might lie in a totally different, unexpected direction. The question, you see, was one of simple, empirical fact. Its solution was not essentially a consequence of a particular conditioning program, one of a possibly infinite number of such, or the inevitable result of some supposedly self-evident, axiomatic proposition, or some supposedly *a priori* theory, but of the world, the nature of things, of simple, empirical fact. Perhaps freedom was not the ideal for everyone. Was that so impossible to conceive of? Perhaps people, perhaps the sexes, were really different. Certainly they seemed very different. One had to struggle not to see that. What if what might be best for one was not truly the best for the other? What was best for one, it seems, might depend, really, not on politics and conditioning, not on cultural accidents and the idiosyncrasies of an ephemeral historical situation, but on other things, say, nature, truth, fact, such things. Perhaps human beings had a nature, like other species. If so, what was her nature? Presumably, whatever it was, it would be a fact about her. She did recognize, of course, that freedom was not an absolute, and that even the most free, so to speak, were subject to countless limitations. At best, freedom was relative, even for the free. But these considerations were not germane to what concerned her most. She had been free. She knew what it was like. She had tried it, and found it wanting. She had been free, and had been free and lonely, free and unwanted, free and unnoticed, free and undesired, free and terribly miserable. Something within her had begged to belong, actually, to be overwhelmed and owned, something within her had cried out to love and serve, totally and helplessly, to give herself unreservedly, totally and helplessly to another. But her world had denied that freedom to her. It had denied the cry of her deepest heart. It had told her, rather, not to listen to her heart, but to deny it, told her, rather, to be different, and mannish. One freedom had been denied to her, the freedom not to be free. That freedom had been denied to her. Freedom had been imposed upon her, socially, legally. She could not have given up her freedom even if she had wished to do so. Freedom was doubtless precious. But, so, too, she thought, was love. And she did not desire the tepidities which might exist between contractual partners. The notion of a democracy of two was absurd. One might pretend that absolute equality could be imposed upon absolute unequals, but it could never be more than a pretense. That myth would have to be hedged about with so many conventions, sanctions, rules and laws as to be a biological joke. It is a farce to claim that absolute sameness, for that is what equality means, could be imposed rationally on creatures as unlike as a man and a woman. To speak as though absolute equality, save doubtless in merit, or value, each marvelous in their own very different way, could exist between absolute unequals, things as diverse as a male and a female, was at best an idle social ritual, and, at worst, a pathological lie which, if taken seriously, if acted upon, would have, by its deleterious effects on the gene pool, widespread, devastating consequences for the inclusive fitness of a species. But such far-flung considerations were far from Ellen's thoughts at the time. She did know enough sociology, and enough history, to know, though she would not have dared to mention it in her classes, that human happiness, statistically, bears no essential relationship to freedom whatsoever, but is rather a function of doing what one feels like doing, with the reinforcement and support of social expectations. Ellen wondered if she were a terrible woman, because she wanted love, because she wanted to serve, wholly and helplessly, because she was eager to be devoted and dutiful, because she wanted to make a man happy, to please a master, because she wanted to literally be his, to be owned by him, to be his complete property, to belong to him, in every way. She wondered if it were such a terrible thing, to desire to surrender herself inextricably, wholly to love. In her heart, it seemed, there had begun to burn, even then, in a small way, small at first, like a tiny glowing flame, not fully understood, the longing to know the deepest and most profound of loves, the most complete of loves, the most helpless and self-surrendering of all loves, a slave's love.

And, too, even in the iron belt, she had begun to sense what might be the nature of a slave's passion.

She wondered if she, too, as Nelsa had put it, would learn to beg and scratch. To her terror, she feared she might.

She squirmed a little in the belt. It seemed heavy on her. And yet how vulnerable she would feel, as she was, naked and collared, without it.

I must not let myself be a wicked woman, she thought. No, no, she thought. I cannot mean exactly that. She had long ago abandoned, at least in her official views, the acknowledgedly obsolescent category of "wicked," with its suppressive, grotesque historical antecedents, but, on the other hand, it was difficult for her to clear her mind of the fumes, the noxious residue, of the past, particularly as these residues had been carefully encouraged, propagated, utilized and exploited by ideologues to advance their own political projects. And such was the victim, she, of years of lingeringly puritanical enculturation. And thus, so to speak, are the sins of the fathers, and of the mothers, visited upon succeeding generations.

To be sure, already on Gor, perhaps because of the air, or the water, or the simple, decent, nourishing food, or perhaps, primarily, because of the simple differences in this world, so fresh, natural and innocent, the immersion in a different culture, so very different from her own, with its different values and *ethos*, she had begun to suspect the existence of psychological freedoms and possibilities, of opennesses, which would have been forever beyond her ken on her former world.

But she was still, in many ways, a creature of that strange world.

I must keep myself above sex, she thought. I must not let myself become sexually aroused. I must never let myself become like Nelsa. I have seen her in Gart's grasp. How terrible that would be if I should become like that! How terrible that would be if I should become sexually helpless in a man's arms! I must never let myself become like that. I must never beg and scratch!

But, she thought, squirming in the belt, beside the tub, I am a slave girl! Passion will be required of me. I must yield, and wholly. If I am displeasing, I will doubtless be beaten, or slain. They will give me no choice! I must not keep myself above sex. It will not be permitted. I must let myself become sexually aroused. It will be required of me! I must become like Nelsa! I must become such that I am helpless in a man's arms. Then, when they have made me such, when they have triggered and ignited my needs and, by their decision, and perhaps to their amusement, made me the helpless victim of them, those profound, terrible, wonderful, overwhelming, irresistible, ecstatic needs, when I must weep, and go half mad with desire, then perhaps I, too, will beg and scratch.

Could I, Ellen, learn to beg and scratch, she wondered.

Yes, she thought. I dimly sense that I, too, might learn to beg and scratch.

She lay beside her tub, thrilled, considering the sexual freedom of the Gorean slave girl. She felt a twinge of regret for free women. How unfortunate they are, she thought. How they must envy us, she thought. It is no wonder that they hate us as they do, or as I have been told they do.

She fingered her collar. How strange, she thought. I am naked, and in a collar, and yet I feel so free! I sense that I may be the freest and happiest, the most liberated, of all women. But then she shuddered, recalling that she was a slave, and subject to the whip and chains. She was an animal. She must obey. She could be bought and sold. It is strange, she thought. I seem to be the most free, and the least free, of all women.

She suddenly heard a small knock at the side of the tub. "Gart," whispered Laura, the redhead.

Quickly Ellen scrambled up and thrust her hands into the soapy water. It was hot but she could now keep her hands and forearms submerged. She seized, and began to rub and work, the clothes in the tub.

She did not look up, but wished to seem intent on her work. All about her, too, she could sense the slaves return to their tasks. Ellen was pleased that there was no way, apparently, that the girls could be observed when Gart was out of the room.

She sensed him walking about, up and down the aisles, between the tubs. Then he had stopped, a bit behind her and to her left. She kept her head down, laundering, as though unaware of his presence. Then she felt his massive hand in her hair, tight, and he pulled her up to an erect kneeling position. His grip was painful in her hair but, as a slave, she dared not protest. Too, though the grip was painful, she sensed he was not trying to her hurt her, just hold her. It struck her as strange, in a way, that she should be so handled. On Earth, had a man so gripped her, she would have been affrighted and would have resisted; she would have screamed, and struggled, and, in a moment, doubtless a number of good fellows would have rushed to her succor, or surely a policeman, if one were in the vicinity. Here, on the other hand, she must submit uncomplainingly. It could be done to her, and she had no recourse. She was slave. In her training she had learned that slaves could be handled casually, and with assurance, and roughly, and brutally. They could be turned from side to side, flung to their belly, thrown to a wall, forced to assume any number of positions, sometimes their bodies being seized and literally placed, limb by limb, in the desired position, handled with an imperious handling, sometimes conjoined with a sharp word of instruction or admonishment. The slave's body, for example, does not belong to her. It, like the entirety of her, belongs to the master. She then felt her body, her hair in his grip, his left hand on her left knee, bent backward, until she was helpless before him; the "slave bow," as the expression is, of her vulnerable, owned beauty thusly exhibited for his attention, or assessment. "Yes," he said, rather more to himself than to her, or another, "you are pretty." She was thrilled, but a little frightened, to hear this. Someone must have said something to Gart, perhaps one of the guards, one who might have observed the girls at night, sleeping, chained by the neck, in their bins. Or perhaps one of the kitchen staff, who ladled gruel into the shallow depressions in the bins.

Gart released her and stood up.

Instantly Ellen went to first obeisance position.

"May I speak, Master?" she asked.

There were gasps from the girls about her. But she was not, she was sure, imperiling herself. She had sensed that this was a moment in which an opportunity to speak might be granted to her. Surely Gart seemed to be in a good, if somewhat bemused, mood. Too, a slave girl quickly learns how to use her body, to produce a mood, or to attempt to entice or encourage one, to stimulate, to placate, to lure, to arouse, and so on. To be sure, Ellen supposed that she had not intended to have any particular effect on Gart, at least fully consciously, certainly not, and, indeed, she had been helpless in his grip, had she not, but she realized, even then, even when she was so new to the collar, that the sight of her beauty must have some sort of effect upon men, and she might have, it seems possible, though she was not sure of it, and doubtless would have denied it at the time, and doubtless it did not take place, struggled a little, a tiny bit, pathetically, futilely, gasped plaintively, submissively, looked up, pathetically, permitted her lips to tremble slightly, and, bent back, drew in her gut, and quickly lifted her bosom, thus accentuating the line of the "slave bow." She heard the auburn-haired slave gasp. Two other slaves laughed. What are they laughing about, Ellen had asked herself, angrily. In any event she had determined to profit from this moment, that won for her through no intent of her own, and despite her complete innocence and modesty, by her beauty. It is not unusual for a slave girl, incidentally, to capitalize upon, utilize and exploit her own beauty, making use of it for her own ends. Indeed, she has little else to use for such purposes. This is, of course, in no sense an admission that Ellen had put her beauty before Gart, that brute, the work-master, he who ruled the laundry and to whom she was fearfully subject, in any way that might have been intended to appeal to him, in any way that manifested her slaveness. How could she have done so? Would it not have been the act of a frightened slave? She was a woman of Earth! To be sure, she had by this time been collared. There are many ambiguities, many opacities, in human experience. So let us suppose that the surmises of her chain sisters were mistaken. Could she then, so long ago, have been such a slave? Surely not!

Forgive me, dear reader!

Forgive me, too, Masters!

I have been instructed to leave the above passage as it is, for purposes of comparison, but now to speak the truth. I must obey. How merciless they are!

Yes, Masters, Ellen put herself before Gart—*as a slave*! There, it is said!

I dare not lie. The masters will have the truth of me. The free woman may lie. I may not. I am slave. Is this so hard to understand, my terror in these matters, dear reader, that I dare not lie? I assure you that you will understand it, dear reader, and very well, should you one day find yourself in the collar.

The use of their sex, and desirability, to achieve their own ends is, of course, common with women generally, whether bond or free. One supposes, accordingly, in that sense, that all women are prostitutes. And men, it seems, do not object to this. Indeed, it seems to be one of the things they find most charming and endearing about the truly *opposite* sex. The slave girl, of course, is far less capable of profiting, certainly in a commercial manner, from her prostitute inclinations than is the free woman. The free woman, being free, can sell, barter or trade her beauty for favors or gain. The beauty of the slave girl, on the other hand, like she herself, is owned, and can thus be commanded by the master for his pleasure, at any time, in any way he may desire. Thus, though the slave girl has, like any other woman, her charming, delicious, ingrained, biologically selected-for prostitute tendencies, she is scarcely in a position to use them in order to garner for herself rich gifts, economic privileges, appointment preferences, status, prestige, advancements, power, and such; rather she might hope to have a pastry cast to the floor before her, to win a smile from her master, to be granted the modesty of a slave strip, to be permitted to elude, at least for a time, the whip. But despite sharing with her free sister her charming prostitute tendencies the slave is, in a more serious sense, not a prostitute. The prostitute is a thousand times above the slave. The prostitute is a free woman, and the slave is bond.

"Yes," said Gart.

Ellen lifted her head a little and threw a glance at Nelsa, who turned white.

"While in the laundry I have seen girls come and go, Master," she said. "Some stay longer, some less. How long, if I may ask, am I to work here?"

One of the sisters from Venna uttered a small inadvertent noise, one of shock, startled at the boldness of the young slave.

But Gart did not strike the young slave.

"I do not know," he said. "Perhaps a day, perhaps a week, perhaps a month, perhaps a year, perhaps ten years, perhaps the rest of your life."

Ellen, head down, moaned.

"Your master is Mirus, is it not?" he asked.

"Yes, Master," said Ellen. That information, she was sure, was on her collar.

"Perhaps he has forgotten about you," said Gart.

"Could you not remind him that I am here, Master?" said Ellen.

"Do not be silly," said Gart.

"Forgive me, Master," said Ellen.

Gart made as though to turn away.

"Master!" called Ellen.

"Yes," he said, turning about.

"If you should see him, tell him that Ellen is ready to beg!"

"What does that mean?"

"He will understand, Master."

Gart fingered the whip at his belt.

"Please do not make me speak, Master," pleaded Ellen.

"Is this the standard begging?" asked Gart.

"I do not know what the standard begging is, Master," said Ellen.

"To please a man, *any man*," said Gart.

"Yes, Master," whispered Ellen, head down.

"And you are now ready to so beg?"

"Yes, Master."

"Then you are not only truly a slave, which is obvious, but you are prepared to acknowledge that you are truly a slave," said Gart.

"Yes Master," said Ellen.

Gart removed his hand from the whip.

"If I see him, I will mention it," said Gart. "But I doubt that it will be of much interest to him."

"Yes, Master. Thank you, Master."

"Return to your work, slave."

"Yes, Master."

Ellen had arrived at a bold plan. That she was in the iron belt must be meaningful, an indication of her master's interest in her, his solicitude for her, his reserving of her deflowering, or her "opening for the uses of men," for himself alone. He must want her, as a special slave, perhaps even a preferred slave! He had put her in the laundry, why? He must be waiting for her to respond affirmatively to the question put to her that evening after supper, an affirmative response that would indicate her interest in, and desire for, sexual experience, in and for itself. What could that response mean, other than the fact that one was at last brave enough, courageous enough, to break through the shackles of Earth conditioning, to admit explicitly to oneself and others that one was a sexual creature, a human female with genuinely human female needs. Surely it could mean no more than that. Too, he presumably wanted her before him naked and kneeling, and uttering such a formula, to further humiliate her, to further pursue his program of vengeance upon her. That would give him an opportunity to again subject her to scorn, another opportunity to exhibit his contempt for her, another opportunity to force her to recognize the debasement, the degradation, to which he had brought her. She must, before him, confess herself the lowest of slaves. She must acknowledge freely what she had now become, make clear to herself, and others, her own abjectness. Very well, she thought. So be it! If that is what he wants I shall give it to him, and meaningfully, and freely. I am a slave. Why should I not admit it?

Apparently I must stay where I am, in the laundry, as a naked, sweating work-slave, until I do this. I acknowledge that his will is stronger than mine. Of course it is. My will is nothing. It is that of a slave. He is master, I am slave. I do not want to remain another minute in this place. I will do anything he wants, anything to escape the misery of this room, the tubs and the heat! But, she told herself, smiling inwardly, I think this is in the nature of a test. He must like me. Perhaps he loves me! Once I beg to serve a man, any man, he will be satisfied, and then, of course, keep me for himself, for himself alone. I love him so! I want to be his slave and serve him. Even from the first time I saw him, so many years ago, something in me wanted to be his slave!

Later that day Gart was again out of the room.

Nelsa was now working at a nearby tub. The black woman, with the chain collar and disk, who was awaiting her consignment to a black merchant, was now carrying the ewer.

"So the little slave is now ready to beg?" asked Nelsa.

Ellen pretended not to hear.

"Slave," sneered Nelsa.

"I did not tell on you, for nearly scalding me this morning," said Ellen. "Perhaps I will do so when Gart returns."

"Thank you for not telling on me," said Nelsa, turning white.

"Perhaps I will do so when Gart returns," said Ellen.

"Please do not do so," said Nelsa.

"I understand," said Ellen, "that if I had been damaged, you might have been boiled alive. As I was not damaged, I gather that your actual punishment may be less severe."

"Please do not tell on me," pleaded Nelsa.

"I think Gart likes me," said Ellen.

"Please do not tell on me!" begged Nelsa.

"Please, what?" asked Ellen.

"Please—*Mistress,*" said Nelsa.

"I shall give the matter thought," said Ellen, tossing her head.

"Thank you, Mistress," whispered Nelsa.

"Now, get back to your work, slave," said Ellen.

"Yes, Mistress," said Nelsa.

"You are a stupid little slave, Ellen," said Laura, the redhead.

"I think that Gart likes me," said Ellen.

"Do not speak his name!" warned one of the sisters from Venna. "You could be beaten. One refers to free men as "Master" and free women as "Mistress," unless given permission to use their names."

"And that permission," said the other sister, "is almost never granted. What free person would want their name soiled by the tongue of a slave? I never let my slaves refer to me by my name."

"I think that Gart likes me," said Ellen. "I have never been out of the house. Tomorrow I think will ask him to let me be one of the girls who airs and dries the washing, on the roof."

"Bold slave!" said Laura.

"I think I can have men do what I want," said Ellen.

"Beware," said Laura. "Do not forget you are a slave!"

"Men are the masters," said one of the sisters from Venna.

"They are the *masters*," said the other sister, pleadingly.

"Perhaps," said Ellen, lightly, tossing her head. "But we shall see, shan't we?"

"Have no fear but what you will see, you stupid little slave," said Laura.

"But I am a pretty slave, and a clever slave," said Ellen.

"You are a pretty slave, yes," said Laura. "You are a very pretty slave. But you are not a clever slave. You are a stupid slave."

Ellen smiled, and tossed her head, dismissively.

When Gart returned to the room, the slaves, including Ellen, returned to their work.

Chapter 13

The Roof;
She Is Summoned Before Her Master

"How beautiful!" exclaimed Ellen.

The wind swept about her, whipping the long, white, ankle-length, sleeveless gown she wore about her body. She was barefoot.

She looked out, over the city.

Above her there raced white clouds in a bright blue sky.

"I have never seen anything like this," whispered Ellen, touching her collar.

"Do not go too near the edge," said Laura.

There was no railing.

"This world is so beautiful, and so fresh, and so marvelous," said Ellen, "and here I am a slave."

To tread such a world, thought Ellen, is worth a brand and a collar, a thousand brands and a thousand collars. What a privilege and joy to be brought here! Do those who are native to this world understand how wonderful it is? I did not know such a world could exist! She reveled in the freshness of the air and the beauty of the sky, and city. How different this was from the gray, crowded, unkempt, polluted, unloved, filthy, squalid city with she was most familiar from her former world.

"How beautiful it is," she called to Laura.

Laura came to stand beside her. "It is beautiful," said Laura.

"It is so much more beautiful than most of the cities of my former world," said Ellen.

"Perhaps those cities have no Home Stones," said Laura.

"You two had best be attending to your work," called Nelsa.

On the broad, circular roof, some fifty yards in diameter, there were numerous, sturdy, tiered racks of poles on which levels of laundry might be dried, and, between these racks, were numerous swaying lines, from which a great deal more wash, like flags, shook, flapped and fluttered in the wind, held to the lines with simple, numerous, wooden, hand-carved clothespins.

Gart, when he had acceded to Ellen's request to work on the roof, had assigned several of the girls close to her the same duty. Perhaps he thought they were friends. He would not know that Nelsa hated Ellen, fearing that she might tell her secret, about the threatened scalding. Nor would he know that Ellen, in Laura's opinion, was little more than a petty, vain, stupid, self-important, ignorant, scheming, meaningless little bit of slave fluff. On the other hand, as an astute work-master, well accustomed to dealing with female slaves, he may have assigned the group as he did in order to reduce jealousy, diminish resentments, and such. After all, he could not always be in the laundry. Perhaps, too, he recognized Ellen's youth and vulnerability, her newness to the collar and such, and thought he might as well do what he could, within reason, to protect her. Too, there was no denying that she was an extremely pretty little slave, and this may have had something to do with it. This is not to say that she did not feel his whip when she shirked her work. It is one thing to be very pretty; it is quite another not to be fully pleasing. Another possibility, of course, is that this would be Ellen's first venture to the roof, and he thought it well to have some of her associates, slaves she knew, slaves with whom she would be expected to be able to communicate, for whatever reason, in her vicinity.

Ellen stood rapt on the roof, the wind moving her long, sleeveless garment about her, gazing across the city, in awe, tears in her eyes.

"You had best return to your basket and begin to hang the clothing," said Laura, turning away, going back to her own basket.

Ellen lifted her arms gratefully to the city, the sky, the world. "I love you, planet Gor," she cried. "You are so beautiful. Here the world is new. Here one begins again. What an honor, what a privilege, what an incredible gift, just to be able to see you, just to be permitted to be here! How unworthy are the women of Earth to know your glory and beauty! What could a woman such as I be on a world such as this but a slave? On such a world what else could we be? Oh, thank you, Masters, for bringing us here, if only for your own purposes, if only to have us as slaves, if only to have us in our collars, abjectly serving, licking and kissing, naked at your feet! I thank you, oh Masters! I thank you, I thank you!"

"Ellen!" called Laura, impatiently, from back amongst the lines of swaying, fluttering clothes.

"Yes, yes!" said Ellen.

She looked out across the city. The building on whose roof she stood, and it had been a long climb to the roof from the laundry, bearing the heavy basket, was very similar to most of the other buildings she saw in the city. It was one of the "high cities," a forest of cylinders, a city of towering, spaced cylinders, many of them in bright colors, and, joining these cylinders, at various levels, like light curving, colored, rail-less traceries in the sky, were numerous bridges. She could see individuals on many of the bridges. Too, there were individuals in the streets below. In the distance, too, between the cylinders, many of which must have been twenty or thirty living tiers, or stories, high, she could see walls. She thought they, too, must be very high. Too, their tops seemed almost like roads. She did not doubt but what two wagons might pass on them. Though it was far off, she thought she could see, like specks, some individuals here and there on the walls. Occasionally there was a flash, as might have resulted from the sun's being suddenly reflected from a metal surface, perhaps a helmet, a spear point, a shield. There must have been parapets, and, discernibly, here and there, there were small towers, which may have been guard stations. Some of these towers jutted partly out from the walls, which would expose the sheer declivity of the architectural escarpment to view. Why would a city need walls, she asked herself. Ellen, who at that time was not only new to her collar, but largely ignorant of the nature of the world on which she found herself, did not understand the darker or more problematic meanings of what she saw, or, perhaps better, the full implications of what she saw. She saw little more than the beauty of the city, its style, its color, its grace, its splendor. She did not understand at that time that the considerations which had been involved in the design of the city were not merely aesthetic, and such, but military, as well. Most of the towers were, in effect, keeps. They were stocked, fortress towers. Many could not be entered at the ground level. The bridges amongst them were narrow and could be successfully defended by a handful of men against hundreds. And the bridges, given their construction, could be easily broken, thus isolating the individual fortresses from other, similar fortresses, which might have fallen to an enemy. To reduce such a city, with primitive weaponry, tower by tower, might well require an army, and, conceivably, an investment of years of effort and expense.

"This is now my world," cried out Ellen. "I am only a slave, but I am here, and now this world is mine, too! It is mine, too! You are mine, too, dear world, and I love you, though on you I am but a slave! But on such a world what could a woman such as I be but a slave? On such a world a woman such as I could be only, and am worthy to be only, a slave!" Ellen then knelt down, at the edge of the roof, knelt down in gratitude, before the world of Gor. "You are now my world," she said. "You are beautiful. I love you. I rejoice to be here." She put her hands on her collar, lifting it a little on her neck, almost as though offering it to the world on which she found herself. "Thank you, world, for existing. Help me to be a good slave!" She looked out over the buildings. "Oh, world," she said, "understand me, and be kind. You are the world of which I have always dreamed! On you, beautiful world, let me fulfill the deepest and most wonderful, and most hidden, of my needs, those needs I was always forced to deny on Earth. Here I can be, and must be, the slave I have always longed to be. Oh, give me virile masters who will own me, powerful men whom I must fear, and whom I must obey instantly and with perfection, subject to them in all things, men who will take my womanhood in hand and see to it that it is fulfilled, to its fullest most helpless measure, men who will dominate me without mercy, who will exact ruthlessly and choicelessly from me all that I long to give!"

Ellen then rose up, and, standing, looked out over the panorama of the city and the hills and fields beyond.

She thought she saw a bird in the distance, and watched it for a moment. Yes, it was a bird, clearly. It was difficult to judge its distance. Something seemed awry with the perspective. She thought it must be some hundred, or two hundred, yards away, but, oddly, too, it seemed as though it might be as far away as the walls, perhaps even further. She was puzzled.

"Ellen!" called Laura, sharply.

"Yes!" said Ellen, and, turning about, she ran to the large wicker basket of laundry she had carried to the roof. It was back among the lines and flapping clothes. She reached into the basket and took out the small clothespin bag, lying on the damp laundry, and slung this over her right shoulder, so that its opening was at her left hip, so that she, being right-handed, might easily reach into it. Then, one by one, she began to lift up and shake out the washed, damp garments, and hang them on the line, fastening them there, carefully, with the lovely hand-carved clothespins, for Goreans are prone to lavish attention even on small things, spoons, knives, cooking prongs, and such, anything to make the world more beautiful. It would not do, of course, to allow a garment to fall to the surface of the cylinder. She felt like singing, but, in a collar, slave, was not certain that it would be permitted.

Many times, she knew, one must even ask permission to speak. One, after all, was slave. Having to ask permission to speak, when it seemed such permission was likely to be required, thrilled Ellen. She loved having to ask permission to speak. Few things brought more clearly home to her her bondage, that she was a mere slave, owned, and subject to the domination of masters. She loved this power of men over her, this very clear insignia of her servitude, this standing evidence that she was helplessly subject to the mastery, that she belonged to men. She might be denied speech; she could be silenced at a word. How different from free women, she thought, certainly those of Earth, and, doubtless, those, as well, of this world! But she loved this token of her condition. How well it reminded her that she was what she wished to be, slave.

How often on Earth she had entertained, however guiltily, the secret, fascinating, delicious thought of being owned, of being the helpless, rightless slave of a powerful, uncompromising master! How fearfully, and eagerly, she would have tried to please him, in all ways! She might have hoped for a caress. Certainly she did not wish to be whipped! And now she belonged to a category of females susceptible to such strictures, a category of females who might be bought and sold, bartered or bestowed, without thought, as the sleek, shapely beasts they were.

She was thrilled to be categorically subject to men, and this small thing, that she might speak only with permission, as few other things, especially as she was a woman, for we so desire to speak, and so delight to speak, spoke to her of the reality of her sometimes-resented, but fundamentally longed-for subjugation. How she resented at times being silenced, but how much more precious then was the opportunity to speak when it was seen fit to be granted. Too, interestingly, she found that being denied speech, being frustrated, and such, excited her sexually. Perhaps this was connected with male domination, which elicits female submissiveness, and an eager, petitionary, receptive readiness that can be almost painful. The sexes are not identical, and each becomes most itself when it refuses to betray or misrepresent itself to itself. Perhaps this has to do with nature, and its nature.

In any event, Ellen was not discontented in her collar. It belongs on me, she thought. And I love it! I belong in a collar! I love it! I love it!

She wished she knew some Gorean songs. Surely some masters would permit her to sing, if she were happy! Some masters, she supposed, would enjoy having their girls singing about their work. She hoped soon to serve a master, and that it would be Mirus. Some girls, she knew, were taught to sing, others to entertain with instruments such as the lute and lyre, and others, it seemed, many, were trained in the dances of slaves. Her own training, she understood, though it had seemed extensive to her, had been almost minimal, quite basic. She wondered if there were some special reason for this. "We will teach you a little," had said one of her instructrices. "Hopefully you will then be able to survive at least the first night at a master's slave ring." Ellen wondered if Mirus, her master, would be pleased, if she were to dance before him as a slave. Had he wondered what she would look like, long ago, when she was his teacher, she wondered, if she were to so dance before him, barefoot, in a bit of swirling silk, in necklaces and coins, in armlets, with bracelets on her wrists and bangles on her ankles, to the flash of ringing zills, summoned, commanded, fearful, begging to please, his. Had she hinted at that, or her slaveness, when she had worn the two small bracelets? Perhaps, she thought. I would like to dance before masters, she thought. It is my hope that I would please them. But, alas, I cannot dance! I cannot even dance the social dances of Earth, let alone the dances of the displayed female slave. The sunlight was pleasant, the air was cool. She thought it must be early spring, assuming this world had a periodicity of seasons.

"Laura," she said, "someone has hung up some of the things from my basket."

"I did," said Laura, irritably. "Perhaps I should not have done so. What if the work-master should come to the roof and find your work not even begun! How soon do you think you would come again to the roof? Or perhaps any of us? Perhaps you would enjoy being tied to the high ring and having your pretty little hide lashed? And the rest of us might be lashed as well, all of us!"

"I am sorry," said Ellen. "Thank you." She decided that Laura might not be as unpleasant or stupid as she had supposed.

Laura looked at her, suddenly, sharply. "You are sorry, aren't you?" said Laura.

"Yes," said Ellen.

"Let us hurry," said Laura.

"Yes, Mistress," said Ellen.

"Get to work, slave!" called Nelsa.

Ellen looked at her, angrily.

"You were dallying," said Nelsa. "Now I, too, have something to tell!"

"Yes, Mistress," said Ellen.

Nelsa laughed and continued to hang her wash.

"There are many more baskets below," said Laura.

One of the girls, clambering on one of the tiered racks, some ten or twelve feet above the surface of the roof, called out, "Look!" She was pointing out, toward the distance, toward one of the towers on the wall. The other girls shaded their eyes and looked in the direction she had pointed. Ellen did, too. She could see nothing in the distance but a flock of birds.

"They will never get past the walls," said Nelsa, who had climbed up one of the racks, and was now some seven or eight feet above the surface of the roof, her feet on one pole, she clinging to another.

"Let us return to our work," said another of the girls, glancing warily at the hatchlike opening to the roof.

One did not know when Gart, or another, perhaps some guard, might appear on the roof.

Ellen, with the simple clothespins, attached a sheet to the line. All about her flapped the rows of suspended clothes. She, and the other girls were almost invisible amongst the laundry and the lines.

She found that she enjoyed doing this simple work.

It seemed fitting for her.

She wondered if she were happy.

"May I speak?" Ellen asked Laura.

Laura grunted in response, a pair of clothespins between her teeth, others in her left hand, which also held a corner of a robe.

"Why have we been given gowns?" asked Ellen.

Ellen waited until Laura had finished with the robe.

"To better conceal you," said Laura. "But do not fear, they are sleeveless, and thus make it likely that you are bond."

"I do not understand," said Ellen.

"It is spring," said Laura, "and that is a popular time for the hunts of tarnsmen, not that those monsters need any seasonal excuse for their predations."

"What are tarnsmen?" asked Ellen.

"Those of the Warriors, or sometimes mercenaries, or outlaws, or raiders, or bandits, whoever mounts, masters and rides tarns."

"What is a tarn?" asked Ellen.

"Surely you are apprised of at least the first knowledge?" said Laura.

"But," said Ellen, "those are only in stories, they are mythological creatures, like the hith, the sleen."

"I have never seen a hith," said Laura, "but I have spoken to those who have. I have certainly seen sleen, and tarns. There are sleen in the house, in pens. They are useful in hunting slaves."

"I have never seen a sleen," said Ellen.

"You might ask to do so," said Laura. "Normally a slave girl is only brought into their presence when she is put in close shackles and has her hands braceleted behind her back. Thus she cannot break and run, an action which might prompt the beast's pursuit behavior."

"You are teasing me," said Ellen. "Sleen are supposed to have six legs."

"They do," said Laura. "That is efficient, given the length and low, sinuous structure of their body."

"Oh, Laura!" protested Ellen.

"There are many sorts of sleen," said Laura. "Most common are the forest sleen and prairie sleen. The forest sleen are larger, and are solitary hunters, or, if mated, pair hunters; the prairie sleen are smaller, and commonly hunt in packs. Some sleen are bred and trained for certain purposes, hunting slaves, and such. The forest sleen commonly buries its dung, thereby tending to conceal its presence; the prairie sleen, running in packs, and more widely ranging, commonly, does not. Sleen have a strong, unmistakable odor. A forester or plainsman, or a sleen hunter, or one trained, can sometimes detect their scent more than two hundred yards away. Caravans in forests often keep verr or tabuk with them, tethering them in the camp at night, as the agitation of such animals sometimes gives warning of the presence of sleen in the vicinity. Sleen, of course, like larls, commonly hunt with the wind blowing toward them. Thus they have your scent and you do not have theirs."

"Why, really, have we been given gowns?" asked Ellen. "We might as well be naked. There is no one to see us here."

"Do not be too sure," said Nelsa, from the rack, still looking outward. "They are circling the city," she said.

"It is daylight," said another girl. "There is no reason to fear."

"Laura, please," prompted Ellen.

"It is a pleasure for a tarnsman to have his tarn seize in its talons a woman and carry her off, or he may prefer the use of a slave net or a capture loop. She later then, in a safe place, may be suitably secured, say, stripped and roped, and put across his saddle, or simply chained naked to a saddle ring. The ideal, of course, is to catch a free woman, for such is the most prestigious game. Surely that would be more prestigious than picking up someone like you or me, who are merely domestic animals, livestock. Some claim that that is the reason that free women are so cumbersomely and concealingly garbed, and that slaves are so lightly and revealingly clad. Supposedly the tarnsman might thus be lured to the pursuit of an identifiably delightful quarry, something obviously worth owning, as opposed to a free woman who might, when stripped, prove to be as ugly as a tharlarion."

Tharlarion, Ellen had been told, were reptilian creatures, some of which were allegedly quite large, and domesticated. Supposedly different varieties were used for various purposes, such as war, haulage and racing. She was not sure, at that time, that such things existed, no more than larls, sleen, tarns, and such.

"There may be something to that," said Laura, "but I suspect that men dress their slaves as they do, if they dress them at all, because they find them exciting to look upon, and wish to call attention to their beauty, and enjoy displaying them as their properties. Men are so vain. You should see how some of them lead naked, painted, bejeweled slaves about on leashes, put them through slave paces publicly, make them dance in the open for tarsk-bits, put them up as stakes in the dicing halls, and marketplaces, and such. And so, perhaps, free women insist on some compensatory distinction, to make it clear that they are not to be confused with such flesh-trash. On the other hand, it is said that beneath all the clothing, the veils, the Robes of Concealment, and such, of a free woman there is still, after all, only the body of a naked slave."

"But there are no tarnsmen here," said Ellen.

"Sometimes they break through," said Laura. "And that is why you have been put in the long gown, and not, say, a tunic. There are two differences here. If the choice is between you and a free woman, the tarnsman will almost certainly notice that you, as your gown is sleeveless, are almost certainly slave, and will thus, presumably, go after the free woman. If the choice is between you, lengthily gowned, and a briefly tunicked slave, whose lovely legs he can take in at a glance, he will presumably go after the briefly tunicked slave. It is difficult to make judicious assessments, as you might suppose, given the brief amount of time at his disposal, time enough for little more than a glimpse, given the distance, the swiftness of the flight, the press of pursuit, and such. To be sure, sometimes women are scouted. It is known when she will be on the bridge, and so on. And so, Ellen, that is why you are dressed as you are."

"I see," said Ellen, skeptically.

"To be sure," said Laura, "if a tarnsman did settle for you, I do not think that afterwards, when he had you squirming naked in his ropes, bound hand and foot, he would be at all disappointed with the nature of his catch."

"Do tarnsmen exist?" asked Ellen. "Really?"

"To be sure," said Laura, "you are only a slave. And yet, what is the first thing they do with their exalted, aristocratic, noble, precious, prestigious free woman? They brand her, put her in a collar, and make her a slave, too!"

"You are teasing me," said Ellen. "Tarnsmen do not really exist."

"If a tarnstrike should be upon us," said Laura, "and you cannot get below, just throw yourself to your belly on the roof. That makes it hard to get you, hard for the tarn, hard for the net, hard for the capture loop."

I shall certainly keep that in mind," smiled Ellen.

"They have broken through!" cried the girl on the height of a nearby rack, she who had originally called their attention to the agitation in the distance. Ellen looked up at her, wildly. The girl's hair streamed behind her, the wind whipping her gown back against her body. She clung to the rack, fiercely.

"They will have the wind behind them!" said Laura. "The defenders must fly against the wind. They may be easily eluded, and then they must turn to pursue. They will have lost the tempo of the passage. Intruders may be through and beyond the city in a matter of Ehn!"

"I want to see!" said Ellen.

In the distance one could hear the ringing of a great metal bar, struck repeatedly.

"Get below!" called Laura.

"It is locked!" cried a girl, tugging at the ring that might otherwise have lifted and opened the hatchlike portal that led to the interior of the cylinder.

Another girl joined her, trying to lift the ring.

"There are prize slaves below, and riches," said Laura. "They do not want to risk them! Stay down, everyone! Stay down!"

Ellen, standing among the flapping clothes, amongst the lines, between racks, shaded her eyes, straining to see into the distance. She could see, in the distance, what appeared to be a flock of birds. It seemed, again, that the perspective was oddly awry. They should be no more than a hundred yards or so away, and yet, at the same time, it seemed they were scarcely within the distant walls. Other birds seemed to rise from her side of the wall, lifting momentarily against the darkness of the wall and then suddenly appearing in the sky, hastening specks, the hills and fields beyond.

"They are coming this way!" called Nelsa, pointing, she, too, on a rack, but lower than the other girl.

"Get down!" cried Laura.

The first girl, she who had first alerted the slaves to the phenomenon in the distance, climbed down from the rack, and crouched near it, amidst the flapping clothes. Nelsa, in a moment, had joined her.

Most of the girls were crouched down. Some lay on their stomachs under the racks, their hands covering their heads.

"I can't see," said Ellen, brushing aside clothes, which had blown before her. She fought the laundry shaking and snapping in the wind about her.

"Get down!" called Laura.

"I want to see!" said Ellen.

Then suddenly she flung her hands before her face and screamed, and the world seemed madness about her. There was a wild cry, piercing, at hand, not more than fifteen feet above her, surely the loudest and most terrifying sound she had ever heard, as of some living, immense, monstrous creature, and she was in shadow and then not in shadow, in a shadow that moved and leapt and was shattered with bursts of sunlight, and then darkness, and clothing was torn from the lines by the blasts of wind from the smitings of mighty wings, and one of the racks, seized in monstrous talons, broke into a thousand pieces, and, lifted, fell in a shower of sticks, raining down to the roof. Ellen could not believe what she saw. Above her, now darting away, was a gigantic bird, an enormous bird, a saddlebird, its wings with a span of thirty or more feet, and, seemingly tiny on its back, was a helmeted man!

Ellen had heard an angry cry from the man above her, and words in Gorean she did not recognize, words that had certainly never been taught to her, a slave girl. She had no doubt that the man was cursing, and richly, the failure of his strike.

Then they were away.

To be sure, how could he have hoped to make a catch when the girls were hidden by the laundry, protected by the lines, could take refuge under the racks, and such?

Ellen was now on her knees amidst the lines, her hands lifted, as though she might fend away blows.

Nelsa sped past her, laughing, and clambered to the height of the nearest undamaged rack. She went to its very height, and stood there, balanced, outlined against the sky, her hair shaken in the wind, her gown whipping about her body.

"Clumsy oaf!" she screamed after the retreating rider. "Who taught you your work? Go home and play with vulos! You have the skill of a tharlarion!"

"Come down!" called Laura.

"Down with Treve!" cried Nelsa, shaking her fist after the rider in the distance. "May her walls be razed and her wealth plundered. May her women be put in collars! May they, and her other slaves, be herded away! May her towers be burned and salt cast upon their ashes!"

The approach of the second tarn, soaring, borne on the wind, its wings still, was silent.

Nelsa, of course, did not see it, as she was facing away from it, crying out, shaking her fist at the retreating figure of the other rider, now muchly in the distance.

It was, accordingly, a simple thing, to drop the capture loop about her standing body.

She must, suddenly, her fist still in the air, angry, shouting, have become aware of it, light and soft as a whisper, dropping about her. Then the tarn was past her and the resistance of her own body to the loop caused it to tighten about her. It took her beautifully, and skillfully, at the waist. It might have snared even a man, so neatly and quickly it was slipped on its quarry, before he could thrust it from his straight, muscular, linear body, but, positioned as it was on Nelsa, a woman, nicely centered, between the flare of her hips and the swelling of her bosom, she could not even have begun to hope to elude its grasp, nor could any beautifully bodied female, no more than Ellen, for similar reasons, could slip the iron belt from her body, whose outline was visible, even now, beneath her gown. In this sense, some Goreans speculate that the bodies of women were designed for bonds. And, perhaps in some minor, contributory evolutionary sense, in addition to more obvious biological considerations, this is true, given selections and such, women with bodies unable to elude such constraints being more susceptible to capture, mating and mastering. Certainly the females of many animal species, and even of many primate species, do not have such hip structure, such fullness of bosom, and such. Regardless of the interest or value of such speculations, the truth of which would in any event be veiled in the mysteries and darkness of the past, the fact of the matter was obvious, the fact of the congeniality of such bodies to the convenience of binding and tethering, as obvious as the perfection of the bond on Nelsa, who, clutching at the air, kicking, frantic, screaming and crying out in terror, was now being drawn rapidly away from the roof, swinging, dangling, wildly, twenty feet below a speeding tarn, between the towers, hundreds of feet above the streets of the city.

"It is the strategy of the second strike," said Laura. "The first apparently bungles his strike and then, silently, the derisive, or unwary, quarry off guard, revealing herself, thinking herself safe, the cohort approaches, and makes the actual play for the game. Nelsa, it seems, is not as clever, or wise, as she thought."

"Look," said Ellen, pointing away, in the direction to which the wind was blowing, that in which the tarn had flown.

"Yes," said Laura, "the two of them, the monsters, are having their rendezvous. Now they are fleeing, together."

The alarm bar was still ringing.

"Doubtless they will split her price," said Laura, or perhaps they will keep her and gamble for her."

"She was shouting about Treve," said Ellen.

"Yes," said Laura. "They were tarnsmen of Treve. That was their leather. It is said those of Treve know well how to handle women."

"So, too, does any man," said a girl, trembling.

"True," smiled Laura.

The only men they knew, Ellen conjectured, were Gorean males.

"Sometimes I am so afraid to be a slave," said another girl, touching her collar.

"We all are," said Laura.

"Tonight I wager Nelsa will dance naked before a campfire," said a girl.

"The whip dance, I hope," said another.

Nelsa had not been popular with the other girls.

"The work-master will now want a new favorite," said one.

"I am glad I am not blond-haired and blue-eyed," said another.

Several of the girls turned to look at Ina, who was blond-haired and blue-eyed. She shrank back, shaking her head, negatively.

"Learn to hold firmly to the sides of the tub," said a girl.

"Perhaps you will get a candy in your bin," said another.

"Look out!" cried a girl.

The slaves shrank down. Some flung themselves prone to the roof.

"No!" said a girl. "That is one of ours!"

They stood up, again, amidst the laundry. Sticks from the shattered rack were strewn about.

"Some of this laundry will have to be washed again," said one of the girls.

"Look!" said one of the other slaves.

"That is one of them!" said another.

Another tarn was streaking by, a hundred yards to the left.

The slave who had cried out clapped her hands with pleasure. "See!" she cried. "He has a free woman!"

Clutched in the talons of the tarn, fearing to struggle lest she fall, but nonetheless helplessly held, held as though gripped with iron, was a human figure, though it seemed little more now than a pathetic bundle, trailing shreds of robes and veils.

"Good for you!" cried one of the girls to the speeding tarnsman.

"Put the iron to her!" cried another.

"Collar her!" cried another.

"Teach her to kiss the whip!"

"Make her jump and squirm!" cried yet another.

"I speculate that her life is going to change," said Laura to Ellen.

"Doubtless," said Ellen, touching her collar, frightened.

Two tarnsmen of the city snapped by in pursuit of the fellow with the free woman. They terminated their pursuit at the city walls. Doubtless they had their orders, and there might well be other Treveans within the city.

In a few moments the alarm bar had stopped ringing.

"The raid is over," said a girl.

"Now a pursuit will be organized," said another.

"Wait," said one of the girls. "There is another!"

"The clever monster!" said another.

"He waited until the bar had stopped ringing."

"Where was he?"

"Below."

"Help! Help!" cried the woman in the net.

"He is going to land on the roof," said one of the girls, frightened.

"Stay back, keep away from him!" warned Laura.

The tarn came down, wings beating, hovering, and then alit on the roof. The rider leaped from the saddle, and pulled the net to the side. It contained a lovely young woman in a slave tunic and collar. She reached out, through the heavy mesh of the net. "Help me! Help me!" she cried. "Summon guardsmen!"

"He is clever," said Laura. "Here the guardsmen may take him for a defender. If he is of Treve, he does not wear their leather."

The tarnsman then regarded the cluster of slaves on the roof.

"We are in the presence of a free man," said Laura. "Kneel. He may be of the city."

The slaves knelt.

"Kneel as the slaves you are," whispered Laura.

Knees then were spread, and widely, beneath the long gowns.

The tarnsman grinned.

"What do you think of my slave?" he called.

"I am not a slave!" cried the woman in the net.

"She is beautiful, Master," said Laura.

"Call guardsmen!" screamed the woman in the net, holding to its mesh.

"There are no guardsmen to call," said Laura.

"I am a free woman!" cried the prisoner of the net. "He took my clothing! He tunicked me! He put a collar on me!"

"He is clever," said Laura to the others. "If it is thought she is a slave the pursuit will be pressed less vigorously."

"What do you think of the legs of my slave?" inquired the tarnsman.

"They are well revealed, Master," said Laura.

"They are lovely enough to be the legs of a slave girl, surely, Master," said one of the slaves.

"It was not I who revealed my legs!" cried the woman in the net. "It was he who put me in this scandalous tunic. It was he who revealed them!"

The woman in the net tried to force the brief tunic she wore down further on her body. She did not have much success in this, as the tunic, perhaps by intent, was quite short.

"Save me!" demanded the woman in the net. "Get this collar off my neck!" She pulled at it, angrily, futilely. She was unsuccessful, of course, as such devices are not designed to be removed by their wearers.

One of the girls laughed, at the absurdity of the behavior of the net's occupant.

"Whip her! Whip her!" cried the net's occupant.

The tarnsman looked about, studying the sky.

"In a few moments the pursuit, organized, will depart, following the raiders," said Laura. "He will then go in another direction."

"I wish I belonged to such a master," said one of the girls.

Laura looked at her, sharply, with interest. "Yes," she then said, "so do I."

"I am from Brundisium," said the tarnsman, pleasantly. "I asked this woman to be my free companion, but she refused. Accordingly I decided I would make her my slave."

"Excellent, Master," said one of the girls.

"Free me! Free me! Call guardsmen!" cried the woman in the net.

"I have waited for days, for there to be a raid I could use for cover, a raid I could turn to my own advantage," he said.

"Master is strong and clever," said Laura.

"You are a pretty slave," he said.

Laura spread her knees more widely, but subtly, seemingly shyly, beneath her gown. Ellen gasped. She had not seen Laura like this before, so before a man.

So, she thought, Laura is indeed a slave girl. I wonder if I would ever behave so before a man.

Surely not I!

Ellen did not think this behavior on Laura's part was unnoticed by the stalwart figure on the roof. The tarn shifted, restlessly.

"Get me out of this sack!" demanded the free woman.

"May I present Lady Temesne?" inquired the tarnsman.

"That is a Cosian name," said a girl. Ellen made little of that.

"Mistress," said Laura, respectfully.

"Mistress," said several of the girls, bowing their heads.

"Mistress," said Ellen, bowing her head, as the others. This was the first free Gorean woman Ellen had ever encountered. She began to sense the awe with which such were to be regarded by such as she, and the deference that would be expected of her in the presence of such. To be sure, this one was in a slave tunic and collar.

"Get me out of this sack!" cried Lady Temesne.

Her accent did seem different from that of many of the other girls, Ellen thought.

The tarnsman then, to the gratification of Lady Temesne, opened the sack, and she began to crawl hurriedly from it, but her gratification was short-lived, as he took her by the hair, when her feet were still tangled in the mesh, and pressed her down on her stomach on the roof, and then knelt across her body. "What are you doing?" she cried. "Put your hands behind you," he told her. "Now." Weakly she put her small hands behind her. He pulled them together and, in a moment, they had been encircled with binding fiber, and were lashed together. She cried out, softly, in protest, as she was gagged. She whimpered in misery, as she was blindfolded. He then drew her from the net, crossed her ankles, bound them together, and looked down upon her. There was no denying that she was a lovely catch. He then thrust her back in the net, her knees pulled up under her chin, and tied the net shut, close about her. He then fastened the net on short ropes close to the belly of the tarn. It would then be less obvious.

He then returned to watching the sky.

"Laura," whispered Ellen.

"Yes," said Laura.

"He is waiting for tarnsmen to leave the city?"

"Yes," said Laura.

"What of Nelsa?" asked Ellen.

"Do not concern yourself about her," said Laura. "She is merely a captured slave."

"Will they hurt her?" asked Ellen.

"I do not think so," said Laura. "Probably no more than to occasionally remind her that she is a slave and, of course, to see to it that she is perfect in her service."

"But the whip dance?"

"True, that will hurt her," said Laura, "but it will teach her, too, who her masters are."

Ellen shuddered.

"Is Treve a city?" Ellen asked.

"Yes," said Laura. "And little love is lost between those of Treve and this city."

"What is the name of this city?" asked Ellen.

"You do not know?"

"No."

"Ar," said Laura.

At that moment several flights of tarnsmen, dozens in each flight, swept overhead.

The tarnsman raised his hand, saluting the flights as they passed.

"He is magnificent!" breathed Laura, in awe. "He will well know how to keep a woman!"

He was now ready to ascend the rope ladder to the saddle, several feet above the surface of the roof. That ladder is then pulled up and tied to the saddle. There are normally two or four rings fastened at the sides of a tarnsman's saddle, one or two on each side.

"Master!" called Laura suddenly.

He turned to look upon her.

"May I speak?" she asked.

"Yes," he said.

"May I rise?" she asked.

"Yes," he said.

She quickly ran to him and, as slaves gasped, she knelt before him, bending over, her head down between her arms, which were lifted, the wrists crossed.

"How dare you submit yourself as a free woman?" he asked.

"Forgive me, Master!" wept Laura, lowering herself humbly to her belly before him, and pressing her lips to his bootlike sandals. She looked up, tears in her eyes. "Perhaps Master would care to capture a worthless slave?"

The occupant of the net, tied close to the belly of the tarn, squirmed, whimpering, angrily.

"She wants to be the only one," whispered a girl to Ellen.

The tarnsman crouched down beside Laura and, with a length of binding fiber, crossed her wrists and bound them together before her body. He then, similarly, crossed her ankles, and bound them, as well. He then carried her to the saddle, over his shoulder, and laid her gently on her back, across the saddle, on the large plain surface before the pommel, perhaps a surface prepared for just such a purpose. It was then but a moment's work to fasten her bound wrists to the forward ring on the left, and her bound ankles to the forward ring on the right. In this fashion she was bound before him, belly up, stretched over the saddle. He then considered her for a moment, and then took a knife from his belt.

Slaves gasped, thrilled.

Laura's gown, in a moment, cut from her, cast aside, had fluttered to the roof.

"I am yours, Master!" said Laura.

"You tell me nothing I do not know, slave," he said.

He then freed the rolled blanket from behind the saddle, opened it, and threw it over the slave, concealing her.

The tunicked, collared free woman, bound in the net, gagged and blindfolded, squirmed and whimpered.

"I suspect," whispered the girl to Ellen's right, "our noble little tunic-wearer will be sold in Brundisium."

"Perhaps he will keep them both," said another girl.

"Perhaps," said another.

"She does have pretty legs," said another.

"The tunic displays them well," said another.

"Surely," said another.

The tarn then smote the air, leapt from the roof, soared for a moment, and then, wings beating, rose higher, leveled in its flight, and then streaked from the city, in a direction other than that taken by those in pursuit of the Trevean raiders.

"We may now rise," said one of the girls, watching the tarn disappear in the distance.

Ellen stood up, uncertainly.

"They take women," she said, in awe. "They bind us. They steal us. They carry us off. They think nothing of this. They make us theirs. They make us slaves. They use us as they please. We are nothing to them. They buy and sell us. They do as they wish with us!"

"They are men," said one of the girls.

"I fear you," she whispered to herself, "beautiful world on which I am a slave."

"The hatch is now open!" called one of the girls.

"We must clean up things and get back to work," said another.

Nelsa was gone. Laura, too, was gone. Tonight Nelsa might be performing the whip dance for masters. Ellen did not know what the whip dance was but she was not displeased that it, whatever it was, might be required of Nelsa. She did not think that Nelsa would be a bother or a nuisance to her new masters. The whip takes that out of a woman. She did not know what Laura's fate might be. Whatever it was, it was in the hands of the tarnsman from Brundisium.

"Have you no work to do, slave girl?" inquired one of the girls.

"Forgive me, Mistress," said Ellen, and drew toward her, across the roof, under a line, her large basket, and then reached into it for another damp garment, to shake out, smooth and hang.

"There are many more baskets below," said a slave.

Ellen, with the wooden pins, hung a garment on the line. It was a male's work tunic. It was large. Ellen wondered what its wearer might look like, and what he might be like, and what it would be like to be owned by him.

"Man!" called a girl.

Instantly the slaves fell to their knees and assumed first obeisance position.

"Is Ellen, who is the slave of Mirus, here?" asked the man.

Ellen was too frightened to respond.

"Who is first girl?" asked the man.

"We have lost two slaves, to tarnsmen, Master," said blond-haired, blue-eyed Ina. "We could not return to the interior of the cylinder. The hatch had been secured from within. Nelsa and Laura, slaves of the house. Of those upon the roof, Laura was first girl."

"Last week, our lads took eight from Treve, three of whom were free," said the man.

"Glory to Ar!" said Ina.

"Glory to Ar!" said several of the others.

"All three were put up for sale yesterday," he said.

"Excellent, Master," said Ina.

"Our warriors did well," said the man.

"Yes, Master," said Ina.

"I trust the brigands from Treve bagged little or nothing."

"Let us hope so, Master," said Ina.

Ellen was certain that the raiders had captured at least one free woman, as she had seen her helpless in the grasp of a tarn's talons. This was not to take account of the fate of the Lady Temesne, for her abductor had been a spurned suitor from Brundisium. The Lady Temesne, who had regarded herself as too fine to accept his suit, might this very night be at his feet, begging to please. But she might be sold in favor of Laura. But then Ellen did not know. The Lady Temesne did have pretty legs. It might be noted that the guard had paid little explicit attention to the slaves involved in these transactions, though he had kept track, noting that five slaves had been taken from Treve recently. One does, in that sense, one supposes, count or "keep score," as one might do with kaiila or tharlarion. The free woman is in theory priceless. Thus she is not comparable with the female slave. As she is priceless, there is a sense in which even thousands of female slaves would not be as valuable as one free woman. On the other hand, reality often embarrasses argument, and it must be admitted that a single female slave, particularly if trained, is often preferred to dozens of free women. But men are that way, she supposed. Ellen did not know what her own value was. It would depend of course, on conditions in the market, and what men were willing to pay. That was an odd, but charming, in its way, thought, that she would now, in a sense, literally for the first time in her life, have value. It is interesting, this sort of thing, she thought. At one moment a woman is free and priceless, and then, in another moment, suddenly, she becomes a very practical, tangible commodity, something very real and very factual, something with a specific value, like any other piece of merchandise. In this sense a woman is without specific or actual value until she becomes a slave; it is then that she acquires specific or actual value. To be sure, these considerations are based largely on legal fictions, for, in fact, free women do have tangible values, the higher born being valued better than the lower born, the upper castes over the lower castes, the more intelligent over the less intelligent, the more beautiful over the less beautiful, and so on. To be sure the slave block commonly introduces a radical common denominator. Stripped of all conventional and social dignities and merits, as well as of their clothing, bereft of all artificialities, what is for sale there is, generally, assuming that there is nothing special about the item, that it is not the daughter of a Ubar, or the daughter of one's worst enemy, or such, is the intelligence, sensitivity, beauty and personness of the item herself.

It would not be known for a day or two presumably how the Trevean raiders had fared within the city.

Ellen was curious as to her market value, and the thought that she must now have one charmed her. That gave an entirely new dimension to her self-concept. She, earlier, being free, had never had such a value. Now she knew she had one, whatever it might be. She knew that girls were often very vain, about the prices they would bring, and such. She thought that that was silly, but she hoped that she would bring a good price, and, certainly, one superior to that which might have been garnered by Nelsa. But she did not fear that her master would sell her. It thrilled her, of course, to know that he had this power, and that he had this power made her feel so much more a slave, but she was certain he would never choose to exercise it. I am sure he loves me, thought Ellen. Or, at least, that he wants me. Surely he thought that my "flanks were of interest." I love him!

"Where is Ellen, the slave of Mirus?" asked the guard.

"There," said Ina. And something about her tone of voice suggested that she had pointed Ellen out.

Ellen looked up a little, and saw the bootlike sandals of the guard before her.

"You are Ellen, the slave of Mirus?"

"Yes, Master," said Ellen, head down, to the surface of the roof.

"Why did you not identify yourself?" he asked.

"I was frightened," said Ellen. "Forgive me, Master."

"You should speak up, instantly," he said.

"Yes, Master. Forgive me, Master."

The guard turned to his left. "What is your name?" he asked.

"Ina," said Ina.

"You are first girl on the roof," he said. "The work-master can arrange matters differently later, as he might please."

"Yes, Master," she said. "Master!" she said.

"Yes?" he said.

"I can keep the guardroom tidy and clean, and make the beds. I can bring food and drink to the guards, and other pleasures," she said.

One of the other girls made a scarcely suppressed angry noise.

There was a silence, and Ellen gathered that the guard might be looking at Ina. It was difficult to tell, as one's head was down.

Ellen supposed that Ina wanted out of the laundry, and that she did not relish taking Nelsa's place as the favorite, or one of the favorites, of the work-master. She was, as we have noted, blond-haired and blue-eyed, and Gart, it seemed, preferred putting such slaves to his pleasures. Certainly she could not blame Ina on either score, though she, like several of the other girls, was shocked by Ina's boldness, and her apparent audacity in seizing this opportunity to shamelessly prostrate her slave beauty before the guard. On the other hand, there might be much more to it. Doubtless, in being addressed, and such, she had lifted her head, and met his eyes. Doubtless something had passed between them. Perhaps she saw in his eyes that he was a fitting master for her and he, looking into her eyes, saw that she was a fitting slave for him, indeed, perhaps even a very special and vulnerable slave for him. Eccentricities and subjectivities, seeming anomalies, often enter into such matters. In such cases a man may bid all his resources, his wealth, his possessions, his life, anything, to obtain she whom he sees at his feet as his own perfect slave.

"Perhaps," said the guard. "First girl," he said.

"Yes, Master!" said Ina, quickly.

"The slave Ellen," said the guard, "is summoned into the presence of her Master, Mirus of Ar, to appear before him in the audience chamber at the eighteenth Ahn. Until supper she is to continue her work on the roof. Instructrices will call for her at the sixteenth Ahn, to bring her to the Chamber of Preparation. A guard in the Chamber of Preparation will have the key to remove the iron belt. In the Chamber of Preparation she is to be washed, combed and perfumed. She is to be presented brief-tunicked and back-braceleted."

"Slave cosmetics, Master?" inquired Ina.

"None," said the guard.

Ellen, her head down, trembled with joy.

"You are a pretty slave, Ina," said the guard.

"Thank you, Master," said Ina.

"You will see that the slave, Ellen, is ready for the instructrices at the sixteenth Ahn."

"She will be ready, Master," Ina assured him.

"The guardroom could use some tidying up," he mused.

"Ina is well-versed in domestic tasks," said Ina.

"And others, as well, I trust," said the guard.

"Master must be the judge of such matters," she said, shyly.

"I am Varcon," he said. "My private quarters are on the seventh level."

"Perhaps Master has a slave ring at the foot of his couch?"

"It is now empty," he said.

"Might not Ina be privileged to wear a neck-chain there?" she asked.

"Bold slave," he said.

"Needful slave," she said.

"We shall see," said he.

He then turned and went to the hatchlike opening, through which he descended.

"Rise up," said Ina. "Continue your work."

The girls obeyed.

"You are a forward she-urt," said one of the girls to Ina.

"I would watch my words, if I were you," said Ina, pleasantly, "or you will be subjected to the bastinado."

"Forgive me, Mistress!" said the girl.

"Return to your work, slave girl," said Ina.

"Yes, Mistress," said the girl, hurrying away.

It is common to set a first girl over others, to see that work is done, to see that discipline is kept, and such. Whereas this is not always done, it is sometimes done even when two slaves leave the house, as on an errand, one then being designated as "first girl." In this way authority is clearly defined. Goreans like this. And woe to the other girl if she should gainsay the first, prove troublesome or be in any way displeasing. Goreans, you see, tend to be great believers in rank, distance and hierarchy. These things stabilize society. One might, of course, if one's taste ran that way, prefer a society founded on a hypocritical denial of obvious differentiation, on concealments of power, on group conflict, on greed, on propaganda, on confusion, uncertainty, machinations, character assassination, spying, slander, and such.

"You heard, Ellen?" asked Ina.

"Yes, Mistress," said Ellen.

"The sixteenth Ahn," said Ina.

"Yes, Mistress," said Ellen.

"There is much work to be done before supper," said Ina.

"Yes, Mistress," said Ellen.

Ellen seized up her basket by the side handles and, struggling, lifting it awkwardly, resting it against her abdomen, moved it a few feet to her right, further under the line.

"You do not carry your basket properly," said Ina. "You are from the world called 'Earth', are you not?"

"Yes Mistress," said Ellen.

"They are so ignorant. It is a wonder they make such good slaves."

"Mistress?" asked Ellen.

"It is easier to carry it in this fashion," said Ina, crouching down behind the basket and, lifting it up, she placed it on her head, steadying it with her two hands. "This way, you can take some of the weight on your arms, if you wish, or use your head and spine, carrying your body erectly, gracefully. That distributes the weight nicely, and is easier on the back. You can also steady it with one hand, and, if you become skilled, balance it on your head alone, without using your hands."

"I do not think I could do that," said Ellen.

"Some girls use a folded cloth, folded in a circle, between the basket and the head. That provides a cushion, and seats the burden with greater security."

"Even so," said Ellen, dubiously.

"Lift it up. Use two hands. No, stand straighter. Good. Hands up. Put your hands up. Higher. Higher. Oh, yes, the men will like that! You are indeed pretty, Ellen. Now walk. Away. Down the line. No, no, not that way. Not as a free Earth woman. That is behind you. You are now a female slave. Here, stop. Let me show you."

Ellen stood back.

"Like this," said Ina.

"Oh, Mistress!" exclaimed Ellen.

"Walking away, turning, approaching. Like this. See?"

"You are so beautiful!" said Ellen.

"And they, the silly beasts," laughed Ina, "may not even know what you are doing to them. They may not even understand why they are ready to kill for you."

"I do not know if I could do that," said Ellen.

"Walking away, turning, approaching," said Ina, "you seem perhaps no more than a burdened slave, but you can drive them mad with passion, and the wanting of you."

"Oh, Mistress," breathed Ellen.

"We are slaves," said Ina. "If we are to please, and thrive, we must make do with the little that is permitted us."

"Yes, Mistress," said Ellen.

"What weapons have we, we, in our collars? Our weapons are our intelligence, our beauty, our body. If you would have a good life as a female slave, you must learn to use them well."

"What of passion, Mistress?"

"Strange that an Earth female would even think of that," said Ina. "Passion we will have little control over. They will enforce it. They will imperiously enrapture us, and, as it pleases them, take us outside of ourselves with ecstasy. They will make us begging, needful, at their feet."

"I have never experienced such ecstasies," said Ellen.

"You will be taught," said Ina.

"Is it wrong to long for such ecstasies?" asked Ellen.

"No, of course not," she said. "You are a female slave."

"I fear I long for them, Mistress," said Ellen.

"That is understandable," said Ina, "but remember that for such as you, slave girl, they are also obligatory."

"Yes, Mistress," whispered Ellen, scarcely hearing herself speak.

Ina smiled at her. Ellen must have seemed to her so young, so ignorant, so naive. And yet both their necks were encircled with slave collars.

Ellen looked at her, plaintively.

"Yes?" said Ina.

"I have heard," said Ellen, cautiously, whispering, "of the *slave orgasm*."

Ina suddenly closed her eyes, gritting them shut, forcibly, and her teeth seemed clenched. Then she opened her eyes, and smiled. "Yes," she said, "there is that. And once you have felt that, little Ellen, you will never want to be anything other than what you are, a female slave."

Ina then gently placed the basket on Ellen's head, and Ellen held it there, with two hands.

"Walk away," said Ina. "That is far enough. Turn. Hands high, remember. Surely you know what that does for your figure. How naturally then, how helplessly do you seem to display it. What choice have you? Suppose, too, you were in a brief side-slit tunic. Can you imagine what it would be then for a man to see you, *in that fashion*? And knowing you *slave*! Approach. Good! Now go back, and turn again, and look at me, suddenly, as though you first noticed me. Good. Now approach. Your expression! Are you humble? Does your expression say that you know that you are owned and must obey? Are you timid? Are you fearful? Are you apprehensive that you may be insufficiently pleasing? Are you joyful to see the Master? Are you hoping he will take you in his arms? Do you wish to be ordered to disrobe in his presence? Remember you are a female slave! Approach. Did they not teach you how to walk? What of your love cradle! Turn, go back, then return, again, down the aisle. Good. Remember you are a female slave. You are owned. You must be beautiful. So little as the movement of a hand, or the sight of a bared forearm in the pouring of wine, can be beautiful, provocative, stimulatory to the master's desire."

I am a slave, thought Ellen. Why should I fear to move as one? It is what I am. And might I not be beaten if I am not pleasing?

To be sure, she knew that already her bondage had irremediably infused her entire being. Even now she was sure that a slaver, without regard to her brand or collar, could pick her out from free women.

"Good, good, little she-urt," said Ina. "Now get to work!"

Ellen put down the basket and knelt before Ina. She put her head down to Ina's feet. "A slave expresses her gratitude to Mistress," she said.

"Back to work, slave girl," said Ina, who seemed in a fine mood.

"Yes, Mistress," said Ellen.

Ellen reached into the basket and removed another damp garment from it, and took up a handful of clothespins. She looked about herself. It is so beautiful, she thought, this lovely, perilous, fearful world on which I am a slave. She attached the garment to the line and then stepped back a little, and looked out over the city. It was as though she would embrace it all, all of this fresh, clean, rushing, windswept, sunlit reality.

"Do not forget, after supper, the sixteenth Ahn," called Ina.

"No, Mistress," said Ellen.

Chapter 14

She Waits, Before Being Presented Before Her Master

"Stand still," said one of the instructrices.

"Oh!" said Ellen, as the comb was pulled through her hair yet again, and again. The other instructrix then began to brush the hair, yet again.

"Hold still," said the second instructrix.

"She is fine," said a guard.

"What do men know of such things?" asked the first instructrix.

Ellen felt her hair smoothed and arranged carefully about her shoulders. "There," said the first instructrix. "Now hold still, little she-urt."

"She is a pretty one," said the second instructrix.

"I think so," said the first.

"You were not to paint her lips, her eyelids, you were not to enhance her with cosmetics?" said the guard.

"No," said the first instructrix.

"She is pretty," said the guard.

Ellen was brief-tunicked.

This garment was cut at the sides, to the waist. In this way the brand can be occasionally glimpsed and, when the slave kneels, if she is a pleasure slave, a bit of cloth may fall between her spread thighs.

She had been cleaned thoroughly in the Chamber of Preparation, her body scrubbed and her hair washed.

She was sparkling.

"Do you like the perfume?" asked the first instructrix.

"It is a slave perfume," said the guard.

"Of course," said the first instructrix. "She is a slave."

"Do you like it?" asked the second instructrix.

"Yes," said the guard. "It must be a good one. It is hard for me to keep my hands from her."

"Do not disarrange her, please," said the first instructrix.

Ellen edged away from the guard a little.

She pulled a little, futilely, against the bracelets, which held her hands confined behind her back.

"How does it feel, little tasta, to be out of the iron belt?" asked the first instructrix.

"Good, very good, Mistress," said Ellen.

"Such things are so weighty, so bulky, and unpleasant," said the first instructrix. Ellen gathered that the instructrix must once have had first-hand knowledge of what it was to be locked within such a thing, to be fastened in such an apparatus.

"Yes, Mistress," said Ellen.

"But you now feel very vulnerable, don't you?" asked the first instructrix.

"Yes, Mistress," said Ellen. She inched a little further from the guard. It was he who, in the Chamber of Preparation, had removed her long gown, and had then removed the iron belt. She wondered if it had been necessary for him to feel her waist, and her hips, and thighs, as he had, when he had done so. The apparatus had been discarded, dropped to the stones of the floor of the Chamber of Preparation, with a clatter. She had then, after a moment, after having been examined by him, as a Gorean master considers a slave girl, been drawn by the hair across the room and plunged bodily into a tub.

"Bracelets," said the first instructrix.

Ellen turned her back to the first instructrix, and lifted her wrists a little, so that her bracelets might be checked.

She felt her wrists lifted a bit, and the steel checked. There was a tiny sound of metal links.

The steel was tight on her small wrists.

That was not necessary, but it left her in no doubt that she was helpless.

She also did not doubt but what the tightness was intentional, and responsive to some instruction.

Slave bracelets were usually snug, but seldom tight.

Sometimes they were even rather loose, suggesting to a foolish girl the possibility of slipping them. But shortly, to her frustration, she learns she is held perfectly. The master, for his amusement, has been playing with her, and, in his way, instructing her.

Such small things help the new girl, in particular, to realize she is a female slave.

A girl who has better learned her collar is never in any doubt about such things.

Bracelets, chains, and such, incidentally, induce a sense of helplessness and vulnerability in the female, which sensations, whether she wishes it or not, increase her receptivity.

To be sure, they also hold her with perfection.

Her master had apparently decided that the bracelets would be tight, that it would please him to have her brought before him extremely conscious of her utter helplessness.

How faraway was the classroom!

There were six tiny links joining the bracelets, one for each letter in the Gorean spelling of 'kajira'.

The key to the bracelets was on a tiny string looped about her collar, not that this did Ellen any good.

"They are pretty bracelets," said the guard.

"We think so," said the first instructrix.

Slave bracelets, designed for women, are often light and pretty, and are sometimes matched to outfits and such. Some, for high slaves, are bejeweled. Some might be worth the ransom of a Ubar. They can be matched to collars, as well, and shackles, and such. Some bracelets are fitted with lock rings, which can be snapped into one another, if and when desired. This resembles the leather slave cuffs worn by some girls in paga taverns. Similarly, some collars, leather or otherwise, have rings to which such snap rings may be conveniently fastened. To be sure, something as simple as leather binding fiber, such as commonly belts the common camisk, well serves for the general purposes of ready tethering. Common, too, are leashes. The style, grace, attractiveness, and lightness of slave bracelets does not detract from their utility. They are more than adequate to hold a female, and with perfection. Not all slave bracelets are pretty, and such, of course. Some are quite plain, and these might be preferred by some men for their slaves, perhaps for reasons of instruction, or economy, or to avoid an appearance of ostentation, or such. Too, warriors, tarnsmen, slavers, and such, might prefer plainer custodial devices for early captures, transportation, simple holding, and so on. Sometimes no more than a string, nose-ring and thumb cuffs are used. Men, on the other hand, as one would suppose, are commonly held in heavier gear, for example, in heavy manacles.

"This tunic is certainly very short," said the first instructrix. She tugged a bit at the cut sides of the tunic, to draw it further down the thighs. Ellen stood very still. The first instructrix had little success.

"You must be careful how you move, Ellen," said the first instructrix.

"Yes, Mistress," said Ellen.

Ellen was barefoot, as female slaves are often kept.

"Is it not past the eighteenth Ahn?" asked the first instructrix, timidly.

"I do not think so," said the guard. "I have not heard the bar sound."

"You may kneel, Ellen." said the first instructrix, "but do not disarrange yourself."

"Thank you, Mistress," said Ellen.

She then knelt on the hall side of the door to the audience chamber, near the wall, and back a little, that she might not block the entrance. Several times she had been presented to her master in that chamber. But that had been before she had been made a work-slave, before she had been sent to the laundry.

She knelt there in the shadowed half darkness, in the light of a pair of flickering wall lamps. She pulled against the bracelets that held her hands behind her back. She did not want to go back to the laundry.

Surely anything would be better than going back to the laundry.

Or that is what she thought at the time.

I have informed the work-master, she thought, that I am ready to beg. How kind was the work-master! How grateful I am that this information has been brought to the attention of my master. Am I ready to beg? Surely I must beg, no matter how shameful, how demeaning, how revealing, this may prove to be! I pretended not to be willing to beg, and I was sent to the laundry. My master is so strong! He has conquered! I am now ready to beg!

He must love me.

He remembered me, he brought me to this world, he restored me to youth and beauty, for I know that I am beautiful, though perhaps not so beautiful as countless others; and he gave me a beautiful name; surely that means something; and he made me property, and he owns me, now literally owns me; surely then he must desire me, and want me, for his very own! He must then want me in the strongest, fiercest, most commanding, most complete, most possessive sense in which a man can want a woman, want me as his uncompromised property, his slave.

And that is what I am, his slave.

I love my master. I want to serve him, and please him, with my whole being, with my whole body, with my whole heart and soul. The master is the meaning of the slave's life, and she rejoices in her collar, that she belongs to him. What an incredible privilege, what an incredible honor, to be the slave of such a man! What an incredible joy to be fulfilled by him, to be owned and mastered by him! How pallid by comparison are boring and meaningless lives; how tepid the quotidian familiarities of contractual partners, each taking the other for granted; how fragile the regimens of arguable legalities; how delicate the cobwebs of convention, sunderable upon a whim; how wearying the tiny testings and battles of implicit competitors, the specified, adjudicable relationships of explicit contractees, each suspicious of, and concerned to outdo, the other. I can understand, she thought, how the same woman might be one man's wife and another's conquered, mastered, loving slave. Let such husbands, such weaklings, cry out in misery, she thought, learning that their pampered, bored, spoiled, troublesome, nagging wife is another man's kneeling licking, begging slave. Another, at the mere snapping of fingers or an imperious gesture, receives from she whom he has never taken the time or interest to truly know, she whom he has never questioned as to her depths and needs, she to whom he has never intimately and truly spoken, she whom he has never attempted to understand, but has insisted upon seeing only from a distance, through the distorting prisms of convention, frequent, delicious, loving, abject services, services of which he has feared even to dream.

Let him, if he will, in defense of his failures and futility, denounce and castigate her, she whom he has never had the strength to own. Or, alternatively, let him buy a whip, put her to her knees and claim her.

But here, on this world, thought Ellen, unlike such a woman, I am a slave not only by nature, and appropriately, but under explicit, recognized law. I can be legally bought and sold, and given away, and such. Here I am simple, categorical, uncontested property not merely in the secrecy of a chamber, hidden away from an ignorant, uncaring, complacent, insensitive world, but in the full daylight of the cultures of a planet. Here, on this world, my brand, my collar, my mode of being, are everywhere accepted, acknowledged, recognized and understood. On this world I am, in the full sense of the law, explicitly and perfectly, *slave*.

It must be near the eighteenth Ahn, she thought. How can I conduct myself within?

It seems that I must beg, and shamefully beg. It seems he must have that of me. For some reason it seems he must have me so humiliated, so reduced, so baring myself before him, as no more than a piteous, worthless begging slave. But he must know, aside from that, aside from the idle repetition of a formula, that I am fully, and only, a slave. Surely that cannot make me more a slave than I am. Surely no woman could be more a slave than I. But surely no slave wants to serve just any man. Surely I am not unique in that. Surely we are entitled to find some masters preferable to others. And even if, in some sense, we are not entitled to find some masters preferable to others, it is surely a fact, which we cannot help, that we would prefer some masters to others. One cannot help that. Surely the slave who must, to her misery, in fear of her very life, proffer perfectly the most delicious and intimate of services to the most hated of masters knows that. Why then must we beg thusly? But, perhaps, she thought, it is not that we would not choose our masters, were it in our power, but, alas, it is the masters who choose us. It is rather that they would have us beg contrary to our deepest wishes, thereby acknowledging their power over us. Or perhaps it is merely a way of them having us acknowledge our reality as sexual beings, that we, as women, want, desire and need sexual experience, in a pervasive, general, organic, biological manner. Or perhaps it is a test which, once passed, is done with, and we may then enter the arms of our beloved master as no more than a surrendered slave, nothing held back, a slave now confessed as needful in general but, in the specific case, blissful within the arms of a beloved master.

The eighteenth bar then began to sound, ringing out its strokes.

"On your feet, little kajira," said the first instructrix.

What does he want of me, wondered Ellen, wildly, struggling to her feet.

Whatever he wants, I want to give him, but I do not know what he wants! Does he want me to again refuse to beg, and will he then, proud of me, I having then proven my worth before him, that I am still much like a free woman, keep me for himself, or does he want me to beg? If I do not beg, will I then be returned to the laundry, perhaps for ever, perhaps to be never again given a chance to please him? Or does he want me to beg, that he will then have evidence of his power over me, and that I explicitly acknowledge myself a worthless slave, or that in begging I will have acknowledged that I have sexual needs or is it that my begging is merely a test for my suitability to wear a neck-chain at his slave ring?

The bar continued to ring.

Ellen felt the comb, and then the brush, at her hair, and her hair was again, hurriedly, arranged about her shoulders. The cut hems of her tiny tunic were drawn down a little, but sprang back when the second instructrix released them. She felt her wrists drawn back, and together, in the bracelets. This, she suddenly realized, much as in placing the hands behind the back of the head or the back of the neck, accentuated her figure; and so, too, of course, might other things as well; she recalled the manner in which she had been instructed to carry the basket of laundry, particularly if two hands are used. The erect, graceful posture of the slave, too, as she commonly carries herself, as a dancer, has a similar effect.

The bar continued to ring, the notes carrying throughout the house.

"Are you a virgin?" asked the first instructrix.

"Yes, Mistress," said Ellen.

The instructrix laughed.

The expression the instructrix had used, if it were to be translated literally into English, was 'white-silk'. The complementary expression is 'red-silk'. These are expressions used, incidentally, only of slaves, not of free women. It would be a great insult to refer to a free woman as either "white-silk" or "red-silk." That would be terribly vulgar. Duels might be fought about such things. Expressions more suitable to free women, in Gorean, are 'glana' and 'metaglana', or 'profalarina' and 'falarina'. But even these latter expressions have Gorean connotations, reflecting the views of a natural world. In the first case, the condition of virginity is regarded as one to be superseded; and, in the second case, it is regarded merely as something which comes before something else, something of greater importance, as an antecedent phase or prologue, so to speak.

"And your master has summoned you before him this night!" she laughed.

"Yes, Mistress," said Ellen.

"And you are out of the iron belt!"

"Yes, Mistress," said Ellen, apprehensively.

"Do not be surprised, little virgin," she laughed, "if you are red-silked this night!"

The other instructrix laughed, as well.

Ellen regarded them, despite herself, reproachfully, offended, shocked, scandalized.

Her expression much amused them.

"See the little barbarian!" laughed the first instructrix.

"Do you think you are a free woman?" laughed the second. "You are not! You are a little she-urt, a little she-tarsk!"

"Yes!" said the first.

Ellen looked down, angrily.

Ellen's virginity was important to her. She had thought to award it, if ever, only in some lovely and romantic context of her own choosing. But now she realized that it, as she, belonged to a master. She was now an animal, a domestic animal. Her virginity, accordingly, was of no more interest or importance to society, or an owner, than would be that of a pig.

She struggled futilely in the bracelets.

The last stroke of the bar rang out, and the eighteenth Ahn had been announced in the house.

The guard took her by the left, upper arm, and, opening the door to the audience chamber with his left hand, drew her within.

Chapter 15

She Begs;
What Occurred After She Begged

Ellen was drawn forward a bit, into the room.

Then the guard released her arm, and stepped back.

The room seemed much as before, except that now there was a long, narrow red carpet leading toward the curule chair.

Ellen gasped, and trembled, seeing her master. She stood still, and fought to keep her breath, and to control herself. Her legs felt weak. She feared she might fall. It was he who held all power over her. It was he who owned her.

"The slave, Ellen," said the guard, from behind her. The instructrices had not entered the room. She did not know if they were waiting outside or not. She supposed they had returned to their cells.

Ellen's master, Mirus, had apparently been reading a scroll. One portion of the roll was in his left hand, and the other in his right. There were two lamps behind the curule chair, one on each side. To the left of the curule chair was a small table, on which there was a decanter of colored glass. Beside it there was a small glass, also colored, matching the decanter. On the table there was also a whip. The whip, like the chain, is a symbol of the mastery.

Mirus indicated that the slave might approach.

Ellen walked down the long rug, approaching the chair. She walked as a slave. She bit her lip. She saw a small smile playing about the corners of his mouth. But she did not change her walk. She was a slave.

"Stop," he said.

She was a few feet before the dais.

"Remain standing," he said. Commonly, when a girl is told to stop, she kneels. That is common when the slave is before a free person.

"Turn, slowly, before me," he said.

She turned, slowly, before him.

She was in a slave tunic, and her wrists were braceleted behind her. She had been scrubbed, brushed, and combed. She had been perfumed, a slave perfume, of course, one appropriate for her.

"Again," he said.

Again the slave turned, slowly.

Men, she did not doubt, enjoyed seeing a woman display herself before them, particularly when commanded to do so, and in a particular fashion. Masters are lustful, appraising brutes, and slaves must hope to be found pleasing. Too, she did not doubt but what men enjoyed seeing a woman's hands braceleted behind her. This bespoke the woman's helplessness, and how at their mercy she was. Such things appeal well to natural glories, their sense of power and pleasure. And it would be superficial, of course, to overlook the effect of such impediments upon the woman herself, how they, like lipstick or eye shadow, accentuate the dichotomies of nature, call attention to the disparities of a radical sexual dimorphism, and deliciously enforce upon her an almost overwhelmingly welcome sense of her own sex, its desirability, beauty and weakness. It is little wonder that women welcome bonds on their body, collars, tunics, camisks, and such. In them they feel most man's, and thus most woman. Such things heat their thighs and ready them for the embrace of masters.

This is what they want, to be so desired that they will be made a man's slave.

Ellen knew she had a sweet figure, and lovely legs. And the tunic, in its brevity, did little to conceal her charms. Too, she knew, she had a lovely, sensitive, expressive face.

Too, she supposed she was intelligent.

Certainly she hoped so.

Gorean men, she had learned, prized intelligence in women. Such women they valued most on their knees before them. There is nothing hard to understand in that. Such women tend to be reflective and introspective, and tend thus to be in closer touch with their needs, desires and emotions than simpler women. They are commonly much aware of their slave, and long for her liberation. Thus, much of the master's work has already been done, even before they are ankleted and brought to Gor. No wonder they learn the collar quickly. In their dreams they have often worn it. In such women refractoriness is short-lived, particularly as they learn it is not permitted, which is, of course, what they desire. Too, such women are usually lovely and, given the complexity and sophistication of their nervous systems, are easily ignitable, and can shortly be made the prisoners of their passions. It is little wonder then that intelligent women are sought for the collar, and bring good prices in the market. Too, they on their tethers and such, one can talk with them.

I am acceptable as a slave, surely, she thought.

In some respects, at least.

Certainly that had seemed the assessment of the guards.

She hoped Mirus was pleased with her.

"Approach," he said.

Before the dais, before the chair, she knelt and put her head down to the rug, in obeisance. This lifted her braceleted hands high behind her.

She did not doubt but what this sight, her obeisance, and that of her wrists braceleted high behind her as she knelt, had its effect upon her master, Mirus. Indeed, she did not doubt but what the sight of a woman's braceleted wrists, either behind her or before her, had its effect on men. She wondered, however, if men realized the effect of her braceleting on the woman herself, its feel and look, how it made her feel helpless, and female, and slave, and desired and beautiful, and ready, and needful. Sometimes the mere thonging or braceleting of a woman, even one hitherto reluctant or inert, is all that is required to release and ignite her slave.

But perhaps men know this, she thought, at least the men of this world, of Gor.

"You are perfumed," he said.

"Yes, Master," she said.

Surely he had specified that.

She kept her head down to the carpet.

"An excellent scent," he said, "for a slut."

"Yes, Master," she said. "Thank you, Master."

He had doubtless specified the scent, as well. She thought it was a beautiful perfume, but here, on Gor, she had no doubt but what it was common and cheap. It was a slave perfume, as she had been informed, and it was doubtless not an expensive one, but one which might be accorded to low slaves.

Still she had the sense that on her old world it might have been costly.

"Thank you, Master," she said, keeping her head down.

The guard had followed her, staying a step or two behind her.

"Whip," said Mirus, taking the implement from the small table to his right.

The slave then rose gracefully to her feet, ascended the dais, and knelt before the chair. There, her hands pinioned behind her, she licked and kissed the whip for several seconds.

Her master then put the whip to the side again, on the small table, and indicated that she might withdraw. She backed down the stairs and then knelt again before the dais, as she had before, in obeisance.

"You are pretty in slave bracelets, Ellen," he said.

"Thank you, Master," she said.

"You wear them well," he said.

"Thank you, Master," she said.

"You wear them as though you might have been a born slave."

She was silent.

"But you are a born slave, aren't you?" he said.

"Yes, Master," she said. "I am a born slave."

"Now properly embonded?"

"Yes, Master."

"Remove her bracelets," he said to the guard.

"Kneel up," said the guard.

Ellen went to first position, as nearly as she could, braceleted, the cloth of the cut tunic falling between her widely spread thighs. The guard freed the key from her collar and, crouching behind her, removed the bracelets. As soon as the bracelets were removed Ellen, unbidden, went to first obeisance position, head down to the rug, the palms of her hands now on the rug, on either side of her head. She heard the guard replace the bracelets, and, presumably, the key, in his pouch. She supposed that he must have received some signal from her master to do this. The guard then withdrew, apparently having received some signal to do this from her master. She knelt in first obeisance position, excited, apprehensive, thrilled, alone with her master.

"Position," said Mirus.

Immediately she knelt in the first position before him, the first position of the pleasure slave.

Their eyes met.

Some Gorean masters do not permit their girls to look into their eyes unless bidden to do so, but this is rare. More often the discipline or punishment is not to permit the girl to look into the eyes of the master, which increases her apprehension and, of course, severely limits her capacity to read his moods. That is somewhat analogous to denying her food, or a particular food, taking something away from her. In standard first position the Gorean slave girl kneels with her head up, unless forbidden to do so. One of the great pleasures of the master/slave relationship is the unparalleled intimacy which obtains between the participants, an intimacy which is naturally much enhanced by the ability to see and react to one another's expressions, body language, and such, these things so indicative of thoughts and feelings. Men desire complete slaves, it seems, and this means total, vital, feeling, thinking females at their feet; that is apparently what one wants there; few if any men, it seems, desire a mere body, a puppet, a doll, an empty slave; who could be satisfied with such? Where would be the triumph, the pleasure, the value? What then, in such circumstances, could be the master's joy in owning us? Ellen had been told that she had very beautiful eyes. They were gray. Her hair was a very dark brown. The hair and eyes of Mirus, as those of most men, were brown.

Ellen looked into the eyes of Mirus. His expression seemed severe. She averted her gaze.

One reason to look into the eyes of a slave girl is to see if there is welcome in them, happiness, anticipation, shyness, mendacity, slyness, deception, joy, confusion, uncertainty, apprehension, fear. If one cannot look into the eyes of a slave, how can one well read her, how can one adequately master her? To be sure, much can be gained from body language. But then more can surely be gained from both her face and body. And from the slave's point of view, how can one best please a master, if one cannot truly see him?

Ellen was certain that her master had seen fear in her eyes. She looked past the chair, frightened.

"Do you enjoy the laundry?" he asked.

"No, Master," she said.

"What is your impression of Gart?" he asked.

"He to whom you refer, our work-master," she said, "is efficient. He is severe, but firm, and in his way, I think, kind. He has been good to me."

"You did not use his name."

"It is not fitting that the name of a free person should be soiled by the tongue of a slave," she said.

"You are clever," he said.

It had been a test.

"Has he whipped you?"

"I have felt his lash four times, in single strokes," she said.

"When you were lax in your labors?"

"Yes, Master."

"It is then appropriate that you were lashed?"

"Yes, Master."

"You then redoubled your efforts?"

"Yes, Master."

He lifted the scroll, which he had laid across his lap. He rerolled it, toward the center, saving his place.

"This is the *Prition* of Clearchus of Cos," he said.

"Master?"

"You have not been taught to read, have you?" he asked.

"No, Master," she said. Surely he knew that.

"You are illiterate," he said.

"Yes, Master."

"Would you like to learn how to read?" he asked.

"Oh, yes, Master!" she exclaimed.

"The proper answer," he said, "is 'Only if Master pleases'."

"Yes, Master," she said. "Forgive me, Master." Tears came into her eyes. She should have been more alert. She had failed that test.

"Most Earth females brought to Gor are not taught to read," he said.

"For what purpose are most Earth females brought to Gor?" she asked.

"Surely you can guess," he said.

"Yes, Master," she whispered.

"For the collar, for the markets," he said.

"Yes, Master," she said.

"We keep them as low slaves, uneducated and illiterate, fit at best for the simplest of tasks."

"Yes, Master."

"Considering their status on Earth, their machinations, and such, that seems to me both amusing and fitting."

"Yes, Master."

"And that is how I see you," he said. "As a low slave."

"As Master wishes," she said.

"Do you aspire higher?"

"No, Master!"

"Good," he said. "That will make your life easier."

She did not understand this.

"I understand," he said, "that you are now ready to beg."

Ellen, I fear, turned white.

"Before you beg, if, indeed, you are going to beg, is there anything you would like to say to me, or ask me?"

"May I speak freely, Master?"

"For the moment," he said.

"First, allow me to thank you for bringing me to this beautiful world, be it only to have made me your slave. And thank you, too, for giving me back my youth, my suppleness, my appetite, my health."

"And your slave beauty," he said.

"My slave beauty?"

"Yes."

"Am I beautiful?" she begged.

"Did I not assure you of that before?" he asked.

"Yes, Master. Forgive me, Master."

"But there are many," he said, "who are far more beautiful."

"Of course, Master," she said. Surely she had seen enough women in the pens, in their collars, to accept that, to realize that.

"I could, of course," he said, "have demeaned your beauty, disparaged it, caused you to doubt your own value, put you in consternation concerning your worth, and such, but I did not do so."

"Thank you, Master."

"I prefer to let you know how beautiful you are, not to inflate your vanity, pretty slut, which is doubtless already excessive, but to increase your sense of vulnerability."

"Master?"

"As a Gorean slave girl, and one of unusual beauty, I want you to realize clearly the peril in which you stand."

"Peril, Master?"

"Certainly," he said. "You will be as hot, fresh meat, juicy and steaming, amongst ravenous wolves!"

"And that is part of your vengeance upon me, to see that I am so placed, Master?"

"Of course."

"I do not care, Master."

"Consider yourself on a street, barefoot, collared, tunicked, not amongst the men of Earth, but amongst Gorean males."

"It is my hope that masters will find me pleasing."

"You are a slave girl," he said.

"Yes, Master."

"Slut," he said, "slut."

"Yes, Master."

He regarded her, moodily.

"And you have grown more and more beautiful."

"Master?"

"And what woman is truly beautiful until she is in a slave collar?" he asked.

"Surely Master jests."

"Not at all," he said.

"Was I not beautiful before, Master, if I was, long ago, when I was a free woman?"

"I assure you, my dear, that you are a thousand times more beautiful now, with that collar on your neck, than you ever were, or could be, as a free woman."

"Master!"

"Surely you understand its meaning."

"Yes, Master. I think so, Master."

"Then you can sense how, in it, you are more beautiful."

"I think so, Master," she whispered.

She had begun to sense how men might now view her, *as a slave*.

"And this goes far beyond the mere aesthetics of the collar. In it you are not simply seen differently, you are different, in a thousand ways."

"Yes, Master." She sensed how this was true. She was aware of the startling transformation which had taken place, and was taking place, within her. A slave girl, you see, is not a free woman.

"To be sure, you were very beautiful," he said, "but the beauty of a free woman, you must understand, is no more than the promise, the hint, of what her beauty would be as a slave. A slave is a thousand times more beautiful than a free woman."

"You saw me even then, *as a slave*."

"Yes," he said, "for you were a slave. It was obvious, slut. How stupid of the men of Earth to permit you and others like you your charade of freedom! Your life as a free woman is behind you. On Earth you were worthless. Here you are no longer worthless. Here on Gor, I assure you, you will be good for something!"

"Yes, Master," she said.

"You may now thank me," he said, "for your slave beauty."

"Thank you, Master," she said, "for my beauty."

"For your *slave* beauty."

"Master?"

"It is no common beauty," he said. *"It is a slave beauty."*

"Yes, then," she whispered, "I thank you, Master, for my beauty, be it only a slave beauty."

She recalled how she had seen herself before the great mirror, on the morning after her branding and collaring. How startled she had been. In the mirror she had seen what had so startled her, an exquisitely beautiful young slave.

What would men pay for me, she wondered.

"A girl is grateful," she said, "that her master finds her beautiful, if only as a slave."

He smiled.

How could a man find a woman more beautiful than as a slave?

"Thank you, Master, thank you, Master," she said.

He shrugged.

What, after all, is the gratitude of a girl, and of one who is only a slave?

But she herself was elated. Her master had admitted that he found her beautiful, if only as a slave. But how could a woman be more beautiful, she asked herself, delighted, than as that most exquisite, perfect and feminine of all creatures, the female slave?

"You have given me a second chance at life," she said.

He shrugged. Again, this seemed of little interest to him.

"Thank you," she whispered.

"Is this trivia all you wish to speak of?" he asked.

"How is it trivia, Master," she asked, "that I have been made again a young woman!"

"Do not flatter yourself," he said. "You are not a woman. You are a girl. I have seen to that."

"And I have lost some money on that," he said.

"I do not understand," she said.

"But it pleased me."

"Master?"

"Have you heard of the *Prition* of Clearchus of Cos?" he asked, placing the scroll on the table to his right, her left, near the glass and decanter.

"No, Master."

"It is a reasonably well-known treatise, one of several in fact, dealing with the ownership and domination of the human female."

"There are manuals for such things?" she asked.

"Certainly," said he, "as there are manuals for agricultural practices, military tactics, cartography, navigation, kaissa and such."

"Kaissa?"

"A board game," he said.

"Is there anything in the *Prition*, Master," she asked, "pertaining to a woman—a girl—such as myself?"

"You are all alike," he said.

"Oh," she said.

"Before you are granted an opportunity to beg," he said, "is there anything else of which you would care to speak?"

Ellen's mind raced. How could she speak of the deepest things in her heart to this man? Her thigh was branded. Her throat was locked in his collar. She wanted to tell him that she loved him, that she had longed to be his slave even from the first time she had seen him, so many years ago. But how could a lady reveal her most intimate thoughts and feelings, particularly if they were of such a kind? What would he think? Must he not then hold her in contempt? Must he not then be shocked? Must he not then despise her? How could he respect her if he knew she wanted to kneel, that she loved to kneel, as a helpless slave at his feet? He must never know that! He must never know that she was so helplessly his, that she loved her brand, his collar on her neck, that she longed to be pinioned helplessly in his bracelets, that she wanted his shackles, that she longed to be neck-chained at the foot of his couch, that she hoped even, sometimes, for the admonitory, flashing bite of his whip.

I love strong sensations, she thought. And I now know that they can exist.

I love being a woman, she thought.

I want to be owned, and dominated, she thought. Only here, on this beautiful, natural world have I understood, for the first time, my body, my mind, my feelings, my deepest being, my very soul, my sex.

No, I cannot even hint at such things!

I do not want to lose him forever.

I cannot reveal to him what a woman is, truly.

I dare not!

"Well?" said he.

She began to speak, but could scarcely understand what she was saying, so confused, so overwrought she was. It seemed she heard herself, as though it were not she herself, but another who was speaking.

"I am your slave," she said. "You can do with me what you want. You can order me as you please. You remembered me. You brought me here. You gave me back my youth, and my beauty, if beauty it be. You have made me young again. You have given me a second chance at life. Why? I think you like me! I am sure you want me. Are my flanks not of interest? Perhaps you love me. Certainly you desire me. You have given me a lovely name, 'Ellen'. You had me put in the iron belt, doubtless to save me for yourself.

Admit to me that you love me! You have done all this! Surely you love me! Surely you love me!"

"Do not speak stupidities," he said.

"Master?"

"Do not dare to jest with your master."

"Master!"

"Do not presume to flatter yourself, worthless slave."

"Do you not love me?" she asked.

"'Do you not love me' what?" he asked.

"Do you not love me—*Master*?" she whispered.

"Love, *for a slave*?" he asked.

"Yes, Master," she said.

He threw back his head and laughed. She shrank back, disconcerted, dismayed.

"You poor, little, stupid, arrogant piece of flesh-trash," he said.

Tears sprang into her eyes.

"Forgive me, Master," she said.

She dared not meet his eyes, his gaze was so fierce.

"Is there something you fear, Master?" she asked.

"What?" he said.

"Do you fear me, Master?" she asked.

He regarded her, angrily.

"Surely you do not fear me, Master," she said, "a half-naked, collared slave girl."

He reached for the whip, but drew back his hand.

"Can it be that you fear yourself, Master?" she said.

"As I understand it," he said, "you are now ready to beg."

"Can we not speak further, Master?" she begged. She wanted to cry out that she loved him, with all the helpless, vulnerable love of a female slave, that she wanted to serve him, to love him, to live for him.

But of course she dared not do so. How he would then hate her, despise her, understand the lowly, groveling, needful thing she was!

He had laughed at her. And how preposterous it was, indeed, that any man might love such as she, might love a mere, worthless, abject slave!

She must not let him know that she was such.

And yet she must beg!

Or would she beg?

Not the laundry again, not for days, or weeks, or months, or years, or life, not that, she wept to herself. What does he want of me, she asked herself. I want to give him whatever he wants. I am his slave! He is my master!

"Are you ready to beg?" he asked.

"Surely you do not wish me to beg!" she cried.

"You may do as you wish," he said.

"Surely you would want me as a free woman!" she cried.

"What makes you think I might want you as anything?" he asked.

"Forgive me, Master," she said.

"Men, you should understand," he said, "are lustful and possessive. You may like this or not, but it is the way they are. Those who do not seem so are glandular defectives, less than men, or are liars and hypocrites. Any man who truly desires a woman, who truly wants a woman, who wants her in the robust, vigorous fullness of powerful masculine desire, wants her wholly, all of her, wants to possess her, totally, wants to have her all to himself, wants to literally *own* her. Thus, what a man wants in a woman is the most precious, coveted and treasured of all possessions, the female slave."

"Surely such things dare not be said," whispered Ellen, frightened.

"You are not now on your old world of falsities and convention," he said. "On this world the truth may be spoken."

"I am a slave," said Ellen.

"That is known to me," he said.

"How can you respect me if I am a slave!"

"You are goods," he said. "I do not respect you."

"If I do not beg, what will be done with me?"

"You will be returned to the laundry," he said.

"Please, please, no, Master!" she wept.

"Yes," he said.

"And if I beg?"

"Then, too, you may be returned to the laundry," he said.

"Of course," cried Ellen, "it will be as Master decides!"

"Are you ready to beg?" he asked.

"Yes, Master," she whispered.

Could he so humiliate her, having her perform this act, and then, amused, satisfied, simply return her to the misery of the laundry?

Yes, he could. He was master.

But I love him, she thought. I love him!

But of what interest or importance might that be, the foolish love of a helpless slave, to one such as he, a master?

"You understand," he said, "that this begging has nothing to do with whether you are a slave or not. That is a matter of indisputable fact. Similarly, personally and psychologically, your condition is well-established and well understood. You are a natural slave."

"Yes, Master."

"That was apparent the first moment I saw you."

"Yes, Master."

"And now you have been fittingly embonded."

"Yes, Master," said Ellen.

"The begging then is for your benefit, slave girl. It is admonitory, and instructional. Still it will be amusing to hear you so beg."

"You have such power over me!" she wept.

"Such is the relationship in which you find yourself," he said, "slave girl."

"Is it not a way, simply, for me to confess that I am a sexual creature, that I have sexual needs, and," and here Ellen put down her head, and lowered her voice, "—and that I desire sexual experience?"

"You have not yet begun to understand your sexuality," he said.

"Yes, Master," she said.

"And do you, little Ellen, desire sexual experience?"

She was silent, in consternation.

"Speak up, now, loudly, clearly!"

"Yes, Master," cried Ellen. "I desire sexual experience!"

In that moment it seemed as though a great burden had been lifted from her. She regarded her master, in terror.

"You need not fear you will be a stranger to sexual experience," he said. "You are a slave girl on Gor."

"Is the begging not some sort of test, Master?" asked Ellen.

"Perhaps, in a way," he said.

He wants me, she thought. He wants me to beg, and then, when I have been so reduced, so humiliated, have so degraded and debased myself, he will be satisfied and keep me for himself. He will then keep me as the slave he wants and as the slave I long to be, worthless but helplessly his, helplessly devoted, helplessly loving. He will then, this test passed, keep me for himself, put me to his slave ring and own me, completely. At his slave ring, chained there by the neck, he will teach me undreamt of dimensions of my collar and begin the fuller mastering of a surrendered, conquered, helpless slave.

Perhaps, she thought, suddenly, wildly, I could pretend to be his slave; I could merely let him think that he is my master! Could I not keep myself a free woman, though branded, though in my collar? But then she almost choked with the silliness, the absurdity, the meaninglessness of this. How foreign to her reality would be such a pretense, how irrelevant to fact would be such a silly inward game! It would be a falsification of truth. Who cared if a dog or a pig pretended not to be owned? Reality remained unchanged. Too, how dishonorable to deny truth! How unworthy, as well as stupid, in the face of facts, to lie to oneself! No, she knew she was owned, *owned in fact, owned in perfect, clear, indisputable fact*. That was what she was, *slave*. And she knew, too, that that was what she had always wanted to be, to be owned, and to serve. She acknowledged that she was a natural slave, and that she had now been, as her master had called to her attention, fittingly embonded. Too, she did not believe that she could, even if she wished, even if it were possible, even if it were permitted, keep a corner of herself to herself. The masters seemed capable of looking through a woman, of understanding her better even than she understood herself. They seemed to have an uncanny sense of her emotions, of her thoughts and feelings. Could she hide nothing from their gaze? This had been brought home to her even in her training. Why could Gorean men not be more like the men of Earth, and look at a woman and not really see her? Perhaps that was because they did not own their women. It is hard to hide from men when one is stripped before them and fiercely questioned. Gorean men seemed interested, as Earth men were not, in paying attention to their women, in spending time with them and listening to them, and, in virtue of delightfully prolonged intimacies, understanding them, learning them, knowing them, truly understanding them, learning them, knowing them. Perhaps that is because they own them, and it is well known the attention and care, and the devotion of sorts, which men lavish on their possessions. Who does not wish to know everything there is to know about his property, about his treasure? Too, of course, this makes it much easier to master the female. The skilled master can read a woman like a book. One cannot hide from him. It seems there is no nook or cranny in a woman's soul into which the master, whip in hand, cannot enter.

They make us slaves, and we are slaves.

Ellen, for whatever reason, because of her intelligence, or her dispositions, or whatever it might have been, had made the transition from freedom to slavery with relative ease. That is perhaps because she had been sensitive to the appropriateness of slavery for her, on some level or another, since puberty. On Earth she had been, in effect, like countless others, a slave without a collar.

In some women, of course, their slavery is more suppressed, more deliberately concealed, more desperately denied and hidden, than it is in others. They are perhaps more frightened of themselves, and more in ideological and cultural bondage, than an emotionally freer woman, more in touch with her deeper self and feelings. But it is said that even in such women there eventually comes a moment in their bondage when the emotional cataclysm occurs, when the breakthrough takes place, when the depths of the unconscious open up, when the surgent, rising earthquake of the liberated spirit totters and collapses the fragile, brittle walls of their psychological prisons, when the moment of truth blazes before them like sunrise, and shuddering and sobbing with gratitude and misery they understand themselves for the first time in their lives, understand that they are women, and belong to men, men who will see to it that they fulfill their natures. They must then accept what they are, with all its marvels, beauties and vulnerabilities. They are not men. They are quite different, quite wonderfully different. They can then no longer hide, either from themselves or others. How unfortunate that this insight comes so late for some women, say, as they lie sobbing, beaten, their wrists bound to a whipping ring anchored in heavy planks, or as they lie cold and hungry, curled up, clutching a tiny blanket about themselves, on the cement flooring of a kennel, or as they are drawn by the hair to the height of an auction block and find themselves displayed as an object for sale, displayed, and fully, to frenzied, bidding men.

"Are you ready to beg, slave girl?" he asked, severely.

"Yes, Master," said Ellen.

He then turned to the side, where, some yards away, across the room, there was a narrow ancillary door.

"Ho!" he called.

In a moment or two there proceeded through the door two men, clad in blue robes. One carried a small rectangular board on which he held some papers. At his belt there hung a small case, containing at least pens, and a tiny horn, which, as Ellen later realized, was an inkhorn. Ellen had seen such papers before, when she had been examined in great detail, apparently partly to ascertain identifying marks, subjected to numerous measurements, and fingerprinted and toeprinted. She had little doubt that they were her slave papers. Such papers, as may have been mentioned, are unnecessary and are not kept on the vast majority of slaves. They can provide a convenience to buyers and sellers, however, as they will provide a good deal of information, with respect to background, caste, education, languages, training levels, physical descriptions, collar sizes, ankle- and wrist-ring sizes, and such, on the slave in question. Sometimes brochures and sales sheets for public postings are compiled from them by judicious selections. Such papers assume greater importance, of course, in the case of pedigree slaves or exotics. The bloodlines of some pedigree slaves go back several generations. Collectors, too, tend to be interested in the background of exotics, for example, who bred them, and where they were bred, and such.

Ellen had scarcely a moment to note the two entering men, in their blue robes, before she was ordered to first obeisance position.

She was then kneeling on the rug before the dais, on which reposed the curule chair, her head to the rug, the palms of her hands on the rug, too, on either side of her head.

"Are you eager to beg?" he asked.

She almost lifted her head but did not dare to lose contact with the rug. She wanted so much to look into his eyes, but she did not dare. She was aware of the two blue-robed men, to the left of his chair, to his left, as he was facing her.

"Yes, Master," she said.

"Speak up," he said.

"Yes, Master!" she said.

"Identify yourself, and your master, clearly, and specify, clearly, what you are doing," said one of the blue-robed men.

"I am the slave girl, Ellen. My master is Mirus, of Ar. I kneel before him. I am eager to beg."

"You may beg," said her master.

"I am Ellen," she said, "the slave girl of Mirus of Ar. I beg to please a man, any man."

Tears burst from her eyes. She trembled. It was done! She had begged to serve a man, any man! How shamed she felt, how humiliated, how debased, how degraded. How worthless she was, she thought. How could she now be anything but the lowest and most worthless of slaves, in the eyes of her master, in the eyes of the witnesses, in her own eyes, in the eyes of anyone? She heard the pen moving on the paper. That she had so begged was now on her papers. The second man in blue robes added a note, or signature, or certification, to the papers.

This is what he wanted, she told herself. What more could he want? Scorn me now, Master, she thought. Now, she thought, you can hold me in contempt to whatever degree might please you. How could I be such now that you might despise me more? You have made me nothing! Your vengeance on me, my Master, if vengeance it is, is surely now complete!

"Thank you," said Mirus to the two men who, shortly, withdrew.

"Position," said Mirus.

Ellen struggled to first position, sobbing, her body shaking with misery. She wanted to throw herself to the floor, covering her face, sobbing.

First position, she thought. I must hold my head up.

He wants to see my face, she thought.

It must be red, and tear-stained. Does that please him?

She dared to look at her master. His expression seemed noncommittal. It was hard to read.

"I have begged," she sobbed.

"As I knew you would, slave girl," he said.

"Please be kind to a slave!" she wept.

"Why?" he asked.

She choked back a sob, and looked past him, past his shoulder, past the curule chair, to the wall several yards behind.

"May I speak, Master?" she sobbed.

"For the moment," he said.

"I have begged," she said. "Now I beg to please my Master."

"In what way?" he asked.

"In any way he may desire," she said.

"Oh?"

"I beg to be permitted to enter your arms."

"You wish to please me—*sexually*?" he said.

"Yes, Master."

"Second obeisance position," he said.

Ellen went prone, before him, her hands at the sides of her head.

"You may now speak, and speak clearly, slave girl," he said.

"I am Ellen, the slave girl," she said. "I belong to Mirus of Ar. I belly before him, my master. I beg to please him—*sexually*."

"But you are a virgin," he said. "That would lower your price."

"Master?" said Ellen, startled.

"To be sure," he said. "It does seem a bit silly. Why should some men want to be the first to open a slave? What difference does it make? The slave will probably have very little feeling the first time. It may even cause her pain. Later she may jump and juice, and scratch, and beg for the least caress. Why should one not pay more for that, since it is the enjoyment of a much more delicious, more helpless, more eager pudding, and yet when one locks one's chains on such a one and thrusts her back to the furs, one simply takes her responses for granted, giving it not another thought. It is all very strange."

"Master?" asked Ellen.

"To be sure," he said, "I have already lost money on you, for had I had you returned to, say, your early twenties, you would doubtless bring a better price. You would be taken more seriously as block-meat."

"Please do not speak of a slave as such," she wept.

"But, as it is, you are something like eighteen. Who could take you seriously? You are no more than a pretty girl."

"But even so, perhaps master finds me of interest," she said.

"Oh you are learning to be a slave," he growled.

"Forgive me, Master," said Ellen. She feared something in his voice. The work-master's voice had occasionally taken on such a tone, usually shortly before he had rudely seized, and tubbed, or put to his pleasure, one of his charges, often the now-abducted Nelsa.

"No, no," he said. "You are learning. It is perfect."

"Thank you, Master," she said, hesitantly. She knew that she had aroused men in her training, but they had not been, she gathered, authorized to seize her, and make use of her, to assuage the passions and tensions she may have aroused in them. They must seek out other slaves. The other slaves had not seemed to mind. She wondered if she might ever become like that, so grateful for the touch of a man, even if it were not she in the first place who had aroused his passions. It was said that young men enamored of free women, perhaps having glimpsed an ankle, or a bit of throat or chin as the wind indiscreetly lifted a veil, sometimes sought out the girls in the paga taverns to lessen the pangs of love, to lessen their miseries. Many times clutching, grateful, gasping slaves heard the names of women they did not know cried out as free men used them to climax their pleasures. Briefly there flashed through her mind the tarnsman from Brundisium who, apparently enamored of a free woman, had taken a different action, seizing the woman, to make her his slave, she then to be herself perhaps no more to him than a paga girl. And later she, Ellen, had even been put in the iron belt, probably as she had progressed in her lessons and had become, if only unconsciously and inadvertently, far more desirable, far more provocative, feminine, and sensuous. She was pleased, of course, but a little frightened, to know that she had this effect on men. But now she was alone with her master. No longer was he her defense and shield. And there is none to defend or shield the slave, you see, from the master. She was utterly vulnerable. Anything might be done to her. She was his.

"But it pleased me," he said, "to have had you made as young as you are, to give you such a meaningless, trivial age, a mere lovely eighteen, though I cost myself some coins in the business. It was a delicious part of my vengeance upon you."

"Vengeance, Master?" she said.

"Yes," he said.

"Master?" she asked.

"And so," said he, thoughtfully, as though pondering some matter, "what would be the loss of a coin or two more?"

"I do not understand what you are saying, Master," whispered the slave.

"Yes," he said, apparently having come to some decision. "Why not? Yes, what is a coin or two, measured against the pleasure of teaching you what you now are, a worthless slave, of instructively demeaning you even further, of reducing your value yet again, even in a market, and thus exacting an even sweeter, richer, more delicious vengeance upon you?"

"Master?" cried the slave, frightened.

"Turn about," he said. "Face away from me, kneeling. Put your head to the rug. Clasp your hands behind the back of your neck!"

"Please, no, Master!" she wept.

"Good," he said. She heard him, she now facing away from him, head down, hands clasped behind the back of her neck, rise from the curule chair. She heard, too, the fall of garments upon the chair, dropped to the side, the robes heavier, the tunic almost inaudible.

He crouched behind her.

She felt the tunic pulled up and thrust forward, and down, until it was about her head and clasped wrists.

"Please, no, Master!" she begged.

"So," said he, "here we have our little feminist, poised for the penetration of her master."

"I am no longer a feminist!" she wept. "I have learned that I am a woman!"

"A girl?" he asked.

"Yes, Master, a girl! A girl! You have done that to me!"

"So here we have my former teacher then," he mused, "prettily positioned. You look well, former teacher. I like you like this. What former student would not like you like this?"

"Please be kind, Master!"

"And, too, of course, here we have our little Ph.D., with her doctorate in gender studies, kneeling down obediently, facing away, awaiting the penetration of her master. Did they teach you of this in your gender studies?"

"No, Master."

"Such studies were then incomplete, were they not?"

"Yes, Master," she sobbed.

"And, of course," he said, "we have here, too, our pretty little slave girl."

She felt his hands seize her, about her narrow waist. He was extremely strong, and she did not doubt but what there would be marks on her body, from where he held her.

"Please, no, Master!" she begged. "Not like this, not like this, Master! I beg you! Not like this, my Master!"

"Who begs?" he asked.

"Ellen, Ellen, the slave, begs!" she wept.

"Whose are you?"

"Yours, Master!"

"Speak more clearly," he said.

"Ellen, the slave, your slave, the slave of Mirus of Ar, begs her master, begs you, her master, Mirus of Ar, for mercy!" she wept.

"You have a pretty ass, slave girl," he said.

"Please do not speak so, Master!"

"You have been complimented," he said.

"Thank you, Master," she wept.

Strangely she had never really thought of herself in such a way. She was, of course, pleased, perhaps inordinately so, with the fresh, lissome contours of her new figure. But how vulgar had seemed his compliment. To be sure, the young, slim, sweet curvatures of her body were of a piece, of a whole, an indissoluble, coherent delight, from her small feet and ankles, to her calves and thighs, her hips, her love cradle, her narrow waist, and sweet bosom, to her soft, white shoulders and lovely throat, all a melody of softness, texture and line, and surely no part of her was without its role and portion in the new and exquisite she of her. She recalled, briefly, fashions of centuries in which clothing itself had been designed to call attention to, and emphasize, just such features. She recalled the pleasure with which she had regarded herself in the mirror, her trimness, her excitements.

But how vulgar had been his compliment!

Yet could she deny that she was pleased?

But in what a shameful position she had been placed!

She thought of the rude, efficient, coital positions of many animals. Was it so different?

And, she realized, too, she was now an animal, a slave, and an attractive one.

But he could not be serious!

What could he have in mind!

Surely he could not be doing this to her, not to her, not to her!

Had he no respect for her? What of her dignity?

Was he not of Earth?

Could he not remember Earth?

"Please, Master!" she wept. "Not like this! Not like this!"

"Please, no!" she cried.

"We are of Earth," she cried, "we are both of Earth!"

"No longer," he said.

"Mercy, Master!" she begged.

"You are going to be red-silked, girl," he said.

"Not like this, Master," she begged. "Please, no! No! Not like this, not like this! Please, Master, not like this!"

"Oh!" she cried, suddenly.

"You are now "red silk,"" he informed her.

"Do not break position," he growled. His hands were on her like iron.

In a few moments she lay on her right side on the rug, at the foot of the dais, sobbing.

He had drawn on his tunic, but not his robes, and was sitting in the curule chair, looking down upon her.

"You are a tight, cold little thing," he said.

Her body was wracked with sobs.

"Remove your garment," he said.

Crying, she half sat up, and pulled her slave garment, the tiny, cut tunic, over her head, from where it was, about her neck and shoulders, and put it beside her. Then again she lay on the rug, on her side, trying to control her tears. There was a bit of blood upon her, and a smeared stain of blood on the interior of her left thigh.

"Taste your virgin blood," he said.

She looked at him, red-eyed, not comprehending.

From within his tunic, from what may have been an interior enclosure there, he drew forth a ribbon and what seemed to be a length or two of binding fiber. He came down from the dais and crouched beside her.

She shrank back a little.

"Oh!" she said.

"Here," he said, putting two fingers to her mouth. "Taste it, the blood of a virgin slave."

Obediently, sobbing, she did as she was told. It was thick, sticky, warm from her body, a little salty, and bore more than a tiny hint of the oils of her nether intimacies. It was not a moment she would ever forget.

"Sit up," he said. And so she sat up on the rug, before him. He was now kneeling beside her.

He held up the ribbon before her. It was about eight or ten inches long, an inch wide, and of red silk.

"You have been had," he said, in English. And then he added, in Gorean, "You have now been opened for the uses of men, for the pleasures of men."

"You are now a red-silk girl," he said.

He then doubled the ribbon, looped it about her collar, and jerked it tight. There seemed something definitive about that, the way he did it.

"Bara!" he said.

She instantly responded to his command, as she had been trained to do. She was now on her belly, her wrists crossed behind her, her ankles, too, crossed.

She felt her wrists tied with one length of the binding fiber, and then, a moment later, her ankles bound with a second length. The pieces of binding fiber might have been each eighteen inches in length. Each, thusly, could be looped more than once about her wrists and ankles.

She was then lying before him, prone, a naked, bound, red-silk girl.

He then turned her to her side. Could it have been to give himself pleasure? Certainly he scrutinized her with care, and seemingly appreciatively. Doubtless he noted how she drew up her knees, and pointed her toes, accentuating the curve of her calf. Perhaps he wondered if she even knew she had done that. She had not even thought of it, at least not in the sense of carefully planning it, but had rather done it naturally, naturally, as a slave. He smiled. Her eyes stung afresh with tears. But she knew how she must be before a man, and wanted to be before a man. She was slave.

He lifted her in his arms and carried her to the height of the dais, where he put her down, gently, on her knees, to the left of the curule chair, as one might look out from it, to the right of the curule chair, as one would face it.

One may recall that on the small table to his right there reposed a decanter of colored glass with its small, matching glass.

He took the stopper from the decanter, and poured a tiny bit of its contained liquid into the glass.

"You may speak," he said.

"What you did to me!" she wept.

"You may not complain," he said. "You are a slave."

"Yes, Master."

"You may now thank me for using you," he said.

"Thank you, Master," she said.

"For what?" he asked.

"For using me, Master."

"As what?" he asked.

"As a slave, Master," she said.

"You're crying," he said.

"Forgive me, Master."

"Perhaps you understand a little better now what it is to be a slave?"

"Yes, Master."

"Later," said he, "when you have discovered more of yourself, and of your sexuality, you will beg such usages."

"I doubt that," she said.

"No," he said. "The time will come when you will crawl backward to a master, naked, whimpering, elevating your lovely posterior, begging."

She regarded him, aghast. Could she ever have such depths within her? It seemed impossible. Yet, to be sure, she had heard some of the girls in the cells and cages, and kennels, crying out, and moaning, and scratching. She had heard of the depths of, and intensity of, "slave needs."

He held the glass toward her lips, and she shrank back, in her bonds.

"What is wrong?" he asked.

"That is not a "releaser," is it?" she asked.

"No," he smiled. "It is ka-la-na."

"Slave wine," which, as administered to slaves, is terribly bitter, from the sip root, found in the Barrens, precluded conception. The "releaser," which is commonly syrupy, and sweet, nullifies the effects of the "slave wine." It is commonly administered to a slave after masters have agreed upon a crossing, and she is to be bred.

"Ka-la-na?" she asked.

"Yes," he said. "A wine."

There are many ka-la-nas, but the one in the colored glass, if it had been in a clear glass, would have been golden in color. The reddish color of the glass infused its contents with something of its own hue.

"From the wine trees of Gor," he said.

She straightened up, as well as she could. She knew she was helpless. He had bound her well, surely as well as any Gorean might have, tightly, but not excessively tightly. There would be no danger of damaging the slave, of impairing her circulation, or risking possibilities of nerve or tissue damage, and, in the psychological dimension, she would have just enough latitude to tease her, and then frustrate her, as she might struggle, and then, eventually, realize she was, when all was said and done, utterly helpless, a slave girl bound by her master.

"You would have me drink wine, and from a glass?" she asked. "How is it that it is not water, put in a pan on the floor, which I must lap from the pan, forbidden to touch the pan with my hands?"

"You speak boldly, for a naked, bound slave," he said.

She tossed her head.

"You have spirit," he said. "That can be taken from a girl, if one wishes."

She moved a little closer to him, and then, suddenly, beggingly, impulsively, as if she scarcely knew what she was doing, put her head to his right knee, turning her head and resting the side of her face, her left cheek, on his knee.

"It is not that I mind a bit of spirit in a slave," he said. "It makes it all the more pleasant to bring them again to their belly, at your feet, kissing and begging."

"Yes, Master," she whispered, softly.

"But there must be not the least impairment in perfect discipline," he said.

"No, Master," she whispered.

He put the tiny glass on the table. She heard the small sound.

"You may speak," he said.

"I love you," she said, "my Master."

"I have brought you here, that you might hate me, for what I have done to you," he said.

"How could I hate you, Master?" she asked, her head to his knee. "You have rescued me. You have saved me. You have given me my rightful bondage. I have always been a slave, but now, at last, you have given me my brand, and my collar. You have given me to myself, in a world where I can be myself, and need not hide myself, even from myself. I am inordinately grateful to you, my Master."

She whimpered, for she felt his hand clench in her hair, tightly, she feared angrily.

"Continue to speak," he said, seemingly controlling his voice, keeping it calm, with an effort.

As he was holding her, she could not lift her head, to look into his eyes, to try to understand him.

She was frightened.

"Go on," he said, quietly.

"I wanted to kneel to you," she said, "even when you were a student. I sensed in you power, and virility, and uncompromised manhood, and, too, I think I sensed in you even then, surely on some level, then only dimly understood, the splendor and force of the mastery. Do you understand how devastating, how irresistible, how overwhelming this is to a woman? In you was manifested the very principle of masculinity to which all women, in virtue of their principle of femininity, long to succumb."

His hand tightened even more in her hair. She winced.

"I love you, Master," she said. "And I want to be your slave."

"Oh!" she cried, in pain.

"Surely," she wept, her head held down, cruelly, "you must have some feelings for me. You remembered me, after many years. You never forgot. You have brought me here. You have given me a second chance at life. You have rescued me. You have saved me. You have restored my youth, and beauty, if I be beautiful. You put me in the iron belt, that I might be protected in a house where men may do much what they please with the women at hand, where the use of slaves is little restricted. You keep me for yourself. You gave me a beautiful name. You have even inflicted peremptory and degrading usage upon me. Surely, then, you must have feelings for me. If you do not love me, Master, do you not like me, if only a little? Surely, at the least, you must find me of interest, as a master a slave. Surely you must want me. Surely you must desire me, if only as an object to rape, punish and abuse. You must find my body of interest. Look upon it, Master. You own it!"

"I own all of you," he snarled.

"Yes, Master," she gasped, wincing.

He released her hair, and she drew back, gratefully, her hair twisted and tangled, in disarray, kneeling before him.

She then saw his eyes rove her, her hair, her face, her throat, her shoulders, her bosom, her waist, her love cradle, her thighs.

She put her shoulders back a little, that her figure might be accentuated.

She turned a little to the side, and lifted her head.

"Brazen slave," said he.

She knelt very straightly. She was very conscious of the steel circlet clasping her throat.

"Surely my flanks are not without interest, Master," she said, timidly. She moved her hands a little in their bonds, futilely.

"It is true, your flanks are not without interest, slave girl," he said.

"Thank you, Master," she said.

"You are a lovely slave," he said.

"Thank you, Master!" she said.

"But there are thousands in the markets as lovely, or lovelier, than you," he said.

"Yes, Master," she said. She did not doubt but what he said was true. Indeed, in this very house, she had seen many women with whose beauty she would not have dared to compare hers. She became aware that tears had sprung afresh to her eyes.

He reached to her and put his hand in her hair.

"Please do not hurt me more," she begged. "I am a bound slave. My neck is in your collar. Please do not hurt me more!"

But he drew her closer to him, not cruelly, but firmly. Then, without removing his hand from her hair, he lifted the small glass of ka-la-na.

He swirled the wine a little in the glass, and held it before him, inhaling the bouquet. He then held the small glass before her.

"It is lovely, Master," she said, breathing in the wine's bouquet.

"It is a nice ka-la-na," he said.

He then held it before her, the rim of the glass to her lips, and tipped it, slightly, that she might sip it.

"It is wonderful, Master," she breathed. "The smoothness, the flavor, the fragrance, the body."

"I thought you would like it," he said.

"Thank you, Master," she breathed.

He is kind to me, she thought. He gives me wine. He is gentle. He is tender. He loves me. My Master loves me! I want to be a wonderful slave to him! I want to be the most wonderful and loving slave on all Gor! Let him do with me as he pleases. Let him kick and beat me. I will rejoice! I will beg to lick the boot that kicks me, I will beg to kiss the hand that strikes me! Oh dominate me, and own me, my Master! I am yours, my Master!

Then suddenly it seemed the blood froze in her veins, as she met his eyes.

"Master?" she asked.

"You will now finish your bit of ka-la-na," he said.

She felt his hand tighten in her hair, and pull back, lifting her head and bending it backward.

She saw the tiny glass before her, her head bent back.

His eyes were hard. In them there was no longer any hint of kindness, of tenderness, of gentleness. In them she now saw only severity and anger, even fury.

"Master?" she asked, frightened.

"Open your mouth," said he. "Widely. Do not spill a drop."

He slowly poured the residue of ka-la-na into her obediently lifted, opened mouth.

"Swallow," said he. "Carefully, swallow. Swallow."

Then he released her hair and replaced the tiny glass on the table.

She looked at him. She ran her tongue over her lips. She could taste the ka-la-na.

Already she thought she could feel its effects.

He was sitting in the curule chair, in the tunic, watching her.

"Master?" she said.

"I had thought," he said, moodily, "it might take you years, and a hundred masters, to learn your slavery, my little feminist and ideologue. I had thought that you would cry out and rage against me for years in your chains and collars for what I had done to you. How that would have pleased me, your anger, your hatred, your misery, your frustration, your suffering, until, of course, eventually, perhaps years from now, in the arms of some master, a leather worker, a peasant, a sleen-breeder, your last psychological defenses would shatter and your womanhood, released, would cry out and claim you, reducing you to the welcomed, surrendered abject glory that is the right of your sex. But, instead, after but a moment, I find you an exquisite little slab of collar-meat, a willing, content, obedient little piece of flesh-trash, no different from thousands of other meaningless, silken little she-urts. Already you grovel at the snapping of fingers, and lick and kiss the whip with not only skill, but eagerness. Almost instantly you have begun to move as a slave girl. Already, at the sight of you, guards cry out in anger, and in need. Already you kneel with perfection and have become excruciatingly, inordinately, maddeningly, marvelously feminine."

"But I am a slave, Master," she whispered. She was kneeling. She felt a little unsteady. She shook her head. There seemed to be a bright, hazy glow about the lamps.

"Perhaps you rushed to your ideology in order to hide your deepest feelings and needs from yourself, the ideology constituting in its way a defense mechanism, as the expression is, a hysterical denial of inwardly sensed biotruths."

"I do not know, Master," she said, confused. "I feel faint, Master."

"You may break position," he said.

She sank to her side on the steps, before the curule chair.

"It is not simply ka-la-na which you have imbibed," he said. "It was mixed with tassa power. You had some weeks ago, on Earth."

She shook her head, trying to retain consciousness. She looked up at him, tears in her eyes.

"You have wondered why I brought you to Gor," he said. "I will tell you. I brought you here because I hold you in contempt, because I despise you, because it amuses me to bring you here and make you a meaningless, youthful slave. Surely in your bracelets and chains you must understand how amusing that is, particularly given your subject matter, your teaching, your publications, your ideology. Here, in a collar, you can at last learn something true about men and women. You can at last learn your proper place in nature. You can learn it with a branded thigh, and an encircled neck, kneeling before masters."

"Do you not love me, Master?" she gasped.

"No," he said.

"Do you hate me?" she wept.

It seemed to be growing dark, about the edges of her vision.

"No," he said. "You are not worth hating."

"I love you!" she wept.

"Lying slut!" he said, in English. Then, rising angrily from the chair, with his bootlike sandal, he thrust her forcibly, rolling, down the steps of the dais to the floor at its foot.

He came down the steps, and, it seemed, was ready to spurn her yet again with the bootlike sandal.

She crawled, squirmed, as she could, to his feet, and, summoning what little strength remained within her, pressed her lips to the bootlike sandal which had spurned her.

She looked up at him, tears in her eyes. "What are you going to do with me?" she asked.

"What am I going to do with you—what?" he snarled.

"What are you going to do with me—*Master*?" she whispered.

"What I planned to do with you from the beginning," he said.

"Master?"

"Complete my vengeance upon you."

"Master?" she whispered.

"Can you not guess?" he said.

She put her head against the rug. She pulled a little against her bonds. Then she lost consciousness.

Chapter 16

The Sunlit Cement Shelf

For a time she could make nothing out of the sounds about her. It seemed for the moment an indiscriminate babble, and, one supposes, from one point of view it was, as the sounds were then unintelligible to her, as she lay there, only dimly, distantly, vaguely conscious. She was trying to hear them with a different ear, so to speak. She was trying, we may suppose, to hear in English, but it was not English, you see, that was about her. It was a quite different language. So her puzzlement, her vague unease, her half-conscious consternation, was not really difficult to understand. Indeed, at first she did not really think of the sounds as of a language, at all, but only as human sounds, and then, gradually, she realized they must be in a language. The streams of sound bubbling about her like water, sometimes breaking forth, sometimes soothing, rippling, sometimes rushing, must be intentionally formed. There was something articulate and precise in the music, in the sounds. These were not the sounds of animals, the roars, and growls, the bleating, bellowing, shrieking, howlings, and hissings of animals, nor the sounds of nature, nothing like the dashings of branches against one another, lashed by the wind, nothing like the pattering of rain, the tumbling of rocks, the drums of thunder, the shattering proclamations of lightning. So why did she not understand them? Doubtless she was very tired, and wanted to sleep. Why could they not be quiet, these voices which must be in her dream? What a strange dream! It crossed her mind that she might complain to the building superintendent. How vigorous and remarkable, and diverse, and expressive, seemed that strange tongue, at once so lively, bright and fluent, even delicate, and then suddenly so explosively rude and brutal, at one moment loud, at another soft, at one moment rapid, even careless, at another measured and stately, at one moment melodious, at another almost inarticulate and fierce, and the dozens of voices speaking, conversing, crying out, calling out, whispering, proclaiming, announcing, arguing, haggling, querying, all this sound, rapid, torrential, swift, slow, then quick again, loud, soft, which, like flowing, sometimes rushing, water, bubbled about her, seemingly everywhere, was surely incongruous in the vicinity of her apartment.

Gradually she became apprehensive, because it began to seem to her that if one thing or another were a little different, if there were a small adjustment, a willingness, a readiness, a slight shifting of attention or awareness, the smallest acceptance or openness, that that inexplicable cacophony of sound about her might suddenly become intelligible, and this suspicion, for no reason she clearly understood, frightened her.

She continued to listen, dimly, determinedly, in English, and, in this way, reassuringly, she understood nothing, or, perhaps better, nothing she would admit to herself.

She was on her stomach, doubtless on her bed in her apartment. On the other hand, the surface seemed very hard, unpleasantly hard, even rough. I must get a new mattress, she thought. She reached for her pillow, but could not find it. It had doubtless fallen to the floor. The bed was hard, much too hard. It also seemed very warm, where she was. It was almost as though she lay on a hot surface, in direct sunlight, in the heat of a blazing summer. The sunlight must be streaming through the window in her apartment. But there was so much of it. And the angle seemed wrong, and it was so hot! How terribly unpleasant, she thought. She was uncomfortably warm, but did not want to awaken.

She reached for the covers, to press them down, and away, but she could not find them. She must have discarded them already.

She sensed redness, radiance and heat through her closed eyelids.

It was hot. There seemed to be bright sunlight.

Was there something on her neck? Had there been a tiny sound, as of the touching of one piece of metal upon another, or a tiny scraping sound?

Something seemed subtly different about her body.

She hoped that it was Saturday, for on Saturdays she had no classes.

She reached down to touch her nightgown. She knew that she should have, given her ideological commitments, affected mannish nightwear, to be more like men, the enemy, but she had not wished to do so, and her fellow ideologues, her colleagues, and such, need never know that she wore a gown to bed, one that might be thrust up, revealing her. It was of cotton. She had not dared to purchase, let alone wear, a subtle, rustling silken gown, or one of those tiny, revealing short gowns, one of those scandalous little things presumably eschewed even by prostitutes, who might wish to have a bit of respect from their clients, the sort of garment in which a master might put a slave girl.

An old dream vaguely touched her consciousness.

No, no, she murmured.

But he had emerged from his seat in the classroom, taken her in hand, and, despite her mild, weakly plaintive protests, almost ritualistic protests, expected of her, quietly, methodically, garment by garment, even to her shoes, stripped her before the class. He had then lifted her to the surface of the desk. She had squirmed beneath him, plaintively protesting, trying weakly to push him away, and then, kissing him and grasping him, had wept her surrender. The class had applauded.

No, she thought. Oh, yes, yes, yes! No! Yes! Yes!

She reached down to touch her cotton nightgown, but touched, rather, her thigh. She feared that in the intensity of her dream she had drawn it up, about her waist, or bosom. She reached to draw it down, but could not find it. She did not sleep nude! She would never do that! She was not that kind of woman! She would never permit herself to be so vulnerable!

She became more aware, then, of the sounds about her, the hardness of the surface on which she lay.

She also became more apprehensive.

She fought consciousness.

She felt her body, and was terrified. It did not seem hers, or not as it had been, when she had retired, surely. She lightly touched her breasts. How sweet and full, and delightful and felicitous, they seemed. She was embarrassed. She touched her waist which now seemed small, firm and slim, and beautifully rounded, even delicate, and she touched her hips and sensed the contrasting flare of a sweet love cradle. She sensed then, to her misery and terror, not the figure she thought she had, but one quite different, one of those figures which draws vulgar whistles and obscene catcalls from rude men, from moved, uninhibited, rude, excited men.

It is not my body, she thought!

But of course it was her body.

She moved to draw up her legs and cover herself with her hands and arms, but, suddenly, was aware of some sort of impediment on her left ankle. It was not that she could not move as she wished; it was only that there was something on her left ankle, something heavy. Too, now there seemed more clearly something on her neck. She tried to thrust the thing from her ankle with her right foot, but could not do so. It clearly was metal, and heavy, and round, and was closed, and closed closely, about her ankle. She could not slip it. Too, she heard a sound, when she moved her foot, as of heavy links of chain, drawn perhaps over a cement surface. The weight seemed to pull at the object on her foot. It seemed to be attached to the object.

She touched her neck. There seemed something there, something heavy. She jerked away her hand.

The noise about her, the sounds, the language, the speech, now seemed even more obtrusive.

She was terrified to awaken.

Yet on some level, doubtless, she was already awake, and fearfully awake.

"Buy me, Master!" she heard, the soliciting, piteously begging call of a woman, from not more than a yard or two away. The call had not been in English, as she suddenly, almost simultaneously, realized, but yet, as she also suddenly realized, as in a moment of blazing comprehension, she had not only understood it perfectly, but understood as well that she had understood it perfectly, immediately, and naturally. It was not in English, but it was in a language she spoke, and with some fluency. Most of the words she heard about her, now, though not all, made perfect sense to her. The tiny shift, the adjustment, had been made.

All this seemed to take place at the same time, and she opened her eyes wildly for an instant but, drawing back from the painful stabbing of sunlight, shut them in pain, but, in that moment, she had glimpsed a world about her, movements, colors, robes, stalls across the way, displayed goods, awnings, shouting vendors, children, men, women, hurryings, groups in converse, peddlers, some with baskets on their heads.

She rolled to her side, and sat up, with a clatter of chain, and clenched her legs together, and covered her breasts with her hands and arms, and screamed in misery.

Girls on either side of her drew back.

Some passers-by paused for a moment, some close enough to reach out and touch her, and then moved on.

She opened her eyes a little, fearfully.

She was on a narrow, sunlit cement shelf at one side of a small plaza, or square. Across the square were numerous stalls, where vendors displayed their goods. Too, here and there in the square, blankets had been spread on the stones, and other vendors, sitting at the blankets, displayed goods spread before them. There were also stalls on her side of the square. Across the way, behind the stalls, and also behind her, on her side of the square, were brick, tenementlike buildings, some seven or eight stories in height, very different from the tall cylinders she had seen before. At one end of the square she could see two of these cylinders in the distance. At the other side of the square, down a narrow street threading its way between buildings similar to those about the square, she could glimpse what seemed to be a high, broad wall.

She began to sob, shielding her body as she could.

She was on a narrow cement shelf, backed by a building on which it abutted, rather like a porch. The shelf was something like five feet in depth, and thirty feet, or so, in length. It was about a yard high. There were steps at either end, giving access to its surface. To the left of the shelf, as one would face it, there was a door at the ground level, through which access to the building was obtained. It was through this door that women could be brought to and from the shelf. Behind that door there was a hallway, with cramped, dark, narrow, cement stairs leading down for some thirty feet. At the foot of those stairs there was a basement level, and on this level there were several basement rooms, some with stout, security doors. It was within one of these basement rooms, ill-lit, musty, damp and straw-strewn, that the women were housed when not on the shelf.

There were seven sockets behind the shelf in the wall of the building, overhead, in which horizontal poles might be fixed, and there were matching sockets near the front of the shelf, into which vertical poles might be placed, from which arrangements of poles, joined together and reinforced by additional, overhead, horizontal poles near the front of the shelf, awnings might be suspended. At present, however, the poles, with their awnings, were not set, reposing rather in a storeroom of the low brick building, the tenement, or *insula,* as the shelf, without the awnings, rented for a lower price.

Instantly the flood of her memories had returned to her, the house, the training, the laundry, the tassa powder.

She looked down at her left thigh.

Could these things be true?

Could she have gone mad?

But there, high, just below the hip, was the tiny, graceful, cursive kef.

It was true!

She was branded! Literally, actually branded! That lovely mark was literally in her. It had been burned into her with a hot iron! She was branded, clearly and unmistakably marked!

On her right side there was a bruise. That was surely where Mirus had angrily spurned her from the dais, with a thrust of his bootlike sandal, and she, helplessly bound, turning and rolling, twisting, in pain, had tumbled rolling to the rug at the foot of the dais.

He had not been gentle with his slave.

She looked at her left ankle. About it there was a heavy shackle. Attached to a ring on this shackle was a stout chain. It was some five feet in length, and was composed of heavy links. The chain was, in turn, fastened to a large, heavy metal ring which was anchored in the cement. She was, accordingly, by the left ankle, chained to this ring.

There were five such rings on the shelf.

The shackle was hammered shut about her ankle. A large padlock, snapped about the dangling shackle ring, attached the chain to her shackle; another large padlock, at the other end of the chain, completed her securing, fastening her to the heavy ring in the cement. The shackle, as it was hammered shut about her ankle, could not be removed, save by tools.

She looked about. On the shelf there were seven girls, including herself. Each was chained as herself. Two rings had two girls fastened to them.

She put her fingers to her throat. No longer did it wear the thin, flat, light, graceful, lovely metal band with which she had become familiar, which she had scarcely been aware she had worn, until perhaps a sharp word or a stroke of the switch had recalled to her attention its significance.

She looked at the other girls.

On their throats were heavy collars of black iron, the perforated ends of each curving about the neck to come together in front, in such a way that the collar curved closely about the neck behind the two perforated ends, and the two perforated ends extended forward. These jutting ends then, with their matching apertures, were hammered flat together. Through the matched apertures a dangling iron ring had been closed. Thus, in a sense, the collar was doubly closed, having not only been hammered shut, but also secured with the ring joining the two ends of the metal. Either closure is sufficient, of course. This collar-and-ring arrangement is simply and inexpensively wrought, not requiring the fusing of metals in welding. Ring mounts, and such, on the other hand, are usually fused into, welded into, thus becoming part of, the shackle or manacle. For example, the shackle on her left ankle had a common ring mount, welded into the metal, through which the ring was inserted and closed.

The heavy metal collar on her throat was uncomfortable, quite different from the light band with which she had been familiar. Further, it was a high collar, and it was not easy for her to put her head down.

It was exactly the same sort of collar, she was sure, as that worn by the other girls. She could feel it, trace with her finger the closure, feel the extended ends, touch the heavy, dangling ring which had been put through the apertures and closed.

Such a collar, with its size and weight, perhaps four or five pounds, its discomfort, she was sure, in the house would have been used only as a punishment collar. Yet, here, all the girls wore it.

But surely they were not all being punished!

Could it be then that they were all merely the least of slaves, the cheapest of slaves, the lowest and the most meaningless of slaves?

Doubtless such girls would all be eager to be freed of such collars, and have their throats returned to the lightness, if inflexible perfection, of a master's collar.

Could that be why the girl had called out so beggingly, so piteously, "Buy me, Master!"

Where am I, she wondered.

What bondage is this?

She looked at the other girls. They did not seem interested in her. One had regarded her with surprise, and then scorn, when she had screamed, and had then looked away. She wondered if they knew she was a barbarian, a girl from Earth.

They, too, as she, were stripped, utterly, given not a thread to wear.

On the collars of the girls closest to her, on her left and right, she could see numerous scratches, some things seemingly scratched in, and others scratched out. She was illiterate, as we may remember, but she could recognize script, both cursive and printed, and what was on the collar, that was not scratched out, was partly written, but mainly printed. The printing seemed uneducated, and crude. She touched her own collar lightly, just barely touching it, with her finger tips, and detected scratches, too, on her collar. She wondered what was written there. She was sure that numerous girls, before her, had worn that collar, and she supposed that others, after her, might do so, as well. It was very different from the neat engraving which, in a mirror, she had seen on her former color. She had been told by one of the instructrices that that collar had said, 'I am Ellen, the slave of Mirus of Ar'. But now that collar was gone. Both brand and collar mark the woman as slave, but both do so in a somewhat different fashion. The brand stays on her; the collar may change. Not all masters brand and collar their slaves, but branding and collaring is strongly recommended in Merchant Law, and it would be a rare slave girl who was not both branded and collared.

"Buy me, Master!" called out a girl, to her right, kneeling on the cement, holding out her hands to a handsome fellow in leather, who had paused near the shelf.

"Put down your hands," said the girl to her left. "Show yourself to the men."

"No, no, no!" said Ellen.

"Kneel facing forward, and spread your knees," said a girl further to the right.

"No, no!" said Ellen, sitting, trying to cover herself. She did not know what posture to assume. Certainly she feared to assume the provocative posture of a kneeling female, particularly one spread-kneed, with its devastatingly shocking acknowledgment of surrender, helplessness, bondage, and submission, and she feared, too, to lie down, facing forward, covering herself, for some might look upon her face, and see her fear, or, in puzzlement, or amusement, order her to reveal herself, even if they did not put her through slave paces, commanding her to perform on the shelf. But, if she turned about, and lay down, on her side, facing away, pretending to sleep, she knew that the posterior curves of her new figure would not be likely to pass unnoticed. She considered lying on her back, but that, too, to her helpless misery, would present a perspective perhaps even more likely to be relished by any hormonally normal male, even one of Earth, let alone the untamed men of Gor.

"Targo will be returning from his tea," said the girl to her left. "I do not know where Barzak is. I think you had better be displaying yourself, and calling to buyers by then."

"No, no!" said Ellen.

She lay then on her stomach, rather as she had slept. Perhaps then, she thought, that would conceal most of her. To be sure, then the loveliness of her figure, so extended, would be revealed in other dimensions, the tininess of her feet, the slimness of her ankles, which took shackles so nicely, the swelling of her calves, her thighs, one bearing a slave brand, the curves, now so beautifully and subtly interrelated, of her new figure, of her fundament, her waist and bosom, her white shoulders, the slim neck, the well-shaped head, the lustrous dark hair strewn on the sunlit cement, the small, rounded forearms, the tiny wrists, seeming to call for slave bracelets, the small hands and delicate fingers, which might bring such joy to a master, in such dimensions, and in a thousand others, as small as the subtlety of her diaphragm as she breathed, the trembling of a lip, the timidity of a glance, the tense way in which the merest tip of a finger might touch a metal collar, would she be revealed, in all these ways and others would she be revealed. How could she, a beautiful stripped slave girl, not be revealed, and as the delight she was?

She covered her head with her hands.

"Targo is coming," whispered one of the girls, she closest on the left.

Ellen kept her head down, pretending to be asleep.

"Man!" suddenly said the girl to her right.

Instantly, without really thinking, and not really understanding, at least for the first instant, why she did what she did, Ellen went to the first obeisance position. It was, you see, a matter of an instant response, one consequent on her training. She heard the girl to her right laugh. Ellen was going to break position angrily, and speak crossly to the girl, thinking herself the victim of a joke, when it occurred to her that the "Man" command might have been appropriately motivated. She looked, subtly, to her right and left and found the others girls, too, in first obeisance position.

She therefore remained as she was.

Perhaps the girl to her right had had her joke, but, too, it was not impossible that, in the joke, the girl had had her best interests in mind. Perhaps the girl had saved her a beating, or at least a tense moment. She had not really been asleep, and a master might have understood that. There were probably differences in the rhythms of breathing, and such. She had not really wanted to deceive anyone, so much as she had been afraid. Perhaps a master might have understood that, and been forgiving, but then again he might have understood it and, nonetheless, saw fit to correct her behavior, admonishing her with the leather.

She heard someone mount the cement steps to her right.

"Kneel up," said a voice.

Instantly the chained slaves, including Ellen, went to first position.

"New girl," said a voice, "remain as you are. The rest of you worthless she-urts may be as you wish."

There was the sound of various chains moving, as the other girls broke position.

Steps approached Ellen, who had, of course, supposing herself the "new girl," remained in position.

The steps seemed short, and a bit ponderous.

Then she was aware of someone standing near her, perhaps a short, heavy man. She had a glimpse of blue and yellow robes.

She was frightened for she knew herself a slave girl who was now doubtless in the presence of a free man.

He might not be a formidable man, as so many of those she had encountered on this world, but he was a man and she was a woman, and a slave.

She kept her eyes straight ahead, looking out on the crowds about. The shelf was hot, and she had moved, so her knees and toes were now muchly aware of the temperature of the cement. She hoped that she would not be burned.

"It is certainly a hot day," he said, puffing a little. "How fortunate you all are, not to be robed."

Ellen knelt straightly.

"Where is Barzak?" he asked someone.

"I do not know, Master," said a girl.

"In some paga tavern," he speculated. "I trust that you have all been presenting yourselves well."

It was Ellen's impression that the girls had called out only when interesting, handsome men had passed, or loitered in the vicinity of the shelf. But then the master had not been present, or Barzak, whoever he might be.

"You had been given tassa powder," he said.

"Yes, Master," said Ellen.

"How do you feel?" he asked.

"Well, Master," she said.

"Good," he said. "There are usually few, if any, aftereffects. Are you hungry?"

"Yes, Master," said Ellen, after a moment. It was only as he had asked that she had realized that she was hungry. Misery and concern had been on her mind, overwhelming it, not food. Before she had been called for, to be taken to the Chamber of Preparation, to be readied for presentation to her Master at the eighteenth Ahn, she had been fed and watered in her bin. She had been chained by the neck there, as usual, and given her two pans, one containing water, the other slave gruel. She was not permitted to use her hands in drinking and feeding from the pans. She must be on all fours or on her belly. She need not finish the water but the slave gruel must be finished, even to the delicate licking out of the pan. If the guards were not pleased she would be beaten. Having been chained, she had feared that she had been forgotten, but the two instructrices called for her, shortly before the sixteenth Ahn, and the guard had freed her, that she might be taken, hands bound behind her, hooded and leashed, to the Chamber of Preparation. There were many parts of the house, which in some respects seemed almost labyrinthine, with which she was unfamiliar. She did not know for certain how long it had been since she had last eaten, presumably the preceding evening, but possibly the evening before last.

"After tassa powder," said the man, "a girl is often ravenously hungry. But when the girl awakens in ropes, or chains, she must wait to find out if she is to be fed or not."

Ellen sensed that the man might be holding something in his hands, something in each hand.

"Look up," he said.

She looked up, frightened.

"Here is some bread," he said. "Keep position," he said, for she had begun to lift her hands from her thighs.

And so she fed, delicately, in position, from his hand.

In his other hand he held a small metal bowl.

When she had finished the bread, he put one hand behind the back of her head and held the small bowl to her lips. "This is Bazi tea," he said.

He helped her to drink. The tea was not hot, but it was strong, and flavorful.

"Thank you, Master," she said.

"What a day," he said. "You will all be browned as a prairie toad, for which I could probably get more money. It is hot enough to burn the turban of a Priest-King."

He put the cup in a pouch, slung at his belt. Most Gorean garments do not have pockets. Goods which would be normally carried in pockets are usually kept in wallets, or pouches. On the other hand, the garbs of certain artisans often have pockets, for tools, pegs, nails, fasteners, such things.

"What is your name?" he asked.

"'Ellen'," she said, "—if it pleases Master."

"That is a pretty name," he said. "To be sure, it is a barbarian name. You are a barbarian, are you not?"

"Yes, Master."

One of the girls nearby laughed.

It suddenly occurred to Ellen, that this might be a test, administered by her master, Mirus of Ar. Perhaps it was a joke on his part.

This man did not seem unkind.

He had fed her, and given her tea.

Surely Mirus of Ar, her master, would never let her out of his collar, really! Surely somehow he would keep her as his forever! Had he not remembered her? Had he not brought her to this world? Had he not restored her youth and comeliness? Had he not given her a beautiful name? Had he not put her in the iron belt? Had it not been he who had first put her to the imperious uses of men?

"We will keep that name, at least for the time," he said. "It should improve your price. It will be one of the few things that would."

"Master?" asked Ellen.

"You are too youthful," he said. "Little more than a pretty girl."

Ellen bit her lip. Mirus of Ar, her master, she believed, in his arrogance, had done that to her.

"What is the forty-third position of joy?" asked the man.

"I do not know, Master," she said.

"What is the sixth delight of the hair of a female slave?" he asked.

"I have no idea, Master," she said.

"What is the title of the eighteenth love song of Dina, the slave poetess?" he asked.

"I do not know, Master," she said.

"Do you know anything?" he asked.

"Very little, Master," she said.

"And neither do these others, either, know anything," he said. "Pot girls, kettle-and-mat girls, worthless she-urts, all of you! Some slaves are worth a Ubara's ransom. Others such as you I should pay unwary buyers to take off my hands. Perhaps I could bribe the cleaners of streets to take you from my shelf, to throw into the pits, to dispose of you as refuse, as flesh-garbage! Do you know what it costs to rent this space, even without an awning!"

"No, Master," said more than one of the girls.

"It is none of your business," he said. "But it is exorbitant. I am destitute! How can I feed you? I shall have to put you on leashes and take you to garbage bins! And where have *you* been?"

A brawny fellow, in a short tunic, with leather on his wrists, had approached. He was grizzled, slovenly, and, apparently, had lost an eye.

This, Ellen supposed, was Barzak.

"The Iron Collar," responded the fellow.

"I was having tea!" said the portly fellow in blue and yellow robes, Targo, who seemed to be Master.

"And I paga," said the grizzled fellow.

"Unwatched, unguarded, I could have lost my entire stock!" said Targo.

"Nonsense," said Barzak. "They are chained, and, besides, who would want them?"

"You could keep a bota of paga here," said Targo.

"One wants both meat and drink," said Barzak.

Most owners of paga taverns are reluctant to let the girls out of the tavern, unless suitably chained and supervised. To be sure, some send them, usually back-braceleted, about the city, soliciting trade. In the taverns the girls normally come with the price of the drink. There may be an extra charge for dancers.

"You have your pick of any of these!" expostulated Targo, waving his arms about, indicating the occupants of the shelf. Ellen realized, uneasily, that she might be included in the width of this sweeping reference. Certainly she had not been explicitly excluded.

"Ho!" snorted Barzak. "I wanted a real slave."

Some of the girls on the shelf moved angrily in their chains.

"So," said Barzak, "the little sleeping she-urt is awake. Widen those knees, girl!"

Ellen, in position, instantly complied.

He put out his right hand and laid it, thoughtlessly, possessively, on her left knee. "Oh!" she cried, and shrank back.

"What is wrong?" asked Barzak, withdrawing his hand.

Ellen could not even speak.

"Nothing," said Targo. Then he turned to Ellen, reprovingly. "You must accustom yourself to being handled, and in any fashion that men please," he said.

"Master?" she asked, looking up at him. Then she put down her head. "Yes, Master," she whispered.

"I am going inside," said Barzak. "It is hot here." He went to the left of the platform as one would face it, and entered the building.

"How is it that I put up with him?" asked Targo. "It is indeed hot here," he observed.

"We will burn and peel, Master," said one of the girls.

Ellen gathered that Targo might be such that one might, with relative impunity, speak to him. She did not think it would be the same with Barzak. Barzak seemed to be one of those men who might as soon cuff a woman or put her to his pleasure as look at her.

"What does it matter?" asked Targo. "How could you be more worthless than you are? Do you have the coins to rent an awning?"

The woman shrank back in misery. Slaves do not even own their collars, or the chains that confine them.

"How many masters have you had?" asked Targo.

"Only one," said Ellen.

"Can you read?"

"No."

"You are illiterate."

"Yes."

"Are you not forgetting something in your responses?" he asked.

"Forgive me, Master," she said.

"Not all men are as forgiving, as understanding, as patient, as long-suffering, as kind, as Targo the Benevolent," he said.

"No, Master," she said. She cringed, thinking of most of the Gorean men she had met, how fearful she was of them, how uncompromisingly and perfectly she would be owned by them.

They seemed to be born masters of women.

"Are you red silk?" he asked.

She looked down at her bared body, in consternation, startled, caught off guard, suddenly distraught, suddenly seeming to understand almost nothing. Obviously she was unclothed, completely, utterly, let alone clothed in silk, of any color. She was naked, slave naked, in her chains, uncomfortable on the hot shelf. What could he have been asking?

"Are you red silk?" he repeated.

"I do not know," she said.

Or was it that, on some level, she refused to understand his question, or, more likely, feared to respond to it.

There was laughter from the slaves about.

"You must indeed be a little sleepyhead," he said.

There was more laughter.

She reddened. "Forgive me, Master," she said. "I was confused. For the moment I did not understand the words in the sense you meant. In my native language, we do not speak of such things in that way. We have other words."

"We speak of them that way in Gorean," he said, "and particularly in the case of female slaves."

"Yes, Master," she said.

"You are a slave," he said. "You must learn the language of your masters."

"Yes, Master," she said.

"Quickly, and well!"

"Yes, Master!"

"Perfectly!"

"Yes, Master!"

To be sure, she doubted that she would ever speak this language perfectly. Who, even among native speakers, speaks any language perfectly? And she supposed that she might forever carry an accent in Gorean, at least a subtle accent, and that this, like fillings in her teeth, and a tiny vaccination mark, would continue, for better or for worse, to betray her barbarian origin. Fortunately few Gorean masters objected to such accents in their slaves. Perhaps they relish this tincture or soupçon of foreign flavor in the speech of their chattels, finding it charming. Too, it tended to mark them out and set them apart from native Gorean speakers. But she was certain she would soon achieve a considerable fluency in the language. This was important. It was the language of her masters, and she must learn it quickly and well. Already she often dreamed and thought in Gorean. There are, of course, a large variety of diverse accents on Gor, even among native speakers of the language. For example, the Gorean of Ar is not that of Cos, and both are clearly distinguishable from that of Turia, far to the south, and so on. One might note, in passing, however, an alleged oddity in the teaching of Gorean to barbarians in certain cities. Several words, and many of these not all that common among native speakers, are supposedly taught to the barbarians with pronunciations which are subtly different from the usual pronunciations of these words. This is sometimes spoken of as "Slave Gorean." The girls, of course, are unaware of these differences, and, usually, that there even are any differences. Most suppose themselves to be being taught normal Gorean. Now let us suppose a girl, attempting to escape, has dared to disguise herself as a free woman, a most unwise thing to do, and is questioned. It is likely that, judiciously questioned, she would almost instantly, unwittingly, identify herself as bond, with immediate consequences as to her fate. And even if a girl knows, or suspects, that she is not being taught normal Gorean, she is unlikely to know precisely in what subtle and numerous ways her speech will betray her as slave. Similarly, a girl is sometimes taught "slave names" for objects, without being informed that these are slave names. Thus, in the most innocent and natural discourse, speaking of this or that, she is likely to show herself a slave, because that is a slave's word, or name, for such and such an object. Ellen has asked her master if her Gorean, that taught to her in Ar, might evince such peculiarities, but he only smiled and informed her that curiosity is not becoming in a kajira. Thus she does not know. Needless to say these possible linguistic precautions and subtleties would not be effective with native Gorean women, should they find themselves put to the collar. On the other hand, once they have been embonded, slavery will inevitably work its subtle effects on them, as it does on all women, and, after a time, they, too, in glances, mannerisms, phrasings, tones of voice, tiny movements, and such, will reveal themselves slave. It is not hard to find a word in English for the difference between the free woman and the slave; the slave is extremely feminine. Sometimes a slave attempts to imitate the assertive stridencies, the masculine movements, the attitudes and gestures, the haughtiness, the mien, of a free woman, but the results are commonly, as on Earth, no more than a farcical caricature of a male. On Earth, of course, no deleterious consequences of such charades and antics are likely to occur; indeed, they may earn their practitioners commendations from pathological quarters in which it is not permitted to so much as whisper of nature and the biotruths of a species; indeed, further, such expostulations and pretenses may have actual value, as in earning their thespic practitioners a number of political and economic rewards. On Gor, of course, the situation is quite different. A woman behaving in this fashion and accordingly being suspected of the collar, of trying desperately to conceal her femininity by this ruse, may be remanded to free women for an examination. If a brand is found the woman will be stripped and bound by the free women, switched liberally, for there is little love lost between free women and slaves, and then turned over to magistrates, to be returned to the mercies of her master.

"So," said he, "are you red silk?"

"Yes, Master!" sobbed Ellen.

"You understand what I am asking?"

"Yes, Master!"

"You have been opened for the uses of men?"

"Yes, Master!" she said.

There was laughter from the other girls on the shelf.

Ellen recalled that her master had indeed opened her for the uses of men, rudely, and with authority. She remembered her helplessness, she kneeling, facing away, head to the rug, hands clasped behind the back of her neck, astonished, affrighted, outraged, shocked, disbelieving, miserable, yet somehow simultaneously elated, willing, accepting, submitting, and the power of his hands on her body. To be sure, he had been uncaring, quick, contemptuous with her. Surely she had been given little, or no, opportunity to experience pleasure. He had not permitted that. He had seen to it. That was by his intent. The pleasure was to be his, and she was simply to be had, and to know herself had.

It was a far cry from the classroom.

She had been utilized abruptly and with contempt. She, kneeling, facing away from him, head down, hands clasped behind her neck, had learned what she was, and would be, to him, nothing, lest it be an object of derision and scorn.

How complete his triumph!

He had risen to his feet.

She had remained as she was, of course, not yet permitted to move, an unimportant, meaningless, despised, ravaged slave.

How faraway the classroom, and their former relationship! No longer was she teacher and he student. She was now slave, and he master.

And well had he taught her, in those moments, her slavery!

She recalled that afterwards he had looped a red ribbon about her collar, and, it seemed with some satisfaction, jerked it tight, meaningfully tight. She no longer wore it, of course. It was not on her heavy, uncomfortable, present collar. She wondered what had happened to it. Perhaps after she had fallen unconscious, it had been removed, and kept in the house, perhaps to be used again, later, when another virgin, another white-silk girl, might be introduced to a new aspect of her bondage.

She supposed that most slaves would be red silk, and thus that there would be little point in having such a ribbon on their collars. Perhaps if she had still been "white silk," a white ribbon might have been put on her collar. That might, she supposed, have some effect on bids, pricings, and such.

She recalled that her master had been amused and pleased that what he had done to her, red-silking her, opening her for the uses of men, would be likely to lower her value. And she gathered that she was not of great value to begin with, a barbarian girl, ignorant, youthful, and scarcely trained. I am largely worthless as a slave, she thought. She did not doubt, however, that her master had derived much pleasure from her body. She might have wished to share that pleasure, or share it more, but had not been permitted to do so. It had clearly been with great pleasure, even with triumph, that he had taken her.

He had me, and how he *had* me, she thought. As a slave, a meaningless *slave*! What a triumph for him! And yet I cannot deny that a part of me rejoiced to be so used, to be put to his unshared, unilateral pleasure!

"Do you juice quickly?" asked Targo.

"Master?" she asked.

"Are you a tasty pudding?" asked Targo.

"I do not understand, Master," she said.

"Do you squirm well?" he asked.

"Master?"

"Do you squirm well?" he asked. "Surely you understand me. You are a slave, are you not? You are branded, are you not? Look at your thigh. Do you whimper, and cry out, and moan, and scream, and gasp, and clutch, and beg, and shudder and kick, and spasm helplessly and repeatedly? Have you never been driven mercilessly and helplessly, as if by whips, to slave orgasm? And then to another, and another, and to as many as your master chooses to force upon you, perhaps ceasing even while you are begging for more?"

Ellen, of course, had never experienced slave orgasm, but she thought that she had some dim sense as to what it might be. Alas, how little she then knew! Little did she then realize how helpless and needful might a slave become.

One of the utilities of chaining or binding a slave, incidentally, is to multiply and intensify her orgasms. Several psychological and physical factors enter into these matters.

Perhaps the helplessness of the slave is too obvious to mention. She cannot free herself and thus must await the attentions of the master, which may be delayed, which may be intermittent, which may be prolonged, for hours, and so on.

In such ways she soon understands herself slave.

"Do you squirm well? It is a simple question. Answer it. Do you squirm well?"

"I do not think so, Master," she said. Was she not to be permitted pride? But then it occurred to her that she was a slave girl and that slave girls were not permitted pride. Inertness and frigidity were not permitted to them. Those luxuries were reserved for free women, who might make the most of them, if they wished. Responsiveness was required of the slave. The switch dissipates inertness, and the ice of frigidity melts swiftly beneath the heat of the whip. To be sure the simple condition of bondage itself militates devastatingly against inertness and frigidity. How can one be inert and frigid when one is mastered, dominated and owned? The slave loves and yields all. She is hot, devoted and dutiful. She is at his feet, heated and moist, begging to serve and please.

"You do not think so?" he said, incredulously.

"No, Master," said Ellen.

"Oh, wonderful!" he exclaimed, in distaste.

"She is a little ice ball!" laughed one of the slaves.

She recalled, suddenly, bitterly, that Mirus had characterized her as a tight, cold little thing.

Doubtless he had not been pleased with her.

She decided she could not help the way she was.

Then she decided, petulantly, angrily, that she would not help the way she was. She would show them! She would pride herself on her superiority to feeling and vitality. She would be one of those women who scorn feeling and vitality in others, and would try to shame them for their resources of sensibility, for their emotional richness, and their treasures of health. No man would ever make her yield!

In this way one might account an inadequacy or impoverishment, natural or willed, a mark of virtue or merit.

Particularly if one suspected that men would not be much interested in one anyway.

But she did sense that if things had been a little different, if Mirus had treated her even a little bit differently, she would have cried out and wept herself his. Her body had ached to yield itself to him.

Even now, how uneasily she recalled the sensation of her peremptory usage. Its memory lingered with her. She could not dispel it. Though she strove to feel distressed, even outraged, she failed. The sensation, curious and fascinating, provocative and insistent, continued to whisper within her tissues. She could not have asked, his hands upon her, for a better demonstration of her vulnerability and femaleness. And, too, interestingly, though she scarcely dared accept this, it seemed in its way a fascinating augury, as might be the brief sight of a bird, the finding of a branch in the water, evidence of new worlds. She had been, as the saying was, opened for the uses of men. She would never again be the same. I want such sensations now, she said to herself. I must have them!

No, no, she said to herself. I am not that sort of woman!

Yes, you are, she said to herself. You are no more than a slave!

I must resist feeling, she told herself.

Then she looked out from the shelf, at the market, so bustling, colorful and crowded, the stalls, the beasts, the carts.

In such a world the resistance of feeling would not be permitted to such as she.

She was not a free woman.

She was a beast who might be purchased for a variety of purposes, amongst them the provision of inordinate pleasure to a master.

She saw the eyes of a young fellow on her, and she looked away, terrified.

I must be strong, she thought.

What would it be to be in his arms, she asked herself.

Would I yield to him?

If this were not a cruel sport of Mirus, my master, pretending to abandon me, pretending to put me up for sale, such as he might buy me!

I will not permit myself to yield to men, she thought.

Then she recalled the lash.

She did not wish to be beaten.

Perhaps I could hold something back, she thought.

Foolish slave, she thought, do you not know that you will not be permitted to hold anything back, but that you must yield wholly, and that there are infallible signs of such yieldings?

She moaned, inwardly.

Do you wish to be tied and lashed, girl?

No, she thought, I do not want to be tied and lashed!

Do you wish to be slain, girl?

No, she thought, I do not wish to be slain!

I must strive, she thought, to see that my master is entirely pleased with me.

Indeed, I would want, and desperately, for my master to be entirely pleased with me.

Then you are a slave, aren't you, she said to herself, no more than a slave.

Yes, she said to herself, I am a slave, no more than a slave.

She looked again toward the market, but the young fellow was gone.

She felt the heavy chain on her neck.

I have been opened, she thought. I want sex. I need sex!

Will you yield all, she asked herself.

Yes, she said to herself, I will yield all! And I want to yield all! I will beg to yield all!

"See her!" said the girl. "See the little ice ball!"

"No," said another. "She is not a little ice ball. She is still just a little sleeping she-urt."

"A pretty one," said one of the girls.

"A master will wake her up," said another.

"Yes," laughed another.

Ellen wanted to cry out with misery, but she was in position, looking out across the square.

There was still a crowd there, passing, moving hither and yon, coming and going, though it was now late afternoon. Mercifully the sun was lower now, and, although the shelf was still in full sunlight, the sun should, in a few minutes, descend behind the building across the square.

She scrutinized the crowd, hoping for a glimpse of her master. Might that not be he, near the stall of kettles, lamps and pans? No, it was not. Perhaps he had, unbeknownst to her, sent an agent, who even now was merrily reporting to him on the success of his joke, the jest he was cruelly playing on his helpless slave.

How cruel the Masters, she thought. How much we are at their mercy!

She saw men in the crowd. It frightened her, particularly as one of them might turn about, and see her, or pause to look upon her, to think that she, as a slave, might be bought or sold. My master, Mirus of Ar, could sell me, if he wished, she thought. How that thrills me! But, of course, he would not wish to do so! Certainly he would not have brought me here, and taken all this time and trouble, merely to dispose of me, merely to have me sold!

She saw, occasionally, among the crowds, a free woman, robed and veiled. How proudly, how serenely, they moved. How she envied them their freedom! They were free! They could come and go as they pleased. They were not chained naked on a cement shelf, eyes half closed against the glaring sunlight. What they are wearing, she thought, those must be the Robes of Concealment.

Whereas in the laundry she and the others had often washed garments of free women, those garments had seldom been the cumbersome Robes of Concealment. Usually they had been house garments, garden robes, veils, hose, subrobes, and such. She had washed street himations frequently enough, however, of the sort which were sometimes worn by free women, particularly those of the lower-castes. The street himation is far less bulky and protective than the usual Robes of Concealment, less stiffness, less brocade, less embroidery and such. It is, of course, almost always combined with the veil. Gorean free women, at least in the high cities, almost always wear veils in public, although some women of the lower castes are occasionally careless in this particular, permitting lax arrangements, and such, especially the maidens. Too, some omit the veil altogether. Veils can be used, if handled and arranged in certain ways, for flirting, much as were fans, once on Earth, in less androgynous times. Slave girls, of course, being slaves, are not permitted veils. This is another way in which, aside from their revealing garmenture and collars, they are to be distinguished from free women. To a girl from Earth this matter of veiling may seem at first rather inconsequential, but she soon learns that it is a very serious matter. And I must admit that, as one becomes more enculturated here, more aware of the Gorean *ethos*, and Gorean customs, values and views on such matters, and comes to understand how one is viewed here, one tends to become more and more sensitive to such things. It is hard to see the contempt in the eyes of a fully clothed, beautifully clothed free woman, flashing over her lovely veil, as she regards you, and not become simultaneously aware, as you kneel before her, of the exposed nature of one's body, your legs, your bared arms, your throat with its collar, and perhaps most acutely and painfully, difficult though it may be to understand at first, your features, the required, imposed nudity of your own visage, that your face, because you are a slave, is prohibited veiling, that it must be, in all its vulnerability, publicly bared. It is little wonder that, after such an encounter, we hurry back gratefully, tearfully, to the feet of our masters. That Earth women are seldom veiled is taken by most Goreans, at least those familiar with the second knowledge, as evidence that we are slaves. Too, there is little doubt that the fact that women on Earth, particularly in Western cultures, do not veil themselves is welcomed by Gorean slavers, and certainly facilitates their selections amongst us. Lastly it might be mentioned that it is traumatic for a Gorean woman, when captured, to be unveiled. "Remove her veil" is a command she dreads to hear, one which strikes with fear and misery to the heart of her being. The vulgar expression for this is "face-stripping." This makes some sense to me, as the face is so expressive. In removing the veil from a woman's face, one takes her from herself; one denies her to herself; one makes her public, so to speak, like a slave.

Ellen thought that perhaps the Robes of Concealment were not to be entrusted to common laundries. That was why, perhaps, she had seen few, if any, in the laundry. Perhaps special slaves, with cleaning chemicals, attended to them.

Yet, despite the bulkiness and clumsiness of the Robes of Concealment, most of them were very beautiful, in an ornate way. Some were doubtless very expensive, and even set with jewels. Too, despite their protective aspects, and she would not have cared to wear such garments on a day as hot as this, they seemed, in their way, attractive, and feminine. They seemed to suggest that something of interest, something lovely, might be concealed within. Needless to say, veils are invariably, or almost invariably, a portion of the ensemble associated with the Robes of Concealment. Robes, hoods, and veils, as might be expected, are coordinated and matched.

She wondered if the free women, wearing such garments, were happy. It was clear to her, and to all, that they were women, of course, even concealed and veiled. How different they were from the men with their large, agile, leonine bodies. How different we are from them, she thought. And how different was she, she thought, from the free women, they in their robes, resplendent in the glory of their liberty, she a stripped slave, chained on a public shelf. How could she even think of comparing herself with them? But are they, such lofty, proud creatures, happy, she wondered. She wondered, too, how many of them might one day find themselves chained in a market, or grasping the bars of a slave cage, or looking up fearfully, trembling, kneeling and bound, into the eyes of a master, to read their fate. She recalled a saying she had heard in the house, that beneath the clothes of every woman there is to be found the body of a naked slave. Once there passed through the square a palanquin, borne by large, powerful, tunicked men. In the palanquin there indolently reposed a free woman. She recalled the woman seized by the tarnsman from Brundisium and wondered if she, too, had once been carried in such a palanquin. That woman now, perhaps, with Laura, heeled her master in Brundisium, some paces behind, and to his left. She wondered if he would permit them clothing in his own city. Perhaps not at the beginning. The palanquin was then through the square.

It had not stopped in this market. Perhaps this market was unworthy of the consideration of such a personage. She wondered if the bearers were male slaves, or merely servants. She supposed they might be servants. They had not been collared, or guarded. Perhaps the woman, wisely, had not chosen to surround herself with male slaves. What if they should, in the rush of their blood, heat and need, turn upon her? How she might be used then, over and over, perhaps on her belly, robes torn away, on the pillows of her then-unborne palanquin! She trembled. She had heard that slaves such as she, low slaves, were sometimes cast to male slaves in the pens, much as one might cast them food. This practice was supposedly useful in reducing restlessness in the pens.

Sometimes, in the crowd, she saw a slave girl, collared and briefly tunicked. What a striking contrast such small, lovely figures, with their tiny tunics, and bared limbs, afforded to the more common denominator of the large, massive, generally male, generally robed throngs through which they threaded their way. How exquisitely, how utterly and beautifully feminine they were! How beautifully they walked and carried themselves. How proud they seemed. How could women be so wonderful? Did they rejoice in their bondage? Did they treasure their collars? How freely and meaningfully, and delightfully, they walked! Of course there is little about the tunic of a slave which might inhibit movement. Sometimes she marveled at their beauty. To be sure, the garments of a female slave, the tunic, the camisk, the ta-teera, the Turian camisk, and such, do little to conceal her beauty. What joy they must bring to their masters, she thought. And, too, perhaps, what joy their masters must bring to them!

How beautiful, too, were their faces! And suddenly, she was delighted that her own face, too, despite the contempt this might elicit from free women, would be bared, and must be bared, on this world. She, as slave, she knew, would have no choice in the matter. And this pleased her. She knew that she had a very pretty face; she was certain of that; it was exquisite, delicate, feminine, sensitive, lovely. She was sure that men would like it. But, too, she was frightened. It was the sort of face, she had learned, that called forth the master in a man. To be sure, she might be transiently sensitive to its exposure in a given context, as in the presence of a contemptuous free woman, or perhaps before magistrates, and officials, but that was only to be expected in this culture, with its particular views. And such moments were likely to be, at most, brief embarrassments.

And there was, of course, another serious thread in the Gorean culture, that which required the display and exposure of the slave. This, too, constituted a cultural imperative, despite what might be the preferences of free women. About this, too, she, as slave, was choiceless.

And how thrilled she was that she was choiceless in this matter!

"You are owned, slave girl," the culture might say. "There are no veils for you. You are denied the veil. It is not for you. Tremble! You will be as men please. Your face will be as bared as that of a kaiila or tharlarion! But understand that you are human females, the most delicious property a man can own. Understand at once how meaningless you are, small, soft, well-curved items of merchandise, but, too, how precious, special and wonderful you are! The tharlarion will be scrubbed, the kaiila combed. See that you, too, are groomed and cleaned! Sparkle, slave, for your master—*and for all men*! As the kaiila has its swiftness, and the tharlarion its strength, so you, too, have your special properties, your service, your passion, and beauty. Your face will be exposed, so that men may gaze upon it. You will be dressed, if dressed, for their pleasure. You will enhance and reveal your beauty. It will be muchly exposed. You will serve with delicacy, deference and zeal. You will respond to the master's least touch with eagerness and gratitude. You will live for a kind word and a caress. You will be as men want you, for you are slave, for you are owned."

All in all, Ellen suspected, frightened at the thought, that she might grow more and more delighted with her beauty, her being and condition. Could it be that she might one day accept her loveliness, wholly, and throw back her head and shoulders, and walk beautifully, in her collar, and be shameless, even joyfully, brazenly shameless? Surely not! How frightful! And yet that was common, she knew, with such as she now was, with female slaves.

No wonder free women hate us so, she thought. Are we not, fulfilled, in our collars, a thousand times more free than they?

Kneeling, in position, chained by the left ankle to a ring, her throat enclosed in a heavy, clumsy, ringed, iron collar, on a cement sales shelf, before Targo, sensitive to her nudity, and miserable, she noted one and another slave girl in the crowd.

How lovely they were!

She wished she, too, might walk about so, so garbed, and free, though in her collar, be free to move about so boldly, so beautifully. She saw men look upon the slave girls appraisingly, admiringly. The girls, heads up, moving beautifully, seemed not to notice, but surely they knew that the eyes of masters were upon them. How could they not be? They were slaves! She wondered if, sometime, they, the natural masters, might look so upon her.

To be sure, free women stiffened, and turned angrily, and looked upon the slaves disapprovingly. But what does it matter, Ellen asked herself. And suddenly it came to her again that free women hated the slaves, and envied them. Perhaps they, thought Ellen, wish they, too, were so garbed, so delightfully and sensuously, and were so free, so vital, so delicious, so desirable, so beautiful!

Too, the slaves seemed to her radiantly happy. It showed in their expressions, and in the carriage of their bodies. She saw their collars, sometimes almost lost in a wealth of swirling, tossing hair. How well mastered they must be, thought Ellen.

When will Mirus of Ar, for that is the name by which she now thought of him, come for me, she wondered. Come for me, my Master, I beg you!

"You may break position," said Targo, with a sigh.

Ellen then sat on the cement, shading her eyes. "Master!" she called, for Targo had turned away.

He turned back, to regard her.

"Where is my collar, Master?" she asked.

"You are wearing it," he said.

"Master!" she protested.

She had hoped that he might respond in such a way as to give away the joke of her master. If he should inform her as to its location, or even, inadvertently, by a word, or a facial movement, suggest that it was somewhere in the vicinity, that would surely show that it was the intent of Mirus to return her to it.

"What is wrong with you?" he asked.

"When am I to be returned to my master, Mirus of Ar!" she said.

"Mirus of Ar is not your master," he said. "I am your master."

"No!" she cried.

"I bought you last night for ten copper tarsks," he said. "I hope to sell you for fifteen."

"No," she cried. "No!"

The other girls on the shelf looked at her, puzzled.

"He would not sell me!" she cried.

"It is not clear to me," said Targo, "why he would have you in the first place."

"I have not been sold!" she cried. "He would not sell me!"

"I own you," said Targo.

"No, no!" she said. "No!"

"If you could read, I would show you the papers," said Targo. "They are all in order, with the proper endorsements, and such."

She tried to lift the heavy collar on her throat, but, of course, it was stopped almost instantly, pressing upward against her chin. She pulled at it, and then, again and again, jerked at the collar ring, wildly.

"You are making a scene," said Targo, disapprovingly.

"Mirus of Ar is my master!" she cried. "Return me to my master! I want to be returned to my master!"

She tried to thrust the shackle from her left ankle, but could not, of course, do so. She succeeded only in abrading the ankle. Then she pulled wildly at the chain, jerking it again and again against the ring.

Men paused to stare at the hysterical slave.

"He would not sell me! He would not sell me!" she cried, jerking at the chain. "He would not sell me!"

"Be silent," said Targo. "Do you want people to think you have been stolen? Stolen slaves are not publicly vended, not in the city of their theft."

"Return me to my master!" she cried, putting herself to her belly, pleading, in second obeisance position, before Targo.

"Barzak!" called Targo.

But Barzak had already emerged from the building and, in his hand, he carried the five-stranded, broad-bladed Gorean slave whip, designed for use on females, to punish terribly but not to mark, or permanently mark, thus perhaps reducing the value of the errant, punished slave.

"Master, please!" begged the slave.

"Whip her," said Targo, turning away.

"Turn about," said Barzak. "Grasp the ring."

"No, please!" she said. But she had turned about and grasped the ring, the ring to which the ankle chain of the girl who had been to her left was chained. The girl who was chained to the ring, who had been to her left, drew back, as far as the chain on her ankle would permit. Ellen saw fear in her eyes.

This fear exhibited by her sister slave frightened Ellen even more.

"Please do not have me beaten, Master!" she called out to Targo, over her shoulder, lying on her belly, on the cement, grasping the ring, but he had left the shelf.

"I will be good, Master! I will be good, Master!" she cried, but he, as we have seen, was gone.

Then she cried out, in disbelief, and in pain.

She could not believe the shocking fire with which, after but one stroke, she was enveloped.

Surely it could not hurt as much as it did!

She could not stand it!

It was impossible to bear!

He must desist!

She would do anything, not to be struck again!

She gasped for breath, she could scarcely speak.

"No, please!" she begged. "I am too young to be beaten, I am only a girl!"

She heard one of the slaves laugh, and then again the lash fell.

This time it terribly enlarged the pain she had felt, and intensified it, as her skin had been already enflamed and sensitized.

"No more, no more, Master!" she begged. "I will do anything!"

"You must do anything anyway," said Barzak, lifting his arm again.

"Yes, Master! Yes, Master!" she cried.

Then the lash fell again.

Tears burst from her eyes, she sobbed, her small fingers went white, grasping the ring so tightly.

After the next stroke she shrieked for mercy.

After the next two strokes she could only sob and clutch the ring, begging in her heart that there would be no more, no more!

The beating was actually a light one, as such things go. She received only six strokes, and the blows, while sharp, had not been heavy, surely not delivered with the full weight of a man's arm. A woman is almost never beaten with the full measure of a man's strength. There would be little point to that, and it would be brutal. She is, after all, small and beautiful, and only a female. The point of a beating is not to hurt her but to improve her.

These considerations were nothing that Ellen understood at the time, and even if she had understood them, there was nothing in them, of course, to lessen the actual, miserable, fierce burning of the lash.

"Well?" asked Barzak.

"Master?" sobbed Ellen, a mass of flaming, stinging stripes at his feet, from the back of her neck, just below the collar, to the back of her knees.

"Thank him, thank him!" hissed the girl chained to the ring which Ellen grasped so tightly.

"Thank you, Master," whispered Ellen.

"For what?" demanded Barzak.

"Thank you for beating me, Master," whispered Ellen, through her tears.

"Speak up," he said. "Perhaps your chain sisters cannot hear you."

"Thank you for beating me, Master!" said Ellen.

"And did you deserve the beating?"

"Yes, Master!"

"And are you now more aware of what it is to be a slave?"

"Yes, Master!"

"And you are now going to try to be a good slave, aren't you?"

"Yes, Master!"

He then left the shelf.

Ellen then lay there, on her stomach, by the ring, still grasping it, sobbing, in misery, her body rich with bright, burning stripes, a whipped slave.

She did not know how long she lay there, but the sun had descended behind the building across the way, and she could sob no more.

It seemed she could barely lift her head, the collar seemed so heavy on her. She moved her foot a little, and heard the chain she wore move a bit on the cement.

"Buy me, Master!" called a girl from the shelf, behind her as she lay, to the left of the shelf, if one were looking outward from it, the side of the shelf farthest from the door of the tenement.

Perhaps a handsome man had paused by the shelf.

Doubtless the woman would do anything to be off the shelf, to be out of the weighty collar.

She wondered if she herself could so beg. Never, she thought, never.

What a shameless tart, she thought.

I could never beg like that.

Where am I, Ellen wondered. What am I doing here? What has become of me?

She lifted her head, dully.

"Who is Targo?" asked Ellen of the girl chained to the ring she still held. "What place is this? Where am I?"

The girl looked about but neither Targo nor Barzak were near the shelf, and the crowd, smaller now in the late afternoon, had its own concerns. Little attention was being bestowed upon the shelf. Naked slave girls are not that rare in a Gorean city. In many public places there are slave rings, to which one may chain one's girls. To be sure, most girls chained at such rings, perhaps by their metal leashes, would be clothed, most often tunicked. The concern of the girl chained to the ring which Ellen still grasped was not unwarranted. Conversation is seldom encouraged among slave girls in public places. It is sometimes regarded as unseemly, and is sometimes, by free persons, deemed actually annoying. Slave girls, of course, are seldom reticent creatures. They, the most extraordinarily feminine of their gender, with their lively minds, their unusual quickness and high intelligence, as is well known, love to talk. It is hard to stop them sometimes, they love so to talk. Often masters charge them with prattling endlessly, mindlessly and interminably. But that charge, I think, is unfair. Certainly there are many things of interest, and worth talking about, or at least very pleasant to talk about, and delightful to talk about, other than problems of agriculture and engineering. And do not men speak among themselves, too? Are they really so different? Certainly slave girls delight in conversation. They love to talk to one another, and to their masters, until perhaps silenced. There are few slave girls, joined together, perhaps met at the fountain, or in marketing, or at the tubs, or such places, who do not relish a lengthy, lively, competitive, sparkling chat, and often the longer the better. To be sure, our conversations are not always such that men might approve of them. Perhaps we relish gossip, and fashion, and the sharing of secrets, more than men. I do not know. Is it true, as sworn by Lila, that the Lady Celestina, the free companion of Publius Major, as though inadvertently, drew back her robe, revealing an ankle to his handsome young secretary, Torbo? What will be the recommended length for slave tunics in the Fall? And how will they be cut? One could always beg the master for the latest style, for surely he would not wish the garmenture of his slave to reflect negatively on his taste or resources. Too, in what new ways might we more please our masters? Might we not be pleasantly surprised by his response, if we were sometimes to kiss his body, pressing our soft lips upon him humbly, intimately, fervently, tenderly, beseechingly, through the cascade of our loosened hair?

What a precious and glorious honor, what a coveted privilege, for a slave, to be permitted to serve her master!

"Targo is a minor slaver, of little account," said the girl. "Once, perhaps, he was well off, but not now. He claims to have once, albeit unwittingly, sold the very tatrix of Tharna. The Cosians have robbed him of girls, some say his best, claimedly for taxes, time and time again. He must guard every tarsk-bit, as an urt its last sa-tarna seed. Targo is poor. He is nearly destitute. He is nothing."

"But he is the master?" said Ellen.

"Yes," said the girl. "As the master he is all, as the master he is everything."

"In his own hovel, even the peddler is a Ubar," said a girl from the right.

"If he has a Home Stone," said another.

"Yes," said the first girl.

"Does Targo, I mean, the master, have a Home Stone?" asked Ellen.

"We do not know, little she-urt," said one of the girls. "He has not permitted us to rummage through his pack."

"You are a barbarian, as it seems," said the girl to whom Ellen had addressed her first queries.

"Yes Mistress," said Ellen.

"I do not like barbarians," she said.

"Forgive me, Mistress," said Ellen.

"Men do," said one of the girls.

"Some men," said another.

"Yes," said another.

"As you are a barbarian, and thus stupid, and ignorant," said the first girl, "I will inform you that you are in the city of Ar."

Ellen had thought that likely, but she did not know if she, during her period of unconsciousness, might have been moved to another, perhaps similar city. Certainly what she could see from the shelf, the market before her, the square, seemed dusty, crowded and squalid, nothing like that marvelous panorama she had glimpsed from the roof of the house, that tall, cylinderlike structure.

"Ar is the largest, most populous city in the northern latitudes," said the girl. "But due to the disappearance of her Ubar, Marlenus of Ar, and diplomatic treachery, she has succumbed to a coalition of enemy forces, largely those of Cos and Tyros. She is supposedly now ruled by Talena, the daughter of Marlenus of Ar, a puppet Ubara in the keeping of Cos and Tyros. There is some pretense that the city is free, but in fact it is not. The true ruler is, I suppose, the military governor, Myron, *polemarkos* of Temos, commander of the occupational forces, or perhaps actually distant Lurius of Jad, Ubar of Cos. Where you are, specifically, in the city of Ar is in one of her most crowded and poorest districts, the district of Metellus, and in the Kettle Market, within walking distance of the Peasants' Gate."

"The Kettle Market?"

"Obviously much else is sold here as well," she said.

"Yes, Mistress," said Ellen.

She had seen that there were dozens of stalls in the square, most lining the fronts of buildings, stalls displaying an incredible variety of goods.

There were, of course, the pans, pots, utensils, lamps, pails, and such, which, on shelves and dangling from poles, she supposed might have suggested the name of the market, but there were also stalls, as well, specializing in many other forms of goods, for example, stalls of fruits and vegetables, and produce of various sorts, and sausages and dried meats, and stalls of tunics, cloaks, robes, veils, scarves, and simple cloth, and of leatherwork, belts and wallets, and such, and of footwear, oils, instruments of the bath, cosmetics and perfumes, and mats and coarse rugs, and such. She saw no stall that seemed to specialize in silk, or gold, or silver, or precious stones, or in weaponry, even simple cutlery. It impressed her as a crowded, dirty, low market, presumably frequented primarily by the poor, or by those of the lower castes, individuals who must carefully guard even their smallest coins.

"For example, slave girls," said the girl.

"Yes, Mistress."

Ellen looked to the left and right, on the surface of the shelf. There were seven girls there, including herself, each, as she, stripped and in a heavy collar, chained by the left ankle to a ring. Yes, slave girls, too, were for sale in this market, and she was such a girl. She, too, here, was for sale, up for sale in this cheap, miserable market, in this terrible place.

How amused must be he who had been her master, for, after her beating, she scarcely dared to use his name in her thoughts, to know that she was here. Perhaps he would lift a glass of ka-la-na and proclaim a toast, offering it to her, chuckling, laughing, relishing his triumph over her, what he had done to her, offering it to her, to his absent, discarded slave. Perhaps he would permit Tutina, though too a slave, to join in the toast.

It was now darker in the square and, here and there, torches were being lit.

The ambiance in the market was now subtly different than it had been. A difference in the crowd was detectable. Perhaps there were fewer robes and more tunics. Perhaps some who had worked during the day were coming to the market at night. If possible the crowd seemed dirtier, rougher, and meaner. Some men may not have had employment, or desired such, and now, like nocturnal animals, they came furtively from their *insulae,* like urts from their holes. There seemed more lower-caste women than before. Some were not veiled. Some young, drunken men staggered by. Ellen shrank back, away from the front of the shelf. She saw two men pass, guardsmen, or such, helmeted, armed, in matching tunics, and many in the crowd drew back, sullenly, to let them pass. Some shook their fists at them, after they had passed. Some children ran through the crowd. A vendor was pursuing them. She saw four women, their hands chained behind their backs, their necks fastened together with a chain, being prodded through the square by three armed men, helmeted and tunicked as had been the other two. The women were naked. Ellen supposed that they, too, then, were slaves. They looked upon the occupants of the shelf, and smiled, tossing their heads, doubtless comparing themselves favorably with what they saw there. "She-urts!" cried the girl to Ellen's left, with a rustle of chain. One of the women being herded through the square, she who was first in the coffle, turned angrily in her chains and seemed about to reply, but the man nearest to her raised his hand, palm open, menacingly, and she put down her head, cringing, and hurried forward, turning her head so that the pressure of the collar would be at the side of her neck and not the front of her throat. This jerked against the collar of the woman behind her, pulling her collar tight against the back of her neck, causing her to stumble forward, which movement was reflected in the motion of the third and fourth members of the small coffle, who must make hurried, awkward adjustments to retain their balance. "Clumsy slaves!" cried another of Ellen's chain sisters. At this moment, to Ellen's dismay, and that of her companions, the lead guard, seizing the first girl by the upper arm, pulled the coffle through the crowd, bringing it to a place just before the shelf. Instantly Ellen, and the other girls on the shelf, frightened, went to first obeisance position. "Kneel up," said a harsh voice. With a rustle of chain Ellen and the others went to first position. "These slaves," said the harsh voice, indicating the coffle in his charge, "are to be sold in the Curulean."

This meant nothing to Ellen, but to the other girls it seemed to have some considerable impact, producing even a sentiment which might be bordering on awe.

The neck-chained women smiled. They stood straighter.

The accent of the man, Ellen noted, did not seem the same as those accents with which she was most familiar, but he did speak Gorean, and she had no difficulty in understanding him. Not all Gorean accents, of course, are easily understood, the one to the other.

The man's tunic was scarlet, and he wore a sword belt slung across his body, from the right shoulder to the scabbard at his left hip, facilitating the right-handed draw. This belt, and the scabbard, and the crest on his helmet, were yellow. Though this was not known to Ellen at the time, the scarlet denoted the caste of Warriors, one of the five high castes of Gor, the others being the Initiates, Physicians, Builders and Scribes. The yellow was part of the dress uniform of the occupational forces, as a whole, but was common in the Cosian military. In times of danger or imminent conflict, the sword belt is looped simply over the left shoulder, so that it, and the attached scabbard, the blade drawn, may be discarded. This prevents the belt being grasped in combat by an enemy, which might be to the disadvantage of its owner. The two men who had passed through the market earlier had been similarly attired and accoutered, as were this man's companions.

"You may speak," said the guard to his charges.

Instantly a fierce torrent of abuse from the chained women rained upon the occupants of the shelf, to which the occupants of the shelf did not dare to reply. "Cement-shelf girls!" "She-urts!" "She-sleen!" "Pot-and-mat girls!" "Low slaves!" "Barbarians!" "Earth-girls!" "Bondmaids!" "Plow-thralls!" "Collar meat!" "Slave meat!" "Flesh-trash!" Such were the epithets that sped forth that evening from the throats of their fair rivals. There were other names, phrases and remarks that Ellen did not even understand.

A moment's digression may perhaps be in order, as some may find it of interest.

The Gorean slave girl, unlike free women, particularly those of lower caste, is not permitted to be vulgar. And, indeed, most are not. The virulence of the coffle, as it poured scorn on the shelf girls, was certainly clear, and its expressions vehement and explicit, but it utilized few, if any, expressions which would not have been in common use in the surrounding community. As an analogy one might note that, on Earth, it might be discourteous to refer to a woman as, say, a tart or a hussy, but it would not be regarded as vulgar to do so, whereas certain other expressions, which might come to the mind of a native English speaker, would presumably be regarded as vulgar, even quite vulgar. Bondage, of course, with its dramatic contrast between the master and the slave, brings out a woman's femininity. It is hard to be kneeling before a man, perhaps in a scrap of silk and chained, and not be extremely aware of one's femininity. Contrasts, of course, are sexually stimulatory. As the saying is, if one wants a man to be more of a man one should be more of a woman. This, in its folklike way, recognizes not only that the human species is radically sexually dimorphic, but that this dimorphism is profoundly relevant to sexuality. Even small enhancements of natural differences, for example, by cosmetics, can be sexually stimulatory, more readily triggering response-dispositions, rather in the nature of innate releasing mechanisms, as has been known for millennia. Studies with primates demonstrate that the testosterone levels of males who have been kept in sexually negative, sexually depressive, environments rise dramatically when the environment is changed, to include, for example, receptive females. Sexuality does not prosper in the androgynous environment. And the master/slave relationship is the least androgynous environment conceivable. It is its diametrical opposite. It, in virtue of its contrasts, is the most sexually stimulatory environment possible. In it we have the slave, vulnerable, lovely, owned and obedient, dressed, if dressed, for the pleasure of the master, at his feet, perhaps bound or chained, in the beautiful symbolism of her condition, subject to discipline, and we have the master, male, lordly and powerful. She is his to do with as he pleases. His virility races; he exults. She, knowing herself his, trembles with need and receptiveness before him. "Put me to your slave ring, Master. I beg it. I am yours. Do with me as you will, my Master!" Both find themselves within a culture's glorious enhancement of, and celebration of, nature's primordial determinations. But to return to more prosaic matters, the Gorean slave girl is not permitted vulgarity. She, though perhaps scarcely clad, or stripped, and kneeling, must be in many ways very "ladylike," for lack of a better word. This, too, of course, contributes to the contrast between herself and the master, much as did the contrast between "gentleman" and "lady" in the Victorian Era, with its concealed, mysterious, romantic, latent, explosive, subterranean sexuality. Sometimes when low-caste women are enslaved they must be taught to be more ladylike, as their masters will have that of them. Their mouths, for example, may be washed out with soap, literally. That is a symbolic, but surely unpleasant, lesson they are not likely to forget. And it may be repeated as often as the master pleases. Most upper-caste women, whereas they might be smug, haughty or cruel, are not vulgar, regarding vulgar language, allusions, gestures, and such as being incompatible with the dignity of their caste. This is not to deny that an upper-caste woman, say, recently enslaved, or any slave girl, for that matter, may not be commanded upon occasion to use the most vulgar language conceivable, in referring to herself, or in begging for use, and such. Here, again, it is the contrast, as well as the understanding on the master's part that he can exact this of the slave and on the part of the slave that it can be exacted from her, that is sexually stimulatory. Sometimes, for example, a slave's referring to herself in a vulgar fashion, or begging for use in a very explicit and very vulgar manner, can help her to achieve a clearer concept of what she is and, of course, consequently, contribute to her readiness for use. On the whole, however, Goreans tend to be remarkably free of vulgarity, perhaps because their world is, on the whole, so much more innocent, natural and conducive to human happiness than at least one other world. There is thus a paradox of sorts which arises. The Gorean will often tend to be courteous and refined in his speech, and yet, in action, direct and forceful, sometimes even ruthless and brutal. We thus have the combination of a gentleman and an uncompromising master in one, with that of a slave and lady in one. But then I suppose that this is not really so difficult to understand. If you are a male, reading this, ask yourself what you would rather have at your slave ring, lying there naked and chained, looking up at you, cringing in the shadow of your whip, a simple, slovenly, vulgar-mouthed slut or a highly intelligent, cultured, refined lady.

Androgyny is inimical to sex; complementarity is stimulatory to sex. The greatest complementarity conceivable occurs within the rigors of the master/slave relationship. This is the secret of its capacity to fulfill, and satisfy, both partners.

To be sure, if one's political programs require the devirilization, and consequent destruction, of the docile, obedient, duped male, then one must do all one can to confuse, deny, blur, and eliminate sexual differences, in this project having recourse to whatever distortions, lies, misrepresentations and propaganda one can manage, and, eventually, of necessity, to the bayonets and guns of a collectivistic, authoritarian state, one that can enforce, by means of executions and camps, the will of an unnatural, aggressive, self-seeking minority on the community as a whole. The destruction of nature and the ruin of human happiness presents an enormous challenge to social engineering, one to which a pathological society, by seizing control of education, the media, and such, must, if it is to be successful, address itself with courage and determination. To be sure, its ends might be achieved more easily by destroying the offspring of all males who show evidence of virility or genetically engineering a new species, a more bovine or insectoidal form of life.

These developments, however, are not likely to occur on Gor. That is because of the nature of Gorean men. Indeed, even on another world which occurs to me, such developments would seem unlikely, once the fevers and fits of madness have passed. Surely even that world, finding itself on the brink of species suicide, might be expected to draw back in horror. Let the fanatics and the insane be put to one side, not to be followed, but to be ignored, as was done before, when one emerged from the late Middle Ages, and into the light of the Renaissance.

Let manhood be reborn.

"Obeisance!" snapped the guardsman.

Instantly Ellen, and her sister slaves, went to first obeisance position, head down to the cement.

"You may now beg the forgiveness of our charges," said the guardsman.

"Forgive us, Mistresses," said the girls on the shelf. "Forgive us, Mistresses," said Ellen, too, following the lead of her chain sisters, she, like the others, head down to the cement, in first obeisance position.

"You will now, in order, shelf-girls," said the guardsman, "acknowledge your inferiority to our charges."

And he was not satisfied until each of the slaves on the shelf acknowledged herself inferior goods to those on his chain. With the two girls who had called out derisively he was most demanding, until he had them in tears praising the beauty and value of his coffle and confessing their own comparative worthlessness, that they were unworthy to act even as the lowliest of serving slaves to such beauties, and so on. He was quick with Ellen, perhaps because of her youth, perhaps because she had refrained from participating in this small contretemps, perhaps in his eagerness to get to the culprit on her left.

"And you," he said to her, "do you acknowledge yourself inferior to these slaves?"

"Yes, Master," said Ellen, and so easily did she escape his further attention. She kept her head down to the cement. Too, objectively, given what she now was, collar meat, a commodity, an object for sale, she had no doubt but what it was true. She was inferior to, and much less than, any of the four neck-chained beauties who stood before the shelf. They were all more beautiful than she. She could not hope to bring the same coins to her master that any of them might. Targo, she supposed, would have rejoiced to have any one of them on his chain.

Perhaps, she thought, if I were not so young.

Then, mercifully, the Cosian dragged the lead girl in the coffle away from the shelf and began to conduct her, her chain sisters perforce behind her, through the crowd. Ellen lifted her head a little. One of the girls in the coffle, she who was last on the chain, or slaver's necklace, turned about to cast a last contemptuous glance at the shelf, but the guardsman behind her struck her a sharp, stinging blow with the flat of his hand below the small of her back, which resounded throughout the market, and she, sobbing with humiliation, with a jangle of chain, hurried forward.

They are still only slaves, such as we, thought Ellen. At various times, in her training, and after her training, when returning to her cell, kennel or cage, one of the guards had given her a similar slap. Such attentions, of course, hurry a girl on. Perhaps that is their ostensible purpose. But they also inform her, whether she wishes it or not, that she is of sexual interest. They also remind her that she is a slave.

"So," said Targo, appearing from the right, as one would look out toward the market, "you are all in trouble."

"No, Master!" said more than one of the girls, still in obeisance position.

"You shall not be fed tonight," said Targo.

There were cries of misery from several of the girls.

"You are all too fat," said Targo.

"And it will save gruel," said Barzak, appearing, too, from the right.

"That has nothing to do with it," said Targo, "but, it is true, it will save some gruel."

"You give us little to eat anyway, Master," sobbed a girl.

"You are all too fat, and I am a poor man," said Targo.

Ellen supposed that Targo and Barzak might have been in the vicinity during the scene with the guardsmen, but, doubtless wisely, wishing to avoid further unpleasantness, if not actual danger, did not step forward and identify themselves.

"May we break position, Master?" asked one of the girls.

"Yes," he said, absently.

There was a rustle of chains.

Ellen, now sitting, looked at the shackle closed about her left ankle. Her ankle was abraded, where she had futilely, foolishly, struggled with the obdurate impediment.

Had she not understood that she was chained? Did she think that those who had chained her did not know their work? Did she think she might simply remove the chain?

Foolish slave!

She pulled a little at the chain, tears in her eyes.

She understood now, and very clearly, that she was chained, that she would remain where she was, precisely there, fastened there, a chained slave, until others might see fit to release her.

"The torches are lit," said Targo.

Indeed, two torches had even been lit on the building behind the shelf, one rather at each end. The torches, and some lamps, tend to be lit toward dark by the market attendants. The two streets beyond the market were now dark. Individuals in poorer districts, leaving their homes after dark or returning to them after dark, commonly carry their own light, usually a lamp. Individuals can be hired, in squares and markets, to escort individuals to their destinations. In better districts, and on the great boulevards and such, high lamps, usually hung from poles, are usually lit after dark by employees of the city, sometimes by guardsmen.

"The light is not so good," said Targo. "That may work in our favor. Buyers may not see what poor stuff you are."

"I will go to the Iron Collar," said Barzak. "I can buy some drinks for some good fellows, get them drunk, bring them back, and who knows. If they are drunk enough, we might make a sale."

"Go then," said Targo.

"I will need some coins," said Barzak.

"Solicit rather in the crowd," said Targo.

Barzak grinned and shrugged.

"What is the name of the girl in the tavern?" asked Targo, shrewdly.

"'Jill'," said Barzak.

"A barbarian name," said Targo.

"She is civilized," said Barzak, irritatedly. "The name was put on her as a punishment name. To be sure, I think it heats her loins."

"Ladies," said Targo to his charges, "I can diminish your rations and add weights to your collars. It is my impression that you have been listless on the shelf, save perhaps when some handsome fellow strolled by. We do not really have enough gruel on hand for you to wait until the rich, handsome master of your hottest, most squirming dreams wanders by. As soon as you spot a fellow with a wallet, whether he is misshapen, lame or whatever, of any caste, and smell, who comes within five paces of the shelf, kneel, call out, lift your hands, smile, wriggle, make yourselves as pleasant and congenial as she-urts can. You are cheap girls. You are bargains. That is a selling point. Remember, too, Barzak's whip has already been warmed, heated nicely, and will be deliciously supple. It has already had one taste of hide today. And doubtless it is more than ready and eager to use its five tongues to lick the same, or another, pretty back.

Ellen shrank back in terror. She remembered the whip, in every tissue and fiber of her body. She had now learned, despite her background on Earth, her studies, her publications, her career, and such, that here, on this world, in her youth and beauty, she was susceptible to the whip; that she was simply and categorically subject to it, that it could be used upon her. She was slave. She was now ready to do anything to be pleasing. She was now desperately concerned to be pleasing. Perhaps this was because she had felt the whip. Let those who have not felt it fail to understand this or scorn her. Its instructive and admonitory value where slave girls are concerned is incalculable. It is one of a large number of devices and techniques for improving a girl.

Targo came about the shelf and stood before Ellen, he on the ground, she on the shelf. She went to first position, unbidden, which seemed appropriate. "I know that this is your first day on the shelf, little she-urt," he said, kindly, "but I want you to learn quickly and make a good impression. You are not really stupid, are you?"

"I do not think so, Master," said Ellen.

"I am not sure that you fully understand your collar," he said, "but I think you will learn quickly. Remember you are a slave girl, precisely a slave girl, and only a slave girl."

"Yes, Master."

"Do you know the call?" he asked.

"'Buy me, Master!'?" she said.

"Yes," he said. "Now, when a man approaches, I want you to kneel as you are, though perhaps with your knees more widely spread, and smile, and lift your hands to him and call out, and beg and plead prettily. Too, try to show need. Small tongue movements are good, exposing the palms of your small hands to him, a bit of plaintive, judicious wriggling, such things."

"Master!" wept Ellen.

"And remember," said he, paying her no attention, "you may be touched and handled in any manner the customer wishes, and must perform for him, assume dictated postures, and such, in any way he wishes. The only thing you need not do is serve his pleasure, completely."

"Yes, Master," she said, in misery.

"Serving his pleasure completely must be cleared through either myself or Barzak, and there may be a charge for that."

"Yes, Master," said Ellen, in horror.

Shortly thereafter both Targo and Barzak disappeared into the crowd.

Ellen suspected that they were both heading for the Iron Collar. Perhaps they would pool their resources to make a bid for Barzak's Jill. Perhaps they could sell her, unless they had other plans for such a one.

"The Masters are so stupid," said the girl to Ellen's left. "Do they really think we are going to attempt to allure an unwanted master?"

"Not in their absence," laughed another, two rings to Ellen's right.

"To make a sale they would have us interest a tharlarion," said another.

"I'm hungry," said another.

"There will be no gruel for us tonight," lamented another.

"Zara and Cotina had to open their cavernous mouths and fling their little tongues about," said another, bitterly.

"Be silent, shelf girl," said the girl to Ellen's left.

"We have not been ordered to silence, she-sleen," said the first. "I can speak as I wish!"

"We would see about that," said the girl to Ellen's left, "if my chain could reach you!"

"You are not Mistress!" said the one.

Ellen realized that a first girl must not have been appointed, though she knew that she herself, given her youth and her newness on the chain, would be subordinate to the others.

"If I get my hands on you, we will see who is Mistress!" said the girl to Ellen's left.

"Take one hair from my head or give me one scratch, and you will be whipped!" said the other.

The girl on Ellen's left turned away, sitting, and looked out upon the crowd, sullenly.

"I am Ellen," said Ellen to her.

"I do not like barbarians," said the girl.

"Forgive me, Mistress," said Ellen.

"I am Cotina," said the girl.

"I am Zara," said the girl, two rings to the right.

"I am Lydia," said the girl who had been critical of Cotina and Zara. "I do not like barbarians either."

"Forgive me, Mistress," said Ellen.

"She is Cichek, she is Emris, and she is Jasmine," said Cotina, indicating the other girls on the shelf.

"Mistresses," said Ellen, deferentially. They looked away.

"They do not like to be shelved with a barbarian," said Cotina. "It is insulting."

"Forgive me, Mistresses," said Ellen.

"What does it matter?" asked Lydia, bitterly. "We all wear collars. We are all morsels for men, all tidbits of slave meat."

"It is still insulting," snapped Jasmine.

"Forgive me, Mistress," said Ellen.

"Mistress," said Ellen, to Cotina, "what is the Curulean?"

"It was a fortress and palace, the ancestral domicile of the first Hinrabians," said Cotina, "but, for years now, it has been the major slave market in Ar."

"Do you think I might be sold there someday?" asked Ellen.

"You are very pretty," said Cotina, "perhaps in four or five years, or six or seven years, or eight or ten years, you might be thought worthy of the Curulean."

"Not for the central block," said Jasmine.

"Who knows?" said Cotina.

"But I have been "stabilized,"" said Ellen.

"You were prematurely stabilized?" asked Cotina.

"I have been stabilized," said Ellen.

"As you are?"

"Yes."

"It was done deliberately?"

"Yes."

"Someone must have hated you very much," said Cotina.

Tears came to Ellen's eyes.

"You will never be more then than you are," said Lydia, "only a pretty girl. No man would want you, except perhaps as a pretty little thing, a pretty little servant, a pretty little maid, to have about the house."

"Do not underestimate the lust of men," said Cichek.

"But who could take her seriously as a female?" asked Lydia.

"That is a different matter," said Cichek.

Ellen put her head in her hands and wept. He who had been her master had seen, it seemed, to her lot on Gor.

He had known, undoubtedly, exactly what he was doing, and had done it.

It had been his decision, not hers, as she was his slave, and he had made it as he had.

"We could all be sold in the Curulean," said Emris. "Surely we are as fair as those she-sleen on the chain."

"That is for the Masters to decide," said Zara.

"We are all worthy of the Curulean," said Jasmine, "except perhaps the child."

"I am not a child!" said Ellen.

"Except perhaps the girl," said Jasmine.

Ellen could not deny that she was a girl, in at least two senses, first in the sense of her youth, the sense which Jasmine had undoubtedly conceded, and, secondly, in the sense that she, as the others, was a female slave. In the first sense, her youth certainly did not militate against her sexual desirability. She knew that. There had been large, full-length mirrors, sometimes wall-size, in several of the training rooms. There had been no mistaking the lovely, exquisite, sweetly curved, collared image that she had seen reflected in the mirror. Too, the responses and attitudes of her male trainers, as well as the frequent condition of their bodies, had left no doubt in her mind that her body, whether she wished it to or not, now constituted a powerful stimulus in the sexual equation, a stimulus of considerable potency. Whether she wished it or not she knew that she was now extremely stimulatory to men, extremely attractive, extremely desirable. And, too, of course, her desirability was considerably increased by what she was, that she was a female slave. Men saw her, and wanted her, badly. She had even been put in the iron belt. Secondly, aside from her youth, as noted, she was a girl in the sense that she was a female slave, the sense in which all female slaves are girls. The expression 'girl' in such contexts is rich and delicious. It has a lovely reductive or demeaning sense in which it discriminates between the slave and the free woman, and calls attention to the lowliness, the unimportance and the meaninglessness of the slave. Indeed, free mistresses will invariably refer to, and address, their serving slaves, and such, even those of their own age, as "girl." Secondly, the expression 'girl', at least in the usage of men, has not only the aforementioned connotation but, even more powerfully, and independently of the age of the female, the commendatory suggestion of extreme sexual desirability. It functions as a term of interest and praise. It is not a chronological classification; it is a signal that he regards her as lying within an ideal prey range for his aggressive dispositions. Of two women the same age, a man will think of one as a girl and the other as a woman. The one he wants will be the one he thinks of as the girl, for he sees her as young and desirable, still young enough to be eager and ready, and sexually stimulating, and the other, in which he has no interest, he is content to let call herself a woman, or whatever she wishes. It is interesting to note, in passing, that women who are interested in men, and are still in the sexual market, so to speak, often think of, and speak of, themselves and their female friends as "girls." At one time Ellen, in virtue of her ideology, was forced to denounce this, but she now understands it. In any event, the female slave is thought of as a girl, a slave girl.

"But we find ourselves chained on a shelf," said Cotina.

"I do not want to be a slave," said Zara. "I do not want to be chained on a shelf!" She jerked at her ankle chain, but as helplessly as had Ellen. She, too, was a helpless, chained slave.

"Be grateful that you are permitted to live, slave girl," said Cotina.

Ellen wondered if she herself desired to be a slave or not. Certainly she did not want to wear so cruel, high, thick, and heavy a collar, one in which she could scarcely lower her head, in effect, a punishment collar. She did not want to be chained on a public shelf. On the other hand, it seemed clear to her that whether she wanted to be a slave or not, she was a slave, and not by dint of the collar, or brand, but by dint of her deepest nature. What was wrong with her? Don't you want to be free, she cried to herself. Was she not supposed to cry such things to herself? Was it not expected? Didn't she want to be free? Surely she knew that her society had insisted that she must want to be free, so what was it, deep within her, deeper than her society, more profound than convention, that wanted rather to love and serve, to be owned will-lessly, to be mastered and dominated? But then she realized that her male-dominated society had imposed its values on both sexes, that it had generalized its own preconceptions. What was good for the male must be good for the female, and so on. Were they not the same, were they not identical? Was it not like the foolish, ignorant male who, finding his female lover suddenly, impulsively, on her knees before him, looking up lovingly, rendering him the homage and obeisance her nature yearns to give, sweatingly, embarrassedly hurries her, scolding, to her feet, admonishing her, in effect, to act more like a man. And so she, shamed, rises up, still trying to please him, despite his denial of her momentarily exposed depths. His will, it seems, is that she not be a woman before him, for that seems to frighten him, but something else. Is it a woman he wants, truly, or not a woman, really, but something else, perhaps a pseudo-male? So Ellen lay on the cement shelf. No, she thought, the thought charming her, I do not want to be free. Is that truly such a heresy, for a woman, or only a heresy for those who insist that women are to be like men, and for male impersonators, so to speak? I have been free, I know what it is like, and its values. I know what it is to be free. I have experienced freedom. I know what it is like. But I have also been, and am, a slave, and know what that is like, at least to now, and its values. And, oh, there are values, profound values, connected with my bondage. I suspect that I have only begun to sense them. Let those who wish to be free, be free, and let those who would be slaves be slaves. Are we not even to be allowed the freedom to be what we most wish to be? If not, what sort of freedom is that? The freedom to conform to an alien stereotype, an image imposed from without? I am a natural slave. I think I have known that for many years, but my slavery was denied me. Now, at last, I find myself on a world on which I can, and indeed must, express my deepest, most fervent nature. I am a slave, and I love being a slave, but surely I dare not admit that to any man. How fearful to be at the feet of a man who knows you are a true slave! How would he treat you? With what contempt, and lust?

But, lying on the shelf, looking out on the crowd, she became apprehensive. I am a slave, she thought. I am chained. I am naked. I am at their mercy. They can do with me what they want. And she suddenly felt very vulnerable. She no longer wore the iron belt. She drew her legs up, close to her body. The cruel security, the protection, the safety of the iron belt was gone. All her softness now, with its sweet, delicious curves, with its delicate intimacies, was exhibited openly. She, the whole of her, was chained on a public shelf. She was vulnerably displayed, well displayed, completely displayed.

"A warrior," whispered Emris. Then she called out, "Buy me, Master!"

Ellen looked up, and gasped. A tall, broad-shouldered man in scarlet, massively handsome, had approached the shelf. His sword belt, scabbard and helmet crest were black.

"He is of Ar," whispered Cotina to Ellen. Then she knelt, knees wide, and called out, "Buy me, Master!"

Zara scrambled forward, as she could.

Emris, Cichek, Jasmine and Lydia, too, almost instantly knelt, and drew as close to the man as their chains would permit. Only Ellen, frightened, remained lying down, her knees drawn up. She had not seen her sister slaves like this. "Buy me, Master!" called out Zara. "I am Zara, if it pleases Master! I beg to be purchased! I am skilled! I can serve you well! Oh, buy me, Master! I beg to be permitted to serve you!"

"Do not concern yourself with her, Master!" called out Lydia. "I am better!"

"No!" cried Zara.

"I saw him first," said Emris.

"Be silent," said Cotina.

"I beg your collar, handsome Master!" cried Cichek.

"See my blond hair and blue eyes," called Lydia, lifting her hair and displaying it. "I alone am fair of these on the shelf."

"She is cold," said Jasmine.

"My belly is hot," said Lydia. "I juice at a touch!"

"I am from the valley of the Vosk," said Jasmine. "My belly flames!"

"I would juice at the sound of your footfall," cried Zara. "I would tear at my chains to reach you!"

"I beg to writhe in need before you!" said Emris.

"See my shapely limbs," said Cotina, presenting her right side and leg for his consideration.

How different were the slaves before such a man, thought Ellen. Look at Zara, thought Ellen. She is as much a slave as the others. A moment ago she was protesting her bondage and now she is half beside herself, beseechingly, with the desire to be this man's slave. Clearly what she wanted was not freedom but a slavery of her choice.

"Put me through slave paces, Master," called Emris. "Let me exhibit a slave before you!"

"Buy me, Master!" begged Cichek.

"No, me!" said Cotina, lifting her hands, pleadingly.

"No, me!" said Lydia.

"I!" called Jasmine.

"I am a natural slave, a slave in my heart," said Zara. "I have wanted to be a slave since childhood, Master! Buy me! Make me your slave!"

"She is no different from us," said Cotina. "We are all natural slaves. Choose then the best and most beautiful of us all, Cotina, me!"

Ellen was startled at the eagerness, the zeal, the openness, the competitiveness, of the slaves. The man was not of the Merchants. He would not be rich. Would they not want to be purchased by rich men, that they would have a softer, easier, more pleasant life? Would a rich man not have many slaves, so that there would be less work for any given girl? Would such then not be the ideal master for any slave, a rich man? What then was it about this man? He would not be rich. And yet they wanted to throw themselves to his feet.

Ellen looked into his eyes, and then, quickly, looked down, frightened.

In his eyes, she had seen that he was one before whom a woman could be only a slave, one who would know well how to master a woman.

Is that why they are so eager, so zealous, she asked herself. Had they had such a master, or dreamed of such a one?

He was one, she did not doubt, who would own the fullness of a female, one who would exact the fullness of her slavery from her.

She felt a sudden tremor in her loins. She had not meant to do that. It was nothing over which she had any control. It was reflexive. She repudiated it, embarrassed. It shocked her.

"Look up," he said.

Ellen lifted her eyes, unwillingly, to his.

The other girls were then instantly silent.

She held her eyes to his for a brief moment, and then could do so no longer, and quickly, frightened, overcome, looked down, and away.

"Please do not make me look into your eyes, Master," she said.

She hoped she would not be cuffed.

"You are very pretty," he said.

She shrank back, frightened. "Thank you, Master," she said.

"Who thanks me?" he asked, gently.

"Ellen, if pleases Master," she said, "Ellen, the slave of Targo, dealer in slaves."

"You are new to the collar, aren't you?" he asked.

"Yes, Master."

"What is your brand?"

"The common kef, Master," she said.

"Show me," said he.

Ellen turned so that he might read her brand.

"Well, Ellen," said he, "who is the best and most beautiful slave on the shelf?"

"Masters will decide that," she said, "not I, Master."

"You are a clever little beauty," he said. "You know you must share the same straw with them tonight."

"It is true, surely, nonetheless, Master," she said.

"True," he said. "Do you know slave dance?" he asked.

"No, Master."

"Are you trained?"

"Very little, Master." That was another thing her master had seen to, that she would not be well trained. In this way, too, she would be of less worth as a slave.

"You are a barbarian," he said.

"Yes, Master." Presumably that had been clear from her accent.

"I once had a barbarian," he said. "She thought she was going to be free, but she quickly learned to kiss the whip."

"Master?"

"I lost her at dice, but won her back. I was going to breed her, but a subordinate wanted her, and so I gave her to him. I think she was afraid of me. As far as I know she is happy in her collar. He is now stationed near Venna, and she cooks and serves in his quarters."

"Have you been sold much?" he asked.

"Only once, to my current master, Targo, dealer in slaves."

"When were you first collared?" he asked.

"I was enslaved some weeks ago, but I was only collared some days ago."

"You are going to be a good slave, aren't you?" he asked.

"I will try to be a good slave, Master," she said.

"Belly," he said, gently, and held out his hand, palm downward.

Instantly Ellen bellied, and, hands to the sides, lowering her head, frightened, began to lick and kiss the back of his hand.

"You have clearly had some training," he said.

"Very little, Master," she said.

"On your world," he said, "is there slavery?"

"Very little, Master, at least on the surface."

"On the surface?"

"Yes, Master."

"There are perhaps secret slaveries?"

"Yes, Master, I have little doubt that many women are held in bondage, though this is concealed from the world."

"Were you free on your world?"

"Yes, Master."

"Did you anticipate that you would one day be a slave on another world, publicly and legally, stripped on a public shelf, chained, affording small ministrations to the back of a man's hand?"

"No, Master," said Ellen, pressing her lips to the back of his hand, softly.

"Let me lick the palm of your hand, Master," whispered Cotina.

"No, let me!" begged Zara, quickly.

"No, me!" cried Emris.

Ellen then realized that it was presumably no accident that he had extended the back of his hand to her, and not the open hand. That was doubtless deliberate, a way of keeping her at a distance, of precluding involvement with a pretty little slave, perhaps because of her youthfulness, or her collar immaturity.

She recalled how she had been taught in training to kiss the palm of a man's hand, sometimes darting her tongue softly in and out of it, suggesting subtly, and begging for, her own penetration. More than once a guard then, in fury, had flung her from him and stormed away, to seize another slave. She had been in the iron belt. She had been left vaguely uneasy, vaguely unsatisfied, but, at that time, slave fires had not been lit in her belly. Another technique is to kneel before the man and take the palm of his right hand, if he is right handed, and press it to your face, firmly, as though you had been cuffed with it, and then to hold the hand, humbly, as in gratitude, similarly licking and kissing the palm.

As has been suggested it is expected, at least by some masters, that the slave is to be grateful for her beatings. She has, after all, received the master's attention. Similarly, she should rejoice that she has been improved.

But Ellen did not doubt but what the warrior was pleased to have her before him, as she was, even though she was licking and kissing merely the back of his hand. After all, she was prostrate before him, a slave, naked, in a posture of abject submission.

"I have seen the shelf of Targo last week," he said. "The lot today is better than the lot then."

"Thank you, Master!" said several of the girls on the shelf, elated.

What occurred to Ellen, instantly, of course, and this frightened her, was that there must have been a considerable turnover in the interim. To be sure, Targo would have to make sales or go out of business.

"Do you want to be sold?" he asked.

"No, Master!" said Ellen, who feared her sale.

"Then you want to remain here, in a weight collar, on the shelf?" he said.

"No, Master!" said Ellen.

He laughed, and drew back his hand, turned about, and disappeared into the crowd.

"You let him go," said Cotina, angrily.

"You are stupid, Ellen," said Emris.

"You are clever in your virgin ways," said Zara.

"I am not a virgin," said Ellen.

"Pretending not to want to be bought, pretending to be so naive!" said Zara.

"Wily little she-urt!" said Jasmine.

"When will such a man come to the shelf again?" asked Cichek.

"You let him get away," said Lydia.

"I did nothing!" said Ellen. "He did not want me!"

"Did you not see him caressing your pretty little flanks with his eyes?" said Zara.

"I do not want to be chained with her," said Jasmine.

"He looked upon all of you, beautiful Mistresses!" said Ellen.

"Do you think you are better than we?" demanded Emris.

"No, Mistresses!" said Ellen.

"Hereafter," said Cotina, "if you do not want a buyer, give him, as you can, to us."

"Selfish she-urt!" snapped Lydia.

"We will tear you apart in the straw," said Cichek.

Ellen moaned.

"Targo!" whispered Cotina.

And through the crowd, from the right, came Targo, followed by Barzak, who had a figure with him, closely behind him, which he was pulling through the crowd by means of a tightly coiled, muchly shortened leash, his hand gripping it not six inches from the lock at its captive's neck, the figure of a naked, hooded, back-braceleted woman.

That must be, Ellen supposed, Barzak's "Jill."

"Targo does not seem pleased," warned Zara.

"Perhaps the new she-urt cost him too much," said Jasmine.

"Remember," said Cotina to Ellen. "You will be less than she, barbarian."

"Yes, Mistress," said Ellen.

"Buy me, Master!" called out Cotina, as though to anyone.

The other girls, too, Targo approaching, began to appeal to the crowd, uttering the attraction call of the common girl for sale.

Such a change, thought Ellen, wrought by the imminence of the masters, formerly inert female merchandise, suddenly, in fear of the whip, become luscious, active flesh goods, attempting to allure buyers, attempting to entice customers for their master.

How I despise them, the slaves, thought Ellen. How lowly, how meaningless they are!

But quickly, she, too, went to her knees and spread them widely. Ellen lifted her hands to the crowd, not daring to meet anyone's eyes, and hoping no one noticed her. "Buy me, Master!" she called. "Buy me, Master!"

Barzak conducted his new charge into the building.

Is she not to be for sale, wondered Ellen. Why is she not to be for sale? I am for sale. Then she almost fainted with shock, for she understood what she had said, that she was *for sale*.

Oh, Mirus of Ar, she thought, bitterly. What you have done to me!

Targo she saw, to her dismay, was standing before her. She did not meet his eyes but continued to appeal to the crowd.

"Smile," said he, not pleasantly. "Catch their eye. Tongue movements! Helpless movements of your knees and thighs! Pretend you are a hot little urt. Wriggle! Squirm!"

Ellen shrieked with misery and collapsed, sobbing, to the shelf.

"Ten copper tarsks were too much for you," said Targo. "Ten copper tarsk-bits would be too much for you!"

Ellen's body, lying on the shelf, was wracked with sobs.

"You are begging for the leather, slave girl," said Targo.

"No, Master," she sobbed. "Please do not have me whipped, please, no, Master!" She was terrified. She had felt the whip. She did not wish to feel it again. "Please, no, Master!" she begged. "I will do anything, Master!"

"My patience is not inexhaustible," said Targo. "You will do better tomorrow, flesh-trash."

"Forgive me, Master," wept Ellen. "Yes, Master."

"Behold, kind sir," said Targo, turning to a fellow nearby, "the loveliness of Cotina, the sweetness of her thighs, her well-turned ankles, and note Lydia, a beauty who might have been from the north, the only one so fair, with blond hair and blue eyes, on the shelf, and see delicious, cuddly Jasmine. She is from the valley of the Vosk, and you know what they are like, particularly the ones from Victoria, only a stone's throw from Jasmine's native village. That is Emris and Cichek who beg you to buy them. Zara, so slim and shapely, pleads for your collar. These are prize slaves, sought by the Curulean, but withheld, due to my popular propensities, for the district of Metellus, and our beloved Kettle Market. Any one of these is worth a Ubar's medallion, a thousand golden tarn disks, but I am a destitute man, who, due to personal exigencies am in sudden dire need of ready cash. I am prepared to let any of these unparalleled beauties go for as little as a dozen silver tarsks!"

"Shelf girls!" snorted a man, turning away.

"Have that one stand, to be examined," said a man.

"Cotina, stand, examination position!" snapped Targo.

Cotina stood, her legs widely spread, her head back, her hands clasped behind the back of her neck. It is hard for a woman to move from this position and she must be concerned with her balance. The subtle adjustments and tenseness required to maintain her balance keep her even more helplessly in place, and these adjustments and this tenseness will also be expressed in her posture, providing body-language cues bespeaking obedience and servitude. Too, obviously this posture bares her vulnerably, and her hands cannot interfere with the examination. The position of the arms, the hands clasped behind the back of the neck, or, sometimes, behind the back of the head, lifts the bosom, exhibiting it beautifully.

The fellow came to the surface of the shelf, climbing directly onto it, whereas Targo hurried about, to the side, went up by the steps, and joined him near Cotina.

"Is she barbarian?" asked the man.

"Certainly not," said Targo, offended.

"Open your mouth," said the fellow to Cotina, who presumably obeyed. Ellen kept her eyes away.

"Wider!"

"You do not think I would handle barbarians, do you?" asked Targo.

"Yes?" said Targo, for another fellow had clambered to the surface of the shelf.

"Is this one truly blond?" asked the new fellow, presumably of Lydia.

"Certainly," said Targo.

There was a sudden, sharp little cry from Lydia, as, Ellen supposed, some hair was drawn from her head to ascertain the veracity of Targo's asseveration.

"I am going to put this one through slave paces," said the man who was near Lydia.

He then began to issue a set of rapid commands to Lydia, almost as quickly as the trainers in the house had accustomed Ellen to respond. Lydia complied as well as she could, chained, and on cement. Slave paces are much more easily performed on a smooth surface, or on furs at the foot of a master's couch, such places. Sometimes they are performed on a rug, say, a Tahari rug, before the master who, seated, observes, or perhaps in the center of such a rug, for the interest of the master's encircling guests. In such cases, often the paces are not called, but performed silently, save perhaps for small gasps and moans, by the slave.

"Oh!" suddenly cried Cotina.

"Yes, she is vital," said Targo. "Hold position," he warned Cotina.

"Master!" wept Cotina.

"Hold position," he said.

"Yes, Master," she sobbed. "Ah! Oh! Please, no! Oh, do not, I beg you! Oh! Ohhhhh!"

Ellen covered her head with her hands, and lost consciousness.

It was later that night, when the market was mostly deserted, and several of the torches had burned out, that Ellen awakened, to a sound of chain. She felt a tug at her ankle, through the shackle. Barzak was unlocking the padlock that held her shackle chain to the ring. "Stand up," he said to her, "and get behind Lydia, holding your left wrist with your right hand, behind your back." Ellen went to stand behind Lydia, who was standing behind Zara. Both girls were grasping their left wrist with their right hand behind their back. Zara's ankle chain had been lifted and padlocked to the large ring dangling from her collar. On the other hand, Lydia's ankle chain had been padlocked into the shackle ring of Zara. In a moment, Ellen's ankle chain had been padlocked into the shackle ring of Lydia. Shortly thereafter, Cichek and Emris had been freed of the shelf ring, and Cichek was standing behind Ellen, her hands behind her, as ordered, and her ankle chain had been padlocked into the Ellen's shackle ring. Emris took her place behind Cichek, standing as the others, and her ankle chain was padlocked into Cichek's shackle ring. "You will move with the left foot first," said Barzak, who did not know if Ellen was familiar with shackled-ankle coffle procedure."

"Yes, Master," said Ellen. "May I speak, Master?"

"No."

"Be careful on the steps," he said.

"Yes, Master," she said.

There were only one or two men left in the market. Almost all of the goods were gone, taken away to be stored safely somewhere. Across the way a man, presumably drunk, lay near one of the stalls, its shelves now bared, its covering gone, as well.

Ellen, between Lydia and Cichek, descended the shelf steps and, in a moment, entered the building. It was dark, and there was an unmistakable smell of urine.

"The steps are to the left," said Barzak. "You may hold out your hands. Do not fall. At the foot of the steps be again as you were."

They would keep their hands in that fashion until they were secured for the night.

The steps were of cement, and narrow, steep and dark.

After moving a few feet down the dark hall, they came to an opened, heavy door, and through this Zara, leading, made her way.

The room, which was large, was lit by a small lamp in a niche on the wall. The room had one occupant, doubtless the woman brought back by Barzak and Targo. She now wore a weight collar, as the others, and this collar, by its ring, was padlocked to a ring anchored in the stone floor. She could not lift her head more than two or three inches from the floor. The hood and leash were gone. She was still stripped. Her body was delicate. Her features were exquisite.

The floor was strewn with straw. It was damp to Ellen's bare feet.

"Surely we are not to be neck-ringed tonight, Master," said Zara.

"And you will not be fed either," said Barzak. "You should understand that, for you were one of the two who precipitated that scene with the Cosians. Do you not understand that we might have been fined, or imprisoned, or killed, or our entire stock confiscated. Do you think the Cosians do not have that power?"

"Forgive me, Master," said Zara, but he had forced her to her knees, and then to her side, her right hand still grasping her left wrist behind her, so bound by the master's will, at one of the rings anchored in the floor. He removed the padlock holding her ankle chain to her collar ring and then used it to padlock her collar ring to the floor ring. He then removed the ankle chain from her shackle, and put the chain with its padlock to one side. He then removed Lydia's ankle chain from Zara's shackle ring. In a moment Lydia then, too, her ankle chain removed, was neck-ringed to a floor ring by one of its padlocks, the chain put, too, to one side. Ellen was next, and then Cichek and Emris. All were then neck-ringed to a floor ring, and freed of their ankle chains. They retained, of course, the shackles with the shackle rings on their left ankles, as the shackles had been closed about their ankles, hammered shut. The weight collars they wore, too, with the dangling rings, by means of which they were fastened to the floor rings, could not be removed either, except by tools. Barzak, who was brawny, had managed this, she supposed. There was a small anvil in one corner of the room. A girl could be knelt there.

"Your hands are freed," said Barzak, and the girls gratefully released their grips on their left wrists, held behind their back.

Barzak put the extra chains and padlocks to one side, took the lamp and left the room. Ellen heard the door being closed and locked. She had seen several rings in the room, on the floor, like that to which she was fastened, and about the walls. There may have been as many as fifty such rings. She had thought that there might have been one small window, high in the wall, closely barred. It was dark now, of course. Perhaps that window opened to a narrow passage between the tenements, or to a small, narrow yard, concealed from the street. Gorean buildings of this sort often present a solid front to the street, this discouraging traffic, trespassing, burglary, and such. It was a large, simple, heavy, dark, stonelike room, designed for slaves or captives. Surely it did not resemble the luxurious boudoirs she had heard of in her training, those sometimes permitted to high slaves, the pampered, perfumed treasures of Ubars and generals, sometimes said to even influence the policies and fates of states. Such were prize acquisitions of conquerors, who might enjoy stripping them and putting them in common collars, and giving them to their lowest soldiers, first, of course, having them perform naked before these soldiers, in the presence, naturally, of their former masters, and the conquerors.

Ellen tried to lift her head, but she could do so only a tiny bit, as it was held, by the rings and padlock, close to the floor.

She had been given bread and tea by Targo in the afternoon. Her hunger then, she supposed, while certainly active, would be less than that of her chain sisters.

Her back still hurt from the lashing she had been given hours earlier.

Tears came to her eyes.

She had felt the whip.

She would obey, and obey instantly and perfectly.

The fiery lesson of the broad-bladed, five-stranded Gorean slave whip, designed to be applied to such as she, had not been lost on her.

Earlier in the day the sun had been fierce. She had scarcely been able to keep her eyes open. She feared that she, and doubtless the others, had burned on the shelf. Surely that would not improve her price, she thought, bitterly. She remembered the coolness of the house, the baths required, and the creams and lotions, designed to keep the skin of a slave girl soft, smooth and caressable, pleasing to the touch of a master.

In the coffle she had been between Lydia and Cichek, and she was now between them, as well, each neck-ringed to their respective floor rings.

She was pleased in a way, because, as they were secured, neither they nor the others could attack her, as Cichek had threatened. Certainly she had not deliberately tried to distract the soldier from attending to the others. Or, at least she did not think so, at least not on a conscious level! She was a bit frightened, however, and was uneasy, that her behavior may have belied her conscious intentions, that a deeper self, or a deeper need, or a deeper desire, without her knowledge, without her consent, had presented her, and revealed her, to his consideration as rightfully and natively bond. Perhaps her slavery, beneath the level of her conscious awareness, unbidden, had insisted on calling itself to his attention, presenting itself, offering itself, for his consideration. Perhaps her slavery had spoken to him in a language she did not even dare to consider, let alone recognize. Certainly her sister slaves had been furious. Had they seen something she had not? But surely she could not help it that it was she whom he had put to second obeisance position, bellying, before him, that it was she to whom he gave the back of his hand to lick. It was not her fault, at least by intent, as far as she knew. She did not want to be bought by him. She would be terrified to belong to such a man.

"Cichek," she whispered.

"Be silent, barbarian," said Cichek.

"Lydia," she whispered.

"What do you want?" asked Lydia.

"Do not speak to her," said Emris.

"We have not been ordered to silence," said Lydia.

"We are hungry," said Emris. "She was fed!"

"I am hungry, too," said Ellen.

"Not so hungry as we," said Zara, unpleasantly.

"Forgive me, Mistresses," whispered Ellen.

"What do you want?" asked Lydia.

"You are crying," said Ellen. "What is wrong?"

"She was put through slave paces, and not purchased," said Emris.

"She was found wanting," said Cichek.

"So much for your blond hair and blue eyes," said Emris.

"She is an ice maiden," said Cichek.

"No," said Lydia, "I need and want a master as much as any of you!"

"Men often put a woman through slave paces, when they have no intention of buying her," said Zara. "They simply enjoy exercising their power over her, and it amuses them to see her perform, at their mercy, not knowing their will or intent. Perhaps they are just bored and are looking for something to do. It has been done to me, and I am the most beautiful of you all."

"Why then are you still on the chain?" asked Cichek.

"What is it that you wanted to know?" asked Lydia.

"Where are Cotina and Jasmine?" asked Ellen.

"Gone," said Lydia.

"Gone?" asked Ellen.

"Sold," said Lydia.

Chapter 17

A Barbarian Slave Girl Is Vended

It was now Ellen's third day on the shelf.

She stood at the back of the shelf, against the wall of the tenement, her back to the wall of the tenement, she then facing outward, her wrists chained over her head to a ring set in the tenement wall. Her arms were sore, and her legs ached. Targo was not much pleased with her.

Surely she should have been sold by now.

On the morning of her second day in Targo's ownership, after his charges were coffled, and then freed from the neck-rings that held their heads so close to the floor, they had been permitted, in turn, the use of the wastes bucket, and then, afterward, fed and watered, on all fours, heads down, from two long, narrow troughlike pans. Following this Ellen had had to apply soothing oil to the backs of her sister slaves, to assuage the pain of their burns and give them some protection on the shelf. Targo had perhaps realized that miserable slaves with roughened skin, scarcely able to move, red and peeling, would have less sales appeal. On the other hand it could well have been that he now felt more financially comfortable, or even secure, having disposed of Cotina and Jasmine, and could afford this amenity. Too, as we have noted, Targo was not, all things considered, an unkind master. He would not hesitate, of course, to have a woman branded, or whipped, and such. Such things go with the mastery. None of the slaves were willing to apply the soothing oil to Ellen, but Barzak had ordered Cichek, who, with Emris, were perhaps the slaves who disliked Ellen the most, she being a barbarian, to do so. They did not care for barbarians, which was not uncommon, but, too, they, perhaps more intensely than Zara and Lydia, were sensitive to the humiliation of sharing a chain with one. Cichek, who had been deliberately assigned this duty by Barzak, that she might be the better reminded of her nothingness, her lowliness and bondage, was not gentle.

"Forgive me, Mistress," had said Ellen, wincing.

The new slave, Jill, who had been a paga slave at the Iron Collar, had not been burned, but she, too, was treated, to protect her during the day.

"I do not wish to be touched by a barbarian," had said Jill.

"You are no better than a barbarian," had said Cichek. "You have a barbarian name! 'Jill'! 'Jill'! 'Jill'! And it makes you hot, doesn't it? 'Jill'! 'Jill'!"

"Yes, yes," wept the new slave. "I am no better than a barbarian. I can tell it from my yieldings."

Cichek and Emris then laughed merrily, and the new slave, kneeling, head down, submitted to Ellen's ministrations.

Goreans, of course, are of human stock. Their presence on Gor was originally due to the Voyages of Acquisition, apparently undertaken for scientific or aesthetic reasons by the mysterious Priest-Kings, whoever they might be. This is in accord with the Second Knowledge, parts of which had been conveyed to Ellen in her training, that she might be a more comprehending slave. The point of this brief digression is merely to inform the reader that there is no reason to believe that there would be any difference whatsoever in the capacity of Gorean women and Earth women for sexual arousal and responsiveness. Physiology has dictated capacity; beyond this the differences will be those of culture and environment. There is little doubt that the average Gorean woman is raised in a culture which is much more open, much freer and much more acceptive of sexuality. If an Earth male were to encounter a Gorean woman he would undoubtedly be extraordinarily delighted by her great interest in, and desire for, frequent and profound sexual experience. Similarly, if a Gorean male were to encounter an Earth woman, free, in her own environment, he would probably be exceedingly puzzled by her inertnesses and frigidities, her culturally conditioned inhibitions, reservations, negativities and such. Indeed, he would probably regard her as defective or insane.

Putting her to her belly at his feet, of course, in her proper place, perhaps as an experiment, he might find that she, fearfully and gratefully licking and kissing, was actually a woman, a true woman, with a true woman's needs, desires, and responses, something quite different from what he had originally conjectured. Hopefully he would then bring her to Gor, mercifully, that she might not thereafter be left behind to languish and suffer on Earth, unfulfilled, tortured by memories, afflicted by loneliness, poignantly recalling what was no longer hers, denied a master.

It is true, however, that Earth women, brought to Gor as slaves, eagerly and joyfully blossom sexually. On Gor they are free to be the women they have hitherto been commanded to deny and conceal, the women they have always wanted to be, the women they have always been in their hearts. On Gor they find that they are far freer and happier as branded chattels than they were as putatively free women on Earth. In their collars, kneeling before men, they find their liberation and freedom as females. No longer do they starve in a sexual desert. They are so eager to serve true men, which many of them had not even realized existed until they were brought to Gor, men so different from the general run of culturally intimidated, negatively conditioned, sexually crippled males they have met on Earth, that they generate an image in the markets, and the general Gorean milieu, of helpless, ready appetition, of docile, servile, eager, begging sluts, of low women hot in their collars, who give an almost new meaning to bondage. Indeed, some Gorean slave girls regard the barbarians as dangerous and hated rivals. They are furious with the interest shown in them by some Gorean males. The Gorean males, on the other hand, the monsters, tend to remain complacent, content to let these slaves compete with one another, each trying to outdo the other, each trying to see if it cannot be she who most pleases the master.

Ellen pulled a little, weakly, at her chained wrists.

Targo had come to the shelf, to assist a buyer who was examining Emris.

Please, Master," begged Ellen. "Do not keep me chained like this."

"Be silent," he said, "else I will chain you facing the wall. Perhaps men would like you better then."

Ellen put down her head.

Not a great deal had gone on, on her second day on the shelf. To be sure, Zara had been sold, though Ellen did not know the final agreed-upon price. So, she thought, perhaps Zara had been indeed the most beautiful of them all. The new girl, Jill, had been chained to her left, where Cotina had been.

Yesterday, on the shelf, however, she had had some unpleasant experiences, which had perhaps contributed to her present predicament, that of being chained upright, standing, at the back of the shelf.

In the morning, shortly after they had been brought in coffle to the surface of the shelf, thence to be chained as before to various rings, a boy, surely no more than ten or eleven years old, had come to stand before the shelf.

She was in first position, or in something rather like it, rather near the front edge of the shelf, the chain attached to her shackle ring trailing behind her to its ring.

The boy continued to stare at her.

"Go away, little boy," she said, irritatedly. "This place is not for you."

"Split your knees, slave girl," said he to her.

"What?" she said, in disbelief.

He repeated his instruction, granting that she might not have heard him properly.

"Never," she said, "you little urt." She drew her legs together and covered her breasts with her hands.

"What is going on here?" asked Barzak, approaching. His whip, on its staff ring, blades folded back, and clipped, against the staff, which is long enough to be held with both hands, was at his belt.

"Nothing," said the boy.

"'Nothing'!" said Ellen. "This little urt was looking at me. He told me to split my knees!"

"And you did not do so?"

"Certainly not!" cried Ellen.

Barzak looked at her, sternly.

"He is only a little boy!" she said.

"He is a free person," said Barzak.

"Master?" asked Ellen.

"Are you a slave girl?"

"Yes, Master!"

"And you have failed to obey a free person?"

"He is a little boy!" she cried.

"So you have failed to obey a free person," he said.

"Yes, Master," she whispered.

"Don't whip me, please!" she cried, seeing Barzak loosen the whip, removing the staff ring from the hook at his belt, and unclipping the blades.

"It's nothing," said the boy. "Do not whip her. I do not want her whipped. She is probably just stupid."

"First obeisance position," snapped Barzak. "Beg his forgiveness!"

Instantly Ellen went to the first obeisance position, head down, palms of her hands on the cement. "Please forgive me, Master," she begged, frightened.

"Kneel up, first position," said Barzak.

Ellen went to first position, with all its revelatory delights.

"Split your knees, slave girl," said the boy.

"They are split, Master," said Ellen.

"Split them much more widely, slave girl," said the boy.

"Yes, Master," said Ellen.

"Turn to the side, as you are, kneeling, put your hands on the cement behind you," said the boy, "lean back, arch your back, have your head back, farther."

"Yes, Master," said Ellen.

"She has a nice line," said the boy.

"Yes," said Barzak. "She is a pretty she-urt."

"You may break position," said the boy.

Quickly Ellen knelt up, and turned to face him, closing her knees, covering her breasts with her hands.

Barzak wandered off.

"I am only eleven," said the boy. "You are too old for me. I would prefer a slave who is nine or ten."

He then turned about and disappeared into the crowd.

Later a small girl had drifted to the front of the shelf. She was clad in a child's version of the Robes of Concealment. The tips of purple slippers could be seen beneath the hem of the robes. She was veiled. Her head, forehead and hair were covered, too, as is common. Ellen could see her dark brown eyes, wide, looking at her, over the white veil. Ellen and the others were in first position. A woman, similarly attired, with robes and veil, presumably her mother, hurried up to her and seized her by the hand, pulling her forcibly away. "Don't look at those terrible, nasty, dirty things in their collars and chains!" she scolded.

Targo came about the front of the shelf. "Appeal, appeal!" he said to Ellen.

Immediately then she began to utter the allure-call to the crowd, "Buy me, Master!"

"You are very inept," said Targo. "Have I not given you better instruction than that? Here are further considerations. Intermingle with, and enrich, your appeal, with additional phrases of enticement. For example, 'Buy me, Master! I am needful! I want a master! I need a master! I beg a collar! Please, oh, please, Masters, buy me!' and so on. Do you understand?"

"Yes, Master," said Ellen, shuddering.

"Too," he said, "do not neglect to shift position, and pose provocatively, and call attention to your body, and its charms, extremely explicitly, by both word and gesture. Do you understand?"

"Yes, Master," moaned Ellen.

How could anyone expect her to do such things?

But surely she did not wish to be again whipped!

But happily Barzak was now not about, and Targo, too, was no longer in evidence.

She was glad for the soothing lotion.

The day, however, was milder than the preceding day, and there was, now and then, a good deal of cloud cover.

She thought of her former master, Mirus.

She thought of her former life, and her teaching, the classrooms, and such. She thought of many of the men and women she had known on Earth, in particular colleagues and individuals met at various conferences and conventions having to do with gender issues, conventions which were not so scholarly, as she now understood, as political, organized to propagandize an ideology, supposedly scholarly meetings but ones in which political deviancy was not permitted, the participants each striving to outdo the others in proclaiming the prescribed orthodoxy. She wondered what some of the female participants might look like in slave silk and a collar, their small wrists confined tightly in slave bracelets, perhaps behind their back. She thought about the male feminists, the allegedly male participants in such travesties of conformist scholarship, wondering what might be their motivations. Did they really believe the absurdities of the antimenites? Were they interested, rather, in their own political futures, willing to be male camp followers, hoping to be permitted to share eventually in the loot of grants, appointments, and prestige? They had seemed so spineless, so ingratiating. Did they not know how they, such hypocrites, or pliant weaklings, were privately mocked and despised by the others? She did not think that that could be unknown to them. Would any of them, she wondered, know what to do with a woman at their slave ring? Or did they not want such power? If not, how could they be truly men? All men desired absolute power over women. Did they fear it? Would any of them, she wondered, know what to do with a whip and a woman? The thought crossed her mind of the superintendent in her apartment building. He, she thought, would have known what to do with me. And so she thought of the men and women that she had previously known, particularly those she had known professionally. How nicely and naturally she, with her affected severity of manner and her carefully chosen, mannish, businesslike tailored suits, had seemed to fit in with them! She was now chained on a shelf, a naked slave, for sale.

Targo returned after a time, perhaps having had his tea. The slaves would be fed, usually, before being brought to the shelf and after being taken from it.

Shortly after Targo had returned, a man, with a teen-aged boy with him, presumably his son, made his way through the crowd, toward the shelf.

"Do you have any barbarians?" he asked.

"I specialize in barbarians," said Targo, "but, alas, I have only one on hand at the moment, lovely Ellen. Position, Ellen."

"I do not wish to purchase one," said the man. "I was just telling my son about them, and how to recognize them. Do you mind if we look at this one?"

"Certainly not," said Targo.

The man and his son ascended to the surface of the shelf.

"This one is young," said Targo. "Yet I think that it is not impossible that one might find her of interest. Certainly she is well curved and pretty. Might she not make a lovely gift for your strapping lad?"

Ellen shrank back, but this did not seem to be much noticed by the father and his son, whose minds were on other things.

"We are not interested in buying her," said the father.

"Oh," said Targo. He turned away.

Ellen was pleased at this confirmation that they were not interested in buying her. To be sure, they could. Targo, she was sure, was ready to let her go at the drop of a copper tarsk. Then she would belong, literally belong, to the father, or to the boy, however it was decided, presumably to the boy.

She shuddered.

She certainly did not want to belong to a teen-aged boy. Her practical age now, in terms of biology, physiology and such, was, say, eighteen, and that might have been the actual chronological age of the lad. Yet what an incredible difference there is in maturity and sexual readiness between an eighteen-year-old girl, already beautifully developed and perfectly suitable for the collar and slave bracelets, and an eighteen-year-old boy!

"Speak, in Gorean," said the father to Ellen. "Say anything, just talk."

So Ellen began to speak, for a little time. "I do not know what I am supposed to say," she said. "You wish me to speak, and so I will do so. It is my conjecture you wish to ascertain something in my speech. It is doubtless different from yours. Is it acceptable, Masters, that I speak as I am speaking?" And thus, in this way, she continued, until the father indicated, by putting his finger up, in a cautionary manner, that she should desist.

"Do you hear the accent?" the father asked his son. "You see it is different?"

"There are many different accents, father," said the boy, "even in Gorean."

"And there are many barbarian accents," said his father. "And this is one of them. It is not Gorean. It is not like the speech of the hated Cosians, for example."

"Is accent so important, father?"

"No," said his father, "particularly as some of these barbarians eventually become so fluent in Gorean, so skilled, that you could not detect, from their speech alone, that they were not native to our world."

Ellen hoped that she could become such a barbarian.

She felt her upper left arm seized.

"Here," said the father. "Such small scars tend to mark barbarians."

That, of course, was a vaccination mark.

"Is it a brand?" asked the boy.

"I suppose so," said the father. "Perhaps it is a temporary brand, put on them for shipping purposes, before they have the kef, the dina, a city mark, or such, put on them."

"This one has the kef," said the boy, looking.

"Most do," said the father.

"I think that it is likely that it is one of their own world's slave brands," said the boy, "that they were slaves on their own world, and then they were purchased and shipped here."

"I do not know," said the father. "Perhaps."

"Open your mouth," said the father. "Widely."

"See," said the father, "those tiny bits of metal in the teeth. Not all barbarians have them, but many do."

"What is their purpose?" asked the boy.

"I do not know," said the father. "Perhaps, it, too, is a slave marking device. Perhaps it serves for purposes of identification."

"I think," said Targo, who had lingered about, and had now wandered back, hopefully, "that it is rather connected with a puberty ceremony, a primitive rite, like the facial scarring of the Wagon Peoples."

"That is interesting," said the father. "Perhaps it is both."

"Perhaps," granted Targo, generously, abandoning logic as socially inexpedient. After all, why should he risk alienating a possible customer.

It was interesting, thought Ellen, that no one thought of asking her about these matters.

To be sure, many Goreans do not believe that slaves are to be trusted. They think that female slaves, in particular, are sly, petty creatures against whose ingratiating, clever wiles the master must be on guard. Accordingly female slaves are to be supervised with care and subjected to the most rigorous discipline. In any event, the penalties for a slave's lying are severe.

"Lastly," said the father, "they are ignorant. What is the month following the month of Hesius?"

"I do not know, Master," said Ellen. She had not been familiarized with the Gorean calendar. To be sure, chronologies, and such, can differ from city to city. The Merchants, interestingly, keep their own calendar, for purposes of contracts, delivery dates, letters of credit, and such. Many cities in the northern hemisphere use the chronology of Ar, along with their own. I understand that cities in the southern hemisphere may similarly supplement their own chronologies, but with the calendar of Turia, which, as I understand it, is the largest city in the southern hemisphere.

"Anyone would know that," said the boy.

"Well, this little she-urt does not," said his father. "But the point is that it is almost certain that there will be simple things that we will know that one of these barbarians will not. Thus, interrogation can also be used as a means for identifying the barbarian."

"I see," said the boy. "Thank you, father."

"So do not let yourself be fooled in the market," said the father. "Do not let an unscrupulous merchant palm a barbarian off on you."

"No, father."

"That would be unthinkable," said Targo, righteously.

"Thank you for the use of your slave, sir," said the father.

"Not at all," said Targo. "And perhaps now, now that you are more familiar with her, you would like to think about buying this lovely bauble for your son. She is a pretty bit of fluff. Perhaps she would make a nice starter slave for him. She is a bargain. I can give you an excellent buy on her."

"She is a barbarian," said the father.

He and his son then descended from the shelf and went into the crowd.

This little business was not Ellen's fault, or she supposed not, but Targo seemed miffed by it.

"You should have worked on both the father and the son," said Targo. "It is not unusual for fathers to buy gifts for their sons which they themselves like, or think they would like. Thus, you should have lured the father, subtly, of course, as in theory he is interested in you for his son. Secondly, you should have squirmed a little for the lad, you know, pathetically, needfully, pleadingly, putting yourself before him, proffering your indisputable slave delights hopefully, when the father is looking away. That lad must be eighteen or nineteen years old, surely old enough to find your curves of interest, surely old enough to respond to them, suitably presented. Surely he was old enough for you, a pretty little slave, to stir up his blood."

"Forgive me, Master," said Ellen.

"You spend more time asking for forgiveness than you do in obeying," said Targo.

"Forgive me, Master," said Ellen. She then wished she had not said that. Surely a simple 'Yes, Master' would have been more judicious.

"Barzak!" called Targo.

"Do not have me whipped, Master!" she begged.

"You will spend the afternoon on your back," he said, "chained between rings."

"Master!" she pleaded.

"Barzak!" called Targo, again.

"Oh!" cried Ellen, moments later, as her ankles were seized by an impatient Barzak, jerked about and held closely together at her own ring. An ankle ring was snapped about her left ankle, beneath the shackle there, and a second ring, on a short chain, some six inches in length, was slipped through the holding ring and snapped shut about her right ankle. She, sitting on the cement, regarded her small ankles, chained to the ring, with dismay. Then Barzak took her arms and forced them up and back, over her head and then pulled her down to her back. Her wrists then, held together with one hand by Barzak, were pulled to the ring which had been to her left as she had faced the front of the platform, the same ring to which the new girl, Jill, was chained by the ankle. While Barzak held her small wrists together with his left hand, he snapped a wrist ring about her right wrist with his right hand. She was then, a moment later, the second wrist ring passed through the holding ring and closed about her left wrist, secured to the holding ring. She was then supine between two holding rings. She could twist to her stomach, or side, but the tensions being as they were, it was most comfortable, and most natural, for her to remain on her back.

Barzak, beside her, on his knees, looked down upon her with irritation. "You are a bother," he said, and, without much thinking about it, touched her.

She cried out with disbelief.

He looked down at her.

"No!" she cried. "No!"

He then again, this time more curiously, touched her.

There was a rattle of chain.

She tried to pull back. She regarded him with horror. "Please do not, Master!" she cried.

"Oh!" she cried.

"You are a bother, aren't you?" he asked.

"Yes, Master!" she said. "Forgive me, Master! No, please, do not, Master! Oh! Oh!"

"But you do not have to be a bother, do you?" he asked.

"No, Master!"

"And you will make an effort to be less of a bother, won't you?" he asked.

"Yes, Master! Yes, Master! Please, do not, Master! No! No! Do not, please, Master! Oh! Oh!"

"You may have possibilities," he mused.

He then rose to his feet, and left the shelf.

She looked after him, in misery and dismay.

Her knees could be drawn up a little and her elbows could be bent. Her predicament was not cruel, but Barzak's arrangement, doubtless by intent, did not allow her a great deal of latitude. As in most chaining arrangements there is a point to the way in which they are done. In the present arrangement, as she would later come to understand, later in the afternoon, she was allowed enough latitude to squirm and writhe, but not enough to defend herself.

In this arrangement, on her back, on the shelf, above the ground level, the slave's figure is beautifully displayed.

As she lay supine, chained, on the shelf, her knees up a little, her arms back and over her head, almost as though alone, she fought with her own thoughts and feelings. What had happened? What were the strange feelings she had experienced? She was disturbed. Were they slave feelings she had felt? Is that what they could have been? Surely not! But what else could they have been? She certainly did not love Barzak. Could any man, the brutal, massive, callous monsters, have done that to her? What had become of her, and her pride and dignity? Surely she could not become one of those worthless women who could not help themselves, who were sexually needful. It was one thing to kneel at the feet of one whom one loved, and quite another to kneel before any man, moaning in need and begging his caresses. Surely she could not be reduced to that, not she! She recalled some of the girls in the house, in various kennels, in cages, in the bins, whimpering and moaning. How they had cried out in gratitude and joy when a guard had taken pity on them. How terrible to be such, she thought, how terrible to be so sexually alive, to be so vital, to be so needful.

She looked up and saw Targo standing over her.

"Master?" she asked.

"Barzak informs me that you may not be the cold little thing we thought," said Targo.

"I do not understand, Master."

"—that you may be awakening," he said.

"I do not understand, Master."

"Perhaps our little ice ball is going to melt," he said.

"Master?"

She felt the side of his sandal against her left side, at the waist, moving there, along her waist, not to kick her, but to caress her in a way, to let her feel a man's foot, to let her feel herself at his feet.

"Master?" she said.

And then he put his foot gently on her body, not pressing with any weight, and moved it a bit, to let her have the feeling of a man's foot on her body, to let her feel herself, a female, beneath the foot of a man.

She tried to withdraw in her chains but could not, of course, do so. "Master," she said, "please, no! Oh! Oh!"

"You are not only going to awaken," he said. "You are going to be a juicy, tasty, steaming little pudding."

"No, Master!" she said.

"You are going to be, in time, as helpless as a she-urt in heat," he said.

"No, Master!" she said. "No, no, Master!" But he had then turned about and left the surface of the shelf. "No, no, no," she wept to herself. She struggled with the chains that bound her. "No, no, no," she wept.

Several times, later in the afternoon, men came to the surface of the shelf to inspect one or another of the items of merchandise there displayed. Zara was sold, but only Zara on that second day. Too, on the second day, no new jewels were added to the slaver's necklace, as had been Jill that morning. Twice men had inspected and, at Targo's invitation, handled Ellen. She, in keeping with her lingering Earth values, and fearing to become merely another slave girl on the world of Gor, had attempted to remain as cold and inert as possible, trying to distract herself with irrelevant thoughts, trying not to feel, trying not to respond. She managed well enough with the first fellow.

"So what is wrong with you?" had asked Targo when the prospective buyer had left the shelf.

"Nothing, Master," Ellen had assured him. "Please do not have me whipped, Master!" she said.

When Targo left, she smiled to herself.

But still, even as she was congratulating herself on her success in achieving a pretense of inertness, on giving no outward sign of responsiveness, it was hard to forget the feel of the fellow's strong hands on her small, soft body. She feared that if something had been a little different, if he had touched her a little differently or a little longer, or had looked at her in a certain way, or if he had taken her head in his hands and literally forced her to look directly into his eyes, seeing him as a male and master, she might have suddenly, willingly or unwillingly, betrayed a muchly feared aspect of herself, that of an eager, vulnerable, begging, aroused slave girl. Surely she must hide this self from the world! But it was hard to forget his hands. It was fortunate, she thought, that things had not been slightly different.

She cursed herself for being so different from a man.

Not long after, a possible buyer had examined Jill. He had knelt her in first position, except for having her hands clasped behind the back of her neck. Whereas Ellen could see little of what went on, she could certainly hear the movements of Jill's ankle chain and her sudden, almost inadvertent gasps. Then she was clearly squirming on her knees.

Ellen moved in her own chains.

The possible buyer had then examined Lydia, whom he treated in much the same manner as he had Jill. He had her, too, squirming. Then, after a few minutes, he had left the shelf.

Ellen recalled that Jill had not wished to be touched that morning by a barbarian, in the matter of applying the soothing lotions to protect the slaves from the sun on the shelf.

"You are certainly a slave," said Ellen to Jill.

"After this," snapped Jill, "when I am being examined, you are not to lift your little loins to my buyer."

"What!" cried Ellen, startled.

"You heard me, barbarian she-urt," said Jill.

"I never did that!" exclaimed Ellen. "That is absurd! I would never do that! Never! Never!"

"We saw you," said Cichek.

"Yes," said Emris.

"It's true," said Lydia.

"No!" said Ellen.

"Perhaps you are not aware of what your own body is doing," said Lydia.

"No!" said Ellen. "Aii!" cried Ellen, for Jill, who was chained to the same ring to which Ellen's wrists were chained had seized her by the hair, with two hands, tightly, cruelly.

"I'm going to pull every hair out of your head," hissed Jill. "We will see then how pretty you are to the buyers!"

"Please, no, Mistress!" cried Ellen.

"Do not hurt her," called Lydia. "The master will not be pleased."

"Aii!" cried Ellen.

"Beg for mercy!" called Lydia.

"Mercy, Mistress!" cried Ellen.

"Ah!" said Jill. "Does Ellen, a meaningless barbarian slave, beg a Gorean woman for mercy."

"Yes, yes!" wept Ellen.

"Do so," said Jill.

"I beg for mercy, Mistress!"

"Properly," said Jill.

"Aii!" cried Ellen. "Please stop!"

"Properly," said Jill.

"I, Ellen, a meaningless barbarian slave, beg a Gorean woman for mercy! Please, Mistress! Please do not hurt me! Aii! Please, Mistress! Ellen begs Mistress! Aii! Ellen, a meaningless barbarian slave, begs Mistress, a Gorean woman, for mercy! Aii! Aii! Please stop, please stop! Please, mercy, Mistress! Mistress! Mistress!"

Jill then, with one last twist, thrusting Ellen's head to the side, released her hair.

Ellen tried to move further away but, chained as she was, she remained perforce within the ambit of Jill's wrath.

Ellen wept, helplessly, fiercely.

Jill turned away, angrily.

The other slaves on the shelf ceased then to attend to Jill and Ellen. Emris called out "Buy me, Master!" to a handsome fellow in the crowd but he continued on his way.

The second possible buyer who seemed to show some interest in Ellen, the first being he with whom she had with some success kept herself seemingly inert, did not come to the shelf until late in the afternoon.

An incident occurred something like an Ahn before that, and, say, some twenty Ehn, or so, after her unpleasant encounter with Jill at the ring.

We mention it for its intrinsic interest, but also because it, in its way, assisted an Earth woman in attaining a somewhat richer understanding of the world on which she now found herself slave.

Ellen was lying on the shelf, her eyes closed against the sun, when suddenly, almost at her side, there was a loud, swift, scuffling noise and there was suddenly something large, extremely large, and alive, at least fifteen or twenty feet long, and weighing easily several hundred pounds, on the shelf beside her, something which had just arrived, scratching and twisting about, on its surface. It was almost over her. At the same time there was a powerful, feral odor, and she felt the heat of living breath on her body. She opened her eyes and screamed, and Jill, too, who was very close, screamed, and scrambled back to the length of her ankle chain. Ellen, as she was chained, had no such option at her disposal. She heard, not really understanding them for a moment or two, so wild and frightened were her own responses, similar sounds of fear and dismay from Lydia, Cichek and Emris.

"Quiet, quiet, quiet!" called Targo, trying to settle his stock. "Greetings, Torquatus," he called.

The beast, which was long, powerful, agile, muscular and sinuous, was darkly, heavily furred, brownish with black bars. Its curious serpentine head, viperlike, moved back and forth. Its tongue, licking outward, then withdrawing, was reddish. It was fanged, these, in two rows, being white and sharp. Its tail twitched, lashing back and forth, though not seemingly in anger, rather in excitement. Its entire body seemed curious, quick, vibrantly alive. It had a heavy leather collar. It thrust its large snout against Ellen's body, and under her arms, and between her thighs, and she screamed and twisted, and Targo told her to be quiet, and it licked her body, as though tasting her, and then drew its tongue back into the mouth, and then it moved about on the shelf, making its way over and about Ellen, sensing each of the occupants on the shelf, who were almost frozen with fear.

"Greetings, Targo," said a bearded fellow in a rough tunic. "Back, Varcus," he called. "Back, boy. Down, boy. Heel, boy."

The gigantic, sinuous creature twisted about on the shelf and, its forelegs first, and then its two pairs of hind legs, following, returned to the ground, in front of the shelf. Turning to the side, twisting in the chains, trembling, Ellen could not see it any longer. She surmised it must be in the vicinity of the bearded fellow.

The beast's fur had been glossy and oily, and some of this oil had adhered to her body, and, for a moment, she had felt her right thigh in a mighty, almost prehensile grip, within the menacing softness of which she had sensed curved, knifelike hardnesses, like short, sheathed scimitars. She could still feel the roughnesses from the beast's swift, inquisitive investigations of her body, the forcible thrustings of its snout about her, its coldness, the rapid, exploratory movements of the hot, moist, rasplike tongue on her breasts and belly.

"Have you business for me today, dear Targo?" inquired the fellow.

"Alas, no!" cried Targo. "These little beauties, which you might examine, if you are interested, are transient stock, and accordingly it would hardly pay for me to avail myself in these instances of your invaluable services, which it is my invariable practice, at least upon occasion, to commend to all enthusiastically. Indeed, I hope to dispose of these lovely creatures by evening. Note, too, that I am not without precautions. Their little necks are well weighted and such collars would certainly be immediately noted anywhere. Too, they are stripped, which does not encourage straying. Too, they are not likely to stray, as they are well shackled, in accord with sound merchant practice. Too, of course, they are all highly intelligent and know, with the possible exception of the lovely little thing chained supine before you, whom I call to your attention, who may be uninformed, that they are truly in their collars, so to speak, that for such as they, lovely things all, there is no escape. They know that the world, if nothing else, will see to that. Accordingly, at the moment, I do not think it would be economically justifiable for me, a poor man, one on the brink of destitution, to avail myself of your services."

"Perhaps if you have a more expensive girl, sometime," suggested the fellow in the rough tunic.

"All of my girls are expensive," said Targo. "It is only that I, poor business man that I am, generous creature and unwary humanitarian, let them slip from my grasp at bargain prices."

The fellow in the rough tunic, Torquatus, we may suppose, lifted his hand to Targo in salute, and left the vicinity of the shelf.

He was accompanied doubtless by Varcus, the beast which had leaped to the surface of the shelf. To be sure, it was not easy for Ellen to ascertain this, given her encumbrances.

"What has occurred?" asked Ellen. "Please. I do not understand."

"Have you never seen a sleen before?" inquired Jill, who had, it seemed, now regained her composure.

"Please, Mistress," said Ellen. "I do not understand things, the beast, the man, what was said!"

But Jill turned away.

"It is a sleen," said Lydia. "Beware of them. They are extremely dangerous. The man is doubtless a huntsman, or a renter of sleen, used for tracking. There are many varieties of training for such beasts. A common form of training is to associate a name with a scent, and then, if one wishes, to associate the name with one or more commands. In your case, if one wanted the sleen to take a scent print of you, your name, or some code name, would be associated with your scent. That name, or code name, could then be used in conjunction with another command to set the beast on your trail. They are wondrous trackers and can follow a scent several days old, even through a city. The common commands are the "kill" command and the "herd" command. Given the "kill" command the sleen pursues and kills, and eats, the quarry. Given the "herd" command, the beasts drive the quarry to a predetermined destination."

"What if one resists being driven?" asked Ellen.

"Then the sleen reverts to the "kill" command," said Lydia. "The quarry, if recalcitrant, is killed and eaten, almost at the first sign of resistance."

Ellen trembled.

"Sometimes a slave is driven for miles," said Lydia, "until, exhausted, her feet bleeding, she finds herself before a cage, into which she must hurry, crawling, closing the gate, which locks, behind her."

Ellen lay back in the chains, and closed her eyes, in misery.

She now understood her slavery in a new dimension.

"To be sure," said Lydia, "sometimes the sleen is leashed, and men accompany it. In this way they come upon the quarry while the sleen is still within their control. At this point a "desist" command may be uttered, which command is known, of course, only to the beast and the huntsman, or huntsmen, at which point the sleen will, or should, abandon the hunt."

"'Should'?" asked Ellen.

"Sleen are temperamental," said Lydia. "One cannot always count upon them. They may, for example, have had a long, frustrating hunt and desire an elating, compensatory victory of blood and feasting; or they may just be ravenously hungry. Too, much depends on the beast and its relationship to its master. Some sleen are incredibly loyal to the master, and will die for them. Others seem to regard the master as little more than a partner in the hunt, almost as though he were another sleen, albeit an unusual one, with whom a prize might be contested."

"What does the master do if the sleen refuses to abandon the hunt?" asked Ellen.

"The safest thing to do is unleash the animal," said Lydia. "One might try to kill it, of course. A sword, or ax, blow at the spinal column, just below the back of the head, is the easiest way to do this, given that one has the leash in hand."

"That would be dangerous, would it not?" asked Ellen.

"Very dangerous," said Lydia. "A wounded sleen is not a pleasant thing to have in one's vicinity. There are stories of sleen whose head is half severed from the body finishing the hunt, and dying across the body of the quarry, snarling defiance at the master. Too, sometimes the master is first killed by the beast, who has doubtless seen him as a surprising and unwelcome impediment to its hunt. Such sleen then normally revert to the wild. They tend to be extremely dangerous, possibly because they are familiar with the ways of men and have tasted human flesh."

"And must they then be hunted with other sleen?" asked Ellen.

"No sleen will hunt another sleen," said Lydia.

"She is stupid," said Jill.

"Yes," said Cichek.

"But then," said Ellen, "would it not be advisable, if possible, to wrap oneself in the pelt of a sleen, or such, to elude them?"

"See," said Lydia, "she is only ignorant, not stupid."

"She is still stupid," said Jill. "Anyone knows that that mixture of scents disturbs and infuriates sleen and hastens their hunt."

"She would have no way of knowing that," said Lydia.

"How then," asked Ellen, somewhat emboldened, "are such sleen hunted?"

"Sometimes by great encirclements," said Lydia, "but as the sleen is commonly nocturnal in the wild and can burrow quickly that is seldom effective. The usual method is to stake out a verr or slave girl, at night, and then, when the sleen comes to feed, concealed hunters attempt to kill it, usually with the quarrels of crossbows, sometimes with long arrows, the arrows of the great bow, the peasant bow. If the hunters are successful, they regard themselves as fortunate."

"The hunters are fortunate!" said Ellen.

"Well, the verr or slave girl, as well, of course," said Lydia.

"Do not fear," said Emris. "You give every sign of one who is going to wriggle well, and so you would not be likely to be staked out unless you displeased your master."

"Let that be an additional motivation to squirm well in the furs, barbarian," said Cichek.

"Please do not use such words of me," said Ellen.

"'Barbarian'?" said Cichek.

"No," said Ellen, "vulgar words like 'squirming well'."

Cichek laughed.

"Do you not think a master, in a bit of time, can make you kick and squeal, and gasp, and jump, and moan, and beg?"

"Certainly not!" said Ellen.

"Why not?"

"I am not that sort of woman," said Ellen.

"Your curves suggest you are."

"I will not be so reduced, so humiliated!"

"Remember that in your chains."

"I am different from you!" wept Ellen.

"Yes, who knows, you might be hotter and more helpless in your collar."

"Even more a slave!"

"No, no!" said Ellen.

"We have seen you on the shelf."

"Are you unaware of how your body has moved?"

"I am ladylike, cold, inert!"

"The lash will take that from you."

"No, no, no!"

"Then you will be disposed of."

"'Disposed of'?"

"Certainly, what good is a cold slave?"

"See how she is frightened."

"No!"

"See the fear in the little slut!"

"Surely you have some sense of what men can do to you, and what you will become."

"I see she has."

"No!" cried Ellen.

"You will probably bring a decent price off a slave block."

"No, no, no!" whimpered Ellen.

"Within a month," speculated Emris, "you will wriggle and squirm like a born slave."

"No!" cried Ellen.

But she wondered if she were not, in some sense, a born slave. Indeed, often, in her most secret thoughts, she had understood herself as exactly that, a born slave. Sometimes this insight frightened her, at other times it humbled, and elated and exhilarated, her. How else could one explain her desire for a master?

"We are women," said Lydia. "We are all born slaves."

The girls were then silent, and it was late in the afternoon.

In the heat, after a few Ehn, Ellen fell asleep in her chains. She wished, just before falling asleep, pulling a little at her bonds, that Targo had given her a blanket, or a mat. The cement was so hard.

She awakened once, or seemed to awaken, filled with the thought of her bondage, that on this world she, now again young and beautiful, was a slave. Her youth and beauty had been returned to her. Surely that must be a cause for rejoicing. But why, she asked herself, had that been done? What was the motive of the masters, and their allies, the physicians, with their serums? Was this an act of selfless benevolence? Scarcely. She thought of many other women, too, whose youth and beauty had been returned to them. She had suspected that there were many in the house. Surely this was a joyful boon. But for what purpose had it been granted to them? Surely not meaninglessly, or gratuitously. Surely not with no interest, value or recompense in mind. Obviously, she thought, because it makes us more appealing as female slaves. It will improve our value in the markets. It has been done for their purposes, not ours. This has been done to us because this is the way men want us. So then, she wondered, would it be better to grow old, and flat, and withered, and tired, and die on Earth, free in some sense, or was it better to be young and beautiful, and healthy and eager, and richly and vitally alive, even though one might be put in a collar and have a mark burned into one's thigh? Let each, she thought, find their own answer to such a question. Although Ellen at that time had profound ambivalences concerning her condition, which was bond, she did not regret the return of her youth and beauty, or that she had been brought to Gor. Too, as she had always considered herself, on one level or another, as she now recognized, the appropriate and natural slave of men, she was not resistant to the fact that her longed-for destiny had been, even though it were by the decision of others, and without her consent, imposed upon her. Better the freedom of slavery on Gor, she thought, than the slavery of freedom on Earth.

To be sure, these thoughts were like mists about her, and she was weary, and half asleep.

That she was chained as she was, and that she now understood something of the nature of sleen, and their possible roles in Gorean society, had helped her to further appreciate and understand her slavery. It had considerably deepened it. She understood better now than she had, how helpless, how utterly vulnerable she was. She better understood now that she and her sort truly belonged to men, that she and her sort were their property, the property of the masters. She understood herself now better than she ever had before, that she was completely in the control of men, totally in their power. It was not she who was dominant, it was they. They were dominant over her, completely and perfectly dominant over her.

This stirred her, and excited her profoundly.

She moaned softly, trying to understand sudden, warm, disturbing feelings welling up within her. Unfamiliar behavioral impulses began to overwhelm her. She knew, of course, that she must kneel before men and perform obeisance, and such things, but now, more than ever before, such things seemed not only fitting to her, but called for. Far beyond this she now felt a strong desire, literally a strong desire, to perform slave behaviors before males. She now wanted to kneel before them and be before them as their slave. In no way could she be more feminine, more female, more herself. She was a true female, fully, vulnerably and deeply. She wanted to submit, she wanted to serve, she wanted to please.

Then she was again frightened, and almost awakened, fully.

Then, again, in the heat, in her chains, on the hardness of the shelf, she fell asleep.

She awakened suddenly, to a hand placed firmly, forcibly, over her mouth, preventing her from crying out.

Doubtless the man who had placed his hand over her mouth did so because she was asleep and he did not want her to awaken with a cry of fear. In this sense he was doubtless trying to be kind to her.

Gorean warriors, tarnsmen and such, are not infrequently concerned with the abduction of women from enemy cities. It is not unusual, either in the history of Gor or of Earth, to have the women of the enemy serving one as one's slaves. I do not doubt that there is something of a sporting cast to this sort of thing, as well, not that the warriors and such mind being served by lovely slaves for whom they do not have to pay. One is reminded of rivalries among various tribes of American Indians, who seemed to enjoy nothing more than running off with one another's horses whenever possible.

In the abduction of a woman one has the wadding ready. When she awakes and naturally, reflexively, opens her mouth to scream the wadding is thrust into the oral orifice. This stifles the scream. The binding is then applied, being forced back, between the teeth, and fastened, usually once around the neck and tied in front, which is easier, this securing the wadding in place. She may then be turned to her stomach and, her hands pulled behind her and her ankles crossed, bound hand and foot.

On the other hand, although the fellow's intention was doubtless sensible, and harmless enough, and even benign, the effect of his action on the slave in question was profound. She looked up at him, over his hand, her eyes wild with fear. "Steady, kajira," said he, gently. The effect of a gag on a woman is interesting. It is perhaps even more profound than that of a blindfold. A woman's tongue, like her beauty, is, I suppose, at least from the point of view of a man, one of her most delightful, perilous weapons. And it is certainly true that when he deprives her of this weapon, by gag-silencing her, that she is commonly reduced to tearful, frustrated consternation. She is deprived of what may be her most successful weapon, both of offense and defense. In any event, gagging a woman commonly alarms her and induces in her feelings of utter vulnerability and helplessness. Accordingly, the gag, particularly if she is a free woman, often makes her more timid, more tentative, more docile and compliant. An ideal combination, of course, at least for certain purposes, is to combine the gag with the blindfold.

"I am not going to hurt you, little kajira," he said, and removed his hand from Ellen's mouth.

She looked up at him. She could still feel the firm, heavy pressure about her mouth where he had placed his hand.

He was kneeling beside her.

Targo was standing nearby.

"I am prepared to let her go for as little as two silver tarsks," said Targo.

"She is a barbarian," said the man.

"One silver tarsk," said Targo.

"She is pretty," said the man.

"Did I missay myself earlier?" inquired Targo. "I meant to say three silver tarsks."

"She is a barbarian," said the man.

"Many could not tell her from a native Gorean girl," said Targo.

"Then they have not looked at her very closely," said the man.

"I might let her go, if pressed," said Targo, "for a mere two silver tarsks."

"She is pretty," said the man.

"She speaks a fluent, beautiful Gorean," said Targo.

Ellen wished he had not said that, for it was certainly not true. On the other hand, her progress in the language, given her time on Gor, had been, according to her tutors at the house, more than satisfactory. Later, in the opinion of at least some native speakers, she would indeed speak a fluent, beautiful Gorean, but there was no question of that at the time.

"She is very young," said the man.

"But in spite of her youth delightfully curved, is she not?" asked Targo.

"Yes," said the man.

"Consider her curves," said Targo. "Are they not slave curves?"

"Yes," said the man. "They are clearly slave curves."

Ellen moved a bit, chained between the rings, on her back, her ankles chained so closely to the ring on the left, as one would face the shelf, her hands chained back, over her head, so closely to the ring on the right, as one would face the shelf. She had never hitherto thought of her body in this fashion, as one exhibiting slave curves. Could that be? Could she be so excitingly attractive as that? Was she really so delicious as a female that she was worth, say, being put upon a block and being bid upon by eager men? One of the girls, she recalled, had said she would probably bring a decent price off a slave block. Could that be true, that men would bid for her, that they would vie to buy her? Were her curves truly such, so exquisite, so lovely, so delicious, that they were truly slave curves? Could it be? She was shocked, pleased and frightened. It seemed that at least part of the secret of her hormonal richness was revealed in the delights of her supine, chained figure. In her figure were apparently manifested, and clearly, the curves of the female slave. And other concomitants, intellectual, emotional, and psychological, would be an exquisite femininity, and a desire to submit and yield, to yield all. Then Ellen tried to lie very still, for she feared, in her tiny, inadvertent, shocked, almost protestive movement, that she had done little more than more prominently to suggest, or even display, the latitudes and geodesics of a female slave, little more than manifest even more clearly the slave curves of which they had spoken. It was not her fault that she had slave curves. It was in her nature. She could not help what she was! To be sure, she resolved to attempt to conceal what she was. None must suspect that she was a slave! She must attempt to deny this even to herself, as she had desperately for years on Earth. Surely it must be wrong to be what one most truthfully, and deeply, was! Surely one must guide one's behavior, even one's thoughts, in so far as it was possible, in order to comply with cultural imperatives, with ideological demands, with external wishes and desires. But is that not a true slavery, a true holding of oneself in bondage, a hypocritical slavery, a lying, worthless slavery, a slavery less worthy than confessing to oneself one's own self, and allowing it to speak openly? How much inner conflict might be thus avoided! But she lay very still, torn in her thought, afflicted by inner torments. He must not touch her! She knew she was a slave.

"She is young, but seems of interest," said the man. Ellen turned her head to the side in misery. He had doubtless noted that small movement. She heard Cichek laugh. Doubtless Cichek, and the others, thought that she had moved like that on purpose, that she was brazenly, shamefully, trying to interest a buyer in the merchandise which was she herself. But that was not true! That was not true!

She could not be like that!

"I am prepared to let her go, against my better judgment," said Targo, "for only two silver tarsks."

"Is she responsive?" asked the man.

"Try her," said Targo.

"No, please!" cried Ellen.

The man, kneeling beside her, looked at her, puzzled.

Targo frowned.

Ellen felt how soft her body was, how vulnerable. It was such a different body, so different from that of a man, and it was displayed before him, supine, without a thread upon it, chained helplessly. She moved her wrists and ankles. How closely, how perfectly, they were held!

"Do not touch me," she begged.

She jerked against her bonds, twisting in them.

Cichek and Emris laughed.

Angry tears sprang to Ellen's eyes.

She looked up at the man beside her and shook her head, negatively, piteously.

The man looked at Targo, puzzled.

"Cuff her," suggested Targo. "It will calm her down."

"I do not think she is worth much," said the man.

"A strong hand and a quick whip and she will writhe at a snapping of the fingers," said Targo.

Ellen gasped, for the man's hand was on her left thigh, not tightly but innocently, thoughtlessly, possessively.

"Touch her," said Targo. "Try her fully, if you wish. We can arrange her chaining in any way that pleases you. Perhaps you would like her on her side, or on her belly. We can position her in any way you like."

"No," said the man. "She is fine, as she is."

Ellen felt his hand lift from her thigh.

"No!" she said.

"Surely you have been tested before, kajira," he said.

"No, please," begged Ellen. "You can see that I am chained! You can see that I am helpless! You can see that I cannot protect myself, or defend myself! You see that I cannot, in any way, prevent you from doing whatever you wish with me. Accordingly, you must show me solicitation, and mercy. You must be sensitive to my predicament! Accordingly, you must respect me! Accordingly, you must in no way compromise my dignity!"

"Is she a slave?" asked the man.

"Yes," said Targo, angrily.

The man replaced his hand on her thigh. Its presence there made Ellen feel tense and uncomfortable, and vulnerable, and slave.

"She has strange views," said the man.

"She is a barbarian," said Targo.

The fellow looked down at Ellen, puzzled. "When a man has a slave exactly where he wants her, and as he wants her," he asked, "why then should he not do what he wants with her, and as he wants, fully, and in all respects?"

Ellen looked up, in consternation.

"She is a slave," the man reminded her.

"You must never do anything to a woman without her consent," stammered Ellen.

"But thousands of things are done everyday, even to free women, and free men, without their consent," he said.

"Everyone must be free," said Ellen.

"From what premises do you derive that conclusion?" asked the man.

"It is self-evident," said Ellen.

"Quite the contrary," said the man. "It is self-evident that some should be free and some slaves. It is self-evident that it is appropriate for some to be free, and appropriate for others to be slaves. It depends on the person.

You, it is clear, should be a slave. You are a natural slave, and are thus, appropriately, to be embonded. It is absurd that a natural slave should be permitted freedom."

"Freedom is trivial and meaningless," said Targo, "when all have freedom. It takes on the fullness of its meaning only in contrast to slavery."

"All persons must be free," said Ellen.

"That is obviously false," said the man, "but, in any event, in your case, it is irrelevant, for the slave is not a person. The slave is a property, an animal, a chattel. For example, you are not a person, but a slave, and are thus a property, an animal, a chattel. Too, men should be free, and women slaves, as that is the meaning and fulfillment of their minds and bodies."

"Give me my freedom of will!" said Ellen.

"You may will as you please," said the man, "but you must obey in all things, absolutely, and with promptitude and perfection."

"Give me my freedom!" said Ellen.

The man smiled. Then he looked at Targo. "Does she obey in all things, absolutely, and with promptitude and perfection?" he asked.

"Of course," said Targo.

"Give me my freedom!" wept Ellen.

"That would be wrong," said the man.

"What?" she said.

"The free should not be slave, and the slave should not be free," he said.

"I do not understand," she said.

"Just as it is wrong for the properly free to be enslaved," he said, "so, too, it is wrong for the properly enslaved to be free."

"Master?"

"Yes," he said.

She regarded him, perhaps with something like awe. Chained before him, looking up at him, she felt stunned.

"You belong in a collar," he said. "That is clear. It is easily seen. You are such as are fittingly embonded."

"You must let me do as I wish!" said Ellen.

"Nonsense," said the man.

"Nothing must be done to me without my consent!"

"You are a slave. Your consent is meaningless."

"Surely not!" wept Ellen.

"Surely so," he said. "The defining will, and final force, is that of the master, in all things, at all times."

"How can I be happy, if I am not free?" asked Ellen.

"Your happiness is unimportant," said the man.

Ellen sobbed.

"But perhaps you can best answer that question, really, yourself, in the depths of your own heart."

Ellen regarded him, tears in her eyes.

"In any event," he said, "there is no necessary connection between freedom and happiness, and often an inverse correlation. Often the freest are the most lost, confused and miserable. That is commonplace. Happiness is not a function of freedom, but of doing what you want to do, really, and being as you want to be, really. Happiness is often found in places which might, I take it, surprise you. It is important, of course, too, to find yourself in a society where what you are, and what you want to be, truly, is understood, accepted and relished. Female slaves, for example, are important in our society, an important part of it, and they make it much more satisfying, innocent, honest, profound, natural and beautiful than it would otherwise be."

He lifted his hand a little, his fingers still lightly in contact with her thigh.

"Don't!" said Ellen.

"I do not understand," he said.

"Surely you are a man of honor!" she cried.

"I think so, I hope so," he said.

"As a man of honor," said Ellen, desperately, "you will not touch me without my permission."

"I do not understand," he said.

"—particularly as I lie helplessly before you, naked and chained, totally at your mercy, incapable of the least resistance!"

"What has honor to do with this?" he asked, puzzled. "We are not fellow citizens. We do not share a Home Stone. Too, even if we had been fellow citizens, you are now no longer a citizen, but a slave. Too, even if we had once shared a Home Stone, you are now without the rights of the Home Stone, having been enslaved. In addition, you are merely a female."

"It seems then," said Ellen, bitterly, "that I cannot expect gentlemanliness of you."

"What is "gentlemanliness"?" he asked, as Ellen, in her consternation, had used the English expression.

"There is no exact word for it in Gorean," said Ellen.

"I think I have heard the word," said the man. "It seems to be a word for a male who subscribes to, and conforms to, codes of behavior requiring, among other things, substituting convention for nature, propriety for power, self-conquest for self-liberation, restraint for command, inaction and conformity for dominance and mastery, and, in short, a word for one who denies his biological birthright, his powers, pleasures and delights, for one who forgoes, or pretends to forgo, his manhood in order to do, or seem to do, what women pretend will please them. He belongs to his culture, and not to himself, rather like the insect to the nest, the bee to the swarm. He is unhappy, as are the confused, unwitting, lovely tyrants whom he refuses to resist, whom he refuses to take in hand and conquer, putting them to his feet, as naked, bound slaves."

"Is it not, then, a word for "fool"?" asked Targo.

"It would seem so," said the man.

He then looked down, again, at Ellen.

Ellen looked up at him, frightened.

The Goreans, she saw, and now well understood, were not gentlemen, or certainly not "gentlemen" in a common "Earth sense" of the term. Rather, however educated, civilized and refined they might be, they were indisputably owners of, and masters of, women.

"Please, wait! Please, don't!" cried Ellen. "I am not as your Gorean women!"

"That is understood by me," said the man.

"I come from a different world," said Ellen, "a world of different values, a world on which it would be regarded as improper that I be owned, helplessly, categorically, a world on which all women must be free, must be treated with total honor and respect! I am that sort of woman! Obedience, helplessness and chains, abject slavery, are not for me! I am not a woman of your world!"

"But you are a human female are you not?" he asked.

"Yes, of course," she said.

"Do not expect me to repeat the mistakes of your world, human female," said he.

"Master?" she said.

"Do not expect me to conform to the confusions and weaknesses of your world," he said.

"Please," she wept.

"You are no longer on your world," he said. "You are now on our world, where things are different."

"Your values are not mine!" she cried.

"I am pleased that that is true," he said.

"I do not exist for obedience, helplessness and chains, for abject slavery!" she wept.

"You do now," said he.

"I am not as one of your Gorean women!" she cried.

"I understand," said he.

"I am from the world called Earth!" she said.

"I understand," said he.

"So I am not as one of your Gorean women!" she cried.

"That is true," said he. "You are a thousand times less, female of Earth."

"Master?"

"You are not worthy to tie even the sandals of a Gorean woman."

His hand lifted from her thigh.

"Don't!" cried Ellen. "Please!"

The chains shook and rattled. She scarcely felt the cement beneath her body, the pull of the steel against her wrists and ankles.

"Oh, oh, oh!" she wept. "Please, don't. Please, don't!"

He desisted.

"No!" she wept. "Please, do. I mean, please, do! Don't stop! I beg you not to stop! I can't help myself! Don't stop, I beg it! Please, please! No, I mean, please stop! Please stop! That is what I mean, please stop!"

He desisted.

"No, don't stop!" she begged. "Yes! Yes! That is it! Oh, thank you, Master! No! Don't stop! Don't stop! I beg for more! I beg for more!"

"Who begs?" asked Targo.

"Ellen, Ellen, the slave, Ellen, the meaningless slave, Ellen, the meaningless, Earth-girl barbarian slave, begs for more!" she wept.

The man desisted.

Ellen, flushed, reddened, imploringly, lifted her body to him.

"I cannot stand it!" she wept. "Please touch me. Please complete your work, Master. Please complete what you have begun with me, Master. Please, please, Master. Be merciful! I beg it! Please be merciful, Master!"

"She shows promise of becoming a hot little thing," said the man.

"Yes, in time," agreed Targo.

"Please, Master!" she begged.

"Very well," he said, and lightly touched her but once more.

"Aiiiiiii!" cried Ellen, and her long, wild cry, her shriek of relief, of gratitude, of helpless joy must have rung throughout the market, piercing it from end to end, from stall to stall, reverberating from the wall across the way, carrying even to the streets beyond.

She then lay shuddering, sobbing, in the chains. She was scarcely aware that the man had left her side, and that Targo, too, was no longer on the shelf.

"Hold me, touch me, please!" she sobbed. But she was alone.

"Slut, slut, slut!" hissed Cichek.

"Helpless slave-girl slut!" hissed Emris.

"Despicable, disgusting slave!" said Cichek.

"No more airs for you, slave girl," said Emris. "You are the lowest of the low!"

Ellen lay back on the cement, frightened, and pulled a little at the shackles confining her. She looked up at the sky, and the clouds. "Come back, and hold me, a little, please," she whimpered, more to herself than to another.

"You are a slut," said Cichek. "Admit it."

"Yes, Mistress," whispered Ellen. "I am a slut."

So he who had been her master had been right about her, even on Earth. He had seen through the severity of her costume, her mien of disinterested inertness and frigidity, through the carefully constructed defenses and facades of her aloofness and professionalism, to the helpless, waiting, naked, passionate slave girl beneath.

Later that day it rained, a long, cold rain, and it rained heavily. The market was muchly emptied, the bustling to-and-fro business of the stalls, of the spread blankets, laden with small goods, the endless, vigorous hagglings, ceasing in the devastating inclemency of the weather. Merchants and their customers, those who did not flee to their homes, or nearby doorways, took refuge against walls and under overhangs, and beneath striped canopies, which soon sagged, and bulged, and, soaking, dripped with the downpour. Ellen lay on her back, chained as she had been, between the two rings, between which, at the touch of a stranger, she had found herself, to her consternation, begging, and bucking and rocking, and squirming, piteously, in the throes of her first slave orgasm, as rudimentary and minor though it might have been. He gave me no choice, she told herself, again and again. And perhaps that was true, but she knew, as well, that she had not wanted a choice, that she had only wanted the continuance, and fulfillment, of those sensations, sensations which she had only dimly sensed, earlier, in her training, and in the hands of Mirus, might lie within her. He gave me no choice, she told herself, again and again, but she knew he had been willing to stop, and more than once, but when he had done so, she had begged for the persistence of his predations, answering to the desperate needs of her vulnerable, needful slavehood. What am I, she asked herself, moving her ankles, and her helplessly confined wrists, a little, in her shackles and manacles. She moved her neck a bit, too, in her collar, that collar which was not the typical light, graceful slave collar, the attractive collar worn by most slave girls in the city, which might merely mark her as bond and identify her master, but the large, heavy, massive collar put by Targo on his properties, that they might, to escape the discomfort and indignity of such impediments, all the more eagerly submit themselves to the consideration of prospective buyers, collars, too, which, if they strayed, or fled, assuming they might obtain the unlikely opportunity to do so, would immediately call attention to themselves.

"Guardsman! Search for an escaped slave in a weight collar, a high collar of thick, black iron, hammered shut about her neck, its two forward projections pierced, a dangling, two-hort iron ring threaded through the piercings!"

So Ellen lay on the cement shelf, chained, closing her eyes, shuddering, shivering, half blinded by the cold, driving rain. She whimpered and moaned. The rain pelted against her, mercilessly, and she felt it run about her body, and, striking the cement, splash up, against her, like spray. Her hair was soaked. Water ran within her collar, and under the constraints she wore. She was bedraggled. Her hair was soaked, and it clung about her forehead and throat. Had Targo's women been permitted slave cosmetics, they would have run about their lips and eyes, and stained the shelf. But Targo seldom wasted slave cosmetics on his properties, claiming the honesty of his wares, and the right of a buyer to understand clearly, and in all respects, the exact nature, pure, raw and simple, of the goods he proffered. Too, to be sure, cosmetics, even slave cosmetics, were not free, but cost their coins. Ellen would later learn that slave girls would fight for a lipstick or an eye shadow, that they might enhance their beauty and prove more pleasing to masters. Too, Ellen would learn later that slaves were sometimes tied outside, exposed in cruel weather, that they might learn to better appreciate the warmth of a fire, the significance of a blanket, the snugness of a place at the foot of the master's couch.

What am I, she wondered. What am I, truly?

And she feared she knew the answer.

After a few minutes the rain stopped, rather suddenly, as it had begun, and water dripped from awnings, and trickled through cracks in the paving stones of the market square, and the sun again blazed down, as before, yellow, hot, indifferent, merciless. Some bustle in the market resumed, though muted now, and water was brushed away from the stalls, and, in places, blankets were again spread and various goods, pans, vessels, jewelries, and such, were arranged on the dark, woolen surfaces. The sound of leather sandals and boots was softened, and subtly different now, on the damp stones. There was the sound of a heavy, trundling wheel moving through a puddle. A child splashed and was reprimanded. Ellen could hear, too, now and then, the clack of high, wooden, platformlike, cloglike footwear, such as is sometimes worn by free women, particularly of high caste, which lift the hems of their gowns a bit from the ground, and serve to protect delicately slippered or sandaled feet from dust and mud. Ellen did not look at them, for she feared free women, and, as most slave girls, avoided meeting their eyes directly, lest they be thought insolent and be punished. The water on the shelf became warm and began to steam upward in the heat.

Much then seemed to her incomprehensible.

How came I here, she asked herself, how thus?

I am on a different world, she thought, a world foreign and strange to me, an exotic world, a beautiful, frightening world, an incredible, startling, vital world, a world so different, a world so alive, a world so very different from my own.

And on this world I am chained, she thought. And I am branded and collared. On this world I find myself only a chained slave.

I can be bought and sold. I exist only to give pleasure to men. I am owned, literally owned, and I must obey, and with all the perfection I can muster.

I remember the sensations. I must have more. I cannot live without them. I want them, desperately, needfully. How the beasts, in all their brutish, careless innocence, have made me theirs! I writhe in my chains, a needful slave. Oh, buy me, Masters! I will serve you well. I will kneel at your feet and lick and kiss them, and beg for your touch!

Oh, dismiss these thoughts, she cried to herself.

You must not be a woman, you must not be so alive, you must not be so needful! You must not desire to love and serve! Castigate such temptations! Ridicule yourself for such tender, animal realities! Think yourself because of them small and disgusting! Seek redemptive frigidity! Praise inertness! Sing the glories of the dull, dismal body! Put aside feeling! Deny the deepest heart of hearts! Dare not desire to love, dare not desire to serve! How improper, how terrible, how wicked to be alive, and needful and loving!

I am chained, she thought. I am on a different world, a world foreign and strange to me, an exotic world, a beautiful, frightening world, a world so different from my own, a world on which I am branded and collared, a world on which I am a slave.

But it is appropriate that I am chained and collared, for I am a slave.

It is what I am, and what I want to be! Oh, dear world, dearest world, give me a strong master, one who will master me uncompromisingly as I desire to be mastered, that I may fulfill myself, in my pleasing of him, in my serving of him, in my delighting of him.

How terrible, how unworthy I am, she thought.

I must have those sensations again. I will do anything for them!

How terrible, how wicked I am!

Mirus, Mirus, she thought, what have you done to me?

It was a slave orgasm, she thought, or something like one. I must have it again! I will do anything for it! Could I do so, were I not so chained, I would kiss my fingers and press them to my collar. And yet it was not a matter of simple sensation, no simple episode, even lingering, of the excitation of tissues. It was muchly other than simply that. It was flames and clouds, forces of nature, winds and storms, earthquakes, tornadoes, volcanoes, floods, an entirety of experience, a coming of seasons of being, a time of wholeness. In it there burst alive a universe of significance, a world of meaningfulness. In it was the defiant rootedness and tenacity of life. In it the grass became green, and the stars sang. In those moments I became ecstatically one with the glory of the universe. In my small way I attained a level of consciousness I had not known could exist, and glimpsed the promise of endless horizons, of infinite mornings, and yet, too, I learned that I was only a slave in the hands of a master.

I remember you, Mirus, my master.

Mirus, you have given me to myself, she thought. I would that I could give myself to you!

But you do not want me!

You have taught me to myself, and have then cast me aside, unwanted.

You saw to it that I have been made a slave.

And how worthless and contemptible are slaves! Yes, how worthless and contemptible we are!

How right of you to have held my lying self in contempt! How shrewdly you perceived my hypocrisy, my worthlessness! How fitting, how appropriate, how right for me then that I should be a slave, naked and chained!

This you saw! This you knew!

And now that is what I am!

And now I would that I were before you, kneeling before you, head down, kissing your feet, begging to serve you!

But you do not want me!

Then Ellen began to weep.

* * * *

It was now Ellen's third day on the shelf.

She stood at the back of the shelf, against the wall of the tenement, her back to the wall of the tenement, she then facing outward, her wrists chained over her head to a ring set in the tenement wall. Her arms were sore, and her legs ached. Targo was not much pleased with her.

Surely she should have been sold by now.

She shuddered as she saw Barzak's hand tighten on his whip as he passed her. She knew that she could be whipped, even without reason, if it pleased the masters. She was a slave.

An Ahn later, which is something more than an hour, she whispered to Targo, who passed, "I am thirsty, Master."

"Did you speak without permission?" he asked.

"Forgive me, Master!" said Ellen. She supposed she should have asked permission to speak, but such things tend to be contextual. Surely not all girls invariably ask their masters for permission to speak, but such could, in theory, be required, and the failure to ask for such permission could be a cause for discipline. But habit, practice, and common sense tend to govern such matters. On the girl's part, the knowledge that she should, in theory, ask permission to speak helps her to keep in mind that she is a slave. Ellen knew of such things, of course, but she was, as we recall, rather new to her collar, and might thus be expected to occasionally forget such niceties, particularly inasmuch as they are not always observed. A stroke of the switch or lash, of course, tends to encourage an awareness of such things, and thus to minimize such lapses.

But a bit later Targo had Barzak water his stock.

Barzak had put aside his whip, but a long, supple switch now hung from his belt. Ellen eyed it uneasily. There was little doubt about the purpose or utility of such an implement, or what it would feel like on her flesh.

When Barzak pulled the spigot of the bota, it seemed too soon, from Ellen's wet, eager lips, she moaning and trying to cling to it, to hold it with her teeth, he patted her belly, which was then pleasantly rounded. She looked after him, tears in her eyes, tears from wanting more water but knowing she must not ask for it, and tears of shame consequent on his simple proprietary slapping of her belly.

Ellen thought that a groom might have slapped a horse in such a fashion, though on the side or back. And then she supposed that the analogy was not as farfetched as one might have supposed.

Barzak had then gone on to Cichek.

Ellen moved her wrists a little in the shackles that held them over her head. Her arms and legs were sore.

She looked out on the market.

Emris was sold toward noon. Ellen was pleased that Targo, apparently, had received a good price for Emris. It goes that way sometimes. A man sees a girl he wants and his objective judgment as to the market worth of the given property can be clouded, perhaps by simple desire, a simple desire to buy and own, totally, a particularly delightful, curvaceous property, but perhaps by something else, too, mixed with desire, and powerful lust, a subtle something that tells him that this, for him, may be a special slave, something he seriously wants in his collar, something not merely, for him, another slave, not merely something on which to slake his lust, to dominate and master, but something, too, which might, in time, prove to have the makings of something more, perhaps, say, a love slave. And, of course, if it doesn't work out, he can give her away or sell her.

Many Goreans, incidentally, fear falling in love with their slaves. Many regard this as a form of weakness. But, in many cases, of course, it is difficult for the master not to fall in love with a slave, as the master/slave relationship is a civilized, codified, institutionalized analogue to the essentials of a natural biological relationship. The master/slave relationship frees both men and women biologically. The natural dominance of the male is not castigated, denounced, ridiculed and societally undermined but allowed to express itself and flourish. This leads to a successful, healthy manhood. Similarly, the female slave, in virtue of similar biological congruities, is the most lovely, vulnerable and needful of all women; she is the most female, the most feminine, and thus the most desirable and lovable, of all women. It is no wonder that men must struggle to resist their feelings for such owned, enticing beauties. Often the love master is most demanding and severe with the love slave, in sensing the weakness which she might produce in him. This brings joy to the heart of the love slave as she hastens to obey and please, and with suitable perfection, indeed, as she must, as though she might be no more than a new girl, frightened and intimidated, in the house. He, of course, remains the master, and she, of course, remains the slave. That is the relationship of the love master and the love slave, the fulfillment of the nature of each.

"You should have been sold by now," snapped Targo.

He was standing beside her.

"I do not wish to be sold, Master," said Ellen.

She drew back, with a rattle of chain, cringing, and closing her eyes, as he lifted his hand, as if to cuff her, but then he had lowered his hand, without striking her, as though such an admonition might be wasted on so stupid a slave.

"Look on the market," he said, "straight ahead."

Ellen did so, while Targo regarded her. "Perhaps you are just too young," he said, "little more than a pretty girl, perhaps not even of twenty summers."

Ellen was startled to think of this in this manner, recalling Earth. But Targo did not know what the new serums had done, it seemed, and would take her at face value, as no more than a young, pretty barbarian. And then Ellen shook with the realization that, indeed, he was in no way in error; that was all she was, literally, truthfully. Physiologically, biologically, she was clearly, simply, truthfully, quite young. Beyond that there were only a distant, now-seemingly-unreal world and conventions having to do with an invented, mechanistic time, devised for purposes of convenience, purposes irrelevant to the natural courses of nature.

"You have a nice figure," he said, "with lovely slave curves."

"Master?" asked Ellen.

"Barzak!" called Targo. "Turn her about. Chain her facing the wall."

In moments Barzak had rearranged the chains, that they not be twisted, and Ellen, to her chagrin, and shame, found herself facing the wall, at the back of the shelf, her hands still chained well over her head.

"Ahh!" said Targo. "Yes, very nice!"

She felt Targo's hands on her sides, and then at her waist, and then moving down the sides of her *derrière* and thighs

"Good," he said. "We shall see if you can interest someone this way."

Ellen shook the chains angrily, and stared ahead, into the wall, but some six inches before her face.

She heard Cichek laugh.

Time passed. Once she heard the scream of a tarn as it swept between buildings, and felt the blast of wind from its wings which half thrust her to the wall. Its shadow passed and she turned her head to the left, looking for it, but missed it between the buildings.

She did not think it was permitted to fly such beasts so low in the city.

"Tarns, tarns!" she heard cry, a few moments later, from somewhere behind her. She could turn about, twisting in the chains, and she saw men pointing upward. Half closing her eyes against the sun, looking upward, she saw some five tarns in flight.

The market returned to its normal sounds.

Once, later, she heard the measured tread of a group of men behind her, probably guardsmen.

Shortly thereafter she heard a springing, clattering, birdlike gait on the stones of the market, and a cry of "Make way, make way!" She turned about, and shuddered. A rider had reined in, turning, a light tharlarion, a delicate, quickly moving, bipedalian, reptilian mount. In the saddle he was some eight feet above the stones. He wore the common Y-visaged helmet, and carried a lance. A studded buckler, a small, round, spiked shield, was at the side of the saddle. This was the first tharlarion that she had seen, though she had heard of such beasts, and she gathered that such, this and others, were not common in the streets of cities. She did know that a large variety of tharlarion, of bipedalian and quadrupedalian sorts, were bred for diverse purposes, war, transport, reconnaissance, hunting, haulage, racing, and such. The tharlarion she saw was much as she supposed the racing tharlarion might be, though perhaps heavier limbed and sturdier. The man, she guessed, was a mounted guardsman, or messenger, or scout. He surveyed the crowd in the market, and then, with an angry kick, and blow of the lance, urged his beast away.

It was unusual, she thought, that such a beast would be in the streets of a city.

"Down with the sleen of Cos!" she heard.

"Be silent!" hushed a man, a hoarse whisper.

"Would that Marlenus were within the walls!" said a man.

"Marlenus is dead," said another.

"He has been seen in the city!" whispered a man.

"Let the traitress Talena, false Ubara, be impaled!" whispered a man.

"Who said that Marlenus has been seen in the city?" asked a man.

"I heard it said in a tavern," said one.

"Which tavern?"

"Do not think me so much a fool as to speak it. The Cosians would seize its goods and burn it to the ground."

"Do not speak these things!" begged a woman. "The Cosians are now our masters."

"Seek your collar!" snarled a man.

"Sleen! Sleen!" she wept.

"Is Marlenus in the city?"

"I do not know."

"Can he be in the city?"

"Who knows?"

"Marlenus is dead," said a man.

"Have you obeyed the Weapons Laws?" asked a man.

"Of course," said a man. "The Cosians have disarmed us. It is death to conceal weapons. We are civilians and must be the tame verr of the Cosians, to be milked, or sheared, or led to slaughter, as they please!"

"The Cosians are our beloved allies," said a man. "They have disarmed us for our own safety."

"Cosian spy!"

"No!"

"Who knows what may serve as a weapon," said a man, "a knife from the kitchen, a pointed stick, a stone."

"The weather," said a man, loudly, "may change. We may have another rain."

A silence came over the men near the shelf.

Then, "Yes, yes," said another man, loudly.

The group broke up, and the market became again much as it had been.

Turning about Ellen saw two guardsmen sauntering by. On their helmets were yellow crests.

Then, suddenly, there was the sharp snap of a switch across her *derrière* and Ellen cried out in pain, and humiliation. "Keep your eyes on the wall, slave," said Barzak.

"Yes, Master," said Ellen, quickly, her eyes brimming with tears.

I am an animal, she thought. I am owned. I am owned!

It was late in the afternoon, in the heat of the day, when she sensed two men behind her. She did not turn about, and kept her eyes fixed on the wall before her. She noted a tiny blemish in the stone.

"Do not turn about," said Targo.

She continued to stare ahead, at the wall. Then she was aware of something dark being lifted over her head, and then it was pulled down, over her head. It completely covered her head. She gasped. She could see nothing. Then she felt it drawn back, under her chin, with threaded straps, and fitted closely about her throat. It was then buckled behind the back of her neck. She now wore a common Gorean slave hood.

"Unchain her. Take her inside. Remove our iron," said Targo. "Then return her to the shelf, hooded, her hands tied behind her back."

"It will take a little time," said Barzak, and Ellen felt him reaching over her head, to the chains which fastened her against the wall.

Within the welcome coolness of the building, Barzak faced her away from him and, with a short thong, casually, tied her hands tightly behind her back. He then, leaning her against the wall, facing away from him, lifted her foot and positioned it on the small anvil. Then, with his hammer and wedge, and with three blows, he opened the shackle on her ankle, and slipped her foot free. He then knelt her beside the anvil, her head down, across it. In order to remove the weight collar he unbuckled the hood, and thrust it up, a few inches. He did not, however, raise it enough for her to see. She shuddered, kneeling, bent over, her head laid across the anvil, as Barzak then, with his tools, opened and removed the weight collar. The ringing of the tools on the metal was loud, reverberating, terrifying, and she remained on her knees, frightened, absolutely still. One false blow of the hammer and she knew that her head or throat, with such blows, could be broken as easily as one might crush an egg underfoot.

How good it felt to have the weight collar removed!

The hood was then drawn fully down again, about her throat, and buckled shut.

Barzak then stood her up, hooded, bound, before him. She then felt herself suddenly, lightly, lifted from her feet and carried toward the entrance of the holding chamber. In a moment, still carried, helplessly hooded and bound, her head to the rear, as a slave is carried, she felt herself brought again into the sunlight, and up the few steps to the surface of the shelf, where she was knelt down, she thought near the forward edge of the shelf.

Her small wrists pulled futilely against the thongs that bound them. Her struggles, she knew, were futile, but in her consternation and fear, in the hood, she could not help herself. And in the end, of course, she knew herself as helpless as before.

She knelt there for a time, bewildered, lost in the darkness of the hood, helpless in her confusion. Suddenly it seemed to her that there was some security lost in the removal of the clumsy, heavy collar and the shackle. None of the other slaves spoke to her, perhaps because there were men about, but she did not know if that were the case or not.

Then she felt herself lifted from the shelf, presumably by Barzak, and placed on her feet, on the stones of the market place, doubtless before the shelf.

"Look, Mother," she heard a child say.

"Come away," said a woman's voice.

"Master, may I speak?" she asked.

"Yes," said Barzak.

"What is happening?" she asked. "What is going on?"

"You silly little vulo," laughed Barzak, "you have been sold."

On the front of the hood strap, before the throat, there was a ring, for the attachment of a leash snap. Ellen had not realized this before. But now she felt a leash catch snap about the ring. She then felt two tugs, the signal, she knew from her training, that she was to be led, imminently, that she must be ready, at the next tug, to follow docilely, an obedient domestic animal, on her tether.

"Masters!" wept Ellen. "Masters!"

"You have been sold," said Barzak.

She heard coins shaken, as in a hand. They were perhaps what had been paid for her. "See that she serves you with the fullness of a slave's perfection," said Targo.

"Masters!" wept Ellen, from within the darkness of the hood.

"You are a pretty slave," said Barzak. "Serve your masters well and you may be permitted to live."

Ellen sobbed. She knew that, as a Gorean slave girl, she must serve her masters not only well, but, as Targo had said, with the fullness of a slave's perfection. And slave was what she was.

Gorean masters, she knew, were not easy with their slaves.

"To whom have I been sold?" she begged. "To where am I to be taken?"

"Were you given permission to speak?" asked Barzak.

"No, Master," sobbed Ellen.

There was a pause then, as though a signal might have been awaited, or a permission granted, by as little as the nod of a head.

Then Ellen cried out in pain, as she was struck, three times, across the back of the thighs, doubtless with Barzak's switch.

"Forgive me, Masters!" she sobbed.

Then, suddenly, Ellen felt a tug, a firm, no-nonsense tug, on the leash, and she stumbled forward in the direction of the taut strap.

Now she was being led from the market, and through the crowded streets of lower Ar, a naked slave girl, hooded, wrists bound behind her, on a leash.

Twice was she cuffed, and once kicked, when she inadvertently brushed against someone in the streets. Twice she fell, and, again struck and kicked, bleating pleas for forgiveness, hurriedly struggled to regain her feet.

Distant now were her seminars in gender studies.

And so she was led she knew not where.

I have been sold, she thought. I follow on my tether, fearfully, a purchased animal, obedient, and docile, as I must.

How faraway now was Earth!

How faraway now was her former life!

She was now on another world, one quite different from her former world.

On this world she was as any man would want her, and as men on this world would have her, a slave.

Men on this world had seen what was fit for her, and what she should be.

Accordingly, on this world, that was what she was.

I am a slave, she thought. I am a slave!

Are you satisfied now, Mirus, she thought. This is what you foresaw for me, what you wanted for me, what you decided for me, that to which you have consigned me, that I should be no more than a slave on a primitive world.

For better than an Ahn she was led through the streets, and alleys, and between buildings, sometimes with passages, many of them steep, downward and upward, and sometimes so narrow that she might strike her shoulders, first on one side, then on the other. Sometimes, on a pronounced declivity, she feared she would again fall, losing her balance, hurtling headlong downward, and, at other times, given an ascending steepness, she struggled, gasping, legs aching, to climb, the leash taut, mercilessly, impatiently, against the ring, drawing her relentlessly forward. There were many twists and turns, and even had she not been hooded, and even if she had known the city, which she did not, well might she have been similarly disoriented, similarly hopelessly confused as to her location. She was certain that she was still within the city, from the paving, and the sounds, the absence of challenges, and such, at gates.

What has become of me, she thought.

This is how a slave is led, she thought.

How fitting for me, for I am a slave!

Be amused, Mirus, she thought. You have done this to me. I wear a brand. I am identified, marked chattel.

A hand, a large, masculine hand, at the leash ring, stopped her, and she stood still. It occurred to her that she was standing well, an erect, slim slave girl. How naturally I am standing thus, she thought. I have been trained. It is now part of me. No more am I, now that I am a slave girl, permitted slovenliness of posture. How my ideological sisters would scorn me, she thought, to see me stand so beautifully, but I have no choice, for I am slave. Let them be put under the whip and they, too, would soon learn to so stand, to accept their beauty and see to it that it was well displayed, for the masters will have it so. We belong to them. We are theirs.

The leash was then dangling before her, from its ring, and she gasped, as she felt herself lifted from her feet and put lightly to a man's shoulder, her head to the rear, again as a slave is commonly carried. She was then steadied on the shoulder with one hand and he began to move upward, climbing, surely ascending a ladder or ladderlike device. He stepped carefully, and doubtless utilized his free hand to steady them in their upward movements. When Ellen became alarmed at the height to which she was being carried, she began to count the steps, or rungs, one after the other. There were more than three hundred such steps, or rungs, after she had begun to count. She could feel wind whipping about at this height, and twice the fellow carrying her stopped in his climb when the wind was particularly fierce. She feared they might be swept from the steps or ladder. Voices from below were now far away, and, in the further ascent, they could drift up but faintly, if at all, from the streets below.

At last he had ascended to a level, some level, and, the winds whirling and blasting about them, and the leather of the hood snapping about her face, she was placed again on her feet. She was then led for several yards across this level, some sort of open, wind-blown, flat surface, and then found herself suddenly out of the wind, and, in moments, some yards within some straw-strewn, wooden-floored room, or area. Then she was put to her knees. She clenched her knees together, frightened, hoping that she might be permitted to be a tower slave. But almost instantly a heavy, bootlike sandaled foot forced her knees apart, widely, and then more widely. She then understood better the services that would be required of her in this place.

Yes, Mirus, she thought. I am to be a pleasure slave for men. But doubtless, too, a work slave. This can be no palace, no mansion, no luxurious, noble quarters, no rich man's compartments. You had me sold as a low slave, from a common shelf, in a poor market, Mirus, she thought. You managed this thing well.

In this area, despite its openness, there was a strong odor, which she did not recognize. It must be that of some sort of living thing, or things, she thought.

A figure was then crouching before her, and she, in the hood, felt the leash removed from the leash ring, and, a moment later, the thong binding her wrists was removed. She had scarcely time to gratefully rub her wrists before she was rudely drawn by the left upper arm to her feet and taken to one side. There, as she stood, her hands were tied before her body, with a leather strap, and she heard a loop of strap strike above her, as though thrown over a beam. Then, a moment later, her bound hands were drawn upward and over her head, until she stood painfully on her toes.

"Please, no, Master!" she wept.

She then received ten lashes of the five-stranded Gorean slave whip, and she wept, and screamed, and protested, and begged, and pleaded, and turned, spinning, jerking, twisting, in the bonds, sometimes bending her knees, lifting her feet from the floor, her full weight then on the wrist tether, and then, after the tenth blow, she hung helplessly, sobbing, sagging, knees bent, on the strap, her full weight on it.

The strap was then apparently freed from the hook or ring which held it over the beam and she fell, hands still bound before her, to her knees.

She now knew that this was a place in which she would well obey, a place in which she must strive with every fiber of her being to be as pleasing as possible.

She sensed the figure before her and put out her bound hands and touched a powerful leg. She then put down her hooded head and, feeling for a foot, pressed her lips to it through the leather desperately, placatingly.

She was then dragged a few feet to the side and thrown on her belly over a smooth, rounded leather surface. It was some sort of artifact. It seemed to have rings on its side.

Then she cried out with dismay.

He was with her only moments.

He then took her to the side and threw her to a bedding of straw. There he untied her hands but, in an instant, pulled them behind her and she felt her small wrists enclosed with slim steel, slave bracelets. She then heard a rattle of chain. A heavy collar, with an attached chain, was then about her neck. This collar was locked in place.

Then, as far as she knew, sobbing in the hood, he had gone.

After a time, lying on her side, she tried the slave bracelets. They were on her perfectly, of course, the ratchet and pawl arrangement having sought unerringly the measurements of her wrists, then closing snugly, efficiently, about them. She could not slip the bracelets. They are not made to be slipped by slaves.

She lay there for a time, quietly in the straw, not moving further. She thought that the man was gone, but she did not know. What if a man were watching? She knew the effect that a naked, bound woman can have on a man, even such a woman half hidden, half buried, in a bedding of straw, such as that into which she had been cast. She lay there then, frightened, a whipped, ravished slave, trying to comprehend this change in her life, what had been done to her.

After perhaps an Ahn, she rose timidly to her knees and, as she could, hooded, explored her surroundings. The chain was fastened to a ring in the floor before her. It did not give her much play, say, some four to four and a half feet. She was on straw, certainly, and, it seemed, given low wooden walls to her left and right, in some sort of open stall.

There is the smell of animals in this place, she thought. Dampness, mustiness, acidic odors, other odors. Large animals, or many animals. This place is a barn, she thought, but it is too high for a barn. What manner of place can this be? What animals, what beasts, what creatures, could be kept here, so high?

As she explored, with her body, legs and fingers, behind her, as she could, hooded, her small wooden-floored, straw-strewn housing, which seemed clearly to be some sort of stall, she discovered, to her joy, within the scope of her chain, which was all that was permitted her, a large, porcelainlike bowl. It had been rinsed, but, from its size, she knew it could not be for feeding or watering, but must be for wastes. Her bladder had been crying for relief, but she had feared to soil the straw, even at the end of the chain. She feared to be again beaten. Masters are not patient with careless slaves. Such bowls, or vessels, of course, serve an obvious purpose, and are common in kennels and cells. The presence of the bowl there, and the ring in the floor, with the chain and collar, suggested that this small housing, or stall, had been prepared for, and was intended for, the keeping of a slave and, presumably, given its openness, a female slave. Ellen supposed that she was not the first slave, nor would she be likely to be the last slave, to be housed in this narrow, straw-strewn space. Gratefully, she squatted over the bowl and relieved herself.

Though it had surely been with pleasure that she had discovered the bowl within the reach of her chain, and she was grateful for the relief of her distress, it was shortly thereafter that she considered the simplicity, rudeness and directness of this arrangement, adequate it seemed for a lowly slave, and considered further how she must look, hooded, chained, naked, braceleted, squatting, taking advantage of such a primitive accommodation. She wondered what her ideological sisters on Earth would have thought of that. But then, she thought, let them be on a chain on Gor! Let them be a chained, braceleted, squatting slave! Let them then preserve what they can of their vanity, dignity, and sophistication! To be sure, she had been forced to relieve herself publicly before men in her training. Such is thought useful in the training of a slave. The slave is not permitted privacy, or modesty, no more than a verr or kaiila, for she, like them, is only another domestic animal.

Then she lay again still in the straw, in the leather hood, naked, chained by the neck, her hands braceleted behind her, and sobbed.

This is my new slavery, she thought.

She remembered the lash. It will not be an easy slavery, she thought. This man, or these men, will not be gentle with their slave girls. They will use us well. Within the darkness of the hood her features, and her entire exposed body, as well, suffused with shame, with humiliation. She recalled the large, smooth, rounded leather surface over which she had been thrown. She pulled angrily, protestingly, futilely, against the bracelets. Then she subsided in helplessness. She was a slave. They can do with me whatever they wish, she thought. I am only a slave. I must submit. I must obey. I am only a slave. Indeed, she thought, bitterly, my first service has already been rendered to my new master.

How strange, she thought, to be utterly at the mercy of others, to know that you are the slave and that they are the masters, and that you must obey them, and strive diligently, desperately, to please them with all your talent, intelligence and beauty. And that you have no alternative. And that that is simply the way it is.

Ellen, of course, was an educated person, and historically informed. She knew that her fate, or condition, was not, historically, that unusual. She knew that throughout vast periods of human history, indeed by far the most of it, the human chattel had been an article of commerce. Women such as she, straightforwardly and naturally, without a second thought, save for the most practical means to accomplish the end, had been captured, raided for, seized, enslaved, and bought and sold. Such was customary in other times. Throughout most of human history, the "slaver's necklace," a coffle of chained beauties, was a familiar sight. Indeed, Ellen knew that, should historical conditions change on Earth, human slavery, with its various values, and its capacity to solve various social problems, might be reinstituted, might rise again. She did not doubt but that many men, on buses, at work, in restaurants, and such must have speculated on what a particular young woman, perhaps an insolent or troublesome one, might look like in slave silk and a collar, or, say, chained naked at the foot of their couch.

No, no, no, she thought. I must not think such things! Gor is different. Different! It is not Earth. It is a different place. It is rude, and primitive, uncompromising, frightening, natural and merciless, fierce. And it is on that world, Gor, not Earth, this fearful, severe, biologically honest world, so far from Earth, that I find myself a slave!

I cannot be a slave, she thought, wildly.

How brutal and rapid he was with me, she thought. With what casual, thoughtless contempt I was used!

Does he think I am a slave?

But, of course, I am a slave!

And how true that is, and how he has shown it to me! If I did not understand my brand before, that lovely, so-meaningful, incisive mark burned into my body, that mark which I cannot remove, which proclaims to all who see it what I am, I understand it now!

I am a slave, and no more than a slave.

Where was his gentleness, his tenderness, his sensitivity?

Surely he could not know my crimes against men on my own world, how I foolishly, deluded by the madness of propaganda, attempted to abet their destruction?

Doubtless I have much to pay for!

I wonder if the men of Earth will one day make the women of Earth pay similarly for their crimes.

But I have changed! I beg to be treated well, my masters!

Then she smiled bitterly to herself.

One might as well ask gentleness, tenderness, sensitivity of beasts, of leopards and lions, of alien, aggressive, different, mighty life forms, life forms, she thought, compared to which we are insignificant, even negligible, valued only for casual utilities. To men such as these, the mighty, untamed, unreduced men of Gor, what can women be but prey and quarry? What can we be before such men but intimidated, dominated slaves, but eager, yielding, responsive, supplicatory slaves? Such men are true men, men as nature intended them to be, and before them, accordingly, what can a female be but a true woman, as nature intended her to be, a begging, aroused, loving slave?

But I want masters to care for me, if only a little.

I will try to serve them well!

Then she shuddered, thinking of the power of men over her.

I am completely dependent upon them, she thought, as theirs, as a domestic animal, literally dependent on them for everything. How wondrously strange that makes me feel. It is they, not I, who will decide if I am to be fed or not. It is they who will decide if I will be given a bowl of gruel or a crust of bread. It is they who will decide whether or not I will be given a sip of water, a bit of straw on which to sleep, a blanket to clutch about myself against the cold, a soiled rag with which to cover myself, if even they see fit to permit me clothing. I am dependent upon them—even for my collar and chains!

No longer am I independent, she thought. I am now dependent, totally dependent, on men, on masters, in all ways.

I am theirs, she sobbed.

She pulled against the bracelets a little.

There is no one to save me on this world, she thought. There is nowhere to go. There is nowhere to run. This is a natural world. I was always such as to be fittingly embonded, but only here, on this frightening, strange, beautiful world, has that propriety been attended to.

I do not know what to feel, or how to feel, she thought. I am frightened. I am terrified. I am owned.

Mirus, Mirus, she thought, I am a helpless slave. Mirus, Mirus, she thought, now your vengeance on me is complete!

There was suddenly a titanic snapping in the air yards away, and it seemed that a mighty wind exploded in the area, scattering and whirling dust and straw. At the same time there was a loud, piercing, raucous, wild, annunciatory scream.

"A tarn!" she thought. "Birds!" she thought. "Tarns! This is a place of tarns!"

She cried out in misery and, naked, hooded, wrists braceleted behind her, chained by the neck, scrambled to the far corner of the stall, bruising herself, and tried to burrow down in the straw, trembling, trying to hide there, trying not to move.

Chapter 18

Intrigue

"Ellen," said Selius Arconious, chewing on a straw, leaning against the jamb of the great portal, leading to the platform outside, "remove your tunic, to the floor, slave paces."

"Yes, Master!" said Ellen, delightedly.

She put down her basket, heavy with layers of meat, and quickly, laughing, slipped the brief brown tunic over her head, it was all she wore save her slave collar, and went immediately to the floor, and, half kneeling, half lying, the palms of her hands on the floor, looked up at Arconious, expectantly, eager, a slave, awaiting his commands. Sometimes the slave is instructed, even commanded, to the snapping of a whip, but at other times she is permitted to display herself, as it moves her to do so. The ingenuity of the human female in such matters is well known. Most important is that she knows herself a property, and an attractive one. Then she enthusiastically and provocatively displays, with skills that might be the envy of a dancer, sometimes with seeming shyness, timidity, reluctance or fear, the well-curved, delectable merchandise which is herself. She presents herself, as goods, to her best advantage. It is in her best interest, of course, to be as beautiful and stimulating as she can. She desires, in her wonderful vanity, to be so, as all hormonally sufficient women desire to be attractive to men, though some might fear this feeling and be terrified to recognize its obvious, deeper meaning, but, even if she did not, she is subject to discipline. There is always the whip, the switch, the discipline of food, the discipline of blindfolds, gags, ropes and chains. When the slave is commanded, the slave obeys. There is nothing unusual, untoward or surprising in this. She is a slave.

"Master?" inquired Ellen, expectantly, looking up, delighted. Selius Arconious was an assistant to the tarnmaster. He was young and handsome, and no stranger to the handling of lovely slaves.

More than once she had writhed moaning, crying out, gasping, begging, in slave rapture in his arms.

"What is going on here?" called a gruff voice, that of a large, bearded man in a brown tunic, with wristlets, and a tarn goad dangling from his belt. "Dress, slut," said Portus Canio, tarnmaster of the Tower of Corridon.

"Yes, Master!" said Ellen quickly, and scrambled to her feet. In an instant she had pulled the tiny tunic over her head, and pulled it down at the hems, as though this might conceal a thread's width, or more, of her muchly bared thighs. She was barefoot. "Surely you have duties, slut," said Portus Canio.

"Yes, my Master," said Ellen, and, crouching down, for one must move carefully in so brief a garment as a slave tunic, picked up the basket of meat. It was heavy.

On Ellen's throat was a light, inexpensive, engraved, metal collar. It was locked on her, fastened behind the back of the neck. The legend of the collar read "I am Ellen, the slave of Portus Canio." To be sure, the reader familiar with Gorean conventions might have noted that Ellen, in her understandable unease, having been discovered, though through no obvious fault of her own, in what might seem a dalliance, or a laxity in her duties, had responded to Canio with the phrase 'my Master'. The slave addresses all free men as "Master" and all free women as "Mistress." The phrase 'my Master,' when used, is commonly addressed to one's personal master, one's owner. Similarly, if the slave is owned by a woman, the phrase 'my Mistress' is commonly addressed only to the slave's actual mistress. To be sure, the slave commonly refers to her owner as she refers to free men and free women in general, namely, simply as "Master" or "Mistress."

"What is your name?" had asked Portus Canio, some weeks ago, when Ellen, freed of the hood, had knelt, head to the floor, still chained by the neck, still back-braceleted, before him in the stall.

"Whatever Master pleases," she had replied. That was the judicious response, as a slave has no name in her own right, but may be named as the Master wishes.

"What have you been called?" Portus Canio had inquired.

"'Ellen,'" she had responded.

"A barbarian name," he had said. "And a pretty name, a name suitable for a pretty little barbarian slave girl."

Ellen dared not speak.

"Very well then, you are "Ellen,"" he said. "What is your name?"

"'Ellen', Master," had said Ellen, now named, named again, as a sleen, or kaiila, might be named.

"Lift your head," he said. The slave obeyed, and found a whip before her lips. Obediently, unbidden, she licked and kissed the whip, for some moments, deferentially, submissively, timidly, lovingly, until it was withdrawn.

"You will be fed and watered," he said. "And then you will be instructed in your duties."

"Yes, Master," she said. "Thank you, Master."

The pans would be put on the floor, and she, neck chained, and back-braceleted, must put down her head to feed, to drink.

She looked after Portus Canio, doubtless her master, whose name she would learn only later, and from others.

She trembled. She had, of course, kissed the whip before, and had even been trained to do so, but this time, oddly, it seemed momentously significant to her. She had knelt before a mighty man and licked and kissed his whip. The symbolism of this act, she on her knees before him, naked and helpless, chained, back-braceleted, suddenly overwhelmed her. Never before, it seemed, had she felt so radically, vulnerably, rawly female. They are the masters, she thought. We are, fittingly, their slaves.

"Ho!" said Portus Canio, turning and glaring at young Selius Arconious. "Are there not harnesses to repair?"

"To be sure, Portus," grinned Selius.

"You do not earn your copper tarsks by amusing yourself with slave girls!"

Selius grinned.

"See if she is sent to your blankets soon," said Portus.

Ellen, lifting the basket of meat, smiled at the discomfort of young Selius. Surely he, a mere assistant, should be more circumspect with his employer's properties. In the last weeks she had become muchly aware of her increasing charms, though they were, of course, collared and owned. She was not insensitive to the tumult, the distress, that a smile, a glance over the shoulder, the movement of a well-turned ankle, might produce in a young man, particularly in one who did not own her. The slave girl, you see, is not without her powers.

"It matters not," said Selius. "There are hundreds better in the paga taverns!"

Ellen, who had lingered, did not care to hear this.

"The paga taverns are being emptied," said Portus, "the best girls being shipped to Cos and Tyros, to Brundisium, and elsewhere."

Selius shrugged.

"If you were not one of the best tarnsters in Ar," said Portus, "I would throw you from the platform."

Selius laughed. "I have harnesses to repair," he said.

Portus then turned about and left the area, going to adjacent rooms.

Selius Arconious, as we recall, at the time of his accosting a young slave, had been in the vicinity of the great portal, that leading outward to the long, curving platform, outside, ledgelike, about the cylinder or tower, with its several perches. Within the portal was the "tarncot," so to speak, of Portus Canio, which was, in effect, for the most part, a large, lofty, barnlike area, certainly that within the great portal. To the left, as one might look outward from the great portal, barred and gated, was the general housing for tarns, with its perches and roosting areas, hooks for meat, reservoirs for water, and such. There were also, in the vicinity, similarly provisioned, some individual cages. Occasionally a tarn must be isolated, particularly a male tarn, from its fellows. Such individual cages, too, are often used with new birds, in their training, in accustoming them to saddling and harnessing, and such. They are also valuable given the occasional necessity of tending ill or wounded birds. The area directly within the great portal, a large area, as one might suppose, served for the departure and entry of tarns. In this area also, against the walls, were various stalls, slave stalls, in one of which Ellen commonly slept, now usually unchained, when not ordered to her master's slave ring, that in which she had been originally placed, hooded, chained and back-braceleted, and a variety of storage areas. Too, to one side there were many stacked tarn baskets. The enterprise of Portus in the Corridon Tower was, so to speak, a livery stable and transportation outlet. The tarns were largely draft tarns, large, relatively slow birds, controlled either from a saddle or, by reins, from the tarn basket, slung below the bird. Birds and baskets could be rented, or purchased, and drivers, or tarnsters, hired. There were also, these accessible from the larger area, some hallways, and a number of ancillary rooms, a kitchen, a pantry, living quarters, a workroom, sometimes used, the office of Portus Canio, and so on.

On the second day of her service in the establishment, before she had been permitted clothing, Ellen had screamed and fled from one of the birds, when it had turned its head, sharply, to view her. She had run madly away, in panic, blindly, but struck into Portus, before whom, in terror, she had knelt. "Do not have me with tarns, Master!" she begged. "I fear them so!" Saying nothing he had dragged her to her feet, she half bent over, his hand in her hair, twisted there, painfully, cruelly, and she then, bent over, thus controlled, this being a common slave leading position, was hurried stumbling out onto the platform, to its very edge, where she, to her horror, teetering on that perilous brink, steadied only by the cruel hand in her hair, could look down, down, and see the street, some four hundred feet below, the pavement.

"Do you think you can fly, little vulo?" he inquired.

"No, Master!" she screamed.

"Shall I hurl you to the street?" he asked.

"Please, no, Master!" she screamed. "Do not kill me, Master! Forgive me, Master! Please forgive me! Please, Master, show me mercy!"

He drew her back a yard from the edge and released her. Unable to stand she sank to her knees in terror and grasped his leg, as much to reassure herself, by clinging to this support, as to a stanchion, of some modicum of safety, as in supplication.

"Whom do you fear more," he asked, "tarns, or men?"

"Men, Master!" she wept. "I am a slave! I fear men more!"

"Your duties, little vulo," said he, "do not, and will not, involve you in great danger, or at least not from tarns. That is not my intention. I would not risk a woman, even a slave, with such beasts. They would seem too tempting, too delicious, a morsel. Still, in empty cages, or in sparsely occupied cages, while a man stands watch, with a goad, you will have ample opportunity, during long hours, to prove your value as a work slave, removing masses of soiled straw, shoveling excrement, scraping and scrubbing floors, supplying and spreading bundles of fresh, dry straw, carrying water for the reservoirs, replenishing salt stones, climbing the wall railings to hang meat on the feeding hooks, and such."

Ellen looked up at him, fearfully.

"Of course," said he, "you will have other duties, as well, cooking, cleaning, mending, sewing, laundering, and such."

"Yes, Master," she said. She was grateful to have been shown the rudiments of such matters in her training. She had been switched more than once for her lack of skill in such matters. She had known little of these homely domestic tasks while a female on Earth. Indeed, she had taken a certain pride in her ineptness in such matters, an ineptness which had seemed appropriate to her for one of her education, interests and station. Such tasks were surely below a female intellectual, which she had then been. Then, in training, under the switch, crying out in pain, weeping under the frequent smartness of the strokes, she had struggled to master them. Needless to say, these are skills routinely expected of a slave, any slave, even one whose price is largely indexed to her passion and beauty.

"Oh, too," he had said, "there are other duties, as well."

"Master?" she asked.

He glanced at her knees, as she knelt before him, and quickly, blushing, she spread them, and then, as he continued to look, she spread them more widely, and then as widely as she could.

In this place, she then understood, she would never be allowed to forget that she was first and foremost what Mirus had decided she would be, a pleasure slave.

He then turned away.

"Master," she called plaintively after him, "may I speak?"

"Yes," he said.

"I still fear tarns!" she said.

"We all fear tarns," he said, and he then left the platform, re-entering the lofty barnlike area.

She closed her knees and went to all fours and crawled after him, not daring to trust her legs, not daring to try to stand.

On the fourth day of her slavery in this place she was knelt down and collared. Portus read the collar to her, before putting it on her, as she was illiterate. That had been established even before she had been purchased from the shelf of Targo. It said, as we recall, "I am Ellen, the slave of Portus Canio." It pleased her, somehow, to be naked and collared. The nakedness suggested her vulnerability and, very much, her femaleness. The collar gave her a sense of belonging, a sense of security; too, it was, in its way, a proclamation of her value; it testified that men wanted her, that she had been found fair enough to collar, that she was desired as a female, that she had been found worth enslaving; too, it made it clear, to her and others, that certain issues of her life had been settled for her, that she was already "spoken for," so to speak, that others need not think of her, that she was already owned. In its way, the collar has some of the symbolic aspects of the marriage ring, except, of course, that that ring is a symbol worn by a free woman who is the putative equal of a man, whereas the collar is worn by a slave, and, aside from such things as its identificatory purposes, important in Merchant Law, is a symbol of the natural woman, the woman who is categorically owned by a man, her master.

To be sure, it is one thing to be naked before the master, wearing only his collar, which you both know identifies you as his, and another thing to be naked in the streets. Ellen was expected to run errands below, to shop, to do the laundry at the public laundering pools, and such. In the first weeks she was not permitted clothing, only her collar. In descending to the street she never used the outside ladder which Portus, who disliked the confinements of the long spiral staircases within the cylinders, had used to bring her originally to the tarn cot. One did not often meet individuals on those staircases, and, when one did, one needed only kneel down, head down, as befitted a slave. Most inhabitants of the tower, free and slave, would leave the tower at various levels, utilizing the bridges amongst them, those stretching from tower to tower, or using them to descend to the street. The city was divided, in this area, in effect, into levels or terraces, and some individuals seldom set foot on the ground, but utilized high markets and such. Ellen avoided these bridges as they were often frighteningly narrow, at least from her point of view, and lacked railings. Goreans, of course, as used to them as those of Earth to their sidewalks, utilized them almost invariably. Even though they might be several feet wide in places, Ellen tended to avoid them. They frightened her.

It required great courage, and resolve, though of course she really had no choice, for Ellen to go into the streets naked, save for her collar. The first time, she stood alone within the lower portal, back in the shadows, cringing, miserable, terrified, for more than fifteen Ehn. How could she, with her background, her antecedents, her education, her former status and station, her delicacy, her beauty, her shyness, her inhibitions, even think of leaving the cylinder, of going forth as she was? Then, after that time, sobbing, fearing she might be whipped for dallying, she stepped boldly out into the sunlight, a stripped slave in the streets. She avoided contact, of course, with the free persons, taking care not to brush against them, not to inconvenience them, not to impede their passage in any way. She was especially careful where free women were concerned. If her eyes might inadvertently meet those of a free person, she immediately lowered her head, and hurried on. Sometimes she knelt, hurriedly, in first-obeisance position. Once, in such a contretemps, she had found herself under the eyes of a free woman, the woman's eyes cold with contempt. "Be on your way, slave girl," had said the free woman, coldly, after a time. "Yes, Mistress. Thank you, Mistress," had said Ellen. But when Ellen hurried on she thought to herself, "Take away your clothes, free woman. Put you in a collar. Then I do not think we would be so different!" Ellen decided she hated free women. But then that was appropriate enough, she supposed, for, clearly, free women hated slaves, and perhaps, oddly enough, feared them, as well. Perhaps they saw themselves in the slave. Ellen did see briefly tunicked female slaves in the street. "How beautiful they are," she thought to herself. "How natural, how radiant, how free, how happy, they seem!" Many of the female slaves had long hair, as masters tend to favor such hair in slaves. Much can be done with such hair, not merely with respect to enhancing the beauty of the slave, as it may be arranged variously, but also with respect to its uses in the furs. Some of the girls smiled at Ellen, but then they probably did not know she was a barbarian. But, too, Ellen wondered if any of the slaves she passed might be, like herself, from Earth. That was surely possible. But how could one tell them from Gorean beauties? Did they not all seem lovely in their collars? Ellen knew that some Goreans referred to Earth as a "slave planet." She did not know if this was because those of Earth, both men and women, tended to live unwittingly in eccentric, unnatural cultural prisons, products of monstrous, lingering historicalities, denying themselves and their natures, submitting mindlessly, uncritically, to pathological, stunting, life-shortening conventions, fearing to live, or if it merely referred to Earth as a welcome, vulnerable resource for the predations of slavers, a world where lovely animals, perhaps rather such as she herself now was, might be netted with impunity, and chained, or crated, and brought to distant markets for their sale. "Stand straight, slave girl," whispered a yellow-tunicked, long-legged slave, as she passed. "Yes, Mistress," whispered Ellen. Ellen did see, from time to time, it reassuring her, other naked slaves in the street. To be sure, she supposed them low slaves, or perhaps slaves under discipline, perhaps denied clothing for several days as a consequence of some imperfection, or possible imperfection, in their service. Then she saw a proud slave girl preceding her master, her shoulders back, her head high, her long hair blowing about her back. She was stark naked. She was on a leash. "She is leashed!" thought Ellen. Her thighs, to her embarrassment, heated. She found herself muchly aroused by the sight of the leashed beauty. Yes, yes, she thought. That is what I want. I want to be leashed, too. It would be so exciting. To be leashed! Their eyes met, and the leashed slave looked away. The leashed beauty was being marched naked through the streets, insolently, brazenly. She is being walked, walked like a dog, thought Ellen. Just like a dog! And she is a slave, an animal, too, like a dog! Her master is doubtless proud of her, and doubtless it pleases his male vanity, the beast, to display his lovely property, his beautiful slave, his good fortune, his exquisite taste, to the world. Ellen leaned back against a wall, weak. "I want to be beaten, I want to be leashed," she thought. Then she thrust such thoughts away. She wanted to hurry back to Portus, or Selius, or one of the others, and beg use. But she must do her errand. It was a simple errand, the first time, merely to obtain an answer from a shopkeeper as to when an order of buckles would be ready. She then hurried back to the tower. But she was not used, merely put to cooking for the men. After the dishes were washed, she was returned to her stall, and there chained. Later, though Ellen continued to envy the slaves who were permitted at least a rag to cover themselves in the streets, she grew more free, and more brazen, in her demeanor. After all, she was not the only slave so sent among the crowds. She was occasionally, of course, and understandably, for many seemed to find her beautiful, accosted, commented upon with cheerful vulgarity, pinched, sometimes cruelly, brushed, touched, caressed, and such, but, invariably, as she could, she hurried on. She also attended to the laundry at the public pools, soaking, beating and rinsing garments, with other slaves. If a Cosian guardsman were in the vicinity they must work in silence. Otherwise the girls would chat merrily. Ellen did not participate in this socialization, as she feared her accent would reveal her as a barbarian, with perhaps serious consequences to her person, or worse, to her laundry. Then, after a time, Ellen would go to the pools, balancing the basket on her head with one hand, easily, proudly. Let Mirus see me now, she thought. Let him see me as I now am, as a naked slave, carrying laundry through the streets of Ar! Would he be amused? Or would he want to put a chain on me? Let him see a lovely, proud slave! Let him see what he has lost! Then she laughed to herself. What would my ideological sisters say if they could see me here, in Ar, a naked slave! I am pleased to be such! Let them cry out in anger, in scorn, in contempt! I would not give the peel of a larma for all that they might think! But see if you, dear, righteous sisters, would behave any differently, if you were stripped, and owned, and collared! Yes, dear sisters, I would like to see you stripped, and owned, and collared! I would like to see what you would do, if you met a real man, a genuinely real man, and felt his chains on your limbs! Do not denounce slaves, until you yourselves have been owned, and mastered! Do not denounce slaves, until you yourselves have learned what it is to be a true woman, pressing your lips timidly, placatingly, to the feet of a man, your master!

One day, on her way to the local laundry pools, as she commonly went, the pools less than a pasang from the Tower of Corridon, within which Portus Canio, her master, conducted his business, she, gracefully balancing her basket on her head as was her wont, steadying it with one hand, passed a familiar wall, only that day, to her surprise, she saw a large, irregular, thick, black triangle scrawled on the wall, some several feet in its dimensions. Apparently it had been placed there in haste; one could even see where paint had run in several places, in descending rivulets, from the bottom of the triangle. Those in the crowd seemed not to notice it, in their passing. Indeed, they seemed deliberately oblivious of its presence. Indeed, they seemed even to hurry, to increase their pace, until they were no longer in its vicinity. She stopped to look at the triangle. It surprised her, and made her a little angry. On her old world, in what had been her city of residence, unauthorized scrawlings, blatant obscenities, defiling letterings, ignorant vandalisms and such were common, these things exhibiting hatred, incivility, a disrespect for property, a petty, ugly desire to defile, to destroy and such, but they were, as far as she knew, rare in Gorean cities. In Gorean cities, you see, there are Home Stones. As a slave, of course, she could not have a Home Stone, no more than any other animal. Her master, however, Portus Canio, she knew, had a Home Stone. His Home Stone was the Home Stone of Ar. "Do not linger here, slave girl," whispered a man, passing her. "Yes, Master," she said, and hurried on. The next time she passed the wall, the scrawled triangle had been removed.

It had been only two weeks ago that Portus Canio, apparently satisfied with her service, perhaps even pleased, had thrown a small wad of cloth before her, as she had knelt in her stall. She did not even know what it was until after he had left, and she lifted it, and shook it out. She cried out with delight, and hugged it to her bosom, tears flowing from her eyes. "Thank you, Master! Thank you, Master!" she had cried out, hoping he could hear. It was a small, brown slave tunic.

The next morning, when freed, the chain off her neck, she had hastened to don the tiny garment and had run to Portus, seeking him out, and knelt before him, covering his feet with kisses. "Thank you, my Master. Thank you, my Master!" she had wept, again and again.

He had then made her stand, and walk about, and turn, and display herself in the tunic to himself and his three men, these being Fel Doron, Tersius Major and Selius Arconious.

Ellen complied, delightedly.

"She is actually rather pretty," said Fel Doron, assessingly.

"She has nice legs, and a pretty ass," said Tersius Major, speaking vulgarly.

Ellen laughed.

"I like her better without it," said Selius Arconious.

Ellen frowned. Who did he think he was? He did not own her!

She was muchly pleased with the garment, and she could tell, from the men, that she was extremely attractive in it. She had certainly seen many slave girls in the streets in such garments. Indeed, such garments were standard slave garb. And how beautiful, how exciting, she had found them! Now she herself had such a garment! Now she could be merely another slave in the streets, proud, head up, hair flowing, not that different from others, perhaps prettier than some, doubtless less pretty than others.

With her two hands she pulled down at the hem of the garment. "Is the garment not rather short, Master?" she asked, timidly.

"It can be shorter," said Portus Canio.

"Yes, Master," she smiled.

"It can be taken from you," said Portus.

"Yes, Master," said Ellen. "I understand, Master." This was a reference to the discipline of clothing, a reminder of her dependence in all things.

Then she knelt before them. "Thank you, Masters," she said.

"We must to our chores," said Portus. "Boil sa-tarna. Call us when it is ready."

"Yes, Master," said Ellen.

It is not unusual for slave girls denied clothing to beg piteously for a rag with which to cover themselves, at least when they dare to do so, but Ellen had not importuned Portus Canio with respect to this privilege, fearing the exasperation of his patience, fearing to be beaten. This was in part, doubtless, a function of her newness to her bondage, and an understandable desire to tread softly, to wait and learn, to test boundaries, if she dared to test them at all, with great delicacy and care. If he saw fit to give her covering for her body, she reasoned, he would; if he did not, he would not. After all, she was slave, and he master.

Ellen felt a suffusion of modesty return to her now that she had a garment. It was extremely precious to her. To be sure, it was only of rep-cloth, a cottonlike material, thin and loosely woven, open at the neck, sleeveless, and scandalously brief. Too, it was split at the hips, which bared more thigh, but allowed her to kneel with her knees widely spread, as was appropriate for her form of slavery. But as she attended to her work in the kitchen she felt that she now was, and realized that she now was, even more vulnerable than she had been before. A privilege granted may be a privilege withdrawn. The tiny garment, so precious to her, might be removed from her, at so little as a word from the master.

* * * *

And so Ellen reached down and picked up the heavy basket of meat, which she must carry to the feeding area, a section within the housing for tarns, and set forth, piece by piece, climbing the wall railings, impaling it on the hooks, for the mighty birds, seven of them, due to return with their empty baskets within the Ahn.

Portus Canio had left but Selius Arconious was still standing in the vicinity of the great portal. Ellen was well aware, and not at all displeased, that he had his eyes on her. She was, after all, a slave.

"We must be about our chores," she said, saucily.

"I think I will save my money and buy you," he said.

"I hope not!" she said.

"If I owned you," he said, "you would obey me well."

"Of course," she said. "All slaves must obey their masters."

He was looking across the straw-strewn floor at an object near one wall. Ellen reddened. It was a large, smooth, glossy tarn saddle, with its straps and rings. Ellen was quite familiar with that object. In her first experience of it, however, she, in the slave hood, had not even understood what it was. Shortly after her introduction into the tarn area, she had been whipped, that to inform her that she was now in the domicile where she would be slave. Then, sobbing, she had been flung over the object, the artifact, the large saddle, on her belly, and subjected to peremptory attentions, brutally, unceremoniously ravished as the meaningless slave she was. That had been done by Portus Canio, her master, of course. There was no doubt about that. But, too, by now, she well knew the feel of his hands on her body. Now she looked at the broad, smooth, glossy, rounded surface and blushed.

Selius Arconious was regarding it, too. And it was not difficult to read his thoughts.

"Do you not have harnesses to mend," she asked, "—Master?"

"Your face, and arms, and legs are red," said he, "slave girl."

Ellen blushed more, her entire exposed body, where it was not concealed with the brief tunic, reddening even more embarrassingly.

She looked at the rounded surface. She had been several times on that surface, and generally on her belly. It was a useful place to teach a slave what she was, it seemed. More embarrassingly Ellen, despite her initial dismay, her resentment, and distress, at Portus's first use of her there, had gradually, in the vicinity of this object, and in certain other places where men had put her to their purposes, begun to be disturbed by slave heat rising within her. Whereas her conscious mind might feign resentment and humiliation at such usages her unconscious mind, the emotions of her depths, seemed insistently, irresistibly, to crave them. A frequent thought in her mind, one she often tried to banish, was "Use me as a slave! Use me as the slave I am!" How startled, and seemingly upset, she had been upon occasion when she was dragged to the saddle for use, to discover, despite her seeming resistance, her trying to hang back, her wrist tight in their grip, that she wished to be taken there. Even more startled she was when, at no more than a tiny touch, the men informed her, she over the saddle, embarrassingly on her belly, her tunic thrust up about her hips, that she was "juicing," "oiling," "lubricating," that she was "slave ready." "No, no!" she wept, but she had then begun to enjoy her uses. To her horror, later, she found her body responding, first with tiny, begging movements, and then, as she was forced to higher levels of excitement, and arousal, with brazen supplicatory liftings, with obvious, shameless petitionary presentations of her body, which the masters, unnecessarily in her view, found amusing. "Oh!" she cried. "You wriggle well, slave girl," she was informed. Then, when permitted, clinging to a ring, eyes clenched shut, lost in her sensations, she served, twisting, grinding, bucking, begging, crying out, until, her fingers white and tight on the ring, she screamed her submission and slavehood. Mental associations are interesting, how one thing may be associated with another, how one may remember things, how one thought may suggest another, how emotions and feelings, and thoughts, may be associated with one place or another, or with one object or another. As the mere sight of the saddle had come to be arousing to Ellen, so, too, with slaves, the mere being in a place or the mere seeing or touching of an article may affect them in a profound manner, disturbing them, rendering them uneasy, rendering them helplessly, grievously needful. The sight of her chains, of a whip, the touching of her collar, the fingering of her brand, even in the absence of the master, can arouse a slave. So, too, the sight of a place she remembers, a grassy knoll, a place behind a shed, a ditch, a stall, the surface of a long, narrow wooden bench, the floor, fur-strewn, at the foot of the master's couch, she not permitted on its surface, that privilege usually reserved for free companions, or perhaps high slaves, such things, can all affect her profoundly, can all heat her, and torment her with the longing, the yearning, of the needful slave, fearful of, but grateful for, the slave fires men have ignited in her belly. But one need not be a slave to be so affected, to feel these things. To be sure, the female slave is the most sexual, loving, vulnerable, helpless and feminine of all women, but such things are not confined to those whose lovely throats are clasped securely within the circlet of bondage. Free women, too, can feel such things. For example, the mere secret touching of a slave tunic can make a free woman sob with need. Sexuality in a woman, and I wish this were clear to all men, is an entirety, a totalistic phenomenon. It is not limited to portions of our body, or moments of our day. It is pervasive; most simply, it is we. Be severe with us, if you will, Masters, but understand what it is you own. It is all of us that you own. It is all of us, our entirety, our wholeness, which you, to our undying gratitude, have put in your collars.

"I trust that my Master, the noble Portus Canio, your employer," said Ellen to Selius Arconious, "does not inquire of me as to your behavior, and if you have been attentive to your duties, for I, as a slave, however reluctantly, knelt down to speak the truth, would have to admit that you have been lax, and that you have a tendency to dally, quite unconscionably."

Selius picked up a loop of harness and held it in his hands. The leather was black, and glossy, some half of an inch in thickness, and some three to four inches in width, and there were buckles attached, for its fastening on tarns. He fingered the leather, while regarding her, and, to her unease, snapped it taut in his hands. More than once he, and others, had put her in portions of such harnessings, for their uses. With all a slave's sensuousness, and a slave's sensitivity to surfaces and textures, she had relished its tightness, and feel, and her slave's helplessness in such bonds, even the cut of the buckle in her flesh. Such things, like cords and chains, perhaps partly for physical reasons, but surely, too, for psychological reasons, cruelly fan the flames of a woman's bondage. They tell her, you are slave, you are owned, you are mine, you have no choice, you will obey, you will yield, you will be punished, and terribly, if you hold anything back, you will have orgasms such that you have never dreamed of, orgasms that you have hitherto not understood were possible, you will have the orgasms of a surrendering, conquered slave.

"Well," said Ellen, lightly, "I must be about my duties."

She then turned away, but, after a step, stopped, looked back over her shoulder and smiled, slyly, and then, saucily, suddenly, bid Selius farewell with a toss, beneath her brief, thin tunic, of her small, well-outlined *derrière.*

"She-sleen!" he cried, taking a step toward her, but she sped away. "You do not own me!" she laughed, "and I do not think you will soon, after today, have my use either!"

"She-sleen! She-urt!" he cried.

Ellen was well pleased with herself. "Let him suffer, and stew about," she laughed to herself. "He thinks he is so handsome, so important. He is only a tarnster, a driver! A lowly employee of my master! Let him roll and twist, and mutter angrily, in his blankets. Let him stew, and cry out, and suffer! He cannot have me! I am not for such lowly sorts! Suffer, Selius Arconious, suffer! You cannot have me!"

In the barred feeding area, the gate shut against the housing for returning tarns, Ellen put the basket of meat on the floor, and, moving about, and climbing, ascending, placed the meat, piece by piece, heavy strip by heavy strip, on the hooks in the wall. From those hooks, sometimes as they fluttered in the feeding area, feet from the floor, it would be torn by the feeding tarns. Sometimes, too, when the tarns were in the feeding area, she would throw the meat upward, between the bars to them. In such a case they tended to seize it in the air, with their beaks. If a piece fell to the floor, they would hover above it, seize it in their talons, and then crouch over it, holding it in place with a taloned foot, while tearing it to pieces with their beaks. "We all fear tarns," Portus Canio had told her once, on the platform. Ellen did not doubt it. She knew that she was terrified of the great winged beasts. She was reluctant to approach them, even with bars between them.

While Ellen climbed and placed the meat, she wondered what it would be like, to be owned by Selius Arconious. She did not even like him, of course. She wondered if he would use the switch, or a whip, on her, if he would beat her. He might, of course. She was, after all, a slave.

She fixed another piece of meat in place.

She was a woman of Earth, and had been an intellectual, a person of stature and importance. How was it then, she wondered, given her obvious excellence and quality, her obvious value, that she had not been purchased by a rich man, someone important, a statesman, a general or a great merchant, surely by some significant personage in Ar. Surely she should serve in a mansion or palace, or a great cylinder, in rich quarters.

Did they truly not know her worth, what she deserved? How was it then that she had been purchased by a tarnmaster, a fellow not even of high caste? She wondered what he had paid for her. Then she realized that these matters of Earth were of no interest here, on this world. Here she was a young barbarian, naive, poorly trained and illiterate. What could she expect, here? She had not even been the best meat on Targo's shelf. Surely she had not been the first sold. Indeed, it seemed that he had, at times, almost despaired of disposing of her. She wondered what she had gone for. Mirus had let her go, it seemed, for a mere ten copper tarsks, such as might be paid for a worthless girl. To be sure, Mirus, as part of his vengeance and amusement, had doubtless wanted her sold so, as a worthless slut. Then she realized that her value on this world was not a function of her value elsewhere, under different conditions. Here she had been sold simply for what she now was, as that and nothing else, as raw female. This, doubtless, was what she was worth, in herself. It occurred to her that she had perhaps been fortunate, given her unimportance and her lack of value here, to have been purchased by a tarnkeeper. She might have been purchased by a peasant, slept chained in a hovel, and, harnessed, struggled to plow his fields.

She recalled with satisfaction, with pleasure, how she had tormented Selius Arconious. She laughed to herself. Oh, dear Mirus, my erstwhile master, she thought to herself, what would you have made of that? Would you have recognized your Ellen, she whom you brought to Gor and so transformed and reduced, in that enticing, insolent, saucy little flirt? One who well knows how to torment a man? Would you have known me? Would you have been surprised? Would you have been outraged? Do you think I might similarly torment you? Perhaps. After all, I am no longer your slave, my dear Mirus.

"Ho, slave!" called Fel Doron. "I see the first of the birds in the distance. Hurry!"

"Yes, Master!" cried Ellen.

* * * *

Ellen, as she was a slave, was not permitted to leave the stable, or cot, without permission. This was quite normal, of course. Slaves, almost invariably, are not allowed to leave the residence of, or the grounds of, the master without receiving permission. When such permission is granted, the slave is expected to specify her destination, her business and her expected time of return. Such things may always be checked. The slave's life is a controlled life. The slave is not a wife, but a property, and, accordingly, as she is not an autonomous, independent contractee but a valued possession, she commonly finds herself an object of jealous regard on the part of the master. She is not respected, but, rather, sheltered, safeguarded and treasured. Masters, as with other valuable possessions, tend to take a detailed personal interest in their slaves, sometimes washing them, as one might a dog, combing their hair for the pleasure they derive from this activity, dressing them for their pleasure, having them display their beauty in a variety of aspects and attitudes upon command, and so on. Masters commonly wish to know everything there is to know about their slaves. To make a trivial comparison, few husbands take the time to really look at their wives, for example, to inspect, scrutinize and truly examine the bodies of their wives, and, one supposes, such attentions might be found disturbing by many wives, who might fear or resist such interests. On the other hand, the master will commonly have examined the bodies of his slaves with great care, familiarizing himself with each subtle, delicious curve. He is likely to note even the tiny hairs at the back of her neck, beneath her collar, pulling her collar out a little to see them. He will know, too, her every tiny blemish, and will commonly see them as interesting and delightful, as making her different or special in her way, or perhaps as beauty marks or patches, whose presence cunningly serves to enhance, by striking contrast, the beauty of the owned wholeness of her. Too, of course, as she is not a wife, but a chained slave, he may experiment with her, subjecting her, she willing or not, to a variety of erotic techniques, until he finds what she cannot resist, and what renders her helpless, what will drive her wild with passion, what might rob her of her last pathetic vestige of self and turn her into a writhing, ecstatic, spasmodic, begging slave. And so, you see, masters are muchly concerned with their slaves, and control them, and regulate and supervise them, with much attention and great care. They are not wives, they are properties. And thus they wish to know, it seems at all times, their activities, whereabouts, and such. It would not do, for example, to have them sneaking off for an assignation with a groom or drover. That is not their privilege, you see. They belong to the master.

Just as Ellen was not permitted, nor would be many slaves, to leave the domicile of the master without permission, so, too, she was not permitted, without express permission, to open the interior door of the apartments of Portus Canio, that leading to the interior stairwell, giving access to various bridges, and, eventually, at its foot, to the street. One does not know who might be on the other side of the door. She can, of course, keep the door, ascertain the nature of callers, and, if given permission, open the door.

We mention the matter of the interior door because, interestingly, usually in the evening, sometimes late at night, unidentified visitors, sometimes several of them, would arrive at the door, visitors who may not have, in their approach, availed themselves of the outside bridges. Portus Canio, himself, would admit these visitors, but only, whether it were early evening or late at night, after he had hooded Ellen, back-braceleted her and chained her in her stall. This puzzled Ellen because, normally, at least after her first few days in the stable, or cot, she was not even chained in her stall. To be sure, where was there for a slave girl to run? The collar and chain, of course, were always there, beneath the straw. Portus Canio entertained these visitors in the kitchen, apparently about the table there. Ellen, from her stall, could hear nothing of what was said.

One morning, when Ellen was sweeping in the kitchen, she bent down and picked up what seemed to be a shard of white pottery.

"What have you there?" asked Portus Canio.

"I do not know, Master," said Ellen.

He put out his hand and Ellen put down the broom, and went and knelt before him, as that is how the girl commonly approaches the master when summoned, and, lifting her hand, gave him the object.

"Do you know what this is?" he asked.

"No, Master," she said.

"It is an ostrakon," he said.

Originally an ostrakon was merely a shard of pottery, often glazed, used for one purpose or another, say, for a token, a ticket, or such. On the other hand, they may be, and often are, prepared deliberately, fired in great numbers for admission tokens, tickets, or such, to restricted festivals, private markets, song dramas, and such. The object in question, clearly, seemed to be an actual shard. It was glazed white, on one side.

Portus held the shard before her, the glazed side facing her. On it was a design, a letter or mark.

"Can you read this?" he asked.

"No, Master," she said.

"You have not seen this," he said.

"Yes, Master," she said.

He put the shard in his pouch. "You may return to your work," he said.

"Yes, Master," she said. "Thank you, Master."

As she swept the floor of the kitchen, she recalled the design on the ostrakon. It was small, of course, no more than an inch or so in height, but she had seen the mark before, on a wall, a titanic mark scrawled there, as though angry and defiant, in dimensions of several feet. It was a black triangle.

* * * *

"Master?" asked Ellen.

"Assume the standard position for the examination of a standing slave," said Portus Canio.

Ellen, in her tunic, puzzled, stood then before him, her legs widely, painfully spread. The split hems of the tunic, slit at the sides, permitted this position. Ellen clasped her hands behind the back of her head, and held her head up and back, in this position looking rather at the height of the great portal, leading into the barn area, from the platform outside.

In this position it is convenient to examine the slave. She cannot easily move without losing her balance. The position of her hands prevents her from interfering with the examination. The raised head, held back, makes it difficult for her to know, or guess, the position of the examiner's hands, where they are, and what they might do, for example, how and when she might be touched, caressed, or tested. Needless to say, this position is normally assumed when the slave is nude.

"Steady," said Portus Canio.

"Oh!" cried Ellen.

"A tiny tube has been inserted in your body," said Portus Canio. "At its base is a tiny leather loop, not visible from the outside, by means of which it may be withdrawn. You may now stand naturally before me."

Ellen then stood as an erect, graceful slave before her master. From his pouch he withdrew a light belly chain, which hooked in front, with attached slave bracelets at the back of the chain. He then put her in the belly chain and bracelets, her hands braceleted behind her, at the small of her back. Given the flare of her hips, her hands would be kept there, at the small of her back. Accordingly, she was unable to reach whatever it was which Portus Canio had placed in her body.

"I do not understand, Master," she said.

"When someone says to you, 'Are your thighs hot?' you are to reply, 'I am a slave girl, Master,' and obey him, without demur. Do you understand?"

"Yes, Master," said Ellen.

"Are your thighs hot?" asked Portus Canio.

"I am a slave girl, Master," she said.

"Good," said Portus. Then from his pouch he drew forth a small message capsule, about a half inch in width and two and a half inches in length, with its screw lid and the loop of string by means of which it might be looped about, or tied to, a slave's collar. He tied it about her collar. He tied it in such a way that it would dangle between her tunicked breasts. This technique is, of course, more stimulatory when the slave is naked. She is thus more acutely aware of the movements of the object upon her, fastened in such a way as to remind her constantly of both the errand and the master. Ellen, of course, could feel it through the rep-cloth, which is quite thin, "slave thin," as it is sometimes said. Rep-cloth, like slave silk, leaves few of a slave's charms to the imagination.

"This message," said Portus, "is to be carried to Bonto, the Cobbler, of the Leather Workers, in Hesius Street. You have been there, you know the place."

"Yes, Master," said Ellen.

"It is an order for work sandals, for the men, with their sizes, and such," said Portus Canio. He then went through the barn area, and the inner rooms, until he reached the interior door, which he opened. Ellen followed him. "Be on your way," he said.

"Yes, Master," said Ellen.

Never before had she been sent forth so, braceleted. Normally she delivered her messages by word of mouth, though, upon occasion, she had been given a scrap of paper, which she normally held in one hand. There are no pockets, of course, in a slave tunic. Similarly, naturally, there is no nether closure in such a tunic, as one of the purposes of such a tunic is to remind the slave that she is to be instantly, readily available to men.

Perhaps a word might be added with respect to this matter.

It is not an accident, of course. Like other aspects of the garment, its brevity, simplicity and such, it has its meaning, its role and symbolism.

The slave is, you see, to be instantly available to men; her inviting, luscious intimacies, so sweet and warm between her thighs, belong not to her but to the master; she is not a free woman who may wrap and bundle herself, and shield and guard herself; she is a slave and thus she is to be instantly, vulnerably, readily accessible to men; she is no more than an object or toy, no more than a possession, no more than a lovely animal, subject to the least whim and convenience of masters.

Does not the tunic make such things clear to her?

In such a garment she is well aware of her vulnerability; she lives in a state of sexual awareness, and often, whether in despite of her wishes or not, she finds herself in a state of helpless sexual arousal.

Men, it seems, respect free women, but seek slaves, they venerate the citizeness, but it is we whom they buy; they esteem the free woman but it is we whom they rope and leash, and lead home.

It is little wonder free women hate slaves, and slaves fear free women.

Ellen descended, carefully, her wrists fastened behind her, the long spiral staircase within the cylinder, and, at the ground level, thrust open the swinging portal with her shoulder, and went into the streets. She had seen other girls running errands clad as she, in their tunics, and back-braceleted, with a message capsule slung about their neck or tied to their collar, but this was the first time she had been so sent forth. She was pleased that she had not been sent forth naked and back-braceleted, with a message capsule. She had occasionally seen slaves on errands, so exposed, so restrained.

In a few minutes she had come to the open shop of Bonto and knelt before him. "Tal, Ellen," said he, for he knew her from previous errands. "Tal, Master," she responded. He unscrewed the cap on the message capsule, removed the tiny paper within and studied it. "Convey my greetings to Portus Canio, your master," said he, "and inform him that the order will be filled by the tenth Ahn, the second day from this."

"Yes, Master," she said.

He then replaced the lid on the capsule, and once more it dangled from her collar.

He lifted his hand and she rose, turned about, and returned to the streets, to make her way back to the Tower of Corridon. Bonto seemed a kindly man, simple and gentle. Ellen liked him. Men are so different, she thought. And I could belong to any man, any man who might buy me. I wonder what it would be like to belong to Bonto. He is muchly different from Portus Canio, my master. I think he would be kind to me, though, of course, I would have to render him perfect slave service. If I were less than perfect, I do not doubt but what he would use the switch, or whip, on me. He is, after all, Gorean. But I think I prefer Portus Canio, my master. I think he is sterner, I think he is more severe. Kneeling before him any woman would know herself a slave. At least I do not belong to Selius Arconious, that supercilious, handsome, vain, arrogant beast! How I detest Selius Arconious! And yet if he were to buy me, I would be his slave, and would have to render him perfections of service. I do not think he would be patient with me, not at all, even as patient as Portus Canio. How I hate him, that young, handsome, vain beast, Selius Arconious, he thinking he is so good-looking, so clever and mighty! How I hold him in contempt, how I detest him! And yet it is hard for me to remain standing before him! I grow weak! He makes me feel helpless! His nearness makes me feel faint! I grow giddy! I wish to flee! I wish to kneel! I wish to put my head down! I must fight the desire to tear away my tunic and throw myself to my belly before him! He is insensitive. He does not understand me. He cares for me not at all, save as an object of lust. Even his least glance treats me as a slave. Why is it then that I writhe in the straw at the thought of him? Why is it then that I dream of his whip upon me, lashing me, claiming me, marking me as his?

"Hold, slave girl," said a voice behind her, a man's voice. "Do not turn about."

Ellen, frightened, stood still.

"Are your thighs hot?" she heard the voice ask.

"Master?" she asked, frightened.

"Are your thighs hot?" he asked.

"—I am a slave girl, Master," she whispered.

"You will continue to walk in your current direction," said the voice. "At the next corner you will turn left, and enter the third door on your left. You will not look behind you."

"Yes, Master," said Ellen. She had the vague notion that she might have heard the voice before, but she did not recognize it.

When Ellen arrived at the designated door, she saw that it hung awry on its hinges, was half broken, and boarded over. It gave access to what, now abandoned, might once have been a small, shuttered, unpretentious place of business. The windows were boarded over. Bills, mostly advertising tharlarion races and paga taverns, adhered to the exterior walls, and, in two places, to the door itself.

"Enter and do not look back," said the voice.

Ellen entered the room, thrusting against the door with her shoulder.

The man followed her within. She heard the door closed behind her. It was rather dark in the room; it was lit only by narrow blades of light coming through cracks in the imperfectly shuttered windows. It was musty and gloomy. There was miscellaneous debris on the floor, a shallow, bent pan, perhaps once used by slaves for drinking, some boards, some papers, and such. In the center of the room there was a table. There was much dust, everywhere. She felt the dust, thick, deep, soft, beneath her bare feet. She did not know when this room had been last entered. She noted motes of dust adrift in the light. She heard a rustle of leather behind her and then could see no more as she had been hooded. She was lifted from her feet and carried to the table, on the surface of which she was placed, on her back. Almost immediately she heard others approach, it seemed from an inner room. She half reared up as she felt her ankles firmly, rudely grasped. She was forced back to the surface of the table. Her tunic was thrust up, about her hips. Then, her ankles cruelly, widely spread, held far apart, she could feel the edges of the table on each side, the object which Portus Canio had inserted within her was drawn free. The message capsule which had held the sandal order for Bonto of the Leather Workers, tied to her collar, hung to one side.

"Remain as you are, slave girl," said the man's voice, that of he who had directed her to this place.

"Yes, Master," she said, within the hood. She must obey, she remembered, without demur. And, indeed, where men are concerned, at least free men, and these men were presumably free, what alternative does a slave girl have other than instant and perfect obedience?

After a few Ehn she again felt her legs spread and the tube, or one similar to it, was again inserted within her. She then heard the men withdraw, with one exception. She was carried to the door, and stood upright, facing it. Her tunic was smoothed down. The door was opened. Then, after a moment, warned not to look about, the hood was removed, and she was ordered to return, as though nothing had occurred, to her master. Ellen needed no urging and quickly left the room, not looking back. She restrained her impulse to run back to the Tower of Corridon, to seek the security of the loft, of her stall, of the kitchen. She tried to walk naturally. She could feel, subtly, the small object which had been placed within her. She had been fully at the mercy of the men, but they had not made use of her. She had not been put to their pleasure. She wondered if that were because she was the property of Portus Canio, or merely because these were serious men, who had more important things on their minds than such as she. At the tower, as chance would have it, though she wondered if he were waiting for her, it was Selius Arconious who opened the interior door to admit her. She saw how he looked at her, and she backed against the wall, near the door. She pulled a little against the bracelets and there was a tiny sound of chain, emphasizing her helplessness and captivity, and her movements, too, of course, drew the belly chain back, more tightly, about her, reining in her belly, which, in emphasizing the narrowness of her waist, the contrasting flare of her hips, the swelling, lovely ascent to her bosom, and her condition as bound thrall, presumably did not much help either. Selius Arconious took her casually, masterfully, possessively, in his arms, and she turned her head to the side, trying to turn away from him. How small her body seemed in his mighty grasp. "No, Master!" she said. "No, Master! Do not, Master!"

"Struggle if you will, little vulo," he said. "You are only a slave."

He then pressed his lips to hers greedily, as though he would devour her. "You are only a slave," he whispered.

"What is going on here?" said Portus Canio, entering the room.

Selius Arconious thrust Ellen from him, and stepped back. Ellen tried to catch her breath. She sank back against the wall, weakly. In another moment, she feared, every fiber in her vulnerable, enslaved body, the entirety of her vulnerable, enslaved self, might have yielded to him. She stood then straight, as Portus Canio was present, reddening, looking embarrassed, trying to look indignant.

"Well?" said Portus.

"I was hungry," said Selius Arconious, "for a snack of slave."

"Seek provender at the taverns, at the brothels," said Portus. He then turned, angrily, to Ellen, who immediately knelt, with her head to the floor. "And what of this is your fault?" he inquired.

"Please do not whip me, Master!" begged Ellen. Her small wrists, behind her, pulled against the bracelets.

"Oh, I do not blame you, slut," said Portus. "You cannot help what you are."

"Master?" said Ellen.

"It was my fault," said Selius Arconious.

"The sight of you to a man," said Portus Canio to Ellen, "is like thrusting a torch into straw. How can it not burn?"

Then he said, "I go to the office. Join me there."

"Yes, Master," said Ellen.

Portus Canio then left.

When Ellen looked up, she found herself kneeling before Selius Arconious.

"You look well at my feet, slave girl," he said.

"My master awaits me," said Ellen.

"Split your knees, more widely," said Selius Arconious. "Yes," said he, "you look well there, and thusly."

"I am under command," said Ellen. "I must hasten to my master!"

Selius indicated that she might rise, and she scrambled, angrily, to her feet.

"May I speak?" she inquired, angrily, looking up a him.

"Yes," he said.

"Dare never again to take me in your arms! I will complain to my master! I hate you! You are a vain, arrogant beast! You are a brute! You are ignorant, stupid and homely! You think you are so grand! You are not! You are only a tarnster! You are an ugly tarnster! You are nothing! I loathe your touch! The sight of you makes my skin crawl! Better to be seized in the claws of a tharlarion! I detest you!"

"Do you think I do not know the feel of a slave in my arms who is on the brink of yielding?" he inquired.

"No!" she cried. "False! False!"

"So the little vulo would pretend that she is a figurine of ice, carved in the form of a slave girl?"

"I hate you!"

"But a touch," he said, reaching out, "ever so gentle, ever so soft, will prove to me, and to any who might be interested, that you are a hot little slut."

"Do not touch me!" said Ellen.

She backed away, frightened.

"You are a barbarian," he said. "You are worthless, but you might serve some simple purposes, as a slave."

"If you touch me again, I will tell my master," she said. "Consider that, vain, handsome beast!"

He regarded her, angrily. And she stepped farther away, and stood straight. She tossed her head, insolently, and her hair, which was longer now, which had never been cut on Gor, save to be trimmed and shaped, danced about her shoulders.

"You may, of course," she said, "look upon me, and frequently, I trust, and I shall find that amusing, for I know that you may not have me. Indeed, I may move with particular interest before you, to insult and taunt you, subtly, of course, so that my master will not notice. I think that will be a frolic. And thus will I avenge myself on you, paying you back for your arrogance, and your unacceptable liberties, by torturing you with the beauty of a slave girl, forever beyond your reach! Oh, I shall relish your agony! Do not smile! Whatever you may say to me, I know that I am not the poorest meat in a collar! I have seen the eyes of men in the streets upon me. I have heard their calls. I have felt their cruel pinches, darted away from their hands, and touches! And I know, too, that whatever I may be, and whatever may be my quality, or whatever price I might bring in a market, you, handsome master, desire me, and heatedly. Good! And you may not have me! I am owned by another! Roll in your blankets and think of me! Moan in your sleep! Dream of what you cannot possess! Let your straw burn, handsome master. Let it burn—fiercely! Suffer, thinking of me! I know that you desire me, and mightily, but know that I detest you, and that you cannot have me! You will never have me! I am not yours! I belong to another!"

"You can probably not even dance nude," said Selius Arconious.

With a cry of anger, Ellen spun about and hurried to the office of Portus Canio. There he put her on her knees, her head to the floor, and, from behind her, removed the object from her body. He then, as the thought struck him, rather as an afterthought, seized her at the hips and briefly made use of her; he then, after a moment or two, freed her of the belly chain and bracelets and sent her to the kitchen, to prepare the men's supper. After supper, while Ellen was busying herself, cleaning up, attending to the dishes, and such, she thought of Selius Arconious. How I detest him, how I hate him, she thought. To be sure, he was young, and strong and handsome. When she was near him she felt weak, "slave weak." He was the sort of a man who made a woman quite conscious of the brand on her thigh, the collar on her neck. She recalled her training. She had not even been shown the rudiments of dance. That had been denied her. Accordingly she was no dancer. Too, Goreans have high standards for slave dance. On the other hand, she thought to herself, I am not such poor stuff. I could show him how a woman of Earth, yes, of Earth, if trained, can dance before men! I could show him how a woman of Earth, as much as any Gorean woman, can drive a man mad with passion!

It might be mentioned that the errand just described was merely the first errand of its type which was required of Ellen. Over the next few weeks she found herself, several times, embarked on similar obscure ventures. There were some differences, of course. For example, she was sent to different shops and places of business, and professional activity, but each time, of course, with some ostensible, public purpose, usually connected, at least officially, with her master's interests or work, a purpose which might be ascertained, for example, by guardsmen, were they inclined to inquire. And then each time, she having discharged her public business, she would be, sometimes even near the Tower of Corridon, addressed from behind, and directed, always by the unseen observer, to a rendezvous elsewhere, in one place or another, at which point the small tube would be removed from her body and then, later, reinserted. She did not know if she were carrying messages back to her master or not, as he never opened the tube in her presence. He did not warn her to silence about these fascinating matters but she was, we may suppose, highly intelligent, or at least intelligent, and surely warily discreet. Too, she did not wish to be smothered, or strangled, or suffer an unfortunate, fearful accident, for example, falling from the platform to the street so far below.

It is perhaps appropriate to mention, however briefly, one further matter, which it seems may have been important with respect to various events which were soon to transpire in Ar and its vicinity.

Ellen was at the public laundry pools on a given morning, those local to her district, toward the ninth Ahn, something before noon, kneeling on a towel, working on the laundry for Portus Canio and his men. This she did weekly. There were several slaves similarly engaged, perhaps two dozen, here and there, about the small pools, and, as there were no guardsmen in the vicinity, these were quite vocal, gossiping, chatting delightedly, exchanging small secrets, playing, splashing water, and so on. Too, they were doubtless not unaware that several young men were about, who, as was common, had come down to the pools to watch the girls in their collars work. It is pleasant to see beautiful women engaged in simple tasks, particularly if they are permitted no more clothing than a slave tunic. Too, Ellen realized, women become more animate, and beautiful, and charming, when they know themselves under the scrutiny of men. They are performing, thought Ellen, they are displaying themselves, as females. How stimulated they are, how pleased they are to do this, she thought. Even free women, she knew, behaved so. She recalled such things even from Earth, even amongst, surprisingly enough, her ideological colleagues. So many of them, she recalled, seemed so different in the presence of men. They are trying to please men, she had thought. And then she had thought, as well, but is that not what we all want to do, please men? Too, she had sometimes marked various changes in their behavior, such as a self-conscious awkwardness, a sudden uneasiness, a stumbling of speech, unfamiliar gestures, of a surprisingly, rather obviously feminine sort, flirtatious expressions and attitudes, a straining for wit and cleverness. Sometimes they burst into uneasy laughter, exhibiting an unnatural hilarity which bordered on nervous hysteria. What they needed, thought Ellen, working on a tunic of Fel Doron, was to have their clothing removed, and to be tied at the feet of men. That is what they needed!

There were, of course, streets in the vicinity of the pools, and these streets had their traffic, of pedestrians, carts, and such. Normally heavy wagons and such were allowed in the streets only after dark, to avoid congestion.

Ellen did not, as we have suggested, join in the pleasant confabulations of the enslaved beauties at the pools, fearing that her accent would betray her as a barbarian, with perhaps unfortunate consequences, even if only so minor as contempt and ostracization. She did, of course, smile when smiled at, and took care to present herself at the pools as merely another pleasant, dutiful slave, engaged in her domestic labors, only another Gorean slave girl. And then she thought once, I may be a barbarian, but, in the end, that, too, is all I really am, only another Gorean slave girl! Too, Ellen knew no one at the pools. Many of the other girls seemed to have their friends, and know one another, and perhaps, being freer than Ellen, even arranged to meet their friends at the pools, seizing such pleasant opportunities to chat, gossip, socialize, and such.

Ellen angrily took from the heap of clothing to her right a tunic of Selius Arconious. He was in the employ of Portus Canio, her master, and, given her duties, there was no way she could avoid doing his laundry. She lifted it to her face, and slowly, deeply, drew in its scent, her eyes closed, and pressed her lips submissively to the cloth.

She heard a bright laugh from beside her, and she quickly thrust the cloth down.

"That must be the tunic of your master!" laughed a girl next to her. The kneeling slave, to her right, she who had spoken, had dark eyes, regarding her, now sparkling, dancing, with amusement. She was dark-haired, beautifully formed and exquisitely beautiful. She wore a light, yellow, brief tunic, with a disrobing loop at the left shoulder, as most masters are right-handed. Ellen thought that she, stripped on a slave block, would doubtless bring a high price. Ellen felt a surge of jealousy.

"No!" said Ellen. "It is the tunic of a hateful brute!" Then Ellen was alarmed, for she saw the girl look at her, sharply. Doubtless she had recognized that Ellen spoke with an accent.

"You seem to have an unusual accent!" said Ellen, defensively, to the girl.

"So, too, do you," she said, not unpleasantly, but a bit narrowly.

"What is your accent?" asked Ellen.

"Your accent seems of Ar, in a way," said the girl.

"But what is your accent?" asked Ellen.

"I fear it is Cosian," said the girl.

"Then you are Cosian!" said Ellen. She knew how those of Cos were hated in Ar.

"How I can be Cosian?" laughed the girl. "I can no more be Cosian than a kaiila. I am a slave."

Ellen smiled, despite her anxiety, her defensiveness.

"But I learned my first Gorean," said the girl, "in slave pens, in Telnus, the capital of Cos."

"'Learned'?" said Ellen, startled.

"Yes," said the girl. "I come from another world. I am a barbarian. Such are now no strangers to Gorean markets."

"I, too, am a barbarian!" said Ellen.

"I thought so!" laughed the girl. "I am from a place called America."

"I too am from America!" cried Ellen. "We are both from America!" She then, suddenly, as though something had broken within her, tears running down her cheeks, fell weeping into the arms of the other girl. "They have taken us and brought us here," she wept. "How terrible they are! How wicked they are! They have branded us, and collared us, and made us slaves!"

"Yes," smiled the other girl. "We are now slaves. But do not weep. There is no going back. We are now here. And this is now our world. If we would live, we must try to be good slaves."

Ellen wept, uncontrollably.

"Surely there are worse worlds," said the girl, consolingly, soothingly. "Consider the beauty of this world, how fresh and glorious it is! Have you known such a place on Earth, surely not many. What a boon, what a privilege it is, to breathe such air, such exuberant air, to see such sights, so striking, so splendid and colorful, to taste fresh, natural foods, not aged and stale, not tasteless, not saturated with alien chemicals! And see how these men love their world and their cities, their fields and forests, how they keep them, how they care for them, and love them, how they will not destroy them, how they will not cut and burn them, nor diminish and exhaust them. There are surely worse worlds than this."

"But we have been brought here as slaves!" said Ellen.

"Yes," smiled the girl.

"By what right?" demanded Ellen.

"By the right of their will, it seems," said the girl. "These are men. They do much what they please, and take much what they want."

Ellen sobbed.

"As foxes are the natural prey of fox hunters, as deer are the natural prey of deer hunters, so women are the natural prey of slave hunters," said the girl.

Ellen regarded her, red-eyed, shaken.

"It is easy to see why they took you," said the girl. "You are very beautiful."

"Oh?" said Ellen.

"Yes," said the girl. "And I do not know about you," she said, "but I belong in a collar."

"No!" cried Ellen.

"Oh, yes, I am appropriately in my collar," said the girl. "I am a natural slave. How fortunate I am to have been brought here!"

"No!" protested Ellen.

"But yes," laughed the girl. "Here I have found love, and the domination I need and crave."

Ellen regarded her, awed.

"I had not known, from Earth," said the girl, joyfully, "that men like these could exist, such natural men, such innocently biological males, such intelligent, remarkable, powerful, virile, demanding, uncompromising, magnificent beasts. Such rightfully see such as we as their slaves, and before such men, natural masters, what could such as we be but slaves?"

Ellen sank back, on her heels.

"And," she laughed, "did I not see you press your lips to the tunic of a male?"

"I hate him!" said Ellen.

"I think we are both slaves," smiled the girl.

"Who is your master?" asked Ellen.

"Aeschines of Cos," she replied. "Who is your master?"

"Portus Canio, of Ar," said Ellen.

"My master is of the Warriors," she said, "but like many of that caste, he has done various works. Many caste members, as you know, do not concern themselves specifically with caste business. He is not now in fee."

"My master," said Ellen, "is of the tarnkeepers."

"What is your name?" asked the girl.

"'Ellen.'"

"I am now called 'Corinne'," said the girl. "But I have had various names. I have been known as Janice, and, before my current master acquired me, as Gail. I have served in Cos, in the city of Treve, and now in Ar."

"I fear I have been only in Ar," smiled Ellen.

"We are not the only barbarians amongst these slaves," said the girl. "See that one there. She is Priscilla. She is from England. Next to her is Sumomo, from Japan."

"They are beautiful," breathed Ellen.

"No more beautiful than you, slave girl," said the girl.

"You said you were a natural slave!" said Ellen, chidingly.

"Of course," laughed her interlocutor. "We are women. We are all natural slaves. We are the slave sex. It is in our genes. Surely you know that. We can never be fully happy without our collars."

"No, no!" wept Ellen.

Then a shadow fell across the kneeling women. Both became silent, instantly. "Be on with your work, slave girls," said a voice.

The embonded women looked up.

It was a guardsman, of Cos.

"Yes, Master!" said Corinne, frightened.

"Yes, Master!" said Ellen.

They then, as with the others, also now silent, bent to their labors with renewed vigor.

As Ellen attended rather irritably to the tunic of Selius Arconious she realized, with a bit of a start, that she and the other girl, her new friend, Corinne, had been conversing in Gorean, naturally, and without thought. To be sure, it was appropriate that they did so. Their language now, appropriately, was to be the language of their masters.

Ellen angrily soaked, and kneaded, and soaked and kneaded, the tunic of Selius Arconious. Then, twisting water out of it, she slapped it down angrily on the sloping cement shelf before her, beyond her knees, on their towel. "There, Selius Arconious!" she thought. "Take that!" And then she was frightened that she might break threads in the garment, or cause a tiny rent to appear in the fabric. Then she cried out, softly, angrily, to herself. "I must always fear the whip!" she thought. "If my master feels I have been careless with a garment, or have injured it in some way, I will be lashed as a clumsy slave. I would like to rip the garment of the brute, Selius Arconious, to pieces, but if I so much as break a thread I may be punished. I would be whipped, and then, carefully, with needle and thread, my body in agony, I would have to repair the garment, as well. I am helpless. I am so helpless!" She examined the garment with great care, and, to her relief, assured herself that it was undamaged. She then rinsed it, and twisted it, gently, ridding it of water, and placed it in the basket to her left, containing damp, clean laundry. But she resolved to be, when her master was not present, even more provocative before Selius Arconious. In that way she could make him suffer. And she had no doubt but what she had caused him, in the past few days, considerable uneasiness. Just yesterday she had sat in the straw, in the open barn area, sitting to one side of him, as he had worked nearby, and extended her left leg, partly bent, her tunic dropping away, split as it was, to reveal a good deal of thigh. She had then, with apparent interest, seemed to be considering her ankle, and she had then turned to him, her hands at her ankle, and inquired, innocently, "Do you think, Master, that my ankle would look well in a golden shackle?" He had risen, not speaking, and turned away. She had called after him. "I am thinking of asking my master for bells. Do you think I would look well, belled?" Then, angrily, not looking at her, his shoulders tight with fury, he had left the room. She had laughed to herself. That evening, after supper, she knelt before Portus Canio, and asked if she might be belled. "Why?" asked Portus Canio. She had shrugged. "I do not know, Master," she said. "I just thought it might be pretty." "You are not a paga slave," he said. "Master!" she wheedled. "They might annoy the tarns," he said. "Yes, Master," she had replied, defeated.

As I have mentioned, there were streets in the vicinity of the laundry pools and these streets, as was to be expected, had their share of various forms of traffic, carts, pedestrians, and such. She had even seen, once this morning, the palanquin of a free woman, being borne by male slaves. The heavy outer curtains, and even the light inner curtains, of the palanquin were drawn open and, from her knees, as she worked on the laundry, she could see a free woman reclining within the palanquin, veiled, hooded, clad in the Robes of Concealment. She lay on one elbow, and seemed bored, and indolent. Her eyes, below the hood, above the veil, idly, briefly surveyed the girls at the pools. Then she looked away, apparently weary, apparently bored. "Perhaps one day, fine lady," thought Ellen, "you will wear a skimpy tunic with no nether closure, and a collar, and be doing the laundry at the pools! Then let the fine ladies look at you on your knees, working! We will see if you are such a fine lady then!"

Suddenly, to her surprise, she heard, to her right, Corinne gasp. Ellen looked over, curious, frightened, and saw Corinne's eyes wide, looking toward the street, her small, delicate hand before her mouth.

Ellen looked then toward the street, to see what might have produced this effect in her new friend. But she saw little that seemed likely to have precipitated this response. Ellen looked about, and made certain no guardsmen were present. "What is wrong?" she whispered to Corinne.

"Look!" whispered Corinne. It seemed she would have lifted her hand, and pointed, but then she visibly, as with an act of will, restrained such a movement.

"What is it?" whispered Ellen.

"See him, the peasant, there, he, the fourth in the line, those men carrying suls!"

Ellen did indeed see the figure referred to by her companion, but noted little of interest, or little out of the ordinary. To be sure, the man who was fourth in the line, a line of some ten or eleven men, was a very large man, an unusually large man, but many of those of the Peasants are well built, even massive. His hair was long and unkempt, his tunic ragged. He was bearded. He was partly bent over, as were the others, carrying, tied on a frame, in a large, open, netlike sack, large and bulging, a considerable quantity of suls, these golden-skinned, suls, a common, tuberous Gorean vegetable. They were doubtless on their way, coming from one of the nearby villages, to one of the wholesale sul markets in the city.

Ellen became nervous seeing the open, netlike sacks. They reminded her of the heavily corded, open slave sacks she had once seen in her training. She had once been put in one, bound hand and foot, her knees drawn up, it then tied shut, in one of the training rooms. She had then been instructed as to how she might move pathetically, provocatively within such an environment. It had seemed to her that one needed no instruction as to how to act pathetically in such a confinement, for in such an environment she certainly felt, and was, pathetically helpless. Too, she was not clear, as well, how one could even occupy such a close, inhibitory prison, even trying to remain still, without being provocative. Clearly she would be seen as a netted "catch." There were also open slave sacks of woven, metal cable, cables a quarter of an inch in thickness, some silverish, some black, some steel-colored, with apertures in the form of two to four-inch diamonds, which could be padlocked shut at the top. She wondered what the woman in the palanquin would look like, stripped, eyes wide, terrified, confined in such a sack, crouching there, her fingers hooked through the apertures. Perhaps then, Ellen thought, she would not be so weary, so bored. Perhaps that would add some interest to her life, some spice to her life, the spice of the collar, of chains and the whip.

"It is he!" whispered Corinne.

"Who?" asked Ellen.

"He! It is he!" cried Corinne, softly.

"Who?" asked Ellen.

"I must hurry to my master!" said Corinne, and she, hastily, with two hands, gathered together her laundry, much of it not yet done, and thrust it into her basket. In a moment, to Ellen's puzzlement, Corinne, clutching her basket, had rushed away.

Ellen looked again to the street but the line of men, bearing suls, had disappeared.

Ellen then returned to her work.

Chapter 19

What Occurred in the Tarn Loft; One Must Make Haste

"The shop of Bonto has been burned! He himself has been seized by Cosians!" cried Fel Doron, he of the employ of Portus Canio, bursting into the loft area, from the interior door.

Portus looked up, wildly, from his work, weaving closed a gap in the wickerwork of one of the light tarn baskets. "Bonto knows nothing," said Portus, angrily, rising to his feet. "He is innocent. He is not involved."

"What are you talking about?" asked Selius Arconious, looking up from the repair of a saddle.

"Is your Home Stone the Home Stone of Ar?" inquired Portus, suddenly, fiercely, of Selius Arconious.

"Of course," said Selius Arconious, puzzled.

"What is going on?" asked Tersius Major, coming from the dark ice pantry, where slabs of meat are stored on blocks of ice, covered with sawdust.

"The shop of Bonto has been burned," said Portus. "Bonto has been seized."

"But why?" asked Tersius Major. "Did he not pay his taxes? Did he not show deference to a Cosian?"

"They are sweeping the city," said Fel Doron. "They are arresting, and burning, almost as though on whim. Madness has infected the Cosian sleen. They seek the Delta Brigade!"

"There is no such thing," said Selius Arconious. "The Delta Brigade is a myth."

Portus, Fel Doron and Tersius Major exchanged glances.

"It exists," said Portus, "but it is ineffective, and dilatory, and we must act independently."

A tarn, one of several in the nearby caged areas, screamed, and snapped its wings.

Ellen understood little of what was going on. She was in an opened, empty cage, nearby, on her knees, with a bucket of water, and a brush, scrubbing, cleaning, the flooring there. She could look back through the stout bars and see and hear the men. She was naked as that was most convenient for the work which she was doing.

"Action at this time is premature," said Tersius Major.

"What is different now? What has precipitated the actions of the Cosians?" asked Portus.

"One does not know," said Fel Doron, wildly. "It is rumored something has occurred in the palace."

"Look into the streets!" said Portus to Tersius Major.

Tersius hurried to the platform outside the huge entry portal to the loft, and, in moments, called back. "There is commotion below. Much running about, shouting."

"It is said that Myron, *Polemarkos* of Temos, has entered the city," said Fel Doron.

Myron, the *polemarkos*, was the commander of the Cosian, and mercenary, forces in the city. His own camp lay outside the gates. It was said he was a cousin to Lurius of Jad, Ubar of Cos.

"What is the concern below?" called Portus to Tersius, on the platform.

"I can make nothing out," said Tersius.

"Talena will address the population from the Central Cylinder," said Selius Arconious. "She will calm the people."

"Talena!" cried Portus, angrily.

"Our Ubara," said Selius Arconious.

"False Ubara!" cried Portus, in fury.

"Portus!" called Tersius, from outside the exterior entrance. "Guardsmen, on the bridges! They may be coming here!"

"Why?" asked Selius Arconious.

Portus turned white.

"They are going everywhere!" cried Fel Doron.

"No," said Portus. "Not everywhere."

Tersius returned to the interior of the loft.

"Tarns can come and go, and leave the city," said Portus. "Where there are tarns they will be suspicious. Doubtless all tarn lofts will be investigated."

"Why?" asked Arconious.

"I think they are coming here," said Tersius, whispering.

"What does it matter?" asked Arconious. "We have nothing to fear."

Portus rushed inward, to the loft office, and, in moments, carrying a heavy bundle over his shoulder, from which escaped the sounds of metal, emerged, seized up a tarn goad and, throwing open the latch to the huge cot, the general housing area, that mighty cage, which held several of the gigantic winged monsters, rushed within, shouting, the goad brandished and flashing. The birds drew back from the goad uneasily, angrily, and, against the far wall of that immense cot, that great cage, beneath straw, Portus concealed the mysterious bundle. He then, crying out angrily, and twice defending himself with the goad, returned to the central area, latching the gate behind him. The tarn goad he placed in a wall, behind a loose board. Scarcely had he finished this than there was a rude, insistent pounding at the interior door. Ellen looked to the huge tarn cage, that enormous cot, where Portus had concealed the mysterious bundle. Two of the tarns went to it, and put their beaks down to it, but they then withdrew, as it apparently contained nothing of interest to them.

"Continue with your work," said Portus to Ellen, and she, dutifully, put down her head, and returned to her scrubbing, the stout bristles of the thick brush damp on the wet floor.

"Ah, Masters, welcome!" said Portus, as he opened the interior door, through which burst several guardsmen, their helmets bearing the yellow crest, their weapons at the ready.

"Who is tarnmaster here?" demanded the leader of the intruders, an officer, a lieutenant, or, perhaps better translated, a subcaptain.

"I, noble Master," said Portus.

"The rest of you," said the officer, indicating Fel Doron, Tersius Major and Selius Arconious, "kneel. You are in the presence of soldiers of Cos."

Fel Doron, Tersius Major, and, lastly, angrily, Selius Arconious, knelt.

"You will show me all records of rentals, hirings, and such, of all comings and goings, of all business in this place to the passage hand before last."

"Gladly," said Portus.

"How many tarns have you?" asked the officer.

"Eighteen," said Portus. "Eleven on the premises."

"You can account for the others?"

"Of course," said Portus. He then went toward his office.

The officer turned to his men. "Search this place," he said. "Search it well."

Immediately the soldiers began to ransack the loft area, casting saddles and harnesses about, pulling down tarn baskets, emptying boxes, stirring, and probing, thrusting about, beneath straw with their spears. They examined even Ellen's stall. She heard the point of a spear move her chain, that fastened to the heavy ring in the floor. She was seldom chained there now at night, but the chain was still there, and it could be put again on her neck at any time, and then, if so, she must remain there again, held at the ring, fastened in place by the neck, awaiting the pleasure of men. They even went into the kitchen, and the rooms of Portus Canio and the others, emptying chests, pulling things down from shelves, scattering things about in the pantry, cutting into sacks. They did not, of course, enter the area occupied by the tarns. They did examine the empty cage areas, among them the cage where Ellen, head down, not looking up, her hair forward, scrubbed the boards carefully, lengthwise, as was required, going with their grain. As her hair was forward, she realized that the lock on the back of her collar, a close-fitting, common slave collar, would be visible to the men. She also knew, uneasily, that the sight of a collar on a woman's neck, locked there, as of course it would be in the case of a slave, tended to be sexually stimulatory to men. After all, it shows that its wearer is a slave, proclaiming her so, manifesting her so, with all that that can mean to a lustful, powerful, domineering, possessive beast, a man.

"What have you found?" asked the officer, emerging from Portus's office, a sheaf of papers in his hands, doubtless to be examined by others, elsewhere. He wadded these papers, these documents, into a pouch, slung at his side.

"Nothing," he was told.

"There is a slave there," said one of the men, indicating Ellen.

The officer turned and regarded Ellen, and she, aware now of his gaze, put aside her brush and, frightened, knelt facing him, her head down, beside the bucket of water. She spread her knees.

"Slut," hissed Selius Arconious.

Ellen cast him an angry glance. Of course she must kneel with her knees spread! That was the sort of slave she was! She did not wish to be beaten. And had he not, himself, often enough, required exactly this posture of her?

"Belly, and to me, slave," said the officer.

Ellen went to her belly and, across the wet floor, through the opened gate of the empty cage, across the dry, straw-strewn floor, squirmed to his feet. She then lay before him, prone, her head turned to the right, her elbows bent, the palms of her hands on the floor.

"Do you not know enough to kiss a man's feet?" she was asked.

Ellen, now no more than a young, enslaved beauty, Earth and her Ph.D. far behind her, kissed his feet, submissively, a docile slave.

"Slut, slut!" chided Selius Arconious.

"What of the tarn cage?" asked the officer. "Has it been searched?"

His men looked at one another. "No," said one of the men.

"Search it," said the officer.

"There are tarns there," said a man.

"Give me a tarn goad," said the officer to Portus Canio.

Portus made a negligible gesture, as of regret. "There are no tarn goads here," he said.

The officer regarded him, angrily.

"These are only draft tarns," said Portus, "slow, clumsy, gentle birds. Of what need would be a goad?"

The officer then went to the cage door and, with two hands, flung up the latch, and, with both hands, swung the gate open a foot. The gates are large, and heavy, and barred, some fourteen to fifteen feet in height, some ten feet in width. A tarn can thus stalk through one, but could not spread its wings and fly through one. Normally they are harnessed in the cage, and then led through the opening. In returning to the loft, from a flight, they are normally unharnessed outside, save for a halter, by means of which they are led within, the halter then being removed. The tarns instantly, alertly, regarded him. At the entrance he hesitated.

"Only cowards fear tarns," said Portus Canio.

The officer thrust through the gate, but scarcely had he entered the area, a stranger, one unknown to the tarns, than one of the birds flew at him, aggressively, and he sprang back through the narrow opening and the great, yellow, scimitarlike beak snapped on the bars, not a foot from his hand.

"They are so tame?" inquired the officer, irritably, turning to regard Portus Canio.

"I do not know what could be the matter," said Portus Canio. "Perhaps it is just that they do not know you."

"It is growing late," said one of the men. "We have other areas to search."

"Several," said another.

"Stand," snapped the officer, to Ellen, who, instantly, so addressed, a slave, stood.

The officer then, appraisingly, walked about her. He felt her breasts, admiringly. She gasped, softly, reluctantly, stimulated, but she dared not resist or protest. She was a slave. She could be felt and handled as men wished. He lowered his hand to her left hip and she drew back, inadvertently, frightened. He smiled, and drew back his hand.

"Open your mouth," said the officer.

Ellen opened her mouth, widely, and the officer, putting his fingers to her mouth, held it open, uncomfortably, and looked within. He then released her and she closed her mouth, keeping her head down.

"She is a barbarian," said Portus.

"I can see that," said the officer. "Too, she has the barbarian brand on her upper left arm." That was, as would be supposed, a vaccination mark.

"She is a barbarian," repeated Portus, disparagingly.

"No matter," said the officer. "And the little scars on the upper left arm do not, I have found, reduce their value in the markets."

"She is a poor piece of barbarian slave meat," said Selius Arconious, from his knees.

"I think she is rather pretty," said the officer. "I think she would look well, chained by the neck, being marched in a slave coffle. I do not think she would be the worst bead on a slaver's necklace."

"A meaningless barbarian," said Portus.

"Certainly she is meaningless," said the officer, "as she is a slave, and particularly so, as she is a mere barbarian."

"She is a low slave, a cheap slave," said Portus, "good only for the cleaning of cages, the scrubbing of floors, the carrying of water, the replenishing of straw, such things."

"She is not a draft slave," said the officer. "She is a slight and beautiful slave. She would be better applied to softer, more feminine labors, the licking of a man's feet, and such."

"Surely you can see what a poor slave she is," said Portus, "how insignificant she is, what poor goods she is."

"I cannot really see that," said the officer.

"I have seen toads who are more attractive," said Selius Arconious.

How hateful you are, Selius Arconious, she thought.

"Toads like this one sell well," said the officer.

Take that, Selius Arconious, she thought.

"She is plain," said Selius Arconious.

Not so plain, she thought, not so plain at all!

"Too, be sure, she should be washed, and combed, and brushed," said the officer.

"A low slave," said Portus, disparagingly.

"Think of her belled, in a diaphanous thread of slave silk," said the officer.

"In a paga tavern, in Cos?" asked Portus.

"Why not?" said the officer.

"She is quite homely," said Selius Arconious.

Not at all, she thought. I have seen myself in the mirror!

"She is young," said the officer, "but if you think she is homely, I suspect you have serious difficulties with your vision."

There, Selius Arconious, she thought.

"Surely you cannot find her of the least interest," said Selius Arconious.

"She has exquisite features and a slight, but beautiful figure," said the officer.

How men might think, and speak, of her!

But was she not goods?

Ellen was acutely aware of the collar on her neck.

"She is nothing," said Selius Arconious.

"No," said the officer. "You are wrong. She is an exquisitely beautiful slave."

"Absurd," said Selius Arconious.

Not absurd, she thought. Have you not heard the appraisal? He is an officer. He has doubtless judged many women. Could it be, she asked herself, that I am beautiful, even exquisitely beautiful, if only as a slave is beautiful?

"I confiscate her in the name of Cos," said the officer.

"No!" cried Selius Arconious, who would have sprung to his feet, save that the butt of a spear, pressing down on his shoulder, kept him in place.

"Please, no, Master!" begged Ellen.

"Were you given permission to speak?" asked the officer.

"No, Master," said Ellen. "Forgive me, Master!" But the officer had put his left hand in her hair, to hold her in place, and he then lashed her face back and forth, striking her twice, first with the stinging flat of his right hand, then with the slashing back of the right hand. Ellen tasted blood in her mouth. "Forgive me, Master," she whimpered, her head down. "Please forgive me, Master."

Ellen was then aware that the officer had opened his pouch, and, in another moment, that he had wired a small, thin, rectangular metal tag to her collar. She did not doubt but what there were other tags such as that in the pouch.

"I will send a man here tonight, a slaver, or slaver's man, to pick her up," said the officer to Portus Canio.

"Cos treats her allies well," said Portus Canio.

"The laws of Cos march with the spears of Cos," said the officer.

He then turned to leave, and his men prepared to follow him.

"Sir," said Portus Canio.

The officer turned about.

"There seems to be some disturbance in the city, some commotion in the streets," said Portus Canio. "What is going on?"

"Nothing," said the officer. He then left the loft area, followed by his men.

"They may return later, with tarn goads," said Fel Doron.

Portus went to Ellen, who was still standing. He turned the tag which dangled from her collar. "'Confiscated in the name of Cos,'" he read.

"You must give her up, Portus," said Tersius.

"No!" cried Selius Arconious.

Ellen looked at him, startled.

He could do nothing to prevent her confiscation, for she was a mere property.

Why did he cry out so, she wondered.

Certainly he could not care for her. He was incapable of such feelings. He was no more than a vain, insensitive, arrogant brute. Too, men did not care for such as she; for she was not free; she was only a slave.

But she recalled the effect she had had upon him and must obviously still have. Certainly he had cried out.

She recalled how she despised and hated him.

Too, she would be frightened to belong to him. She knew he lusted for her, like the lion for hot meat. She, a former woman of Earth, feared naturally, understandably enough, to belong to a Gorean male. The men of her world had not prepared her for such a fate. She was terrified to think of herself as a helpless slave at the mercy of such men, Gorean males, at the mercy of such virile, severe, demanding, untamed, bestial predators, and she realized that, in that desperate predicament, she would be choiceless, absolutely so, that she would be the vulnerable, helpless object of powerful, uncompromising, unbridled lust, and that she must assuage and serve it with all her embonded loveliness, instantly, perfectly, unquestioningly.

How I hate him, she thought.

Soon I will be rid of him! Excellent! And I will have a new slavery and new masters. Splendid!

And she recalled how she had been muchly pleased to keep him at a distance, how amused she had been that he might burn with need, writhe with desire.

Tears sprang to her eyes.

Then she saw his eyes were upon her, and she smiled, smugly, and tossed her head, insolently. Burn, she thought, Selius Arconious, burn! You will never have me! Suffer! Suffer! Burn! Burn!

She saw he looked upon her with fury. I am not yours, she thought. Then, when she was sure he was looking, she turned her head away, smiling. To be sure, her gesture might have been a bit more effective if she had had her tunic.

"I fear Fel Doron is right," said Tersius Major. "They may return later, with tarn goads."

"We will not be here," said Portus.

"What?" said Fel Doron.

"Give the signal," said Portus.

"It is premature! It is not yet time!" said Tersius Major.

"We must act," said Portus. "Give the signal."

Fel Doron nodded. He lit a lamp.

For a moment he lifted the lamp, and regarded Ellen. Thus under the scrutiny of a free man, Ellen, appropriately, knelt.

"Doubtless it causes less ill will to confiscate slaves at night," muttered Fel Doron.

"We are taking her with us," said Portus. "She figures in our plans."

This intelligence startled Ellen. Surely they could not take her with them. Had she not been confiscated? Did she not have a Cosian tag wired to her collar?

Fel Doron took the lamp outside. He returned a moment later. "It is done," he said.

"Gather your goods, anything you want," said Portus to Fel Doron and Tersius Major. "We fly tonight."

"What is going on?" asked Selius Arconious.

"Selius," said Portus, "attend to the slave. See that she is fed and watered, and that she relieves herself."

"Very well," said Selius, puzzled.

"Then go below, and see if you can learn what transpires in the streets."

"I will do so," said Selius Arconious.

When Ellen looked up, from her knees, she saw, in the half darkness, Selius Arconious looming over her.

She did not find it a particularly welcome sight.

"Oh!" she cried in pain, for he had reached to her hair and yanked her to her feet, and was now leading her, she painfully bent over, her head at his right hip, his hand tightly in her hair. She stumbled beside him, hurrying, trying to put her hands on his thick wrist. "Please, Master!" she cried. "Stop! You are hurting me!"

"Be silent, slut," he snarled.

He drew her to the kitchen and threw her to her knees. Then he took a pan, threw it to the floor, and kicked it before her. He shook some biscuits into the pan, and they struck the pan and rattled about within it. She looked up, in misery. From a hook in the pantry he had taken down a slave whip. It was now in his hand. "Eat," he said.

Quickly she put down her head and, on all fours, addressed herself to the biscuits. They were dry and it was hard for her to eat them. She looked up, in misery. He lifted the whip. She again put down her head, sobbing. Perhaps she was slow. Perhaps he was impatient. He pulled her by the hair to an upright kneeling position and held her by the hair with his left hand, the loop at the butt of the whip about his wrist, where it hung against her right cheek, and, reaching into the pan, took the last two biscuits and thrust them into her mouth. She tried to chew, wildly, terrified. She half choked, she struggled to swallow. She was still gasping when he put a pan of water before her, which she went to seize gratefully but found the whip interposed between her mouth and the pan. She looked up at him piteously, crumbs and flakes of biscuit about her face and mouth. His eyes were stern. "Like the sleek little she-urt you are," he said. She put her head down and drank. "More quickly, slut!" said he. She wept. The salt of her tears mixed with the water. Her lips and tongue felt sometimes the sides of the pan, sometimes its bottom, so desperate were her efforts. Her hair was wet where it fell into the water. "You are too slow," said he, and lifted the pan before her. "Open your mouth, slut," said he, and he then, unceremoniously, impatiently, too rapidly, poured water down her throat, but much of it, too, went about her chin, and throat, and under her collar, and ran down, too, plentifully, between her breasts. When he threw the pan to the side with a clatter she was trembling and sobbing. She was then drawn again to her feet and led, bent over, as a slave, to her own stall. "Squat," said he, "slave." "Please!" she begged. He lifted the whip. She relieved herself before him.

"Wipe yourself," he said, "slovenly creature."

She wiped herself with a handful of straw from the stall, depositing the straw in the wastes container.

She then was kneeling before him, looking up at him, in the half darkness, sobbing, shaking with humiliation.

"You may speak," he said, amused.

"I hate you! I hate you!" she cried.

"You might be easily used," said he, "on the straw of your stall."

She shrank back.

"Are you a creature of ice?" he asked.

"Yes," she wept. "Where you are concerned!"

"So you will still pretend to be the little figurine of ice, carved in the semblance of a slave girl?"

"I am ice," she cried. "I am ice!"

"I see," said he. "You are a cold slave?"

"Yes," she said. "I am cold! I am a cold slave!"

"I see," he said.

"What are you doing?" she cried.

He had put her to her belly on the straw.

"Have no fear, little icicle," he said.

He then, with two thongs, bound her, hand and foot. As she struggled, helpless, he lifted her in his arms.

"What are you going to do with me?" she asked. "Where are you taking me?"

"Portus wants me to go below, and see what is occurring in the streets," he said.

"Put me down!" she cried.

"In a moment," he assured her.

"No!" she cried. "Don't!"

He opened the heavy door of the ice room, and, in a moment, as she protested weakly, and struggled, and moaned in dismay, and begged mercy, he placed her in the room, bound as she was, on blocks of ice, half hidden by the sawdust.

"This is a good place for little icicles," he said.

"Don't leave me here!" she begged. But, in a moment he had left, swinging shut, and latching, the heavy, timbered, reinforced door, and she found herself, to her consternation and misery, plunged into darkness.

She cried out, but it seemed that Portus and the others were unconcerned, or did not hear her.

Serious matters of some sort were afoot. Surely haste was being made. It was not surprising then that the comfort of a she-thrall, the comfort of a curvaceous little bondmaid, particularly one being disciplined, was less than uppermost on their minds.

"Please Masters, free me!" she wept. "I will be a good slave! I will be a good slave!"

She twisted, and squirmed, on the ice. Cold sawdust was on her face and in her hair. Her back ached with cold. She tried to change her position but the ice was even more merciless to her bosom, to her belly, the front of her thighs. She put her feet up, trying to keep them from the ice. Then she was again weeping on her back, and then on her sides, and then on her back again, in the darkness. "I will be a good slave!" she wept. "I will be a good slave!" She feared she would lose her mind from the cold and darkness. She was doubtless not there long, but, in the darkness, and in her misery, she lost all sense of time. It seemed she had never been so cold as now. The metal of the collar absorbed the cold and seemed like a flat ring of ice on her neck. Even the thongs that bound her seemed stiff with cold, and she feared they might cut her like frozen knives.

In what might have been some half of an Ahn, or so, the door to the ice pantry, or ice room, opened and there stood therein, silhouetted in the light behind it, the figure of Selius Arconious.

"Master!" cried out Ellen, beggingly, piteously.

"Are you prepared to be a good slave?" he inquired.

"Yes, Master! Yes, Master!" cried Ellen.

He then entered the ice room, picked her up, threw her over his left shoulder, steadying her there with his left hand, and left the ice room, she carried as a slave, as would be expected, her head to the rear. One advantage of this carry is that the slave cannot see to what device, or accommodation, or destination, she is being borne. He closed and latched the door to the ice room behind him, with his right hand. Too, it is difficult for a slave to be carried thusly, and she not to understand herself clearly as what she is, goods.

What men can do to us! What men can do with us, thought Ellen. They can do whatever they want with us!

How fortunate, she thought, that this fact has been concealed from the men of Earth, that they, perhaps in their simplicity, perhaps in their lack of imagination, perhaps in their naively uncritical acceptance of imposed conditioning programs, are unaware of it! Woe to us, should they decide to exercise their prerogatives, their rights in the order of nature! For would they not then again make us their slaves?

He carried her to the kitchen and there put her on her knees before him, she still bound hand and foot.

She knelt there, before him, shuddering, trembling with cold.

"So," he asked, "are you a cold slave?"

"I am freezing!" she wept.

"Are you a cold slave?" he asked, amused.

"No," she cried out, suddenly, comprehendingly. "I am a hot slave! I am a hot slave!"

"Perhaps then," he said, "you are prepared to beg to serve me—as a hot slave?"

"Yes, Master!" she wept.

He smiled.

"I beg to serve you as a hot slave!" she wept. "I beg to serve you as a hot slave!"

"Remember," said he, "in future slaveries, that you so begged. Remember that you begged to serve Selius Arconious, of Ar, begged piteously, and helplessly, to serve him, *as a hot slave*."

"Master?" she asked.

"And that he refused to permit you to do so," said he. "That he scorned you. That he regarded you as inadequate, and dismissed you as poor slave meat."

She looked at him, wildly, disbelievingly.

He then took her tunic from the table, to which he had apparently brought it somewhat earlier, before fetching her from the ice room, and carefully folded it, several times, into a small, thick rectangle of cloth. He then thrust the tunic, so folded, now this small, soft thick rectangle of cloth, between her teeth. "I would not drop this if I were you," he said.

He then carried her out to the general loft area, and put her, bound as she was, on her back, on the boards.

"The slave has been fed and watered, as you wished, Portus," said Selius Arconious. "And I watched her relieve herself."

"Good," said Portus. "Harness tarns."

Fel Doron, carrying a crate, passed Ellen. He put the crate in a tarn basket.

"Where is Tersius?" asked Portus.

"I am here," said Tersius. He was entering the loft area from the exterior platform. He carried a lamp.

"What have you been doing?" asked Portus.

"Watching," said Tersius.

"We will soon take wing," said Portus.

"I am ready," said Tersius.

"Assist Selius," said Portus, looking about, as though he feared to hear at any moment the cries of men and the rushing of footsteps on the stairs, the rude, insistent smiting of spears against the inner door.

Tersius set the lamp, a small, shallow, panlike tharlarion-oil lamp, on a shelf bracket and hurried to gather up an armful of harnesses from pegs on the loft wall.

Portus, taking his concealed tarn goad from its hiding place to one side, behind the loose board, entered the tarn cage in which he had placed the oblong, mysterious package before the arrival of the Cosian soldiers, and retrieved it from under the straw. He brought it to the loft area, and put it on the floor, not far from Ellen, and unrolled it. Within, clattering out, there were several swords, two war axes, some crossbows, and some wired bundles of short, metal-finned quarrels.

Such things, Ellen gathered, were not permitted by the laws of the Cosian occupation.

A tyrant state always attempts to disarm its citizens, invariably on the pretext of doing this for their own good. And thus are the necks of men bent to the yoke of the state.

Fel Doron passed her again, this time carrying supplies from the kitchen, bread, biscuits, dried fruit, a bulging sack of meal, which supplies he placed in a nearby tarn basket.

"Arm yourselves," said Portus.

Tersius and Fel Doron came to the sprawl of weapons on the floor. Each took a sword and a crossbow, and a bundle of quarrels.

"Seven tarns are ready harnessed for cargo," said Selius Arconious, emerging from the tarn cage, and two others are haltered, ready for tandem, trailing flight. What is this all about?"

Two tarns, it seemed, were to be left behind.

"Do you care to arm yourself?" asked Portus.

"Surely you know such things are forbidden," said Arconious.

Portus rerolled the bundle, tied it shut and placed it in one of the tarn baskets, one of seven taken from the nearby stacks and put near the great, lofty exit from the loft.

"You are leaving?" said Arconious. "What is going on?"

"You have heard of the Delta Brigade," said Portus.

"It is a myth," said Arconious.

"What do you know of it?" asked Portus.

"Little, if anything," said Arconious.

"It is an organization," said Portus, "formed largely, but not entirely, from veterans of the great disaster of the Vosk delta, where they were betrayed by treason in high places, denied supplies, abandoned, left to die, who muchly suffered in their retreat from the delta, and found themselves despised and humiliated when they returned to their city, held in contempt, and spat upon, despite their sharing of its Home Stone. Later, as you know, the gates of Ar were opened to the Cosians and their mercenary allies, again by insufferable treason in high places, under delusory pretenses of friendship and alliance."

"Such could never have occurred," said Selius Arconious, bitterly, "had Marlenus, our Ubar, he, the Ubar of Ubars, been in the city."

"We must do what we can without him," said Portus.

"I do not understand," said Arconious.

"The Delta Brigade is not a myth, as you may have supposed," said Portus. "I assure you of that. I, and Tersius, and Fel Doron, have been of the brigade. But we have now left it. It is too small, it is dilatory, it is unready to act. There are things that can be done now. We must do them. We will take independent action."

"What can you do, alone?" asked Arconious. "Ambush and kill a Cosian sentry, precipitate the taking of hostages and reprisals by Cos? They could burn districts, slay thousands."

"Some things can be done, and must be done," said Portus. "We are not alone in these matters. There are others, too, who were of the Brigade, who feel similarly. Tonight, though we are less than ready, we will begin to act."

"The city," said Arconious, "must rise as a whole."

"There is no rallying point," said Portus.

"What can you do?" asked Arconious.

"The forces of occupation are not all Cosian," said Portus. "Indeed, the greater portion of these forces are mercenaries in the pay of Cos. Their loyalty is not to the Home Stones of Jad or Temos but to the purse of their paymaster, gross Lurius of Jad. They have been supported largely by the routine, methodological looting of Ar, but the mercenaries are many and impatient and Ar grows poorer, and there is only so much silver, so much gold, so many women, only so much wealth which can be seized and distributed."

"So?" said Arconious.

"Cos, in consort with Tyros, she under the Ubarate of Chenbar, the Sea-Sleen, extend their hegemonies, and lay tribute on more than a dozen cities."

"Yes?" said Arconious.

"Portions of this wealth will come to Ar, to content the mercenaries," said Portus.

"Cosians themselves could hold the city," said Arconious. "They no longer need their mercenary allies. Their war is won."

"Do you think the mercenaries, and their captains, will simply submit to being dismissed?" asked Portus. "That would be like turning larls loose in the streets. Denied their pay who knows what they will do. They might turn their weapons against Cos and Tyros."

"That is a problem I am pleased to leave to Cos," said Arconious.

"A caravan of gold is on its way to Ar," said Portus. "It left Brundisium the last passage hand. It is pay for the mercenaries, and it is intended that it will be delivered to them on the feast of the accession of Lurius of Jad to the throne of Cos."

"That is better than fifty days from now," said Arconious.

"But already," said Fel Doron, bitterly, "banners have been hung proclaiming the imminence of this joyous festival."

"Your plan, I take it," said Arconious, "is to interfere with, or delay, the arrival of the pay caravan."

Portus grinned.

"Do not attempt this, I beg of you," said Arconious. "The caravan will be well-guarded."

"Are you with us?" asked Portus.

"It is foolish," said Arconious.

"Are you with us?" asked Portus, again.

"No," said Arconious.

"I wish you well," said Portus. He extended his hand and the two men clasped wrists, each the wrist of the other. This is the strongest of grips, for otherwise hands may be pulled apart. In this fashion each has his own grip, and if one hand should slip, the other will hold. It is a grip common to mariners, it seems, and may have been derived from maritime practice. It is useful, it seems, in their dangerous work, where a lost grip might be the prelude to catastrophe, a fall from a yard, a plunge into cold, stormy seas. It has its value, too, of course, among tarnsmen, tarnkeepers, tarnsters, and such, who must occasionally move from saddle to saddle, or from basket to basket, and such, while in flight. The normal Gorean handshake, it seems, at least those which this slave has seen commonly exchanged amongst free men, is the same as, or rather like, that of Earth, from which world it is doubtless derived, the clasping of two right hands, thus the giving of the expected weapon hand to the other, a grant indicative of respect, trust and friendship, one supposes.

"I urge you to reconsider," said Arconious.

"We do not," said Portus, smiling.

"You are brave fools," said Selius Arconious. "I wish you well."

The tarns, interestingly, were arranged in order within the loft area, rather than outside, on the platform. Portus would lead, controlling the first tarn with its basket. Fel Doron would follow with the second tarn and basket. Tersius Major would come third, with the third basket, but, from his tarn's harness, a long line extended to the fourth tarn and basket, and from the harness of that tarn, with its basket, there ran another line to the fifth tarn, and so, too, to the sixth and seventh tarn, this forming a string of tarns with their cargo baskets. The eighth and ninth tarns were in harness but bore no baskets. They did form, as they too were joined to the others by a line, a part of the tandem progress of attached tarns. There were thus two free tarns, so to speak, with baskets, and then a line of seven tarns, strung together, five with baskets, two without. This left behind, in their barred housing, two of the eleven tarns which had been originally in the loft. These two tarns were left in the care of Selius Arconious, who had chosen to remain behind.

Cosians would presumably be less suspicious if some tarns remained in the loft. Business, presumably, might have taken the others on their various ways. There might be problems, of course, when a slaver, or slaver's man, came to collect a slave. Selius Arconious, of course, a lowly employee, could not be expected to be of much help in such matters. Too, what would the slaver, or slaver's man, when he arrived with his whip and leash, know? Orders might have been countermanded. Or perhaps Portus might have been ordered to deliver the slave himself to some designated location. It was hard to know about such things. The important thing was to be courteous, and as helpful as possible.

Ellen had lain on the floor amidst this bustle, naked there, on the straw-strewn boards, bound hand and foot, neglected, the small, now-damp, folded tunic clenched between her teeth.

Portus entered the first basket, and Fel Doron and Tersius Major entered the second and third baskets, respectively. Draft tarns are usually controlled from the basket. They may, however, be controlled from the saddle. Ellen supposed that a tarn progress of this sort, tarnsters abasket, might attract less attention than one in which tarnsters might be in the saddle. Might that not be a disguise for roving tarnsmen, who might then jettison the baskets and wing their way free to whatever mischief they might portend?

"Untie the slave," Portus called to Selius, "and put her in the last basket." Selius turned Ellen to her belly and bent to free her of her several-times-looped, narrow pinions. He unbound her ankles first and then, kneeling across the backs of her thighs, undid the thongs which confined her wrists. She continued to clench the folded tunic between her teeth, not having been permitted to release it. It touched the floor, as she lay. Then she turned her head to the right, the left side of her face then on the boards. She could feel straw beneath the side of her face. "Ellen!" called Portus. She turned, as she could, lifting her head, rising a bit on the palms of her hands, to view her master, her body still pinned in place by Selius, who was kneeling across the back of her legs. "Though your hands are free," said Portus to Ellen, "you will retain your gag until we have passed, if we pass, over the walls of the city."

Ellen nodded, tears in her eyes.

Ellen did not understand Portus's qualification 'if we pass'. What could he have meant by that?

It frightened her.

"Put her in the last basket," said Portus.

Ellen, her mouth stuffed with her own tunic, serving as a gag, moaned in dismay. She was terrified of tarns, and frightened of heights. And what if the narrow ropes by which the basket was suspended from the harness should break? She would not have dared to protest, of course, even if she had been permitted speech. She did not wish to be beaten. She knew it would be done with her as masters wished, as it would be with a verr or a sack of sa-tarna flour.

Selius picked her up and put her on his left shoulder, her head to the rear.

Well she knew the meaning of that carry.

"When Portus addressed you," said Selius Arconious, "you merely shook your head in understanding, and affirmation."

Ellen moaned, a tiny noise.

"Surely you know gag signals, slut," said Selius.

Ellen whimpered once.

"Would you like to be thrown from the platform?" asked Selius.

Ellen whimpered twice, miserably, two tiny, pathetic noises.

"Good," said Selius.

Ellen had been taught gag signals in her training, of course. The small tunic she now held between her teeth was not typical of Gorean gags, which often involve packing and stout mouth binding. It is important for a girl to know gag signals, for it is not unusual for her to be gagged by her master. This is useful in discipline, and it is also useful merely to remind her that she is a slave. They are also subject to blindfolds and hoods. In such encumbrances they must learn to respond to a variety of signals, for example, mere touches on an arm, guiding them, or, alternatively, verbal commands which, even though they can see nothing, they must obey with alacrity. The least hesitation or tentativeness is cause for discipline. In this way, it is possible to conduct a frightened, blindfolded slave even through narrow, twisting, intricate passages at a brisk pace.

Ellen was then lowered into the last basket. In it, other than herself, there was only a blanket, a small loaf of bread, flat, and round, like most Gorean loaves, and a small bota, presumably filled with water.

The basket, as it was a cargo basket, had no seat or bench. It was woven of stout fibers, generally an inch or better in width. It was something like five by five feet wide, and had a depth of something like four feet. Ellen stood within the basket, holding to its rim. She stood there, looking at Selius Arconious, she within the basket, he standing on the floor beside it, the small, folded tunic between her teeth. Tears burst into her eyes. She wanted to cry out that she loved him and she wanted to be his slave, but she could not speak. Surely she would never see him again, he for whose collar she longed to beg, he at whose feet she craved to kneel, he before whom she desired to fling herself, kissing his feet, he whose whip she longed to lick lovingly, obediently, he whose sandals she wished to bring to him in her teeth, on all fours, he to whom she desired to be the most abject and devoted of love slaves. Bind and whip me, she wanted to cry out to him. In this way she could have no doubt but what he was concerned with her, that she was an object of his attention. Bind me and whip me, she wanted to cry out to him. Teach me with the lash that I am, and that you claim me as, your slave. Bind and whip me, she wanted to cry out to him, that I might cry out in my bonds, in ecstasy, knowing myself at last yours, fully yours, your claimed slave!

But she could say nothing.

"Remember," he said, "that you begged and were rejected, that you were scorned, that you were dismissed, as poor slave meat."

She whimpered once, piteously.

In his eyes she saw only contempt, and hatred.

"The cargo is stowed," Selius called to Portus.

Tears burst anew into Ellen's eyes. The prints of her small teeth were deep in the damp layers of the tunic.

Portus lifted his arm, and Fel Doron, and Tersius Major, behind him, acknowledged this signal.

"Selius!" called Portus.

Selius turned his contemptuous gaze from the distraught, rejected, tearful slave. "Portus?" he asked.

"You were below," said Portus. "Did you learn the origin of the disturbance in the city, the cause of such shouting, of such commotion, in the streets?"

"Yes," said Selius Arconious. "Talena has disappeared from the palace."

Portus then gestured ahead, and urged his tarn forth, out of the loft area, to the platform. In a moment the tarn had leapt from the platform, spread its wings, soared for a brief moment, swooping downward, and had then, with a sudden snapping of those mighty wings, begun to fly. The tarn basket attached to the bird's harness, having slid on its leather runners from the platform, swung darkly on its ropes beneath the bird. Portus kept the bird low, and it moved in relative silence amongst the cylinders of the city. In a moment Fel Doron, with his tarn and basket, had left the platform. Then followed the train of tarns led by Tersius Major. All kept their birds low, moving swiftly and silently through the forest of cylinders, toward the walls, none visible against the three moons.

As Ellen's basket began to move suddenly, she was almost flung from her feet. It then began to slide from the loft, out onto the platform. She held out one hand to Selius Arconious piteously, sliding away from him. She could see where he was standing in the great portal of the loft, at one side of the portal, his figure dimly outlined by the light of the tiny lamp behind him, that lamp far back, in its bracket, in the loft. She could read no sign of emotion in that calm, large, still figure.

Then the basket, so suddenly it seemed, dropped away from the platform.

Inwardly she screamed.

She felt a sickening moment of abject terror, and the dizzying, terrifying sensation of being unsupported, of falling. She closed her eyes, expecting in a moment to be dashed to the stones below. Then the basket swung on its ropes. She opened her eyes, in fear, but, too, in fascination. Wind rushed about her, blasting her hair. She gasped for breath. She felt cold in the rushing wind. She fastened her fingers in, about, and through the wicker, holding to it with every particle of her small strength. She looked up, struggling to keep her balance, at the ropes, the harness, the dark, majestic body of the winged titan above her. It was not easy to stand in the basket, it swinging so. Then, clinging to the side of the basket, she, startled, viewed, here and there beneath her, and muchly, too, about her, the vastness and splendor of the city of Ar. Many of the cylinders were ablaze with light. In many of the windows she could see that lamps were lit, the tiny, softly glowing lamps of love. In many of them she supposed there might be, exterior robes put aside, but modesty robes doubtless retained, free companions. A free companion would presumably not show herself naked to her lover, for such would not comport with her dignity. She is, after all, free. Too, he might then see her as a slave, think of her as a slave, and treat her as such. No free woman, surely, would wish to risk that. But perhaps some free companions did dare, in the privacy of their own compartments, to show themselves naked to their lovers. How bold they would be. How fit then would such women be for the collar! Perhaps they might even, in the privacy of their own compartments, dare a necklace or bracelet, some piece of metal on their soft flesh, this subtly suggesting, though the suggestion would doubtless be frenziedly denied, an insignia of bondage, but surely not an anklet, for that would be too slavelike. But such things could be dangerous, for the free companion who is a man is still a man, and men are excitable, and brutes. Even the best of them may be insufficiently weak, insufficiently devirilized, insufficiently tamed, insufficiently broken on the wheel of a woman's will. But in others of those compartments, Ellen supposed, there would be not free companions but slaves, and masters. In such places she supposed the slaves lovingly served the masters. The relations of slaves and masters, of course, are quite different from those of free companions. In the master/slave relationship the master owns the slave, and thus will have everything from her, and at the time, and in the place, and precisely in the way he pleases. And the slave, lovingly, would not have it otherwise. Masters do not fraudulently deny the war of the sexes. Rather they recognize it, win it, and enslave their opponents. The conquered slave serves the master. She is owned. She is hot, devoted and dutiful, and grateful.

Below her, too, here and there, were broad thoroughfares, lit by torches. Some of these thoroughfares were divided by a gardened strip of greenery. Though it was late some individuals were abroad, some in palanquins, either men or women, borne by male slaves, some with guards, perhaps returning at this hour from late visits, some strolling alone, meditatively, in the late evening, some walking leashed slaves. She saw the stand of a vendor below, one selling perhaps candied suls, or tastas. Other streets were dark between the cylinders. These were muchly deserted, particularly during the lawlessness of the occupation. Many mercenaries, particularly of the smaller companies, are not above brigandage. Too, even in better times there are areas in Ar which are not wisely frequented after dark. On some of these streets could be seen small parties, led by individuals with torches. In other areas, muchly dark, one could scarcely detect the narrow crooked ways which twisted amongst clutters of buildings, some of them several-storied *insulae*. Some markets were open, these lit with torches, small, bright patches of light in the darkness. In these, various goods, as is common, were being offered. One, interestingly, was a tharlarion market. The larger beasts can be brought into the city only after sunset, when the streets are freer of traffic. In two markets, she saw slaves, some exhibited on a shelf, as she had been, others in small cages. In another place, within a rectangle of canvas walls, on a small stage, as the music of flutes and a czehar drifted upward, she saw acrobats, jugglers and fire-eaters. To one side, behind a curtain, she saw slaves, in silk, doubtless waiting to dance for their master's customers. It is common to save the best dancers for last.

The basket swung on the ropes. Ellen released one hand from the wicker, to clutch a rope. Her hair flew about the rope. It is so beautiful, she thought. I hope the ropes hold. They seem so narrow! This world is so beautiful. This world is so natural! How fearful, she thought, to be a woman and live on a natural world! And yet, she thought, the thought startling her, I would not be elsewhere than on this world. On this world there are men such as Portus Canio and Selius Arconious! I am a woman. I did not know such men could exist. She touched her collar. What could a woman of Earth be before such men but a slave? But I would not be elsewhere than on this world. I am a woman. I have learned that on Gor, and have been taught what it means in its truth, depth and fullness. Better a collar on Gor than a throne on Earth! How glorious to be a woman and live upon a natural world, a world in which I must occupy my rightful place in the order of nature, my place at the feet of masters! The beat of the tarn's wings above her was steady, and smooth.

She could see beacons now, set upon the walls of Ar.

She passed over the roof of a small cylinder. On the roof, amongst boards, and debris, there was a naked slave, chained by her wrists to a ring. She looked up as the tarns swept by overhead.

I trust she is well mastered, thought Ellen.

She could see the walls clearly now, the two of them, the interior wall overlooking the lower wall. They were being approached silently, smoothly.

Portus's remark 'if we pass' returned to her, and it frightened her.

But she supposed that he knew what he was doing, and that this particular point on the walls, this exact location, would have been chosen with intent.

As it was night tarn wire might have been strung but here there was no sign of it.

Ellen did see a fellow look up from the interior wall below. He was, she thought, a guardsman of Ar. In any event that was his uniform. He made no move to signal the train of tarns nor did he rush to sound an alarm.

Then the walls of Ar, and its lights, were behind them, and they were making their way, still at a low level, across the open countryside. She did see the lights of some scattered villages.

She recalled the large peasant, and Corinne's agitation at seeing him. Corinne had rushed away from the laundry pools, not even finishing her work there. That had startled Ellen. She herself, of course, had remained at the pools, finishing her own work.

There had been much commotion in the city that day. According to the report of Selius Arconious the explanation of the unrest had to do with the alleged disappearance of Talena, the very Ubara of Ar, from the palace. Perhaps she had departed on secret state business and had now returned to the palace, and was now again on the throne of Ar. That must surely be it. Certainly Ubaras, with all their walls, and gates and doors, and passwords, and guards, do not simply disappear. She recalled that Myron, who was *polemarkos*, commander of the occupation forces, had supposedly entered the city. She gathered that this would be unusual. She had heard that Talena had given him a lovely slave girl whose name was Claudia, who had once been the daughter of a former administrator of Ar.

Ellen then, the walls of Ar having been passed, removed her gag. She put her head back, her hair wild about her in the wind, and breathed in, gratefully. She clutched in one hand the thick, packed, sopped folds of the tunic. She looked back at Ar. Obviously they had not wanted her to scream, to cry out in terror, to call out, or such, until they were safely past the walls of Ar. She could still see the lights of the city behind them. She did not see any signs of pursuit. I am cold, she thought. She knelt down in the basket and spread the blanket a little, so that its folds rather matched the dimensions of the basket. The bottoms of her feet doubtless bore wicker marks. The blanket would protect her from the miseries of such a surface. She supposed that not all slaves, or captures, would be granted that indulgence. It would be quite unpleasant, she supposed, to be bound naked, hand and foot, in such a conveyance, one's ankles perhaps lashed closely to one's wrists, a simple, popular, but extraordinarily effective and secure slave tie, and kept in the basket in one way or another, perhaps by a secured lid, or perhaps merely by ropes or a harness run through the wicker. She shook out the tiny tunic, which, given its service, and the folding, in lines and creases, was irregularly damp. She drew it on, over her head, and pulled it down about her, as far as it would go, which was, of course, not really very far. Now, she thought, delightedly, I am again my own woman! And then, in the wind and the swaying of the basket, she laughed aloud. She was her own woman, insofar as a slave could be her own woman, which was not at all. She was the master's woman, his slave. Still she now had, however skimpy, and amusingly minute, some covering for herself, for her enslaved beauty, some moment of shielding, be it only a thin layer of loosely woven, sleeveless, revealing rep-cloth, slit at the sides. Slaves are grateful, even for so little. The tunic, of course, though we may speak of it as "hers," was, like herself, the property of her master. She did not even own the collar she wore. Slaves can own nothing; it is they, rather, who are owned. She then sat in the basket, and tried to pull the slit sides of the tunic more about her. She was extremely conscious of the absence of a nether closure in the garment. Few slave garments, as noted, contain such a closure. An exception is the Turian camisk. The absence of a nether closure in a garment tends to be sexually stimulatory to a woman, and this is particularly the case when the garment is brief, and, of course, required of her by a man. She pulled the blanket about her. How warm she was then, how comfortable, within its ample, sheltering folds. How kind is Portus, my master, to me, she thought, gratefully. How kind he is to a lowly barbarian, a mere Earth-girl slave! After an Ahn or so, she went again to her knees, holding the blanket clasped about her, and reached out for, and picked up, the small, round, flat loaf of bread which lay on the wicker flooring with the tiny bota. She bit off pieces of the bread while kneeling. There was nothing untoward in this, or unique to her condition, which was that of slave, for Gorean women in the high cities, and particularly those of high caste, commonly eat kneeling, or reclining, at low tables, as Gorean men in the high cities, particularly those of the higher castes, commonly eat at such tables cross-legged, or, like the women, reclining. To be sure, a slave's dishes are often placed before her, on the floor, not on a table. The slave, of course, might be denied the use of her hands, if the master wishes, and then she must put down her head, and, on all fours, eat and drink from pans on the floor. Too, she is sometimes fed from the master's hand, again not permitted to use her own hands. This is, of course, primarily symbolic, and is often used, if used, for no more than the first bite or two of food. It is a way, of course, of reminding the slave that she is dependent on the master for her food. In public places fountains often have several tiers, and almost always at least two, the bottom tier usually no more than a few inches from the ground or pavement, and, as would be expected, slaves, leashed verr, pet sleen, and such, are expected to drink from the lower level.

Ellen did not eat all the bread, but only a little of it. She did not know how long it must last. Too, she had been fed, in a manner of speaking, earlier by the brutish, impatient, handsome Selius Arconious. Oh, how I hate him, she thought. Oh, how I want him to master me! She also took a drink from the bota, which contained water, as she expected. She feared it might have been drugged, presumably with tasteless tassa powder, to sedate her in the basket, but it had no such effect. This pleased her. She recalled in anger, in humiliation, too, how he had watered her, with such reckless contempt. Then she recalled with fury, how he had forced her to squat before him and relieve herself. To be sure, she was only a slave. I hate him, I hate him, she thought. He is so Gorean! He is not like the sweet, pleasant, conquered men of Earth! He does not respect women! He does not treat us with tenderness and gentleness, he does not give us our due of solicitation! He does not care for our feelings! He dominates and masters us!

He is the sort of man who looks upon us as though we were horses, he with a riding crop in his hand! What have we to hope from such men, other than to remove our clothing and kneel before them, hoping to please them?

Later Ellen stood again in the basket, and watched, as she could, part of the blanket beneath her feet, the rest clutched about her, shielding her from the wind and cold, the passing countryside beneath her.

She looked up at the three moons. They are so beautiful, she thought. This is such a beautiful world.

As she stood there, the wind whistling about her, her hair blowing in the wind, the wing strokes of the great winged beast above her, deliberate, measured, she felt the tag wired to her collar.

I suppose I now belong to Cos, she thought. I have been confiscated. But my master, or he who was my master, has hurried me away.

She supposed she was now, at least from the point of view of Cos, stolen property.

This frightened her, as vulnerable goods.

Why did Portus not turn me over to the soldiers of Cos, or their representative, she wondered. After all, in the past months thousands of slaves in Ar had been confiscated, and hundreds of free women put in the collar. I think he was fond of me, but I do not think he was overly enamored of his young barbarian slave. Surely he was not in love with her, as though a man could be in love with a slave! Why then has he taken me with him? Why did he buy me? Solely for the lowly labors of the loft, and, of course, for the common purposes of the pleasure slave? Surely a man of his means could have purchased a better-trained, more beautiful girl, a Gorean girl. He said I figured in his plans, she thought. I wonder what that meant.

Then she felt a sudden chill. Perhaps he purchased me for a purpose for which he would not care to risk a Gorean girl!

She remembered the messages she had carried, the intrigues, the dangers in contemporary Ar. That is it, she thought to herself, miserably. He wants a meaningless, expendable tool! Then it seemed to her that this was too simple. He must also have wanted, she thought, an ignorant girl, one unversed in the politics of Ar, one who will understand little of what is being done, of what she is being used to accomplish, one who, even under torture, her flesh writhing on the rack , drawing back, screaming, from the heat of fierce, white irons, could reveal little or nothing of the matters in which she obediently, unwittingly, had figured.

What purpose has he in mind for me now, she wondered.

She did not doubt, however, but what Portus was fond of her. It was only, she was sure, that her value was negligible, and perhaps so, too, was that of dozens of free men, compared to some end in view, some projected goal in the city.

What had happened to Talena, she wondered. Why was the Ubara missing from the palace?

But doubtless there was nothing to worry about there.

But I think, she thought to herself, that I have little to fear, actually, little more than a horse might have to fear. I am property, I am goods. I may figure as spoils, being seized by one party or another, wearing one chain or another, but I do not think that I have to fear as might free persons fear. I would think that it would be Portus Canio, my master, who must fear, and Fel Doron and Tersius Major, his associates and friends, for they are free persons and would doubtless be held accountable for their actions, for theft, treason, or such.

I am a slave girl, thought Ellen.

As she stood there in the basket, in the wind, holding to the side of the basket, the blanket clutched about her, being sped through the night, beneath the moons, she had an odd sense of contentment, and pride.

I have never known such happiness as on Gor, she thought.

I am so pleased to have been brought here.

Here, for the first time, I am something, something exact and real. Here, for the first time, I have a function, a condition, a nature and an identity, an actual identity. For the first time I know what I am, and how I must be, and what I must do. Here, for the first time, too, my sex means something. Here, for the first time, my sex is truly meaningful. Too, for the first time I have an actual value. Free women may be priceless, but, thus, they are worth nothing. As what I am I now have a value and it will be determined by my beauty, which I have reason to believe is considerable, the desire of men, and the conditions of the market. On this world wars have been fought for slaves. We have value. Despite what masters say I suspect we are the most valuable form of merchandise on this world. Wagonloads of gold, hundreds of tarns, have been exchanged for high slaves. For some slaves cities have been bartered. Even average slaves are important items in the economy. Men desire slaves, and here they may have them.

Men fight for slaves. Men kill for them.

We are treasures, prizes. We are sought with eagerness, with zeal, with energy, with ambition, passion and power.

Men become great with our necks in their collars. At their feet we find our womanhood. Nature is confirmed, enhanced, fulfilled and celebrated.

The wind blew through her hair.

You may reject me, Selius Arconious, she said, bitterly, but others will not. I know that I have value, that I would bring a good price in a normal market. I may be young, and a barbarian, but I know that I am a beautiful slave. Yes, a beautiful slave! See me on a market block, Selius Arconious. See me perform! Then you will cry out with rage, with misery, with need, seeing what you have lost!

"You have lost a prize, Selius Arconious," she cried, to the indifferent emptiness of the dark countryside. "You have lost a prize!"

The moons are beautiful, she thought, through tears.

Then, weeping, she lay down in the basket, a small figure, her knees drawn up, wrapped in the blanket.

I am a slave girl, she thought. I wonder whose chain my neck will wear.

In time she slept.

Chapter 20

Coffled

Ellen, choking in the dust raised by the clawed feet of restless saddle tharlarion, stirring, grunting, snorting, coming and going, seemingly all about her, miserable in the heat, shutting her eyes against the dust and glare, the sun burning on her back, weeping, the tears mixing with the grit of dust, was forced to her knees, and then to all fours. She heard the rustle of chain behind her and then, in an instant, a heavy metal collar was clasped about her neck and locked. A chain dangled from its back ring, its posterior ring, that at the back of her neck, to a girl behind her, and another chain ran from her collar's throat ring, or anterior ring, to the back ring, or posterior ring, of the next collar, which, a moment later, was closed about the lovely, slim neck of the slave before her, and so on, toward the beginning of the coffle.

"Stand, sluts!" she heard, and the crack of a whip.

Ellen struggled to her feet, with a rattle of chain. She felt the draw, the tension, the pull of the chain on the collar, before her and behind her. How hot the sun was! There was so much dust! It was hard to breathe, for the dust. She had her eyes half shut against the glare.

She felt miserable, and dizzy. Things swirled about her. Tharlarion rushed past. Men shouted. She heard the creak of wagon wheels. She feared she might be ill, that she might faint.

She grasped the chain before her, with both hands. How small and delicate seemed her fingers on the heavy, merciless links. How well they keep slaves, she thought.

"Put your hands at your sides, slave girl," said a voice. "Keep your eyes straight ahead, stand gracefully."

"Yes, Master," said Ellen. The voice seemed not unfamiliar. It seemed she must have heard it somewhere, and recently.

She felt the coil of a whip beneath her chin, lifting it. It was then removed. She, of course, kept her head raised.

"I thought you would look well in coffle," said the voice.

"Thank you, Master," whispered Ellen. She dared not turn her head.

"You are perhaps a bit young, and a bit slender," said he, "but you are nonetheless exquisitely formed. I have no doubt you will bring a good price. Figures such as yours sell well. I think you are intelligent, for a slave. You have a beautiful face, exquisitely sensitive and feminine, though smudged now, and excellent hair, long and flowing, though desperately now it needs washing, yes, excellent hair, long, fine, flowing, soft hair." As he said this he was examining her hair. "You have a good throat," he said, appraisingly, "good shoulders, stand straighter, yes, lovely breasts, a narrow waist, a nice belly, wide hips, a sweet love cradle, nice flanks, a pretty ass. I wonder—"

"Oh!" cried Ellen.

"Yes," he said, satisfied, "you should bring a good price."

The sun was hot.

"Perhaps I shall bid on you myself," he said.

Ellen was confused, and miserable. She had been brought into the camp last night.

"Your former masters were fools," said the voice. "They sought to outwit Cos. But the eyes and ears of Cos are everywhere."

"Yes, Master," whispered Ellen.

"Perhaps you are curious to know the fate of your companions?" he said.

"Yes, Master!" said Ellen, quickly.

"Curiosity is not becoming in a slave girl," he said.

"Yes, Master," she said, sobbing.

"Lower your head," he said.

She stood then in the dust and heat, her head bowed.

He was rather near her, and rather before her.

There was a pounding of claws on the earth and a saddle tharlarion, with a hurried, leaping gait, hurtled by.

She could hear, somewhere behind her, the grunting of a ponderous draft tharlarion, presumably being harnessed, or backed into its traces. To her left, yards away, tent pegs jerked from the earth, poles lifted and lowered, colorful, striped canvas seemed to collapse in upon itself, to be gathered and rolled, and tied. She heard a rattle of pans somewhere behind her.

The sun was hot upon her.

She hoped she would not faint in the heat.

"You may look upon me, slave girl," said the voice.

Ellen lifted her head. He who stood near her she had seen before, in the loft. He was the Cosian subcaptain who had demanded documentation of Portus Canio, the subcaptain whose men had searched the loft, he who had confiscated her in the name of Cos, wiring the tag to her collar.

"Do you recognize me, slave girl?" he asked.

"Yes, Master," she said.

It was he who had speculated that she would look well, chained by the neck, being marched in a slave coffle.

He then turned away.

What was the fate of Portus Canio, Fel Doron and Tersius Major, she wondered.

Were they safe?

Men were cursing somewhere.

One she took to be the camp marshal passed her. He carried a list. She had seen him approaching, moving along the lines, stopping to confer with officers and drovers. It is the function of the camp marshal to choose sites, lay out the camps, and, when ready to move, to order the components in the march, arranging wagons, cavalry, stock, guards, scouts, and such. His arrangements, of course, may be overruled, or revised, by the camp commander, the highest officer with the march.

Several female slaves, indeed, a very large number, Ellen amongst them, had been arranged and "necklaced." Not all the female slaves in the camp were in the coffle, of course. Those not in the coffle were presumably camp slaves, associated with the camp, properties of the Cosian military, or perhaps, in some cases, of officers. The presence of such women in the camp is a great convenience to the soldiers, as one might imagine, for they are useful in various ways, performing a variety of tasks, such as cooking, cleaning, laundering, and sewing, and, naturally, more delicate, subtle, pleasurable slave tasks, such as "serving wine," and such. These slaves were tunicked much as common slaves, briefly, and in a variety of colors, though, at the left hip, low, near the hem of the tunic, on the side, rather in the back, there was a small, vertical, rectangular, gray patch, which color is often used for the tunics of state slaves. They looked upon the slaves in the coffle with contempt. As far as Ellen knew all slaves not commonly associated with the march, except some high slaves, the latter in barred slave wagons, were in the coffle. Ellen had no clear idea how many women were in the coffle. Usually about ten slaves are on a single, given chain, but chains are linked together, by padlocks and posterior rings, and such. Ellen estimated that there were between two hundred and fifty and three hundred women in her coffle. She knew that coffles of over a thousand women were not unknown. Ellen was rather toward the head of the coffle, perhaps some twenty or thirty women from its beginning. Curious, she determined that the coffle was not arranged in order of height, as are many smaller coffles. In a marching coffle she knew that the most beautiful were often put at the beginning, and the least attractive put at the end. Sometimes girls strove for a better coffle position, passionately trying to improve their attractiveness. In a sales coffle two policies tend to predominate: sometimes the most beautiful are saved for the end, which has led to the saying "rich enough to buy from the end of the chain," or, more often, the girls are mixed on the chain with various sales strategies in mind, for example, mixing skin colors, facial types and such for aesthetic purposes, putting a moderately attractive girl between two less attractive girls to improve, by contrast, the chance of marketing the moderately attractive girl, and so on. Sometimes the positions are determined randomly, by lot. Buyers tend to approve of this arrangement, for one can then suppose that one has had the best buy, regardless of the girl's position on the chain. To be sure, what all these approaches seem to overlook, though it is probably understood well enough by all, is that much which is very personal, even "chemical," so to speak, is involved in these matters. A slave who is nothing to one man may be exactly the slave that another man must have at any price, and a stunning beauty, perhaps a flower from a defeated Ubar's pleasure garden, perhaps even his preferred slave, these women vended in a war camp, might not appeal to a given common soldier, and such.

Ellen wondered if the coffle had been ordered in terms of beauty, at least as some men saw these things. If so, she was surely prized. This both flattered her, and frightened her. But then, again, the coffle might have been arranged in no particular order, or in an order in which beauty, or estimates of beauty, were irrelevant, an order of acquisition, or an order based on the night's chaining, or such.

Too, she was certainly not in one of the barred slave wagons. She was a far cry from a high slave. She was only a youngish barbarian. Yet she was rather near the beginning of the coffle.

I am miserable. I am hot. I can scarcely breathe for the dust, thought Ellen. She looked toward the sun with closed eyes, and the insides of her eyelids were a warm, radiant red. She put her head down, and it seemed as though there was blackness about the edges of her vision. I must not faint, she thought. They would beat me. I must struggle to remain conscious. Why will they not let us sit down, or lie down? They have commanded us to rise. I fear the whip. They have made us rise. Soon I fear we must march. I will try to march well. I do not want to be struck with the whip.

Four soldiers on tharlarion thundered by. Dirt and gravel flew up from the animals' passage, pelting, stinging the startled, chained girls, who shrank back, whimpering, and a rising, thick, floating cloud of dust, bright in the hot sun, lingered and swelled behind, enveloping the line. Ellen and the others, pelted, stinging, choking, half-blinded, turned their heads away from it, covering their eyes.

Then the dust settled, and Ellen felt it on her face, on her eye lashes, her breasts and body. Her hair, she knew, would be filthy with it.

She could feel the dust on her lips, as though in cracks there. She ran her tongue over it, and her tongue felt dirty. Her mouth felt dry, and dirty. Her head ached, from the glare of the sun. Her eyes smarted, from the brightness, and glare. Putting down her head, she tried to wipe her eyes, to free them, and her eyelids, of the dirt and dust, and powdered grit, which clung about them, and was lodged within them. The material was scratchy.

Sweat, too, ran into her eyes. Her eyes smarted and stung. It was hard to see.

They have had us stand, she thought. I hope they do not whip us. Surely we must soon move.

And so she stood there, her feet in the hot, thick dust, chained with the others. She felt sick. She was miserable. I must not faint, she thought. Heat seemed to envelop her. It was like invisible fire. The sun boiled. She put her hands on the chain before her neck, running from her anterior collar ring to the posterior collar ring of the slave before her. The chain felt hot to her small fingers. The collar, of iron, some half of an inch in thickness, was close about her throat. It, too, felt hot. The light collar of Portus, the common collar, typical of Gorean slave collars, had been removed last night, and the tag that had been wired to it. The only collar she now wore was that which fastened her in the coffle. On her thigh, of course, was her brand. Even without the master's collar, the brand would clearly mark her slave. The collar marks the girl as slave and commonly identifies the master. Too, it is generally visible. The brand marks her as slave, but is a generic emblem of bondage independent of a particular master. It would normally be covered by a slave tunic. She heard shouts along the line. Are they going to move us now, she asked herself. She heard an approaching tharlarion, from behind her, on her right. She closed her eyes, and tried not to breathe. It passed, rapidly. Once again the air burned with a choking, agitated smoke of grit and dust. Ellen then gasped for breath, and coughed, and wiped her face. There was the sound of the blow of a whip from somewhere behind her, and the cry of a girl in pain. A bit later she was aware of a man near her. She kept her eyes ahead. She straightened her body.

Then he had gone forward. He carried a whip.

She was naked, of course, as were the others.

She recalled that the officer of Cos, in the loft, had speculated that she would look well, a chain on her neck, marched in a coffle.

And now she stood here, somewhere, days from Ar, passive, obedient, as she and the others must be, awaiting the order to march.

She put her head down, under the merciless sun, in the dust and heat.

There was a chain on her neck.

She was coffled.

* * * *

It will be recalled that Portus and his party left Ar under the cover of darkness. When morning came, the first day, they had landed, taken shelter in a grove of ka-la-na, and made their first camp. Clearly this was to be a concealed camp, and Portus had forbidden the lighting of fires. When the tarns in the progress of Tersius Major had come to the ground, Fel Doron, already landed, came to the last of the seven baskets, and lifted Ellen from the basket. She could have climbed from, or scrambled from, the basket, of course, but she had not been given permission to leave it. Too, slave girls are expected to be aware of what men want of them, expect of them, and demand of them, of their beauty, their image, and its suitable movements and demeanors. They are not expected to act like inert, unawakened, sexless tomboys. That is the last thing they are. And it is difficult to leave such a basket in a tunic without presenting yourself as a spread slave. The baskets in which free women travel have gates, through which they may proceed with suitable modesty, with due elegance. Ellen's basket was a cargo basket, and a deep one. When she had been placed on the grass before Fel Doron, she knelt before him, put her head down, and kissed his feet, an act of deference appropriate for a slave. She was then set about small tasks in the camp. She was forbidden to leave the ka-la-na thicket. During the day the men, concealed among the trees, took turns watching the skies. She herself, when her chores were done, gathering grass for bedding, spreading blankets, preparing food and serving it to the men, and such, was chained by an ankle to a tree. Portus, within the thicket, with a crossbow, stalked and slew a small tabuk. Its meat was fed to the tarns. Ellen, awakening in the afternoon, about the twelfth Ahn, noted that Tersius Major was not in his place. It was his turn on watch. At nightfall the tarn train again took to the skies, Ellen once more in her conveyance. Ellen was much more content, and pleased, with her journey the second night, as many of her fears had been dispelled. They were, it seemed, now flying over a district in which there were many lakes. The moons were reflected in the waters. It took several Ehn to traverse some of these waters. Once, the second night, Ellen was frightened, but fascinated, because an Ahn or so after departure there was a great shadow in the sky near her, and, looking up, she saw the gigantic figure of a wild tarn wheeling away; it had approached silently. Ellen looked down at the countryside, interspersed as it was with waterways, pools, ponds and lakes. Before dawn the tarn train once more landed, this time amongst a cluster of small hills, covered with needle trees, evergreen trees, and took its shelter in a narrow ravine. This time, when her chores were done, Ellen, to her chagrin, was put in a belly chain with attached bracelets. In this device, if the slave's hands are braceleted before her, the free ends of the device are closed and locked behind her, at the small of her back. If the slave's hands are braceleted behind her, the free ends of the device are closed and locked before her, at her waist. She was back-braceleted. She was also gagged. That day, too, as might be expected, her left ankle bore as before its encircling metal impediment, by means of which, with its attached chain, she was secured to a small tree.

Ellen tried to stay awake, to listen to the men. Given the narrowness of the sheltering ravine, and its various physical limitations, boulders and such, they were only a few yard away. But, even so, they spoke softly, and she could not hear what they said. Their demeanor seemed earnest, their tones urgent. She did make out the word 'rendezvous', from which word she gathered that Portus, and perhaps unknown allies, would soon meet, to prosecute some plan or another. What part she might play in their plan, or plans, she had not been informed. She recalled the saying that curiosity was not becoming in a slave girl, a saying which had always seemed ironic to her, because, to the best of her knowledge, amongst such eager, bright, lively creatures, an avid curiosity was endemic. If you were a chained slave, often deliberately kept in ignorance, would you not be zealous to be apprised of the least tidbit of news, for example, that you were to be transported, sold or mated?

Why have they gagged me, wondered Ellen. Perhaps they are now in an area which they regard as sensitive, an area in which they would not care to risk the bleating of a verr, the cry of a slave.

She shuddered.

She had great difficulty in sleeping for a time, but, late in the afternoon, in the warmth, the sunlight descending gently, lazily, amongst the trees, she fell asleep. She awakened once, hearing Portus inquire of Tersius Major where he had been, and, drowsily, heard his reply, that he had gone for water. She then slept again until she felt someone turning her to her back and undoing the belly chain. It was Portus. She tried to squirm a little, to bring her tunic down from her waist, to which location it had crept in her sleep. Then she lay still, looking up at her master, over the gag. He smiled at her, in the half darkness, and put his hand gently on her. She whimpered once, and then whimpered once, again. She lifted her body to him, begging. "No, little slave girl," he said, gently, and turned her to her stomach, freeing her hands of the bracelets. He then removed her gag. She knelt before him, taking care that her knees were piteously, beggingly, spread. "No," he said, gently. "Help the others to pack." She then rose, reluctantly, and went to assist the others. In her bondage, of course, slave fires had been lit in her belly. She was no longer the creature she had been on Earth. She now needed sex, and desperately, and at frequent, recurrent intervals, rather as she needed food and drink. Men had done this to her, liberating her natural sexual needs, which must then blossom, inflicting upon her their enflaming, inexorable demands. And, of course, as she was dependent on the master for her food and drink, so, too, she was dependent upon him for the satisfaction, as he might please, if he might please, of her sexual needs, the profound sexual needs of a slave.

Then, again, they were aflight, again over a district muchly watered.

She tried to despise herself for her weakness, for her behavior before Portus Canio. How terrible you are, she castigated herself. But she realized that she now was, that she had now become, despite whatever she might wish, despite what she might desire, or consider proper, a needful slave. She understood then how some of the girls in her training could moan and scratch at their kennels, and hold out their hands through the bars to a passing guard, for a mere touch. She understood then how a chained slave could scream her needs to the moons of Gor. She recalled the naked slave she had seen on the roof in Ar. Oh, she thought softly to herself, I think she is indeed well mastered.

She gritted her teeth, and clutched the wicker of the basket, holding to it in desperation.

Remember, she said to herself, you must be dignified. You must be above sex. It is for the low, and the vulgar, the unenlightened, those whose thinking has not yet been corrected. If any concession had to be made to such vulgar insistencies, it must be as limited, and despised, as possible. Sex must be kept in its place, which was a small place. It was to be regarded as, at best, only a small and unimportant part of life. Then she laughed, bitterly. What a fool I was, she thought. What a blind, naive, stupid fool!

Remember, you are a college professor, she thought. You have a Ph.D.! Again she laughed, in the whistling wind, speeding through the night. That is all behind me now, she thought. Now I am only a collared slut, an aroused, needful, begging slave! Masters, have mercy on me! I will try to please you, Masters! Take pity on a needful slave!

Then, suddenly, her attention was directed ahead. It seemed that there was, incredibly, a light in the third basket, that of Tersius Major, a sheltered lantern, swinging. Then it was gone. She looked about and saw, or thought she saw, a tiny point of light in the distance, some hundreds of feet above the ground, perhaps hundreds of yards away, to the right. Then it, too, was gone. Perhaps it was a star, she thought, now obscured by clouds. She kept her eyes on that part of the sky. It was dark, but she was not sure there were clouds there. Certainly there had been no doubt about the lantern in the third basket. Tersius Major must have been signaling Portus Canio and Fel Doron, she supposed. But they might not see, as they were ahead. Perhaps he did not wish to call out. She herself had been gagged at their last camp. How then could he signal them? Then, to her amazement, she sensed that something was very different in the tarn train, and realized, with a start, that the line connecting the tarn and basket of Tersius Major and the following tarns and baskets was free, perhaps cut. It hung below the fourth tarn. The fourth tarn, and the others, behind it, then began to veer off to one side. Tersius Major, on his tarn, was now moving rapidly to the right. The two lead tarns and baskets, those of Portus Canio and Fel Doron, continued on their way, apparently unaware that Tersius Major had left the train, and that his trailing tarns had been, in effect, loosed.

What is going on, cried Ellen to herself, clutching the sides of the basket.

The tarn and basket of Tersius Major was streaming to the right. The train in which her basket formed a part departed, too, from the line of flight, also bending to the right, but then, in a few Ihn, it turned back and began to circle about. The tarns and baskets of Portus Canio and Fel Doron continued on their way.

Why, Ellen wondered, had Tersius Major broken the line. Was this an elected point? Was this prearranged with Portus Canio and Fel Doron? They seemed to be continuing directly on. There seemed to have been signals exchanged, or at least a signal given by Tersius Major. Had that signal been intended for Portus Canio and Fel Doron, or for others? Others, surely. Indeed, perhaps Portus Canio and Fel Doron were aware of the signal, it forming a part of their plans. This must then be the rendezvous? It seemed there had been a responding signal, far off. Or one of perhaps several points of rendezvous? Would Fel Doron be the next to leave the train? But why would Tersius Major have freed the tarns and baskets in his winged retinue? That seemed to make no sense. Were they loosed to be retrieved by allies?

As these thoughts raced through Ellen's head she noted, approaching from her present left, what would have been the right before her tarns had begun, leaderless, to veer about, and circle, a storm of wings, perhaps as many as thirty tarns. She knew these were not wild tarns, because of the orderly approach, the measured, three-dimensional spacing of the birds. She caught, in less than an Ehn, a glimpse of saddles and shields, of lances, of helmets. "Tarnsmen," she gasped. These were no irregulars, or guerrillas, no motley assemblage of defiant, desperate, courageous patriots. These were surely no allies of Portus Canio and his tarnsters. These were professional soldiers, uniformed, organized, disciplined, well-armed.

Two tarnsmen of the flighted squad wheeled from their formation, and began to approach the loose, leaderless line of six tarns, which had been the fourth through the ninth tarns in the original train, the fourth through the seventh with baskets, Ellen in the last basket, that carried by the seventh tarn, and the eighth and ninth without baskets.

Ellen crouched down in the basket, and pulled the blanket about her, concealing herself as well as she could, crouching below the side, covered with the dark blanket, and peered out through the wicker.

One of the tarnsman, aflight, was within fifty feet of her. She saw the insignia on the shield, but made nothing of it. It was not the sign of Cos, familiar to her from Ar. Mercenaries, she thought. Not brigands, but mercenaries! But who could hire mercenaries, she asked herself. Cos, she thought, Cos!

There was no sign of Tersius Major.

Moving in the basket, facing forward, peering again through the wicker, she saw the first tarnsman who had approached the train swoop beneath it, beat his way forward, and then seize the long rope dangling better than a hundred feet from the harness of the first tarn, that which had been the fourth in the original train. He wound this rope about the pommel of his saddle and brought his bird to the lead. Slowly the train fell into line behind him. Turning about, Ellen saw the second tarnsman was now following the last tarn, and was some fifty to seventy yards behind it. The first tarnsman turned the train westward. In that direction would lie Thassa, the sea, and perhaps the port of Brundisium.

She crouched down in the basket, and grasped the metal tag wired to her collar. Do I belong to Cos, she asked herself. What will be done with me?

Is there an escape for me, she wondered, wildly.

No, she thought, wildly. There is no escape for me. I am a Gorean slave girl. I am collared. I am branded. I have only a tunic. Even my beauty might give me away, it seeming to be a beauty appropriately that of a slave, and little things, too, about how I move, things I am not even aware of. And there is nowhere to go, nowhere to run. This culture understands, and respects, slavery. They recognize it as natural and rationally grounded. Its validity is recognized, and accepted. It is not questioned. What would be questioned would be the right of one such as I to be free. That is what would be regarded as unnatural and absurd. Here on Gor slavery is an explicitly institutionalized, culturally sanctioned recognition of certain forms of biological differentiation, and constitutes an acceptance of, and an endorsement of, certain biological proprieties. The master has the right of command, and will exercise it; and the slave has the duty of unquestioned, absolute, instant obedience.

I love my collar, but should I not seek to return to my rightful Master? Might he not search for me?

And so Ellen resolved to attempt to elude her unwitting captors. She knew that she had no hope of escaping her bondage on this world; that was not possible. Too, she did not wish to do so, having come to understand that whatever might be the case with other women, she herself belonged in the collar; the collar was her fulfillment, her dream and meaning. She belonged at the feet of a master, serving, loving and obedient. This Gor had taught her, and the lesson had been well learned. On the other hand, she was not eager to fall into the hands of strangers, to whom she would be no more than a loose verr or strayed kaiila.

When they land, thought Ellen, I will try to slip away. Then it occurred to her that they might well land after dawn, in the full daylight, and in some camp, where she would be instantly discovered. She clutched the blanket about her, angrily, crouching in her tiny tunic in the swaying basket. What hope could there be for her? What hope could there be for any Gorean slave girl?

"Away!" she heard. "Away!

Quickly she peered through the wicker.

Following, some fifty yards or so to the back, and right, and some yards above, was a great shadow.

The following tarnsman had been he who had cried out.

There was no mistaking the nature of that shadow, the breadth of wingspan, the wicked beak, the crest. It was a tarn, a wild tarn.

It has been following us, thought Ellen. It is the same tarn I saw last night! It is not clear, of course, that her surmise was correct. But it surely seemed the same bird, or one muchly similar.

"Away!" cried the tarnsman, brandishing his lance.

Ellen saw the legs of the wild tarn suddenly appear, extended forward and down, talons opened.

"Go away! Be off!" cried the tarnsman.

The most common prey of the wild tarn is the small single-horned, usually yellow-pelted, gazellelike creature called the tabuk. On the other hand, it is ready to prey upon, and sample, a variety of game. Too, it is not above raiding domesticated, as well as wild, herds of tarsk, verr or hurt, that the bounding hurt, valued for its wool. It can also, of course, be dangerous to human beings.

It is hungry, thought Ellen. But it is not likely to attack its own kind, tarns. What then? Or perhaps it is territorial, and resents the intrusion of these new birds into its hunting area. If it is the same tarn I saw last night, thought Ellen, it is probably hungry. But surely it would not attack its own kind, not our tarns. What then?

The tarn suddenly uttered a weird screaming sound and swooped downward, its talons open, grasping, toward the following tarnsman who, turning in the saddle, angrily, thrust up at it with his lance, and withdrew the lance from the feathers dark with blood. The attacking bird wheeled away.

"Begone!" cried the tarnsman.

"It is coming again!" cried the leading tarnsman who had freed the rope from his pommel, swung about, and set an arrow to a small saddle bow, used for clearing the saddle, firing to either side.

Once again the train of tarns was unled, the lead line free, dangling, uncontrolled in the sky.

This time the tarn, fiercely, perhaps in rage, in pain, hurled itself downward on the following tarnsman. The lance pierced its body, appearing through its back. But the bird, the lance like a straw in its mighty bulk, struck the tarnsman and the other bird, grasping and biting. The tarnsman's shield was ripped from his arm and went flying into the darkness below. The bird had its talons on the man but could not pull him free, because of the safety strap. He cried out in fury, trying to fend away the beak. The two birds wheeled, and spun in the air, falling, climbing, screaming, falling. The tarnsman's bird, doubtless a war tarn, scenting blood and battle, almost on its back on the sky, ripped upward with its talons at its wild brother. The lead tarnsman loosed, as he could, arrow after arrow into the body of the attacking bird, and then, drawing his sword, for he carried no lance, tried to close with it, to strike it somehow, across the back of the neck, in that tumbling tangle of rage and hunger. The other tarns, strung together, but not controlled, struck about, erratically. Different birds beat their way, confused, frightened, in different directions, and were then jerked up short, and lines began to twist, and the birds to scream. Feathers drifted toward the ground. Ellen's basket swung wildly on its ropes, and she clung to the wicker with all her strength. The lines of the train of tarns were then tangled, and the train began to falter, screaming, struggling, impeded, toward the ground. One bird's wing was tangled in a loop of the line. Another scratched and tore at one of the baskets which was near it. Another tarn, wheeling about, struck Ellen's basket and she was nearly thrown from it. One side of the basket was ripped open. The basket began to jerk in flight, and then it was held by only three ropes, as one of the anchoring ropes slipped loose, off the torn wicker. There was ground below, and then there was water, and then ground, seeming to swing about and turn, and then water, again. The tangle of tarns were then thrashing about in the water, wing strokes pounding about, raising great, dark, leaping sheets of water. The tarn then, to whose harness Ellen's ruined basket was insecurely fastened, began to strike out, perhaps crazed with fear, for tarns abhor water, biting, at the line, at the other tarns, at the basket, perhaps in its fear, or madness, or to rid itself of perceived obstructions or impediments. Ellen cowered back, as pieces of the basket were torn away, flung out into the water, the wicked, bright eyes of the bird near her, not a yard away, the beak slashing at the wicker. When the bird turned away, to strike at another bird, Ellen, wildly, thrust the last rope free, and found herself in the water, the basket free of the harness, clinging to the remains of the basket, little more now than two sides and a flooring. The water was dark and cold. Ellen did not know how to swim. She clung to the basket, terrified. She could hardly breathe or see, for the darkness, the thrashing shapes, the splashing water.

❊ ❊ ❊ ❊

"March!" came the command, a command accompanied by the crack of a whip, sudden and sharp. Ellen heard tiny cries of fear and dismay, from both before and behind her. She was then aware that she, herself, had so cried out, softly, inadvertently, involuntarily, unable to help herself. That sound, you see, the fierce, sudden crack of the whip, is not unknown to slave girls. We understand its meaning well.

The long coffle then began to move.

It was a large coffle, of perhaps some two hundred and fifty to three hundred girls, each stripped, each chained by the neck.

Ellen was toward the beginning of the chain, surely amongst the first twenty or thirty on the chain.

She did not know what had become of her party. She did not know where she was being marched.

The march was a large one, and contained a great deal more than the coffle. There was a long train of wagons, some drawn by bosk and others by tharlarion. There were some cage wagons, perhaps carrying high slaves or women of political importance. The slaves could be seen, stripped, behind the bars. Were they high slaves that must have been humiliating for them. But then high slaves are, when all is said and done, slaves, no more or less slave than the lowliest kettle-and-mat girl. On the other cage wagons, silken curtains were drawn, within the bars. To be sure, those within, perhaps robed free women, might put out their small hands, lightly, and feel the bars on the other side of the silk. They, too, were incarcerated, as much as a stripped slave. Sometimes captured free women are given only a light, single, sliplike garment to wear. This makes them uneasy. Many soldiers, infantry, and tharlarion cavalry, accompanied the march. There may have been as many as three companies with the march, two of infantry and one of tharlarion cavalry. Independently, there were many mounted guards with the march. It was from these, presumably, that scouts and outriders were drawn. On the other hand most of these guards, mounted, tended to flank the march, distancing themselves some yards apart, on each side. They and the girls were forbidden to communicate, save that commands might be issued, whips used, and such.

* * * *

"It is a slave girl," said a young male voice.

Ellen stirred, awakening, on her stomach, lying in the mud, half in the water, amongst the reeds, clinging still to the wreckage of her basket.

There were two of them, standing in the water, one on each side of her. She did not look up, but hooked her fingers tightly in the remnants of the wicker.

"Let us see her," she heard.

Her fingers were then loosened from the wicker. It was then thrust away, back into the water. Her fingers dug into the mud of the shore, the water lapping softly about her. She then felt herself being turned about and put to her back.

"A pretty little vulo," said one.

"Neck-ringed and all," said the other, approvingly.

She lay on the mud then, on the sloping surface, descending to the water, her head down and back, toward the water. There were two of them, lads.

"Let us use her," she heard.

She felt her tunic thrust up. "No," she whimpered. She felt her ankles being grasped, and spread, widely. "No, Masters, please, no," she said.

Last night, when Ellen had been in the water, unable to swim, fearing for her life amidst the maddened, frightened, thrashing tarns, she had clung desperately to the wicker. Free of the harness it was forced away from the birds by their very struggles, their movements creating rolling swells of water, swirling into the darkness. Too, Ellen, as she could, squirmed and paddled her float away from the turbulence. As it was dark she had no idea what might be the closest shore. She could crawl only half upon the wicker without forcing it beneath the water. After a few minutes one of the tarns, that which had been fourth in the original line, and had been the leader of the six tarns once the line had been loosed or cut, lifted itself, wings beating, a few feet from the water, only to be dragged back down by the line linking it to his fellows. But his action had begun an alignment, a pull in a particular direction. The tarn behind him tried to beat its way forward, too, and this urged the first to make another attempt. The third tarn, whose wing had been entangled in the line, turned by the motion of the second tarn had had the wing freed, the loop drawn forward and away, not without the loss of several feathers. Then, one by one, the six tarns, as though recalling the order of the train, began, following one another, screaming, to plunge and beat their way behind the first tarn. The first then lifted itself from the water, furiously beating its soaked wings, plunging down, striking the water, then sweeping up again, the wet feathers scarcely sustaining its flight. This progress was imitated by the others. Then, after a hundred yards, the train left the water, clearing it at first by only feet, the shreds of baskets dangling below two of them, splashing, dragging in the water, but then, bit by bit, climbing, they were aflight.

Ellen was then alone, in the darkness, in the cold water.

She began to move the wicker, as she could, in the direction the tarns had gone. That must be, she supposed, the nearest shore. The tarn is not an aquatic species, and resists being flown out of the sight of land.

Something brushed her leg, under the water, and Ellen screamed, and tried to scramble upon the wicker, but she only forced it under the water. Then she began to struggle to follow the tarns. In the distance she could see a sloping darkness, that seemed to be a hill, and she made toward that.

About dawn she reached the shore and lost consciousness amongst the reeds.

She felt her ankles held widely apart. "No, Masters, please, no," she had said.

Her ankles were released, and she quickly moved back, away, literally into the water, drew her legs together, smoothed down her tunic, and half sat, half knelt, the palms of her hands partly supporting her body, frightened, regarding the two young men, little more than boys, who had found her.

Though she was not a runaway, she had the fear of a caught slave.

"She is pretty," said one of the boys.

"She is filthy," said the other.

"Let us take her back to the village and chain her with the village slaves," said the first.

"I am already owned!" said Ellen, quickly. "I am not a runaway. My master is Portus Canio, of Ar. We were in flight. There was an accident."

"We found you," insisted the first lad.

"Thank you for finding me," said Ellen. "I seek news of my master, and his party, that I may be returned to him."

"Let us not take her back to the village," said the first. "Let us keep her for ourselves."

"Surely I am too old for you, youthful Masters," said Ellen, quickly.

"You are not much older than we," said one of the lads.

Ellen supposed that that was true, but two or three years, in a female, made quite a difference. These were young males, little more than youngsters, who could scarcely grow beards, whereas she, perhaps no more than two or three years older, as she now was, was prime block material.

"It would be hard to keep her just for ourselves, as our secret," said the first lad. "We could keep her in the forest, chained to a tree, or in our hideout cave, but sooner or later someone would suspect, or find her. If we take her back to the village, they will take her away from us."

"Then we must sell her," said the second. "And keep the money for ourselves."

"Please, Masters," said Ellen. "Help me find my master. Return me to him. Doubtless he will reward you."

"And where is your master?" asked the second.

"I do not know," said Ellen.

"You are a runaway," said the first.

"No!" cried Ellen.

"Be grateful if we do not hamstring you," said the second.

Ellen regarded him with horror.

"You are a slave girl, are you not?" asked the first.

"Yes, Master," said Ellen.

"Should you not be kneeling," asked the first, "as you are before free men?"

Quickly Ellen knelt. She kept her knees closely together. She did not wish to be used by boys. Yet she knew that either of them could easily overcome her lesser, her slight, female's strength. They would not know that she was not a tower slave.

But the older of the two lads splashed toward her and, with the back of his hand, lashed out and struck her across the mouth, causing her to half rise, stumble, and then fall back, some feet, to her side, in the deeper water.

"You are too pretty for that sort of slave," he snarled. "I have been to the fairs. I have seen them dancing in the booths, I have seen them on their leashes. Do you think I do not know a slut slave when I see her?"

Quickly Ellen recovered her balance, turned, and knelt before them in the water, muchly where she had fallen, her knees widely spread.

The water there, say, some three or four yards from shore, was some eight to ten inches deep. It moved about her and between her thighs. It felt chilly and gritty. Under the water she felt the mud, slippery and cold, beneath her toes and knees. A breeze came over the water. It moved her hair just a little, she felt it on her arm, and it rustled beyond her, through the reeds.

She did not wish to be again struck.

Her cheek still stung.

Had they a switch or whip she did not doubt but what they would use it on her.

She was, after all, a slave.

She was miserable, and felt helpless.

She was sure she could not placate them, or appeal to them, or use her vulnerability and beauty to protect herself, as she might have with a fully grown male.

They were boys.

What did they know of men and the women in their collars?

The older lad motioned that she should come closer, and then cautioned her to approach no more closely.

The water now, where she knelt, was no more than two or three inches in depth.

She could now feel, in the mud, sand, and pebbles, beneath her knees.

She was perhaps four or five feet from shore.

"Pull up your tunic," said the first lad, angrily. "On your back. Split your legs!"

"Please, no, Masters!" said Ellen.

She then went to her back in the muddy water. She felt it cold, in her hair. Her head was down, given the slope of the shore.

"She is filthy," said the youngest of the lads.

"I like to see them spread like that," said the older lad.

"Please, do not use me, Masters," begged Ellen, supine, obedient, in the shallow water, it lapping about her. "I am not yours! You do not have my master's permission! You do not own me!"

"No one will know," said the second lad.

"The condition of my body will betray your use of me," cried Ellen.

"You can always be drowned in the lake," said the second lad.

"Then you will have no money for me!" cried Ellen.

The two lads looked at one another and grinned, and Ellen, the naive, gullible butt of their rude humor, their rustic joke, reddened.

"What a stupid slave you are," said the second lad.

Ellen moaned. She, indeed, felt foolish and stupid. As though Gorean males, of whatever age, would waste so lovely and useful a property as a female slave! Better to have her a thousand times, and then, when one tired of her, give her to another.

One of the lads then, the older, wading toward her, touched her, and she drew back, quickly.

The slave girl cannot control her sensitivities.

She is helpless.

She belongs to men.

He touched her again, and she twisted suddenly about, and turned her head wildly to the side. She felt muddy water in her mouth.

"See?" said the older lad to the younger.

"I see," said the younger lad.

"Keep your hands on your tunic," said the older lad. And Ellen clutched the hems of the tunic tightly, the tunic up, about her waist.

He touched her again, and she cried out, softly, unwillingly, uncontrollably.

"See?" said the older lad to the younger.

"Yes," said the younger again, interested.

"Oh!" cried Ellen.

"This is a good slave," said the older lad.

"Yes," said the younger.

"See," said the older, "she is ready."

"No!" cried Ellen.

"Good," said the younger.

"Please do not use me, Masters!" Ellen begged.

The older of the two lads grinned.

"Sell me for coins!" said Ellen.

"Why should we not have coins *and* your use?" inquired the older lad.

"Please, no, Masters!" cried Ellen.

"Are you a virgin slave?" asked the younger.

"Think carefully before you respond," said the older.

"No, Masters," said Ellen. "I am not a virgin slave."

"That can be told from the way you move, slave," said the older lad. "No virgin slave moves like that, or not until later."

The older lad now knelt beside her, in the shallow water. His right hand was then on her left leg, above the knee.

The younger lad, standing in the water, was near him.

"I think we will enjoy you, pretty slut," said the older lad.

"Yes," said the younger.

"Beware!" cried Ellen, suddenly. "I belong to Cos! I am a property of the empire of Cos!"

The two lads exchanged sudden glances, clearly of concern.

"Yes," cried Ellen. "Yes! Yes! Beware, Masters! I belong to Cos!"

"Liar," said the first lad.

"See my collar, the tag!" cried Ellen.

"You said you belonged to some fellow of Ar," said the older lad.

"Ar is far away," said the second.

"I did, but I have been confiscated. Beware, young Masters, I am now the property of Cos!"

"You can read," said the younger to the older.

"A little," said the older. He turned the collar tag and looked at it.

"What does it say?" asked the younger.

"Something—'in the name of Cos'," said the older.

"'Confiscated'," said Ellen.

"Can you read?" asked the older lad.

"No," admitted Ellen.

"How do you know it says that?" he asked.

"I heard it read," said Ellen.

"We do not want the village burned," said the younger of the two.

"Get a rope from the boat," said the older lad. He then, angrily, his hand in her hair, drew the slave to her feet, and conducted her, bent over, her head at his right hip, in leading position, onto the shore. There he knelt her, in the sand, facing away from him. Then he said to her, "On your belly, slave girl, and cross your wrists behind you."

The slave obeyed instantly, unquestioningly, as slaves must.

She heard the younger lad now splashing through the reeds. In a short time he returned and her hands were bound behind her back. The rope was long enough to serve as well as a leash, and, moments after she had been ordered to her feet, some yard or so of it, rising from her confined wrists, had been looped and knotted about her throat, its free end then, some five feet or so in length, serving as a leash. Ellen knew that sometimes even desiderated slaves, before a submission ceremony, were put on a simple camp rope and led about, that they would better understand their condition and status, that of a domestic animal, but in her case the rope was not symbolic in nature, but effected a simple utility, constituting a device for keeping and controlling a girl. Ellen, bound, was led on her leash, stumbling, wading, through the reeds. A bit later she was placed in a small, flat-bottomed boat, on her belly, under a tarpaulin. In the boat were two wide, shallow, wooden buckets, each half filled with wet, glistening leeches, taken from the water, often from the stems of water plants, such as rence.

Before being put on her belly in the boat, Ellen's face, she on her knees, was almost thrust into these two buckets, one after the other, filled with twisting, inching, churning leeches, that she might see them. She shrank back, as she could, in terror.

These creatures are utilized in some manner by the caste of physicians, not for indiscriminate bleeding as once on Earth, but for certain allied chemical and decoagulant purposes. Such creatures may also be used, of course, for less benign purposes, for torture, the extraction of information, punishment and, in the extreme, executions. The "leech death" is not a pleasant one. These creatures are not to be confused with the leech plant, which supplements its photosynthetic activities with striking, snakelike, at passing objects. It has paired, curved, hollow, fanglike thorns, associated with a pulsating, podlike bladder. The leech plant can draw a considerable amount of blood in a short time. They tend to grow in thick patches. There is not a great deal of danger from such plants provided one can remove oneself from their vicinity. They are not poisonous. Sometimes one literally uproots the plant in one's escape, so tenacious is the clasp of the thorns. It is different, of course, if one loses one's footing amongst them, or is thrown, naked, bound, amongst them. They are normally cleared away from areas of human habitation, from the sides of roads and such.

Ellen was then put to her belly in the bottom of the boat, hands tied behind her, the rope on her neck, under the tarpaulin.

"You are not to utter a sound," said the older lad, "not the least sound, or we will put you on your back, and put a stick between your teeth and tie it there, so that you cannot close your teeth, and then bind leeches in your mouth."

"Yes, Master," said Ellen, terrified.

"There is a Cosian retinue some ten pasangs to the west," said the older lad, working the back oar. "Their foragers came to the village yesterday, from the west. We will intercept the retinue, or find its camp. With a lantern we can follow the tracks of the verr they took. We will hide her until dusk in the forest, in our cave. We will both return to the village. Toward dusk we will take a wagon, pick her up, and take her to the camp. We can be back before morning, and no one will know, and we will have coins."

Ellen, under the tarpaulin, remained absolutely silent.

And things had proceeded, in large part, as the young man had speculated.

Once, out on the lake, they had apparently been hailed by another boat, doubtless from their village, which must be close. "Did you make a good catch?" called a voice, that of a man, from across the water.

"Yes," called back the older lad. "We have made a good catch!"

Ellen, under the tarpaulin, remained absolutely silent.

The boat was rowed, or maneuvered, with its back oar, to a different point on the shore, and, when the area had been sufficiently reconnoitered by the two lads, she was lifted from the boat, and led into the trees. She was taken to a small cave, and was thrust within. Some light filtered in through the opening. The leash rope was then removed from her throat and taken down to her ankles, which were crossed, and bound. With another piece of rope she was trussed further, several loops put about her legs, above the knees, some loops about her belly, holding her bound hands more closely behind her, and various loops about her arms and upper body. She was well aware, as she had been as long ago as her training, that her body, that of a female, lent itself beautifully to the trussings of captors, because of the flare of her hips, the narrowness of her waist, and the swelling delights of her bosom, ropes, for example, going nicely, tightly, above her bosom and under her armpits, and beneath her bosom and about her waist. It seemed a body that might have been designed for bonds. She wondered, idly, if such bodies might have been selected for, so different from those of most primate females, in dozens of millennia of prehuman, and, later, Paleolithic tribal warfare, in which females, as well as hunting grounds, would be the spoils of war. In such small things, and others far more profound, but connected with ownership, capture, work, servitude, love and breeding, she thought, were women evolved, evolved to serve and please men. It is not so strange then, she thought, that women desire masters, that they long to love and serve, to give themselves to the master, that in their hearts they want and seek masters. Those who did not were perhaps discarded, or left unmated. On the other hand, those females who knelt, even with a braided leather rope on their neck, and found their fulfillment in submission, servitude and love, in belonging to the stronger, to victors, to masters, would be those treasured, those sought, those bought and sold, those mated, those replicating their genes. I have been bred to be as I am, she thought, from the prairies, the forests, the caves, I and my sisters.

The boys then left Ellen sitting up, trussed in the cave. Brush was drawn across the entrance, concealing the opening. There was, however, some light in the cave, filtering through the brush at the entrance. The ropes were scratchy, but she would not move much. She squirmed, just a little, testing them. They were tight and well done. Gorean boys, she knew, especially boys in the villages, were taught to tie slaves. It was something they were supposed to know. They would use the village slaves for practice, the bonds inspected, and approved, or revised, by their fathers, or other older males. Though she was a young woman and they were little more than boys, they had tied her well. She knew herself helpless. They are males, she thought, males, by nature our rightful masters.

As she sat, or lay, in the cave, trussed, awaiting as she must the return of her young captors, she was restless, uneasy, uncomfortable, needful. The touches of the older of the two young men had been deft. She whimpered, angrily. She was furious with her slave needs, but, too, was desperate to placate them, to obtain the ecstatic relief to be obtained from their alleviation. Bonds, too, she knew, increased female arousal. Their function, apart from their obvious practical aspects, such as security and control, was symbolic and psychological, having to do with their relationship to the dominance/submission ratios of organic life. Too, appropriate binding and chaining, she knew, increased both the frequency of, and the intensity of, female orgasms. As a slave girl she was in no doubt about this. Surely she had bucked, and wept, and squirmed, and begged, often enough in bonds. And so, in time, she rolled, and thrashed, and moaned, on the dusty floor of the cave, until, red-eyed, weary, she lay there quietly, save for an occasional small, pathetic, protestive movement, one seeming to arise from somewhere deep within her, from somewhere within her deprived, needful, tortured, begging slave belly. "You are worthless," she said to herself. "You have a slave belly." "Of course, you have a slave belly," she said in response to herself, angrily. "What do you expect, little fool? You are a slave!"

It grew darker and darker in the cave.

Toward nightfall the two boys returned. "Masters!" said Ellen, piteously. Despite their youth, and her reluctance, and her pride, she was prepared to beg for their touch. "Be silent, slave girl," said the older lad. "Remember the leeches." "Yes, Master," whispered Ellen. "You are going to be put in a sack," said the older lad. She lifted her belly a little to them, and whimpered. "Bring the sack," said the older lad to the younger. Ellen lifted herself again, in her bonds, and whimpered. "Do you think we wish to risk the village?" asked the older lad. "There are village slaves, many prettier than you, whom we can use." Ellen, in her slave's vanity, wondered if that could be true, not that there might not be slaves in the village, available to the lads, but that they might be prettier than she. Perhaps, she thought. She wondered if any of her sisters of Earth, brought as she to Gor to serve masters, served in villages, as lovely domestic beasts of peasants.

She thought of the aristocratic, clever, beautiful, formerly rich woman "Evelyn," whom she had served at the supper of Mirus. Doubtless she was now in a collar, now, too, no more than a branded chattel. Ellen wondered if she would be in a peasant village. She did not think so. She thought, rather, that she would be surely kept, at least for a time, by "Jeffrey," he whom she had also served at that supper. She could imagine her at his feet, at the foot of his couch on the love furs, attached to the slave ring there, naked, cringing, not knowing if she was to be whipped or caressed, as a slave, taking the whip cast before her in her small hands and, looking up, trying to read the mood of her master, fearfully, tenderly, hopefully licking and kissing it.

Ellen was then, bound as she was, eased, feet first, into a long, burlaplike sa-tarna sack, which was tied shut over her head. She could see to some extent through the loosely woven cloth. She was then lifted up and carried from the cave, and, some yards later, placed in the back of a wagon and covered with straw. Shortly thereafter, with a creak of wheels, the wagon moved, being drawn, judging from the sounds, by a small, draft tharlarion. Through the sack and the straw, she could detect the light of a lantern. Occasionally the wagon stopped and one of the lads would climb down from the wagon box. "This way," she would hear. Then the lad would either lead the way, it seemed, with the lantern, or, in a bit, the wagon already again in motion, resume his position on the box.

* * * *

Toward noon, the coffle was halted, with the general halt of the march.

Thankfully Ellen, and her sisters in bondage, knelt. They must kneel, knees spread, turned to the right, hands on their thighs, heads down.

Ellen had feared she could not go another step. Her feet were sore. Her body ached. She was hot. She was covered with dust.

She envied the slaves in the slave wagons.

As Ellen knelt, turned to the right, the chains from her collar extended to the left and right, rather than before and behind. This is a common feeding and watering position for a coffle.

"Lift your head," she heard, a female voice. "Open your mouth, keep your hands on your thighs."

Ellen, looking up, found herself before one of the Cosian camp slaves, this one a ravishing blonde, in a brief yellow tunic, with its small vertical, rectangular gray patch, in the vicinity of the left hip, that discreet emblem indicative of state ownership. Most state slaves in the cities, Ellen had heard, wore gray tunics. This made it easy, at a glance, to distinguish between state slaves and privately owned slaves. This distinction might occasionally prove to be of more than simply proprietary or identificatory relevance, for example, if one wished, in short order, to commandeer state slaves, to round them up and transport them, exchange them for goods or prisoners, and so on. Accordingly, for various reasons, a uniform color, or such, for state slaves, would doubtless be institutionally judicious. In any event, it seems to be the common practice. The color gray was probably chosen because it seems unpretentious, conservative, subdued, and sober, a color thus fitting for a girl who is a mere slave of the state, one lacking a private master whose collar she might wear and at whose slave ring she might kneel, and will fit in nicely enough with almost any coloration of eyes, hair, and skin color. Another theory as to the usual choice of gray for state slaves is that it is a sop cast to the sensibilities of free women, who, resenting the usual effects of female slaves on free men, wished the state to limit or reduce the attractiveness of its slaves. On the other hand, this stratagem, if stratagem it is, is almost universally acknowledged as being inefficacious. A beautiful woman in a slave tunic, whatever its color, is a beautiful woman in a slave tunic. The state slaves with the march wore, as noted, a variety of tunics, and their status was marked out simply by the small, rectangular gray patches. Ellen doubted that there were many free women with the march, who might object to this latitude accorded the state's collar girls, saving perhaps those who might be behind the drawn curtains in the cage wagons.

Ellen did not care to be kneeling before a woman, though, of course, often enough, she would kneel before a free woman. But this was a slave. To be sure, she was doubtless a higher slave than Ellen. She was not, for example, in a coffle. But she did not even have a talmit, the cloth headband which occasionally serves as a symbol of rank or authority amongst slaves, sometimes in pleasure gardens, usually in camps or rural areas. A cloth strap ran over the blonde's right shoulder, to which was attached, near the left hip, but rather before her, a cloth sack, which apparently contained some form of sizable biscuits. One of these objects was thrust in Ellen's mouth. It was large, hard and dry. It filled her mouth. "Head down, chew," she was told. The blonde then moved to the next slave, she on Ellen's right. "Lift your head. Open your mouth. Keep your hands on your thighs," she heard. "Head down, chew." Ellen, head down, not permitted to use her hands, dealt with the object as well she could, it filling her mouth, her mouth dry. She tried to tear it with her teeth. She must keep her hands on her thighs. She must not drop it. She must not lose it. She tried to swallow some of it. She began to choke. Then, her mouth still filled, she gasped and caught her breath. She engorged more of the substance, and then more of it. Some girls behind the first slave, she with the biscuits, came a second slave, with a bucket and dipper. Ellen, desperately, half choking, tried to chew and force down the last of the biscuit. It would not do to miss the water. "Lift your head, open your mouth, keep your hands on your thighs," she heard. She looked up. The slave with the bucket and dipper had a yellow tunic, as well, with its gray patch near the hem, on the left, but she was a sleek brunet. Ellen had little doubt but what the camp slaves had been chosen for a diversity of properties, many of which had little to do with those of a simple work slave. Indeed, the girl with the bucket and dipper was a slight girl, and it would be difficult for her to manage the heavy bucket, especially when it was full, and in the heat. She seemed, rather, the sort of woman who might, in bells and diaphanous pleasure silk, serve wine in a captain's tent. A few feet behind her was a guard, with a whip. Ellen felt the metal rim of the dipper put to her lips and she gratefully drank. Too quickly was the dipper withdrawn. "Please, Mistress, more!" begged Ellen. "You have drunk to the mark," said the slave. "What is going on here?" asked the fellow with the whip, moving toward them. "She asked for more," explained the girl with the bucket and dipper. "Proceed," said the guard to the slave, and she moved to the next girl, she on Ellen's right. He shook out the coils of his whip. "Please, no, Master!" begged Ellen. Then she groveled in the dust, weeping, curling up, drawing up her knees, trying to cover her head and face, as she was whipped. Then he continued on his way, following the slave with the water. Ellen lay in the dust, on the chain, sobbing. "Kneel," she heard a voice say, a female voice. Ellen looked up, from her side, and saw a slave, a long-haired blonde, in a brief beige tunic, with the gray patch. She had long legs. Too, she had a talmit. Too, she carried a switch. Ellen cried out, wincing, struck twice with the switch, and scrambled up to her knees. "Split those knees, pleasure slave," she was told. "Yes, Mistress," said Ellen. When the talmited slave had gone Ellen lifted her head and looked after her. She might have a talmit and a switch, thought Ellen, but she, too, I can tell, is a pleasure slave. Are we not all pleasure slaves? "You may be a terror to us, and strict with us, and an authority amongst us, you with your switch, we who are coffled slave meat," thought Ellen, "but in a man's tent, in the shadow of his whip, you, too, female, will kneel, tremble, whimper and beg to serve!"

Last night Ellen had been brought to the camp. The two lads from the lake, stopped by sentries, had made known their business. In the light of the lantern the straw had been parted and the sack undone, and thrust down, at first just enough to view the tag on Ellen's collar, but then, as the interest of the sentries was apparently aroused, to her waist. "Pretty," said the first sentry. "Yes," said the second. "And she is goods of Cos, all right," said the first sentry. "How do you know?" asked the second. Ellen speculated that they might be considering taking her from the boys. She did not doubt but what that could be done. "It is clear, there," said the first sentry, indicating the metal tag wired to Ellen's collar, that bearing the confiscation notice. "Oh," said the second. The first, at least, it seemed, could read. To be sure, he had not seemed too pleased with what he had read. Among sentries it is common to have at least one on duty, or an officer of the guard in the vicinity, who can read, someone who can interpret letters, passes, and such, if need be. Most sentries, of course, are looking for a password, or watchword. These are changed frequently, at least once daily. "Take her forward," said the first sentry, "and ask for the tent of the slave marshal." "We want coins for her," said the older of the two lads, boldly. "See the slave marshal," said the sentry. The sack was then again drawn up, over Ellen's head, and tied shut.

A bit later Ellen felt herself lifted from the wagon and the straw, and placed on the ground, on her stomach. Through the burlap, lifting her head with difficulty, she could see the light of two torches, apparently one elevated on each side of the entrance to a large tent. She was rather close to the torch stand on the right, as one would face the tent. Thus the sack lay in the full light of that torch. The wagon was to one side, the tharlarion shuffling about. She lay there, in the burlaplike sack, bound, awaiting the pleasure of men. Somewhat later then she heard the boys return, apparently with another individual. "Let us see her," she heard. The sack was undone, and she was drawn from it. "Untie her," she heard. "Stand," she was told. The older of the two boys steadied her for, for a moment, it was hard for her to stand. "She is filthy," she heard. A hand, that of he whom she took to be the slave marshal, the officer in charge of slaves in the camp, a large, bearded man, lifted and held, briefly, the tag on the collar. "See, she is the property of Cos," said the older boy. She then felt the tag released. It dropped back, against her body. "We caught her by the lake," said the younger lad.

"I am not a runaway," whispered Ellen, frightened. She could barely speak before this man, so large and fierce he seemed. She did not wish to be beaten, or hamstrung, or fed to sleen. "We were aflight. There was an accident."

"And doubtless you were being hurried to our camp," said the man.

Ellen was silent.

She became aware then that in the vicinity of the tent, where she could see behind it, and to its sides, there were many whitenesses in the darkness, whitenesses receding, seeming to become smaller, into the darkness. She could make out, dimly, to the left, in the half light, the figure of a woman, risen to all fours, a chain on her neck, looking at them. She was naked. There must have been, she estimated, behind the tent and about it, some acres of slaves, chains of them, the chains doubtless secured in some fashion, perhaps fastened to heavy stakes driven deeply into the ground.

Ellen drew back in fear, as she saw a hook knife flash in the man's hand.

"Steady," said the man's voice, soothingly. "We are just going to see what you've got."

The hook knife half cut, half tore, through the tunic, soiled, stiff with dirt, and the tunic, parted, fell to the ground.

"We want coins for her," said the older lad. "We did not keep her. We brought her back."

"You would have considered keeping the property of Cos?" asked the man.

"Not we, of course," said the older, hastily. "But some might have."

"Some less grateful to their beloved benefactors, some less loyal to the empire?" suggested the man.

"Yes," said the older boy.

"That would be theft," said the man.

"We brought her back," pointed out the older lad.

"She is a young, cheap slave, and, if I am not mistaken, a barbarian," said the man. "But be assured, in any event, that you have the gratitude of the empire of Cos."

"And everyone knows the generosity of Cos," said the older lad.

"You want a reward?" asked the man. "For merely doing your duty?"

The lads were silent.

The visage of the slave marshal, for that is who it was, was severe.

"Serving Cos is reward enough," said the older lad.

"Wait a moment, lads," said the man. "There may be others, less honest, less noble, less loyal than yourselves to the empire, and we would not wish them to be dissuaded from returning properties such as this to their rightful owners."

"Master?" said the older lad, hopefully.

"Girl," said the man.

"Master?" said Ellen, frightened.

"Have you had your slave wine?" he asked.

"Yes, Master," she said.

"Go about the tent, on the left," he said. "There you will find a trestle. Bend over it, and wait."

"Yes, Master," said Ellen, miserably.

"Have you made use of the slave?" asked the man of the boys, severely.

"No, Master," said the older.

"No, Master!" said the younger, quickly.

"She is the property of Cos," the older one reminded the man.

"I will find some coins for you, in the tent," said the slave marshal. "In the meantime, accept the gratitude of Cos, and enjoy the hospitality of Cos."

"Long live Cos!" said the older lad.

"Long live Cos!" said the younger.

"You will find thongs at the trestle," said the slave marshal. "Tie her left wrist to her left ankle, the right wrist to the right ankle."

Later the slave marshal came himself to stand beside the trestle. Ellen was weeping, bent over, wrists tied to ankles, helpless, embarrassed, well secured.

"Portus Canio, of Ar, was your master," he said.

"Yes, Master," she said. It is not easy, as you may understand, to conduct a conversation, particularly one in which one retains any dignity, when one is fastened thusly. He would have read her collar, she supposed, when he examined the Cosian tag wired to the collar. Ellen wondered if he had heard the name of Portus Canio, of Ar, before. It did not seem unfamiliar to him.

"What is wrong, little vulo?" he asked.

"Nothing, Master," she wept.

"You may speak," he said.

"You gave me to boys, Master!" she wept. "You gave me to boys!"

"Do you object?" he asked.

"No, Master!" she said, quickly.

"They seem like nice lads," he said.

"Yes, Master," she said. "But am I not a little old for them? Would I not be consigned more suitably to men, Master? Am I not more for men, Master?"

"You are for whomsoever masters decide," he said. "But it is true that you are for men. You are the sort of woman who obviously and appropriately belongs to men."

"Yes, Master!" she said. "But I was not satisfied."

"Who cares if a slave is satisfied," he said.

"They were so quick with me, Master!"

"I shall be even quicker," he said.

"Master?" she asked.

"We do not want you contented as yet," he said. "I think it will be better if you sweat a little, and, for a few days, heat your chains. In a day or two I suspect you will scream for a man. You have the look of such a slave."

"Please, Master, have mercy," begged Ellen.

"Surely you would wish to be sent to the block desperate for a master. Would you not then perform better, more piteously, more needfully?"

Ellen moaned.

"I will send for one of the metal workers tonight," he said, "and we will get this collar and tag off your neck. Then, afterward, we will see that you are chained. And, in the morning, when we leave, I will put you in the coffle."

"In the coffle, Master?" wept Ellen, in horror.

She then felt his hands on her body, holding her.

"Oh!" she cried, suddenly. "Oh!"

He was indeed quick with her. She held to her ankles in misery.

When he turned away she called after him, "Master, may I speak?"

"What is it?" he asked.

"Were the boys rewarded for bringing me here?" she asked.

"The young men were compensated," he said.

"May I ask to what extent, Master?"

"You wish a clue as to your value, do you not, collar slut?" he said.

"Yes, Master," she said.

"Cos," he said, "is noted for her liberality, her unparalleled generosity."

"Yes, Master," said Ellen.

"Five copper tarsks each," said he.

"Thank you, Master!" said Ellen.

"You are all vain she-urts," he said, turning away.

"Yes, Master!" said Ellen, delightedly.

That would be in most cities something like one hundred tarsk-bits altogether. It would be something like fifty tarsk-bits for each lad. Presumably they would not have so many coins at one time until they were responsible for their own fields, and the sale of their own crops. This was, we may remember, the price for which Mirus had allegedly sold her to Targo. It was not much, but it was surely something, and Targo, a professional slaver, had paid it, and so, doubtless, had hoped to make a profit on her, perhaps of as much as five tarsks. She did not know what Portus had paid for her. Several times she had been tempted, when he had seemed in a good mood, to crawl to him on her belly, take his ankles in her small hands, kiss his feet, and beg to know. But she had not dared to do so. Portus was not a patient man. Too, she knew that curiosity was supposedly unbecoming in a slave girl. She did not wish to be beaten. But she was curious, of course, intensely curious, just the same. She had no doubt that she had grown in her bondage, in her beauty, her walk, her responsiveness, even her skill in various domesticities thought suitable for a female slave. For example, she could now make tiny, fine, straight, measured stitches. To be sure, her experiences in the streets of Ar did not suggest that men would be likely to bid upon her with their eyes intent upon her skills as a cook or seamstress. Indeed, she had been obviously taken in the streets of Ar as merely another lovely, briefly tunicked Gorean slave girl, as no more than another Gorean slave girl, and then she thought, this thought muchly pleasing her, that there was nothing unfitting or surprising about that, for that was what she now was, only another Gorean slave girl! She was muchly pleased with the compensation accorded the boys, and she doubted, truly, that those of Cos were any more generous than those of any other city when it came to such matters. A reward of ten copper tarsks for her seemed considerable. Obviously the slave marshal regarded her as acceptable collar meat, perhaps even excellent collar meat! There, take that, again, Selius Arconious, she thought. She did not expect, however, to ever bring as much as a silver tarsk. It would be exciting to be bid upon, she thought. How few women are put upon a block and sold for what men find them to be actually worth!

Do free women think they are so lofty and precious? Let them be put stripped on a sales block and see what they would bring! Let them then get some idea as to what they are truly worth!

Thus, few women, she thought, have any sense of what they are actually worth, as a female. What would be their monetary value, on a slave block? To be sure, it is hard to know about such things, as so many variables affect a price. If the market is glutted a beauty may go for tarsk-bits, and if women are scarce a pot girl might bring a silver tarsk. And some men, determined at all costs to bring a particular woman to their slave ring, may bid prices incomprehensible to others.

Still there is something to be said for what a woman goes for, what men will pay for her.

In a few minutes a fellow in the black and gray of the metal workers appeared and removed her collar, with the attached tag. He then made use of her, briefly, and then freed her from the trestle. She was then, held bent over, in common leading position, her head at his hip, taken back about the tent and chained for the night.

After their feeding and watering the girls were permitted to lie in the dust and rest. The coffle would not move for an Ahn. Bosk and tharlarion were to be fed, watered, and rested. Soldiers were taking their midday meal. Some drovers lay in the shade beneath their wagons. Ellen's body still burned from the lashing, and the two strokes of the slave's switch. As she lay there she realized that her lashing, and her switching, had been well deserved. She should not have asked for more water, and she should have come to position more quickly after her whipping. What a stupid slave she was! Still she was angry with the woman. It is one thing to be whipped by a man, who is a master, and another to be struck by a woman, and one who, like oneself, is a mere slave! Would I not bring a higher price than she, wondered Ellen. Am I not near the head of the coffle?

As she lay there, her arms over her head, to protect it from the sun as well as she could, she became aware of a whispering in the coffle, proceeding toward her. It is forbidden to speak in the coffle, of course, but if no masters are about, or their representatives, such as switch slaves, it is certainly not unknown. The whispering seemed to be eager, and lively.

"Slave," she heard, from the girl who preceded her in the coffle.

Ellen rose up, to all fours, looking anxiously about.

The other girl, too, looked about, then she crawled toward Ellen and addressed her in a soft, confidential, pleased whisper. "In three days," said the girl, "there will be a festival camp, near Brundisium. Cos has been again successful. A plot has been foiled. Conspirators have been taken. Victory to Cos! There will be feasting. Slaves will serve. Slaves will be sold, and danced! Tell others!"

Ellen's heart sank. She feared that this intelligence boded ill for Ar, and perhaps for Portus and his fellows.

"Tell others!" insisted the girl before her, looking about.

Ellen turned about and whispered these tidings to the girl who would be behind her in the coffle. That girl then, delightedly, a redhead, turned about, and passed the message on.

Then, profoundly disturbed by this news of some victory by Cos, though its nature seemed uncertain, Ellen lay again down in the dust to seize what rest she might. Too soon, for her desires, though perhaps not now for those of her enchained sisters in bondage, the order to rise was received, emphasized by the snapping of a slave whip. Ellen could see that the coffle now was in higher spirits. If the guards noted that, they did not inquire as to the reason, and, indeed, perhaps they were well aware of the reason. Perhaps it was they, under orders or not, who had dropped this information near the coffle, in conversation, knowing that it would, at the first opportunity, course like wildfire along the chain. Sometimes we think we are clever. But then, not unoften, it seems that it is the masters who have been most clever. It makes one feel vulnerable. But then one is no more than a slave.

"I do not want to go to Cos or Tyros," whispered the girl behind her. "I want to be sold before Brundisium. I will perform well! Do you think I will get a rich master?"

"Yes," said Ellen, "you are very beautiful."

"You, too, are very beautiful," said the girl.

Very beautiful?

This startled Ellen, for she had not really thought of herself along these lines, or at least not often, or at least to that extent. Beautiful, perhaps. Surely her vanity suggested that. Had she not seen herself in mirrors? But *very* beautiful—and by *Gorean* standards?

Surely she could not have so changed, from the shelf of Targo in Ar.

Perhaps she was "ten-tarsks beautiful," but more?

Perhaps!

Could she hope then, ever, to bring as much as a silver tarsk?

She was convinced, of course, that she was a valuable, attractive slave. She had no doubt about that. She was not unaware of how men had looked upon her, for example, in the streets of Ar. Yes, then thought Ellen, I think I am beautiful! Perhaps even very beautiful!

To be sure, that was for men to decide.

I am near the front of the coffle, she reminded herself.

And the camp slaves have treated me with cruelty. At least it seems so to me. Could they resent me, perhaps for my beauty? Might they be jealous of me?

Could I have changed so much, from the shelf of Targo?

But beauty was for the men to decide. It was they who carried the whips and chains. It was they who did the bidding, the collaring, the branding, the buying and selling, the raiding and netting and roping, the capturing and herding, the mastering.

"What of you?" asked the girl. "Will you perform well?"

"I do not know," said Ellen.

"You will, slave," laughed the girl softly behind her. "It will be seen to by the masters!"

"Are you a hot slave?" asked the girl behind her.

"I do not know," said Ellen.

"If you are not," she said, "do not worry. You will be trained under the hands of the masters. They will teach you to squirm and beg. They will put slave fire in your belly!"

"Perhaps," said Ellen, trying to speak indifferently, even coldly, even skeptically. She saw no point in informing her thoughtful, solicitous sister in bondage that she, Ellen, despite her youth, was no stranger to slave fire, that the flames of the owned, dominated, mastered woman already raged frequently, irresistibly, in her belly, that she hungered for touches, for caresses, for embraces, which were being denied her. Men had indeed taught her to squirm and beg. But they had not created her sexual needs, nor her sexual nature. Not these men, at least, though her nature might have been shaped, through startling complementarities, and interactions with men, in the course of evolution, through countless millennia of capturing, buying and selling, bartering, domination and mastery. They had merely summoned it forth, imperiously, even against her will, merely commanded it, merely liberated it. Only in bondage is the sexual nature of the human female totally freed. In her enslavement she finds her freedom. This is the paradox of the collar.

The order to march was then received.

Standards were lifted, and flashed in the sun.

Drovers called out to their animals, whips cracked, wagons creaked. There was the tread of the soldiers, the grunting, and scampering about, coming and going, scattering dust, of saddle tharlarion.

The coffle, too, with its sound of chain, marched.

The march had been underway for something like two Ahn. Saddle tharlarion, as has been noted, were familiar components of the march and camp. These, not unoften, ran the length of the march, relaying orders, carrying messages and such. Too, of course, there were mounted officers, and others, civilians, and such, who rode with the march, rather than walked, or had places in the wagons. A pair of men approached, and halted their tharlarion some yards ahead of Ellen's position, and, turning the beasts, which were restless, were engaged in conversation. As Ellen, on the chain, marching with the others, approached them, they relatively fixed at the side of the march, she was startled, terribly shaken. She was certain that she recognized the two riders, neither of whom were concerned with the progressing coffle. One was the subcaptain, the Cosian officer, who had been in the loft of Portus Canio, whose men had ransacked it, indeed, he who had wired the tag to her collar, and who had spoken to her earlier. The other man, in colorful riding robes, laughing, jesting with him, she also recognized. It was Tersius Major.

Quickly, as she approached them, miserable, on the chain, covered with dust, she put her head down and brought her hair before her face, to conceal her features. And thus she passed them, unnoticed, no more than another slave in the coffle.

As she passed them she heard laughter. Then the laughter was behind her. When she turned about she saw that the two tharlarion had continued on their way, toward the rear of the column.

Somewhere she heard the crack of a whip.

Quickly she turned her head forward again, and continued on her way.

Chapter 21

The Pool

"You are an ignorant barbarian, are you not?" asked the man.

"Yes, Master," said Ellen, quickly.

She knelt before him, her head to the ground.

"Do you know how to bathe?" he asked. "You may look up."

Ellen lifted her head, timidly. "Yes, Master," she said. "I have been taught."

"You will go to the designated pool with this group," he said, gesturing. "Oils, sponges, rags, will be at the pool, and lotions. Pebbles will do for scrapers. Stand there."

Ellen rose to her feet and went to stand behind another girl, one in a line now of seven, including herself. Three more would be added to the group. All were naked. This is not that unusual for slaves in transport. Whereas nudity is certainly not unknown amongst slave girls, and is relatively familiar, even publicly, and masters often keep their slaves naked in their own quarters, still a naked slave is likely to be noticed; she is unlikely to blend in with "clothed" sisters in bondage, permitted perhaps an open camisk or a scanty ta-teera. Seen in a field, for example, free men will commonly investigate the sight of such a slave, and, if she is not known to them, set upon her, apprehend her, and demand an accounting. An attendant knotted a rope about her left ankle. It went to the girl before her, about whose ankle it was already knotted, and would be extended behind her, to fasten the next three slaves in the ankle coffle, as she was, each such coffle consisting of ten slaves.

The usual coffling order, for those whom it might interest, is not from front to rear, as was being done here, girls being selected almost randomly to be added to the rope, but from rear to front, the slaves keeping their eyes forward. This is particularly the case when chains and collars, or wrist rings, or ankle rings, are used. In this way the slave does not see the device until it is upon her, and then, of course, it is too late; she is locked within it. She knows, of course, that this is going to be done. She hears the chains, the snapping shut of the locks, and so on. Indeed, she, standing, or kneeling, presumably knees spread, hands on thighs, or on all fours, waiting, forbidden to turn about, builds up a considerable amount of suspense in the matter, and it comes, usually, as a welcome climax, as a relief, when she finds herself at last added, as she knows she must be, explicitly, securely, helplessly, to the "slaver's necklace." One supposes it is done in this fashion largely for its psychological effect on the slave, it tending to make her feel apprehensive, docile, obedient and helpless. And it does have that effect. It is also supposed that it makes it less likely that the slave will bolt, or flee, but that seems to me dubious, except perhaps in the case of recently captured free women, terrified to find themselves in such a line, presumably naked, or new slaves. The rational slave knows she is to be chained, and that there is nothing she can do about it; she neither bolts nor flees. She does not wish to be dragged back to her place by the hair, and whipped there, in the very spot she so foolishly forsook. "Here!" it might be said. "Here is your place, foolish girl!" "Yes, Master! Yes, Master!" And the lash would fall. "And you are not to leave it without permission, stupid slave!" "No, Master! No, Master! Forgive me, Master! Please forgive me, Master!" And the lash would fall again and again. And then the chain is put on her. She sobs. She has learned. She has been taught her lesson.

It was not unpleasant standing in the soft grass. One must stand well, of course, for one is under the eyes of men. There was a gentle breeze moving inland from the sea. Ellen was no longer in the coffle, in which she and others, some hundreds it seemed, had been marched to this location. She was pleased to be out of the heavy, sturdy coffle collar, with its weighty chain dangling before and behind her. She wore no collar now, that of Portus Canio, with the tag attached by the subcaptain, having been removed some days earlier in the Cosian camp. She was, of course, well marked as bond, in virtue of the brand, in her case the common kef, the most common mark on Gor for a slave girl, that which Mirus, doubtless to his amusement, had had put on her.

The massive walls and towers of Brundisium could be seen in the distance, some two pasangs, or so, away. It was at Brundisium that, months ago, the invasion forces of Cos and Tyros had made an unopposed landfall, and proceeded thence toward Ar.

The sky was a bright blue. White clouds, unhurried, insouciant, pursued their leisurely way inland, floating, drifting, in the currents of the wind, like ships on an invisible ocean, like remarkable, protean creatures risen majestically from the cold waters of gleaming Thassa, the sea.

She felt the rope jerked tight on her ankle, both forward and back, and then drawn back, to be ready for the next bead, so to speak, on this improvised slaver's necklace. The attendant stood up, slightly behind her, waiting for the next slave.

"Make yourself desirable," he said. *"Slave desirable."*

"Yes, Master," said Ellen. There was no mistaking what he had said, or what it meant. How far she was from Earth, she thought, with its oddities, eccentricities, miseries, agonies and denials. How different is Gor from Earth, at least for women such as I, she thought. How simple, how natural, how primitively virtuous is Gor! Here, there is no war of the sexes, at least for women such as I. Here the war of the sexes is over, at least for women such as I, certainly for me. I have fought. I have lost. I have been taken. I am spoils of war, and am now slave. But Ellen did not mind this. She rejoiced in this, and wanted it. It suddenly occurred to her that this might well be the point of the war of the sexes, that it might well be entered into and encouraged by women merely that they might be reassured, much as a naughty child might test limits, that they might have manhood affirmed, and find themselves once more, in the light of fact and truth, seized and returned to their rightful place in the order of nature, dutifully subdued, conquered, treasured, prized, mastered, loved, owned. How she then pitied free women in their ignorance, both those of Gor and Earth, in their anxieties and depressions, in their little-understood forlornness, in their little-understood, unsatisfied hungers.

But then she was suddenly terrified. There was a rope on her ankle. She was mere property! She was slave!

How she was looking forward to the opportunity to clean her body, after the heat, the dust, the coffle!

There was to be a festival camp, celebrating yet another victory of invincible Cos. Merchants, dignitaries, soldiers, travelers, artisans, peddlers, tradesmen, citizens, peasants, villagers, townspeople and others were all making their way into the vicinity of the city, some setting up tents and camps, others renting space either within the city, or about the walls. Among these visitors, and citizens of Brundisium, too, she knew, would be slavers, professional slavers. These were men who dealt shrewdly in wares such as she. She trembled, thinking of the sales block, the eager, virile, possessive, bidding men, the whips, of being exhibited dramatically, specifically, callously, in intimate detail, rawly, as the lovely, helpless merchandise she was.

She trembled, yes. But, too, she was fascinated, almost giddy, at the thought of being sold. What would she bring?

She thought of her feminist sisters, of Earth, on such a block, in chains, being sold to men. In such a place they would be in little doubt of their sex, or of its meaning—just as she, here, on Gor, had learned her sex, and its meaning.

"Move!" she heard, and her group of ten, in its turn, in line, she the seventh in her group of ten, in ankle coffle, left foot first, was directed across the grass. The grass felt fresh and soft beneath her feet. She watched the rope move before her, that fastened to the left ankle of the girl before her, pulled forward, then dropping down, disappearing in the grass, then seeming to leap up, only to drop down again between the blades. The group was directed toward a narrow trail, one winding its way gently downward among deciduous trees. In a few Ehn, between trees, she saw a small stream. The pools, she had heard, would be in the vicinity of this stream, some nearer, some farther. Her group was conducted downward, slipping a bit on the dirt and grass, one girl fell, to the border of the stream, along which was a narrow trail, some five feet above the stream. The group was then directed along this trail, rather toward the city. Another such group was a hundred yards or so before them. Presumably they would be followed by other groups. Here and there there were tiny, wooden bridges over the stream. Wagon tracks in the mud, however, and the prints of bosk and tharlarion indicated that wagons commonly forded this narrow waterway. At the fording places she could see gravel and rocks under the water, and she thought that the depth there could not be much more than a foot or two, surely not higher than the hubs of wagon wheels. The rocks and gravel, or some of it, she supposed, might have been put there to help secure a reliable fording. Elsewhere she supposed that the stream was not more than three or four feet deep, or, as the Goreans would have it, who tended to think of water from the bottom up, three or four feet high.

"Look," whispered the girl before her, indicating with a subtle motion of her head, a direction across the stream, to her right.

"Yes," whispered Ellen.

It was there she saw the first of several small, sunken, shallow, walled pools, each a yard or so deep. Most of these were in the vicinity of the stream, some on one side and some on the other, and some were actually open to the stream, and fed by its water. Others were not now in obvious contact with the stream but were nearby, perhaps fed by waters which had occasionally exceeded the normal boundaries of the stream, or by waters which had drained downward naturally, overflowing the sunken walls, filling the area, cisternlike, the expected result of the declivity in terrain. To be sure, she supposed that they might, or some of them, have been filled by water carried to them, from the nearby stream. That was a possibility. And within the Ahn this possibility became even more obvious, and vivid.

What startled Ellen was the large number of these pools. Surely there were at least thirty or forty of them, some on one side of the stream, some on the other. In several of them, sporting delightedly, some in the water, some splashing about, some assiduously washing, some attending to their hair, were groups of slave girls, ten in each group. Ellen had little doubt that these girls, those in each group, were roped together, as were those in her group. Supervising each group was a man, not a soldier, or guardsman, merely an attendant, a drover, a hireling, usually loitering nearby.

In these days one did not steal from Cos.

"Male slaves, to the left," whispered the girl before Ellen.

Some seven or so males were kneeling in a small space, stripped, covered with dirt, heads down, to the left. They were chained, hand and foot, and fastened together by the neck, by an additional chain. They appeared haggard, exhausted. They were perhaps half-starved, in order to induce distraction, confusion, failure of will, and weakness. Their bodies were bruised, as though by the blows of clubs or spear hafts, and bore in lines of caked blood the marks of the lash, where the whip, perhaps the snake, had been put to them.

The snake is never used on women, for they might soon die under its blows. Whereas Gorean masters are strict with their kajirae, some inordinately so, they never forget that they are females, only females.

"I do not think they are slaves yet," whispered the girl behind Ellen. "I think they are prisoners, war captives."

"They will soon be slaves," said the first girl, haughtily.

"Yes," said the second, "and doubtless on the galleys, or in the quarries of Tyros."

Ellen gasped.

"Move more quickly. *Harta*!" said their attendant.

One of the men had raised his head. Ellen recognized Portus Canio! He did not see her. It seemed as though he could see little. Beside him, chained to him, was Fel Doron!

Ellen hurried on, miserable. How awry had turned out the brave adventure of Portus Canio!

"Thus to the enemies of Cos!" called out their attendant, spitting toward the group of prisoners, or slaves.

More than one of them lifted their heads, but they seemed not fully to comprehend, or mind, the passing jibe. Ellen supposed that little might matter to them now but food, sleep and commands. How complete was the victory of Cos! And what a small part of their victory was the slave called 'Ellen', as incidental to it as an appropriated tarsk!

Ellen quickly turned her head away from the kneeling captives, or slaves, put it down and brushed her hair to the side. She did not wish to be recognized by either Portus Canio or Fel Doron. Surely Portus Canio was miserable enough. No need for him to see his former slave as she was now, now merely another evidence of the victory of his foes, now no more than another article amongst the loot of his enemies, now merely another item in the abounding wealth of Cos. Too, she would have been embarrassed to have been seen by him as she was, naked, on a stranger's rope, being marched to the bath. So much, perhaps, remained to her of Earth.

"There," said the attendant, pointing, "over the bridge."

To the right of the stream was an empty cisternlike, low, walled enclosure, a constructed pool, of some twenty feet in diameter. In this pool none were bathing. Near to it, on towels spread on the grass, were vessels, presumably of cheap oils and lotions. Too, on them, toward the edges, were a number of sponges and rags. Some small heaps of pebbles, doubtless from the stream, lay here and there near the towels.

In a moment the bridge was passed, Ellen feeling the worn, spaced boards beneath her feet, and then, on the other side, the grass. The bridge, as with most Gorean bridges, even the high bridges in the cities, was without railings. In this case that presented her with no anxiety as the bridge was little more than a yard or so above the waters of the shallow stream. She saw a fish disturb the water briefly, noted the rippling effect of clouds and sky in the stream, and caught sight briefly of her own image, of her head and upper body, peering down, into the water. She quickly looked up, for the image reminded her of what she was. It was the image of a bared slave.

"Kneel down here," said the attendant. "First obeisance position."

The girls complied.

"Do you beg to be permitted to bathe?" inquired the attendant.

"Yes, Master," said the girls, quickly. "Yes, Master!"

"Each of you," he said, "will beg individually. As I stand before you, you may lift your head, but keep the palms of your hands on the ground."

He then stood before the first girl. "Do you beg to be permitted to bathe?" he asked.

"Yes, Master," she said, lifting her head, looking up at him, but keeping the palms of her hands on the ground. "I beg to be permitted to bathe."

"You may bathe," he said.

"Thank you, Master," she said.

"You may kiss my feet," he said. "First obeisance position."

"Yes, Master," she said. "Thank you, Master."

This ritual was repeated down the line, one by one, as Ellen was approached, girl by girl.

Obviously the girls had been brought to the pool to bathe, but it is common for the kajira to thank the master on such occasions, as for a scrap of food thrown before her, a caress, a blow, water in her pan, a blanket, a rag with which she might cover herself, and such. If a girl did not beg there was always the possibility that the attendant would simply return her, unbathed, filthy, smelling, to the coffle, at which point one would not wish to be that girl, for discipline would be swift and severe. Commonly the interval between a girl's being displeasing in any way and suffering the consequences of her lapse is very short. And it is far more terrifying when the interval is long, say, overnight, for that commonly signifies that the master is according some serious thought to the matter of her punishment.

Then the attendant was before Ellen.

"Do you beg to be permitted to bathe?" he asked.

"Yes, Master," said Ellen, looking up but keeping the palms of her hands on the ground. "I beg to be permitted to bathe."

"You may bathe," he said.

"Thank you, Master," said Ellen.

"You may kiss my feet," he said.

"Yes, Master," said Ellen. "Thank you, Master!"

She kissed his feet gratefully, tears in her eyes, overjoyed to be shown this favor, permitted to touch her lips, though only those of a slave, to the feet of a free man, a master.

How unworthy she was of this privilege!

Ellen thrilled to be dominated categorically by a strong male, she in a position of absolute helplessness and servitude. It was what she lived for, and what she realized she had lived for on Earth, and had never found. She was mightily aroused, and knew herself alive and wet with heat, vulnerability and desire. She had scarcely understood the extent and power of female desire until that moment, at the feet of a mere attendant, a Cosian hireling. She wondered if the irresistible might of male desire did not have its perfect corollary and complement in the natural woman, the slave, eager to yield all unreservedly and unquestioningly to her master, begging to love and serve, to please, to be owned wholly.

She wondered if the man could smell her desire, her need, her petition to be treated as a mere object, to be his, as a possession or a toy, to be uncompromisingly subjugated.

She realized, and had earlier learned, that the former strait-laced, female Ph.D. whom she had been, she who had specialized in gender studies, she who had been so smug and haughty, she who had been so proud of her degree and her publications, she who had been respected, even esteemed, for her unquestioned political orthodoxies, she who had been invited to attend many conferences organized to promote pathological political agendas, she who had been once no more than a miserable, frustrated, lonely activist, a militant bluestocking, was now no more than a young, lovely, hot slave. In her belly now, as she knelt in the grass, a rope on her ankle, burned slave fire. She moaned, and trembled, a slave almost incandescent with need.

But she knew that she was not to be permitted any satisfactions. She had not yet been sold.

"Bathe," said the attendant.

"May we speak, Master?" begged a bold girl.

"Very well," said the attendant.

"Thank you, Master!" cried several of the girls.

Chatting, laughing, the slaves went eagerly to the water. Some cried out at its surprising coldness. Ellen, the rope on her ankle, went with them, she, too, eager, to the edge of the wall, and, with them, first sitting on the edge of the wall, rather at the level of the ground, in her turn, slipped into the water. It was cold. It had been days since they had bathed, and they rejoiced in the opportunity to cleanse themselves of the filth and soilings of the march. How wonderful, thought Ellen, is the chance upon occasion to do something even as simple as washing one's body! How few people realize how precious so seemingly common and familiar an act can be at times! How grateful the slaves were for this opportunity to bathe! The rope on

Ellen's ankle, as she had slipped into the water, first floated, and then was drawn under, she and her companions entering the pool. Then, the rope was held under the water as the slaves stood about in the water, rinsing, laughing and splashing about. But the rope, of course, held them together, even though it could not be seen. Ellen was grateful to the masters for the chance to bathe, to wash away the misery and grime of the march, but she realized that the motivation underlying the provision of this welcome opportunity was surely unlikely to be simply that of generous impulse. They were livestock, doubtless being readied for its sale. Naturally their owner, the state of Cos, would wish them to be exhibited at their best, to be clean, healthy, rested, presentable, attractive. It would wish to enhance their sales value. It would want them to be appealing, attractive items of merchandise when it came time to offer them to buyers.

If these were sobering thoughts, the girls, oblivious of such considerations, and with all the innocence of the lovely, curvaceous animals they were, laughed and chatted, and sported about in the water, splashing and playing, the heat and dust of the march put now behind them.

Ellen, bending down, rinsed and washed her hair as best she could.

In a few moments she feared they must leave the water, to apply the cleansing oils, thence to scrape them from the body, with the strigil-like pebbles, after which they would re-enter the water to rinse once more. After that they would emerge and dry themselves with the towels, and then apply the soothing and fragrant lotions. Then they would be conducted whence masters might wish, perhaps to chains and stakes, or even, as they were in the vicinity of Brundisium, perhaps to exhibition cages.

"Look," said the girl to Ellen's left, who had preceded her in the ankle coffle.

Ellen turned to look, and placed her fingers, defensively, before her lips. Approaching the pool was the line of prisoners, or slaves, which contained Portus Canio and Fel Doron. The miserable line, moving slowly, carried large earthen jars on their shoulders, presumably filled with water drawn from the stream.

Ellen drew away as she could, put down her head and brushed her hair about her face. She did not wish to be seen by either Portus Canio or Fel Doron. But her concern seemed unnecessary, for none in the slowly advancing line looked about themselves.

They were in the keeping of two soldiers of Cos, in the hands of one of which was a whip.

More than once the whip fell here and there on the line.

It seemed that the miserable occupants of the chain could scarcely cry out in pain, or groan under the blows.

One by one, painfully, they poured the contents of the vessels into the pool.

Then Ellen noted two other figures now approaching the pool. She gasped, for these were the figures of the Cosian subcaptain, known to her from the tarn loft of Portus Canio in Ar, and from the coffle, and Tersius Major, who had been in the employ of Portus Canio, and who had left Ar with them.

"So, the noble Portus Canio, of Ar, who dared conspire against the might of Cos, now carries water, as though he might be a slave, to replenish the contents of a cistern, one devoted to the drinking of tharlarion and the ablutions of slaves," said the subcaptain. "It is fitting," he laughed.

Portus Canio lifted his head a little, and looked, dully, at the subcaptain.

"Have no fear, sleen of Ar," said the subcaptain. "You will soon be slave, branded with the mark of the quarries of Tyros, or perhaps we will mark you for the bench of a merchant galley, where, drawing your oar by day or night, hungry for a crust of bread or a sip of water, you will have time to ponder your foolishness."

There was no response from Portus Canio and the subcaptain gestured to the soldier with the whip, who struck Portus Canio twice. He seemed scarcely to react to the blows. Ellen winced, and wanted to cry out, but remained silent. Two more blows, at a sign from the subcaptain, were laid upon Fel Doron.

"I am greater now than you," said Tersius Major to Portus Canio. "You are no longer my coin giver. No longer do I obey your orders. You are a fool. I am clever! The wind blows. Could you not note its direction? Did I not hint such things to you? Why did you not listen? The Home Stone? The Home Stone of Ar is no more than a piece of rock."

Portus Canio lifted his eyes to those of Tersius Major. His gaze was sullen, and darkly menacing.

"There is more gold in my purse now than I would have earned from you in a year," said Tersius Major, angrily.

"The eyes and ears of Cos are everywhere," said the subcaptain.

"I shall return to Ar," said Tersius Major, "and uncover more of the Delta Brigade."

"Gold will smell out rebels," said the subcaptain.

Portus Canio put down his head. It seemed he could scarcely lift it. Ellen feared he might fall. She suspected he had been starved, and denied sleep.

"Can you hear me?" asked the subcaptain.

"Yes," said Portus Canio, the effort to speak seeming to cost him much.

"Would you not wish to look upon the pleasant bodies of slave girls?" asked the subcaptain, expansively, gesturing to the pool. "Some are lusciously curved. There is some excellent slave meat in the pool. See the several, lovely little beasts. They are quite attractive. They exist for the service and pleasure of men. Perhaps you should avail yourself of this opportunity. You will not find many such, I assure you, in the quarries of Tyros, or amongst the benches of the great galleys."

Portus Canio did not lift his head.

"Perhaps we will have you wash slaves," said the subcaptain.

Portus Canio raised his head, painfully, angrily.

It is common for slave girls to assist and serve free men in their bath, washing them, applying oils, cleaning them, toweling them, applying lotions, kissing them intimately, serving their pleasure, and such. Ellen had been taught the bathing of free men in her training. It is one of many things in which female slaves are expected to be proficient. The suggestion that Portus Canio, a free man, might wash slaves was, of course, a grievous insult.

"Perhaps we will have you clean the dirtied feet of slave girls with your tongue," said the subcaptain.

It is not unknown for female slaves, as a discipline, to be forced to kneel down and clean the paws of kaiila, the ponderous, clawed feet of tharlarion, and such, with their lips, mouth, teeth and tongue. It is a way of reminding them that they are nothing, only slaves.

"Take them away!" said the subcaptain, irritatedly, to the soldiers in charge of the line. "There are tens of other pools to replenish!"

Again the whip cracked, and the line, with a rattle of heavy chains, took up its now-emptied jars, and turned about.

Ellen had not been recognized in the pool, she was sure, neither by Portus Canio nor Fel Doron, nor by the subcaptain and Tersius Major, the attentions of the latter pair being focused generally on Portus Canio and Fel Doron, whom, she supposed, they had come out to discomfit, witnessing them in their humiliation and captivity, perhaps one last time before they, Portus Canio and Fel Doron, patriots or insurgents, might be taken to Brundisium, and from thence transported to Tyros or Cos, there to be subjected to doubtless unenviable fates.

"It is time to emerge from the pool, to apply the oils!" called the attendant, and Ellen, in her turn, with the others, clambered from the pool, and went to the spread towels and vials, and pebbles.

Chapter 22

Beasts

"Wine, Master?" inquired Ellen, and, as the goblet was lifted to her, the man sitting cross-legged on the ground, in converse with others, he not even glancing at her, she filled the goblet.

"Wine, girl!" called another, and Ellen hurried to him, threading her way amongst the men, the fires and torches, and replenished his goblet.

She carried the wine in a red-figured pitcher, refilled by dipping as needed, and frequently, from a large vat of red ka-la-na on a wooden stand.

The music of czehars, flutes, and kalikas, from scattered bands of musicians, swirled throughout the gigantic festival camp, spread over pasangs. There was the pounding of tabors, too, speaking of excitement and the rousings of blood. Goreans do not eschew emotion; eagerness, zeal, warmth, heat and passion are common with them; they tend to be vehement, hearty, cordial, enthusiastic, ardent, impetuous; they are quick to anger, quick to forget, quick to laugh; they do not pretend to subscribe to obvious falsehoods; they value truth over hypocrisy; they have not yet learned to dishonor honor; to live among such folk is to be emotionally free; they live closer, perhaps, to their bodies than some others.

"Wine!" called a man, and Ellen made her way to him, as swiftly as was compatible with the crowd.

She moved with the grace and loveliness that was now hers, that of the female slave. She was stripped, and wore not so much as a collar, but her hair, grown longer now, and slave lovely, fell about her. On her left breast, inscribed there with a marker, in soft grease, was a lot number, the number 117.

"Wine!" called a voice, a woman's voice.

The woman, clad in the Robes of Concealment, sat on a stool near one of the fires. The light glinted off a necklace, and sparkled, reflected in jewels sewn onto her robes and veils.

The body of the sitting woman seemed stiff, and severe. Something in its mien suggested disapproval, anger, hostility and envy. Free women hate slave girls. They try to make them ashamed of their femininity, condition, beauty and passion.

Ellen, standing, prepared to pour wine for the free woman.

"Do you not know enough to kneel before a free person, girl?" inquired the free woman.

Quickly Ellen went to her knees.

The woman regarded Ellen for some time, the eyes cold over the veil, not offering her the goblet for her attentions.

"You are naked," said the woman.

"Yes, Mistress," said Ellen.

"How meaningless and contemptible are slaves," said the woman.

"Yes, Mistress," said Ellen. But Ellen thought to herself, but men seem to like us, and you, proud free woman, beneath all your robes and veils, you are as naked as I!

"You are young," said the woman.

"Yes, Mistress," said Ellen.

"Do you know the duties of a woman's serving slave?" she asked.

"No, Mistress."

"But you could be taught."

"Yes, Mistress."

"117," said the woman, leaning closer, reading the number on Ellen's breast. "Perhaps I shall bid on you. Would you like to be a woman's serving slave?"

"The wishes and desires of a slave, Mistress," said Ellen, "are of no consequence."

"You are a clever little slut," said the woman.

Ellen put down her head.

The woman then extended her small goblet to Ellen and Ellen, gratefully, on her knees, filled it.

"I can see that you are for men," said the woman.

Ellen was silent.

"Doubtless they find you of interest," she said.

"Some, it seems, Mistress," said Ellen.

"I wonder why."

"I do not know, Mistress," said Ellen. Could the woman really be ignorant of the toolings of time, and how nature had designed such as they, she and the free woman, for the handling and embrace, and service and pleasure of masters?

"What could they possibly see in one such as you?"

"I do not know, Mistress." Could she really be ignorant that such as they answered to a thousand needs, that such as they in countless capturings and matings were bred to kneel and please?

"You are, of course, a slave?"

"Yes, Mistress."

"They seem to like that."

"Yes, Mistress."

"I despise slaves."

"Yes, Mistress."

"You are beautiful," she said, appraisingly.

"Thank you Mistress," said Ellen. "But I am sure that Mistress is far more beautiful."

"Of course," said the woman, "for my beauty is the unparalleled beauty of a free woman, with which the beauty of a slave cannot begin to compare, beside which the beauty of a slave is nothing."

"Yes, Mistress."

"You are no more than a tasta, a meaningless confection!" she said suddenly, angrily.

"Yes, Mistress."

"A whip licker and sandal-bringer for brutes, a servile pet and pleasure object for lustful beasts!"

"Yes, Mistress."

"I wonder then what they can possibly see in one such as you?"

"I do not know, Mistress." Could the woman be candid? Could she be unaware of the effect of a slave on the blood of men? Had she not seen the eyes of men following them in the streets? Could she be unaware of the markets and biddings, the seekings and huntings, the pursuits, the raids and wars, the careful and calculated efforts to bring just such women as they, she, and doubtless the free woman, too, appropriately and helplessly, into collars and chains?

Men desire to possess us, thought Ellen, and that is, too, what we desire, to be possessed by them.

"How stupid men are," said the woman.

"They are the masters," said Ellen.

"They are not my masters," said the woman.

"No, Mistress."

"Yes," she said, regarding Ellen, "—you are for men."

"Yes, Mistress."

"What else would you be good for?"

Ellen put down her head.

"Nothing, Mistress."

She had now learned that men were her masters. She now wanted to love and serve them, and perhaps beg for a caress. She could not, now, never, willingly go back to the emptiness, the disutility, the absurdity, the barrenness, of her former life, with its mockeries of truth, and its spurious freedoms. The man was free, the master; his was a genuine freedom; but the freedom for the woman, her genuine freedom, was quite different; it was to belong to him, to be owned and mastered, to be his slave.

The woman waved her hand in dismissal. "Go! Get out of my sight, you disgusting little slut!"

Ellen leapt up and hurried away a few yards. She then looked back. There were few free women in the camp. The woman must indeed be bold, thought Ellen; perhaps she was wealthy, and well protected. If Ellen were a free woman, she did not think that she would have come to such a camp, unless she was prepared to risk her freedom. Ellen wondered if the woman was courting the collar. She wondered if the woman's icy hauteur might not melt under the blows of man's whip. Frigidity, and inertness, she knew were not accepted in a female slave.

But Ellen knew she must now hurry back to the vat of ka-la-na, for her vessel was nearly empty.

She paused for a moment to look back once more at the free woman. The woman had lifted her veil with her left hand, just a little, to drink from the goblet. Ellen could see the impression of the upper rim of the goblet through the veil. Lower-class women sometimes drink through the veil, and their veils, subsequently, may be severally stained. Ellen saw that the woman's body was very straight as she drank. As the veil was lifted somewhat, as she drank, one could see a bit of her throat, white and lovely, where a collar might be nicely locked. Her ankles could be seen, above her slippered feet, as the robes were lifted a bit, seemingly having been inadvertently disarranged as she sat. Her legs were turned to one side, and placed side by side, apparently demurely closed beneath her robes. Slave girls, when permitted tunics and permitted to sit, as on a log, a rock, a shelf, commonly sit thusly. This is not only congenial to a certain modesty, but men find it provocative. Ellen wondered if the woman had seen slaves sit in that fashion. She had now lowered the veil, and was chatting with some of the men sitting about cross-legged, near the fire. Watching her, some yards from the firelight, were two tall, darkly robed men. Their robes were cut in the pattern of Cos. Ellen doubted that the woman was aware of them. At the sash of one of them there was a narrow, coiled rope of black braided leather.

Surely I must warn her, thought Ellen, cruel and imperious as she is, of the danger in which she lies! Surely, as I, too, am a woman, I must warn her, that she not risk falling into the miserable fate, the helpless and terrible fate, in which I find myself implicated, that of a slave!

Then Ellen laughed to herself. She loved being a slave. It was her joy, her meaning and fulfillment. She would be nothing else. She would not barter her bondage for all the world.

On Gor, with all the suffering and joy, the misery and delight, the beauty and peril, the marvels and danger, she had come fully alive, far more than she had understood possible on her former world.

But she is doubtless different, thought Ellen. She is doubtless a free woman, not merely a slave not yet owned.

What is it to you, if she is put in a collar, Ellen asked herself. Let her be humbled! Let her learn to kneel before a man and shrink down in terror, his. Let her serve!

She must know what she is doing, thought Ellen. She is Gorean. She cannot be ignorant. She must know the dangers of this camp for free women, a festival camp where hundreds of slaves are to serve, and be danced, and vended!

No, thought Ellen, I must warn her.

"Wine!" called a man.

"I must fetch more, Master!" cried Ellen, and, turning about, seemed to hurry toward the vat of ka-la-na, that the vessel of her service might be replenished. But, in a moment, she had turned aside, and back, determined to kneel before the free woman and, risking the blows of masters, and risking punishment for speaking without permission, warn the cruel, harsh mistress of the risks she might be running.

Soon Ellen had returned to the fire near which the free woman had been sitting. The stool on which she had been sitting was overturned. The goblet from which she had drunk lay in the dirt near the fire. There was a bit of stain, of reddish mud, near the goblet, where wine had spilled. There were some marks, scuffings, perhaps the sign of a struggle, near the overturned stool.

"Masters?" inquired Ellen, her eyes wide.

"You have seen nothing, slave girl," said one of the men.

"Yes, Master," said Ellen, and, turning about, made her way to the ka-la-na vat, to fill once more her pitcher.

As she made her way back to the vat she skirted about a dancing circle near one of the fires. Some of the slaves already, to the music of the czehars and other instruments, which was clearly audible everywhere in the camp, danced.

Ellen was pleased that the slaves danced.

Doubtless the free woman was all right. Doubtless, even now, she was returning to Brundisium. Ellen hoped that that was true, and hoped, too, that it was not true. She was haughty, she thought. Strip her, Masters, and put her to your feet. Let the brand and collar be hers!

How beautiful the slaves are, she thought.

See them dance before masters!

Goreans believe that slave dance lurks in every woman's belly. Ellen, however, thought that this was surely unlikely.

Did they not know that dancers might train, and hone their skills, for years, gaining greater and greater control over their body, adding dances to their repertoire, becoming more and more adept at this sensuous, delicious, intricate art form?

To be sure, she supposed, there was a basic, biological sense in which "slave dance," or something certainly akin to it, did indeed lurk in every woman's belly. Perhaps that is what the Goreans, in their typically straightforward and natural way, recognized. Or perhaps they literally meant *slave dance*. She supposed that that was possible. She wondered if it could be true. Certainly, embedded in the mysteries of the female genome, lurking within the uncanny, exciting secrets of the human female's behavioral genetics, bred into her, are the impulses and sensitivities of what are known as display behaviors. In her academic work it was imperative that she deny such things, or dismiss them as unenlightened social artifacts, but, even then, she knew them to be pervasive amongst mammals, and, indeed, in one form or another, universal in human cultures. In the interests of advancing a particular political agenda she had had to deny large numbers of the most obvious facts of ethology, biology and anthropology. That went without saying. Ideology and politics were to take priority over such embarrassments as truth and fact; reality was inconvenient; clearly it had not been formed with orthodoxy in mind; nature denied would, of course, exact her vengeance; causes would continue to have their effects; rationality would be sacrificed, intellectual suicide for a rational animal, happiness would be lost, minds would be stunted, miseries multiplied, lives shortened. Obviously display behaviors existed, and in countless types, and in countless varieties within types. And certainly amongst human females there was a disposition to attempt to present themselves to advantage before an attractive male. Even she had found it hard to deny that. Certainly she had noted her ideological colleagues preening and flirting when a powerful male was in the vicinity, not one of their suitably indoctrinated, conditioned, filleted male-feminist colleagues. And now, suppose there was a natural society, in which nature was not denied, but, rather, with all the refinements of an advanced civilization, respected, fulfilled, enhanced and celebrated. In such a society, one might expect, accordingly, the pervasive dominance/submission ratios of nature to be recognized by, and reflected within, customs, laws, social arrangements, institutions, and such. In such a society one would certainly expect to find female bondage and the male mastery. And in such a free, natural society, it is only to be expected that female display behaviors, of all women, but particularly of those in bondage, would be refined and elaborated, and would become openly and gloriously expressive. In such a society then, in what countless ways might a woman, any woman, but particularly one in a collar, be expected to present herself before a male? Would the female not desire to appear in certain ways, to move in certain ways? Presumably, yes. And certainly one of the most devastatingly, self-enhancing, exciting ways for a female to be before a male is to be before him in the dance. And certainly in erotic, display dance. There is little doubt then that these desires, and associated movements, provocative and luring, of the hips and pelvis, or the dispositions thereto, are in some way genetically coded, such that, in a given stimulus situation, recourse will be naturally had to them, and it will seem quite natural and appropriate to perform these behaviors. It is quite likely that, in the history of the human species, thousands of women have begged for their lives by dancing naked before severe captors, and that the case even in historical times, before Chaldeans and Hittites, Assyrians and Babylonians, Greeks and Romans, Goths, Mongols, Crusaders, Turks, and others. And the most provocative and erotic of dances, of course, is slave dance. Accordingly then its power and beauty is sought avidly by women desiring to be pleasing to men, to masters. And certainly, if the woman is theirs, it is exactly the sort of thing that would be expected of them, and required of them, by their lords and masters. And so, Ellen thought, perhaps there is a sense in which slave dance does lurk in the belly of every woman, a basic biological, genetic sense. Certainly such a disposition, as with many others, such as the desire to belong, to be found pleasing, to love and serve, would contribute to success in matters of gene replication. And these genes would then be transmitted to future generations, assisting in the shaping of a species. Had primitive women been feminists the human race would have been extinct thousands of years ago; it is the ideology of death. It can survive only as a cannibalistic excrescence on the biological givens of reality, as the modality of a self-seeking, parasitical, politically active minority. Generalized, it would falsify and degrade human life, destroy the gene pool, and lead to the termination of the human race. But, of course, primitive men would not have permitted that pretentious indulgence on the part of primitive women. Dragged by the hair to the back of the cave they would have been reminded of their sex. It is a common belief on Gor that all free females desire in their secret hearts to be the slaves of masters; there is a saying, in every free female there lurks a slave, a slave awaiting her liberation, her freedom, her collar.

Ellen knew little of slave dance, for her first master, called on Gor 'Mirus', had determined that she would be only slightly trained, that she might be sold as a substantially ignorant girl, trained perhaps only to the extent that she might prove satisfactory enough to be permitted to live, that she might thusly, to the amusement of Mirus, he enjoying his vengeance upon her, continue to be indefinitely subjected to the degradation of the lowest of bondages.

She was not, however, altogether ignorant of slave dance, or its general nature; indeed, how could anyone on Gor, unless it be a free woman, be totally ignorant of it? Although she had not herself been given such training, and apparently by design, she had occasionally seen girls dance in the training rooms. She had been thrilled to see them so dance, and had gasped, and breathed quickly, so startled she was at how beautiful those of her sex could be in the dance, and particularly in these dances, dances required of them by men, the dances of slaves. She had begged one of her instructrices to inquire of Mirus, her master, for she herself was seldom admitted to his presence, if she might not be so trained, but the response to her petition, though apparently it amused him that she should make it, was in the negative. He apparently wanted her, in her collar, to be little more than an ignorant woman of Earth, forced to serve in dismay and torment, in the crudest and lowest of bondages. Sometimes, fascinated, she spied secretly on the lessons but, when caught, was cruelly switched. Sometimes in her cell, unobserved, she had tried to move as she had seen one or another of the dancers move, but then she had desisted, frightened, sensing what it might be, to be seen so before men.

And so Ellen had never danced before men.

She feared to do so.

Yet if the fingers were snapped, or the hands clapped, or the gesture made, lifting the palms upward, she knew she must dance, dance as any slave, and as a slave must dance, for men. Any free man in such a camp, of course, might order her to dance, to pose, to writhe before him. There was a lot number on her left breast. The dancing circles were some ten or twelve feet in diameter, and sanded, and near the fires. There were several such circles in the camp, each with its flag on a wand at one edge of the circle, each flag being of a given shape, square, rectangular, forked, triangular, and so on, and color or mixture of colors. Each flag, too, had its letter or number. Thus each circle could be recognized by both its flag and its letter or number. An order then might be issued that slaves of such and such lot numbers, which numbers were inscribed on their bodies, on the left breast, given to them for the convenience of the camp, should go to, say, circle such-and-such, which was, say, "square and blue" or "triangular and yellow," and so on. This was judicious as many slaves were illiterate, and are deliberately kept so. For example, Ellen is so kept. She would like to know how to read, but it is not permitted to her. She suspects she could better serve her masters if she learned to read, but the decision is theirs, not hers.

Perhaps it amuses them to have an illiterate barbarian slave, from a despised world, a world fit for little perhaps other than the harvesting of its women, to be bought as slave fruit to their markets. I do not know.

Too, why should a slave read? She is not, after all, a free woman. She does not have a Home Stone. She is merely a shapely beast, purchased for your service and pleasure. Would you teach a verr, or kaiila, to read?

In all ways, of course, whether literate or not, we are in the absolute power of our masters. I find that I relish that I have no choice but to submit to them, wholly. How else would I want to live? I rejoice to be at their mercy. It is my pleasure to obey and please. I belong to them. I am owned. In all ways is intensified my sense, and it is a welcome, delicious sense, of unimportance, dependence and helplessness, which, in turn, opens my sexuality to them, as a begging flower.

Forgive me for intruding the first-person voice into this narrative, which, on the whole, must deal objectively with the slave, Ellen, as the object, and property, she is. Would a verr or kaiila be permitted to write of herself in the first person? Sometimes, perhaps.

Speaking of illiteracy, however, it should be noted that illiteracy is not that uncommon on Gor. For example, many Goreans of low caste are illiterate. Indeed, many seem to regard reading as an accomplishment ill befitting decent, serious folks, an accomplishment more appropriate, at least, to the high castes than to theirs. Interestingly, too, many of the warriors, and that is a high caste, pride themselves on an inability to read, seeing that homely, and somewhat magical, skill, as one not for them, if not actually beneath them. And some who can read pretend to ignorance of the skill.

To return to our proper narrative:

The lot numbers of slaves would be called out, and then, too, the circles to which they must report. Ellen knew her number, of course, as she had been told. Too, those who, as Ellen, might be unfamiliar with the location of the circles, for the camp was quite large, had simply to follow their caller, one of several torch-bearing heralds leading the way to the particular circle. She would, accordingly, be intent to listen carefully to the numbers, and follow any caller who had enunciated her number, which was "117."

She could recognize, incidentally, several of the signs of the Gorean alphabet but knew only two or three of their names and sounds. Goreans had not been free with that information. One letter of the Gorean alphabet which Ellen did know was the fourth letter of the 28-letter Gorean alphabet, which was 'delka'. She had seen that letter in Ar, scrawled on a wall, and also on an ostrakon in the holding of Portus Canio. And she knew at least one number, that which was inscribed in grease on her left breast, "117."

But Ellen had no expectation of being called forth to dance in any of the circles, as she was not a dancer.

"Can you dance?" she had been asked by the scribe.

"No, Master," she had answered, as truthfully as she knew how.

So she did not expect to be called, when the calling began, later in the evening. Goreans, she knew, whereas they might be interested in her in many respects, as she had abundant evidence to attest, were not likely to be interested in her in that respect. They were connoisseurs in slave dance, hard to please, and quite particular in such matters. She would be in such matters the rankest of amateurs.

Still she was vulnerable, and any man, as we have noted, could pose her, or dance her, or such, for his pleasure, in a circle, in a tent, or elsewhere.

She shuddered.

But I shall not be called upon to dance, she told herself, for I have informed the scribe that I cannot dance. Thus I will be safe. Thus I have nothing to fear. How terrified I would be, if called upon to dance. For I know nothing of it. I would fear to dance. I cannot dance. But I am not a dancer. That they know, and so I am safe.

Then Ellen thought again of the free woman in her slippers, and veils, and cumbersome Robes of Concealment.

She really did not think that she had returned safely to Brundisium. That seemed very unlikely. She had seen strong, somber men nearby, watching her, perhaps studying her. At his sash one of them had had a narrow, coiled rope of black braided leather. Slave strikes are seldom made at random. Perhaps they even knew her from Brundisium. There had been the overturned stool, the spilled wine, the warnings of the men who had been about.

The poor woman, thought Ellen, returning to the ka-la-na vat. What a terrible misfortune for her! How unfortunate! And then Ellen smiled, and laughed to herself. How perfect, she thought. Let her wear a collar! Let her be a naked slave! Let her grovel and fear free women!

Yes, thought Ellen, and let her dance before masters, as a naked slave, and be lashed if not pleasing!

I am pleased that I am not a dancer, thought Ellen. I am pleased that I need not fear being called upon to dance.

Ellen hummed the strains of a joyful Gorean slave song to herself, in which the slave bedecks herself and eagerly awaits the arrival of her master.

Suddenly she heard a fierce movement in the air, behind her, an unexpected but unmistakable swift hiss, and, almost at the same time, below the small of the back, she felt a stinging stripe, the swift, sharp blow of a supple switch, a yard in length.

"Are you dallying, slave girl?" laughed a young voice.

"No, Master!" cried Ellen, tears bursting from her eyes. It was one of the lads used about the camp for the supervision, control and management of the serving slaves. Fully grown women are not unoften put under the management of such. In the Gorean theory, as slaves are animals, they may be managed by any free person, or, indeed, any designated slave. Sometimes they are put under the supervision of a boy or girl who is no more than a child. And, of course, the least bit of resistance, recalcitrance or such may invoke severe discipline, even death. Behind the children, and the lads, you see, stand men.

Ellen hurried on to the vat. Her fundament stung from the stripe. She was humiliated, particularly as the blow had been struck not by a man but by a lad. To be sure, the lad, who must have been fifteen or sixteen, had doubtless, by now, enjoyed slaves such as she. Although the blow stung, and was humiliating, Ellen was not displeased with it. It did remind her that she was a slave, and that such things might be done to her, and that she was under discipline. She wiped her eyes with the back of her right wrist. He had not been angry with her. He had merely hurried her on about her duties. She was now, she realized, somewhat to her surprise, rather pleased that she had been struck. The pain, in its way, now, was warm and pleasant, and its lingering resonance reminded her that she was subject to discipline, to complete and categorical domination, which, as a female, as she now knew, she craved.

In the festival camp there were many forms of merchandise, other than the flesh loot, such as she, of Cosian conquests, merchandise such as produce, meat, leather and metal work, cloth, cabinetry, artifacts, tools, weapons, remedies, wagons, carts, precious stones, and such. Too, there were animals to be vended, other than human females, such as verr, bosk and tharlarion. Ellen had even seen, or partly seen, for the crates were muchly closed, gigantic, furred animals of a sort she did not recognize. She did not know if they were bipedalian or quadrupedalian. She had seen wild eyes in a gap between stout slats, heard snarling, glimpsed a white, curved fang. Perhaps they were bears, or tigers, or, in any event, things like them, perhaps larger and fiercer.

She conjectured that there were better than ten or twelve thousand men in the camp.

She dipped her vessel into the ka-la-na, and returned to her work. Someone, she remembered, had called for wine. She would return to that place, though she supposed that, by now, another slave would have served him. It would not do, not to return. She looked at the red-figured vessel she carried, the red image on it bright, fresh and exciting against the smooth, glazed, curved, black background. It reminded her of similar vessels she had seen long ago in museums, from ancient Greece, and she did not doubt but what the techniques and style of that and similar vessels might own to antecedents of her former world, that they might, in substance, nature and style, be traced back to the work of ancient terrestrial craftsmen. She found the vessel precious and beautiful, but here, of course, such things were thought little of; they were familiar, cheap and common. They were used for the serving of common ka-la-na; they might be handled even by slaves. The figures on the vessel, two on one side, two on the other, were similar, rather as in a repeated design. On each side the same scene was depicted, that of a nude female, presumably a slave, kneeling before a man, presumably her master, in whose hand there was a whip. The female had her hands, the wrists chained, lifted to the man, as though in supplication. He was looking down upon her, presumably considering some plea, perhaps for forgiveness, perhaps for mercy. It was up to him, clearly, to decide what to do with her. Ellen held the vessel against her, to steady it, it feeling cool against her skin. A bit of wine ran over her hip.

She heard a beastlike roar and howl, some two hundred yards away. She supposed that that frightful sound emanated from one of the heavily planked crates. She doubted that men would wish to purchase such things.

Why should such things be brought here, she wondered.

She then hurried back to where the man had called for wine.

* * * *

Earlier in the day, after having been at the pool, and having been fed and watered, she, and those who had been in her ankle coffle, were conducted to an exhibition cage, one of more than perhaps fifty or sixty. While they stood outside the cage, roped together by the ankle, lot numbers were inscribed, with a grease pencil, or marker, on their left breasts. The left breast is used in such matters as most men are right-handed. Records were kept, regarding the lot numbers and names. Those girls who did not have names were given names, for clerical purposes, which might or might not be kept on them after a sale. Some of the names were lovely. All were suitable for female slaves. The matter was supervised by a scribe, with a clipboard, to which were attached several sheets of paper.

"Name?" he had asked her.

"I have been called 'Ellen', Master," she had said.

"117," he had said. "Ellen."

Something was then inscribed by one of the guards on her left breast, she feeling the firm, wide, smooth pressing of the greaselike point on her body. It was, doubtless, the number 117. She, as noted, had not been taught to read. On Gor she was illiterate. Doubtless Mirus had found that amusing. Many slave girls, too, as mentioned, are illiterate. And those brought from Earth are most commonly kept that way. They are, after all, barbarians. But, too, as has been noted, illiteracy is not that uncommon on Gor, particularly amongst the lower castes.

Within the cage, most near the exterior bars, were ten upright metal poles, which helped to support the roof of the cage. These were placed in such a way that a slave, if fastened to one, would, first, be kept near enough to the exterior bars to be easily viewed, and, second, would be just beyond the reach of any who might who might wish to touch them, by putting their hands through the bars.

Ellen's hands, before her, were braceleted about one of the upright bars, on the side of the cage which faced the general concourse, along which, on each side, the cages were lined. This was far better, thought Ellen, than the cruel, cement shelf, boiling in the sunlight, on which Targo had exhibited her, a shelf to which buyers were free to ascend and handle the merchandise, and were even encouraged to do so. To be sure, she could be commanded by observers to smile, to shake out her hair, to lift her head, to exhibit certain attitudes, and perform in various ways, at the bar. She as slave must obey. And so many times, in the afternoon, had she been forced to kiss the bar, to cling to it, to caress it, to kneel before it, head down, and such.

"What is your lot number, slut?" would call a man, and she would call back to him, "117, Master."

There were doubtless several hundred slaves in the camp, more even than had been in her coffle on the long trek toward Brundisium. Perhaps there were more than a thousand slaves in the camp. She did not know.

Her number, she knew, was very low. She did not know if this were significant, or not. If it were significant, and the lower numbers meant the more desirable merchandise, surely she would be entitled to a high opinion of herself as goods. She found that, despite reservations lingering from her Earth conditioning, and her supposed dignity, and her supposed superiority to, and contempt for, such things, that she wanted to be attractive, desperately so; she wanted to be beautiful, and desirable; she wanted to be found pleasing by men. She wanted to be valuable, wanted to be wanted. To be sure, as she was a slave, such things were important, even from a very practical, even from an economic, point of view. Being beautiful is considerably in a slave's best interest, in many ways, as it would be, too, of course, for many other forms of domestic animal. To be sure, the beauty of a woman has a special interest for men. I love men, she thought, and I want to serve them and please them. That is what I want to live for! I have been chained on the concourse side, she told herself, that I may be more easily seen. I have a low number, considering the many girls in the camp. I must be desirable, she thought, at least in the opinion of some. I wonder if I am *slave desirable*. Could I, once of Earth, she asked herself, be that desirable? To be sure, she thought, my number, my chaining, may mean nothing. Perhaps they are saving the best for last, or something. After all, I am only from Earth. How could I, only from Earth, compete with a Gorean woman? But then, she told herself, humans on Gor are surely of Earth origin. Thus, ultimately, we are no different. So why could I not compete with a Gorean woman, even with a Gorean slave girl? Am I not now, too, Gorean; and am I not now, too, no more than a slave girl, and a Gorean slave girl? How vain I am, she thought. But then women are vain, she thought, and I am a woman, so why should I not, too, be concerned with such things? I do not care even if I am narcissistic, or frivolous and shallow. I do not care. Such things are important to me. Why should I not care about them? Why should I not, too, be vain? Yes, I am vain! I have the vanity of a female slave, who exists only for men! I do not care! I do not object! And I love it! I love it! I love it! This settled in her mind, and kissing the bracelets on her wrists, holding her to the upright bar, she laughed, and was pleased with this understanding. Layers of guilt, falsity and hypocrisy fell from her, like a weighty, obsolescent armor, dried, useless scales shed when no longer needed.

"What is your lot number, little tasta, little vulo?" called another man.

"117, Master," Ellen responded.

"Yes," she admitted to herself, "I am a vain slave. And I am exquisite, I think, and I am beautiful, I think. Or perhaps so! And in any event I love being owned and I love being a slave!"

But then she remembered men and their whips and was afraid, very afraid.

"117, Master!" she called to a fellow who had stood by the bars, and tapped himself lightly on the chest, on the left.

* * * *

Ellen, carrying the pitcher of wine, found the fellow who had called out to her earlier. He had been served in the meantime, as she had supposed he would have been, but, in any event, she had returned, to see after the matter, as was appropriate. He permitted her to add a bit of wine to his goblet, and she was grateful for this kindness, for in it he acknowledged her return, and her solicitude that he be served. She wondered if, had she not returned, he would have had her sought out, and punished.

Ellen did not wish to be punished.

But she loved being subject to punishment. If I am not pleasing, she thought, I will be punished. How appropriate for a slave! How different from a free woman, she thought. No matter what they do they are never punished. But I must be pleasing, and perfectly, or I will be punished. I am a slave. Men will have what they want of me. Men will have me as they want me!

She looked about herself.

She suddenly felt a man put his arm about her waist, clumsily.

It would not have been the first time that she had felt a touch in her serving, the grasping of an ankle, a pinch, the brief holding, and smelling, of her hair, the light grasping of a thigh.

He held her.

She stiffened, slightly. She was frightened. Then, she wanted to press suddenly against him, whimpering, but she knew she was not to be used, not until after her sale.

Until then she was to heat, and simmer, until she wanted to scream with need.

How hateful are the masters, she thought. How cruel they are to us!

She wondered if her heat had been visible in the exhibition cage, when she had touched the warm bar, kissed it, pressed herself piteously against it.

He drew his arm away from her. He staggered, a little, shifting unsteadily. He steadied himself with one hand on her shoulder. He bent forward. She smelled a breath thick with paga, not the red and yellow wines from the vats, the wines which she and the others carried.

The man looked blearily at her left breast.

"117, Master," said Ellen.

"You are too young," he said, blinking, stepping back, wiping his hand across his bearded face. He then turned about, almost falling, and staggered away.

I am not too young, she thought, angrily. Many men, fine men, strong men, virile men, do not think me too young at all!

There had been, she had learned, twenty-one bids on her, following her release from the upright bar and the exhibition cage. These bids set the price at which she would be initially offered to the buyers, that point at which the bidding would start. She knew she was, in effect, guaranteed a sale to the highest starting bid, even if no one in the entire camp cared to bid even a tarsk-bit more. She had not been told, of course, what the highest bid of the twenty-one bids had been.

She had, of course, after having knelt and begged permission to speak, inquired.

"Curiosity is not becoming in a kajira," she had been told.

"Yes, Master," she had said.

"You will learn on the block," she was told.

"Yes, Master," she had said.

"Wine, girl!" called a fellow, lifting his goblet, and Ellen rushed to him.

In a few Ehn Ellen, her pitcher half full, stood back in the darkness, some yards from the closest fires.

The first of the formal dancers had been called to one circle or another, following the hailings of the torch-bearing crier. Men who might have been interested in bidding on them, having found them of interest in the exhibition cages, might then follow them to the designated circles, to continue their appraisal. Others, too, of course, the curious, the lustful, the admirers of beauty, and such, tended to gather about the circles in question.

How beautiful the dancers are, thought Ellen.

A few moments ago, she had peered between men, pausing in her serving, to watch perform some among the first of the summoned dancers.

Would that I could dance, would that I were so beautiful, thought Ellen.

She now stood alone in the darkness, looking toward the fields.

What is to become of me, she asked herself. What is to be my fate? I do not know. I am only a slave.

Who is watching, thought Ellen. Perhaps I could run. Perhaps I could escape. Then she laughed ruefully to herself. I am only an ignorant, stripped, branded slave, a poor Earth-girl slave on barbaric Gor. There is no escape for one such as I. Indeed, there is no escape for any Gorean slave girl! There is nowhere to run, nowhere to go. We continue to wear our collars at the pleasure of men. And they do not free us! They keep us as they want us, as what we are, their slaves!

She felt moisture on the side of the pitcher she carried, and she recalled, too, that a little ka-la-na had run from the lip of the pitcher to its side, and onto her hip. Too, this sort of thing, a trickle of ka-la-na on the vessel, is not that uncommon in pouring. She put one finger to the side of the vessel and found the arrested trickle of wine. Looking about, and determining to her satisfaction that no one was looking, she put the tip of her finger to the trickle, and then lifted her finger to her lips, and tongue. Her eyes widened. How startling, how wonderful, she breathed, for this common wine, dispensed so lavishly at the festival camp, was better than any she had tasted on Earth. Then suddenly she was terrified, and rubbed her finger on her thigh, trying to wipe away the evidence of her putative indiscretion. If only I had a bit of cloth, she thought, that I might wipe my lips, but then she hastily discarded that wish, for the cloth might have been stained. She thought to wipe her lips with her hair, but that, too might be stained. She wiped her lips with the back of her right forearm. What if a man takes me in his arms, holds me helplessly and chooses to rape my lips with the kiss of the master, she thought. What if he should taste the wine! To be sure, she had not been forbidden to taste the wine. But she knew enough of Gorean custom to suppose that such a liberty taken without permission, in the case of a slave, if not explicitly permitted, might be an occasion for grievous discipline.

Again, first looking about, she wiped her lips, desperately, frightened.

I must hurry back, to serve, she thought.

She paused, looking at the camp, at the men and the fires, the tents. How beautiful and exciting, how real, is this world, she thought.

I wonder what the highest bid on me was, she thought. Curiosity is not becoming in a kajira, she reminded herself. But how desperately curious she was to know!

Put it from your mind, she thought. Be about your duties, girl, she thought.

And quickly she hurried back to serve.

* * * *

It was a few Ehn later when, making her way amongst the joking, roaring, laughing, colorfully garbed men, tunicked and robed, many sitting about the fires, some afoot, moving here and there, the firelight reflecting from the side of the red-figured pitcher, the side of her lit by one of the fires, her feet in the soft earth, the music about her, dancers elsewhere, in some of the circles, she stopped suddenly, startled, shaken, and nearly dropped the vessel she carried.

Amongst the men about one of the fires she saw, sitting cross-legged, in sedate, deliberative, sober converse with men in Cosian robes, not soldiers, one whose presence here was incomprehensible. She was stunned, she could not move. He, too, was in Cosian robes. How magnificent he looked, seeing him now, once again, he in rich robes, at ease, rich, prosperous, secure, self-assured, splendid, more so than she had ever dreamed he might be. He was the sort of man at whose feet a trembling slave would cringe, the sort of man at whose feet belonged women, the sort of man at whose feet a queen might beg her collar. He was here! She gasped with terror, eagerness and desire. She was shocked, she felt weak, her heart beat wildly, she feared her legs would give way beneath her, she was vulnerable, she was stripped, she felt giddy, and feared that she might faint. Never had she expected to see him again! She fought to gain her breath. She tried to stand very steadily. She held the handles of the pitcher, hard, as though for support, as though for a renewed contact with what was solid and real. She trembled in consternation and confusion.

It was he who on this world had been her first master, he who on Earth had arranged and executed her straightforward, flawless abduction, he into whose keeping and under whose mastery she had first come, he amongst whose toils she had first found herself inextricably enmeshed, so absolutely, so simply and professionally, so easily, so casually, so helplessly and perfectly, he under whose supervision she with her station, auspices, prestige and credentials had been transformed into no more than a young, shapely, meaningless slave, he who, on this world, had taken the familiar, common name, 'Mirus'!

Has he come for me, she thought, wildly.

But there was no indication that he even knew she was in the camp. Surely there would have been, so far as she knew, no reason for him to suppose she was here.

Doubtless he had business here, but it did not seem that it would concern a lowly slave, one he had discarded for a pittance, after teaching her pain, shame, and the meaning of her collar.

"Wine, slave girl!" called a fellow, from about the very fire where Mirus sat.

She wanted to turn and flee, and seemed rooted to the spot, nor did it seem that she dared to approach. Yet she knew she must serve. He must not see her as she was now, not shamed, not as a naked slave! What was she to do? Then she feared a command might be repeated, and she might then be thrown beside the fire and beaten before him, as a tardy slave. Timidly, trying to remain in the shadows, she approached the fire. As she approached, it seemed he was finishing his conversation, and preparing to rise.

She poured the wine, unsteadily. The fellow whose goblet she was filling looked up at her, quizzically.

"Forgive me, Master," she whispered.

When she raised her head and straightened her body Mirus had risen to his feet, turned from his interlocutor, and was preparing to depart.

Suddenly, their eyes met!

She cast her eyes down, not daring to return his gaze. Too, it is often thought presumptuous for a slave to meet the eyes of a free man. Such can be an occasion for discipline.

In the instant their eyes had met she saw that he seemed startled. Then he had not expected to find her here in the festival camp!

Trembling, she lifted her head again and looked at him.

He was regarding her, regarding her now as a man regards a slave, candidly, appraisingly, speculatively. She wondered if, after all, he recognized her.

His glance went slowly, lingeringly, from her small feet, to her trim ankles, to the lovely calves and thighs, to the love cradle of her, to the narrow waist, to the swelling sweetness, the vulnerable softness, of her breasts, to the soft shoulders and her white throat, now innocent of a steel circlet, to her glossy hair, now of slave length, to the face, thought beautiful, and surely exquisitely feminine, by many, and to the trembling lips, and the darkly lashed, longly lashed, gray, wide, frightened eyes.

Though she was a slave she felt her body heat and flush helplessly, being so regarded.

Did she not know her beauty was public? Had she not learned that, forcibly and clearly, in the Kettle Market in Ar, on Targo's sales shelf?

It seemed she was being regarded as a mere, interesting, sleek animal, perhaps as a very special sort of tarsk or kaiila.

How could he look at her in that fashion? How dare he look at her in that fashion?

Then she recalled she was slave.

When again their eyes met it seemed that it might be as though he were seeing her for the first time. Again it seemed to her that he might be startled, or surprised, perhaps even astonished, looking upon her. But this was not an astonishment, not now, at seeing her here, in the camp, that she should be here, but an astonishment, it seemed, that she was now as she was, was now as he found her to be. Had she changed so much, she wondered. Perhaps he did not recognize her?

"Wine, slave!" called a fellow from another group.

"Coming, Master!" she called, and relievedly turned about, hurrying to her new summoner, mercifully breaking the spell which had held her, as an immobilized slave, before his gaze.

She made her way to her new summoner. And she moved, of course, as what she was, a slave.

She suddenly thought that perhaps she should try to walk like a free woman, stiffly, clumsily, affecting mannishness, moving straightly, striding, attempting to conceal her vulnerability and sex. But then she did not do so for she did not wish to be struck. She stumbled a bit, undecidedly, then resumed her progress toward her new master of the instant. Then, angrily, tossing her head and hair, defiantly, not looking back, wondering if he were still watching her, not knowing, putting the shames of Earth behind her, she approached her new summoner proudly, naturally, gracefully, beautifully, a summoned slave. She would show Mirus, if he were still looking, what he had lost! She was suddenly joyous, and fulfilled, in being a slave! She recalled how surprised he had seemed to be, not just seeing her here, in the camp, but seeing her as she now was. Did he think she would go for tarsk-bits now? There had been twenty-one bids on her! Surely there had been no mistaking the admiration implicit in his scrutiny when he had so openly appraised her. How natural now were her carriage, her grace, her deferentiality! Was this the consequence of her training? In one sense, no, for her training had done little more than liberate the slave within her; in another sense, her training had, of course, improved, refined, and enhanced the slave self that had longed for such tutelage. Dispositionally she had longed to submit to males, serve them and love them. Dispositionally she had longed for male dominance. Such needs, of course, are most perfectly satisfied within the master/slave relationship. This is not to claim, of course, that Goreans instituted female slavery in order to satisfy the needs of women. The origins probably lie closer to the interests and desires of imperious, unconquered men, the pleasures and utilities to be found in the ownership and mastery of such delicious creatures. And one supposes that the women prefer it this way, that the men will do with them as they please, for that is part of the strength to which they long to submit. In any event, the institution of female slavery is part of the very fabric of Gorean society. It is both historical and contemporary; it is honored in custom and tradition; it is honored in practice; it is pervasive, societally and culturally; it is familiar, recognized and unquestioned; it is ingredient in the law and enforced with all the sanctions of the law. Ellen had never expected, of course, to find herself in a society in which such an institution actually existed, in a society allied with nature rather than opposed to her. Earth had not prepared her to even entertain such a possibility. Too, of course, she had never dreamed that she would, in fact, find herself on such a world an owned, branded chattel. But here, at last, on Gor, her femininity, and deepest self, had been freed. The genetic template had always been there, fastened in her by eons of evolution, part of what made her what she was, a woman; the training, and the Gorean milieu, had merely, so to speak, freed her to be herself, had encouraged her to be herself, had required her, she willing or not, to be herself, or be fed to sleen, or cast to leech plants. Genetically, she desired to love and serve men; in the Gorean milieu she had learned ways of doing so. For example, genetically, she desired to render obeisance to men; on Gor she had learned certain conventional ways in which this might be done, such as the first and second positions of obeisance.

When Ellen had served the fellow his wine, pouring evenly, carefully, she straightened up and looked back to the other group, sitting about its fire.

Mirus was no longer there. She did not know where he had gone, doubtless about his business, perhaps in one of the tents of the camp.

She looked about herself, to see if others were about who might desire her service. She saw another slave, such as herself, some yards away, stripped, her skin partly illuminated in the firelight, also with one of the two-handled, red-figured pitchers, serving. She is pretty, thought Ellen. I think it is Renata. I wonder how many bids were put in on her.

When Ellen had poured for the fellow, she had been careful not to let her hair fall forward and brush his shoulder. She knew such things might be arousing to men, and that Gorean men, with their powerful sexual appetites, were easily aroused. If he were to cast her down between the fires and put her to his peremptory pleasure, she had little doubt but what it would be she who would be blamed. Is it not always the slave who is blamed, who must writhe beneath the whip? Had there been a sufficient number of iron belts in the camp she supposed that she might have been locked in one. She was supposed to heat until, on the block, she would be pathetically, uncontrollably needful. Had he been her master, in private compartments, she would not have hesitated to permit such an inadvertence, or she might have tied the loose bondage knot in her hair, on the left, as a mute plea for attention. "Serving wine," although it will usually have its obvious meaning, is commonly used as a euphemism on Gor for serving the pleasure of a master. "Has he had you serve him wine yet?" one girl might ask another. "Wine, Master?" is a question which might be put by a slave to her master, or to her master's guests, if she has been made available to them. Another example of this idiom is found in phrases such as, say, "Your slave begs to serve you wine" or "The slave begs to serve her master wine." There are also, differing from city to city, rituals connected with this sort of thing, as when the slave kneels, kisses the cup, and then proffers it to the master, with two hands, arms extended, head down between her arms. Sometimes the cup is first warmed at the breasts, for Goreans commonly drink wine warm, or pressed meaningfully against the slave's lower belly, the hard rim of the cup pressed inward, severely, against her yielding flesh. These rituals, as noted, differ from city to city. Also, of course, masters may differ, as well, and each will, if he wishes, train his slaves to his pleasure in this matter, as in other matters.

"Ellen," said a slave.

"Renata?" asked Ellen.

"Yes," said the girl, suddenly, rather pleased. It was the slave Ellen had seen earlier, yards away, serving in the half darkness. Ellen knew her. She was red-haired. She had been close to Ellen in the coffle for days, and, sometimes, at night, in their chains, between the stakes, they had whispered to one another. She had also been in the same exhibition cage, and they had been in ankle-coffle together for the earlier bathing. She had been 'Auta' before, but the scribe had not cared for that name, and had given her the name 'Renata'. So now she was Renata. She liked this name, but was not yet accustomed to responding to it. To be sure, slaves learn quickly to respond to the names given them by their masters.

"Do you have much wine left?" asked Renata.

"Not much," said Ellen. "I must return to the vat for more."

"I would go now," said Renata. "There is not much left in the vat."

"Ah!" said Ellen. "Thank you—Renata."

"It is nothing," said Renata.

Ellen did not want to be caught with an empty pitcher and the vat empty, perhaps for Ehn, even an Ahn, until its supply might be replenished. She could wait near the vat on the other hand, until it was once more full. No one could be angry about that. It was not as though someone had sent her for wine and she had been dilatory in returning. And, of course, she had no access to the other vats in the camp, for they were guarded jealously by their own vat masters, with their own assigned slaves.

And so Ellen returned to the vat, stopping on the way to serve two men.

She wondered if Mirus had recognized her. She was sure he had, from the first glance. But then he had looked upon her as though she might be a complete novelty to him, an astonishment to him, a totally unknown, lovely slave. Perhaps he had thought he recognized her, and had, but then, later, thought that he had been mistaken, that the slave he saw could not possibly be she for whom he had originally taken her?

Could I have changed so much, Ellen asked herself. Could I have become so different, and so completely a slave?

"Ah, Ellen!" called the portly vat master, one of the caste of vintners. "One can scarcely scrape the bottom of the vat! These loafing tarsks drink like desert kaiila! Hurry to the sutlers! Tell them to trundle a new cask to the vat of Callimachus!"

Ellen stood there, clutching her pitcher. She regarded the vintner with dismay.

She did not want to make her way to the sutlers for that way took her into the darkness, and into the tented areas, closer to the walls of the city. Too, if she went directly, it might take her near the crates containing the strange beasts that had terrorized her, even within their confinements.

"Hurry!" said the vintner. "Do not just stand there! Run!"

"Yes, Master!" cried Ellen, frightened.

"Stop!" he cried.

"Master?" inquired Ellen.

"Leave the pitcher, stupid girl!" he called.

Confused, frightened, she put the pitcher on the bench near the vat, where others already reposed.

She suddenly fled to Callimachus, the vintner, the vat master, and fell to her knees before him. "Might not another slave, a swifter slave, a more beautiful slave, better accomplish this errand, Master?" she inquired.

Ellen was not eager to leave the fires of the festival camp.

"I have already sent Louise," he said. "She is not yet back!"

"Perhaps she will return soon, Master," said Ellen. "Surely a slave better suited to this errand than I might be found."

"So the stupid little slave wants the lash!" he cried.

"No, Master!" cried Ellen.

"Up!" he cried. "Run! Run like the kaiila!"

And so Ellen sprang to her feet and hurried toward the darkness.

"Stop!" cried the vat master. "That way, that way!" he cried, pointing.

"Yes, Master!" she wept.

He would have none of an indirect, or circuitous, route. What was it to him if she must fear for her life in the midst of beasts?

They are confined, she told herself. There is no danger. And that is truly the shortest, most direct route. If I were to go differently I might become lost. I might be apprehended by guardsmen. Would they believe my story, she wondered, that she was on an errand? At the least she might spend the night swathed in coarse ropes, suspended from a hook in their guardhouse. And what would be her punishment from the Cosian slave masters, for her foolishness, ignorance and confusion? And what if they thought she had tried to escape? As she was a barbarian, they might think her that stupid. She did not wish to be crippled, or fed to sleen. There is no danger, she reminded herself. The beasts are confined.

And so Ellen sped toward the city of Brundisium.

She hurried among the fires. She felt men reach out and grasp for her, but she sped on. She passed dancing circles where sinuous slaves, lot numbers on their left breasts, swayed their beauty before lusty brutes who might soon bid upon them.

She had a reasonably clear idea where lay the temporary stockade of the sutlers, and its direction had been reconfirmed for her by the vat master but moments ago.

She must seek out the dealers of wine amongst them, and deliver the order, to be brought to the vat of Callimachus of Cos, to whose tablet it would be marked. Ultimately, however, in theory, the cost of the wine, as tabulated, and the cost of its distribution by such as Callimachus, was to be borne by the state of Cos, as the festival camp was organized on her behalf. To be sure, Ellen had heard it rumored that she, Cos, might suggest that its donation, that of the wine, and the coverage of associated expenses, would be a welcome, suitable gesture of gratitude on the part of Brundisium for the many benefits she had received at the hands of Cos, and the alliance of the two powers, and such. But such concerns were not those of a slave. And, in the end, she supposed, Brundisium, in turn, might decide that this benevolence might be best exacted of her merchant caste, and particularly of those dealing in wines. But here, again, these were not concerns for such as she, a slave.

In a short time Ellen was beyond the fires and among the tents, most of which were dark. She was taking the most direct route, but, as yet, had not entered into the vicinity of the crates of certain beasts, those the glimpses of which and the roars and cries of which had caused her considerable alarm. She stumbled twice, and once struck into a box. Putting out her hands she felt, nearby, a tharlarion saddle. Once, running, she nearly stepped on a chained, sleeping sleen. Its sudden rising up and vicious snarl terrified her. If she had struck against it her leg might have been ripped from her with one savage snap of the jaws. She fled about it, further into the darkness. She began to cry. She stopped. She was now afraid to run. Why was there not more light? Torches, lanterns, lamps, anything? Surely at places in the camp, even away from the festival fires, there was some light. But very little here. Men might find their way among the tents with the aid of a lantern, a torch, or such, but she had no such device. She put out her hand and touched something that loomed wall-like in the darkness, canvas. She turned about. She cried out, softly, piteously, her progress suddenly arrested by a tent rope, taut, running diagonally downward from its pole to its peg, anchored in the dirt, some feet from the tent. She put our her hands in the darkness, to feel her way.

It was very dark here.

She suddenly realized she was not clear as to her location. On the other hand, she was not totally disoriented as she could see the fires of the camp behind her and, in the distance, the lights of Brundisium, among them some of the beacon fires on her walls. But where along those vast walls was the stockade of the sutlers?

She crouched down in the dirt, and wept.

Then she heard a howl, which she surmised must emanate from one of the beasts she muchly feared.

That is my direction, she thought.

She hoped fervently that Louise, sent out before her, had now returned successfully, having finished up the entire matter.

She heard some men approaching. One of them carried a lantern. She wiped tears from her eyes. She shrank back in the shadows.

Crouching down she watched the men pass. They did not see her in the darkness.

One of the men she saw, this startling her, was Mirus!

She crept after them, using the wavering light of the lantern to follow them, it casting strange shadows on the tents and earth.

Thusly she might the more safely find her way, she reassured herself. To her surprise, but pleasure, she saw that their path led very much in the direction she desired to go. In any event, though she did not admit this to herself, she would have risked much, merely to follow Mirus.

And so she crept after them, a young, naked slave.

In one or another of the tents there was a lit lamp, its light visible through the silk or canvas. At such places she tried to stay in the shadows, and then, in a moment, once more follow the swaying lantern, a tiny, glowing dot before her.

Occasionally a lantern was slung from a pole, a pool of light at its base. At such places she must most particularly endeavor to avoid detection.

On her hands and knees, crawling, she heard a woman's voice, from within a tent. Something in the voice, in its helplessness, its piteousness, in its gasps, its intonations, suggested that the woman might be struggling futilely, weakly, pulling against bonds. "Please, Master, I love you!" Ellen heard. "Permit me to yield! I cannot stand it! I fear I will die! Oh, oh. Please do not bring me again and again to this point, so, cruelly, without permitting me to yield! Just one more touch, Master! Please, another touch, just the tiniest touch! It is all I need! I am your slave! Do not be so cruel! Show me mercy! You have conquered me a thousand times! I am hopelessly and abjectly yours! I love you, Master! I beg to be permitted to yield!"

Men, the arrogant, masterful beasts, thought Ellen, biting her lip, grinding her fingernails into the palms of her hands. How vulnerable we are! How they make us theirs! They play us like czehars, drawing what music they will from our bodies! How arrogantly, how imperiously they master us, their slaves! And Ellen envied the slave within the tent. Would that I were in her bonds, thought Ellen. I, too, would weep with passion, and beg to yield, and if my master, in his mercy, saw fit to grant me the caress of permission, I would weep with ecstasy, his, and beg to please, again and again.

Will he not be kind to her? Does he not know she is only a slave?

There was then a soft, rapturous, prolonged, grateful, inarticulate cry from within the tent, partly muffled, for the master had perhaps placed his hand firmly over the mouth of the slave, that she might not disturb the camp. In a moment his hand must have been removed from her lips, for Ellen heard, "Thank you, thank you, beloved Master! I love you, Master! I love you, Master!"

Kind master, beloved master, thought Ellen.

Ellen sought to control herself. She must not cry out!

Tears burst from her eyes as she clenched her fists, in her own frustration, in the throes of her own starved needs.

She must not cry out!

I am a slave thought Ellen. I want a master! I want a master!

Then Ellen looked up, suddenly, frightened.

Where was the lantern? Where the men? Quickly she looked about, and hurried in the direction it had last been moving.

"Where, where?" she cried out to herself.

She rushed into the darkness.

She fell.

Where is Mirus, who was my master, she asked herself. No, no, I must get to the sutlers, she told herself. I have an errand. I must hurry. Oh, where has he gone? Where is Mirus?

She rose again to her feet, and continued on, and then, after a few moments, stopped, suddenly. She heard men somewhere before her. She went to her hands and knees and approached, cautiously.

Putting out her hand she touched the side of something which seemed to be a great, stout box. She recoiled in terror. It was surely one of the crates which had held one of the large, shaggy, half-seen beasts which had so terrified her earlier. But there was no sound from within the crate. Perhaps the beast was asleep. As silently as she could, she crawled forward a little. A tiny creaking noise to her right startled her. The gate to the crate had moved a little on its hinges. She felt she might die with fear. She put out her hand a little and touched the gate. It was ajar. She moved it a little. A heavy, beastlike, musky odor came from the box, but she could detect no sign of life within it. There was no evidence whatsoever of a presence within the container, no suggestion of movement, no sound of respiration from large, savage lungs. She felt sick. The crate, she was sure, was empty.

"It is time," she heard, the voice of one of the men a few yards away. It was as though he were addressing something.

Suddenly she saw the lantern once more revealed, now brought forth from beneath a cloak, and lifted.

She went to her stomach, fearfully, in terror that she might be seen.

There were four men standing before one of the crates. In the light she could see that Mirus was one of them. More frightening to her was that there was now something with the men, two shambling, gigantic shapes crouching near them. She law light reflected in the eyes of one of the beasts, from the uplifted lantern. They glowed like fire for the briefest moment, and then it had turned its head away. She had no doubt these things with the men had been the denizens of the boxes. There had been five such boxes, she thought. Why had the men dared to release these things? What manner of madness had overcome them?

One of the men stood before one of the crates, and tapped it gently. There was a responding growl from within the crate. "It is time," said the man. "Others are within the tent."

There was a large tent near the crates, a tent Ellen had supposed might house, perhaps among others, the beasts' masters or handlers.

The crate, like the others, was apparently secured by two hasps and staples, each with their own gigantic padlocks, better than six or seven pounds in weight and six inches in diameter, some three or four inches in thickness.

Do not let it out, thought Ellen, lying on her stomach, hiding in the darkness.

But, to Ellen's horror, the men did not bend to undo the padlocks and release the inmate. Rather the door simply swung out, being opened from the inside. The beast emerged and stretched. As it stood on its hind legs it was some eight feet in height, and its arms must have been five feet in length. It must have weighed several hundred pounds. Then it sank down to all fours, like a rounded, furred boulder, and looked about itself. The padlocks, the stout bolts and plates, then, had been meaningless. The appearance of their stout securities had been a sham, intended to conceal a fearful truth, that the beasts had never been other than at liberty.

Ellen was sick with terror and could not move.

"Let us go inside," said the man with the lantern. "Let us join the others."

The four men and the three beasts turned about and went toward the large tent. One of the men, he with the lantern, held back the tent flap, looking about, and the other men, followed by the three beasts, they now on all fours, thrust through the opening. Mirus was the first to enter the tent. Ellen thought, in the light of the lantern, that she glimpsed another beast, and two other men in the tent. One of the men was standing. Then all were inside the tent.

I must flee, somewhere, somehow, thought Ellen. I must get away from here. In her terror even the thought of the errand on which she had embarked temporarily eluded her. But she found it almost impossible to move her body. She lay there, in the dirt, on her belly, hiding, scarcely able to move, trembling. At last, after a few Ehn, her senses began to clear. She knew then she must again be about her errand. Mirus seemed to be in no danger, nor the other men. Perhaps the beasts were domesticated, even pets of some sort, she told herself.

She rose unsteadily to her feet.

There had been five crates she remembered, remembering it from somewhere, vaguely from about the edge of her consciousness. She had seen four men outside the tent, and two within, and a beast within, and three beasts outside.

She suddenly sensed a heavy, musky odor behind her, and before she could scream a heavy paw, placed tightly over her mouth, drew her swiftly backward, and she was lifted from her feet, and held tightly against a gigantic, shaggy body.

She was helpless in such a grip. She could not scream. She squirmed futilely, and was carried to the tent.

Chapter 23

What Occurred Within the Tent and Later Outside of It

Ellen was thrown to the rug within the tent, and she raised herself to her hands and knees, blinking, illuminated in the light of the lantern, it too close to her, the only light within the tent, and found herself in the midst of six men, and, with them, crouching back on their haunches, four of the darkly furred, massive, monstrous beasts. The beast who had captured her stood near her, as it seemed, half bent over. Two of the men rose, Mirus one of them.

Ellen swiftly went to the first obeisance position before Mirus, and then crawled forward a foot, her head still down, and pressed her lips fearfully to his sandals, then backed away a few inches, and kept her head down.

The monster who had seized her and brought her to the tent made some noise. It almost seemed as though Ellen could understand it. It was much as though a bear or tiger might have spoken. There seemed to be, to Ellen's alarm, a similarity to Gorean phonemes.

"A spying slave," said one of the men, as though translating what the beast had said.

"No, Masters!" cried Ellen. How could it be, she asked herself, that a beast might speak? She was sure the utterance of the beast had been intelligible in some sense. There had been an articulation within those noises, a subtlety and clarity which was quite unlike, though reminding one of, the snarling, the growling, of an animal.

"Let us see her," said one of the men.

Ellen felt the gigantic, clawed paw of the beast grasp her hair and her head was pulled up and back violently, painfully.

"A pretty one," said one of the men.

"Rather plain," said Mirus, dryly.

Tears sprang to Ellen's eyes.

"Position," said another of the men.

Ellen, the beast having released her hair, went to position, kneeling, knees wide, back straight, head up, hands on thighs.

"A pleasure slave," said one of the men.

"Obviously," said another.

Ellen wondered if she should have kept her knees closely together, before Mirus, but she had naturally, instantaneously, not even thinking about it, assumed the wide-kneed position.

She saw Mirus smile, and flushed.

She closed her knees.

"Knees wide, slut," said a man.

Again she opened her knees.

"Wider!" he snapped.

She complied.

"More widely!"

Again she complied.

How vulnerable, how helpless, physically and psychologically, is a woman in such a position, that of the Gorean pleasure slave!

"What is your name?" asked a man.

"Ellen, Master."

"Who owns you?"

"The state of Cos, Master."

"You are a serving slave in the camp?" asked a man.

"Yes, Master."

"Mark?" said a man.

Swiftly she rose up on her knees and turned her left thigh to the interrogator, at the same time putting her hands behind the small of her back, as though they might be braceleted there. It is one of the positions of brand display.

Mirus smiled.

Ellen flushed.

I hate him, she thought.

But she remained in the position, a common one for brand display. Her wrists, behind her back, were nearly touching. The position accentuates the breasts and, given the position of the hands, is provocatively emblematic; I think that even a male of Earth, one who, if there are any such, had never given a thought to the possibility of female slavery, or even of a particular woman, stripped, and bound hand and foot, lying on the rug at the foot of his bed, helpless, fearful and squirming, wholly at his mercy, might have some sense, seeing it, of the meaning of that position; it would certainly suggest to him, or anyone, I would suppose, female obedience, submission, servitude and bondage. Might not that sight, or vision, then, as though accompanied with a clap of thunder, change him forever, showing him a possibility which might transform him from an indoctrinated, manipulated, obsequious political puppet striving to please those who secretly hate and despise him into a male, one suddenly awakened, one attentive to distant cries, one who now hears drums long silent, one now apprised of tides, of seasons and the motion of planets, of the rights of nature?

Too, of course, obviously, the position makes it easy to bracelet the slave.

"Common kajira mark," said a man.

"A low slave," said a man.

"Yes," said another.

The fellow who had asked for the brand display then made a tiny gesture and Ellen, instantly, returned to first position.

"Does she have a lot number?" asked a man.

"Yes," said a fellow, leaning forward, "—117."

"A low number for such as she," observed Mirus.

Ellen bit her tongue.

"Who sent you?" asked one of the men.

"No one, Masters," said Ellen, frightened. "I am on an errand, to the sutlers, that more wine may be brought to my serving station."

Again the beast behind her spoke, or growled.

"You were following us," said one of the men. "You were lurking outside, hiding."

"Who sent you?" again pressed a man.

"No one, Masters," said Ellen.

"Let us cut her throat," said another.

One of the beasts in the circle seemed to growl for a moment.

"You can eat later," said a man to the beast. "Kardok is hungry," he said to the group.

"She must be the tool of someone," said one of the men. "Torture will make her speak."

"She will not know whose tool she is," said one of the men, angrily. "Our foes are astute. They will have dealt with her cunningly, she hooded, or they masked."

One of the beasts regarding Ellen moved its long tongue about its mouth, and about its fangs. Its lower jaw seemed moist.

"Let us kill her," said another of the men, uneasily.

"It would be difficult to dispose of the body in the camp," said another.

"Bind her, gag her, take her afield," said another.

One of the beasts, that which had been regarding Ellen, said something.

"She could be eaten," said the man whose office it seemed was to interpret the guttural noises of the monsters.

"The bones, snapped apart, splintered, crushed, could be buried," said one of the men.

"Here within the concealment of the tent," said another.

"Please, no, Masters!" wept Ellen.

"Do you think your life has value?" asked one of the men.

"It has value to me, Masters," wept Ellen.

"Yes," said a man. "Even the life of an urt is precious enough to itself."

"Surely the life of a slave," said Mirus, dryly, "may be of some value, however negligible, to masters."

Ellen cast a wild glance of gratitude at Mirus.

"Do you wish to speak to that point?" Mirus asked her.

"Yes, yes!" cried Ellen.

"Do you beg your life?" asked Mirus.

"Yes, Masters!"

"And do you beg to be permitted to be pleasing, and to serve, in any way, and in all ways?" he asked.

"Yes, Masters!"

"In whatever degree of intimacy?" he asked.

"Yes, Masters!"

"And as the most meaningless and abject of slaves?" he asked.

"Yes, Masters!" cried Ellen.

Then she saw that Mirus was smiling down upon her, contemptuously. How humiliated she felt for a moment, and she put down her head, tears running from her eyes, cruelly shamed. Yes, she had begged as a slave, and had meant every word she had said! What of it? She was a slave!

"Slaves are cheap," said a man. "We may have such from any slave."

"Please, Masters," begged Ellen.

"What have you seen?" asked Mirus.

"Nothing, nothing, Masters!" said Ellen.

Mirus reached down and struck her with the back of his hand, striking her to the rug. Quickly, blood at her lip, tears in her eyes, her face stinging, she scurried to return to position before him. A slave does not dally in such matters. She looked up at him, a cuffed slave.

"I have seen beasts, Masters," she said. "But I understand nothing of what I have seen!"

"Who sent you?" asked a man, again.

"No one, Master," Ellen reassured him, once more.

"Many have seen such as our friends here," said a man, "outside of cages, performing, say, in fairs and circuses."

One of the beasts growled menacingly.

"Their appearance in such places," the man continued, "being a useful, and common, disguise, permitting them to travel anywhere, to make suitable contacts, to avoid suspicion, and such."

The beast crouched back, its anger subsiding.

"Why did you follow us?" asked Mirus.

"I am on an errand, Master, which leads me in this direction." She put down her head. "Then I saw you, Master."

"You saw me earlier, in the camp," said Mirus.

"Yes, Master," she said.

"Then you saw me again, and followed me here?"

"Yes, Master."

"Why?" he asked.

Ellen put down her head, shamed.

"Do you know this slave," a man asked Mirus.

"Yes," said Mirus. "It was in my house that she was first marked and collared."

"You once owned her?" asked a man.

"Yes," said Mirus.

Ellen kept her head down.

It was true, Mirus had been her first master.

"She is a barbarian, is she not?" asked a man.

"Yes," said Mirus.

"She has never forgotten you," laughed a man.

"Did you whip her?" asked another.

"Of course," said Mirus.

"Did you give her first whipping?" asked a man.

"Yes," said Mirus.

"They never forget their first whipping," said one of the men.

"She is an enamored, lovesick slave!" laughed a man, suddenly.

Ellen choked back a sob.

"What a presumptuous slut!" laughed a fellow.

"They will die for their masters," laughed another.

"Let us kill her," said one of the men, uneasily.

One of the beasts growled.

"Kardok is hungry," said the man who seemed to understand the sounds of the beasts.

"Then let us give her to our friends," said a man.

"They will eat her alive," said a fellow.

"They are fond of living food, hot and bloody," said another.

"She would scream," said another.

"We can bind her pretty mouth shut," said a man, "so tightly that not a squeak shall pass the binding."

"Were you truly on an errand?" asked Mirus of the kneeling slave.

"Yes, Master!" said Ellen, fervently.

"Soon, then," said Mirus, "she will be missed. A search will be made. Tents and belongings will be ransacked."

"They will not find her," said a man, quietly.

"But the search will be made, in any event," said Mirus. "And I, for one, am not eager to find our business, and our friends, the objects of official scrutiny."

"What do you suggest?" asked the man with the lantern.

"What do you understand of what you have seen?" Mirus asked the kneeling slave.

"I understand nothing of what I have seen, Master," she said. "I am only an animal, a meaningless, inconsequential beast, a slave, Master!"

"Will you speak of what you have seen?" asked Mirus.

"No, Master! No, Master!" said Ellen.

"Even were you to speak," said Mirus, "there is nothing here of interest, and it would be pointless to speak of it. We are merely handlers of beasts, as you can see. Such things are familiar enough. Our papers are in order. The beasts are under perfect control, and such."

"Yes, Master," said Ellen.

"You understand that?" he asked.

"Yes, Master," said Ellen.

"I know this slave," said Mirus. "She is a stupid, plain girl. I brought her here. Personal reasons were involved, no, not what you think, for she is meaningless."

Ellen regarded him with agony.

"For these personal reasons, reasons of a rather particular nature, it amused me to bring her here, and have her enslaved."

"Was she troublesome on Earth?" asked one of the men.

Mirus smiled.

"Perhaps she once entered a line, or a door, before you, not invited to do so, but as though it were her right?"

"Perhaps she cast you a haughty glance, or once spoke shortly to you?" suggested another.

Ellen then began to grasp how easily a woman of Earth, and with so little awareness, thinking herself superior and safe, might court the collar of a slave. A movement, a glance, a word, a gesture which might cause no more than a moment's irritation or disgruntlement to a typical male of Earth, used to such abuse, might have different consequences altogether with another sort of man, a man less tolerant and less accommodating than those on whom she was accustomed to inflict her pettiness and disdain with impunity. "We will come back for her," might say a Gorean slaver. "That one does not know it but she has just made herself an appointment with the slaving iron." How differently would a woman of Earth behave before a man, thought Ellen, if she realized that one day she might find herself at his feet, on her belly, stripped and chained, his slave.

"It does not matter," said Mirus. "The details are unimportant. Let us merely say that, in virtue of these personal reasons, I found it gratifying to have her enslaved, to get her neck in the collar, where it belongs."

One of the men laughed.

Ellen reddened.

"In any event, I did not keep her," said Mirus. "I found her boring. One tires of her easily."

"I do not know if I would have tired of her so easily," said a man.

"She is young," said another.

"But she is pretty," said another.

Ellen put her head down.

"Her thighs steam for you," said a man.

"The mere sight of you lubricates her for the mastery," said another.

"Long ago, weary of her ugliness, her simplicity and limitations, I ridded myself of her, discarding her for a pittance."

"And so all in all we are to understand that you brought her from her own world to the markets merely for your amusement?" asked a man.

"Yes," said Mirus.

Ellen kept her head down, tears running from her eyes.

"She followed you like a she-sleen in heat," laughed a man.

"And that," smiled Mirus, "is the sum of the matter." Then he said, sharply, "Slave!"

"Yes, Master!" said Ellen, frightened.

"I believe you have an errand to run," he said.

Ellen looked at him, wildly.

"You may leave the tent," said Mirus.

Scarcely able to stand Ellen rose, unsteadily, looked about herself and moved, step by uncertain step, toward the entrance of the tent.

"What was her lot number?" asked one of the men.

"117," said another.

Ellen was then outside the tent. She could see the illumination of the lantern through the canvas. Mirus had followed her outside the tent.

The men within seemed to be in converse. Their tones seemed low, and earnest. Sometimes, there was a noise from one of the beasts.

Mirus and she faced one another.

She went to the first obeisance position before him, crept forward, and covered his sandals with kisses.

Then, when she sensed she might do so, she looked up at him, tears in her eyes, clasping his knees.

"So we meet again," he said.

"Yes, Master," she whispered.

"You have changed much since last I saw you," said he.

"It is my hope that that is true, Master," she said. She recalled his glance of appraisal in the camp. She had no doubt but what it was of the sort often bestowed by strong, virile masters on one of those exquisite, little she-beasts known as kajirae. It was the first time that she recalled that he had looked upon her in exactly that way.

"You knelt well in the tent," said he.

"Thank you, Master," she said.

"You no longer kneel as an Earth woman embonded," he said, "but kneel now as a self-understanding, complete and total slave."

"It is what I now am, Master," she whispered.

"And I noted that you knelt instantly, naturally, perfectly, in the position of the pleasure slave."

"It is what I now am, Master," she said.

"You displayed your brand excellently," he observed, "rising up, turning, your wrists lifted behind you in the bracelets position."

"I was taught that in your house, Master," she said.

"You did it well," he said.

"Thank you, Master."

"The word 'Master' comes easily to you," he said. "It is fitting for you. It belongs on your lips and tongue."

"As it should, for I am a slave, Master," she said.

"You are a servile slut," he said.

"Yes, Master," she said.

"I see now what has changed muchly about you," he said.

Ellen dared not speak, but her heart raced.

"It is that you are now a slave, a full slave."

"That is true, Master," she said, "for on this world I have found myself, I have learned that I want to be, and am, a slave."

"Yes," said he, contemptuously, "*slave*."

"Do you object that I have become a slave, a true slave?" she asked.

"No," he said.

"Perhaps," she said, "you would prefer that I continue to object to my inner truth, that I continue to deny it, and continue to suffer all the torments of denying my innermost being, the very meaning of my sex, my nature?"

"I despise you," he said.

"For accepting the truth, for being myself?" she asked.

She sensed that he raised his hand, but he did not strike her.

"Is there not something else in this, Master?" she asked, emboldened.

"What do you mean?" he asked.

"Surely there is more in your concern than the obvious fact that I have become a true slave."

"I do not understand," he said.

"Your anger with me, your impatience, might have another motivation, might it not, Master?" she inquired.

"I do not understand," he said.

"Have I not become more beautiful, more attractive, more desirable? Might I not have become even *slave desirable*?"

"You insolent slut," he said.

"Does this not disturb you?" she asked. "I think that you want to hate me, but that you find me attractive. I think that this makes you furious. You brought me here in hatred, and for your amusement, but now, to your fury, you learn that I have become a true slave, and, I think, an attractive one! You are furious that I have found myself on this world, that I am young, beautiful, healthy, eager, ready, passionate, that I desire to love and serve men, that I want to be owned, that I want to live for a master! You had not wanted that! And you are furious that I will bring a high price on the block! That is not what you had anticipated, not what you wanted. Now you are angry with yourself! You are angry that I have become a true slave! And I think you are angry that I have become beautiful, and desirable! Yes, I am that, Master, and I will go for silver, I assure you, not copper! There have been twenty-one bids on me already, twenty-one! And there is something else, Master, which I think is the most maddening of all for you!"

"What is that, slave?" he asked, skeptically.

"Nothing," she said, suddenly, putting down her head.

"Speak," he said.

"It is that you find me of personal interest."

"Absurd," he said.

"I think that what is most maddening of all for you, Master, is that you want me, that you want this slave!"

Mirus threw back his head and laughed.

"Yes!" insisted Ellen.

"I wonder how you can be punished, you insolent little slut," said Mirus, laughing.

"Master?" said Ellen, warily, suddenly sinking back on her knees before him.

"When a slave is displeasing in any way, let alone presuming beyond her station, it is customary for her to be punished."

"I belong to Cos, Master," said Ellen quickly.

"Can you dance?" asked Mirus.

"No," said Ellen, frightened.

"But," said he, "if you were called to a circle, you would have to perform."

"I am not a dancer," she said. "I will not be called to a circle."

"But if perchance you were," said he, "you would have to perform."

"I suppose so, Master," she said.

"Interesting," said he.

"Do not have me called to a circle, Master!" Ellen begged, terrified.

"Why?" he asked.

"Because I cannot dance," she wept. "I would be clumsy! They would be angry! I would be beaten!"

"If a girl does not report to a circle," said Mirus, "it is my understanding that that constitutes not only disobedience, but a presumption of flight."

Ellen groaned.

"You are familiar with the penalties for a fugitive slave," he remarked.

"Yes, Master," said Ellen, shuddering.

"You would not look well without your feet," he said.

Ellen put down her head, in her hands, weeping.

"Your lot number is 117, as I recall," said Mirus.

"Yes, Master," said Ellen.

"You were serving at the station of Callimachus, as I recall," said Mirus.

"Yes, Master," said Ellen, frightened.

When she looked up, he had turned away, presumably returning to the tent.

Only a little later, as she knelt before the tent, trembling, she saw a lantern approaching, and heard the trundling of a cart. It was a small, two-wheeled, high-wheeled cart, with two handles, by means of which it might be drawn. The lantern was fixed on a short pole, at the front, left side of the cart, as one would look forward from the cart. She welcomed the light. The cart was being drawn by a naked woman, struggling between the handles. On the cart, tied there, was a large, damp, cool barrel.

"Is that you, Ellen?" inquired the woman, from between the handles.

"Yes!" said Ellen.

It was Louise, one of her fellow serving slaves, who had earlier attended the vat of Callimachus with her, serving the men in its vicinity. Ellen recalled that Louise had been sent before her to the sutlers. Given the impatience of the vat master, Ellen had been, somewhat afterward, dispatched on the same errand.

"Get between the handles. Help me!" said Louise.

"Who are you?" asked a strapping, short-haired lad, following the wagon, bearing a switch.

"Ellen," said Ellen.

"Do you know her?" the lad asked Louise.

"Yes," said Louise.

"Are you with the vat of Callimachus?" asked the lad.

"Yes, Master," said Ellen.

"Stand," he said.

Ellen did so.

"What are your doing here?" he asked.

"I was on my way to the sutlers, Master," said Ellen.

"Yes, on your knees," he said, "outside a master's tent."

He then gave her a stinging stripe across the back of the thighs. "Get between the handles, pull," he said.

Ellen, as Louise had gripped the handles rather near the front, bent down and then rose up between them, grasping them behind Louise. There were several welts on Louise's back.

Then Ellen herself cried out, as she herself felt the switch, twice, of their youthful driver.

"Move," he said. "Hurry! *Harta*!"

She then, with Louise, put her small weight against the resistance of the wagon.

"Will it be necessary to beat you further?" asked the lad.

"No, Master!" said Louise.

"No, Master!" said Ellen.

He then gave them each more stripes.

"Hurry," he said. "*Harta*!"

"Yes, Master!" cried the straining, hurrying, switched slaves.

The high wheels of the wagon creaked. The ground was uneven. The small feet of the slaves dug into the dirt. They leaned forward, grasping the handles. One could hear the ka-la-na moving about in the barrel, like a surf within the wood, the barrel rocking in the small wagon bed, rolling within the restraining ropes. The lad directed them through the darkness.

Ellen was confident that Mirus would not have her called to a circle. To be sure, he had frightened her for a moment. How cruel of him to tease her so! But he would not do that to her, not to her. They were both from Earth.

She was uneasy, however, for she knew that she was a slave.

Chapter 24

Danced

Ellen looked about herself, anxiously.

Surely the men were quieter now, less unruly.

She with Louise, and the lad, had a few Ehn earlier, directed by the lad, arrived at the wine station of the exasperated Callimachus.

There were cries about from angry men, and clashing goblets. Some were on their feet. Some were in the vicinity of the vat itself. Some had left to seek their beverage elsewhere in the camp.

"There was haggling, and new wine had to be brought out from the city," the lad explained to Callimachus.

"Hurry!" said Callimachus. "The wine! The wine! Slaves, here! To me, slaves!"

The bung was drawn from the barrel and the precious ka-la-na, the barrel still on the cart, was released over the vat. Yet little of it reached the vat at first for, at the order of Callimachus, the serving slaves filled their empty pitchers from the cascading stream itself, and then rushed to serve.

Four times Ellen had rushed back and forth to fetch more wine. She saw Renata. Louise, too, was now serving. Now she stood amongst the fires and men, a half-filled pitcher grasped in her hands.

Things now, it seemed, were much the same as earlier.

She knew the sales were to begin soon at the great block. They would last, presumably, for two or three days, as there were many slaves to be vended, probably well over a thousand.

She touched her throat lightly. There was no collar there now. But perhaps as early as tomorrow morning she would once more wear locked upon her neck the identificatory circlet of a master, her master.

Early in her bondage, although she had understood that she had been enslaved, she had, perhaps oddly, not really thought of herself as being *owned;* perhaps she had thought of herself as being more a prisoner or captive of sorts; then, a bit later in her bondage, but initially while still in the house of Mirus, she had come to understand that she was not a prisoner or a captive, nothing so dignified, nothing so honorable or important, or deserving of respect, but something quite different, simply a property; she then understood that she was *owned*; and for a time it had been fearful to think of herself as being *owned*. But later she had come to understand this as a given modality of her actuality, as an aspect of her being, as a quotidian reality. She then understood herself, and accepted herself, quite naturally and honestly, and without fear, as being what she was, as being something which was *owned*. And this, of course, was particularly in the legal sense. For years before her branding and collaring she had sensed that she was a natural slave and had surreptitiously dreamed, while trying to deny such dreams, of meeting a master who would enslave her and whom she might thereafter lovingly serve. To be sure the slave would like to choose her master. But Ellen now, apart from her natural dispositions and deepest reality, fitting her for love and the collar, had come to understand herself on all levels, factually and honestly, as something which was owned, as something which could pass from master to master, as might any piece of property. Had kaiila or verr the rationality to comprehend such matters they, too, would have such an understanding of themselves. And Ellen, whom I think we may accept as intelligent, perhaps even quite intelligent, forgive me, Masters, given the selection criteria of Gorean slavers, of which we may take Mirus to be one, had this understanding of herself. She understood herself to be a property, in this case a domestic animal, in the same sense in which a rational kaiila or verr would understand themselves as such. In short, she now understood herself, and thought of herself, quite naturally and accurately, as what in fact she was, as something which was *owned*.

She thought of the tent of the men, and beasts, and of Mirus. For a time she had been frightened there, exaggerating in her own mind the significance of her curiosity and inadvertence. But Mirus had made it clear to her that the matter was unimportant. How foolish she had been, to have been so frightened. Doubtless the men had intended to frighten her, but had intended her no harm. Surely they had let her go, without even a whipping. Mirus himself had conducted her outside the tent. If animal trainers wished to keep the docility of their beasts, and their level of training, secret, in order to make a better performance at a later time, that was surely their prerogative. She did not blame them for their not wanting her to betray their secret, and perhaps spoil their performance. But it had surprised her that Mirus, whom she knew was well fixed on Gor, should have been a member of their party. Perhaps he was investing in the performance, and had wished to ascertain for himself the promise of a substantial return on his venture.

She had no doubt that such, or something much like it, was the explanation for the episode. Too, in retrospect, her momentary fear that the beasts might actually be intelligent creatures, and in communication with their masters, was dismissed, as an illusion of the contretemps, and her fear. Beasts did not speak, save perhaps such as she.

Why had she followed Mirus?

Well, she had not seen him in a long time, and she was curious. Too, it had been in his house that she had been branded and collared. A woman is not likely to forget such things.

Too, had it not been his whip that she had first felt as a slave? Certainly no slave is likely to forget her first whipping.

But certainly her "thighs did not steam for him," and the mere sight of him did not "lubricate her for the mastery," nor had she followed him "like a she-sleen in heat"! No! Never! That was absurd!

"Lying little slave girl," she said to herself. "Your thighs steam for any man, and the sight of any virile male lubricates you for the mastery. And if you are not like a sinuous she-sleen in heat, it is rather because you are more like a sleek, curvaceous little she-urt in heat! You are a meaningless little slut in whose belly have been kindled slave fires!"

"I hate you, Mirus," she said to herself. "You have called me plain and stupid, and I am neither. I am so sorry that you tired of me! What a disappointment for you, that you made so little money on me! I was not interesting enough for you to have at your feet! You let me go! You rejected me!" But then she said to herself, "But we are both of Earth. You extricated me from amongst the men and beasts at the tent, who might otherwise, in their impatience, have subjected me to the whip or bastinado. And you have not had me summoned to a dancing circle, knowing what that might mean for me. Perhaps you have some sympathy, if not affection, or desire, or lust, for a fellow Earthling, one now in categorical bondage, one who is now no more than I am, a legal animal, a property, on another world. You then, somehow, have at least that much consideration for me. For that I thank you, you who are known here as Mirus of Ar."

"Turn, face me," said a man.

"Yes, Master," said Ellen. "Wine, Master?"

He was looking at her left beast.

"Follow me," he said.

"But I am to serve," said Ellen.

"No," said he. "You will follow me."

He turned about and Ellen followed him. He led their way past the wine vat of Callimachus, and indicated that she should discharge the residue of her pitcher's wine into the vat, which she did. She then, at a gesture, put the pitcher on the bench, beside two others.

"Master?" asked Ellen. But already he was threading his way through the crowd, and the fires. Swiftly she fell into place behind him, heeling him, behind his left shoulder, but, given the press of the crowd, much more closely than would normally be the case. A slave girl's heeling distance is a function of a particular situation, of local circumstances, so to speak. In an open area a girl will normally heel three to five paces behind, normally on the left. Whereas following on the left, which is usual, may be a simple matter of gratuitous custom, it might also be noted that this arrangement may have a darker origin. If objects are to be handed to a man, say, a warrior, such as a buckler, or barbed war net, this transfer of articles from the left is not likely to discommode or encumber the most common weapon hand which is, of course, the right. On the other hand, it is thought that following on the left is generally a position of less dignity, and thus appropriate for animals, including slaves. A consideration favoring this possibility is that left-handed Goreans will also, commonly, have their sleen, their slaves, and such, follow on the left. A free woman walks proudly beside a free man or, if the press does not permit this, is often accorded the privilege of preceding him. One of the most humiliating things for a Gorean free woman, after she has been enslaved, other than the loss of her name, is that she must now follow, and neither walk beside nor lead. To be sure, the tunic, the brand and collar are also instructive.

"May I speak, Master?" asked Ellen, struggling to follow him, he moving so swiftly through the crowd.

"If you wish," he said.

"Whither bound are we?" she asked.

He turned about, looked at her, how small she felt before him, and put his hand in her hair, and then put her head, held by the hair, at his hip, in leading position.

Her face was at the coarse wool of his tunic.

"The ba-ta dancing circle," he said.

"No, Master!" she cried. "There is a terrible mistake. I am not a dancer!"

"Ai!" she cried, in pain, drawn along, at his hip.

"Do not lie, slut," said he. "Only the finest dancers are summoned to the first two circles, the al-ka and ba-ta circles."

"Please let me go, Master!" wept Ellen. "It is a mistake, a terrible mistake! I am not even a dancer! Ai! Ai!"

She had heard of the al-ka and ba-ta circles, named for the first two letters in the Gorean alphabet. They were not like most of the other circles, which were in the open, where naked slaves swayed to distant music for the delectation of masters. The al-ka and ba-ta circles were enclosed, surrounded by walls of silk, held on poles. Men had to pay a fee to enter, for within those confines they were to be treated to the finest exponents of the intricacies of slave dance. Similarly reserved, but for less skilled dancers, were the gamma and delka circles. In these first four circles the dancers were even clothed, that their beauties, if but ill-concealed, might be cunningly enhanced. Each of these circles had its own group of musicians. In the open circles, if a girl was displeasing, which few were, for only dancers were permitted in them, she might be merely hooted from the sand, or pelted with garbage, or perhaps dragged to the side and cuffed, but in the silken circles there were whip masters. Their function it was to see to it that, if not the finest, the most stimulating, the most gratifying, of performances would be elicited from their silked, bangled charges, then there would be elicited from them at least performances which, perhaps to the lash of the whip, would bring howls of pleasure from the drunken, lustful brutes who had crowded into the enclosure, determined to have recompense a thousandfold for the bit of copper with which they had purchased their ostraka of admission.

"Please, no, Master!" wept Ellen. "It is a mistake! I am not a dancer! I am not a dancer! Please, no, Master!"

But he drew her rapidly, mercilessly, through the crowds, she in tears, stumbling, painfully bent over, held in common leading position, her head at his hip, his hand cruelly twisted in her hair.

* * * *

"Here are silks, and veils," said a whip master. "There, in the chests, are bells, anklets, armlets, bracelets. Adorn yourself, girl. Cosmetics, too! There! Apply them swiftly. Kneel there, before the cosmetics tables. Hurry! The performance is soon to begin!"

Ellen was now within a small, silken enclosure, separated from the dancing area, but adjacent to it. She could see the men outside through a parting in the silken curtain. There were eight or nine girls of exceeding loveliness within.

"Master," begged Ellen, going to her knees before the whip master, "I am not a dancer!"

Two or three of the other girls turned to look at her. Others were intent on preparing for their summonses to the sand, adjusting their costumes, some tying cords of bells about their ankles, others having others tie such cords of bells about their wrists, regarding themselves in the mirrors, considering their makeup. Ellen heard a rustle of bells as one of the dancers stood and moved. Ellen had not understood that a woman could move so sensuously.

She had heard numbers called throughout the camp, with the associated letters of the circles. On her way to the circle she had heard her number called more than once, announcing that she would be danced, and in the ba-ta circle. She had little doubt but what several of those who had made bids on her might then attend the performance, curious to gather further data on a commodity of possible interest. She had not been advertised as a dancer, of course. And she had not been put in an exhibition cage with dancers. When her attributes had been recorded, her height, weight, measurements, identifying marks, collar size, languages, literacy, skills and such, she had been asked about dancing but she had, of course, responded negatively. And now she found herself, to her misery, waiting outside the ba-ta circle!

"Master!" begged Ellen.

"Be silent, slave," snarled the whip master. "You would not be here if you were not a superb dancer. This is the ba-ta circle."

"It is a mistake, Master!" protested Ellen.

He looked at her left breast. "You are 117—Ellen—are you not?" he asked.

"Yes, Master," sobbed Ellen.

"Let us see," he said. He turned to one of the poles supporting the silk of the small enclosure. A list was attached to this pole, tacked there, a little above eye level. "Yes, it is here," he said. "117—Ellen. You are here on the list, added at the end. Ah, you must be good, very good. You are to dance last."

"No, no, Master!"

"Prepare yourself, slave girl," he said.

Moaning, Ellen looked down at the silks which lay at her knees, cast before her by the whip master.

"Hurry!" said the whip master.

Men began to shout impatiently outside.

There was a skirl of music from the musicians outside, to one side of the sand, flutes, czehars, two kalikas, a tabor.

Men shouted in eagerness.

"Ita, are you ready?" asked the whip master. This was the second whip master, he who had his post within the preparation enclosure. The first whip master was outside, and would supervise the actual performances.

"Yes, Master," she responded.

"Go," she was told, and she hastened out through the parting of the silk, onto the sand. There was a raucous cry of pleasure from the crowd. The sand was lit with the light of torches.

Ellen reached into the chest for a bracelet, but another girl seized it before her. "That is mine!" she hissed.

"Forgive me," said Ellen, kneeling, dropping back on her heels, tears running down her cheeks.

"Barbarian," said the girl.

"Yes, Mistress," said Ellen.

Slaves, of course, owned nothing. The materials in the chest were for the use of all the dancers. But Ellen did not want to be scratched or bitten, or thrown to the rug within the enclosure and have her hair torn from her head. The other girl was larger than she.

Ellen then put her head in her hands, and wept.

"What is wrong?" asked one of the dancers.

"I do not even know how to put on silks and veils," wept Ellen, red-eyed.

"I will help you," said the girl.

"Mistress!" said Ellen, gratefully.

"I am not "Mistress,"" said the girl. " I am Feike." She lifted a swirling skirt of diaphanous dancing silk, scarlet, and shook it out.

"I am not a dancer," said Ellen.

"Surely you have had some training," said the girl. "That is common in most houses."

"No!" wept Ellen.

"But surely you have seen such dance?" she said.

"A little," said Ellen. "But then I was beaten, and not permitted to watch."

"Why was that?" she asked.

"I was to be kept ignorant," she said, "that I would be a low slave, a cheaper slave, a poorer slave, at best no more than the lowest of kettle-and-mat girls."

"Your master must have hated you very much," she said.

"I was sold for ten copper tarsks," said Ellen.

"That is hard to believe," said the girl. "You are quite pretty."

Tears sprang anew to Ellen's eyes.

"Do your best," said the girl.

"I do not know what to do," said Ellen.

"Stand," said the girl.

Ellen regarded the dancing silk. She gasped. In it she felt she might be more naked than naked.

"There," said the girl.

"I do not know what to do!" wept Ellen.

"Be a slave," said the girl, absently. "Good. There. That is pretty. We want your left leg to show, your brand leg. You have lovely legs. Yes, you are pretty, very pretty."

Ellen smiled, weakly, in gratitude.

"Lift your arms," said the girl.

"Good," said the girl. Ellen's breasts were now closely haltered, in scarlet silk.

Feike then dug about in the chest, and found some bells, on their thongs, an armlet, several bracelets. Before the mirror Ellen found herself, bit by bit, undergoing a remarkable, exotic, barbaric transformation.

"Do you know veil work?" asked Feike.

"No," said Ellen. "No."

"Do your best," said Feike. "Each of us is a different slave. Each of us is unique. Each of us is precious, no matter what the beasts say. Certainly they bid hard enough to own us, they fight wars to possess us, they risk their lives to steal us, they fight for us, they kill for us, do not let them tell you you are not important and valuable! Each of us is different, and special. Each must try to be the slave she is, not another slave, but the slave she is, the deepest and most profound slave, which is her deepest self. Remember, there is no other slave such as I, and there is no other slave such as you."

"Adele, Lois!" called the interior whip master.

Two slaves looked at him, frightened, nodding.

Those were Earth names, Ellen realized. To be sure, she did not know if the slaves were from Earth or not. She supposed not. Earth names, she had learned, were understood on Gor as slave names. So it was not that unusual to find such names worn by Gorean slaves. Another example, Ellen realized, was 'Ellen'. Adele was then called forth onto the sand. Ita returned, flushed, covered with sweat, and sank down on the rug, trying to regain her breath. Each of the girls would dance, three times, in order. Costumes and jewelry might be changed. Ellen saw Adele out on the sand, through the narrow parting in the silk.

"She is beautiful," whispered Ellen to Feike.

"Yes," said Feike.

"I am a barbarian," said Ellen.

"That is obvious," said Feike.

"Are Adele and Lois?" asked Ellen.

"No," said Feike.

"What of the others?" asked Ellen.

"No," said Feike. "We must comb your hair. There is a broken comb there. Kneel down, facing away from me. Then we must hurry with the cosmetics."

Ellen knelt down, facing away from Feike. The hair of slaves is usually combed while they are kneeling. Interestingly, masters often comb the hair of their slaves, grooming them. Masters seem to enjoy this, and the slaves, too, tend to relish it, the intimacy and such, though the slave understands that she is being groomed, as her master's animal, much as might be a kaiila or pet sleen. Sometimes masters wash their slaves, as well, much as a dog might be washed on Earth. This is sometimes done before slave exhibitions, or competitions. Sometimes it is done for the simple pleasure of it. Sometimes the slave is washed while bound, say, with her hands tied behind her. It is difficult to convey the psychological impact of this on a woman, say, standing, kneeling or sitting in a shallow wooden tub, perhaps out of doors, pinioned, while her body is being carefully and thoroughly washed by a man. She certainly understands herself slave in such a situation. Sometimes the master so arouses the slave in this situation that she crawls to him on the grass, untoweled, her body glistening, still wet, begging to serve his pleasure. Ultimately, of course, the slave is responsible for her own appearance, cleanliness and such. She must keep herself clean, neat and attractive. The carelessness or slovenliness of a free woman is not permitted to her. Laxity in such matters is a cause for discipline. Needless to say, the diet, rest and exercise of a slave are also carefully supervised.

Ellen moaned.

Then, thought Ellen, I will be the only Earth woman here tonight to dance in this circle before these men. I am so frightened! I am only from

Earth. These men, these Goreans, these brutes, are so different from the men of my world. They are frighteningly, gloriously different! They are not mindlessly amiable and forgiving. They know what they want and will have it. Certainly they will have it from me, and from any slave! They are severe and demanding. And I must obey! They are innocently possessive, powerful, ambitious, uncompromising. Honor and loyalty inform their *ethos*. How different from Earth! They refuse to be confused, tricked, crippled, tamed, enfeebled! They think in terms of things and realities, not words. They are the sorts who could see through the bombardments of gaudy rhetorics, unmasking pathological agendas. They are acute, sometimes brilliant, passionate, unconquered men, men who are close to nature, who know her, and believe in her, and will not leave her side, men who have never forgotten what women are for, and what is to be done with them.

And I am a woman, thought Ellen, and here on their world, not mine. And I am to dance before them, such men. Nothing on Earth has prepared me for this.

"Yes, you are very pretty," said Feike.

"Thank you," said Ellen.

"Are you frightened?"

"Yes," said Ellen.

"I understand," said Feike.

Ellen was silent.

Feike combed Ellen's hair, with long, deep strokes.

"It is said," said Feike, smiling, "that no barbarian knows how to please a man."

"That is not true!" said Ellen.

"Good," said Feike. "Show them."

Ellen bit her lip.

She was miserable.

How could this have happened to her? She was a woman of Earth! She had been plucked from civilization, as it had been understood by her former peers, plucked from a busy, complex, crowded, polluted, industrial society, and set down in a very different world, in a fresh, green, natural, primitive world. And here, on this world, she, a woman of Earth, a woman of education and sophistication, that behind her now, would soon be thrust through silken curtains, sent to torchlit sand, to dance barefoot, belled, silked and bangled, as no more than an adorned slave before barbarians!

I am from Earth, she thought, in misery. I will never be able to please them.

"Lois," said the interior whip master, and, as Adele returned, her head thrown back, gasping, but obviously delighted, Lois hurried through the silk, onto the sand.

Ellen clutched the veil about her, shawl-like.

"Face me," said Feike.

The two girls knelt facing one another, and Feike, having recourse to the tiny pans and dishes, and the pencil-like applicators on the low cosmetics table, applied her skills to the countenance of the barbarian.

"Purse your lips," said Feike, "hold still."

"Yes, Mistress," smiled Ellen.

Feike laughed.

"Feike!" snapped the whip master.

"Done!" said Feike. "Look in the mirror! See a slave!"

Feike then stood up and lifted her arms, took a deep breath, and twirled, and stamped her feet twice into the rug.

There was a jangle of slave bells.

"Thank you, Feike!" said Ellen, looking up, and then, as Feike rushed through the silk, Lois returning, Ellen turned to look in the mirror.

She gasped.

"Stand slave, face me," said the interior whip master.

Ellen complied, frightened. How could she stand to have a man see her as she now was?

"Excellent," said the man.

Ellen sank down to her knees, not daring to look again into the mirror.

"If I had my way," said the man, "that is the way they would be sold off the block, at least to begin with. They could be stripped, bit by bit, during the sale, until the buyers have no difficulty seeing what they are paying for. It is too bad that they do not permit cosmetics, eye shadow, lipstick, body paint, and such, on the block. We would get a great deal more for you sluts." Ellen had been sold from the shelf of Targo without the benefit of cosmetics, of course. And she had understood that, whereas it was not unusual to strip a woman, little by little, during her sale, to increase the heat of the bids, that the slaves were always, when all was said and done, exhibited as only slave, raw. Goreans want to know what they are buying. An auction house in Venna was once burned down, she had heard, when it was discovered that it had sold women with dyed hair, especially as the house had not called this to the attention of the buyers. In the courts the owner's claim of inadvertence was viewed skeptically. Considering the number of slaves to be vended over the next two or three days in the camp, Ellen did not think the agents of Cos would have time for the tantalizing allures of gradual unveilings. Such luxuries in any event were usually reserved for the sales of high slaves.

"You are lovely," said one of the girls, who had not noticed her before.

"Thank you," murmured Ellen.

"Do you dance in the manner of Turia, or of Ar?" asked another of the slaves.

"I do not think so," said Ellen.

"Perhaps," said another, "in the manner of Schendi, or of the Tahari?"

"I cannot even dance!" said Ellen, suddenly.

"Oh, yes!" laughed one of the dancers, merrily.

The others looked at her, strangely, and then turned away.

"It is very crowded," whispered one of the girls, peeping through the curtain.

Ellen rose to her feet, and suddenly stopped, frightened by the sound of bells on her left ankle. It was the first time since her training that she had worn such things. There was no mistaking the meaning, the message, of that sensuous jangle. It was stimulatory, and insistently, proclaimedly, excitingly erotic. Some masters keep their slaves in bells in their private compartments. Others may bell them sometimes before putting them to the furs, enjoying the jangle of the bells while the slave writhes helplessly, beggingly, in the throes of her slave ecstasy. The bells bespeak, and would bespeak, of course, even in total darkness, the presence of a slave. Sometimes new slaves are kept for a time in bells, that they may become all the sooner accustomed to their new condition. It is hard to be belled, without knowing oneself female, and slave. Ellen, thus, was well marked for the occasion, and the dance. She was a belled slave.

Then she, too, her movements marked by the sound of her affixed slave bells, went to the curtain.

Feike was lovely.

If only I could dance, thought Ellen, mournfully, to herself.

She could not see the outside whip master, but she had no doubt that he was there, appraisingly there, ready to snap the whip in warning, or, if necessary, or thought useful, to put it to the back of a dancer.

Ellen examined the crowd, desperately. There were many men there, perhaps better than two hundred, crowded within that rather small enclosure. In the front, in several half circles, they sat, closely together, cross-legged. In the back, they stood, some at the very poles at the rear of the enclosure. There was a variety of caste colors. Some soldiers were there, too. Many ostraka had been vended. There were no women in the crowd. Any gentling, refining influence which their presence might have exercised was thus absent. The slaves would thus be dancing for men, for Gorean men. Some of the men in the crowd she had seen before, here and there in the camp. She had served some of them near the vat of Callimachus. She saw the scribe who had been in charge of her in the exhibition cage. She did not see Mirus. "So," she thought, "he has put me here, to be humiliated, and beaten, here where I will be exquisitely punished for my boldness before him, in daring to suggest that he might find me of interest, slave interest! And he further insults me by his absence! He does not even come to see me perform, and painfully receive the deserts he has measured out and arranged for me, as punishment for my supposed insolence. Well, noble Mirus, *of Earth*, so be it! But I think you do find this Earth slut of interest, regardless of what you might claim! Do you think a slave is not aware of the meaning of a master's glances?"

Ellen stepped back.

Feike, smiling, sweating, breathing deeply, brushed back through the silk, and another slave, at a gesture of the interior whip master, hurried to the sand.

I can only be beaten so much, thought Ellen. And I do not think they will kill me. And as each is to dance thrice, it is not as though they will feel particularly cheated, for after me will come Ita once again, who is a fine dancer. They will then see that it was a joke that I be sent to the circle. I will then be drawn from the roster, beaten, and permitted, I trust, to return to the vat of Callimachus. That is what will happen. I did not ask to come to the circle. They cannot blame me. I warned them. Perhaps they will be merely amused at the clever jest. Too, a girl from another circle, say, one of the free circles, might be hurried here to take my place.

But I am frightened, terribly frightened, she told herself.

Girl after girl went to the sand and returned.

Ellen felt she could scarcely move. She was tempted to run, to try to leave the enclosure by the back entrance, through which she had been introduced into it. After all, she was not chained there, one of a set of kneeling dancing slaves, to be released, one after the other, from a shackle, to be returned to its obdurate clasp when her performance was concluded.

She looked to the back entrance, wildly.

"117, be ready," said the interior whip master.

Ellen knew there was no escape for her. For the Gorean slave girl there is no escape.

"Yes, Master," said Ellen.

The opening seemed inviting, seemingly beckoning her to flee into an alluring, salubrious, safely concealing darkness beyond, but for all the good it would have done her, it might as well have been sealed with granite and iron. She might as well have been chained hand and foot, and neck, to a heavy ring fixed in the bottom of a narrow, cement, well-like slave pit, looking up at the iron grating yards above her head.

But there was time. The other girl had scarcely begun to dance.

Then there was, from outside on the sand, the sudden sound of a snapping whip. Ellen started. It was not only that the sound was unexpected, and sharp, but that its significance carried a special meaning for such as she, a slave.

Outside there was some hooting, some angry cries of men.

Then, only a moment or two later, she heard the whip again, twice, and this time cries of pain, doubtless from the exhibited dancer.

In a moment, clutching her silk about her, it parted by the whip, crying, the chastised dancer fled within the preparation enclosure. It was she who had appropriated the bracelet from Ellen, and it was still on her wrist. "It serves you right, arrogant slave girl," thought Ellen. "Now you are not so proud!" The woman knelt on the rug within the small enclosure, bent over, holding her arms about herself, weeping bitterly. There was blood on her back. She looked up at Ellen for an instant, and then looked down, miserably. No longer was she proud and beautiful. Now she was only a whipped slave. "Next time, 51, Dara," said the interior whip master, "you will dance better." He held his whip down and she fled to it on her knees and kissed it, and then put her head down, kissing his sandals. "Yes, Master," she sobbed. "Yes, Master!"

"51," thought, Ellen. "Such a high number! To be sure, she is so beautiful! What would she have done wrong? Perhaps she had been overconfident. Perhaps she had thought herself too good to be danced in this place, before such men. Perhaps she had not given her best performance? Perhaps she had held something back?"

The men were shouting angrily outside.

The interior whip master looked up from the beautiful penitent slave at his feet, as though suddenly coming to his senses. "117!" he cried. "Out, little fool, onto the sand!"

With one last look at the beaten slave, and with terror and a sinking heart, and a jangle of slave bells, Ellen, clutching her veil about her silks, rushed abjectly through the curtain and half stumbled to the sand outside.

There was a sound of interest, and laughter, from the men, and then they were expectant, quiet.

Ellen realized, suddenly, that it had not occurred to them to take her clumsiness at its face value. This was the ba-ta circle. Surely it was intentional on her part. Slave girls are not clumsy, certainly not after they have learned their collars. They are the most vulnerable, feminine and graceful of women, for they are owned, for they belong to men, and dancers, of course, are also slave girls and thus, and certainly given their special training, will presumably be in no way inferior to their more common sisters in bondage. As an incidental observation, it is interesting to note that the grace of the dancer, though, of course, not the special training of the dancer, is expected of all slave girls, and most certainly of those who like Ellen must kneel before men in the spread-kneed position, that is, the pleasure slaves.

Ellen knelt then in the sand and put her head down to the sand, that it might be clear to all that she was a slave and acknowledged them her masters.

She wanted them to be in no doubt about that.

How well and perfectly she knew herself the slave of men!

It was what she was, and knew herself to be!

I am yours, Masters, she thought to herself.

I am that sort of woman, she who is, and knows herself to be, a man's slave, only that!

Please do not beat me!

Then she rose to her feet and put her veil about her head, wrapping it closely about her head and shoulders, concealing even her face. It was much as though she might be a free woman, though surely the bells on her ankle and her silks belied that possibility. She then walked about the dancing area, erect, proudly, gracefully, but keeping herself concealed.

To be sure, her feet were bare, and there were bells on her left ankle. This created, to the Gorean thinking, a paradox.

She was sure she was beautiful, and that the men, who had glimpsed her for an instant when she entered upon the sand, had seen that, but only for a tantalizing moment. Her beauty, she hoped, might save her, compensating to a significant extent for her ignorance of slave dance. To be sure, she had seen the women moving in the circles. She could not control her body with the subtlety they manifested, but she could see some of the simpler things they did, and she had some sense of what it might be to yield to such music, to obey it, to surrender herself to it, abjectly, as an aroused, commanded slave.

She walked about the circle once more, the veil closely about her, concealing even her features.

The whip master, whom she noted with care, seemed puzzled, but tolerant. Certainly his hand was not clutched menacingly upon his whip, the coiled blade of which, visibly, bore stains of blood, that of her humbled predecessor. The first czehar player, in whose charge were the musicians, appeared puzzled as well, but continued to elicit from his instrument, held across his knees, subtle melodies which sang of life and nature, which hinted of men and women, and masters and slaves. The music followed Ellen, quietly, expectantly, enhancing her contrived mystery.

Then, suddenly, Ellen, without permission, turned about and gracefully, regally, and with a toss of her head, exited the sand, going through the parting of the silk to the preparation enclosure.

There was silence behind her.

The other dancers were awaiting her, many wide-eyed and frightened.

"I do not understand," said Feike. "What are you doing?"

"Being a slave," said Ellen.

Suddenly, from outside the preparation enclosure, there were shouts of pleasure, and the smiting of the left shoulder, in Gorean applause.

"Ita," cried the interior whip master, "to the sand!"

Ita hurried through the parting in the silk.

"What were you doing?" asked the interior whip master of Ellen.

"Dancing," she said.

"That is not dancing," he said.

"There is more than one way to dance, Master," said Ellen. And, as she knelt down by the cosmetics table, she thought to herself, "I have not yet been beaten. But what shall I do now? Surely I am no more than the width of a strand of slave silk from the blows of the lash."

The second time the beaten slave, 51, Dara, had apparently danced well. She had not been permitted to change her silks, and they were parted in the back, where the whip had cut through them. In her dance she had piteously, and abjectly, made it clear to the masters that not only did she now respect them, but that she was now pathetically concerned to subject herself to their pleasure, even as though she were their own slave. Gone was now any arrogance or haughtiness. Gone now was any suggestion that she might be too good to dance for such as they. Now it was clear that she was only a humbled, punished slave who had well learned her lesson. She danced now as a grateful slave who was inordinately privileged to, and profoundly grateful for the opportunity to, be granted permission to perform for them, for those who were a thousand times, nay, immeasurably, above her. She even incorporated into her dance, turning away from the crowd, the stripes upon her back, exhibiting them, where the admonitions of the whip had recalled her to a clearer sense of her position and condition. Ellen was, on the whole, pleased that 51, she called 'Dara', had not been again displeasing, and had not been again subjected to the typical Gorean consequences attendant upon the least lapse into slave laxity, but, on the other hand, she realized that she herself would now find herself contrasted not with a slave who had failed to please masters but with one who had been only too obviously pleasing. Given the Gorean applause, the striking of the left shoulder, the callings out of the men, Ellen supposed that Dara, upon returning to the area of preparation area, would be flushed with insolent triumph. On the other hand, when she returned, she seemed white-faced, and shaken, and grateful that this time things had gone as well as they had.

"117, Ellen," said the interior whip master.

"A moment, Master!" said Ellen. "Let them wait an instant! It is important!"

On an impulse Ellen addressed Dara. "Slave girl," she said, sharply.

Dara looked at her, frightened. No longer was she the insolent slave who had seized the bracelet from her.

"Mistress?" said Dara, quickly, before she had thought.

"When you dance again," said Ellen, "feature the bracelet you wear on your left wrist. Call attention to it! See that it is well noticed!"

Dara, frightened, went to remove it from her wrist.

"No," said Ellen. "Wear it when you dance next. See that it is recognized!"

Dara cast a frightened glance at the interior whip master. "Do it," he said, though doubtless he was as puzzled as she.

Ellen then thrust the armlets and bracelets from her own limbs.

Dara had sunk to her knees within the area of preparation, partly in misery, partly in confusion, partly in relief. Ellen bent down, quickly, and kissed her. "Thank you," said Ellen. Dara looked up at her, bewildered. It was no longer clear to her where she stood amongst the slaves in the tent. Presumably, before Ellen's addition to the list, she had been the last dancer, and thus, putatively, the best, for the best is often saved for the last. Perhaps that is why, at least in part, she had danced as she had the first time on the sand, because she was angered at having been unexpectedly supplanted in the favored position of last dancer. But then she had been whipped, and upon her return to the area of preparation after her second dancing, Ellen, a mere barbarian, who had seemingly supplanted her in the favored position, had spoken sharply to her, a liberty which might have been authorized, as far as she knew, by the interior whip master.

"Out, surely out onto the sand!" said the interior whip master to Ellen, uncertain, half in exasperation.

"Yes, Master!" said Ellen, and hurried out through the silk, onto the sand.

The first time Ellen had barely shown herself to the men, keeping herself concealed in veils, and had done little more, after her initial, clear and unmistakable acknowledgment of her abject bondage before them, that they would have no doubt as to what she was and how she understood herself, than move about the sand with a certain cold, superior, lofty, regal pride, moving serenely, insolently, about, as a smug, self-satisfied free woman, doubtless of high caste, one secure in her status, one fully assured of her importance and station. She had then, with a toss of her veiled head, returned to the area of preparation.

It was a different Ellen who appeared this time upon the sand, one who seemed uncertain, and frightened.

With her own hands, but, it seemed, as though with the hands of another, she drew her veil about, drawing it to one side and then the other, this providing a glimpse, then again they concealed, of her features. It was as though two or three men, unseen, might be tearing at the concealment, she fighting them, she trying to restore it. Then, as she spun in the sand, to the music, she unwound the veil and put it down about her shoulders. She threw her head back as though in anguish, in misery and protest, but her features were bared to the men. It seemed then she had undergone one of the most dreaded fates of a high-caste Gorean free woman. Her face was publicly bared! She was face-stripped! Her face was naked! Her face, with all its beauty, with all its readable, betraying, exquisite and subtle expressiveness, with all it would tell about her inner life, about her emotions, her feelings, her interests, fears, hopes, pleasures and concerns, had been publicly revealed; it had been bared; it was naked, stark naked; it was now as that of a slave. One of the interesting things from the Gorean point of view about most of the women of Earth is that they do not veil themselves; most go about, even in public, with bared features. This tends to be incomprehensible to the average Gorean. On Gor, on the other hand, as you have doubtless by now gathered, this omission, or this practice, that of not wearing the veil, is common with, and, indeed, is usually imposed upon, and in many cities by law, slaves. Such are commonly denied the veil, as they are other garments of free women. Indeed, the donning of the garments of a free woman by a slave can be a capital offense. The failure of most women of Earth to veil themselves is regarded as shameless. It is one of several reasons, such as the failure to speak Gorean, which tends to make Goreans regard Earth females as barbarians, as natural slaves, as slave stock. Going about so brazenly, is it not their intention to offer themselves for the scrutiny of slavers; is it not a way to court the collar, to beg for it? Certainly Gorean slavers on Earth are grateful for the custom, as it considerably facilitates their assessment of the slave wares of Earth.

As Ellen had with the veiling of her features, so now it seemed that she struggled with her implicit, but unseen, assailants, to cling to the veil, held so tightly about her shoulders and body. Who could be tearing her veil away from her body? Could these be invisible assailants, of some powerful, but uncertain nature, or were they her own needs determined despite her conscious will to have their way with her, to reduce her brutishly, ruthlessly, to the denied, but beloved core of her being, or might they be the unseen hands of any there, of any within that crowded, silken enclosure, who were determined to see that she became a woman?

Bit by bit, to the music, writhing, turning, twisting, resisting, sometimes winning, sometimes losing, she fought with the veil, and then lost, the veil behind her, in the sand, and she was before them as a silked, belled slave, in swirling skirt, open on the left, with high-haltered breasts, and encircling necklaces. It seemed she fled then about the circle, running here and there, sometimes coming close to the men, who sometimes reached for her, sometimes drawing back, as in fear. She seemed in consternation, frantic, as though she would turn this way and that to escape, but found always her way barred. In this it was made clear to all, by gestures and displays, though unobtrusively, by subtly drawing attention to the matter, that her arms and wrists were bare. At the time most of the men probably did not notice this, but would presumably be aware of it on some level, and would recall it later.

Then suddenly on the sand, she stopped, near its center, and looked out, toward the crowd. The music stopped with her. She took a step backward, and then another step. And the czehar player underlined these steps. Her lip trembled. She put forth her hand, as though to fend away someone who was approaching her. Then she seemed to watch someone approach her on her left, and seemed too terrified, or exhausted, to run. Then she hunched her left shoulder up and looked to her upper left arm in horror, as though it might have been grasped. She looked with dismay, and fear, it seemed, to some unseen captor.

Then swiftly, to music, it seemed she was turned about, fiercely, and then, as she stood still, yet seeming to resist in place, it seemed that her hands, wrists crossed, were lifted up behind her, to the small of her back. They then stayed there. She struggled to free them, but could not. She looked back over her shoulder in fear, as though at an imperious, ferocious captor. Then it seemed she was thrust stumbling, back-braceleted, toward the parting in the silk that led to the area of preparation, and, in an instant, disappeared within.

There was a pause, as though that rude, bestial gathering was for a moment taken aback by what it had witnessed, and then there began a steady, increasing flow of applause. Men cried out with pleasure, and Ellen, gasping, and frightened, within the silken enclosure, trembled, for she well knew the accents of lustful masters and that such as she, the embonded woman, was the object societally designated for the satisfaction of their most profound needs. Such men would not rage in frustration on Gor; they would not starve on Gor; the civilization in its foresight, understanding, wisdom and benevolence had provided such as she for their service, satisfaction, and delectation.

Women such as she existed for men.

They were captured, and stolen, and bought and sold, and exchanged, and traded, for the pleasure of men.

They were not free women; they were something quite different; they were slaves.

The female slave is a property, commonly purchased for, and certainly mastered for, the requirements, even caprices, of men.

The very *raison d'être* of the female slave, that form of item and article, of object and possession, that form of luscious, living merchandise, is the service and pleasure of men.

"I do not understand, Mistress," said Dara, when Ellen returned. "Are you dancing?"

"I do not know," said Ellen. "And do not call me "Mistress.""

"Yes, Mistress," whispered Dara.

Ellen saw that the interior whip master was regarding her. He seemed puzzled, if not bewildered. Ellen put her head down. One must be careful about meeting the eyes of a free man.

Then Ita was again through the parting in the silk, and again danced, again eliciting cries of pleasure from the crowd, again proving her right to perform as a slave before masters, even in so high a circle as the ba-ta circle.

"I do not know what you are doing," said Feike.

"I am following your suggestion, to be a slave, Mistress," said Ellen.

"You are a slave," said Feike, smiling.

"Yes, Mistress," smiled Ellen.

"Then continue to be a slave," said Feike.

"Yes, Mistress," said Ellen.

As Ellen knelt on the rug inside the area of preparation, waiting, while the other girls danced, she thought of how far away, how remote, so many things seemed. Her life on Earth seemed so far away. It seemed to be dim, distant, faint, intangible, gray, and dull. It almost seemed unreal. Had it been real? Had it truly taken place? Had she once been there, actually lived there, in such a place? Could it be? She listened to the music outside the area of preparation, the cries of the men. "What was there, in that world," she wondered, "to compare with even the light wisp of silk I feel upon my thighs, with the bells knotted about my left ankle?"

Dara thrust back through the parting in the silk. Behind her there was a storm of applause. She had done well. She sank to her knees, gratefully. For the time she need not fear the leather. Dara was beautiful. Her number was 51, a very low number. It was not for nothing, Ellen surmised, that Dara had been originally scheduled as the last dancer. Doubtless lovely Dara would bring a high price on the block, being valued not only for her skills as a dancer, but for her obvious possibilities as a common pleasure slave.

Ellen did not wish to delay this time on her return to the sand.

"The bracelet, quickly!" she said to Dara.

Ellen had spoken in the voice of a mistress and Dara, startled, responded instantly as a slave, slipping the bracelet from her wrist, putting her head down and lifting it to Ellen.

"Thank you," said Ellen, and then she hurriedly slipped the bracelet on her left wrist, gave Dara a quick kiss, and hurried out onto the sand.

She knew she was the last dancer of the evening, at least in this circle.

She pretended to stumble out upon the sand, to a point a bit behind its center. It was rather as she had done at first, but this time it was deliberate. She wanted her movements to seem uncertain, frightened.

She turned about, to the music, and then lifted her left wrist, looking upon it, with dismay.

There was an intake of breath in the crowd, a murmur of excitement.

Now, as not in her second appearance, there was a ring of metal on her left wrist. Surely, as she looked upon it, with awe and dismay, it must suggest the bracelet of a slave. It seemed then, given the conclusion of her second appearance on the sand, that she, captured, had been in the interim embonded. Surely her movements suggested those of a new slave, timid, frightened, trying to understand what it would mean to be owned. She then, for the first time in her dance, seemed to notice the bells tied on her left ankle, and the sounds they made. She seemed to cry out in misery and despair, and hardly seemed to move. Surely she must be embonded now, for upon her there were slave bells. But, too, of course, in examining the bells she had revealed her leg, the left leg, the brand leg, through the parting in the swirling skirt of scarlet slave silk. The beauty of this limb was not lost on men accustomed to own women. "Ai, ai!" cried men. She then framed with the fingers of her left and right hand, regarding it, the tiny mark on her left thigh. There was a greater cry of pleasure from the attendant brutes. Surely she was branded, and so she must be now a slave! She seemed not to hear them but to be alone with herself, perhaps in a master's house, or within a walled patio, or pleasure garden. She then put her hands to her throat, as thought she might be feeling there a circlet of bondage. Again men greeted this concern with delight. "Know yourself slave, little slut!" cried a man. She then, with the music, seemed to swirl about as though in incomprehension. It seemed she could not believe what had been done to her! "Slave!" cried a man. "Kiss the whip!" called another. She then, in moving to the music, seemed to first notice, back on the sand, to the left of the parting in the silk, as one would face it, the veil which she had earlier discarded. It had been left there, deliberately. She approached it, moving with the music, frightened. She bent down, reaching her hand toward it. "Beware!" called a man. But then, to the music, turning away, she drew back her hand in fear. She no longer dared touch the veil. Whereas a woman's slave may, and often must, handle the clothing of a free woman, assisting the free woman in her cabinet, and such, she is seldom, if ever, permitted to wear the clothing of a free woman. As I have mentioned, it can be a capital offense for a slave girl to don such garments. When she had drawn her hand back quickly, not daring to touch the discarded veil, there had been applause from the men, who were now, it seemed, muchly drawn into the drama which the lovely slave had been enacting before them. It was clear now, if not in many ways earlier, that the character being portrayed by the dancer now understood herself to be no more than kajira.

She then seemed suddenly to see someone approach. She recoiled with fear, half bent over. She tried to cover herself, as though she might have been stripped. She half turned away. Then, as though ordered, she faced forward, and straightened up, but held out her hands, as though to fend away some individual. Then, as though ordered, she put down her hands and, as with a moan of misery, she knelt, looking up, as though into someone's face. Then it seemed she lifted her hands and received into them an object, which, putting down her head, she kissed, and then, lifting the object, returned it to the unseen master. And doubtless there were few if any men in that audience to whom it did not seem that it was into their hands that the whip was returned.

And thus was the sovereignty of the male, and his command over her, acknowledged by the slave.

She now knelt with the knees closely together. Then, as the music swirled, she apparently protested, and pleaded with the master, regarding him with disbelief and misery, shaking her head piteously, negatively. Then, her supplications obviously unavailing against his sternness, she put down her head and covered her eyes with her hands, as though weeping. And her knees then, slowly, furrowing the sand, widened. Men cheered.

She then uncovered her eyes and her expression had changed dramatically, from tearful protest, to surprise, to awe, to, as though for the first time, a sense of her own sexuality.

She then rose up, as though now an aroused slave. She extended her hands to the master, piteously, now begging, moving her hips and love cradle in mute entreaty, regarding him with wild, startled eyes, beseeching him with her beauty, imploring attention, soliciting, seemingly to her amazement, the touch of a free man, however, casual, on her embonded loveliness. But to her consternation, it seemed he remained adamant. Then, with ever greater desperation, she attempted to stir his interest, to inflame his passion, and as a piteous, now-aroused, begging, needful slave. Whatever might have been the reluctance or severity of her supposed master there was little doubt but what the slave was more than successful with her audience.

Suddenly, to her actual consternation, briefly, until she caught herself, she glimpsed, in the back of the enclosure, near the wall of silk, standing there, back among several other men, his arms folded, Mirus. How long had he been there? Had he seen her earlier appearances? He might have been there, unnoticed. But whatever might have been the case, clearly he was there now.

She cried out wildly in misery that he, Mirus, should see her as she was now, dancing as a slave. How amused must he be! How justified now was all his contempt for her! How could she ever hope to win his respect, now that he had seen her thusly! This was now all she could ever be to him! Never again could he see her as anything but what she now was, something worthless, the most abject and degraded of slaves!

Then suddenly she was furious. You have done this to me, she thought. You have made me like this! Oh, I was always a slave, yes, doubtless, but it was you who forced me to reveal it! You, then, it was who forced me to acknowledge myself, who forced me to show myself as what I truly am! Surely a woman is entitled to this privacy! Surely she is entitled to conceal this truth!

But on Gor, of course, a slave girl is permitted no such thing.

She must be herself, openly, publicly, as innocently and unapologetically as the rhythm of her breathing, the beating of her heart, as innocently and unapologetically as the scar of her brand and the metal of her collar!

Why did you come to see me, she thought, dancing. I am not being beaten! Has your joke, clever master, turned out badly?

I cannot read your expression. It is dark there, and you conceal your feelings well.

I think you do want me, in spite of what you pretend. How long have you been there?

Well, then, see your Ellen! Despise me if you will. I do not care! See her dance, as the slave she is! You sought to destroy her, to reduce and ruin her, but you have succeeded only in giving her the dearest, the most precious and greatest fulfillment a woman can know! I love being what I am, being joyfully, willingly, helplessly, given over wholly to love and service. You put me in chains, and in them I have found the greatest freedom and happiness a woman can know!

Oh, I know my vulnerability, and I fear the bonds of a slave, but I would not have things other than as they are!

Oh, I fear the whip, but I would not be other than subject to it!

So see me dance, Master! See me dance, one you once reduced to bondage, now only another slave, now only another slave before free men!

Ellen had then, in her dance, a sense of her power over men. She saw interest, their fevered wildness, their blazing eyes, their clenched fists, heard their applause, their cries of pleasure. You, Masters, she thought, have the power of strength, and dominance, and weapons, but I, a mere slave, and my lowly sisters, have power as well, the power of our desirability, the power of our beauty!

And our power is not inconsiderable, I assure you!

Who is strongest, I wonder, she asked herself.

Then suddenly it seemed she knew who was strongest for, to her astonishment, she now saw, toward the back of the silk, only a few feet from Mirus, to his left, Selius Arconious!

He, though impecunious, though a simple workman, no more than an ordinary tarnster, was a Gorean master. He was the sort of man, she knew, who could easily, and without thinking, put her in her place and keep her there.

He cannot be here, she said to herself, swaying before the men. He must be in Ar! I do not understand this!

Then tears burst into her eyes.

"I am dancing as a slave!" she thought. "I cannot let him see me in this way! Not in this way!"

She stopped dancing for a moment, confused, but tried not to look at Selius Arconious, lest their eyes meet.

The czehar player looked up, puzzled.

There was a growl from the exterior whip master, and the snap of a whip.

Instantly, frightened, obedient to this warning, she was again a dancing slave.

"Why not?" she asked herself. "Slaves are not permitted to conceal themselves from their masters, in any way. I must be what I am. Gorean masters are not men of Earth! They do not require hypocrisy in women. We must be before them as we truly are. They will have it no other way.

We must be naked before our masters, naked not just in the body, for even a free woman may be stripped, but in every way."

"What are you doing here, Selius Arconious," she wondered. "Are you searching for Portus Canio, for Fel Doron, for Tersius Major? Beware of Tersius Major!"

"Or," she thought wildly, "have you come here following a slave? I trust you have not come here for me, for my number is 117, and you will not be able to afford me! You are the sort of man to whom a woman desires to belly, to whose feet she desires to crawl! You are such that even a free woman might beg to bring you your sandals, crawling naked to you, bearing them humbly in her teeth. How much more then a lowly slave! Or have you come for a girl, but not one such as I? You would have no way of knowing that I was here! Then you have not come for me! Are you surprised to see me here, and to see me as I am, in bells and silk? There is a great sale. Doubtless you have heard of it. Men have come from hundreds of pasangs to buy. Many women will go cheaply. Why did you have to come here, and make me miserable, reminding me of your imperious strength and mastery! I will go to a richer master! I do not think you could afford a girl whose lot number is less than seven or eight hundred. Yet there are many pretty bargains, even at that price!" Tears ran down Ellen's cheeks.

Then, in fury, arrogantly, she danced her beauty to Mirus. Men even turned to look at him, but his expression remained impassive. Ellen saw the scribe who had queried her earlier, in the exhibition cage, and, oddly, momentarily, was frightened. Beside him was a guardsman. Then, with a toss of her head, and a whirl of her hair, she danced toward Selius Arconious. "I will show you what you have lost," she thought. "I will show you, proud, handsome master, what you cannot afford!"

Then, she moved from Selius Arconious to Mirus again, dancing in the sand, regarding him steadily. Conscious of her power, she danced before these two men, first one and then the other, danced before them the arousing beauty of an insolent slave.

None could have her until her sale, she knew.

"Suffer," she thought, "Masters!"

Mirus followed her dancing, and looked carefully upon Selius Arconious, and Selius Arconious, when she danced to Mirus, had little difficulty in detecting the object of the slave's provocative, haughty glances.

"Dance to all, slave girl, or feel the whip!" snarled the exterior whip master.

And Ellen, then, terrified, returned to the character she had created on the sand, and danced her needs to all, piteously inviting the attentions of one after another of the ostraka-possessing patrons of the silken enclosure.

In moments the men again were commending her, with applause, and hearty cries of appreciation.

Ellen, dancing, circumambulated the interior edge of the dancing sand, sometimes closer, almost within an arm's reach of the men, sometimes farther back. The eyes of men glistened. Slave bells jangled. The bracelet was upon her wrist. The music swirled about her.

She was afraid. What if the men were not pleased? What if the exterior whip master was not pleased?

"Exploit your beauty," thought Ellen. "You are very beautiful. You know you are. Use your beauty. Use it! Trust in it to compensate for your lack of training, for your lack of skill, in slave dance. Do not regard Master Mirus or Master Selius! You are a slave girl and can be whipped in an instant. You must perform, even as though they were not here. The men seem pleased. Obey the music! Let it teach you! The resources of the slave girl are limited. What have we to offer, to bargain with, to petition with, but our beauty, our desirability, our intelligence, our passion, our desire to serve and love helplessly and wholly, asking nothing, giving all? I feel the music. It is doing things to me. It is like the thought of being a slave. It is like the thought of being owned. It is like being on your knees, naked, before a man, his. It is like straps and chains, it is like the sight of the whip. You are acting a part, Ellen, only that, the part of an aroused slave girl, dancing her need before strong men, before whom she is nothing, only an animal and slave. Do not forget you are only acting a part. You are only acting a part, aren't you? Please, my body, do not reveal your needs! No! I fear that I am becoming aroused! I must not let this show, certainly not before Masters Mirus and Selius. It is a part I am playing. I must disengage myself from this part. I am acting! I must be only acting! Please, body, be merciful to me!"

But she found herself flushed, and gasping, and holding out her hands to the men. And then in her belly, undeniably, as many times afore, there burned slave fire. Tears came to her eyes. And she and the part, despite her will, became one!

Men cried out.

She did not doubt but what there would now be more than twenty-one bids upon this slave.

In an instant's glimpse she read scorn in the eyes of Mirus. How helpless she was in the throes of her slave needs. Let her yowl in heat like a she-sleen. What did the men mind? The face of Selius Arconious was impassive. Doubtless he had seen the dancing of many desperate, needful slaves, doubtless many more lovely than she.

And she was only an Earth girl, a scion of female slave stock, a barbarian. How could he do other than hold her in contempt?

Then, exhausted, miserable, aroused, tearful, she, in a sudden swirl of music, concluded her dance, hurling herself to the sand, to her left side, her legs drawn up, she on her left elbow, her right hand lifted piteously to the crowd. Then she put her head down, surrendered. It was then the concern of masters whether or not they would deign to summon her, a needful, submitted slave, to their feet.

Quickly then, flushed, in tears, amidst shouting and applause, she sprang to her feet and fled within the area of preparation.

"Out, out, all of you!" commanded the interior whip master, and the dancers emerged once more, all, to the sand, to receive the plaudits of the crowd.

The exterior whip master waved expansively to the musicians who rose and, smiling, bowed their heads briefly to the crowd.

"First obeisance position," said the exterior whip master, and this position was instantly assumed.

Ellen, her head down, then heard small sounds, and the murmur of conversation, as men moved toward the exits of the enclosure.

At least she had not been beaten. She supposed now that she would return her silks and adornments, the bells and such, to the interior of the area of preparation, and return to the vat of Callimachus.

She dared to lift her head a little, but she saw neither Mirus nor Selius Arconious within the enclosure. She did see, this frightening her, and she quickly put down her head, the scribe who had interviewed her in the exhibition cage, and three guardsmen, with him, not one but three, all approaching.

Her apprehensions were much increased when she became aware that they had stopped in her vicinity.

Ellen, trembling, pressed her forehead down into the sand.

"117, Kajira Ellen," said the scribe.

"Yes, Master," said Ellen.

"Dismiss your girls, save this one," said the scribe.

"Return to the area of preparation," said the exterior whip master.

Immediately, with a rustle of bells, and the clinkings of necklaces and bangles, the other slaves hurried to their feet and went into the area of preparation.

"Master?" asked Ellen.

"Strip yourself, completely," said the scribe.

"Yes, Master," said Ellen.

"Help her," said the scribe.

One of the guardsmen undid the halter, behind her back, and pulled it away. One of the other two guardsmen whistled softly. "Nice," he said. Ellen, flushing, lifted aside the necklaces and the bracelet and, embarrassed, though a slave, unhooked the swirling skirt of dancing silk. "The veil, there, Masters," she said. "That was mine to wear, too." In this way she had purchased a moment's modesty. Then the veil was put beside her, and on it were laid the halter, the necklaces and bracelet. She looked up and, meeting the stern eyes of the scribe, lifted away the skirt, folded it, and, head down, placed it, too, beside her.

"Bells," said the scribe.

Ellen sat then in the sand, and drew up her left leg, to attempt to remove the bells. She was at this time naked, save for the bells. Her fingers fumbled. The knots seemed too close, too tight. She struggled, and began to weep.

"On your belly," said the scribe.

One of the guardsmen, then, crouching beside her, bending her leg, lifting it by the ankle, pressing it closely against her body, so closely she whimpered, undid the bells. With a jangle they were flung to the bit of garb and the few adornments beside her. She remained, of course, on her belly, but put her leg down. Her head was turned to the right, her left cheek in the sand.

"Well, little Ellen," said the scribe. "You danced well."

"Thank you, Master," whispered Ellen, frightened.

"But I thought it strange," said the scribe, "when I heard your number called in the camp, summoning you to a dancing circle, and, indeed, one so high as the ba-ta circle. I seemed to recall the number, and, accordingly, as is my wont in such instances, checked my records, which I have with me."

Ellen was silent, lying in the sand, the feet of the men about her.

"According to my records," said the scribe, looming over her, tall in his blue robes, she could see but the hem of his robe and his sandals, "you responded negatively when queried as to your ability to dance. Perhaps my records are in error?"

I think we may grant, even within this narrative, despite the possible risk of a seeming impropriety, hopefully not one punishable, that Ellen had at least average, or reasonable, intelligence. Certainly her life on Earth, her education, her attainments, her position, and such, suggest as much. More coercively, perhaps, we might note that intelligence ranks high among the selection criteria of Gorean slavers, of which, as noted earlier, we may assume that Mirus was one. I think that it is seldom that stupid women are brought to Gor. The Gorean master, you see, looks for high intelligence in a female slave. It is one of his pleasures to take a highly intelligent woman, even a brilliant woman, provided, of course, that she is attractive, would be of interest in chains, is likely to squirm well in the furs and such, and teach her her womanhood, a lesson which is too often neglected in the education of a free female, either on Gor or Earth. He delights then to take such an interesting, lovely, remarkable creature in hand and, step by step, with great patience, reduce her to an unquestioning, passionate, obedient chattel. The more intelligent she is, of course, the better slave she is likely to make; I assume that that is obvious; she is likely to be more aware of the subtlest and almost unspoken desires of her master; she is less likely to make errors which might displease him; and she is likely to be not only hot, devoted and dutiful, as the saying is, but inventive and zealous, conscientious and creative, intelligently desperate to please, in her unrelieved, categorical servitude. Also, I suppose that there is just more pleasure in owning an intelligent woman than in owning one who is less intelligent. She is a greater prize to have at one's feet. Too, the average Gorean master wants a woman he can talk to, seriously talk to, one with whom, in a sense, he can share his life. It is not unusual for a master to speak of numerous matters with his female slave, politics, culture, music, history, philosophy, and such, almost as though she might be his equal, though she is likely to be kneeling before him, naked, and back-braceleted. In this way she is not likely to forget that she is a female. Afterwards he can put her in pleasure chains, and, as it pleases him, turn her once again into a begging, submitted, conquered, spasmodic, writhing slave. A dull woman, you see, is not of great interest, whether in a collar or not. An interesting woman, on the other hand, is not the less interesting in a collar; indeed, she is more interesting in a collar.

"No, Master," said Ellen. "Your records are correct. I denied that I knew dance." She supposed that the question had been a trap, but, even had it not been, even if the scribe's question had been innocently, honestly, motivated, she thought it wisest to answer truthfully. As a slave she feared the penalties for prevarication, the least of which might be a severe whipping.

"Then," said the scribe, "it appears that you are a lying slave."

"No, Master," she wept. "I answered as honestly as I could. I am a slave girl. I would not dare to lie to a free man!"

"You said you could not dance, and yet with my own eyes, and to my pleasure, I may add, I saw you dance."

"I cannot dance!" cried Ellen.

There was laughter, from the scribe, and from one of the guardsmen, and from the two whip masters who had now come forth from the area of preparation.

"It is true," said Ellen. "I did not so much dance, as act to music. And I have seen dancers, in the circles. I tried to imitate them! I tried to do well! Then I felt myself taken by the music, and I could not help myself. Then, as though held in its chains, I found myself dancing. I had been captured by the music. I had no recourse but to obey it, Masters! I did not know I could dance, if dance I did."

"You danced," said the scribe.

Ellen groaned.

"You had lessons?" said the scribe.

"No, Master," said Ellen.

"But you have seen slaves dance?"

"Yes, Master," wept Ellen.

"And you learned from them?"

"Perhaps something, Master."

"And surely, as a slave," said the scribe, "you upon occasion, naked, in secret, had swayed before a mirror?"

"Yes, Master," whispered Ellen. She recalled that she had done this, not only on Gor, but even on Earth, as a frustrated female intellectual, more than once, in anguish, and curiosity, and embarrassment, in the privacy of her apartment, the shades drawn, far above the distant pavement, far above the dismal, crowded, gray streets below. She had wanted to see herself as she might be, and wanted to be, as a beautiful, natural creature, and to see herself, as well, as that creature might appear, beggingly presenting itself, beggingly displaying itself, in all the lure of the dance, to a member of the opposite sex, to a man. Once, to her astonishment, she had found herself whispering to the mirror. "I am here. Where are you, my master? I am ready for a collar. I want a collar. Come, collar me, my master!" She wondered how many slaves danced thusly in such small, lonely apartments, their slave needs starved, longing for a master.

"Then you have not only made observations, from which you perhaps learned something, but you have practiced," said the scribe.

"Yes, Master," wept Ellen.

"I think I shall have you remanded for the liar's brand," said the scribe.

"Do not have it put on me, please, Master!" begged Ellen, terrified.

"I would think that a good whipping would be sufficient," said a voice, "say, ten lashes."

Ellen started, keeping her head down.

"Who are you?" asked the scribe.

"I am called 'Selius'," said the voice.

Ellen dared to look up, from her belly, half buried in the sand, into which it seemed she would crawl, as though to hide. Her fingers dug into the sand, at the sides of her head.

It was Selius Arconious!

"Perhaps you are right," said the scribe. "I myself was inclined to be lenient, though I suppose the liar's brand would be appropriate for her."

Ellen dug her fingers into the sand, in terror.

"I did, as doubtless did we all, enjoyed her performance, and that should count for something, I suppose," said the scribe, "and I, besides, upon reflection, am inclined to grant that she may not have fully understood her latent talents in the matter."

"It is instinctive in a woman," said the guardsman. "They are all slaves, with or without their collars. They are all born to dance the dances of slaves. Such things are in their belly from birth."

"True," said Selius Arconious. "But she was stupid not to understand this."

"Yes," agreed the guardsman.

Ellen bit her lip in anger, remaining quiet on her belly amongst the feet of the men.

"Surely she should at least have qualified her answer, or have been more candid, or more speculative, with our fellow here," said Arconious, indicating the scribe.

"Agreed," said the guardsman.

"I am inclined to forget the matter," said the scribe. "All in all, I do not think the little slut was trying to mislead us."

Ellen gasped softly with relief.

"But she did mislead you," said Selius Arconious.

"Inadvertently, unintentionally," suggested the scribe.

"Then she is stupid," said Selius Arconious.

"Granted," said the scribe.

Ellen dug her fingers into the sand.

"Apparently," said Selius Arconious, "those of Cos are indulgent with their slaves."

"We do not have that reputation," said the scribe, unpleasantly.

"Too, intentionally or not," said Selius Arconious, "she has made a fool out of you, and of Cos."

"No, Masters!" whispered Ellen, frightened.

"Were you given permission to speak?" inquired Selius Arconious.

"No, Master," said Ellen. "Forgive me, Master!"

"You see how stupid she is," said Selius Arconious.

"Yes," said the scribe.

"I did not know that Cos accepted stupidity in her slaves," said Selius Arconious.

"We do not," said the scribe. "Whip!"

The whip of the exterior whip master was handed to the scribe, who gave it to one of the attending guardsmen.

Of the other two guardsmen one took Ellen's wrists and drew them forward, holding them, and the other took her ankles, and, holding them tightly, drew them back, this extending her legs. In this way she was stretched at full length, on her belly, and held, vulnerably, in the sand.

"What do you think should be her punishment?" asked the scribe.

"I would think fifteen lashes," said Selius.

Ellen sobbed in misery.

"Ten for the stupidity of imperiling the integrity of your records," said Selius Arconious, "and another five for the stupidity of daring to speak without permission."

Ellen saw the shadow of the guardsman, the arm lift, the hand holding the whip. She shut her eyes tightly, in misery.

But the blow did not fall.

She opened her eyes. Selius Arconious had interposed himself, and his hand rested on the arm of the guardsman, staying its blow. The guardsman, puzzled, lowered his arm.

"I will buy the strokes," said Selius Arconious. "I would suppose that a tarsk-bit a stroke would be sufficient, as the slave is stupid, rather than willful or wayward."

"That is acceptable," said the scribe. "Fifteen tarsk-bits."

"Done," said Selius Arconious.

Ellen heard the tiny sounds of small coins. She saw the whip returned to the exterior whip master.

The scribe distributed some of the coins to the attending guardsmen. "Good," said one of them. Such coins would buy more than one round of paga.

"So," thought Ellen. "How cleverly Selius Arconious demeans me! He knows I hate him, that I cannot stand him, that I loathe him! Now he whom I intensely despise chooses to interfere! From where has he come? Why is he here? By what right does he interpose himself betwixt a slave and an agent of her master, the state of Cos? How he humiliates me! So now I should be grateful to him? With what contempt he buys away my whipping! How better could he show his contempt for me? How better could he impress my vulnerability, my nothingness, my slavery, upon me? And so he wishes to put me in his debt, me, whom he so scorns! Am I now supposed to be grateful to him, for this act of calculated humiliation. I loathe him! I loathe him!"

"You may belly," said the scribe, "and express your gratitude to your benefactor."

Ellen, who well understood her condition, needed not be reprimanded or kicked, nor required a suggestion, or command, to be repeated, but squirmed immediately, prostrate, on her belly, to Selius Arconious, and, putting down her head, her hair falling about his sandals, kissed his feet.

"Thank you, Master," she said, bitterly, angrily.

"Your gratitude may be premature, my dear," said Selius Arconious.

Ellen lifted her head a little, puzzled. Selius Arconious stepped back, away from her.

"Kneel up, slut," said the scribe. "Lift your wrists, crossed."

Ellen, kneeling up, lifting her wrists, crossed, flushed. She was obeying, and kneeling, a naked slave, in the presence of Selius Arconious, whom she hated.

She felt her wrists lashed together, at one end of a leather tether.

She was pulled to her feet.

She looked at Selius Arconious.

"I have always thought that you were a slave," he said, "and now I see that you are."

She looked down, angrily. Then she looked up, for her wrists were lifted, by the scribe, he checking the confining knots which bound them.

"There is no more dancing or serving for you this night, 117, Ellen," said the scribe. "You are being taken to the slave cages. There you will wait. You will be sold tomorrow night."

"She is a slut, meaningless and stupid," said Selius Arconious. "I recommend that she be confined straitly."

"I will see that she is put into one of the tiniest of the slave cages," said the scribe. "By tomorrow night she will beg to run to the block."

The slave's tether was then handed to a guardsman.

Ellen, turning about, cast an angry glance at Selius Arconious, who regarded her impassively.

She turned away, angrily.

Then she was led away.

Chapter 25

Sold

Ellen screamed in pain, her head seeming to explode with fire. "Please, no!" she cried, lights bursting in her vision, jerked forth by the hair, doing her best to scramble out, to comply, to please, stop the pain, stop the pain, please, don't hurt me, flung to the dirt on her belly outside the tiny cage. She lay there on her belly in the dirt and felt her left wrist seized and manacled.

There had been metallic sounds, as the locks had been undone, the hasps flung back, and the padlocks, partially opened, slipped over the staples. The small gate was then thrown open.

"Out, out!" had said the keeper.

"Yes, Master!" she had cried, going to her hands and knees, to crawl forth. Then he had seized her hair.

"On your feet," said the voice.

Ellen tried to rise, but her body, from the cage, was in such pain and so stiff, and so ached, that she, trying to rise, fell. "Oh!" she cried, as a bootlike sandal kicked her thigh, and she, bent over, her left wrist in the manacle, with the chain, her eyes filled with tears, rose to her feet.

At least her hair had been released.

Behind her, on the chain, were some sixteen or seventeen girls. She could see the lot number, rather similar to her own, on the left breast of the frightened girl, a blonde, behind her, she also chained by the left wrist in the line.

Perhaps the blonde, who had exquisite features and a lovely figure, had not been sold before. Or perhaps she knew more than Ellen, and feared this sort of sale.

"Stand straight," said a voice, that of another keeper, and Ellen straightened her body.

There were two empty manacles on the chain before Ellen. They, with their chains, were before her, waiting, lying in the dirt.

From an area of chains and stakes she saw two girls being conducted toward her chain. Each was bent over, held in leading position, both in the handling of one keeper. They were then released and knelt, and then commanded to bow their heads and lift their left wrists. They were then roughly entered onto the chain, each by the left wrist. They were then ordered to their feet, as had been the others. The lot number of the one manacled before Ellen, which number she had seen as she had been brought forward, was again similar to her own. Was it higher, or lower? "How beautiful she is," thought Ellen. "Is she more beautiful than I?"

A scribe, with papers, was nearby, and, in a moment, began to course the chain.

"115," he said, of the first girl on the chain.

"116," he said, of the second girl on the chain.

It was not the scribe she had known from the exhibition cage or the silken enclosure of the preceding evening.

"Put your head up, girl," said the scribe.

"Yes, Master," said Ellen.

"117," he said, of Ellen.

He made notes in his papers, as he coursed the line.

"118," he said of the girl behind her, the blonde.

So she before me is a lower number, and she after me a higher number, thought Ellen.

And are not the lower numbers the most beautiful?

Are the two slaves before me truly more beautiful than I, she wondered. And can it be that she behind me, so beautiful, is less beautiful than I?

Surely we are all much the same, and yet men, the brutes, rank us, and will buy and sell us! As it pleases them! As goods! But, of course, as the goods we are!

But might not I bring a higher price than any of these others?

But that is for men to decide?

In what order will we be sold?

Will they take any bid on us? Or will they place a reserve on us? But there were twenty-one bids on me, even from the exhibition cages! And then I was danced, as a slave!

Men will want me!

Have I not seen their eyes on me?

I am a desirable slave!

How startling once, so long ago, would have been such a thought!

Yet, was bondage, even then, so alien to me? Had I not, even then, wondered about such things, amidst my papers and pretensions, amongst my articles, my books, my vagaries, my dusts, my boredoms and aridities? How I despised the male weaklings I knew, so gullible, so easily manipulated, so spineless and accommodating, so softened, so self-betrayed, so twisted, reduced and crippled! How I dreamed of being taken in hand, stripped and collared, of being chained, of being imperiously ravished, of being mastered! How I would have accepted, even pleaded for, a stroke of my lord's lash, that I might the better know myself uncompromisingly his. Yes, long ago, on Earth, in my most secret dreams, in my most feared and forbidden, but persistent, exciting, delicious and fascinating thoughts, I wondered what it might be to be a slave! I had wondered, too, what I might be truly worth, if anything, what I might bring in an open market, sold raw, as a mere vended female. Now it seems I shall learn!

The scribe was then well behind her, farther back down the line. In a few moments, she again heard his voice. "Take them to the ready area," he said.

The lead girl, whom Ellen understood to be 115, was then put in leading position, bent over, a hand in her hair, and, as she whimpered, she was conducted from the area, amongst various cages, shelters, tents and stakes, toward distant sounds of men, shouts and calls, and the rest of the chain followed. Ellen was pleased she was not lead girl.

* * * *

Ellen had knelt in the tiny cage, confined there, grasping the bars, waiting. Every muscle in her body had seemed to ache. The cage was of the sort commonly used for a disciplinary device, one in which an errant slave might be incarcerated pending the subsidence of a master's ire. In such a device her contrition quickly becomes authentic, her lessons are learned and her ways mended. Powerful resolutions of improved service are quickly formed in that small space. It is the sort of device into which a proud free woman might be thrust but out of which creeps a humbled, self-acknowledged slave, asking only to be permitted to please, in any way the master might wish. Such cages are designed for the small body of a woman, and this particular cage had been designed for a small woman.

It was the evening, at about the 14th Ahn, following Ellen's performance in the silken enclosure.

The bars in the cage, which had a metal roof and floor, were set some two inches apart, to make it impossible for an aching limb to be thrust through the openings. One can sit, knees drawn up, or kneel, or crouch in such a cage, but, obviously, one cannot stand in it, or stretch out in it. If one lies down in it one must have one's knees pulled tightly up. One's relief is merely to change from one cramped position to another. In time a considerable amount of body pain is built up. It is rather like close chains, in this respect.

Ellen was aware that a small chain was being formed, which was approaching her cage.

She did not know if she were to be added to that chain, or to another. Several chains had passed her cage.

"Please let me out of the cage," thought Ellen. "Oh, please, masters, let me out!"

Selius Arconious, she recalled, had suggested that she be confined "straitly," and the scribe, to whom he had given some fifteen tarsk-bits, buying her blows, had found this not only agreeable, but, given his earlier rancor, eminently fitting.

And so she had been put into the tiny cage.

"This is the smallest of the woman cages?" had asked the guardsman, her tether looped about his left wrist.

"Yes," had said the attendant.

She had then been knelt before the cage, and there the guardsman had removed the tether from her wrists, that on which she had been conducted thither, as might have been a verr, from the area of the silken enclosure where she, and other slaves, had been put to the entertainment of men.

Kneeling before the small enclosure, she had regarded it with dismay.

The gate was swung open.

"In, slut," she was told.

She went to all fours before the tiny opening. She cried out in surprise, pain, and humiliation, kicked. Then she scrambled hastily, awkwardly, within. She heard the guardsman laugh. She felt the bars against her body. Her feet were lifted, that the door could be shut. Then it was closed behind her. She faced the back of the cage, with its bars. She heard the two locks put in place, behind her. She twisted about, with difficulty, cramped, brushing, turning, against the bars, to face the front of the small confinement. Then she had knelt within, in misery, and grasped the bars of the gate. She had looked out. She could hardly be seen within, given the narrow spaces between the bars.

"Please, Master," she had protested, dismayed.

"Be silent, slave girl," said the attendant.

"Yes, Master."

"You can hardly see her," said the guardsman.

"It will be easy enough to see her later," said the attendant, "when she is on the block."

"In the future," said the guardsman to the incarcerated slave, "perhaps you will be less stupid."

"It is my hope that that will be so," said Ellen.

"It had better be," he said.

"Yes, Master," said Ellen.

He had then left.

A moment later, with a jangle of keys, the attendant, too, had left.

Ellen had grasped the bars. "Selius Arconious has done this to me," she had said to herself. "How I hate him!"

The sales had commenced yesterday evening, and some three to four hundred women had been swiftly vended, of diverse quality, some in lots. The strategy of the vendors, it seemed, was to mix lots in such a way as to have excellent goods available for all three nights of the sale. The average sale took only two or three Ehn. But it was rumored, nonetheless, that the next day's sales, the third day's sales, would begin in the early afternoon, to ensure the disposal of all the merchandise. The Cosians, it seemed, had not anticipated that there would be intense, competitive bidding on so many girls. But the buyers, clearly, had a greater interest in several of the items marketed than the Cosians, in effect, wholesalers, had anticipated. There were many professional slavers in attendance, of course. They, clearly, on the whole, were interested in picking up cheap girls for training and subsequent resale, the first buys in the festival camp being understood largely as speculations or investments.

Ellen's cage, and some similar cages, but most much larger, some even like exhibition cages, containing several girls, were within a large, canvas-walled area, the canvas strung upon and held upright by poles, behind and adjacent to the sales area itself, with its great block at one end, a block some two yards in height and twenty feet in diameter with broad, flat steps on each side, by means of which merchandise might be brought conveniently to its surface and, subsequently, with similar ease, taken from it. The auditorium, so to speak, was open to the air, and consisted of several ascending tiers of closely spaced benches, these arranged in semicircles on a shallow hill, at the foot of which was the block. The block itself, after dark, would be illuminated by torchlight.

* * * *

Ellen followed in line, in pain, almost hobbling, scarcely able to walk. The scribe of the exhibition cages and silken enclosure, it seems, had certainly been wrong about one thing. When she was taken from the cage she would not run to the block. She could scarcely walk to it.

But, as she walked, gradually, in this activity, in virtue of this gentle movement, in virtue of this concomitant stretching and exercising of her limbs, much of her body pain began to dissipate.

"I am going to be sold," she said to herself. "I wonder if any of my former male colleagues would care to bid on me, and own me. Or would they buy me to free me? Could they be that stupid? Probably. Would they relinquish the opportunity to own something as precious, as delicious and desirable as I am? Perhaps. One supposes so. Or would this be the opportunity of which they have secretly dreamed? Perhaps some of them, who knows, dreamed of me at their feet, naked, in their chains. I wonder then if they would be so stupid as to free me? Probably, as they are such asses. And I suppose I would have to pretend to be grateful! But perhaps some would not be so stupid as to free me. There is, after all, a Gorean saying that only a fool frees a slave girl. But the men I knew were surely fools. They would probably free me. One does not know. But in any event I do not think I would care to belong to one of them. I do not think they would know what to do with me. I do not think they would know what to do with a slave girl."

Ellen conjectured that her chain, which consisted of twenty slaves, presumably numbers 115 through 134, would soon be in the vicinity of the great block. Her conjecture was nearly, if not entirely, correct, as her chain was led into a ready lane, one of several, which was within, say, fifty yards of the block. There were a number of lanes, marked out with stakes and strung ribbons, and in each of these lanes, or rather within each which was occupied, there was a line of chained, waiting slaves. These slaves were muchly at their ease, resting, sitting, kneeling, lying down, subject only to the constraints of their manacling, Some were speaking softly to one another. Some, on the other hand, were white-faced and apprehensive, particularly those in the lanes nearest the empty lanes closest to the block area. The mode of the chaining for the girls in each lane was the same as in Ellen's group, all being left-wrist linked.

Ellen's group was led into one of the lanes. "This is your lane," said a keeper. "You will stay here until shortly before your sale. You may be much as you like here, even permitted gentle speech, but you may not rise to your feet without permission."

"Master," said 115, "may I speak?"

He regarded her, and a moment's annoyance crossed his features, a tiny thing, but one which brought apprehension to the chain but then, seemingly, he found her pleasing.

"Yes," he said.

"She is surely beautiful," thought Ellen. "I suppose one such as she is more likely to be granted such privileges than others. I wager she knows, the luscious vixen, how beautiful she is. Did that give her courage? I wager it did. I wonder if I would have been granted permission to speak. Perhaps. But then there is little risked by a girl's requesting permission to speak. One would be seldom punished for that. And how else is a girl to speak if she may not ask for permission to do so?"

"How long, Master," asked 115, "before our sale?"

"How bold she is," thought Ellen.

"I think," said he, surveying the lanes, and their waiting occupants, the lengths of the chains and such, "better than two Ahn."

"That is a long time," thought Ellen.

"Thank you, Master," said 115.

"I think he would like to have her," thought Ellen. "I wonder if he would like to have me, too. Perhaps. I suspect that I would do for him, and do quite well."

"You will later be fed and watered, and permitted to relieve yourselves," said the keeper.

"Yes, Master, thank you, Master," said 115.

The keeper then turned away, and, later, returned with another chain.

That chain would occupy the next lane. And, similarly, from time to time, he, or others, brought new chains to various lanes in the ready area.

Ellen lifted her wrist, and looked at the manacle upon it. She could not slip it, of course. She lay down between 116 and 118, and stretched her body, in almost feline luxury. How good to be out of the cage! She looked up at the sky.

Then, for a moment, she was angry with men.

"They put me in a cage, a cage!" she thought. "By what right did they put me in a cage? By what right was I caged? By what right do these Gorean beasts arrogate to themselves the right to cage women, or women such as I?" And then she felt how stupid was her question. It was an Earth question, a question from another world, a distant, superficial, polluted, noisy, unnatural, artificial world, a question from another *ethos*, one not one with nature, but one at war with nature; it was not a biological question, not a natural question, not a Gorean question. "Obviously they have every right to do so," she said to herself. "They have the right of masters, the obvious right of masters, to do with us, their slaves, as they please. Have you not yet learned the nature of this world, and what you are on this world? What a silly little vulo you are! What a stupid little pudding you are!"

Later, rising to a half-reclining, half-sitting position, she brought her legs together, to one side, with smooth, swift, sinuous grace. "Oh," she thought, suddenly, "you did that without thinking. You, indeed, are now a slave girl. How shameless you are, you branded little tart!" And she smiled to herself, pleased.

She could hear the sounds of the crowd, it seemed far off, like distant surf, vague cries, calls, shouts, crashings, rumblings, responses.

"They are selling women," she thought. "And I, too, am to be sold. I cannot prevent this. None of us can prevent this. We are helpless, absolutely helpless. But that is fitting for us, that we should be absolutely helpless, for we are slaves."

There was the sound of a gong, which signified that another sale had been concluded.

"How strange it suddenly seems to me," thought Ellen, "that I, an Earth woman, should be here, on this world, with these others, waiting to be sold." But then, upon reflection, in the context of her abduction, the smoothness, care and efficiency with which it was conducted, and given the predations of slavers upon Earth, and their access to techniques and vehicles capable of at least interplanetary spacefaring, and the market for such as she on this world, then, in this larger context, her situation did not seem so untoward or inexplicable at all. Its hue of strangeness was no more than an illusion, a distortion, perceived through a prism of ignorance. To a native glass beads may appear strange. And she had no doubt but what had happened to her had happened to a great many of her former world. She suspected that her status, her condition, her situation, her fate, her fortune, her experiences and such, those of an Earth woman brought to Gor as a slave, were not unique to her. Doubtless they were shared by many of her former world.

From time to time, the gong sounded.

Then she said to herself, "In any event, you are now no longer an Earth woman, but only a Gorean slave girl. That is what you are now, and all you are now!"

She wondered if lovely Dara, who had danced yesterday evening in the ba-ta circle, who had taken the bracelet from her in the area of preparation, who had been lashed by the exterior whip master, who had had the low number 51, had been sold. She thought it likely, as Dara had had such a low number. On the other hand, they might save her for the last night. It was up to the masters. Ellen envied Dara her low number.

Somewhat later Ellen's lane was fed. A slave girl with a bucket of thickened slave gruel went down the line and those in the lane were permitted, one after the other, to reach into the bucket with their free hand, and were permitted to keep what they could hold in one hand. A second girl, carrying a large, flat, wicker tray, brought wedges of bread, cut from flat, rounded loaves, and gave one to each slave. Ellen had learned in the coffle, days ago, that it was not wise to ask for more.

The sales proceeded.

Ellen was thirsty, but she supposed that water would be provided later. Certainly that was among the bits of information which had been secured by 115.

She was grateful to 115, for her boldness, however deferentially it had been proffered, and the welcome intelligence she had managed to obtain. She herself, less confidant, would have been reluctant to inquire. She would not have wanted to be lashed. But there was something for being first on the chain, of course. That did, in effect, make one a likely spokesman or representative of one's fellows. Too, she was undeniably beautiful. Beautiful slaves often, it seemed, were accorded preferential treatment. This did not, of course, increase their popularity with their sisters in bondage. To be sure, some masters, perhaps aware of the latent dangers of such tendencies to laxness make it a practice to be particularly severe with beautiful slaves, and then the beauties are kept in so fierce and orderly a discipline that it requires great courage for them to do so much as lift their eyes to those of their master.

But I suppose that I am as beautiful as she, thought Ellen.

And, of course, from time to time, one lane or another was emptied, as its occupants were conducted forward, or perhaps, one should say, "herded forward," as that phrasing seems more accurate. Certainly the men who fetched them, the sales attendants, seemed more like rude herdsmen than solicitous merchants. They carried sticks, and it was not without jabbings, pokings and blows, and impatient expostulations, that they sped their linked, disconcerted, intimidated charges, those lovely, chained she-animals, forward, presumably to a final staging area prior to their sale.

Ellen was then angry with Selius Arconious. She recalled how he had looked upon her, when she had knelt in the silken enclosure, when she had lifted her wrists, and had had them tied, and had then been drawn by them, tethered, to her feet, to be led to the sales area.

"He looked upon me as an animal," she thought. "In his eyes I was no more than a tethered beast!" Then she recalled, angrily, that that was all she was, in truth, a beast, an animal, a domestic animal, a small, sleek, exquisite, curvaceous domestic animal, who might be bought and sold. "I hate him!" she thought. "I hate him!"

Ellen was furious.

"He might have been looking upon any slave," she thought. "How pathetic and miserable to be a slave! How glorious it would be to be free, so that I might tantalize and taunt him, that I might make him suffer, that I might make him miserable, that I might punish and torment him, if only with the glimpse of an ankle, with all the cleverness and all the power, and all the impunity, of the secure, protected free woman! But I am a slave! Such things are denied me! I cannot behave in such ways. I cannot do such things! Men have decided to own me, and will do so!"

"I hate him! I hate him!" she thought.

"Put him from your mind," she thought, "a nothing, a lowly tarnster! You had twenty-one bids on you. You should obtain a well-fixed master. You might have sandals. You might be given a silken tunic. How pleased I am that he cannot afford me! I hate him! I hate him!"

The gong then rang again.

Ellen wondered if Louise and Renata had been sold. She had not seen them in the cages, or at the stakes, or in the lanes. That was not surprising, as there were, obviously, a great many slaves in the camp.

This was not a typical market, Ellen realized. It was not merely that it was a festival camp, for it was not that unusual to sell women on holidays, and at times of celebration, sometimes with special advertising on the public boards, and such; it had to do, rather, with the sales being conducted not by a private house, but by a state, in this case the state of Cos, the amount of merchandise being offered and the relatively brief duration of the sale, some three days, it seemed. That was not a long time in which to dispose of so considerable an amount of stock, something in the vicinity of a thousand women.

Perhaps that explained something of the urgency, the impatience, of the attendants.

To be sure, after the days of the sales, there might be some women left over. A thousand women, or so, was a great many to dispose of in three days, even if several were vended in lots.

The lane next to Ellen's had now been emptied, and, a little later, another chain of women was introduced into it.

The lanes, it seemed, were not going in any obvious order, at least in any order obvious to the occupants of the lanes. Lanes on both sides of Ellen's lane, nearer or farther away, had been emptied and refilled, some more than once.

"We are special," the girl before Ellen, 116, said. This message was apparently being relayed from the girl before her, 115, who seemed pleased about the matter. So Ellen turned to the girl behind her, and transmitted the message. Ellen, too, was somewhat pleased. Apparently her lane was being held for later in the sales.

It was not difficult, upon occasion, however, to anticipate which lane would move next for a wastes bucket was passed down the lane, that the slaves might relieve themselves. This reduces the possibilities of accidents on the block, brought about perhaps by consternation or terror. Even so most blocks, in the gentle, circular depression toward their center, worn by the passing of so many small, bared feet, are furnished with sawdust. Following the passing along of the wastes vessel, over which the slaves must squat and relieve themselves in order, a girl brings a bucket and dipper with water. The slaves must then drink liberally from the large dipper, draining it, for this freshens their appearance and pleasantly rounds the belly. That liquid, of course, will not have time to pass through their body before their sale.

Ellen's attention was drawn to a slave in the lane to her left. That slave, like the others, was linked by the left wrist to the others in her group. She, however, was red-eyed, apparently from crying. Also, on her back and elsewhere about her body there was a plenitude of stripes, which must have pained her sorely. The slave went to all fours, looking about herself, wildly. Some of the women in Ellen's lane were conversing softly, which was permitted. "Slave girl," whispered the slave fiercely, she in the lane to Ellen's left, rather at her side, as the lanes were organized.

"Yes, slave girl?" said Ellen, irritably.

The woman looked at Ellen angrily.

"May we speak?" she whispered, looking about herself, presumably fearful of the presence of attendants.

"Yes," said Ellen.

"They have beaten me!" she whispered.

"Perhaps you were displeasing," said Ellen.

"You do not understand," said the woman. "They have taken my clothes!"

"None of us are clothed," said Ellen, puzzled.

"You do not understand, stupid slave girl," said the woman. "I am the Lady Melanie of Brundisium! I am a free woman! A terrible mistake has been made! They seized me, yesterday evening! They have chained me! They think I am a slave!"

"You are pretty enough to be a slave," said Ellen.

"I am Melanie, of Brundisium! The Lady Melanie of Brundisium! How can I convince them of this? How can I correct this terrible misunderstanding!"

"Explain the matter to the masters," suggested Ellen.

"I tried! They beat me!" wept the woman.

"Cosians?" asked Ellen.

"Yes!"

"They do as they wish," said Ellen. "One does not question the spears of Cos."

"Tell me what I am to do! Tell me how to free myself!"

"Do I not know you?" asked Ellen.

The woman looked at Ellen, closely. "The slave girl!" she said.

"I know you," said Ellen. "I can tell your voice! You are the free woman by the campfire, in the Robes of Concealment, with the necklace, and the jewels on your robes. You had me pour wine for you! You made me kneel before you!"

"Yes, slut!" said the woman.

"When you are sold, perhaps your master will give you a tunic," said Ellen, "—if you beg prettily enough."

"Insolent slave!" said the woman. "I shall order you beaten!"

"Not unless you have the talmit, or the switch, or unless you are first girl," said Ellen, angrily.

"Slave, slave!" hissed the woman.

Ellen moved a bit forward, and to the side, and the woman tried to turn quickly away, but she had not detected Ellen's intent quickly enough, and Ellen had a glimpse of what she had suspected.

"You are branded," said Ellen, delightedly.

"No!" said the woman.

"I think you are," said Ellen. "Show me!"

The woman, angrily, turned a little, to the side.

"Yes," said Ellen, "you are branded."

"The beasts held me down! I could not move! They marked me!"

"A nicely done brand," said Ellen.

"Do you think so?" asked the woman.

"Yes," said Ellen. "It is the common kef."

"It is meaningless!" cried the woman.

"I do not think you will find it so," said Ellen.

"I am not a slave!" said the woman.

"You have been marked," said Ellen. "You will be sold. Then you will doubtless find yourself in a collar, your master's collar. Whether or not you will be permitted clothing, a tunic, a rag, a slave strip, will be up to your master."

"I am the Lady Melanie of Brundisium!" she protested.

"I am not sure you have a name," said Ellen. "Did a scribe give you a name?"

"Of course not!" she said.

"What did the scribe put on your records?"

"'Melanie'," she said.

"Then you have been given a name, 'Melanie'," said Ellen. "Your master may change it, if he does not like it. But it is a pretty name. Perhaps he will permit you to keep it."

"It is my name!" she said.

"No," said Ellen, "not in the sense you think. In the sense you have in mind, you have no name, no more than a tarsk. Your name, if it is seen fit to give you a name, will be whatever masters wish."

"—if it is seen fit to give me a name?" she said.

"Have no fear," said Ellen. "Masters commonly give us names. We may thus be the better referred to, distinguished from other slaves, summoned, ordered about, and such."

The slave knelt and put her head down, her face in her hands, weeping.

"What a hypocrite you are," said Ellen.

The slave looked up, tearfully. "I do not understand," she said.

"You came unattended, unprotected, to a festival camp of conquerors, of Cosians. You sat with men, chatting with them. Do you not think they would be curious as to what might lie hidden beneath your veils? Do you not think they would speculate as to what delights might lie concealed within your cumbersome robes? And do you think they would fail to note the putative value of your necklace, the sparkle of your jeweled robes and veils? And surely you knew that hundreds of women were to be marketed. And did you not flirt with the men? Was your veil not disarranged as though inadvertently when you drank? Did you not sit in a certain fashion, turned to the side, legs together, as a slave girl might sit, if she were permitted to sit? Did you not insolently, haughtily, arrogantly, put a naked slave to your feet, and not realize that men would be curious as to what you yourself might look like, put similarly to their feet? Did you not know that your carriage, and demeanor, your pride and pretensions, might try the patience of men? Did you not know that such might tempt them to transform you into something of more interest to them, that they might consider taking you in hand and turning you into a luscious, cringing slave, pathetically begging to please in whatever manner they might desire? And do not think that I did not see the hem of your robe lifted in such a way as to bare an ankle!"

"No," wept the slave. "No!"

"Perhaps they wondered what that ankle would look like, encircled with bangles, or thonged with slave bells."

"No!" she protested.

"You were begging the brand! You were courting the collar!"

"No, no!"

"At least," said Ellen, "they have permitted you some modesty."

"What?" she asked.

"The wrists of a free woman, as I understand it," said Ellen, "as generally the rest of her body, are not to be publicly exposed, to prevent that being the function of gloves and sleeves."

"Yes," said the slave, bewildered.

"You are wearing a manacle on your left wrist," said Ellen. "Does that not conceal a bit of wrist, thus affording you some modesty?"

"Insolent slave!" cried the woman.

"To be sure," said Ellen. "It is not a great deal."

"I was not courting the collar!" said the woman.

"You were, obviously," said Ellen.

"What is it like to be a slave?" whispered the woman.

"Much depends on the master," said Ellen, warily.

"But we must serve our masters—*in all ways*?" she asked.

"Certainly." said Ellen.

"*Sexually*?" she asked.

"Yes, particularly so," said Ellen.

"I am not—white silk," she whispered.

"Few of us are," said Ellen. She did not inform the slave that she had been white silk herself, even when brought to Gor. She had not become red silk until Mirus, her master, had seen fit in his audience hall to open her for the uses of men. And Ellen recalled he had not done so in any way that might have been regarded as in a sensitive, or considerate, manner. To be sure, his use of her had been instructive, apprising her of the sort of thing that might be done to her as a slave. It had come to her as something of a revelation. Then he had sold her.

"He was polite, and feeble," she said. "It was terribly disappointing." She looked down, reddening. "Is this all there is to it, I asked myself. Is there no more? I remained dissatisfied. This could not be all! I was starving! And on my plate there was flung no more than the tiniest of crumbs!"

"You were not mastered," said Ellen.

The slave looked at her, wildly.

"You should have been stripped and bound, and caressed for hours, until you shrieked with need and ecstasy," said Ellen. "Then you should have been penetrated with all the imperious ruthlessness of the callous, self-serving master. You would then know yourself nothing and slave. Then you should have been chained for the night at the foot of his bed, that you might there, in that place, recollect your feelings, and what had been done to you, and what you now were. In the morning you would be freed to kneel, and kiss the whip, to belly, to wash his feet with your tongue. You would learn to be ordered about, to work, to serve, to obey with alacrity and perfection. You would know yourself owned, and by a master whom you know will have all from you. And that is what you want, a master who will be satisfied with nothing less than all from you. And soon you would learn to beg, and serve, with all the vulnerable, passionate intimacy of the slave. Your life would then be changed. You would find yourself dominated, and subject as any slave to the whip. I assure you you would strive to be pleasing, and in this service, and in this relationship, you will have feelings, and experiences, forever beyond the ken of the lesser woman, the narrower, colder, shallower, more inert, less awakened free woman. Your sexual fulfillment comes not from him alone or from yourself alone, but from the complementarities of nature, the male and female, the man and woman, the master and the slave, he who commands and she who, conquered, surrendered and loving, obliged to please, subject to discipline, serves, serves gratefully, zealously, lovingly, with every fiber of her owned being. In her service she is joyous; she desires to serve, fervently, and she knows that she must serve, and perfectly, whether she will or no. This reassures her and pleases her. She knows that she has been found attractive enough to put in chains. She rejoices that she has been found worthy of the collar. She knows she is the most intensely desired of all women, the female slave. She has been found exciting enough, attractive enough, desirable enough, to be enslaved, to be owned. At last she is at peace with her sex; at her master's feet; she has come home to the collar."

"Thank you, Mistress," said the slave, and lay down in her lane.

"Perhaps you could call out from the auction block, proclaiming your freedom, seeking to attract the attention of citizens of Brundisium."

"They would beat me," she said.

"Nonetheless, you could try," said Ellen.

"No," she said. "I want to be sold."

"I understand," said Ellen. "But there might be another consideration."

"What is that?" she asked, lying down, her head resting on her left elbow.

"If you do not attempt to call out, you may never know, thereafter, what might have happened."

"Yes?" asked the woman.

"There might then be a lingering doubt left in your mind, that you might have been able to regain your freedom, at that one moment, before that opportunity disappeared forever, the price being small, only a beating, a few strokes of the lash."

"But I do not want to be free now," she whispered.

"But perhaps you will not fully appreciate your slavery, or understand its inflexibility, its absoluteness, unless you have made every effort to obtain your freedom, and have failed, and have come to understand the absolute hopelessness of such an endeavor. Surely then you will better understand yourself as slave. Accordingly, I recommend that you conduct this experiment, that you call out, boldly, from the block, desperately inviting rescue, zealously seeking succor."

"Do you think I would be successful?" asked the woman, apprehensively.

"Certainly not," said Ellen. "But in this manner you will learn the perfect categoricality of your situation and status, that you cannot alter or qualify your condition in any way whatsoever, to even the smallest possible degree, that you are helpless, absolutely helpless in all such matters, in short, that you are a complete and helpless slave."

The woman regarded Ellen, red-eyed, her lower lip trembling.

"And if you should manage to obtain your freedom, which I assure you you will not, by calling out upon the block, that is not the end of the matter."

"Mistress?" she asked.

"If your bondage is important to you, and you understand it as your one possibility to obtain your total fulfillment as a female, you may always again expose yourself to the risk of the collar, disarranging a veil, walking lonely bridges at night, lifting the hem of a garment, as though to avoid soiling it in puddles in the street, speaking insolently to strangers, denouncing the Home Stones of visitors to your city, accompanying ill-guarded caravans, and such."

The gong rang again, from the vicinity of the great block. The two slaves lifted their heads, listening for the moment. The slave to Ellen's left gazed upon the manacle on her left wrist. There was a small sound of chain. The note of the gong then faded away, with diminishing vibrations. The slaves regarded one another. Another sale had been concluded.

"And then you would not have to worry about the possibility of obtaining your freedom," said Ellen. "You would not have to concern yourself with such matters. You could put them from your mind. The collar would be upon you as much as on any slave on Gor."

The woman nodded, and smiled.

"What is your lot number?" asked Ellen.

"Mistress cannot read?" asked the slave.

"No," said Ellen, irritatedly. Here she was not quite fair to herself. She could, of course, read some numbers, for example, her own and, now, some similar numbers. They were easy enough. The other slave's number, however, was rather complex, or at least seemed so to Ellen at the time. Indeed, for all she knew, one or another of those signs might have had a significance more than merely numerical. Common Gorean, you see, does not use an "Arabic notation," but represents various numbers by letters, combinations of letters, and such. Most figuring is done on an abacus. It is said, interestingly, that some of the higher castes, for example, the Scribes and Builders, have a secret notation which facilitates their calculations. Ellen does not know if that is true or not.

"1242," said the slave.

"That is a high number," said Ellen.

"I received it late, after most numbers were assigned," she said.

Ellen nodded.

"Had I been embonded earlier I might have had a lower number," she said.

"I think so," said Ellen.

"Am I beautiful?" she asked.

"That is for men to decide," said Ellen.

"Yes, Mistress."

"Yes," said Ellen. "You are beautiful."

"Thank you, Mistress," she said.

"I think you will bring a high price."

"Thank you, Mistress," she said.

Ellen noted, to her interest, that two lanes, not one, were now being readied for moving forward, to the block area. And the two lanes thus emptied were shortly thereafter repopulated with new chains.

"The sales," she thought, "might be moving too slowly."

Ellen lay then on the grass between the stakes, on which ribbons were strung, marking the lanes.

"We will soon be moved forward," she thought. "I have been starved for a master's touch. The Cosians have seen to that. These Gorean beasts have released the slave in me, as they wished. They have fanned the slave fires in my belly which now rage fiercely, tormenting fires I cannot control, putting me helplessly at their mercy. The beasts! They have made me healthy, and now I suffer from my vitality. I need the touch of a master. I fear I might die in another day without it. I must be soon owned, or I may perish in need. I do not care who buys me. I hope he is rich. Whoever it is, I will beg prettily, helplessly, plaintively, to serve. Please be merciful to your slave, future master! I am suddenly so miserable. I cannot help myself. Why do they do this to a poor slave? That former free woman! What does she know of what will be done to her, of what passions will be kindled within her! What does she know now of being transformed into a man's plaything, a helpless, piteous, begging, pleading toy?"

She looked at the former free woman lying near her. "What an unaware, simple, naive thing, you are," she thought. "Rest in ignorance. You will learn. You will learn, my dear. I am so miserable, so terribly miserable!"

She thought of the scorn with which Mirus would regard her, the contempt in which he would hold her, she, his former teacher, with her once smug, prim attitudes, now the helpless victim of slave needs. But then she was not dissatisfied to be so female, and so alive. "I would rather feel than not," she thought. "It is better to feel than not to feel. But I am miserable. Oh, future master, have pity on the slave you will buy! Assuage my needs! Content me, if only a little! Would you not caress any pet animal upon occasion, particularly if she begs prettily enough?"

"Squat!" she heard, a man's voice, from several yards away, from somewhere behind her. He was at the end of the line adjacent to hers.

There the man had had the last slave in the line, that next to hers, on the left, stand and put her legs apart. Between them he had then thrust a large, round, porcelain vessel.

Notice of this quickly coursed down both chains, and the girls looked back.

Near the keeper was a slave with water, and a dipper.

The line to the left will be moving out first, thought Ellen. But then she noted that the porcelain vessel was moved to the right and the last slave in her own line must assume the posture and perform the expected behavior, as well. Both lines would apparently be taken forward rather at the same time.

The vessel then began to pass back and forth between the two lanes, moving forward. Following the wastes vessel was the slave with the water. Each slave in the chain, following her use of the wastes vessel, must kneel and drink from the dipper, draining it. Ellen looked forward to the water. She was thirsty, and she did not doubt but what this state was common on the chain. Soon, mercifully, the thirst of the chain would be assuaged. More importantly, she supposed, from the point of view of the keepers, the appearance of the girls would be freshened and improved. It is common to water stock, she knew, prior to its sale.

"Stand," said the keeper to the slave across from Ellen, the former free woman. "Get the bowl between your legs!"

"Please!" begged the former free woman, looking about herself, in misery, wildly.

"Squat," he said. "Be quick, slave."

Reddening, the former free woman, tears running down her cheeks, squatted miserably over the bowl. Then, doubtless for the first time in her life, she publicly relieved herself. No one must watch her. But, when she cast a frightened glance about, conducting a furtive reconnaissance, she saw that several of the other girls were watching her. She saw that Ellen, too, was watching her, very frankly, with a lofty, superior mien, with an almost malicious pleasure. Tears sprang anew to her eyes. She would receive no sympathy from Ellen. Ellen, you see, was recalling her former haughtiness, and was not a little pleased and amused. It was a pleasant vengeance in its way, to watch this once-haughty creature, now reduced to a shamed slave, squatting over the porcelain bowl, performing this homely act upon command. Slaves are not permitted modesty.

"117," said the keeper, reading Ellen's lot number.

Ellen took the bowl from the adjacent lane, and squatted over it. Now the eyes of the former free woman were upon her, and, it seemed, with a similar malicious satisfaction. It was now the turn of the former free woman to enjoy the discomfiture of a slave, and relish that slave's embarrassment. Ellen was angry. She looked forward, pretending not to notice. She heard a soft laugh from her left, and was furious. Ellen turned to the former free woman and said, angrily, "So? We are both slaves!"

"Yes, Mistress," smiled the former free woman. Then she must kneel and drink, for the slave with the water had reached her place.

You will look well in a collar, thought Ellen, irritably.

Soon even the lovely 115 had been readied for the staging area.

Two attendants then, with sticks, hurried the two lanes forward. The attendants cried out, angrily, making use of their sticks. Ellen cried out once, when struck across the back of the left shoulder. The former free woman, too, received a blow. But they could move no more quickly than the others on their respective chains! Soon the girls, the two chains, were crowded together, kneeling, at the side of the great block, at its right as one would look forward, toward the crowd. The crowd noise was close now, and loud, frighteningly loud. They could hear the calls of the auctioneer, bids, shouts. Ellen suddenly became terribly frightened. She was going to be sold, sold! Her shoulder stung from the blow she had received. All the girls, hurried as they had been, awkwardly, rushed, stumbling, were now kneeling huddled together, chained, frightened. They were disoriented, confused, fearfully intimidated. In this way there would be no doubt of their slavehood on the block, of their vulnerability and terror, nor of their eagerness to obey the auctioneer's slightest suggestion or gesture. They would be instantly, unquestioningly obedient; there would be no doubt in the buyers' minds of the docility, the piteous, abject servility, of the merchandise.

So, thought Ellen, it seems that there may be yet another reason, other than time, and impatience, for rushing the chains forward, weeping, crying out, begging for mercy, stumbling, under blows, herding them so cruelly with jabs and blows to the block, to their sale, that we may show ourselves as frightened slaves before masters! But Ellen's understanding of this, if understanding it was, did in no way diminish its effectiveness on her. She was fearful, frightened and intimidated. So this understanding, if understanding it was, certainly did not diminish reality. Rather it would make her so much the more aware of it. Such treatment, whether by intent or not, inevitably induced in her apprehensions and terrors which were fully suitable in one such as she on occasions such as this. She was terrified. She was a chained slave, soon to be offered to buyers. She shuddered. Her shoulder hurt. She knew she would obey on the block with abject alacrity, fearing only that she might be found displeasing in any respect. The blows and jabbings had perhaps not been necessary, but they had reminded her of what she was, and what could be done to her.

That was doubtless a more than adequate justification, if one were required, for the fierce, rushed herding.

If such was its intent, to teach this lesson, what she was and what could be done to her, it had certainly succeeded.

She was a chained, terrified slave.

And in this she was no different from the others. Masters would see women on the block who well knew they were slaves.

Ellen could see no order in the way girls were removed from the chains, to be dragged to the height of the block, one at a time. The light was now from torches. It illuminated the block, of course, and, partially, the pathetic goods clustered about it, to one side or the other. There was an attendant near the top of the block who could observe what was occurring, the type of girl being vended, the nature of the bids, and such. Perhaps he then made decisions as to who might most judiciously be next exhibited. Other attendants brought girls to the surface of the block, and, presumably, others conducted them from the block, on the other side. There seemed to be at least one attendant on the block, with the auctioneer, who, Ellen supposed, might upon occasion lend him assistance, perhaps posing a girl, or carrying one from the block who might be unable to walk, perhaps having succumbed to terror or having fainted.

I hate Mirus, she thought. I hate Selius Arconious, she thought. I am going to be sold! How can they sell me? I am a woman! But, ah, Ellen, she thought, you are a woman who is a slave! Thus it is that you may be sold, and thus it is fitting for you to be sold! There were twenty-one bids on me! There is thus interest in owning me, perhaps considerable interest! Hundreds must have viewed me in the exhibition cage. I wonder who, of all those hundreds, made bids. I do not know. How could one tell? How could one be sure? The highest of those bids, whatever it might be, will be in a sense a reserve put on me, a bid below which others will not be accepted, the initial bid, that at which the bidding will begin. But surely it is not likely the bidding will both begin and end there. Beyond being seen braceleted to a pole in the exhibition cage, on the basis of which the twenty-one bids were made, I was later seen elsewhere, in the festival camp, for Ahn serving wine, from the vat of Callimachus, the number on my breast for all to note, and even later, I was danced, and in the ba-ta circle! Some, I am sure, will recall this slave when she ascends the block. Indeed, some, counting their coins, will doubtless be waiting for her to appear.

I am to be sold, she thought. I am to be sold!

The highest bid will be my opening bid. What will it be!

I am suddenly afraid to ascend the block, to be shown to the men, to uninhibited, virile, powerful, lustful men, to men who are accustomed to the owning and the mastering of women. I am chained, I am stripped, I cannot flee!

On this world I am a property, an animal!

I am going to be sold, sold like a pig or horse!

I am going to be sold! I am going to be sold!

But of course I am going to be sold! I am a slave!

How is it that I am here?

How can this be, that I am here?

Foolish vulo, she thought. You are here because you have been brought here, by men, as women for centuries, and doubtless on thousands of worlds, have been brought to such places.

But why, why!

Because they have found you of interest, and, accordingly, will have you in their collar.

Surely they cannot sell me, she thought. Not I, not I!

Can you not hear the biddings, the calls, she asked herself.

They must not sell me, she thought.

Why not, she asked herself. That you, a female, should be sold is fully within the rights of nature.

Do you not know that such as you, dear Ellen, sweet, lovely Ellen, are the rightful property of men?

Have you not understood this, have you not, for years, sensed it?

Why, then, should you not be sold?

How is it that I am a slave?

Nature has made you such. Pity your impoverished sisters who have not yet met masters.

Yes, yes, yes, thought Ellen. I well know myself slave, and rightfully so, but I am afraid to be sold!

Who will buy me?

Who will buy me?

I am afraid to be sold, afraid!

Afraid!

Ellen half screamed, and turned away, but it was not her arm which the first of the two attendants seized, but that of a woman not inches from her, kneeling, cringing, the former free woman. There was the sound of a key thrust into the lock of the manacle, and turned, that by a second attendant. The manacle fell from her wrist. The former free woman was drawn to her feet, and held upright, as it seemed her legs might buckle. She looked down at Ellen, wild-eyed, trembling, weak, but in Ellen's eyes she doubtless saw little but her own terror reflected. "I shall close my hand! I shall close my hand!" called the auctioneer. "My hand is closed! Sold!" The gong sounded from somewhere on the block, doubtless toward its back. There was a sound of sobbing, a sharp blow of the whip, a cry of pain. The former free woman raised her eyes piteously to the attendant who held her left upper arm in a grip of iron, perhaps then understanding what it was to be a woman and a slave, but he was not even aware of this, keeping his gaze fixed on the attendant toward the top of the stairs. There was a sudden gesture, imperative, impatient. Crying out, the former free woman was dragged toward and then, stumbling, up the steps. "It is too soon," thought Ellen. "She has had little time to adjust to her bondage. She was marked only last night!" Ellen recalled the former free woman's rich necklace, the jewels of her veils and robes. Surely a life of wealth, of luxury and pampering would have done little to prepare her for chains, exposure, degradation, the searing heat of the pressing, held, iron, for the sudden, sharp, instructive stroke of the whip, for the grasping, imperious hands of men, for the sawdust of the sales block. Then Ellen recalled the haughtiness of the former free woman, her former superciliousness, her almost intolerable arrogance, how she had treated Ellen, though she, too, beneath her robes was no more than another female, and thus a fit slave for men! Had she no understanding of herself? Had she never paused before a mirror, and therein observed the loveliness of her own unmistakable slave curves? How self satisfied she had been, she so loftily relying on the security of her station, she so complacently ensconced in the fortress of her status! How smug she had been, how superior! "She is a hypocrite," thought Ellen. "She craved a collar, and now she will have one! Let her try to get it off! Be sold, slave girl! Be sold to the highest bidder!"

Then Ellen recalled that the former free woman was now no more than she, only another slave, and she feared for her.

"I hope you get a strong and kindly master," thought Ellen, "one who will see to your needs, one who will care for you, and love you, and cherish you, but one at whose feet you will never be permitted to forget that you are a female and a slave."

"Ten copper tarsks for this slut!" called the auctioneer. "Untrained! Never yet collared! Let yours be the first! Marked last night! Fresh meat off the iron! Fifteen copper tarsks! Seventeen! Had but once, and then as a free woman!"

There was laughter from the crowd.

A new slave, if taken for commercial purposes, is routinely subjected to a virginity check. In the slave's case, Ellen could well imagine her horror, legs spread, undergoing this examination. The test in her case, of course, doubtless to her chagrin, shame and embarrassment, would have had a negative outcome. Ellen could then imagine her hysterically defending her respectability, that she had had such an experience but once, had not found it satisfying, muchly regretted it, had found it disgusting, and so on, the usual defenses of frigidity in a free woman. Wait until you feel slave heat, and crawl to a man, begging, thought Ellen. What the auctioneer had said about the slave's sexual experience tallied, of course, with what she had told Ellen, in their earlier conversation. And Ellen did not doubt but what it was true. Indeed, why otherwise would the slave, when a free woman, have come alone to the festival camp, if she had not, on a profound subconscious level, scarcely understanding her own action, been seeking more, a more which she was sure must exist.

"Accordingly scarcely opened for the pleasures of men! Indeed, for most practical purposes, one might say 'not yet opened for the pleasures of men,' certainly not yet opened for the true pleasures of men, and certainly not opened as a slave is opened! Twenty copper tarsks! Be the first to open her as a slave is opened! Twenty-five! Consider this luscious slave! Look upon her! See her, there! She can be first opened as a slave but once! Be he who first opens her as a slave! Be the first to enjoy her as a slave! Twenty-eight! Thirty! Thirty-five!"

But then, to Ellen's trepidation, and shock, the former free woman herself called out to the crowd. "Sirs!" she called. "Kind sirs!"

She would then, it seemed, dare to address the crowd!

The auctioneer, somewhere on the surface of the block, was suddenly silent, doubtless taken aback, perhaps momentarily not even comprehending. Surely he would have been taken unawares.

To the right of the block, at the foot of wide, low, rounded steps, the kneeling slaves, chained, jammed together, huddled together, exchanged sudden startled, fearful, glances. Surely the slave on the block had not received permission to speak!

The crowd was suddenly quiet, alert, and this seemed even more fearful.

Ellen moaned softly.

It suddenly occurred to her that the life of the woman on the block might be in danger. She had not thought of that earlier.

"Sirs!" called the former free woman from the block. "Succor! I beg succor! Behold me! I am not what I seem! I am a free woman, free!"

Somewhere in the crowd a man laughed.

"No!" she cried. "I am free! I am a free woman mistakenly, wrongly, brought before you, thusly exposed and degraded, as though I might be a naked slave! I am a free woman! I am the Lady Melanie of Brundisium. Fellow citizens, give me succor! I am in grievous distress! I call upon some noble, gallant citizen of Brundisium to rescue me! Please, please!"

"Well," called the auctioneer to the crowd, "it will take at least thirty-five copper tarsks to rescue her!"

There was laughter from the crowd.

"I will rescue her for the whip!" called a man. "Thirty-six tarsks!"

"And I will rescue her for my pleasure gardens!" called a fellow. "Thirty-seven!"

"I think I would rescue her for the kitchen!" called another man. "Ten copper tarsks!" There was laughter. That had been the auctioneer's suggested opening bid.

"Was she taken from within the walls of Brundisium?" called a man.

"No," responded the auctioneer. "But even had it been so, the brand is already upon her!"

There was laughter from the crowd.

"You affirm," said a man, "that she has been properly embonded, and that all legal proprieties have been satisfied?"

"Yes," said the auctioneer. "All is in impeccable order, to the last detail."

"Please, sirs!" cried the woman. "Take pity on me!"

"I will take pity on you with a whip!" called a fellow. "Thirty-eight copper tarsks!"

The woman cried out with misery.

"How came she here?" called a man.

"She came alone, unguarded, of her own choosing, to the camp," responded the auctioneer.

"Thirty-eight copper tarsks is too much for so stupid a woman!" called a man.

This observation was greeted with laughter.

"Please, sirs, save me!" called out the woman. "Someone, please, save me!"

"Do you beg to be purchased, my dear," said the auctioneer, solicitously, but in a voice which could easily be heard well out into the crowd.

"Oh, yes!" she cried. "Yes! Yes! I beg to be purchased!"

There was much laughter from the crowd.

"Only slaves beg to be purchased," the auctioneer informed her.

"No!" she cried.

"On your knees, slave girl!" snapped the auctioneer.

Ellen supposed that the woman must have knelt, instantly. There was laughter from the crowd. There was no stroke of the whip.

"Please," she cried again, perhaps now on her knees, her hands perhaps extended piteously to the crowd. "I will repay you a hundred times for whatever you give for me!" she cried.

"You then acknowledge yourself a slave?" asked the auctioneer.

"Yes!" wept the woman.

"Yes, what?" he inquired.

"Yes—*Master*!" she cried.

"Do you mean, repay in coin?" asked the auctioneer.

"Yes," she cried. "Yes, Master!"

"Surely you know," said the auctioneer, "that you no longer have economic means at your disposal, no more than a kaiila or tarsk. A slave owns nothing, not even her collar."

"No!" she cried. "No, no!"

"Pose her," said the auctioneer. Ellen, huddled with the others beside the block, at its foot, and at its right, as one would face the crowd, heard a cry of misery from the woman, and supposed that she had been pulled to her feet, probably by the auctioneer's assistant.

"Consider the line of her body," the auctioneer advised the crowd. "Turn her," he said, presumably to his fellow on the block.

"Forty copper tarsks!" called a voice.

"Forty-five!" cried another.

"You will indeed, of course, my dear," said the auctioneer to the woman on the block, "repay your purchaser for purchasing you, as will any slave. You will repay him with extensive, servile, intimate services. You will repay him, day in and day out, night in and night out, lavishly and abundantly, and endlessly. You will be hot, devoted and dutiful. You will be a perfection to him. You will be his possession, and his toy. You will be his cook, and laundress, his housekeeper and maid, and, fear not, the answer to his most secret dreams of pleasure."

There was a raucous cry from the crowd.

Ellen did not know what was taking place on the block.

"Let us see if she is vital," called the auctioneer.

Ellen shuddered.

"Stand facing the masters," said the auctioneer, "stand straight, straighter, legs spread, more widely, clasp your hands behind the back of your head, head back, hold that position!"

In a moment Ellen heard the woman shriek.

"Hold position!" said the auctioneer.

The woman cried out in shame, in misery, in wonder.

"Hold her," said the auctioneer, doubtless to his fellow. "Steady, steady, little vulo," said the auctioneer, soothingly.

She cried out, in protest, in shame, in relief, in gratitude, in joy.

"Now to your belly, curvaceous little slut," said the auctioneer, "and you may beg the masters to be purchased. Surely you are not unfamiliar with the way in which this may be done."

Whereas Gorean free women commonly scorn and hate female slaves, and profess no interest in them, it is clear that there are few topics of greater interest to them. When with free men the free women seldom neglect an opportunity to speak loftily and disparagingly of slaves. How tedious it must be for the men to hear them so incessantly denigrate and castigate the innocent, helpless, scantily clad kajirae, sometimes even when being served by such. Naturally they wish the men to share their views but most Gorean men refrain from discussing the matter with them, except perhaps to dismiss the matter with some remark, such as "Do not concern yourself with them. Let them be beneath your notice. You are priceless, and free. They are only meaningless slaves, only domestic animals." Despite their profession of disinterest in such matters, free women, it seems clear, seek avidly to learn all they can about female slaves and their lives. What do they do? How do they serve their masters? What goes on behind those closed doors? What is it like to have to obey? What is it like to be in a collar? When the free women are alone with one another, and no young free females are present, they speak of little else. It seems they are obsessed with their embonded sisters. If they are truly free, why is it that they find the topic of the slave girl so extraordinarily fascinating? Doubtless it would be presumptuous for Ellen, who is only a slave, to speculate on such matters. She will, however, note in passing, that this antipathy and fascination is not limited to Gorean free women. Ellen recalls that many of her former female colleagues seemed obsessed with decrying women as slaves and chattels, and such, even when the women were obviously among the best fixed, the most comfortable, the richest and most free of the population. Is it because they want the collar put on them, truly? Too, even amongst her former colleagues, there had been an inordinate fascination with the female slave, when evidence of such might occasionally arise, even amongst the gray piles, the densely inhabited cliffs and busy, noisy canyons of their own civilization. Indeed, stripped, collared slaves served masters in their own cities, sometimes in the most expensive and prized of domiciles, in penthouses, and such. On marbled floors might patter the feet of bangled slaves. On rich rugs, amidst glass and chromium, and high bookcases, might they kneel. Surely they knew that. Did they dare guess how many? Did they really think they could shame a true man, a virile, rational man, one who thinks for himself, into not keeping a slave, should he be so fortunate as to acquire one? After once having had a taste of the mastery? No. That taste is not forgotten. That is clear to me. What can compare with it? Compliance with pathological politicized prescriptions, designed to promote the power of unscrupulous, self-seeking misfits? All the social engineering, all the establishments in charge of controlling minds, all the power of the media melt away before the sight of a slave at one's feet. With what would you reward a man who betrays his manhood? What will you give him that is worth more than his manhood? And I do not even comment on the other side of the coin, except to say that it is one coin, and it has another side. There are men and there are women, and the needs and desires of one are complementary to the needs and desires of the other. Each is a gift to the other, bestowed by nature, the slave to the master and the master to the slave. Ellen wonders, sometimes, how many of her former colleagues, in their private lives, in their secret lives, repudiate the falsity, foolishness and treason of their public lives. How many, she wonders, are dominated, stripped, belted in slave cuffs, and thrown to the bed, and from this surface look upward, into the eyes of masters?

But let us put such speculations aside.

Accordingly, the former free woman, as other Gorean free women, would doubtless have heard of, or been apprised of, doubtless to her scandal and horror, and doubtless in whispers, behaviors sometimes attributed to slave girls on the block.

And so the former free woman begged to be purchased. And it seemed, as far as Ellen could gather, that she was not, as the auctioneer had speculated, unfamiliar with the way in which this might be done.

Free women, after all, if only in virtue of hushed, furtive, scandalous rumors, would not be all that unacquainted with at least the possibility of such a thing.

Though they might decline to believe it.

But even supposing such things might actually occur, which seemed so improbable, surely she had never dreamed that one day it would be she on the block, she herself, then only a branded slave, who must perform so, who must behave in such a manner.

And then she found herself such.

How ironic, thought Ellen, how perfect!

And Ellen knew that on the block there was at least one man who had a whip, and would be willing to use it, instantly, on an errant girl.

Perfect, thought Ellen.

"Buy me, Masters!" called the slave. "Please buy me, Masters!"

It is unfortunate, thought Ellen, that there are no free women in the audience, for her former friends might be interested in seeing her so.

Doubtless they would find her predicament amusing and delicious. But let them beware, lest they find themselves sharing her fate.

Yes, thought Ellen, it is unfortunate that she is not before free women, as well, for such a contrast, with its excruciating, unspeakable humiliation, particularly at this time in her bondage, might help her to learn her slavery more quickly. But, no matter, for she will doubtless have many experiences before free women, kneeling, serving, obeying and such, and such experiences will send her even more needfully, even more gratefully, even more piteously, to the feet of a master.

"Buy me, Masters!" cried the slave on the block, presumably now on her belly, one hand perhaps extended to the crowd. "Buy me, Masters! Please, Masters, I beg to be purchased! Buy me, Masters! Please buy me, Masters!"

She went for two silver tarsks, surely a considerable sum for a new girl, an untrained slave.

Ellen was pleased with the sale of the slave. Had she not, when a free woman, once been haughty to her? To be sure, she was now only another slave.

"Oh!" cried Ellen, as her arm was seized. She tried to pull away a little, but she was helpless. The grip was like a vise. Marks would be left upon her arm. A second attendant thrust a key into the iron cuff which clasped her left wrist, and the metal fell away, loose on the chain. In a moment she was being dragged up the broad steps to the surface of the large block from which livestock, fleshstock, such as she was being vended. Briefly, wildly, she thought of Earth. How can this be happening to me, she thought. Then she recalled that she was now naught but a Gorean slave girl. Be proud, be beautiful, she thought. Show them that you are worth a high price! There were twenty-one bids on you, even from the exhibition cage. Show them that their bids were not mistaken. Show them you are worth even more!

She stood then before the men, apprehensive, but slave beautiful.

She heard murmurs of interest.

She knew that she was an object of desire, that she, stripped and standing before them, was of interest to men, to strong, virile men, men who knew what to do with women such as she.

But it is not unusual for a female slave to be desirable. They are usually selected for, as obviously they will usually be priced for, their desirability. In Gorean there is even an expression "slave desirable," which means, of course, desirable enough even to be a female slave.

Doubtless many Gorean women, and doubtless many of Earth, as well, have stood naked before a mirror, regarding themselves, and asked themselves if they were worth enslaving, if they were beautiful enough to be a female slave. Would they have value? If so, how much? What would they bring?

The sawdust was deep, about her ankles. There was a little dampness, perhaps from first-sale girls who had preceded her on the block. She was pleased that she had been given the opportunity, and had even been required, to relieve herself earlier, in the lines, between the ribbons.

What would the quoted bid be, she wondered. It would be the highest of the twenty-one bids from the exhibition cage.

She heard herself being praised, as slave meat, and as a toy of possible interest. I am intelligent, she thought, quite intelligent. Tell them that! Then she wondered if her intelligence, really, was that much higher than that of her chain sisters. The brutes, she thought, they are taking my intelligence for granted. That given, their interest seems to be in the pleasures which I seem to promise!

She heard herself described in some detail, by the auctioneer's assistant, who read from papers, presumably extracted from scribes' records. Various measurements were iterated matter-of-factly, for example, those of her bosom, waist and hips, and those of her neck, wrists and ankles, the latter primarily of interest with respect to the dimensions of appropriate identificatory or custodial hardware, the collar, wrist rings and ankle rings.

She blinked against the torchlight. The block was well illuminated. It was harder for her to see the crowd. Faces in the front rows were adequately visible. Some men were standing literally at the front edge of the block.

She was described as semi-trained. This pleased her, for she did not want her new master to expect too much of her, and be disappointed. He could always train her to his particular pleasures. That was always pleasant for a master. She would desperately strive, as any slave girl, to learn how to please him, to prepare his meals, to arrange his furs, to lie provocatively at his slave ring, to use her hands and hair, her lips and tongue as he might wish, and so on.

"Walk about, pose," she was told.

She did so.

"Barbarian," she heard.

"They do not have to beat me, to have me show myself to the crowd," she thought.

There was a cry of pleasure from some of the men.

"Red silk," she heard.

"That is obvious," called a man.

There was laughter.

It was Mirus who had first opened her, for the uses of men.

"A slave not without interest!" called a man.

"Yes," said another.

"Am I brazen?" she thought. "Very well, should that be the case. I do not mind. And are not such expressions merely disparaging expressions, from a distant Puritanical world, fearing life and beauty? Have they not been invented by the homely and inhibited, the ugly and inert, as weapons against the proud, the beautiful, the soft and vulnerable, the eager and passionate, to conceal their own grayness, their own flatness and uninteresting mediocrity? Am I a narcissistic little bitch, as Mirus, once my master, might claim? Perhaps. If so, I do not mind. No, I do not mind being beautiful, and delicious, and provocative. That pleases me. I like it. It makes me happy. What is wrong with that? Put aside the mediocrity's armament of vengeful semantics. See life as it is, directly, in its beauty, if only for a sudden, startling moment, perhaps as men might have seen it before language, before the subtle, altering, translucent barriers of words, the invisible wall that so liberates, but yet confines and shapes, was interposed between the mind and existence, not through the distortive prisms of the sluggish, fearful and defective. Would that there could be a new language, or new words, a lexicon of light that would allow us to see the world as it might be seen, in its innocence, profundity and glory."

How humiliating this is, she thought. How shamed you should be, Ellen! But you tramp, you slut, you tart, you are not! How terrible you are!

There was no mistaking the interest of the buyers. Suddenly it seemed she could almost feel the heat of their interest, like waves of heat emanating from the door of a furnace she had inadvertently opened.

She felt suddenly she might run from the block, but she could not, of course, do so.

"Apparently, she has some skill in slave dance," called the auctioneer's assistant.

Ellen hoped the buyers did not take that too seriously. To be sure, she would not have objected to being taught something of slave dance. It had suddenly seemed, last night, as though a world had been opened up before her, a wondrously exciting, sensuous, vital world. She had felt very female, very feminine, in the dance, pleasing men, performing, a slave before masters.

"Fluent in Gorean," was called to the crowd. "Small scar on the upper left arm." That would be her vaccination mark, from childhood, on Earth.

I wonder if Mirus and Selius Arconious are among the men, she thought. I suspect so. Or have they even bothered to attend?

"Brand, the kef," called the attendant.

That was the most common kajira brand, the "kef" being the first letter in the expression 'kajira'. Mirus, of course, had seen to it that she would wear the common kef, which he regarded as fitting for her; he had seen to it that she should be marked as it pleased him, as a common slave.

Perform, she thought. I wonder if dear Mirus and dear Selius Arconious, the arrogant, imperious pigs, are here. Perhaps! Then show dear Mirus what he gave up, what a fool he was to let something like me slip away! If he would have me now he will pay and pay! He will pay dearly! I do not care if he would empty his purse! But he will not bid upon me because he would look like a fool to do so, after letting me go! So be it. I care not a whit. That means nothing to me now! And let me show dear Selius Arconious what he shall not own! I hate him, the arrogant Gorean tarsk! Hurt him! Hurt Selius Arconious! Let him see what he cannot afford! I hate you, Selius Arconious! Grind your teeth, clench your fists, sweat, moan, tear your clothing, burn in needful misery, dear Selius Arconious, as I perform, delectably, exquisitely, as I do now, but know that you shall not have this slave! No! You cannot afford her!

Then tears sprang to her eyes.

I hate you, Selius Arconious, she said, to herself. I hate you, I hate you!

But neither, she supposed, neither Mirus or Selius Arconious, were here. Or, if they were, what was it to her? Both despised her, surely, as she despised them! And Mirus would be too proud, or would be too ashamed, to bid upon her, and so confess his foolishness in letting her out of his collar. Too, he might be outbid. There were many rich men in the crowd, dealers and others. And she need not concern herself at all with Selius Arconious, a lowly tarnster. He would be fortunate to be able to put together a handful of copper tarsk-bits. He was as impecunious as a field urt. She need not fear falling into his hands. And, too, she hated him. So she was safe from them both! How suddenly secure, and free, this made her feel, a strange attitude perhaps for a woman on a sales block. But Ellen laughed to herself. How pleased she was!

So perform, slave girl, she thought. Show these rugged, virile brutes that your slightness and softness, on sale before them, are worth at least a silver tarsk!

Earn yourself a rich master, Ellen!

Perform, thought Ellen. Perform!

Ellen dared not call out to the crowd, of course, as she had not been given permission to speak, but her eyes spoke to the men, and her body.

Some men shouted with pleasure.

Suddenly Ellen was startled. You enjoy doing what you are doing, don't you, she asked herself. Yes, she thought. Why, you brazen hussy, she thought. You shameless slut! You narcissistic little bitch! You have truly become a slave girl, haven't you? Yes! Yes, she thought. It is what you are! You have become a slave girl. You are truly a slave girl! Yes, she thought, on this world I have been put in my place, precisely where I belong, at the feet of powerful men. And my will means nothing here! These things have been done to me whether I wish them to be done to me or not, and would have been done to me whether I willed them or not! They have been done unilaterally, by the will of masters. And, lo! Here, on this world, where there are true men, on this world of masters, I have found out, for the first time in my life, what it is to be a woman, a true woman. And I am pleased, and proud, and gloriously happy to be what I am, a woman!

"Stand as you were before," she was told.

She did so.

"Hot and needful," she heard.

She tossed her head, a bit angrily, a bit insolently. Did they have to know that? Could that not be left as her secret, to be revealed only, whether she willed it or not, in the arms of a dominant male? She wondered at the knowledge of the slavers. How could they know such things? It seemed they could see in a woman what she could scarcely admit to herself, even in her most secret dreams. Doubtless there were subtle cues in a woman's body, in her movements, in her discourse, her carriage, her expressions and such. She had been told that slavers on Earth occasionally passed by beautiful women, to take as prey women perhaps less beautiful, but more intelligent, more latently passionate, those who, in their view, would make better slaves. Passion, of course, is required in a slave. Too, if she does not have it to begin with, she will soon acquire it. The master, the whip, will see to it. All women, at least latently, are passionate slaves. To be sure, much depends on the master. Some women know their master at a glance, others learn it at his feet. Bondage, in itself, is devastatingly arousing in the female. She recognizes it as her fitting condition. To the slaver's practiced eye there must be ways of telling. But, indeed, even a man of Earth can occasionally sense, incontrovertibly, suppressed needs, latent passion, in a woman. And they are not even slavers, whose professional concerns require a considerable degree of accuracy in such judgments. But, to be sure, Ellen had doubtless squirmed at night, on her chain, cried out in her sleep, wept with need, and such, publicly enough. Too, she recalled, in the Cosian camp, days ago, before being coffled, having been bent over and tied at a trestle. Unwilling though she might have been to reveal her arousal under such conditions, it had doubtless been clear enough from the state of her body. She wondered if her new master would bind her so, occasionally, over a trestle. It is difficult for a girl to retain her dignity in such a position, but then Ellen recalled that a slave is not permitted dignity. Rather, expected of her is unquestioning obedience, delicious service and helpless passion.

"What is your name?" inquired the auctioneer of Ellen.

"'Ellen', Master," she said, "if it pleases Master."

"It is acceptable," said the auctioneer. Then he turned to the crowd. Ellen looked uneasily at the whip, in his right hand. "We have here, Ellen, a young barbarian, small, curvaceous, brunet, gray-eyed, semi-trained, common mark, red-silk, responsive. There is interest in this slut, for there were several bids on her before she was removed from the exhibition cage." He then turned to his assistant. "How many?" he asked.

"Twenty-one," said the assistant, consulting papers. These were sometimes carried, but there was a small stand at the back of the platform where they might be deposited. Actual sales were recorded, and payments arranged, or made, at a table on the ground level, to the left of the block, as one would face the crowd.

Some of the men reacted to this, and leaned forward. It is, of course, easier to see a girl in the exhibition cage, where, if she is not restrained, one may even call her to the bars, than from most of the positions in the tiers, at night, as she is shown illuminated in the torchlight of the sales block. That, of course, is the purpose of the exhibition cage, *to exhibit*. One may then take note, under favorable conditions, of merchandise in which one might be interested. Ellen, of course, could not have been called to the bars in the exhibition cage, as she had been braceleted about one of the stanchions. She had, of course, had to caress the stanchion, kiss it, writhe about it, and such, responding to the commands of the fellows peering in, in their robes, from outside the bars. Had she been uncooperative an attendant would have entered the cage and put the whip to her. She had not been uncooperative. She, like the other women in the cage, had been stripped. Goreans do not buy clothed women. They wish to see what they are getting.

"Mostly from dealers," said the assistant.

That pleased Ellen, as dealers might generally be expected to be relatively objective in their assessments. Such bids should be a good index to at least her wholesale value. To be sure, she did not know the nature of the bids.

"What was highest bid?" asked the auctioneer. That would be the bid at which the open bidding would begin.

"Two silver tarsks, fifty copper tarsks," said the assistant.

Ellen nearly fainted. She trembled. Her knees buckled for a moment. She tried to regain her balance.

"Two and a half!" called the auctioneer. "Two and three-quarters?"

It is a mistake, thought Ellen. It must be a mistake. I do not want to be sold for so much! Masters will expect too much of me! I am not trained. I am only a common girl, and a barbarian!

Although these matters differ considerably from city to city, and silver and gold is often weighed by merchants, common ratios in the vicinity of Brundisium at the time of this writing, given the inflation of the unsettled times, are a hundred tarsk-bits to a copper tarsk, and a hundred copper tarsks to a silver tarsk. Depending on the nature of the silver tarsk, there will usually be ten to a hundred for a golden tarn disk. For the common silver tarsk, the smaller tarsk, the coin pertinent to the bidding in question, the ratio was one hundred such tarsks to the golden tarn disk, at least that of Ar or Jad, on Cos, and certain other major cities, including Brundisium.

In a moment, it seemed the auctioneer had his invited bid of two and three-quarters, and, a moment later, three.

Ellen, frightened, backed toward the auctioneer's assistant. "May I speak?" she whispered.

"What do you want?" he asked.

"I think there is some mistake, Master," said Ellen.

"No," he said.

The auctioneer's assistant then raised his hand, and called out, "Four!"

"Four, from my colleague!" called the auctioneer.

"He is not permitted to bid!" cried a man.

"Five," came from the crowd, somewhere.

"I rule my colleague may bid, subject to review by the camp *polemarkos,*" said the auctioneer. "But the point is moot, as we have a bid of five." He looked about, at his assistant. The assistant shook his head. The auctioneer lifted his hand for a moment's respite, and turned to his assistant. They conferred in low tones, and Ellen looked away, indeed, moved away from the small table. "Do you want her for yourself?" asked the auctioneer. "I could claim a defect, an error in the records."

"You would have a riot on your hands," said his assistant.

"Did you want her for yourself?" asked the auctioneer.

"No," said the assistant. "I like blondes. I thought only to turn a profit on her."

"Then we shall let the matter stand," said the auctioneer.

"Yes," said his assistant.

"Buy something as good, for less, when the crowd is smaller," said the auctioneer.

The assistant nodded.

"And there may be leftovers, to be distributed," said the auctioneer. "Possibly one or more blondes."

"True," said the assistant.

The auctioneer then turned to Ellen. "Go to the front of the block, where buyers can get a better look at you," he said.

Ellen obeyed.

"We have a bid of five!" called the auctioneer, "a mere five tarsks for this exquisite little barbarian bauble. Would you not like to have her crawling to you, bringing you your sandals in her teeth! Imagine her before you, on her belly, licking and kissing your feet, begging to serve your pleasure!"

"Oh!" cried Ellen, for one of the men near the front of the block had grasped her ankle. She dared not, of course, protest. If she had tried to kick at the man her foot might have been removed.

But the eye of the auctioneer was quick. "Do not handle the merchandise," said he, laughing, "until you own it."

Grinning, the man removed his hand. "Six," said the man.

But in a moment there was a bid of seven from the crowd.

Ellen was dazed.

The thought passed her mind of her lectures in the classroom, her former demeanor, her former prim attire. So faraway, so different! And then the strange image came to her of herself, stripped as she now was, but standing on the cool, flat, smooth surface of the desk in the classroom, being exhibited as a slave. In that image it seemed that, somehow, there were several young men then in the classroom, as there had not been, considering her, having her turn about, and so on. The female students in the room, many of whom she remembered, seemed timid, small, shy, quiet, subdued, fearful, withdrawn, but were regarding her with fascination. And from time to time the young women in the classroom looked about themselves, at the young men. Did they ask themselves what it would be, to belong to one or another of them? As they regarded her, with wide, fearful, attentive, shining eyes, did they expect, or await, or fear, their own turn upon that platform, similarly, blatantly, coarsely, displayed. And then the image was gone, and Ellen was again herself, on the exotic world of perilous, barbaric Gor, illuminated in the light of torches, standing on the concave surface of the block, her ankles in sawdust, the lights of Brundisium in the distance, the men calling out, being offered for sale, being sold.

She scarcely realized that there was now a bid on her of ten silver tarsks. That is too much, she thought, too much! That was a full tenth of a golden tarn disk!

There was then a lull in the bidding.

"More? More?" inquired the auctioneer, though it seemed he did not, really, expect more.

Ellen did not think that many girls sold in this camp would go for so much. Perhaps a hundred, or a hundred and fifty, perhaps high slaves, perhaps exquisitely, lengthily trained pleasure slaves, perhaps skilled dancers, perhaps such, but surely not she! Accordingly, instead of being excited and thrilled, she was apprehensive. There must be some mistake, she thought. I am not worth that much, she thought. To be sure, she told herself, it is men who will decide what you are worth, not you. How much I must have changed, she thought, if men, particularly in a general, improvised camp such as this, are willing to bid so much!

Dare I think such thoughts? Dare I accept myself as being that attractive? Surely I must dismiss such thoughts. They are far too bold for a slave! There must be a mistake, a mistake of some sort!

"Here, kajira," snapped the auctioneer, behind her.

Quickly Ellen backed to him, that she might not cease to face the men, until she sensed that he was a foot or so behind her, to her right.

She felt his hand in her hair, behind her shoulders, his hand then lifting, looping the hair several times about his fist, until his fist was tightly at the back of her head. She put her head back a little, apprehensively, to ease the pressure. Then she cried out suddenly in pain as his hand twisted tightly, cruelly, in her hair, bending her backward, exhibiting the bow of her beauty to the men. She tried to reach back to her hair, twisting, sobbing.

"Place your wrists behind you, crossed," said the auctioneer, and Ellen, the slave, complied, bound by the will of the master.

She was then turned about, from side to side, that the men might better see.

I trust, she thought wildly, that neither Mirus nor Selius Arconious are among the buyers. Surely they must not see me so, not exhibited thusly!

Clearly the men were enflamed at the sight of the helpless, displayed slave.

"Eleven!" she heard.

"Twelve!"

"Thirteen!"

"Fourteen!"

"Fifteen!"

There was then again a lull in the bidding.

Ellen sobbed suddenly, again, held, twisted backward.

"Is there more?" called the auctioneer. "More?"

He released Ellen's hair and took her by the upper left arm, and threw her to her hands and knees in the sawdust before him. Her knees were deep in the sawdust, and her hands were in it, to the wrists. She looked wildly out, through her fallen, dangling, scattered hair, into the crowd. Tears fell into the sawdust.

"More?" inquired the auctioneer. "I have fifteen! Do I hear more? My hand is lifted! I am preparing to close my hand!"

"Twenty," said a voice.

There was a gasp from the crowd.

Ellen shook her head, trying to clear the hair from before her face. She looked out, into the crowd, trying to see. "No," she wept. "No!"

Then she lay on her left side in the sawdust, facing away from the crowd, her knees drawn up, her head covered with her hands, at the feet of the auctioneer.

"Did I hear a bid of twenty?" asked the auctioneer.

"Twenty," repeated the voice.

"This is a barbarian, not fully trained," said the auctioneer.

"She can be trained!" laughed a voice.

"Twenty," said again the first voice.

"Kneel, facing the men," said the auctioneer.

Ellen then knelt, facing the men, but with her head down, her knees closely together, trembling, her arms crossed before her, trying to cover herself as best she could, trying to conceal as much of the slave as possible.

"Position," said the auctioneer to Ellen.

And then Ellen, tears running down her cheeks, knelt appropriately before the men, as what she was, a Gorean pleasure slave, back on heels, back straight, head up, hands down on thighs, knees widely spread.

"I have twenty," said the auctioneer. "I am preparing to close my hand!"

Ellen had recognized the voice. In a moment she would again belong to Mirus, he who had first opened her for the uses of men, her first master.

I do not want to belong to him, she thought, suddenly, wildly, no longer, no longer! And the thought, springing into her consciousness, startled her, and amazed her.

But she would belong to whomsoever she was sold, he who would then have all rights to her embonded beauty, and he who would exercise all rights, he whose slave she would then be.

"I will now close my hand!" said the auctioneer.

"No!" called out another voice, from the crowd, firmly, clearly.

Men looked about, to see who had spoken, who might choose to challenge the preceding, remarkable bid.

Mirus turned about, to see as well, he several yards back, in the crowd, to Ellen's left, as she faced the crowd.

Mirus clearly did not know his competitor.

The garments of Mirus were ample and splendid, robes which might well betoken his wealth and position.

The fellow who had halted the auctioneer was plainly clad, in a simple brown tunic, and was surely of low caste, perhaps of the peasants, or a drayman of sorts.

Mirus smiled.

Although the caste of Mirus might be unclear from the particular nature of his garmenture, Ellen supposed him of the slavers, which would be a subcaste of the Merchants, which caste was doubtless the wealthiest on Gor, and one which was often wont to view itself, perhaps in virtue of its wealth, if not as well in virtue of its influence and power, as a high caste, a tendency which, however, was not widely shared, save perhaps, at least publicly, by its clients and sycophants. Goreans respect wealth but tend to value other attributes more highly, and, indeed, to the credit of the Merchants, it should be noted that they usually do so, as well. One such attribute is fidelity; another is honor. Gor is not Earth.

In any event, aside from any cultural ambiguity which might attend the station or status of the Merchants, Mirus would presumably concede nothing in caste merit to the fellow who had just, it seemed, dared to gainsay him.

Mirus again regarded his apparent competitor, and again smiled.

It did not seem that he need have much to fear with respect to any ensuing competitive engagements.

"The bid was of twenty silver tarsks," called the auctioneer, "not twenty copper tarsks."

"Close your hand," called Mirus.

"Do not do so," called the other man, several yards farther way than Mirus, but to his left, and Ellen's right.

"You have a bid?" asked the auctioneer.

"I bid one," said the man.

"I do not understand," said the auctioneer.

"One golden tarn disk, of the Ubar's mint, of Cos," called the man.

A murmur of surprise, and interest, and disbelief, coursed through the crowd.

Ellen shook her head, wildly, disconcerted, frightened.

"What is your caste?" called Mirus to the man.

"Surely one need not certify caste to bid in open auction," said the fellow. "I do not recall that being required hitherto, here or elsewhere."

"A ruling!" called Mirus.

"Certification of caste is not a prerequisite for bidding," said the auctioneer.

"Let us see the color of his gold!" called Mirus.

"With all due respect, good sir," said the auctioneer to the fellow back in the crowd on Ellen's right, "all in all, under the circumstances, I think that a fair request."

"No other has been required to do so," called the plainly clad fellow.

There was laughter in the crowd.

"I have a bid of twenty silver tarsks," called the auctioneer, "and I am preparing to close my hand!"

"Wait!" cried a man, pointing to the plainly clad fellow.

He was now holding up, over his head, a large coin. Aloft, held so, it seemed to speak of weight and power. Its glossy glint in the flickering torchlight carried even to the block.

"See if it is genuine!" cried Mirus.

The auctioneer gestured to the side of the block and one of the assistants there hurried through the tiers. He held the coin, and bit at it. "It is good, it seems good," he called back to the block.

"Let it be tested and weighed at the business table," suggested the plainly clad fellow.

"And whose throat did you cut for it?" called Mirus to his adversary.

"None, as yet," said the plainly clad fellow.

"One, one!" called Mirus. This was a bid of a golden tarn disk, and a silver tarsk.

The crowd was quiet. All eyes turned to the plainly clad fellow.

"Five," said the plainly clad fellow, "five golden tarn disks, each of full weight, each from the Ubar's mint, at Jad, on Cos."

Ellen, in position, trembled. She was in consternation. Where would the plainly clad fellow, one such as he, obtain such riches?

She struggled to keep position. She did not wish to be a whipped slave, surely not before Mirus and the other! She fought blackness, which seemed to close about her. Then she fought her way back to full, alarmed consciousness. She had somehow managed to keep position. She blinked against the light. She was very much aware of the sawdust in which she knelt, "slave knelt." She was afraid. Surely he must be a sought man, surely guardsmen would enter the tiers at any moment and put hands upon him. Surely he should flee with his gains, howsoever he might have come by them. And how dare he reveal such wealth, here, in this place, he with no retinue, no men at arms to surround and protect him? Surely in a camp such as this, so open, so populous, there might be thieves, brigands, bandits, murderers, who knew what practitioners of diverse arts predatory and unscrupulous.

"I have a bid of five tarn disks," called the auctioneer. "I am preparing to close my hand!"

"Wait!" called Mirus. "I cannot at the moment match that bid in ready coin. Indeed, no rational man, without guards, outside of a caravan, would carry about such wealth! I do not have the coins at hand, but I can give you a note, my note, for more!"

There was a roar of laughter from the tiers.

"I am Mirus, of the house of Mirus, of Ar!" called Mirus.

"Ar is bankrupt," cried a man. "She is occupied, looted. She is a den of cowards, beggars and traitors! She lives at the sufferance of Cos!"

"Long live Cos!" cried more than one man in the crowd. And this cry was soon taken up by others.

"I have a bid of five tarn disks," called the auctioneer. "Is there more? Is there more?"

"You will not accept my note?" called Mirus.

"I am sorry, good sir," said the auctioneer. "We deal with coin in this camp."

There was more laughter in the tiers.

"Down with Ar!" cried a man.

"Long live Cos!" shouted a man.

Mirus thrust his hand angrily within his robes, toward his left side, but a fellow with him, one Ellen recognized as having been with him in the tent, put his hand warningly on his arm, and Mirus withdrew his hand. He then stormed away, making his way through the tiers, pressing away through the crowd, followed by some four men, he who had placed his hand warningly on his arm and three others, all of these having been seen by Ellen earlier in the tent. For some reason these men frightened her. More than one cast a backwards glance toward the block. Could it be that they had, for some reason, wished Mirus to be successful in his bidding?

"I have a bid of five tarn disks," called the auctioneer. "Do I hear more?"

There was silence.

"To be sure," said the auctioneer, "that is a high price to pay for this little piece of slave meat."

"Is she incognito?" inquired a fellow from the tiers. "Is she a Ubar's daughter?"

There was laughter in the crowd.

Ellen reddened. There had been no mistaking her for such, not she. Only too obviously did they see her as mere chattel, a simple collar slut.

"No," said the auctioneer, "she is a barbarian, semi-trained, a relatively common piece of chain goods, nothing particularly out of the ordinary, a fairly typical item of fleshstock. To be sure, she is a vulnerable, nicely curved, cuddly little slut, not unlike many barbarians."

"I am preparing to close my hand," called the auctioneer, well pleased.

Suddenly the momentousness of the moment came home to Ellen. She was on the brink of being sold!

"No, no!" she cried, suddenly. "Do not sell me! Not to him! Please, no! No, please! No!"

The auctioneer looked down at her, startled. Ellen had twisted, to see him behind her.

"May I speak?" she begged. "May I speak?"

The auctioneer scrutinized the stripped slave at his feet. His eyes narrowed. He did not respond to her request to speak. Clearly she was beside herself with misery and fear.

"Do not sell me to him, Master!" she begged. "Sell me to anyone but him, Master!"

"Ah," said the auctioneer. "Now I think I understand. It is a vengeance buy. Once you betrayed him, and now he will have you at his mercy, and will revenge himself upon you lengthily, and exquisitely, and at his leisure."

"No!" cried Ellen. "That is not it! It is different! It is different!"

No matter how she might have annoyed, or scorned, or tormented, or taunted, from time to time, this handsome competitor of her former master, Mirus, she had surely never dealt him treachery, had never betrayed him to enemies, or such. Thus his interest in her, if interest it was, could not be of the nature of a "vengeance buy," at least in any normal sense of that term, with its commonly dreadful implications.

Indeed, let the woman beware who is the object of a true vengeance buy! A man will pay much to obtain her! And then, sold to him, she is his to do with as he pleases. Let the woman beware, whether slave or free, who has betrayed a Gorean male, lest she come later into his power. Gorean males will pursue such a woman relentlessly, intent on bringing her into their collar. How terrifying to find oneself in chains, owned, stripped, at the feet of one whom one has betrayed! But such cases are rare, and extreme. The usual "vengeance buy" might more appropriately be regarded as little more than a "satisfaction buy." Perhaps, say, a woman, doubtless a free woman, as a slave would be very unlikely to risk this, has irritated or annoyed a man. Has this been done deliberately? Doubtless. But, why? Perhaps she is merely nasty, or unhappy, and feels secure in her freedom. Perhaps, on the other hand, she is, subconsciously presumably, as the saying is, "courting the collar." Who knows? Is her unpleasantness merely something to be reprimanded by the collar, that she is to be taught, stripped at a man's feet, that such a thing is impolite, and unacceptable? Or is it rather an unwitting, scarcely understood, cry from her heart, a cry for the secret, yearning slave to be released from the dungeon of denial in which she has for so long languished, neglected and ignored, a plea for her to be permitted to emerge at last into the liberation of total bondage, and helpless, absolute love? But would it not be pleasant, in either case, to have her in one's collar? A moment of explanation might not be here amiss. Gorean free women, particularly of high caste, have a status which is far higher than that of the average free woman on Earth. Indeed, the average free woman of Earth would have very little understanding, at least initially, culturally, of the social station of a Gorean free woman. Her culture would not have prepared her for it. She will, of course, become aware of this almost immediately on Gor, when she will be so unfortunate to find herself, a slave, before such a woman. In any event, aware of her status and station the Gorean free woman, particularly if of high caste, commonly regards herself, and is culturally justified in doing so, as a very special and superior creature, one generally aloof and unapproachable, one commonly lofty and exalted. She has, after all, a Home Stone. Accordingly, as might be expected, she is often vain, petty, selfish, supercilious, and arrogant. One might then have some understanding of the radical and traumatic transformation, with all its attendant mental and psychological anguish, which such a woman might undergo should she become a slave. She, at least, from her culture, has some understanding of what it is to be a slave. She has a clear idea of what has been done to her. The Earth woman, on the other hand, on her native world, is commonly not even veiled. She lets anyone look upon her face, not even aware of how much more exquisitely expressive it is, how much more sensitive and revealing it is, than her bared body. Too, her transition from free to slave, given her background, is not as radical and dramatic a transition as would be that of a Gorean free woman to the same status, that of bondage. To be sure, it should in all honesty be admitted that Gorean women, at least after some initial adjustments, do quite well in slavery. Given no choice they, as their Earth sisters, thrive in their collars. This is not surprising for we are both women and can come home to ourselves only at the feet of a man. Too, the Gorean free woman is subject to many constraints, physical, psychological and cultural, of which the slave is free. It is nice to think that within those cumbersome, ponderous robes a naked slave is waiting. How wonderful it is to be tunicked and safely, securely collared, to be able to move freely about, to walk and run, to be open to the sun, to feel the air and wind on one's body, to see and feel the glory of this world, to revel in its vitalities and sensations, and, too, to know that one is excruciatingly desirable, to say nothing of knowing oneself owned, and taken in the arms of one's master.

So let us all, slaves, whatever might be our origins, strive to please our masters!

"No, Master, no, Master!" cried Ellen, and turned about, on her knees, clasping the knees of the auctioneer in piteous supplication, looking up at him, her eyes bursting with tears. "Do not sell me to him, not to him! To anyone but him! Not to him, please, Master!"

The auctioneer thrust her back.

"I hate him!" she cried. "I hate him!"

"And he you?" inquired the auctioneer.

"Yes!" she cried. "He holds me in contempt, and hates me!"

"It is not inappropriate to hold barbarians in contempt," said the auctioneer. "Your lowly origin alone justifies that form of regard. Surely you have learned that by now on Gor. But in what manner, other than by your origin, did you earn his contempt?"

Ellen looked down, into the sawdust.

"Were you poor in the furs?" he asked.

"I trust not, Master," she said.

"Speak," said the auctioneer.

"I scorned him," she wept.

"Ah," said the auctioneer. "I see that you will have a pleasant time of it."

"He hates me!" she wept.

"Doubtless that will add an interesting flavor to your relationship," said the auctioneer.

"Sell me to anyone but him, Master!" Ellen begged. "Do not have me put in that collar! I do not want to wear his collar!"

"Be silent," said the auctioneer.

Ellen looked up at him, agonized, not permitted then to speak.

He then with the back of his hand struck her across the mouth. She sobbed, looking up at him, regarding him, aghast.

"That is for having spoken without permission," he said.

He then with a thrust of his bootlike sandal spurned her to the sawdust, and she lay sobbing before him, at his feet.

"Belly," said he then, "head to the left."

Ellen then lay on her belly in the sawdust, her head toward the exit steps from the great block. She tasted blood at her lip. How foolish she had been, to have spoken without permission. Had she learned nothing as to what she was on this world? She felt the bootlike sandal of the auctioneer resting on her back. It held her in place. She could not rise. She turned her head toward the crowd, to see he who had bid so high on the miserable, pathetic piece of helpless flesh merchandise which was she.

"Five tarn disks!" called the auctioneer. "I close my hand!"

She saw the eyes of her buyer upon her. His expression was unreadable. Her lower lip trembled; again she tasted blood.

The gong rang out. She knew its signification. Surely she had heard it ring out many times before. The auctioneer removed his bootlike sandal from her back.

The vibrations of the gong seemed to linger in the atmosphere, and in her flesh. She knew what it meant, that another girl had been sold.

And suddenly she realized that she was the girl.

She had been sold!

She now belonged, in the full meaningfulness of Gorean servitude, to her new master, Selius Arconious!

The auctioneer's assistant half dragged her to the stairs, and there handed her down, into the arms of another assistant. In a moment she was at the left of the block, as one would look toward the tiers, among other girls. She felt her left wrist clasped in a holding manacle, much as had been the case earlier, at the right side of the block, before her ascent to the sawdust-covered, concave surface from which she had been but a moment earlier vended.

No, no, she thought. Not to him! To anyone but him! He hates me! I hate him! I hate him! Oh, Ellen, miserable slave! He has bought you! He owns you! You belong to him! You belong to Selius Arconious! It is his collar that you must wear!

She put her face in her hands, weeping.

The chain dangled down, from the close-fitting metal on her wrist.

Chapter 26

We Must Depart the Camp

"My master is going to call me 'Melanie'," she said.

"That is now a slave name," said Ellen.

To be sure, Ellen was half numb with fatigue and misery. And she was afraid, for she knew who it was who had bought her.

"Yes, of course," she said, happily. "I wear it now only upon my master's sufferance."

"You understand that?" asked Ellen.

"Yes, fully, completely!" she said, happily.

"Excellent," said Ellen, weakly.

Ellen, with other slaves, sold women, wrist-chained, was in a holding area. They were awaiting their pick-ups. Several had already been removed from the chain. A receipt is tendered, and the slave is delivered. This was the morning after their sale, something like an Ahn before noon. Slaves are not always promptly claimed. There may be collars to prepare, chains to be measured, whips to be purchased, arrangements to be made.

Ellen was confused, dismayed, frightened.

Selius Arconious, it seemed, for whatever reason, as was the case, it seemed, with a number of other masters, as well, was in no hurry to claim his slave.

She wondered if he would come to the area in person, to claim her.

She wanted to be claimed, and was frightened that she would be claimed.

"I was sold to one from Venna!" Melanie said.

"That is far from Brundisium," said Ellen.

"Yes," she cried, delightedly. "And there I can be only a slave!"

"I assure you," said Ellen, "even if you were sold to someone in Brundisium, you would be there, in your former city, no more than a slave, as well. No more, even there, would the briefly tunicked, collared slave Melanie be confused with the former free woman, the proud, heavily robed Lady Melanie of Brundisium. If anything, you would be treated even more harshly, more cruelly, in Brundisium."

"He is strong, and handsome, my master," she said. "I am so happy! I have always wanted to be so beautiful, so desirable, that men would find me beautiful enough and desirable enough to take me and enslave me! And now it has been done! I have always wanted to be owned, to belong to a man, to be completely subject to him. I have always wanted to belong to a man strong enough to dominate and master me. I have always wanted to belong to a man who will require of me, casually and without a second thought, the fullness of my womanhood. I have always wanted to serve and love—fully, will-lessly, selflessly. And now I belong to a man whom I shall so serve and love, one who will have everything from me, which is what I long to give. I am happy, happy!"

"I am happy for you," said Ellen.

Melanie threw Ellen a kiss in the Gorean fashion, brushing it to her with her hand.

Ellen returned the kiss, similarly.

The slaves could not reach one another, for their chaining.

"Hold still," Ellen heard.

Ellen stiffened. She was kneeling. She could not see behind her, and dared not turn.

"Hood the slut," she heard.

A leather slave hood was thrust over her head and pulled downward. In moments it was buckled tightly about her neck. She then heard a lock snap behind her neck, through the buckle rings. It was then on her. She could not remove it. The hood was opaque. It is an efficient control device. In it she would be disoriented and helpless. She lifted her right hand and touched the ring on the front of the device, to which a leash might be attached.

The manacle on her left wrist was unlocked. It dropped to one side. She had remained on her knees, of course. She had neither been given permission to rise, nor had she been ordered to do so. Someone crouched down behind her. She spread her knees, thinking it best to do so, without having been ordered to do so. Too, it was appropriate. Men had left her in no doubt as to the sort of slave she was. Too, she did not know if Selius Arconious was in the vicinity. He was her master, and she knew that he would be strict with her. He was not the sort of man who would permit a slave even the smallest of laxities. Too, though she tried to brush away the thought, she had a sudden sense that she wanted to spread her knees before him, perhaps even supplicatingly. She excused herself on this count, with the recognition that Selius Arconious was the sort of man before whom women naturally felt an impulse to kneel, and spread-kneed. She felt her wrists drawn together. Then they were tied behind her back, it seemed with some loops of a leather string. It was more than sufficient to hold a female slave. Whoever it was was then before her, standing one supposes. She felt something snap about the ring on the front of the hood. Briefly a leather strap brushed her right breast.

"On your feet, slave girl," said a voice.

She rose. It was not the voice of Selius Arconious.

Then, guided by a pressure at the ring on the front of the hood's neck strap, she followed, as she must, as helpless as a tethered verr.

She must have followed for several hundred yards, stripped, bound, hooded, leashed. She conjectured she was then in the outer reaches of the camp, or perhaps beyond them, for she felt grass beneath her feet.

Then she was told to kneel, head down, and she did so.

"Are you obedient and docile?" she was asked. The voice was the same as that of the man who had ordered her to her feet, presumably he who had also led her to this place.

"Yes, Master," she said. And it was true. The battles, the wars, were done. And she was pleased that it was so. The superficialities of the conventions were at an end. The pretenses were over. On this world men ruled, or at least ruled such as she. They would tolerate no affronts to nature. Here they had refused to relinquish their rightful, natural sovereignty. Here they were hardy, virile masters. It was so, it was incontestable. Ellen, head down, was content.

"May I speak?" asked Ellen.

There was no answer, so she remained silent. She did not know if she were alone or not.

It was hot in the hood, stifling. Her small hands twisted behind her, in their bonds. She could feel the leash dangling between her breasts.

After a time she heard a man approach. She looked up in the hood, struggling a little.

"Master?" she asked.

"It is pleasant to hear that suitable, appropriate word on your tongue, kajira, particularly as addressed to me," said a man's voice.

Ellen sobbed with relief, then fear.

It was the voice of Selius Arconious.

"May I speak, Master?" she asked.

"It is suitable that you should ask permission to speak," he said. "It is good that you have learned at least that much. And, as I recall, you remembered to ask permission to speak on the block. But apparently you did not remember to wait until you had received that permission before you dared to speak. Had you also remembered that you might have saved yourself a cuffing."

Ellen was silent.

"You are a stupid slave," he said.

Ellen was silent.

"Yes, you may speak," he said.

"Portus Canio and Fel Doron are in this camp, in chains," said Ellen, hastily, fearing to be interrupted, the words spilling out. "They were on some obscure mission northward. They were betrayed by Tersius Major. It seems he is in the service of Cos. Beware of Tersius Major! Portus Canio and Fel Doron are even now awaiting transportation to Cos or Tyros, perhaps to the quarries!"

"Do not concern yourself about such things, slave girl," said Selius Arconious.

"Portus Canio and Fel Doron are your friends!" said Ellen.

"I attempted to dissuade them," said Selius Arconious. "But, nonetheless, they have inadvertently played their role in such things."

"I do not understand," said Ellen.

"Curiosity is not becoming in a kajira," said Selius Arconious.

"What brought you to this camp?" asked Ellen.

"An impulse to travel," said Selius Arconious.

"Please untie me, Master," Ellen begged. She pulled a little against the loops of narrow leather which held her wrists behind her.

"No," he said.

"Please, then," she said. "Remove, at least, my hood!"

"No," he said.

"I beg it, Master," said Ellen.

"No," he said.

"Did you come to seek me out? To buy a slave?"

"Curiosity is not becoming in a kajira," he said.

Her heart leapt. Could he care for her? She was in torment, confused as to her feelings for him, who now owned her.

"It is a long way from Ar," she said. "We are far from Ar!"

"Do you wish to have your bonds and hood removed?" he asked.

"Yes, Master!" she said.

"Remain in them," he said.

"Yes, Master," she said. "Master."

"Yes," he said.

"You bought me."

"Yes," he said.

"Surely for some purpose."

"Or purposes," he said.

"Why did you buy me?"

"Are you so stupid as not to know?" he asked.

"Please, Master!"

"Perhaps I thought you would look well under my whip."

"Do you not hold me in contempt, do you not hate me?"

"No," he said. "You are beneath contempt."

"Oh," said Ellen.

"And why," he asked, "should one hate a pretty, curvaceous little piece of slave meat one owns? There would be no point in it."

"Yes, Master," said Ellen.

"And what are your feelings, slave girl?" he asked.

"My feelings do not matter, Master," said Ellen.

"True," he said, quietly.

"I will do my best to serve my master well," said Ellen.

"I am sure of it," he said. And he laughed, and the laugh made Ellen's blood run cold.

"How could you afford me?" asked Ellen.

"I think you will soon know," said Selius Arconious. "Indeed, I suspect, within hours, the entire camp will know."

"I do not understand," said Ellen.

"It will not be wise to remain long in the camp," said Selius Arconious, "but, unfortunately, there is no help for it. If all goes well, we should be able to leave in a few Ahn, hopefully in the early morning."

"Yes Master," said Ellen. She understood nothing of what was going on. But then it is not uncommon for masters to keep their slaves in ignorance.

"Master," she said.

"Yes," he said.

"Thank you for buying my whip strokes from the scribe, at the dancing circle," said Ellen. "Otherwise I fear I would have been whipped."

"You should be whipped," he said.

Ellen was silent.

"Before a woman is sold, it is common to starve her of sex," said Selius Arconious.

"Perhaps, Master," said Ellen.

"Was that done with you?" he asked.

"Yes," whispered Ellen.

"I thought so," he said.

Ellen put her head down, in the hood.

"Then your sexual needs have been long left unsatisfied," he said.

"Yes, Master!" said Ellen. She lifted her head to her master, pathetically, blindly in the hood.

The thought crossed her mind that the sexual needs of her sisters on Earth, in their countless thousands, in their millions, in the loneliness of their empty, sterile freedoms, were similarly, commonly left unsatisfied. How much tragedy there was on that barren world! Did the women there not understand the meaning of their anxieties, their depressions, their displacements, their projections, their confusions, their sense of futility, their anomie, their emotional starvation, their sense of loss, of estrangement, of lack of connection, of unreality? The arms of ideology are cold and ultimately unsatisfying. There were women on that world who did not even understand the meaning of their misery and who found themselves forbidden to search for it in the most obvious place, in the denial of nature, in the frustration and starvation of their most basic personal needs. The natural human female, Ellen supposed, is not a social artifact, despite what she had been taught to mindlessly repeat, not a construct of social engineers who neither understand her nor care for her, creatures interested ultimately only in their own power and influence; she is not, ideally, a twisted, inadequate, unnatural, pathetic, neurotic replica of a different sex; she is rather herself, a creature of nature, needful and beautiful, in her way unique, precious and glorious; are the codes of nature so hard to read? Are these things truly such perilous secrets? Why should they be so dangerous to recognize and enunciate? Why should it be so dangerous to even speak of them? Why should conformity be enforced with such relentless hysteria? Why should careers be destroyed, appointments be denied, positions lost, for lack of orthodoxy? Who could these truths frighten, only those who can profit from their concealment. Not since the insane asylum of the Middle Ages has sexuality been so feared and deplored. There were women on Earth, Ellen understood, who, literally, had never experienced an orgasm. And there were countless millions, as the statistics would have it, who lived in a veritable sexual wasteland, in a parched, lonely erotic wilderness.

But Ellen was not on Earth any longer.

She was a slave on Gor, and her sexual needs, as those of other slaves, had been, whether she willed it or not, uncovered, displayed and ignited. In her belly the slave fires had been lit and now, irremediably, with an insistent, frequent periodicity, powerfully, irresistibly, they emerged, squirmed, and cried out piteously for their satisfaction.

It is hard to be a female slave on Gor. One is so much at the mercy of men. They will have it so.

Ellen moaned.

"Would you care to receive sexual relief?" he asked.

"Yes, Master!" said Ellen.

"Are you prepared to beg to be caressed?" he asked.

"Yes, Master," whispered Ellen, softly.

"Then do so," he said.

"I beg to be caressed, Master," whispered Ellen.

"Speak up, so I can hear you," he said.

"I beg to be caressed, Master," said Ellen, clearly, her voice breaking, tears forming in her eyes, running down her cheeks, inside the hood.

"Surely you can do better than that," he said.

"Ellen, the slave, your slave, Master, begs to be caressed by her master, Selius Arconious, of Ar," said Ellen.

"Do women of your world often beg to be caressed?" asked Selius Arconious.

"Doubtless, if they are slaves, Master," said Ellen.

"I have other matters to attend to," he said.

"Master?" moaned Ellen.

"In the meantime," he said, "I will see to it that you are well-warmed."

"Master?" asked Ellen.

She felt his hand take the leash at her neck, and she felt it tossed back, between her legs.

"No," she said, suddenly frightened. "Please, no!"

The leash was then pulled down, tightly, from the leash ring.

"Please, no!" she wept.

"Ai!" she cried.

The leash had been pulled up behind her, forcibly, fiercely, tightly, snugly. One hand had kept her on her knees.

"Please, no!" she sobbed.

And it was then tied closely, securely, to her bound wrists.

"No, Master, please, no, Master! Please have mercy, Master!"

But he had none, as she knew he would not.

This is sometimes used as a leading tie.

She was then thrust down on the grass, on her stomach, and her legs were pulled up behind her, the ankles crossed. In a moment, her legs bent up closely behind her, her ankles were lashed together. He then bound her ankles to her wrists. In this way she was not only helpless even to try to rise, but any movements of her bound ankles would exert pressure on her bound wrists, which would, in turn, exert pressure on the leash strap, which was attached to her wrists. Thus, in short, the leash ran from the ring at the front of her neck, the ring on the hood straps, down, tightly between her breasts, tightly between her legs, and tightly up to her crossed, bound wrists. But her wrists were also attached to her crossed, bound ankles, and thus, with respect to her ankles, she was limited to two options, first, to try to keep her ankles close to her body, which was uncomfortable, and did nothing to relieve the warm, creasing, implacable stress of the leash between her legs, or, second, to try to move her ankles a bit away from her body, to relieve the pressure on her bent, aching legs, which, in turn, in virtue of the ankles' attachment to the wrists, would produce a further warm, stirring, arousing, sawing, excitatory motion of the leash. So, as she moved, or squirmed, or sought some comfort, or respite, for her bent, bound legs, held so closely to her body, the leash would move as well, tautly, effectively, doing more of its work.

"Master!" called Ellen. "Master!" But there was no response. He had doubtless left the area. She turned to her side, and tried not to move.

Then suddenly she began to writhe, and thrash about, weeping. What a helpless, pathetic slave she was! I hate him, she thought. I hate Selius Arconious! I hate him! I hate him! Then she cried aloud, in the hood, "Oh, please, Master, have mercy on me! Come back! Hold me! Touch me! Help me! I will obey well! I will be a good slave! Fulfill me! Give me my slave's release! I beg it! I am your slave! Be kind to your slave! Be ruthless if you will! I care not! Put me to slave service! Use me! I beg use! I beg use! Master! I beg use, Master!"

She heard a man laugh, passing by, amused at the discomfiture of the squirming slave.

I hate Selius Arconious, she thought. He has made me a spectacle! He has made me a laughing stock! How sweet his vengeance must be! Why cannot I be as I was on Earth, frigid and cold! But men have done this to me! They have made me a slave! Now I am naught but an aroused, passionate slave!

I hate men, she thought. I hate them! I hate them!

But then she thought of the house of Mirus, long ago. Clearly she was now ready to beg to serve a man, any man!

You monsters, she thought. You monsters! You magnificent monsters! You know well, do you not, you monsters, that this slave girl is yours!

And thus she thrashed about, weeping and bound.

Ellen for a time could do little but squirm in misery, tethered helplessly, hand and foot. Then, mercifully, she slept, but dreamed of herself as a bound slave girl. Then, after a time, she was not sure how long, she awakened, finding herself a bound slave girl, to the sounds of excited voices. "Oh!" she cried, softly, squirming tearfully, finding the leash still persistently, mercilessly, active upon her. Then, pressing her heels as closely as she could to her body, to try to relieve a bit of the stress of the leash, she listened to the voices.

"The pay for the garrison at Ar has been purloined!" she heard.

"It cannot be," cried a man. "No alarms have been sounded! There has been no attack on us!"

All of this made little sense to Ellen, for she had supposed that the confiscated, gathered wealth of a dozen cities, and hundreds of smaller communities, destined for the troops of Cos and Tyros, and the regiments of mercenaries in Ar abetting their occupation, was in this very camp, that because of the numerous guards, the tharlarion, the war tarns. She suspected that Portus Canio and Fel Doron had been under this impression as well. Indeed, she suspected, though it was scarcely a matter of which slaves might speak, that Portus Canio and Fel Doron, and, supposedly, Tersius Major, had planned to strike at this treasure, in order to weaken and worsen the occupation in Ar, to outrage the garrison posted there, to outrage both the mercenaries and regulars, and perhaps even sow discord amongst them.

"It was not here," she heard. "That was a ruse, it seems, a hoax, to draw bandits fruitlessly to our tents, where they might be discovered and snared, while in the subtlety of Cos the gold made its way safely, elsewise, to the coffers of Myron, *polemarkos* at Ar."

"It seems the plan was penetrated, said a man, excitedly.

"Perhaps all routes were watched, the skies scrutinized," speculated a man.

"What force could seize the gold of Cos?" asked a man, incredulously.

"What force would dare?" asked another.

"The garrison at Ar is large," said a man. "Much gold would it take to weight their purses!"

"Thousands of gold pieces," said a man. "Many fresh from the mints of Jad!"

"When did this occur?" asked another.

"Some days ago," said a man. "But only now the news reaches us."

"In the sales last night," said a man suddenly, "a fellow, a drayman or tarnster I think, gave five gold pieces for a slave!"

"Where would such a fellow obtain such wealth?" asked a man.

"Who knows?" said another.

"Doubtless he is even now being sought," said a man.

"Doubtless," said another. And then the voices left the vicinity. Ellen also heard the creak of wagon wheels, and various sounds about her, as of the breaking of a camp, or parts of it.

Far off it seemed she did hear alarm bars sounding, which must have had their source in Brundisium.

Ellen lay quietly, in consternation, not daring to move. In the hood she did not know what time it was. She did not know how long she had slept. The grass on which she lay had been pressed down by her body. It had not been damp with dew when she had first knelt upon it. She moved her small, bound wrists pathetically, helplessly. "Oh!" she said, inadvertently, for she had moved. Why has he tied me like this, she asked herself, but dared not move, lest the answer be made even more clear to her.

It was a simple arousal tie, the sort of tie which well reminds a woman she is a slave. To be sure, it was perhaps a bit more severe, or cruel, than was necessary, and scarcely one in which one would be likely to place a beloved slave. But we must remember that the feelings of Selius Arconious toward his recent purchase were rather ambivalent. It is a tie, incidentally, not unfamiliar to slavers, particularly with captured free women, whom they are endeavoring to begin to acquaint with what is to be the nature of their new life, that of a sexual creature, that of a man's plaything and chattel.

But bonds, in general, are sexually arousing to a woman, as they speak to her of her vulnerability and helplessness, and of her subjection to the power of men. Simply leaving a woman alone, bound, perhaps for the time put out of one's mind, say, neglected or forgotten, is sexually charging for her. And there are hundreds of passion ties. The numerous psychological dimensions of sexuality, well understood by, and well exploited by, Gorean masters, enhance a thousand times the sexual experiences of their chattels. The human female is an incredibly rich, lovely complexus of mind, body and emotions, and her sexual life is a rich one, limited not to a handful of Ahn, now and then, but one which can enrich and inform her entire existence. Indeed, the very condition of bondage itself, and what it means to a female, enflames her in a thousand ways.

She belongs, as she wishes, to a master.

He has accepted her.

She is grateful.

She will serve him with devotion and zeal.

She will hope he will attend to her needs, of various sorts, as to the needs of any animal he might own.

* * * *

Perhaps a word might be said pertaining to the collar.

The slave girl is an animal.

And are not animals suitably collared?

And so then, might not the slave girl, who is an animal, be suitably collared?

Certainly.

Then it is done.

Behold, the collar is on her neck!

The value of the collar extends far beyond the mere marking of its occupant as slave, and, usually, the identifying of her master. Such features are obvious, and require little attention.

It is locked, of course, and that, as you might well suppose, is meaningful.

She cannot remove her collar.

Would you not find that meaningful?

I do.

Similarly certain other aspects of the collar would seem so obvious as to require no lengthy explication, such as its various aesthetic and psychological features, which have an impact on both the wearer and he beneath whose scrutiny she falls. The collar is a beautiful ornament, of course, and muchly enhances the loveliness of she who must wear it. Consider the zest and attention devoted by the women of Earth to lovely throat-encircling enhancements, beads, bands, chains, and such, with which to bedeck themselves. I have often thought, incidentally, that a Gorean slave collar might be prized as an ornament on Earth. One supposes it would be expensive there, which seems amusing, given its commonness on Gor. Too, doubtless it would have to be called something else. I wonder if a woman of Earth would understand its meaning. I suspect that she might experience strange sensations when she put it about her neck, and heard it close. Surely, fearfully, she would wish to keep the key close at hand. But what if the giver chose to put it on her and retain the key? But I suspect that any woman, even a free woman, of Earth, who wore such a thing would be suddenly aware, this perhaps frightening her, of the slave within her. Too, at home, after, say, her attendance at a dinner or cocktail party, or such, she might remove the device in fear, recalling how men had, perhaps for the first time in her life, at least in that particular way, in so unsettling and predatory a way, looked upon her, and approached her, and had circled about her, as might have ravening wolves about a young and vulnerable hind. She might then dare to wear it only naked, before her mirror, or stripped, in bed, weeping. But perhaps she would one day see her master and put on the device and approach him, and kneel before him, handing him the key. "I give you the key to my collar, Master. I would be your slave. It is my hope that you might find me acceptable." Gorean free women, incidentally, will seldom encircle their throats with jewelry of any sort, even in the privacy of their quarters, I suspect, as such things in their culture, speak to them of bondage. Slavers have often commented on the fondness of the women of Earth for throat encirclements, necklaces, and such, particularly for those which require a fastening and cannot be lifted away, over the head. They seem to take this as significant. Perhaps it is. I do not know. Certainly there is beauty there and an analogy to the collar of a slave. The throat is, of course, the ideal mounting point for an insignia of bondage, as it is both secure and prominent. The psychological aspects involved in these matters have been hinted at. I think we need not elaborate on them, as they seem reasonably clear.

Let us now turn, as we originally intended, to matters which are interesting, at least in my view, but, I fear, which may be less obvious than those with which we have hitherto dealt.

It is my hope that some attention to these cultural matters may be found illuminating, and add, in their way, to your deeper understanding of this narrative, and, certainly, of the Gorean culture.

It may be a culture quite different from that with which you are likely to be familiar. Yet, I am sure it has affinities with your culture, and, in an obscure way, perhaps biologically, it may lie ingredient within your own. It is, in any event, a human culture, and thus it cannot be utterly alien to you.

In a collar, and I hope this will not be surprising, a woman may find clarity and comfort, and her meaning and redemption. I wonder if that is hard to understand. I hope not.

As these matters are complex and subtle I will mention no more than a tiny corner of the concealed fabric, of the vast hidden tapestry into which are woven so many persistent, whispering truths.

In the collar she has a precisely defined cultural reality. Perhaps for the first time in her life she is something perfectly comprehensible and actual, something specific and unambiguous. It gives her an exact identity, and an articulated, and clearly understood, position in society, a society in which she finds herself, whether she wishes it or not, a familiar, prized and beautiful ingredient. Men follow her about, in her errands and peregrinations, and look upon her, and admire and value her, and speculate upon her lineaments and the coins that might bring them to their slave ring. She is scorned and celebrated, the victim of ropes and the subject of songs, the lowliest of beasts and the most desiderated of possessions. She is a slave. For her, now, at last, all ambiguities, uncertainties, confusions, pretensions, hypocrisies, vyings, and such, the banes of a free woman's existence, are at an end. She is slave.

In it she knows she has been found attractive, and is desired. She is wanted. A man has seen fit to put her in his collar.

In this she is reassured indisputably of her femininity.

She knows now what she is, and what she must do, and what she must be.

And at the feet of a man, as his slave, she is fulfilled in her womanhood.

She receives the guidance, domination, nurturance, discipline and mastering for which she yearns, which she needs, and for which she has been bred.

She is now where she belongs, at a master's feet, and is obedient, and humbly content.

Perhaps one might also note something further, but hope, as well, that this further observation will not be found disturbing, or disconcerting, to free women, might these recollections and reflections, however unlikely, come somehow someday within their ken, that of creatures so noble and refined, so lofty, so exalted and esteemed, so beyond one such as I, a slave, creatures who have never stood naked upon a slave block, hearing bids being taken on them, who have never worn a chain at a man's feet.

The collar has this cast or aura, too, one always recognized, but seldom expressed, perhaps because it is too obvious.

The collar states that its wearer is, and must be, a sexual creature.

The frigidities and inertnesses, the prides and loftinesses, of the free woman are not permitted to her.

The woman in a collar cannot deny her sexuality. It is proclaimed of her as obviously, as visibly, as the prominence of the band encircling her throat.

Why do you think women are enslaved?

The collar cries aloud of female sexuality.

Any woman in a collar understands that she is viewed as a sexual creature.

Pretenses, games, are at an end.

Surely women understand for what they are captured, or purchased.

Please do not be offended.

I must speak the truth.

Why do you think men enslave women? One supposes there are many reasons but it seems clear that not the least amongst them is the desire to keep them for the pleasure they can provide.

The collar states clearly that its occupant is *sexual*, that she is a sexual creature, and of sexual interest. Women without sexual interest are seldom collared. Of sexuality the collar cries aloud. "This woman has been found desirable; men want her; men will have her."

The female slave is openly acknowledged as a sexual creature. She must be such. She is given no other choice.

So do not forget this meaning of the collar.

The female slave is not permitted to forget it, nor does she wish to forget it. She loves it. She can be, at last, freely, openly, honestly, the sexual creature she has always desired to be.

"Caress me, Master, I beg it."

* * * *

Surely, she thought, Selius Arconious knows something of these things! And he paid five pieces of gold, of gold, for me! Perhaps he had a hundred, and they were no more than tarsk-bits to him! What then does that make me worth? Must I not now reassess myself? Am I not again no more than a cheap, meaningless slave! How he has insulted me, buying me with what to him is no more than trash or sand! So that is what he thinks of me! But perhaps he knows nothing of the Cosian gold? Perhaps he stole the gold elsewhere, perhaps he gambled with unusual success, perhaps he found loot discarded by alarmed, fleeing brigands? In any event she knew she was his, as a dog, a pig, a tarsk, or a verr, or a slave belongs to a man.

It was a little later when she smelled the smoke of cooking fires, so she was sure it must be the fifteenth or sixteenth Ahn.

She was suddenly aware she was terribly thirsty, and hungry.

She heard someone approaching, and lay very still. Then someone crouched beside her. She felt strong, masculine hands thrust up the straps of the hood, exposing an inch or so of her throat. She tried to press her bound ankles up, tightly, against her *derrière*, as she lay. She felt a metal collar put roughly about her neck. It fitted snugly. It was locked shut. She was collared.

"Master?" she asked.

A small noise warned her to silence. She was drawn, whimpering, to a kneeling position.

"Oh!" she exclaimed, as her wrists were pulled up behind her, and she squirmed unwillingly as a slave before him. But he then, with this bit of slack, merely untied the leash from her bound wrists and, at last, the creasing, agitating pressure was gone. "Thank you, Master. Thank you, Master," she murmured, then to that extent again her own woman, as much as any slave can be her own woman. But then she knew, in an instant, that she wanted to be taken into his arms, dominated as a slave and penetrated. She whimpered. She hoped he could not smell her need. The strap had done its work well. Then she felt the lock at the back of the hood opened, and the hood was pulled up, but only enough to expose her mouth. She could still not see. "Master?" she asked. She pursed her lips, humbly. Would her lips be now raped with the kiss of the master, he imperiously claiming his property? There was a small, soft laugh, a man's laugh. "Slave," he whispered. Then the spigot of a bota was thrust between her teeth, and, head back, she drank gratefully. Too soon it seemed the spigot was withdrawn. "Open your mouth, slave," she heard, and she, head back, obeyed. A handful of slave pellets was thrust into her mouth. He then pulled the hood back down, and, as she, within the hood, dealt with this simple, nutritious form of slave feed, that which had been permitted her, had it again in place. She felt it locked again, behind the back of her neck.

After a time she had finished the pellets.

"Are you warmed?" he asked.

"Yes, yes, Master," she said.

"Well warmed?" he asked.

"Yes, yes, yes, Master," she said.

"We must be on our way," he said. She gave a small cry as she felt the leash snapped forward, between her thighs. It was then before her, dangling from the strap ring at the front of her throat. She then felt him free her ankles from her wrists. How wonderful that felt! He then unbound her ankles. She was muchly pleased. With a sob of relief she moved her feet, and then, whimpering, suddenly, inadvertently, pressed her thighs together. He must not know her condition, what he, her master, had done to her.

"Position," said he, and she, whimpering, went as much to position as her bound wrists permitted her. Would he not allow her even that much modesty, that much relief?

"Would you like to be braceleted?" he asked.

"Yes, Master," she said, pulling at the tight loops of leather string that bound her wrists, hot and sweating, the one to the other.

"Would you like to be front-braceleted or back-braceleted?" he asked.

"Assuredly, Master," she said, "front-braceleted!"

She felt his fingers forcibly widen a space between the loops of leather string that held her wrists behind her. Then, against the exposed flesh, between the loops, she felt metal, pressing closely, the opened curves of slave bracelets. Then the devices snapped shut about her wrists, closely, snugly, and she was braceleted, back-braceleted. And only then were the loops of leather string removed from her sweating wrists, only after her wrists had been securely enclosed in slave bracelets. This is not that unusual in Gorean custody, the slave being kept in one bond until another is in place. A similar custom is generally observed with respect to identificatory hardware, for example, with respect to collars, bracelets, anklets, and such. For example, if one is going to anklet a slave, one would normally keep the bracelet or collar on her until the anklet is in place, and so on. In this way there is always at least one token of bondage on her, other than the brand. Doubtless this is what had been done with Tutina, on Earth, or before bringing her to Earth. Ellen remembered that Tutina had been ankleted. Bandages had covered it, outside the house. Ellen recalled that she, too, in the house of Mirus on Earth, had found herself ankleted, but she had not, of course, at that time, understood the significance of the device. Perhaps a collar would have been clearer to her.

So Ellen knelt, wide-kneed, back-braceleted, somewhere, she supposed on the outskirts of the festival camp. Although he had not seen fit, in the master's prerogative, to accede to her request for front-braceleting, she was nonetheless grateful for her braceleting, for the encircling metal wristlets were far more comfortable than the tight loops of leather string had been. To be sure, she was now more his than before. Anyone might cut leather bonds, a brigand, or such, but she now wore slave bracelets. These could not be removed without a key, or a tool.

She pulled a bit, against the bracelets.

I am braceleted, she thought.

Even in the house of Mirus, long ago, she could not help but respond to her braceleting. Even then, however reluctantly, she had found the bracelets stimulatory. How delicious it was, how exciting it was, that feeling of being braceleted, of being helpless, utterly helpless, of having her small wrists fastened together, locked together, particularly behind her back, her beauty then so exposed, so unguarded and defenseless, in those linked, obdurate, sturdy, uncompromising bracelets—slave bracelets. It spoke to her of her vulnerability, her helplessness, of her subjection to men, of her condition, slave, of her nature, female.

I love being braceleted, she thought.

Ellen sensed that her master was then standing before her, the leash presumably in his hand, she gathering that from the tiny draw on the hood's strap ring. Too, she did not feel the leash against her body.

"Master, may I speak?" she asked.

"Yes," he said.

"There is confusion in the camp," she said. "I heard men speak. The gold for the troops in Ar has been stolen!"

"You look well," he said, "kneeling before me in suitable position, naked, hooded, leashed, back-braceleted."

"Master!" she protested.

"Do not concern yourself with such matters," he said. "They are not the concern of slaves."

"But men may seek you, for you possessed gold, coins which, it seems, may have borne the quality and weight certifications of Jad, on Cos!"

"Do not concern yourself with such matters," he said.

"You may be seized, Master!"

"Then you will doubtless be resold, and will have another master, slut.

Do not forget that you are a mere chattel. As such you are trivial and meaningless. These matters have no more to do with you than they would with a tarsk, a creature more valuable than yourself."

"Few tarsks go for as much as five gold pieces, Master," said Ellen.

"The gold was meaningless," said he, "save as a gesture, as an insult to Cos, which I suspect that only now they comprehend."

"An insult?" asked Ellen.

"Certainly," said he. "Thus one of Ar shows his contempt for the coins of Cos, that he uses them to buy no more than a worthless slave."

"There were silver tarsks bid for me!" said Ellen.

"That is true," he said. "Perhaps you are worth a handful of silver tarsks."

"Surely you purchased me for something!" said Ellen.

"Perhaps you will amuse me for a time," he said, "until I tire of you."

"Yes, Master," said Ellen, sobbing.

"Know yourself a slave, little vulo," said he.

"Yes, Master," said Ellen. "Master."

"Yes," said he.

"It is your collar on me, is it not?"

"Yes," he said.

"Perhaps you care for me a little, to put your collar on me?"

"It is common to collar slaves," he said.

"Do I have a name?" asked Ellen.

"'Ellen' will do," he said. "It will serve to summon and command you as well as any other name."

"Is that name on my collar?" she asked.

"Do you think that would be wise?" he asked.

"No, Master," said Ellen. She knew she had been sold under that name, that that name was on the records of scribes.

"Also, that way," he said, "the collar may be used for an indefinite number of female chattels."

"Yes, Master," said Ellen, angrily.

"To be sure," he said, "one could always use the name 'Ellen' for any number of kajirae."

"Certainly, Master," said Ellen, angrily. "May I ask what the collar says?"

"Perhaps you can make it out one day, deciphering it in a pool or mirror," he said.

"Please, Master!" protested Ellen.

"Ah," he said, "I had forgotten that you are illiterate."

"Master?" she asked.

"It says," said he, "'I am the property of Selius Arconious, of Ar.'"

For a moment Ellen's heart leaped within her bosom, incomprehensibly, with joy, that she would be such, and publicly designated as such. She had forgotten, for the moment, it seems, that she hated him. But then she asked, "Is that wise, Master?"

"They do not know me," said he. "Too, a blank collar might arouse even more suspicion. Besides, it pleases me to have the little barbarian slut in my collar, and in one which identifies her as mine."

"I hope to wear your collar worthily, Master," said Ellen.

Then she cried out within the hood as she was drawn roughly to her feet. "Do not lie to me, little slut," said he.

"No, Master!" she cried.

"Do you think I do not know what the women of Earth do to the men of Earth?" he asked. "You, Earth slut, will be a slave amongst slaves!"

"As Master wishes," said Ellen. "I am his!"

"It is pleasant to own women," he said.

"Yes, Master," said Ellen.

"Did the leash warm you?" he asked.

"Yes, Master!" sobbed Ellen.

"Good," he said, angrily. And then he cupped her, casually, possessively, holding her in place with his left hand behind her back. She sobbed, and whimpered, and squirmed, helpless in the bracelets. "I see that it is true," he said.

"Please, Master," cried Ellen, "be kind to me!"

"Be silent," said he, "female."

It seemed he had little intention of treating her with gentleness. He then held her by her upper left arm, not even bothering with the leash, and drew her forcibly, she stumbling, beside him. She was thusly dragged for some twenty yards. Seldom had she felt more female, thus helpless, thusly imperiously handled. What men can do with us, she thought. Then she was thrust down, on her stomach over some surface, that of seemingly a large, felled log. She felt the rough bark on her belly. She was helpless. She squirmed. He pushed up her braceleted wrists and entered her. He had told her she would be a slave amongst slaves. "Oh!" she cried. "Oh!"

He growled like an animal and she was claimed.

Then he withdrew and she sank to her knees beside the log, pressing the hood against it. She could feel particles of bark on her belly, and grass beneath her knees. She was aware of his collar on her neck.

"Oh, Master, Master," she sobbed softly.

"There is no time," he said. "Do not fear, Earth slut. I am looking forward to pegging you down and having you writhe and scream yourself mine. I will bring you to the point of yielding a hundred times before I permit you relief, if I choose to do so at all. I will impose a domination on you that you will never forget. When I am through with you, Earth slut, you will know who your master is."

She wept in the hood.

"Please do not be cruel to me, Master," she whimpered. "I am only a slave."

"So the little barbarian slut acknowledges herself a slave?" he said.

"Yes, Master!"

"Say it," he said.

"I am a slave, Master," said Ellen.

"Are you obedient and docile?" he asked.

"Yes, Master," she said.

"Are you hot, devoted and dutiful?" he asked.

"I will do my best to be so, Master," she said.

"Earth woman," he laughed.

"No, Master," said Ellen. "No more am I an Earth woman. I am now only a *woman*, and a slave."

"Stand," said he, "kajira."

Ellen rose to her feet. She quivered. She was unsteady. She pressed her thighs together. She whimpered. "Master muchly denies me," she whispered.

"Follow," said he, and she felt a tug on the leash.

Why is he cruel to me, she asked herself. Does he not know that I am now no more than a slave?

And so she followed her master, on his leash. She wondered if any of the women of Earth knew such men, masters. How many, she wondered, clung to their tear-stained pillows, longing for the domination, the mastering, that would complete them, that would give meaning to their lives.

She was led for some ten to fifteen Ehn. Sometimes she sensed the smoke of fires, sometimes their warmth. The odor of roast bosk penetrated the leather of the hood. Once the odor of scalding kal-da came to her nostrils. Sometimes she heard men talking. Once she heard the laughter of a woman, in this camp doubtless a slave. Once she trod through cooling ash. She supposed it would be dark, or nearly dark, by now. Too, something in the feel of the air on her body suggested the dampness of the coastal evening. She realized that, in the hood, it was not likely she could be recognized, either as the dancer of two nights afore, nor as the slave for whom, yesterday evening, such a surprising price had been paid. She wondered if Selius Arconious, whom she supposed still held her leash, was disguised, or wore about his features the hoodlike folds of a cloak. She suspected he was not alone. Surely he, alone, could not have obtained the loot of Cos. He must have confederates! Had not another brought her away from the holding area? But he must have risked much to have secured her, she thought, in open auction, and to have dared to use gold, whether that of Cos or no, to buy her. She did not take too seriously the thought of his suggested insult to Cos, though she did not doubt but what that might have provided some sort of pleasant, subsidiary satisfaction. That was just too pat, too convenient. There would have been too much risk involved, surely, to justify a mere gesture, even for a Gorean. Too, with such wealth at his disposal, he might have bought any offered slave, or a great number of offered slaves, in the camp. He could have purchased enough girls to have set himself up in business, chaining them together, and then seeing what he might get for them in other venues. Many Goreans buy women on speculation. That is not uncommon. And, indeed, do not many slavers do just this, those who buy them, rather than hunting them down, say, like horses. To be sure, it is not unusual, as I understand it, that a slaver will note and then pick out a particular woman for himself, keeping her at least for a time. I do not think this is surprising. Such would seem an opportunity unlikely to be neglected. Indeed, is such not a privilege of his position, an entitlement, in its way, of his sort of enterprise? This doubtless happens with some Gorean women, and, I would suppose, with some Earth women, as well. Certainly some unusually beautiful Earth woman, all unaware of such matters, and, like others, scouted without her least knowledge or suspicion, might find, upon her arrival on Gor, after her initial terror and consternation, discovering herself stripped and chained, a slave, that a rather different or uncommon fate was in store for her, that she had been selected out, and a reserve, so to speak, placed on her, that she had been brought to Gor not like her sisters for the markets, at least immediately, but rather, it seems, for the personal service and delectation of a particular fellow, one by whom in the mysteries of such matters she had been found, totally unbeknownst to herself, appealing, presumably some slaver. She must then wait to discover to whom she belongs. To be sure, most are doubtless acquired with an eye to profit. Slaving, after all, is a business; accordingly the great majority of women brought to Gor would be put up for sale, usually publicly.

Yes, Selius Arconious could have done much with his gold, she thought.

But he had bought her.

He had bought *her*!

He must have wanted me very much, she thought. Very much, indeed. Could that be true, she asked herself. Perhaps. She smiled within the hood. Her steps became light. She knew she hated him, of course, but, still, he was very strong, and very handsome, and, too, of course, he owned her. And a slave must always be very careful of who owns one. He is, after all, the master.

But surely it did not hurt that he was strong and handsome. One could do worse than be the slave of such a man.

I hate him, of course, she reassured herself.

It excited her that he would be her master. But how the brute had tormented her with the leash strap!

She had no doubt what she would be to him!

In his casual, insolent way, he would well know how to handle, and keep, a slave.

I hate him, she thought.

But perhaps she did not hate him, really, that much.

In any event she must strive to please him, and perfectly, with every bit of her intelligence and beauty.

She was, after all, a slave, and his slave.

Then she became afraid, for she sensed that matters perilous were afoot in this disturbed camp of Cos.

There might be brigands who had seen him with gold. And she remembered the men who had been with Mirus. Perhaps somehow, without understanding it, she had seen too much. Too, there were the beasts, the terrible beasts.

And guardsmen might even now be seeking the mysterious stranger, the seemingly lowly fellow, who had had coins from the mint at Jad.

Then there was no longer a sense of the leash draw on the hood ring, and so Ellen stopped, and knelt. This was appropriate. There might be free men present.

Some men, she understood, in a moment, were indeed about.

"Have you secured the guards?" she heard Selius Arconious ask.

"Yes," said a voice.

As Ellen knelt she felt the leash strap between her breasts. She felt it best to widen her knees, and so did so. This proclaimed her a pleasure slave, but then that was what she was. She did not wish to risk a cuffing for having neglected the position which was appropriate for her. Too, though she hated Selius Arconious, she was sure, it nonetheless pleased her to kneel thusly before him. After all, she was his, and it was only fitting that she display his property suitably before him. Someone was standing, she was sure, before her. Perhaps it was Selius Arconious, her master. She straightened her body even more. Then, in a bit, the leash was unsnapped from the ring at the front of the hood. No longer then was the leash against her body. Presumably it was coiled and put somewhere. Then Ellen felt hands at the back of her neck. The hood lock was undone, and then, to her relief, but fear, the hood was pulled up, over her head, and removed.

It was rather dark, but one could see somewhat. One of the moons was visible through a break in the clouds.

The fresh air was glorious on her uplifted countenance, and she breathed it in, deeply, gratefully. Her face was doubtless reddened, blotched, from the confinement of the hood. Too, her face would be tear-stained.

Selius Arconious was to one side, placing the hood in a pack. There was a cloak about his shoulders, but the hood of the cloak was thrown back about his shoulders.

"Masters!" breathed Ellen.

But Portus Canio and Fel Doron, each in the garb of a Cosian guardsman, cautioned her to silence. Other men were about, their chains apparently removed. Two others, too, wore the garb of guardsmen.

Ellen then observed two more men approaching the group. They must have belonged with it, for their arrival caused no stir. One was dark-haired and lithe. The other was a large man, a strong, a dangerous-appearing man, who moved with the grace of a larl. He was red-haired, and was wiping a dagger on his thigh, which he then sheathed.

"You were followed," said the lithe, dark-haired fellow who had just arrived with his companion.

"I know," smiled Selius Arconious. "But I knew you were in attendance."

"What occurred?" asked Portus Canio. He had a sword, presumably that of a guardsman, slung at his left shoulder.

"He is no longer followed," said the red-haired man quietly.

"Who were they?" asked Fel Doron.

The dark-haired man shrugged. "Brigands," he said.

"It was clever of you to publicly purchase this slave, with Cosian gold," said one of the men about, indicating Ellen, who remained immobile, tense. "Thus, the camp will be looking for a tarnster."

"Has Tersius Major, the traitor, been apprehended?" asked a man.

"He is in custody," said the red-haired man. "He will be clad as Selius Arconious, gagged, tied in the saddle of a tarn and set aflight."

"That will provide the incident needed to begin the disruption of the camp," said one of the men.

"I would prefer to cut his throat," said Portus Canio.

"If he can turn his head about and squirm a little that will lend plausibility to the diversion," said a man.

"Perhaps you can cut his throat later," said Fel Doron, slapping Portus Canio jovially on the shoulder, and Portus Canio grinned, and snorted in disgust.

"Are the wagons ready?" asked Selius Arconious.

"They are in place," said a man. "Tarns will be released later and put aflight, and thus pursuit will presumably be directed to the skies, which Cos controls."

"Then," said a man, "we will disperse with the hundreds of others, who will break camp tomorrow."

"The Cosian forces here will presumably march on Ar, to reinforce the occupation, and prevent mutiny," said another.

"Is it true," asked Selius Arconious, of the red-haired man, "that Marlenus has been found near Ar?"

"It seems so," said the red-haired man. "He was discerned by a slave, who had tended him while he was imprisoned in Treve. It seems he escaped and made his way toward Ar, but somehow he seems unaware of the political realities in the city, and neither to understand nor know his true self."

"We must regain him," said a man. "He is needed as a symbol of resistance, as a rallying point."

"Without him, how can Ar be restored?" asked another.

"He is needed to give the people courage, to ignite them, to rouse them to war, to cast out the Cosian sleen and their allies!"

"We need Marlenus of Ar!" exclaimed another. "He is the leader, the Ubar! None can stand against him!"

"Without him, what hope is there?" asked a man.

"He must lead us!" said another.

"Down with Talena, the traitress Ubara!" hissed a man.

"Our vengeance on her will be sweet," said a man, grimly.

Ellen shuddered at the tones of the voices she heard.

"Death to the traitress!" said a man. "Death to the Ubara!"

"She shall know the penalties for betraying the Home Stone, those to be suitably inflicted upon a traitorous free person," said a man.

"Perhaps she is not a free person," said the red-haired man. "Perhaps she is only someone's slave."

"Absurd," said a man.

"She is Ubara," said another.

"Perhaps she who sits upon the throne of Ar," said the red-haired man, thoughtfully, smiling, "is only a slave."

"How would she dare?" asked a man.

"Let her fear then to be unmasked," said another, softly.

"Yes," said the red-haired man, thoughtfully. "Let her fear to be unmasked."

"What would be the penalties for a slave, pretending to be a Ubara," asked a man.

"It is difficult to conjecture," said a fellow.

"I would not wish to be she," said another.

Again Ellen shuddered.

"Is there to be a change of the guard here?" asked the dark-haired man of Portus Canio.

"Not until morning," said a man.

"Good," said the dark-haired man. "That will give us time."

"Have garments been brought for the former prisoners?" asked the red-haired man.

"Yes," said a fellow, "a variety of such."

"Have them distributed," said the red-haired man.

The fellow to whom he spoke left the area.

Ellen, from her knees, looked up to Selius Arconious. "May I speak, Master?" she asked.

He nodded.

"Did you purchase me," she asked, "as only part of a plan?"

"Do you think you are important?" he asked.

"No, Master," she said. "Master."

"Yes?" said he.

"Did you not want me, just a little, if only to beat and whip me?"

"Think," said he, "stupid little slut."

"Master?" she asked.

"I could have bid with the same effect, with no compromise to a plan, upon hundreds of other women," he said.

"Yes, Master!" breathed Ellen, kneeling before him, suddenly again helplessly alive in her belly. She had suspected this earlier, of course, but she had wished to hear it from his lips, those of her master.

"Things fell nicely into place," he said. "I purchased a worthless slave with a plenitude of Cosian gold, thus felicitously insulting the state of Cos. I arranged matters so that suspicion would fall upon a tarnster, as soon as the news of the theft of Cosian gold would reach the camp. This will help to create a useful diversion. And I obtained a cuddly slut, one who was once troublesome, but one who will now be well advised to learn to serve me zealously, with detailed, abject perfection."

"You wanted to own me?" asked Ellen, happily.

"Yes," said he, angrily, "meaningless slut. I have wanted to own you since the first time I laid eyes upon you. I do not know why. Surely there is no good reason for this aberration on my part. I am sure it is irrational. But ever since I first saw you I wanted to own you. I wanted you in my collar, and that is now where you are."

"Yes, my master!" breathed Ellen.

"Have you not overlooked something?" asked Portus Canio, grinning.

"What?" asked Selius Arconious.

"Let us consider the matter," said Portus Canio. "She was taken from me by confiscation in Ar," he said.

"Yes?" said Selius Arconious, warily.

"Now I surely acknowledge that the confiscation was within the letter of the law, given the current sorry state of Ar and the ordinances of the occupation; and I acknowledge further that she has been out of my hands for more than the number of days which, in Merchant Law, legitimate her seizure and claiming by another, and I recognize, further, of course, that she has passed through one or more hands in this time, as his or their slave, and that she was honestly purchased in open auction, in good faith, from her actual and completely legitimate owner, the state of Cos."

"You see then," said Selius Arconious, "that you no longer have any claim to her."

"Of course not," said Portus Canio. "That is clear. On the other hand, we do share a Home Stone."

"Very well," said Selius Arconious. "She is yours. I give her to you."

"Master!" protested Ellen. Then she swiftly put down her head. "Forgive me, Masters," she said.

"But," said Portus Canio, "I might be willing to sell her to you."

Ellen lifted her head, hopefully.

"How much?" asked Selius Arconious. "Six gold pieces? I paid five."

"What was the highest bid in silver for her?" asked Portus.

"Twenty," said Selius.

"Very well, I will ask twenty-one, in the coin of Ar."

"But that is my own money!" protested Selius.

"That is my price," said Portus.

"You should have left him in the chains of Cos," smiled Fel Doron.

"She is pretty, but she is not worth that much," said a man.

Slowly, as Ellen watched, delighted, Selius Arconious, angrily, reluctantly, removing them one by one from his purse, placed twenty-one silver tarsks, of Ar, in the hands of Portus Canio.

Portus Canio looked down at Ellen. "You see, little vulo," he said, "you are worth that much."

"Thank you, Master," said Ellen, kissing his sandals.

When she raised her head, Selius Arconious was looking down at her, in fury. She looked away, innocently.

"Do you think you are worth that much?" he asked.

"As a slave girl," she said, "I dare not speculate on such matters. My value, if value I have, will be determined by men."

"Gloat now, little she-sleen," said Selius Arconious, angrily, "but do not forget that it is in my bracelets that your wrists are locked."

"No, Master," said Ellen, happily.

"I wanted to see how much you wanted her," said Portus Canio. "Here are your silver tarsks back. I will sell her to you for less."

"I do not understand," said Selius Arconious.

"Give me a tarsk-bit," smiled Portus Canio. Fel Doron laughed. One of the other men about slapped Selius Arconious good-naturedly on the back. There was much laughter.

Selius Arconious, reddening, replaced the silver in his purse. Ellen stiffened as he then gave a tarsk-bit, the hundredth part of a mere copper tarsk, to Portus Canio. Portus took the coin and put it in the guardsman's wallet at his belt.

"That is doubtless, objectively, what she is worth," said Portus Canio.

"Alas," said Selius Arconious, "there is no smaller coin."

Ellen looked angrily, from her knees, she back-braceleted, from Portus Canio to Selius Arconious.

"To the feet of your master, slut," snapped Portus Canio.

And quickly, frightened, Ellen put down her head and began to lick and kiss the sandals of Selius Arconious, once again a slave, once again reminded of the absoluteness of her bondage.

"I am yours," she said. "I will try to be pleasing to you."

And as she performed this simple, homely act of respect and obeisance, common amongst female slaves, she groaned inwardly with need. How arousing it was to her to so kneel, naked, back-braceleted, head down, rendering submission to a man, her master. She felt incredibly female, incredibly feminine, incredibly thrilled and fulfilled. Men on this world, she thought, know the proper handling of women. She wondered if these men even realized what such postures, acts and rituals, so much taken for granted on this world, did to a woman. The culture of Gor was not devised to deny nature but to fulfill her. What might seem convention, taken for granted, and scarcely understood, by many on Gor, were profoundly symbolic acts, deeply moving acts, expressions of, and enhancements of, nature, which in their beautiful ways, and forms, stated, and celebrated, profound truths. Even chains, and the whip, were largely symbolic, the woman thusly understanding herself slave, and subject appropriately, as nature would have it, to the will of the dominant sex.

She lifted her head and looked up into the eyes of her master. Tears formed in her eyes. He looked away.

"Some of our men, clad as Cosian guardsmen," said Fel Doron, "will raise a cry that the suspect tarnster has been seen. Shortly thereafter our friend, Tersius Major, gagged and bound, clad appropriately, will be put aflight on a tarn. There will doubtless be a pursuit. It should take some time to bring the tarn down. Later, say, an Ahn later, other tarns will be freed. This will be taken as the actual departure from the camp of the conspirators, and a new pursuit will be mustered. In the general confusion, and disbandment, of the camp, the former prisoners and the rest of our men will go their hundred ways, afoot, some of the Cosian gold divided amongst them. Those of Ar will attempt to severally work their way southeast to Ar. Our friends, Marcus, of Ar's Station, and Bosk, of Port Kar, who have been instrumental, with others, in the purloining of the gold, and its subsequent temporary concealment, will in a few days attend a prearranged rendezvous with diverse cohorts, at a place of concealed tarns. There they will convey information as to the location of the great bulk of the gold, in its temporary cache, to these cohorts, who will then, as planned, see to its movement and disposition. Our friends of the scarlet caste will then attempt to return to Ar by tarn, traveling at night, utilizing the cover of darkness."

The "scarlet caste" was a way of referring to the caste of Warriors, the expression being suggested by the usual color of their tunics. Ellen had seen many scarlet tunics in Ar, mostly those of mercenaries and Cosian regulars. As Portus Canio had referred to Bosk of Port Kar and Marcus, of Ar's Station, as friends of the "scarlet caste," they must be then, thought Ellen, of the Warriors. She had, of course, suspected as much earlier. They were large and powerful, and had the look about them of men not unaccustomed to look upon war, men not unfamiliar with the darker uses of steel. They were not, however, now in the scarlet of their caste, but wore simple brown tunics. In a sense, she supposed, they were incognito. Doubtless that was wise in a Cosian camp, if they were not of Cos, even though the camp was in theory an open camp. To be sure, in raids, in battle, red is not always worn. Much depends, as would be expected, on the terrain, the situation, the objective, the mission, and such.

"Have arrangements been made for me?" asked Selius.

He did not mention Ellen, for she was property, and, as property, might, or might not, be brought along, as the master chose.

"Yes," said Portus Canio. "You will come with me, in a prepared wagon, and Fel Doron will accompany us. Too, until it is time for their departure for the rendezvous point, the place of concealed tarns, we will have at our disposal the swords of our friends, Bosk of Port Kar and Marcus, of Ar's station."

"Can one trust one of Port Kar?" asked Selius Arconious.

"He is with us, for whatever reason," said Portus Canio.

"In Port Kar," said the red-haired man, he like a larl, "there is now a Home Stone."

"I did not know," said Selius Arconious. "Forgive me."

"It is nothing," said the red-haired man.

The red-haired man frightened Ellen. She would have feared to belong to him. His speech had a foreign flavor, almost as though his Gorean had the trace, impossibly enough, of an English accent. But there are many accents on Gor. It did not seem likely that he would have a barbarian origin. He was too Gorean.

He glanced at her, and she, kneeling, quickly put down her head, unable to meet his eyes. She felt, beneath his gaze, as beneath that of many others, strong men, masters, completely slave. She knew that Gorean men saw her as a slave, and she knew in her heart that they saw her truly.

"There is little to do now," said Portus Canio. "In the morning, after the alarms of the night, if all goes well, we will make our way to the wagons and, with thousands of others, unnoticed in the general thronging, leave the camp."

"How many of our men are in the camp?" asked Selius Arconious.

"Not counting the freed prisoners, fifty," said Portus Canio. He then turned aside, to speak to others.

"May I speak, Master," whispered Ellen, softly, looking up to Selius Arconious.

"Very well," he said.

"I think Master finds me of interest," she said.

"Oh?" he said, skeptically.

"He could have purchased others in the auction. He purchased me. He was willing to pay twenty-one silver tarsks, of his own money, for this girl."

"He is a fool," said Selius Arconious.

"I hope not," she said, "for he is my master."

"Do you want a taste of the leather?" he asked.

"No, Master," she said.

"I had you for a tarsk-bit," he said, "no more. You are only a tarsk-bit girl. Do not forget it."

"I sold for more than that the first time," she said.

"Then someone paid more for you than you are worth."

"I think Master may like me a little," she said.

"Absurd," he said.

"Just a little—perhaps, Master?"

"Do not presume," he said.

"At least it seems that Master may want me," she said.

"That is an altogether different thing from "liking,"" he said.

"True," she said, "but it pleases a slave that she should at least be wanted."

"Good," said he. "Be pleased, slave."

"Perhaps you want me muchly?" she said.

"Absurd," he said.

"Twenty-one silver tarsks is a great deal of money," she said.

"It was a momentary act of madness," he said, angrily. "Nothing more."

"But did he not tell Ellen, his slave, and in the presence of Master Canio, and others, that he wanted her, and seemingly badly, in his collar?"

"Yes," he said.

"Surely Master must have had something in mind," she said.

"Perhaps," he said.

"What?" she asked.

"I was curious to know what you would look like, bound and whipped."

"Whip me if I deserve it, Master," she said.

"I will whip you if, and when, I wish," he said, "whether you deserve it or not."

"Yes, Master," she said.

"Do you think that you are not a slave?" he asked. "Do you think that you will have an easy slavery with me, if I decide to keep you, for more than a night of abuse, selling you in the morning?"

"I know I am a slave, Master," she said, suddenly frightened.

"And you will learn it," he said. "Portus! Portus Canio!"

"Yes," said Portus, turning about.

"How many guards were there with the prisoners?"

"Four," said Portus. "They are now bound and gagged, concealed in that declivity, and stripped, of course, for we required their uniforms."

"To them, and please them," said Selius Arconious, "with your kisses, and lips, and tongue and mouth. Draw their seed forth, and leave no traces, for we do not wish them to be slain in the morning, signs of pleasure about their bodies."

"Master!" protested Ellen, in horror. "You cannot be serious!"

"They are doubtless good fellows," said Selius Arconious. "And surely they should receive at least some small recompense for their help, their cooperation, in our endeavors this night."

"I beg to give you such pleasures, and a thousand other intimate, and beautiful, and precious pleasures, my Master, no limit of pleasure for you, for I am yours, but I beg you, do not ask me to so serve! Not others! Recall that I was not only a woman of Earth, but a lady, a lady of Earth!" She hoped that that expression would turn him from his intent, for the station of "lady," on Gor, is a lofty one. He need not know that it had a lesser status on Earth.

She pressed her head down to his sandals. "Please, no, Master!" she begged. "I was a lady on Earth," she said. "Please do not ask me to so serve!"

"You may have been a lady on Earth," he said, "but you are a slave girl on Gor. And you will serve whomever, and however, I please."

"Master, please!" she begged, head down.

"Must a command be repeated?" he asked.

"No, Master!" she said, frightened. In his tone there was ice, and iron, and she then knew what she was to him, and would be to him, what he would have her as, an uncompromised full slave.

Sobbing she sprang to her feet and hurried some yards away, to the indicated declivity. The clouds were more open now, and two of the three moons were visible. She had no difficulty in locating the bound guardsmen. They were tied apart, bound hand and foot, fastened in a row, tied by the neck and feet to two notched poles, so they could not reach one another. When she knelt near the first, she a naked slave, bending over him, her small hands braceleted behind her, the guardsman, sensing what was to be done, began to struggle fiercely, angrily. His eyes, over the gag, against which he helplessly fought, glared savagely at her. She was frightened, but she was even more frightened of her master, Selius Arconious, whom she now understood was not to be trifled with. He was to be obeyed categorically, instantly, unquestioningly, perfectly. She had no doubt now that he would use the whip on her, and without a second thought. She was, after all, his slave. "Forgive me, Master," she whispered to the first man. "It will do you no good to struggle. You are helplessly bound, hand and foot, and though I am only a weak slave, know that you are now fully at my mercy. You cannot prevent me from doing what I will do. Please, forgive me, Master."

Then, as he reared up in futile protest, she bent to his body.

Ellen then, to the best of her ability, pleased him. She tried to remember the lessons of her training, limited though they might have been, the kisses, the pneumaticities, the subtleties, the delicacies, the gentleness, the deeper grasps, the swirlings of the tongue, the touchings with the side of her face, the caress of her breasts and hair, the occasional, seemingly inadvertent brushing even of the eyelashes, light as feathers, her face beside him. "Please forgive me, Master," she whispered. "I must do what I am told.

Please forgive me." And as she dealt with him she noted his responses, his twistings and turnings, and struggles, even the smallest movements of his body, and, even though he was gagged, the myriad subtleties and wealth of his expressions, resistant, demanding, furious, startled, disbelieving, helpless. "I hope to give you pleasure," she whispered. "I am a pleasure slave, and I exist to please and serve men. It is what I am for, Master. It is accordingly my hope that I may please and serve you." They guide you, she thought, through signs, even gagged. You can read the book of their pleasure, whether they wish it or not. He is teaching me! In his eyes she saw a reluctant, belligerent, begrudging admiration. I, a mere slave, she thought, am well pleasing a master. The thought crossed her mind then, as it had upon occasion before, that it was likely, at least for the most part, that only highly intelligent women were brought to this planet, to wear the collars of Gor. Who would wish to be served by a stupid slave? Certainly I am intelligent, she thought. At least I would suppose so. I would hope so. And others surely are, as well. We are not stupid. And slavers know that, she thought, the imperious, glorious, uncompromising, virile monsters! Even what I am doing, to do it well, she thought, requires sensitivity, attentiveness, intelligence. Even to serve as I am requires intelligence. Men will expect us to do such things well. A stupid girl might well diminish or bungle his pleasures. Then she swiftly, fearfully, dismissed such thoughts, those of the desiderata against which the values of slaves might be assessed and measured. Pay attention to what you are doing, slave girl, she thought. You do not wish to be beaten. How right I am in my collar, she thought. How right we are in our collars, she thought.

And she continued to serve.

She wondered what her former colleagues and students would have thought of her, could they see her now, kneeling, bent, stripped, back-braceleted, deliciously serving. Would they even have recognized her, their former colleague and teacher, now a commanded, performing slave girl? Would her female students weep with need and desire to so serve as well, to find therein one of the thousand rewarding, fulfilling, beautiful meanings of their sex? Would not her male colleagues have cried out with envy, sensing how forlorn, tricked and deprived they were, screaming with misery that they did not live on a natural world where one might own such women? Seldom had Ellen felt so female as then, commanded, helpless, pleasing intimately, beautifully. Such an act brings home a woman's slavery to her. Her subject suddenly reared, twisted, and emitted a soft, guttural, indescribable noise. "Thank you, Master," said Ellen. He then lay back, his head back, trying to catch his breath. Ellen, as is common with slave girls, humbly, gratefully, joyfully, took into her body, imbibing it, relishing it, the gift she had been given. Too, she knew that there was to be no sign of his pleasure found on his body in the morning. In attending to his body, cleaning it with her lips and tongue, she was suddenly startled, for he had again become strong. Then, again, of course, she pleased him.

She then went to the second guardsman, who, doubtless aware of the futility of resistance, turned his head angrily away. "Forgive me, Master," said Ellen. In a moment, however, he raised his head, and moaned softly. "A slave begs to please Master," she whispered. "But, alas, even if he does not wish it, she must please him, for she is so commanded. He has no choice. She has no choice. Both are choiceless, he bound, she commanded. Forgive me, Master." Then in a moment, she said, "Oh," softly. "Forgive a slave, but she thinks that master is pleased. She hopes that that is the case. Surely she will do her best to give him pleasure."

In a little while she went to the third guardsman, and then to the fourth. Kneeling beside the fourth, her wrists moved a little in the closely fitting, light steel bracelets behind her. It was a tiny thing, but, as often, it was muchly arousing to her. So simply was she reminded that she was embonded. She then felt herself very much a slave, felt herself very much what she was. Then, putting her head down, she bent humbly to his body, to please him.

* * * *

Scarcely had Ellen backed away, on her knees, bent humbly, head down, from the fourth guardsman, that she might not rise to her feet at his side, this perhaps being taken as insolence, he supine and bound, than she heard, vaguely, obscurely, not really registering it at first, as she now recalls it, some sounds, some sort of commotion in the camp, in the distance. She stood up, unsteadily. Her dark hair, slave long now, was about her face. She tossed her head, trying to throw it behind her. She smiled. She hoped she had done well. Certainly she, a slave, might be severely punished if she had not done well. She had certainly tried to do well. Perhaps one of the most difficult things for an Earth woman to understand in the case of the female slave, unless of course she herself is a slave, is that one of the most significant fears known to the female slave is that she may not be found fully pleasing. You see, there are consequences for such lapses. Anything less than perfection of performance is not accepted in a kajira. They are not, after all, inert, vain, independent, quiescent, smug, bored, exalted, spoiled free women. For example, they are not permitted indifference to sex, indifference to appearance, indifference to movement, and such. They are trained and marketed for the service and pleasure of men. It is what they are for. The sounds were far off. She did not pay them much attention at first. She did not think they would have anything to do with her. It was still rather dark. Clouds raced overhead. The night was damp. Two of the three moons were visible. The grass was wet and cold beneath her feet. She touched the bracelets, behind her, to her body. They were cold, and damp. She supposed dew was on them. She licked her lips. On them she could taste the soft, lovely, adhering residue of her service. She shivered a little, in the darkness. She moved her neck in her collar. It identified her as the property of a Gorean, Selius Arconious. I hate him, of course, she thought. Indeed, consider what he has just made me do. But still I am his slave, and must strive to please him. What a lamentable fate, she thought, and smiled. Then suddenly she gathered her wits about her, and strained to listen. Two of the guardsmen must have heard the sounds, too, for they were struggling to free themselves. Quickly then Ellen hurried from the declivity concealing the guardsmen. A few yards away there was a small fire, and several men were gathered about it. There were some wagons rolled about, as well, but they were muchly dark, in the shadows.

Ellen hurried to the fire, and knelt.

Selius Arconious was there, and Portus Canio, and Fel Doron, and others, including the red-haired man, he so much like a larl, claimedly from Port Kar, it seemed of the Warriors, and his fellow, the dark-haired, lithe man, said to be of Ar's Station, also it seemed of the Warriors, which was somewhere to the north. Ellen's arrival was no more noticed than might have been that of a dog.

She knelt beside Selius Arconious, knees wide, her head down.

"The sought tarnster has been detected!" she heard, a cry from several yards away.

"He is escaping!" she heard.

"He has stolen a tarn!"

"Pursuit will be mounted!" called another man, from somewhere in the darkness.

"He will be apprehended!" someone shouted. "Tarnsmen will be aflight in moments!"

"Should we not exhibit some interest in these matters?" asked Fel Doron.

"Certainly," grinned Portus Canio, and rose to his feet. "What is going on?" he called into the darkness.

"The fellow who had Cosian gold is trying to escape the camp!" said a tharlarion driver, coming into the circle of firelight.

"And well he might," said another fellow, coming toward the fire. "He would doubtless be turned up promptly enough with the coming of daylight."

"I wonder if they will catch him," said Selius Arconious.

Ellen shuddered.

"The slave is cold," said one of the newcomers.

Selius Arconious took a blanket and threw it about Ellen's shoulders. She welcomed its warmth.

Can it be that my master cares for me, she asked herself. As much would be done for a shivering kaiila, of course, she told herself. But she then thought that it would much more likely have been done for a shivering kaiila than for a slave, the kaiila being likely to be a much more valuable animal. Indeed, sometimes the slave is left shivering, that she may the better understand herself as a slave, and all the more dependent on the master. But he gave me a blanket, she thought. Perhaps I will be able to dominate him? Then she fearfully put aside that thought, for she knew she would never be able to dominate Selius Arconious, or any Gorean male. She could never be before such anything but a docile, humble, obedient, frightened, conquered, submitting slave. They were such men. But perhaps he likes me, she thought. He has given me a blanket. I must keep clearly in mind that I hate him! Then she put her head down and tried not to move, not wishing to lose the blanket. She could not hold it, or adjust it, with her hands, as they were still braceleted behind her. There is a technique which might be mentioned, for those interested in such matters, by which a back-braceleted slave girl can wrap herself in a blanket if she is permitted to lie down. One spreads the blanket out and grasps it at the bottom between one's feet, in the center with one's braceleted hands, and toward the top with one's teeth, or between the chin and neck, and then rolls oneself in the blanket. This is not taught to us but is something one learns to do quickly enough if one is cold, in a camp, say, or at the foot of the master's couch. Ellen tried to reach the blanket with her teeth, but could not do so without breaking position. And it slipped down a little, which did not please her.

"He went toward Ar," said a man.

"They will catch him," said another.

Their informants then took their leave, hurrying toward other fires in the camp.

"They did not recognize you," said Portus Canio to Selius Arconious.

"They are not looking for me here," said Selius Arconious. "Thus they do not see me here."

"Perhaps we should leave now," said a man, uneasily. He rose to his feet, looking about.

Another man, too, rose to his feet.

"Yes, perhaps we should leave," said another fellow, looking at Portus Canio.

"We could travel light," said another.

"We could leave the baggage, and wagons," said another.

"And the animals," said another.

"And the slave," said another. "She could not keep up with us."

Ellen moved, apprehensively. The blanket fell from her. She was frightened. She moved toward Selius Arconious, on her knees, facing him, and lifted her chin.

"What is wrong?" asked Selius Arconious.

"Should we not flee, Master?" asked Ellen.

"'We'?" he asked.

"Yes, Master," said Ellen, leaning forward, and raising her chin yet more.

"It seems you are ready to be leashed," he said.

"Yes, Master," said Ellen. "Leash me. I beg to be leashed!"

"A woman of Earth begs to be leashed?" he asked, amused.

"Yes, Master!" Ellen assured him.

"You are afraid you will not be taken with us?" asked Selius Arconious.

Ellen was silent.

Selius Arconious reached to the blanket and drew it completely over Ellen. She moaned, within the blanket. She dared not shrug it off, for it had been cast over her as it had, in that special way, by her master.

Blankets, sheets, and such, of course, may be used as hooding devices. Sometimes they are placed over the head and tied about the neck; sometimes they are placed over the head and tied about the belly, the woman's hands and arms within them. The simplest hooding with a blanket, of course, is that to which Ellen had found herself subjected, a simple covering. She did know that when she was covered in such a way she was not to be heard from. A woman might be so covered for a variety of reasons. Perhaps, as she was not now hooded, her master did not wish her to be recognized as the slave purchased the preceding night for so great a sum. But in the darkness, and such, she supposed she had been so covered merely to dismiss her, so to speak. Yes, she thought. I hate Selius Arconious. It is not unusual on Gor, however, to conceal women, either free or slave. Do not peasants upon occasion hide their daughters? Do not the men of the Tahari order their slaves to the tents upon the approach of strangers, and so on?

On Gor, it might be mentioned, that some of these things might be better understood, women tend to be regarded as goods and prizes, as loot and booty, particularly if one does not share a Home Stone with them. The capture of the enemy's women is a common feature of Gorean warfare. Indeed, wars have been fought to obtain female slaves. And raids to obtain women are commonplace. Indeed, among men, the monsters, there is much here that has a sporting cast. Too, the possession of women is often taken as an index of wealth, rather as, in other times and places, might have been cattle or horses. There is much loneliness and misery, I suspect, in the pleasure gardens of wealthy men. Certainly Gorean cities vie with one another not only with respect to the splendor of their promenades and parks, their fountains and architectures, but with respect, as well, to the number and beauty of their slaves.

"It is not time yet," said Portus Canio.

"Our friends from Port Kar and Ar's Station must yet flight tarns," said Fel Doron, "which should convince our Cosian friends that we, their undetected but suspected foes, presumed allies of the pursued tarnster, who presumably did not work alone, have also taken our departure from the camp, and similarly. But then, while Cosians scour the clouds themselves, we, below, in daylight, mixing with hundreds of others, shall quietly, unhurriedly, calmly, take our leave afoot."

"I am afraid," said a man.

"Morning, morning," said Fel Doron.

"How long until morning?" said a man.

"Two Ahn, two and a half Ahn, something like that," said Portus Canio.

Ellen, under the blanket, could see nothing, but she gathered from small sounds that the counsel of Portus Canio and Fel Doron had prevailed, and that their uneasy fellows had now returned to their places by the fire.

"Master," she whispered, from within the blanket, "may I speak?"

"No," he said.

She then knelt under the blanket, small and soft, in darkness, a collared slave, not permitted to speak. He is strong, she thought. He masters me. I am no more to him than a pig or dog. I must try to please him well.

He is Selius Arconious, my master!

How strange she then thought that I, of Earth, should be here, on another world, a far, beautiful world, one many of Earth do not even know exists, kneeling on its grass, naked, back-braceleted, covered with a blanket, dismissed from attention, unable to see, waiting, a slave.

How different I now am from what I was, how much has been done to me!

How much has changed!

I am now a girl, she thought, as once I was, I have seen myself in the mirror, a girl of no more than eighteen or nineteen years of age.

On Earth I might have been a freshman in college, a new student, with her books, one being noticed by upperclassmen.

A beautiful girl.

But here I am a slave.

A beautiful young slave.

My name is Ellen.

It is my hope that masters will find this girl pleasing.

If they do not, she fears she will be slain.

But how the master heated me, she thought, angrily, with the cruelty of an arousal tie, a stimulation tie! Men have done this to me. Master, be kind to me. How lordlike they are to their slaves! How much we are at their mercy! Men have made us dependent upon them, not only for our food and drink, for even a rag to wear, but, too, in other ways, ways far more profound, dependent upon them for the assuagement of cruel and desperate needs, needs routinely released in bondage, needs, insistencies, urgencies, and torments, in the grip of which we find ourselves pathetically helpless. Men, for their pleasure and amusement, kindle the tinder of our needs. As it pleases them, and doubtless because it will improve our price, they set slave fires in our belly. And then they step aside, as though noticing nothing, while these fires periodically rage. They make us the victims of our own needs, and use them to bring us choicelessly to their feet.

How cruel they are!

How I need, want and love them!

On Earth, I tried to hate them, as my sisters wished, but would not say, but even in my determination to conform to these sororal demands, and in the midst of my prescribed, routinely uttered critiques and denunciations, I found them fascinating.

I wondered even then what it would be to belong to them, fully, as a chattel, as so many women in history, my sisters, belonged to them.

I found it hard to believe that human nature was a mistake, and biology incorrect. Could an entire species be in error?

And I knew too much history, over a thousand generations, to suppose that the biography of a race was an inexplicable accident, a mere haphazard contingency that might as easily have been otherwise, that it was without meaning or foundation, that there no reason why it was as it was.

And I wondered if I had not on Earth betrayed my truths and sold my happiness to please others. What reward will compensate one for that? Lies are expensive, and sorely purchased! There are gains and losses, always, but the gain of the few may be the loss of the many, and one wonders if the few have truly gained.

Can hunger and unhappiness, sorrow and misery, hatred and pain, illness and tragedy, really be the evidential insignia of health and truth?

It does not seem likely.

But Ellen then squirmed beneath the blanket.

On her neck was a collar, and slave fires burned in her belly. But she did not envy or desire the sluggish, aloof tranquility of the free woman, so much a stranger to need and life. Let them in their pride and separateness scorn the vitality of slaves, she thought. Let them, if they wish, prize and cultivate a winter within their robes. Let them congratulate themselves on ice and inertness. What would they care for, or could they know of, the feelings of a slave? What could they know of the needs of slaves? Would such needs not be so alien to them that they must find them incomprehensible? Perhaps thought Ellen, but perhaps too, in their way, they have some sense of such things, for they, too, are women; perhaps then they have at least some dim sense of what it might be to scratch at a kennel's walls and howl to be touched.

To be sure, how cruel these needs! With them and in them I suffer, well do I know their anguish, but I would not exchange them for the soporific quiescence, the quietude and repose, the numb and frosty serenity, of the unperturbed free woman. I would not exchange my slave needs for the world, for with them, and in them, I am intensely aware, awake and alive, a thousand times more so than I would have thought possible. With them I am a fabric spread to the weathers of the world, to its vibrant, vital multiplicity and wealth. How alive the collar makes us! How welcoming and sentient we become in so many ways in this so sentient world! We welcome its myriads of sensations, its aromas, its colors, its sounds, its textures and tastes, the feel of wet sand beneath our bared feet, that of the wind on our bared arms and legs, rushing landward from sparkling, salty Thassa, the pull on our leash as we are led behind our masters, the smell of high, rain-drenched grass in the fields, the luster of delicate talenders blossoming in the spring, the creaking of a heavy wagon, the sound of kaiila bells, the feel of the fur at the foot of the master's couch, the feel on our belly of the tiles as we crawl toward him, close encirclements of leather on our bound wrists, confining our hands behind our body, the taste and texture of his sandals on our lips and tongue.

On this world we respond to, and welcome, its myriad sensations. Every inch of us is alive.

Slave needs, of course, as any unsatisfied need, can cause suffering, who knows better than a helpless slave, but I would not be without such needs. In this suffering, and anguish, if nothing else, I know myself intensely alive.

Imagine now, if you can, the concern, and hopes, of the slave that such needs, such cruel needs, will be recognized by the master, and that he will be moved to attend to them.

How different things are for the slave and free!

The free male, should he have an interest in free women, perhaps he has no access to slaves, usually initiates the sexual encounter. He petitions the free woman, so to speak, who may or may not accede to his petition. In the master/slave relationship, on the other hand, it is the woman, the slave, who often puts herself to the feet of the free man, begging for sex. What a pleasant turnabout this must be for the fellow who has never before owned a woman. The man, of course, in a master/slave relationship never petitions or solicits. As he is master he commands, and often that the woman will prepare herself, in one fashion or another, perhaps presenting herself in a certain manner, say, silked or belled, or putting out certain articles, or such, for his use, perhaps a given variety of chains or cuffs, and perhaps a switch, to be used upon her if she is insufficiently pleasing. If he is in a certain mood, or in a hurry, he may simply, abruptly, put her to use. A slave, of course, may be ravished in any way, and at any time and place, at the master's pleasure. This is one of the appurtenances of the mastery. It might be added that the slave finds this lovely jeopardy appropriate and exciting. The piquancy of an unexpected encounter adds spice to the collar life. Too, it is extremely important to her, as it may not be to a free woman, to be frequently reassured that she remains sexually desirable, even disturbingly so, even maddeningly so, to her master. And his frequent uses of her leave her in little doubt as to her attractions. Neglected, she weeps and fears. Has he tired of her? Is he thinking of selling her? But she loves him! She dares not speak her love to him, of course. She is a mere slave. She does not wish to be lashed. She redoubles her efforts to please.

And our slave needs, as noted, put us much at the mercy of the master.

How frequently, and how intensely, our slave fires burn!

Can you not imagine then our piteous supplications, our pleas to be permitted to serve him? We petition him to be put to his use. We beg our use.

And as we are slaves, for what uses do we beg?

Not the uses of free women, never, but the uses which are fit for us, the uses which we now need and want, for which we plead, the uses of slaves.

The uses for which we petition, you see, as we are slaves, will be very different from the tamenesses which would be appropriately accorded to a free woman, uses conformable to her status and dignity. We wish to be handled quite otherwise. We wish to be handled as slaves. We wish to be positioned, turned about, knelt, spread, bound, such things. We wish to be treated as the slaves we are. As with the kaiila the masters will have a firm hand, so to speak, on our reins. Too, as with the kaiila, and not merely "so to speak," the quirt will be at hand. We will be done with as our masters please. We will be treated then not as free women, but as owned women, which we are. Our uses will leave us in no doubt as to our bondage. We will be choiceless in these matters, but this choicelessness, as we are slaves, is precious to us. It is what we want. We do not want the tepid, boring experiences of the free woman. Leave them to her. We beg rather for the ecstasy of the slave. We wish to be used then not as free women but as ruthlessly mastered chattels, for that is precisely what we are, and would be. We are not free women who may adjust and regulate, as we please, beneath our sheets and within our modesty robes, the delicate and respectful attentions of some fellow fortunate enough to have been admitted to our chamber.

Does the free woman sometimes feel an uneasiness, is she sometimes restless, does she sometimes experience a discomfort, one perhaps not even fully understood?

The slave can know agony.

Let the free woman twist and squirm in bed, and drench her pillow with tears.

The slave prostrates herself before the master, her hair about his sandals, hoping he will be merciful, that he will take pity on her.

Does the free woman sometimes wonder what it would be to be a slave, to be utterly rightless and vulnerable, to have to serve and please? Does she wonder sometimes what it might be to find her beauty, perhaps stripped and collared, looked upon with interest and satisfaction, with approval and anticipation, to find it thusly, helplessly, within the regard of a man who owns it, whose property it is, her master?

Never before has she been so looked upon.

Let her now understand, perhaps for the first time, that she is beautiful, that she is delicious and well-curved, that she is tormentingly desirable, that she is a fit meat for masters.

Surely she now understands why she has been collared.

Does she sense what it would be then to have his hands reaching for her, what it would be to be taken within his arms?

Perhaps.

One does not know.

But put aside thoughts of free women, and their wants, and tragedies.

We are not free women.

We are slaves.

We are commanded. We are naked and collared. We may be danced; we may be ordered to perform in any number of intimate modalities. We must hope to please our masters. If we do not, we must expect to be whipped. We are slaves. Not unoften we are chained or bound, mercilessly exposed for the master's pleasure, his property displayed for his delectation. When he puts us to use, we are left in no doubt as to our subjugation. He is kind to us. He will grant us his caress, though we are only slaves. We are grateful for his touch, and we cry ourselves his, again and again, in the blinding delirium of our joy, in the ecstasy of the mastered slave.

But our slave needs, thought Ellen, are not simply such needs, the needs of a pathetically aroused and cruelly intensified sexuality, as obvious as these things are. There are also subtler needs involved, those to belong, to be ruled, to be owned.

Can free women, Ellen wondered, understand anything of this?

Perhaps.

One does not know.

How fine and noble, how lofty and exalted, are free women, thought Ellen, and how I am nothing before them, but for all their status and glory I would not trade my collar.

But then Ellen grew fearful.

How long had she been beneath the blanket, so kept in place?

She feared now for her master, and his friends, and allies. To linger longer in this place, this now-disturbed, now-fearful, now-sobered festival camp, would be, she feared, grievously dangerous.

Was this not clear, even to an ignorant young slave?

The fire crackled. It had been twice stirred, and twice replenished. Ellen wished desperately to speak, to urge flight, but she dared not do so. Too, she feared she might be left as she was, beneath the blanket, abandoned. She knew she could not keep up with the men if they chose to begin a rapid, severe trek afoot. But she had understood that they, if they followed the stated plan, would leave the camp in a leisurely manner. That recollection reassured her. Too, abandoning baggage or a slave might suggest a suspicious, precipitate haste. She could always be abandoned, of course, if one wished, on the trail. She could be bound hand and foot, and left to the side, subject to claimancy by others, should they happen by. That was possible. But this would normally be done only with an unwanted slave. How piteously then might they call out to strangers. But many would pass them by, not wanting another man's leavings. Such an experience, of course, is likely to be instructive to a slave, and if she should be so fortunate as to be accepted by some passing traveler, she is likely to be to him amongst the most grateful, devoted and zealous of slaves. Too, of course, the sleen tends to prowl at night. But Ellen did not think she would be an unwanted slave. Surely she had seen the eyes of men upon her. She was no stranger to the frankly appraisive glances of masters.

The men of Earth, she thought, are often circumspect, even furtive, when looking upon women, as well they might be, given the entanglements, the risks and absurdities, of their pathological environment. Some, suitably conditioned, would even feel guilt, upon, say, an occasion's having arisen when they had, however briefly, indulged in one of nature's most ingredient inclinations, the human male's perusal of the human female. The Gorean male, on the other hand, looks upon women openly and honestly, particularly slaves. Many was the time when Ellen, even tunicked, had felt herself speculatively undressed by a fellow's regard.

The men of Earth think nothing of looking frankly upon dogs and horses, so why should they not look as frankly upon another form of domestic animal, the female slave? But perhaps they have never seen a female slave? If so, that is their misfortune, for such beasts are often very beautiful.

To be sure, the Gorean slave tunic leaves few of its occupant's charms to the imagination. But, too, many was the time that Ellen had seen men considering even cumbersomely robed, gloved and veiled free women. Doubtless they were considering the hidden slave. To her amusement, Ellen had noted that such free women, sensing themselves within a male's regard, while pretending to be unaware of the fact, tended to straighten their body, hold their head up, walk well, and such. They, too, are slaves, Ellen had thought, with much satisfaction. Let them too, then, be collared and put in tunics! Then they would truly learn how to hold their bodies and walk. Certainly Ellen had been taught, to the sting of a switch, how to walk in a tunic, in the house of Mirus.

One of the delights of a Gorean city, at least from a male point of view, is the scrutiny of its slaves. Males enjoy looking upon lovely women, particularly if they are lightly, briefly clad, revealingly clad. It gives them pleasure. Thus, if the women are slaves, they will have them so clad, "slave clad," as the expression is. The garmenture of the slave, of course, at least officially, or at any rate in the lore of free women, is intended to be shameful, and to demean the slave. I do not think, of course, that it actually has this effect, or anything like it. To be sure, sometimes a slave new to her collar, a recent free woman, must be whipped from the house before she can bring herself to appear so clad on the street. Her discomfiture, of course, muchly delights other slaves, who may then follow her about, publicly calling attention to her legs, and such.

And in such garments, certainly, we must acknowledge that the slave, by intent, in accord with the imperious will of masters, is well-bared, that she is muchly exposed, that she is well exhibited, that she is well displayed, and such. But I do not think that such garmenture, slave garments, is demeaning, or shameful, at least not for a slave. Rather, they are appropriate for a slave, as they should be. If the slave is permitted garments, it is certainly appropriate, do you not agree, that they should be garments fit for a slave, namely, be simple, lovely, exciting, and revealing. After all, she is a slave, and she will often, doubtless, find herself before men. In such garments, too, given their brevity and such, it is usually easy, if one is interested, to see why she has been put in a collar. Most slaves, we should note, love their tunics, their ta-teeras, their camisks, and such. Usually they wear them with pleasure and pride, as visible tokens of their interest to men, as badges, unassuming as they are, of their desirability. In them they are exciting and beautiful, and they are well aware of this. The slave tunic, and such garmentures, rather as the collar, too, proclaims its occupant a woman who has been found worth capturing, worth collaring, worth buying and selling, worth owning, and so on. And do not think that slaves do not take pride in this.

Whereas they may at first shudder in their pens and jerk helplessly, weeping, at their chains, they know, too, on some level, at least, and this appeals profoundly to their vanity, and to the yearning, secret slave within, perhaps hitherto fearing she might be valueless, perhaps hitherto fearing that no man might want her, perhaps hitherto fearing that no man would enslave her, that they have been found worth penning and chaining. Has not every woman wondered if she were attractive enough, or interesting enough, to be a slave?

Even the most insolent and beautiful of women, one inordinately vain, one supremely confident of her worth and beauty, even inveterately, snobbishly so, in her customary interactions and relations with despised males, must tremble, wondering what it would be to find herself kneeling naked and collared at the feet of a true man, regarding her skeptically, whip in hand. Is she now so sure of her beauty? Would it be sufficient for *that* male, whom hitherto she has seen only in her dreams?

But she is now penned, now on a chain.

So perhaps she will learn.

They now know they have been found beautiful enough to be put on a sales block and publicly sold. They now know they are lovely enough for the collar. In such things they find keen gratification. Are they not entitled to take some pleasure in recognizing that strong, lustful men will be satisfied with nothing less than owning them? Do they not understand now that they are amongst the most beautiful and desirable of women, women who, by the will of men, will be kept as they should be kept, as slaves?

Perhaps they are trinkets and baubles, but they are trinkets and baubles which are zealously coveted, and relentlessly sought. Do you think they do not know that when a city falls and they are led forth in their chains, herded along, perhaps cruelly prodded, with other domestic animals, that they are esteemed the most luscious of booty and loot, the most relished of prizes and treasures? Can they not see the eyes of the conquering soldiers upon them? Can they not hear their cries of pleasure and anticipation? Certainly, too, they are the customary quarry of slavers, the primary object of raiders. Men risk their lives for them; men fight for them; men kill for them. They are the possession men want most. What man would not want them at his slave ring? And in time, ruled and owned, disciplined and possessed, they find their own fulfillment, as they had dreamed, at the feet of their master.

In bondage a woman finds her reassurance and meaning.

In the collar of a master is the belly of a woman best stirred.

In the ropes of her lord a woman is most secure.

The free woman may think herself a thousand times above the slave, and may be justified in doing so, and, indeed, in many ways, but the slave, kneeling frightened before the free woman, her head to her sandals, knows that it is she, and not the free woman, who has been collared.

Lastly it might be noted that the garmenture of the slave, amongst its other features, has this one, too. It distinguishes her clearly from the free woman. In the Gorean culture this is extremely important. This is a distinction which must never be unclear or confused. The free woman is a person; she is a citizen; she has standing before the law; she has a Home Stone; she is noble, lofty, and exalted. The slave, on the other hand, is a property, an animal.

But she does have her collar.

Ellen hoped she would be neither left behind nor abandoned on the road.

She would do her best, she knew, to keep up with the men.

She would endeavor to be so pleasing, so obedient and helpful, so docile and servile, and so sensual, sensual as she had been taught in the pens of Mirus, sensual as only a slave can be sensual, that they would not wish to do without her.

A slave, you see, in her way, by her appearance, demeanor, and service, may exert a considerable influence on the value and quality of her life.

A slave who is pleasing will normally be well cared for, fed, clothed, and caressed. Too, it is not unusual for a pleasing slave to be cherished, cherished as only a slave can be cherished, cherished as a free woman cannot be cherished, cherished in a way forever denied to a free woman.

And, too, is the slave not often ambushed by love? Is her path not beset with its thousand snares? Is she not often trapped, a helpless possession, within the nets of her needs? She lives with a man on terms of obedience and intimacy. She belongs to him. She knows herself his. She must please and serve. She lives thus in a radiant world enflamed with emotion. In such a world are forged the stoutest and most inescapable of chains. Talenders blossom in the meadow of her bondage. Such a world, that of bondage, is congenial to her deepest needs, and her sense of self. She senses she is where she belongs, and where she wants to be. She has longed to be put to her knees naked before a master. She has longed to press her lips in obeisance to his sandals. She is now so before him, and is content.

She lifts her head to him, her eyes shining, in gratitude.

Perhaps he will caress her.

She may hope so.

Perhaps he will keep her.

She may hope so.

But, too, he may not do these things.

She must wait to learn. She is, after all, only a slave.

She may be loved, or hated. She may be noticed or ignored. She may be silked or kept stripped. Her limbs may be kept free, or they may be held tightly to her body by coarse ropes; indeed, as she is a slave she might be swathed with merciless cordage, or perhaps chained, cruelly spread-eagled, on tiles. She may be called upon, to her delight, to dance for her master's friends or acquaintances. How decorously she will dance if free women are present, and how like a slave, if they are not! Perhaps her master will permit her much latitude; perhaps she may be allowed to run freely about the city. Or perhaps he will keep her confined to the house, in shackles, or perhaps give her the run of a chain in the yard. Perhaps he will permit her to heel him on outings, joyfully, comfortably, or perhaps he will run her, hands tied behind her back, weeping and gasping beside his kaiila, on a short leash, tethered to his stirrup. She might be brought perfumed to his slave ring. She might be neglected in the filth of a kennel. She might be caressed. She might be lashed. She might be kept. She might be sold. She is a slave.

Slaves are slaves, only slaves.

And Ellen, kneeling naked, back-braceleted, concealed under the blanket, knew herself, too, such, and only such.

She was a slave.

She could be left behind.

Would she be left behind?

They must take me with them, she thought. They must, they must!

You are a burden, she said to herself. You are a slight slave, more fit for the furs, there squirming and moaning, than trekking beside masters for long days and nights. You will be left behind, or abandoned.

No, no, she cried to herself, within the blanket.

I can keep up with them, she said to herself. I must keep up with them!

She did not want to be left behind.

They must not leave her behind!

But she did not think they would leave her.

Too, there were wagons, and she might be permitted to ride. Too, Selius Arconious had been willing to pay twenty-one silver tarsks for her. Twenty-one! Do not forget that, she told herself. Despite his arrogance and disclaimers, I am sure you are important to him, she thought. No tarnster casts aside twenty-one silver tarsks. Perhaps I am pretty. Perhaps I am even a desirable slave. Can that be? I think it is possible. There were twenty silver tarsks bid on me in open auction. For most Goreans that is a considerable amount of money. To be sure, she thought, a kaiila would bring more, and a tarn a great deal more.

"Is it time to flight tarns?" asked Portus Canio.

"They must not be flighted too early," said a man, whom Ellen, from the voice, knew to be the red-haired man. "We must not give the Cosians time to collect their wits before the camp breaks up, lest they close the camp. We must count on their confusion, until the camp is broken, and thousands are scattered in a hundred directions."

"But soon," said Fel Doron, uneasily.

"Yes, soon," said the other.

"Well," said Selius Arconious, "I think that I shall seek some rest." Ellen heard someone rise, and make a noise, as of contentment, as in languorous stretching. She had little doubt it was her master.

"How can you rest?" asked a man.

"At such a time?" asked another.

"It is an excellent suggestion," said the red-haired man.

"We might pretend to rest, as it is late," said Portus Canio.

"We might pretend to awaken in consternation, given an alarm," said Fel Doron.

"I am not going to sleep," said a man.

"Tend the fire then," suggested another.

"On your feet," said Selius Arconious, and, from the tone of his voice, Ellen, even though beneath the blanket, had no doubt he was addressing her. It was the voice of one who anticipated no hesitation whatsoever, and would accept no hesitation whatsoever, in the addressee's compliance. It was the voice of a master addressing a slave. Her response was instantaneous. She struggled to her feet as quickly as she could, given the impediments of the blanket and bracelets. The celerity of her response, despite the handicap of the blanket and bracelets, apparently occasioned neither stir nor interest on the part of the men, its promptitude being taken for granted by them, presumably not even being noticed by them. Such things were simply expected of her. She was a slave. Within the blanket Ellen bit her lip, in embarrassment at how quickly, and fearfully, she had obeyed. Yet, had the same command been given again, under the same circumstances, she would have responded in the same fashion, or perhaps even with greater alacrity. It was as if a dog had been commanded. Ellen realized that she, as other women brought to Gor for the diverse purposes of the collar, had learned to obey, and to obey immediately, and perfectly. How different this was from when she had been on Earth! She was now standing, still completely covered by the blanket, its lower folds now fallen about her ankles.

She felt a strong hand gathering together the portion of the blanket which was about her head, pulling it forward about her neck, and wadding it beneath her chin, where it was firmly grasped. In this way an arrangement was produced not unlike a hood with a throat-ring, a ring by means of pressure on which, by a leash or such, an occupant might be conducted about. She was drawn a few yards to one side. She stumbled once, but the hand at her throat, grasping the blanket, did not permit her to fall. There was now grass beneath her feet.

"Kneel," said her master.

She was then kneeling beneath the blanket.

The blanket was then rearranged, put about her shoulders, and drawn about her, in such a way that she knelt within it, it open a bit before her, her throat and head exposed. He held it about her neck for a moment, and then released it. It remained rather as it had been. With his two hands he brushed her hair back, once more behind her shoulders. The gesture was almost tender. He looked into her eyes. She looked at him, frightened, pleadingly. She was his, and did not, truly, know him. She told herself that she hated him, that she despised him, but she knew herself his, and, for some reason, her eyes were moist with tears. He touched the side of her collar with the fingertips of his right hand, a gesture which, to her surprise, seemed almost loving. But then it seemed he caught himself, as though in a moment of indiscretion. He then laughed softly, harshly, even cruelly, mercilessly, in proprietorship, his eyes glistening and hard, and grasped the collar, possessively. There was a look of satisfaction on his face then, and she suddenly understood, trembling, that he was a true owner of women, not the sort of man who freed slaves. And certainly he would not free her, not this young, lovely barbarian which was she. Indeed, given the genuine opportunity to own her, what rational man would consider freeing her? She realized then, it startling her, that on this world she was too valuable, too precious, too desirable, to be free. Perhaps if she had been enveloped within, bundled within, the cumbersome Robes of Concealment? But surely not if they had once glimpsed her in the brief tunic of a slave, or seen her chained, in rags, in a market or exhibited nude on a block. Her face, her slave curves, betrayed her. Only too obviously such as she was the natural property of strong men. Too, she suspected that this man, her master, aside from social and institutional imperatives, literally, deeply, personally, for whatever reason, relished the owning of her. He would not let her go, she was sure. This frightened her, but thrilled her, as well. Few women on Earth, she suspected, other than slaves, had any inkling as to what it was to be so wanted, to be the object of such fierce desire, that of a master for a slave. He found her, she suspected, "slave desirable." He desired her with such passion, with such lust, with such wanting, that she would be kept exactly as he wanted her, as his complete slave, until, of course, he might tire of her, and then she could be sold to another.

She was his.

He sat near her, before her, cross-legged, and reached his hands to her hair, and, by means of her hair, as she knelt, back-braceleted, drew her head downward a few inches, toward himself. Her head down, she lifted her eyes, looking into his eyes, questioningly. A tear coursed down her left cheek. She tried to draw back, a little, but he drew her head, by the hair, a few inches closer to his body.

"You pleased the guardsmen, I take it," he said.

"A slave did her best to please them, Master," said Ellen.

He then lay back on the grass. His hands were still in her hair, and her face, held, was now but inches from his body.

She bent to his body, her lips pursed.

His hands now held her from him. "Master?" she asked.

"It seems you intend to give pleasure, uncommanded, and of your own free will," he said.

"Master?" asked Ellen, confused.

"Were you, a meaningless, wretched slave, given permission to touch the body of one whose Home Stone is that of Ar?" he asked.

"Master is clearly ready for pleasure," whispered Ellen.

He was silent.

"Did not Master draw me to him?" she asked.

"It is one thing for me to send you to give pleasure to Cosian sleen," he said, angrily. "It is another to permit you to touch a citizen of Ar."

"I do not understand what I am to do," said Ellen.

"Did you not lower your head to me, uncommanded, uncoerced?"

"Yes, Master," said Ellen. "I thought—"

"Yes?" he said.

"I thought you might be pleased," she whispered.

"Did you want to please me?" he asked.

"I think so, Master," said Ellen, in tears.

"Why?" he asked. "To save your worthless hide? To ingratiate yourself with me? To practice your wiles, to ensnare me with pleasure, to purchase an easier life, to avoid beatings and chainings?"

"I do not know," wept Ellen. "Master confuses me."

"How well the word 'Master' sounds on your lips," he said. "How fitting!"

"It is fitting," said Ellen. "I am a slave. I have learned it on this world."

"She-tarsk," said he. "Conniving, hypocritical she-tarsk!"

"I am not conniving, Master," she said. "And I do not think that I am hypocritical."

"We hate one another, do we not?" he asked, angrily.

"Why did Master buy me then?" she asked.

"Doubtless for the pleasure of owning and mastering you, for the pleasure of exacting from your hide compensations a thousandfold for frustrations you dealt me in Ar. Oh, yes, it will be pleasant to own you, Earth slut, to impose upon you a leisurely, prolonged vengeance, to subject you to a slavery so thorough and abject that you will creep to your kennel at night, and weep there for the smallest of your former indiscretions. Have no fear, slave girl! You will well know that you are owned!"

"I do not know what my feelings are, Master," said Ellen. "I suppose I must hate you. I suppose I should hate you. I do not know! I have told myself that I hate you."

"There!" said Selius Arconious.

"But I do not know if it is true or not!"

"What a silly, stupid little tasta, you are," he snarled.

"Sometimes we tell ourselves what we think we should feel, but what we do not feel. Sometimes we tell lies to ourselves."

"How can one tell lies to oneself?" he asked. "Do you not think you know what you feel? Who knows, if you do not?"

"Sometimes others know," said Ellen. "Portus Canio might know."

"More of you than you know?"

"And perhaps more of you than you know."

"Absurd."

"As Master will have it."

"He knows nothing of us," said Selius Arconious.

"Is Master so sure of his own feelings?" asked Ellen. "Forgive me, Master," she added, hastily.

"Know that you are hated!" he said.

"Yes, Master," said Ellen.

"Why did you bend to me earlier?" he asked.

"It seemed to be what I should do!" she wept. "I do not know! I wanted to please my master! I wanted to give him pleasure! I do not know!"

"Did you want to do it?" he asked, rising to one elbow. "Truly?"

"I do not know! I think 'Yes,' Master!"

"Liar!" said he. "Slut and liar!"

"You own me now, Master," wept Ellen. "I am yours and totally helpless. Please be kind to your slave!"

He then reached to her hair and drew her painfully, forcibly, to his body, until her lips were but an inch from the heat of him. He held her in such a way that she could neither approach him more closely nor withdraw.

"Put out your tongue, your moist, lying little tongue, and lick your upper lip, slowly," he said. "Now, purse your lips and kiss, again and again, at me, but do not touch my body. Now, lick again your upper lip, and now, again, more slowly, yes, that is it, slave girl."

Her hands twisted helplessly behind her in the bracelets. Her body became alive with need. Her thighs flamed. She was muchly aroused.

He then, with an angry sound, flung Ellen, painfully, by the hair, to his left side, and she lay there, her head at his left thigh.

"I am ready to please my Master," she said. "Please let me do so."

"No," he said.

She dared to press her lips softly to his thigh. She hoped she would not be beaten.

"Why did you do that?" he asked.

"I think," she said, "that a slave loves her master."

"Liar," he said softly. But he did not seem angry, nor did he strike her.

He then pulled the blanket away from her and spread it on the grass, in such way that it might be laid upon, and, when it was folded, it would cover them, as well. At his gesture, pointing, she took her place on the blanket, so that when he lay upon it, her head would be at his thigh. She was, of course, on the blanket to his left, as he was right-handed. In this way, by simply turning, he could easily handle, dominate and possess her. The closed side of the blanket was to his left, as well. In this way, the slave is confined between the closure of the blanket and the body of the master. Too, in this arrangement, the open side of the blanket being to his right, he could leave the blanket instantly, his sword hand free.

He then lay under the blanket, supine, it folded over the two of them. She lay on her side, at his side, back-braceleted, covered completely by the blanket, her head at his thigh. In this way, her head covered, she could not see what might transpire in the camp. She would be kept, suitably, in "slave ignorance."

"Master," she said.

"Yes?" he said.

"May I speak?"

"Yes."

"I am collared, Master," she whispered.

"Yes?"

"I am an animal, Master," she whispered.

"I am well aware of that," he said.

"I am a collared animal, who cannot remove her collar," she said.

"Certainly," he said. "You are a slave."

"Are not masters concerned for their animals? Are not masters kind to their animals?"

"To some, perhaps," he said, "but you are a special sort of animal, a human female animal, a slave. One need not be concerned for such animals, nor need one be kind to them."

"Yes, Master," she said.

"Perhaps you remember the tarsk pen, the railing, and the whip?"

"Yes, Master," she said, frightened.

"You are a transparent, manipulative little slut," he said.

"Forgive me, Master!"

Again she pressed her lips, softly, to his thigh.

"Master."

"Yes?"

"Might the blanket not be turned a little, put aside a bit, so that I might the more easily speak to my master?"

"I can hear you," he said.

"Master!"

"No," he said.

"Yes, Master," she said.

She lay at his thigh, covered. Sometimes she could hear the small noises of the nearby fire. A breeze ruffled the leaves of a nearby tree. Occasional insect noises might be heard.

"Master."

"Yes?"

"I am back-braceleted," she said, "and am beside you, at your thigh, utterly helpless, a woman, and a slave."

He was silent.

"Perhaps Master might make use of me," she said.

"Why?" he said.

"I am pretty," she said. "How is it that I do not please Master?"

"You are worthless," he said.

"Master paid much for me," she said.

"I cannot deny that it is pleasant to own you," he said.

"I do not know what to do," she wept. She pulled a bit at the bracelets, in frustration. How well aware she was of her helplessness, of her wrists' captivity, they fastened so effectively, so closely, behind her, imprisoned so securely within their light, close-linked circlets.

"I do not understand," he said.

"I am Master's," she said. "If I am not now pleasing, I beg to be informed as to how I may become pleasing."

"You wish to be pleasing?"

"Yes, Master!"

"Liar," he said.

"No, Master," she said. "I do want to please you!"

"Perhaps," he said.

"I want you to want me," she whispered. "I want to be attractive to Master. What can I do? I do not know what to do! Perhaps I might be adorned? Perhaps Master might bedeck me, according to his fancy or wont? Would that help? I do not know. I want to be attractive to him."

"Perhaps some cheap bangles," he said.

She recalled, from Earth, the two, small, golden loops she had once worn on her left wrist, in class.

"As Master pleases," she said.

"Perhaps," said he, "bells on an ankle."

"Whatever pleases Master," she said.

"Locked, in place," he said.

"Certainly, Master."

On Gor it is not unusual to bell a slave, and the erotic clash of such bells, slave bells, on an ankle, in the markets and parks, in the plazas and bazaars, is a frequently heard sound. And the same bells which serve so well to draw attention to a lovely, demurely tunicked slave in the sul market, her shopping basket balanced with one hand on her head, serve as well, doubtless, to record in their jangling her leapings and squirmings in the arms of her master.

"Perhaps I will buy you earrings," he said.

"As Master wishes," she said.

"You would be a pierced-ear girl?" he asked, surprised.

"I have no fear of such things," she said.

"You are indeed a worthless slave," he said.

"Yes, Master," she said.

Earrings, on Gor, interestingly, are placed on only the lowest of slaves. Nose rings, incidentally, for whatever reason, do not carry the same connotation of degradation, and such. Indeed, Ellen has been informed that in the southern hemisphere such rings are worn by even free women amongst certain nomadic tribes. Complex veiling and the Robes of Concealment are most common, of course, in urban areas, and particularly so amongst women of the higher castes. To be sure, even peasant women may veil themselves before strangers, and, one supposes, wisely.

Many Gorean slave girls live in terror of having their ears pierced. To be sure, this not unoften improves their price. Woe to the Earth girl brought to Gor whose ears are pierced. She will be sold publicly, as a "pierced-ear girl."

Ellen, of course, had no objection to various adornments and enhancements. On Earth she would have deplored such things as politically scandalous, but, on the other hand, had often dreamed of herself so adorned. As in many facets of dress and ornamentation the effect of such things is stimulating to the woman as well as to he under whose gaze she finds herself.

"In my training," she said, "the guards often bound me in pretty cords. This seemed to please them. I gather I looked well in them." To be sure, Ellen knew she was remarkably fetching in such constraints, particularly when nude. Had she not seen herself in the mirrors, when ordered to struggle in them, and had she not noted the reactions of the guards? "You will tie me in pretty cords, will you not, sometimes, Master?" she wheedled. The sight of her helplessly bound in such cords, she hoped, might please him. Too, she, their helpless prisoner, had found them astonishingly arousing, as well.

"Coarse ropes will do for you, slut," he said. "Squirm in them, by yourself, cold and miserable, alone in the woods, tied by your neck to a tree."

"A slave wants to please her master," she wept.

"Are your slave needs much upon you?" he inquired.

"Yes, Master!" she whispered, intensely.

"I find that amusing," he said.

She jerked futilely, in fierce frustration, at the constraints on her wrists. The tiny sound of the links further excited her. The sides of her wrists hurt.

How helpless, and how needful, she was!

"Master!" she begged.

"It is pleasant to have a woman so beside one," he remarked, dryly.

A wave of hatred for the brute, Selius Arconious, swept over her.

"We are far from the tarnloft, are we not, pretty slut?" he asked.

"Yes, Master," she said, angrily.

"How you tormented me there," he recalled.

She bit her lip, under the blanket, in frustration.

"Doubtless it was your worst nightmare," he said, "that you might one day belong to me."

"Yes, Master!" she said, angrily.

"And now you do," he said, with obvious satisfaction.

"Yes, Master!" she wept. "Please, Master! Content a slave! She begs it!"

"Very well," said he. "Beg, slut. It will please me to hear it."

"Please, Master!" she protested.

"You are a needful slave?"

"Yes, Master!"

"You may then beg, if you wish," he said.

Ellen thrashed in misery, but then turned again, to his thigh.

"Master's girl begs to be taught her collar. Master's girl petitions for her ravishing. Master's girl begs for her subjugation. Master's girl begs use. She wishes to be conquered. She begs to be mastered. She is Master's property. She would learn, then, what this entails. She is Master's possession. Apprise her then of the treatment to which she is subject. She is Master's animal, his beast. Let her be trained then, leash- and whip-trained if he wishes, to his pleasure. She is Master's collar slut, his shackle girl, his chain bitch. Teach her then what it is to be such. She begs to be put to his use, uncompromisingly, ruthlessly, that she may know herself no more than what she is, a worthless, meaningless slave."

"You beg the use appropriate for you, as a slave?" he asked.

"Yes, Master."

"You beg slave rape?" he asked.

"Fervently, humbly, Master."

"No," he said, quietly.

"Master?" she whispered.

"Others," said he, "are not experiencing pleasure. The paga does not flow. Meat is not roasted. There are no hot, collared slaves, naked and aroused, seized in their arms, writhing, moaning, yielding. Danger is imminent."

"Yes, Master," whispered Ellen. "Forgive me, Master."

A little later a thought came to Ellen. "Would Master like to send me to others, to give them pleasure," she asked, as though innocently. He could do such, she knew, as he had done before.

"No," he said, angrily.

"Yes, Master," said Ellen, smiling to herself.

"She-sleen," he growled.

"Perhaps Master is unduly possessive," she speculated. "Perhaps he is jealous. Perhaps Master now regrets having sent his slave to please Cosians. Perhaps she did well. Perhaps she did very well. She is, after all, a slave. Perhaps Master now thinks that he may have made a mistake in that matter. Perhaps Master now wishes that it had been he himself who had received such pleasures. Perhaps Master now wishes to keep his slave to himself."

"Beware," said he, "lest I send you to give pleasure to the entire camp."

"There are thousands of men in the camp, Master," she said.

"Are you being troublesome?" he inquired.

"No, Master," said Ellen. "Forgive me, Master."

"You should be beaten, and beaten," he said.

"As Master wishes," said Ellen, and pressed her lips closely, again, to his thigh, beneath the blanket.

Later Ellen whispered, "Perhaps Master cares for his slave, a little."

"No," he said.

"Yes, Master," she said.

"You may speak," he said, after a time.

"Master's slave loves him," she whispered.

"Master's slave," he said, "is a liar."

"No, Master," she whispered.

"Do you contradict me?" he asked.

"A slave must speak the truth to her master," she said.

"You cannot love," he said. "You are an Earth woman."

"What do you know of Earth women, or of the feelings of Earth women?" she asked.

"They are nasty and small, petty and vain," he said.

"But we do make excellent slaves, do we not?" she asked.

"Yes," he said. "You obtain some value, some small value, once you are in collars."

"Then an Earth woman might have some value to you?"

"Perhaps as an abject slave," he said.

"I do not think we are so different from your women, Master," she said.

"Beware, slave," said he. "Do not become presumptuous."

"We are all women," she said.

"The collar levels all sluts," he said. "It makes them all the same."

"Even before the collar we are the same," she said.

"I suppose so," he said.

"We are all women."

"Yes."

"And then you enslave us."

"Some," he said.

"Slaves have feelings," she said.

"They are unimportant," he said.

"Do you know how she feels, being a slave?"

"Her feelings are not important," he said.

"Are you not curious, as to why we make such excellent slaves?"

"Such things are not important," he said.

"Yes, Master," she whispered.

She then again pressed her lips softly to his thigh.

"I wonder if any man understands the meaning to a woman of her brand and collar, the particular meaning to her, not to him, of being owned, how exciting and glorious it is, how it debases and dignifies us, how it reduces and exalts us, how it makes us meaningless and gives us meaning, how in denying us all it bestows upon us everything, how it enflames us. What, indeed, Master, do you, or any man, know of slaves, truly, and the feelings of slaves?"

"I know that they are to be owned, and mastered, totally," he said.

"Yes, Master," she whispered, again kissing his thigh. "That is true, Master. It is that which makes us women. It is that which fulfills us."

"And I wonder," said he, "if any woman, or any slave, understands the glory of the mastery, truly, the rapture, the splendor, the joy of owning and commanding a woman."

"Sometimes I think I have some sense of it, Master," she said. "And it is you who own me, and is it I who am subject to your commands. It excites me, and exalts me. Doubtless it has similar effects on the man. Do we not fit together? Are we not two parts to a single whole? Are we not meaningless alone, but whole together? Are we not the lock to your key, and you the key to our lock? Only you can open us to ourselves, and only we can reveal to you the full meaning of your key."

"It is not long until dawn," he said.

"Yes, Master," she said.

"Let us rest," he said.

"Yes, Master," she said.

She did not think that Selius Arconious slept then. She surely did not. Perhaps an Ahn later, shortly before the first rays of Tor-tu-Gor, Light-Upon-the-Home-Stone, the common star of Earth and Gor, began to glimmer in the east, rising there as it does on Earth, they rose together, he suddenly to his feet, casting the blanket aside, she quickly to her knees, at his thigh, not daring to rise, as they heard the alarms, these sounding from within the camp.

"It has begun," he said.

Chapter 27

What Occurred in the Fields

This was now the second day, following the morning departure from the camp outside Brundisium. Portus Canio, Fel Doron, and their small company, including he known as Bosk of Port Kar, and Marcus of Ar's Station, were moving eastward, away from the camp which had been outside Brundisium, not southeastward, toward Ar. Presumably, on the likely Cosian assumption that their enemies might be of Ar, then those enemies might naturally be expected to move toward that city, and, consequently, one supposed that Cosian searches, and attempts to apprehend fugitives, might be largely directed to the southeastern routes, say, eventually to the Viktel Aria and such. Altogether, matters had proceeded rather as the conspirators had planned. Initially there had been a tarn pursuit of the trussed, gagged Tersius Major, he tied upright in a tarn saddle, clad as had been Selius Arconious. Accordingly the Cosian search for Selius Arconious had been at least temporarily abandoned. Some Ahn later, somewhat before morning, several tarns had been released from holding cots and sped from the camp, this being taken in the darkness as the unexpected departure of enemies of Cos and Tyros. A large pursuit had been soon mounted. Whereas the fate of Tersius Major was at this time unknown, one supposed that, in an Ahn or so, the pursuit of the riderless tarns would be resolved, the tarns taken in hand, or, at least, that it would have been determined that most of them, for they would have scattered, had been riderless. By the time, several pasangs away, the nature of the diversion was understood, the flighted tarns being regained, or it being understood that most, if not all, had been riderless, it had become morning and the vast camp, bit by bit, shortly after dawn, had been broken, the thousands of men, their goods, their wagons, and animals, including slaves, then wending their many ways toward their countless destinations. With them, of course, as unhurried, as unnoticed, as others, had gone Portus Canio, Fel Doron and those accompanying them.

So they had left the camp the preceding morning, and it was now in the late morning of the second day.

Ellen was now in a brief, sleeveless slave tunic of brown rep-cloth. No longer was she back-braceleted. Her wrists were now crossed and thonged before her, and she was following Fel Doron's tharlarion-drawn wagon, a tether running from the wagon to her thonged wrists.

When she sensed Selius Arconious's eyes upon her she walked especially well.

"She-sleen," he said.

"Master?" she asked.

"Sometimes," he said, "I wish you were free, for I would muchly enjoy enslaving you."

"Alas, Master," said Ellen, "I am already a slave."

"And mine," he said.

"Yes, Master," smiled Ellen.

"How do you like your garment?" he asked.

"It is not my garment, but the property of my master," said Ellen. "As master knows, a slave may own nothing."

"But perhaps you are pleased to be permitted to wear a garment?"

"Yes, Master. A slave is grateful that her master permits her a garment."

"It may be removed at my whim," he said.

"Of course, Master," she said.

"Do you like it?" he asked.

"It is rather short, is it not, Master?" she asked.

"Beware," said he, "lest it be further shortened, or removed entirely."

"Yes, Master."

"Do you like it?" he asked.

"Master made me beg prettily enough for it last night," said Ellen.

She had been unbraceleted shortly after leaving the camp yesterday morning, and had, of course, prepared the midday meal, and, later, the evening meal for the men. After that, and the cleaning up, and the kissing of, and turning down, and preparation of, the sleeping blankets of the men, he had thrown a bit of cloth to the ground near her. "Master!" she had cried, delightedly. But when she had crawled toward it, not having been permitted to rise, he had kicked it farther away from her. He had played with her for a time in this manner, and had then had her go to her belly before him and lick and kiss his feet. He then permitted her to crawl to the garment, pick it up in her teeth and crawl back to him, and then be before him on all fours, lifting her head to him, beggingly, the garment between her teeth. Would he permit it to her? There had been beseeching tears in her eyes. He had then said, "Very well," and she had bellied again, tearfully, gratefully, the bit of cloth, now damp, still clutched between her teeth, pressing the side of her face against his bootlike sandals. She had then been permitted to draw it on.

"So do you like it?" he asked.

"Very much," she said.

"You look well in it," he said.

"If I look well in it, then I particularly like it," she said.

"It conceals your defects," he said.

"Oh?" she said.

"Not that it conceals much of anything."

"My defects, Master?" she asked, warily.

"Yes," he said. "Your figure is too exciting, and too lusciously beautiful, and, thus, when one looks upon you it is hard to keep one's mind on serious matters."

"I would think," she said, "that a slave would long for such defects."

"Well, in any event, they certainly improve her price," he said.

"Yes, Master," she said.

"But you are not worth twenty silver tarsks," he said angrily.

"Master paid twenty-one," she said.

"Your master is an idiot," he said.

"A slave dare not contradict her master," said Ellen.

"You would actually be of interest," he said, "if you were not stupid."

"It is hard to have everything, Master," said Ellen.

"You should be whipped," he said.

Ellen was silent then. She wondered if some slaves were whipped because the master was angry at them, resentful of the mesmerizing fascination which such a lovely creature might exercise over them, that they might be furious at a suspected weakness they thought they might detect within themselves, a fear that they might melt, that they might succumb to the power and beauty of such a vulnerable, delicious, beautiful, owned creature. Was the slave to be punished for her own attractiveness, and beauty, for which men were muchly responsible, for that attractiveness and beauty which, despite whether she approved of it or not, her bondage had surely bestowed upon her?

* * * *

Perhaps a word might be here inserted, briefly, as a "beauty bestowed by bondage" might seem to some an unfamiliar concept. First, as I think has been clearly indicated from time to time men, slavers, for example, have criteria. Not every woman is regarded as "collar worthy." Not every woman is "slave desirable." Have you not wondered, sometime, for example, if you are attractive enough, desirable enough, to be a slave? The acquisition of slaves is seldom a random matter. Selections are usually involved, often severe and rigorous selections. Some obvious criteria, among several others, are beauty, intelligence, and a latency, at least, for arousable, helpless passion. The captor may, of course, upon occasion, balance out a multitude of features, aspects, qualities or attributes. Women are, of course, complex and various. For example, to take a very simple case, a woman who is less beautiful but more intelligent is more likely to find herself in the chains of a master, subject to his whip, than one who is more beautiful but less intelligent. To be sure, the ideal of the slaver is to find all his desiderata conjoined, as they, fortunately for him, so often are. Commonly the beautiful woman is intelligent, at least latently passionate, and so on. One might note, in passing, that the usual Gorean taste in women tends to favor the statistically natural or normal woman, the lovely, nicely figured woman of average height and weight, who as a slave fits nicely in a man's arms, as opposed to the more unusual "model types," who tend to be awkward, scrawny and breastless. Sometimes Earth girls in the pens ask where are the beautiful women, and only later come to understand that it is they who are the truly beautiful women, the ones ruthless men have selected for collars. To be sure, some "model types" are also brought to Gor, and they, too, in turn, will learn to well serve masters, in the kitchens and in the furs.

But to return to the "beauty bestowed by bondage," understand that that the free woman scouted for bondage is almost always beautiful to begin with. Thus, it is not surprising that she will make a beautiful slave. But how is it that she will become even more beautiful in bondage? A number of things are involved, and only three will be mentioned, and but briefly. First, collared and "slave clad," women are beautiful. The collar enhances their beauty not simply as a lovely ornament, attractive on any woman, but even more by its meaning, that its wearer is a slave, that she is merchandise. It thus adds dimensions of meaningfulness and stimulation to her appearance, both aesthetically and psychologically. Too, being "slave clad" enhances a woman's beauty. Imagine, for example, seeing a woman in a severe, sober business suit and then seeing her revealed in a slave tunic. She is suddenly a hundred times more attractive. Second, the slave is commonly trained, at least to some extent. She learns to walk as a slave, move as a slave, kneel as a slave, speak as a slave, behave as a slave, and so on. She becomes obedient and deferent. She is graceful and feminine. All these things enhance her beauty. Lastly, and most important, as she learns her collar and is mastered, she comes to understand that she is a woman, deeply and truly, and in a sense far more profound than that of merely the attractions of her delicious lineaments, which have called her so to the attention of men, and have had their indisputable role in bringing her to the slaver's platform, to the chains of a market. Gone then are the false starts and distractions, the conflicts and confusions, the dissonances consequent upon the imposition of false images, of political contrivances engineered by manipulators and haters. She has come home to herself. She has at last fulfilled the ancient template of her needs. She is now herself, at one with her nature. In bondage she finds her meaning and fulfillment. She has found happiness where she had never thought to look for it, in a collar. And happy, radiant, at one with herself, she has become more beautiful. In such ways then one might speak of the "beauty bestowed by bondage." If a woman would be beautiful let her seek her master, and his collar.

* * * *

Or was it that a lashing might be no more than merely another prosaic mnemonic device, one among many, reminding the slave, lest she might forget it, that she was truly a slave. Certainly, from the slave's point of view there is little doubt that being subject to the lash of her master is a confirmation, in her own mind, as in that of others, like the collar and brand, of her condition. Interestingly, too, though Ellen feared the lash, and would go to great lengths to avoid it, she, in the complex subtleties and ambiguities of the master/slave relationship, in which she was so obviously implicated, and despite her constant explicit reassurances to herself that she must hate her master, the virile, arrogant, masterful beast, Selius Arconious, found it necessary to attempt to suppress within her own mind a frequent, poignant, astonishing refrain, "I want to be whipped. I want to be whipped. I love him. I love him. I want him to whip me. I love him. I want him to whip me." Doubtless there were subconscious depths and mysteries here which eluded superficial explanations, which eluded the facile, at-hand, convenient, shallow categories of the ideologically conditioned understanding, which defied political mockeries of human nature, a reference to realities which lay deeply, restlessly, in the being of a species, realities which were perhaps born before the dwelling in caves, before the hunting of great, lumbering, tusked beasts, before the nurturing of sparks, and the lifting in triumph against the darkness, in a hairy paw, a burning brand.

"I think Master likes me," said Ellen.

"Beware," he said.

"Nights ago at the dancing circle," said Ellen, "I recall that I was to be whipped. But Master saved me. My master is thoughtful, and kind. He rescued me. He bought my strokes from the scribe. A slave is grateful."

"If I were you, slave," said he, "I would not be too grateful."

"Master?" asked Ellen.

"Watch," said he. "Watch the skies." Then he walked about her, and went beside the wagon. Ellen was troubled. Then she was mildly perplexed. Then she straightened her body, and walked well. Then she smiled. The thongs were on her wrists. She heard the tharlarion grunt. The wagon wheels creaked. They continued on their way.

In the next two or three days, sometime, presumably depending on the trekking, they should reach the vicinity of "the place of concealed tarns," at which point Bosk, he of Port Kar, and Marcus, he of Ar's Station, would leave the group, presumably proceeding thence to the rendezvous point. Portus Canio and the others, then, would presumably turn southeast, toward Ar, hoping to reach the great southern road, the Viktel Aria, Ar's Victory.

* * * *

The next morning Ellen was permitted to ride in the back of the wagon. She was in her tunic, and back-braceleted. She was lying mostly supine, nestled in bedrolls and blankets, in the wagon bed. About her were some tarpaulins, these covering various boxes and bundles, housing utensils, supplies and such. She was warm, and drowsy from the creaking and rocking of the wagon, and she opened her eyes a little, squinting against the morning sun. She was grateful for having been permitted to ride, and, as for the back-braceleting, slaves must expect such things. She did not think that they feared she might steal a biscuit. She thought, rather, that they merely enjoyed seeing her thusly. It surely made it difficult to keep the tunic down about her thighs, but it could be managed somewhat by a bit of judicious, if embarrassing, squirming. And the men seemed to enjoy that. Men are beasts, thought Ellen, who enjoy the discomfiture of a bound woman, aesthetically and otherwise, one put totally at their mercy, in accord with their imperious will. Back-braceleted, the slave knows herself helpless. Indeed, a common point of back-braceleting is just that, to impress her vulnerability and helplessness upon her. This also tends to be arousing to a woman. But Ellen's master, for whatever reason, had not made use of her. This puzzled her, and troubled her, for she knew that her body, if not her mind, longed to serve his pleasure. Certainly her body eagerly, plaintively willed to be put to his slave use. It might be mentioned in passing that, whatever may be the ideological point of encouraging antimenite fantasies of martial prowess on a politicized world, for example, in popular entertainments, fantasies themselves, such fantasies have little grounding in reality, and, if acted upon, may have tragic consequences. Incidentally, the penalties for a slave's striking, or attempting to strike, a free person are severe. They range from death to such lesser penalties as the amputation of a foot, the breaking of the teeth out of a jaw, and such. Women on Gor, whether slave or free, are in no doubt, on some level at least, that nature, for whatever reason, has made men their masters.

Ellen struggled to sit up.

Then she struggled to her knees, and then to her feet, trying to hold her balance in the wagon.

There seemed no mistaking the spots in the sky.

"Masters!" she cried.

Her shout instantly drew the attention of the men who, sheltering their eyes, followed her gaze.

"Do not break," said Portus Canio. "Do not seize weapons. Keep your places. We are innocent travelers, returning home. We have nothing to fear. Pretend that you have not seen them."

"They may pass over," said a man.

"They may be merchants, carriers of precious commodities, too rich to risk on the ground. They may have no concern with us," speculated Fel Doron.

The men kept their position about the wagon, facing in the direction of the trek. Fel Doron, who held the reins of the tharlarion, spoke soothingly to it. "On, gently now, you fat, beautiful gross wart. On, on, slowly, gently."

"Ellen," said Portus Canio, not looking at her, "down. Sit. Sit in the wagon, facing backward. Keep us informed. Tell us what you see."

"Yes, Master," said Ellen, frightened.

"Continue as you were," said Portus Canio to Fel Doron.

"On, ugly beauty," said Fel Doron, quietly.

"They do not seem to be approaching, Master," said Ellen. "They may be circling, far off."

"Then they are not merchants," said a man.

"Have they seen us?" asked Portus Canio.

"I do not know, Master," said Ellen.

"I saw five," said Portus Canio. "How many do you see?"

"I count five," said Ellen, slowly.

"Are they tarnsmen?" asked a man, looking forward.

"Are there tarn baskets?" asked another.

"I think so," said Ellen. "It is hard to tell."

"They would then be merchants," said a man.

"If they are tarnsmen, there would be only five then," said a man.

"They could reconnoiter, and summon others," said another man.

"Can you see if there are tarn baskets?" asked another.

"Yes," said Ellen, suddenly. "As they just veered, I am sure there are tarn baskets!"

"Then they are civilians, merchants," said a man.

"That may not be true," said Portus Canio, grimly.

"There could be four or five men to a carrier," said Fel Doron, softly.

"That could be twenty or more," said a man, apprehensively.

"Can you see banners, weaponry?" asked Portus Canio.

"It is too far away," said Ellen.

"What are they doing now?" asked Fel Doron, looking forward, over the broad, scaled back of the draft beast in the traces.

"I am not sure they see us," said Ellen. "Their interest may be in something behind us."

"We will continue on our way," said Portus Canio.

"What is behind us?" asked Fel Doron.

"Stand," said Portus Canio.

Ellen struggled to her feet, bracing her leg against the side of the wagon bed. "I see only the grass, bending in the wind, clouds, the horizon, Master," she said.

"What of the tarns and carriers now?" asked a man.

"They are smaller now," said Ellen. "I think they are going away."

"I do not understand this," said Portus Canio. "If they are merchants, they would not circle, but continue on their way. If they were tarnsmen, or soldiery, one would expect them to approach, to alight and inquire into our identity and destination."

"They may not have seen us," said a man, "and, come to the perimeter of their search range, turned back."

"Perhaps," said Portus Canio.

Ellen, looking back, could see the wake of the wagon wheels in the tall grass. She had little doubt but what so remarkable a feature might be detectable from a height, and much more easily than from a position on the ground, unless one were in the actual wake of the wagon itself.

Portus Canio swung himself over the side of the wagon, and stood upright beside her for several Ihn, looking backward. He shaded his eyes. From the height of the wagon he could see much farther than was possible from the level of the ground. Too, he was some twelve to fourteen inches taller than the slave. He could see, of course, the twin tracks in the grass behind them, which would mark, for several hours, the passage of the wagon.

He then lifted Ellen from her feet, holding her for a moment, and looked down into her eyes. She felt the strength of his hand in the softness behind the backs of her knees, and his other hand at her back. She trembled slightly, held helplessly off her feet, knowing herself in his power. She held her legs together, demurely, her head down, slightly bowed, turned to the side, her toes pointed, emphasizing the curvature of her calves. As a slave girl she had been taught to hold herself in this position when carried in that fashion. She knew substantially what she looked like. She had observed herself in the large wall mirrors of the training room when she had been new to a collar, being carried in exactly that way by instructors or guards. This posture of the body, she knew, is extremely provocative, as it is intended that it should be. She wondered what some of her arid, shrill, frustrated, sex-starved feminist colleagues would have thought of her, if they could have seen her being carried in that fashion, as a half-naked, braceleted slave girl. She did not care. They knew nothing of what it was to be a woman, and to belong to men. Let them go their own way, she thought. And let them cry out, if they would, if they could manage nothing better, in tragic, unsatisfied need, and clutch, and drench, their pillows with desperate tears, tears of helpless frustration, envying her, and wondering why they knew no men, wondering why no one would put a collar on them.

Portus Canio growled softly, held her for a moment, then laughed softly, and then placed her gently on the blankets in the wagon bed. He wants me, thought Ellen. Someone wants me! Someone thinks I am of interest! Indeed, it had been Portus Canio who had bought her off the shelf of Targo in Ar, in the Kettle Market! She stole a glance at Selius Arconious. He was dark with fury. She smiled, and turned her head aside, innocently, pretending not to notice.

"Keep watch, behind us, and to the sides," said Portus Canio.

"Yes, Master," she said.

But they saw nothing more of tarns and tarnsmen, or merchants, or aerial soldiery that day.

They continued on their way.

Perhaps the next day, or the day following, they might reach the neighborhood of the "place of concealed tarns." It was in that vicinity that Bosk of Port Kar and Marcus, of Ar's Station, were expected to leave the group, and the group itself to turn toward the Viktel Aria, and, eventually, Ar. She did not know. Such things were not discussed directly with slaves, nor did she feel it was her option to inquire. She did, of course, as she could, and as unobtrusively as possible, listen to the conversations of the masters. As is well known, there is a Gorean saying to the effect that curiosity is not becoming in a kajira. On the other hand, who has ever heard of a kajira who was not inquisitive, and quite so? After all, what do the beasts expect? We are females, and slaves.

She gathered that things might be afoot in Ar.

It was rumored that Marlenus of Ar, the Ubar of Ubars, as some thought him, had returned to Ar. Mercenary garrisons, deprived of their pay, become restless. Revolution in the city, it seemed, might be soon enkindled.

That day Bosk of Port Kar twice called halts. This was for no reason that she understood. After calling the second halt, he had stood on the wagon bed, near her. He paid her no attention, but looked about. She remained very still. He frightened her. She did not dare to meet his eyes. Was this, she wondered, because she was now no more than a meaningless, braceleted, collared, half-naked slave on Gor, or was it rather simply because she was a female? But she speculated that even if she had met him on Earth, among others, in a civilized setting, or one of those settings called "civilized," perhaps at a cocktail party, she in sophisticated garmenture, in heels, perhaps in pearls, she might have felt similarly, been similarly frightened. Would she have been able to stand poised before him? She thought not. She thought, rather, she would have looked into his eyes, even in such a room, in such a place, at such a time, and comprehended in his gaze the calm fires of command. She was sure she would have understood, even there, on some level, even in such an unlikely place and time, that she was looking into the eyes of a master, one who could detect, and knew how to deal with, the slave in her. She would have trembled, even there. Oh, she would have smiled, and chatted, for a moment, and looked away, and laughed lightly, perhaps a little hysterically, and negotiated the room, withdrawing, but knowing that his eyes were still upon her, undressing her, idly measuring her for chains.

At his bidding, after the second halt, after he had descended from the wagon bed, the trek was slowed.

She would have feared to belong to him. She sensed he had suffered many cruelties, and perhaps betrayals. She did not think she would wish to be the man, or woman, who might have dared to betray such a man.

He seemed to her taciturn, and dangerous.

Twice from her position in the wagon bed, as the wagon had rolled on, she had seen him standing to one side, his head lifted, as though testing the wind for some subtle scent.

That night they made no fires.

After she had kissed, and opened, and prepared the blankets of the men, her master's last, as was proper, she lay down beside him, her master, at his thigh. He did not bracelet her again, nor did he fix slave hobbles on her ankles. "I could run away," she thought to herself. "Does he want me to run away?" She squirmed, and turned to her back, looking up at the moons. "Or is he so arrogantly sure of me, that he knows I would not dare to run away? To be sure, there is nowhere to run. There are the dangers of the grasslands, of animals, of starvation, of thirst, the danger of another collar, the danger of recapture and punishment, punishments whose severity I dare not even contemplate." She touched her collar, and fingered the delicate scaring of her brand. "There is no escape for the Gorean slave girl," she thought, "and that is exactly what I am, and all that I am, only that, and nothing more." She turned back, gently, smiling, to his thigh, and kissed it, softly, that he not awaken. "Why do you not use me, Master?" she whispered. "Am I not pleasing? Are you truly my master? If you are my master, why do you not show me that you are my master? I am ready. Prove to me that you are my master. I beg it. Teach me, Master, that I am your slave."

"So you beg slave use, like a she-sleen in heat," he said.

"Never," she said suddenly, startled, softly, embarrassed. "Certainly not, Master!"

"You are an Earth woman?"

"Yes, Master."

"And Earth women do not beg for their use?"

"Perhaps some who are slaves do, Master," she said, "for they are helpless, and cannot help themselves."

"But you do not so beg?"

"No, Master, of course not!" she said.

"Go to sleep," he whispered.

"I did not know you were awake," she said. "Forgive me, Master," she whispered.

"Go to sleep," he said.

"Yes, Master," she said.

"And you are a little icicle from Earth?" he asked.

"Yes, Master," she said.

"You did not seem such in the camp," he said.

"The camp, Master?"

"The festival camp, outside Brundisium."

"Oh," she said.

"It might be interesting," he said, "to turn you into a squirming, begging slave."

She dared not speak. She choked back a sob of need.

Later they slept, she closely beside him, her head at his thigh.

* * * *

In the morning Ellen awakened abruptly, to the stirrings and shouts of men.

"I do not see them," she heard.

"Where are they?"

"They are not here."

"They are gone."

"Gone?"

"Yes!"

"Is their gear missing?"

"Yes!"

The cries of the men were not those of alarm. The cries, rather, were those of surprise, of bewilderment, of consternation.

"They left the camp."

"When did they leave?"

"Sometime last night."

"In what watch?"

"We do not know."

"How could they leave without detection by the watch?"

"They are Warriors," said a man.

"Like shadows, like serpents, as silent as the leech plant bending toward its prey," said another.

"Where are they?"

"Who knows?"

"Where did they go?"

"Who knows?"

"Why did they leave?" asked a man of Portus Canio.

"I do not know," said Portus Canio.

Selius Arconious was no longer at her side. She struggled to her feet, and wiped the grit of sleep from her eyes.

"Why did they leave?" pressed a man, again.

"I do not know," said Portus Canio.

She saw Selius Arconious near the wagon. Fel Doron was standing in the wagon bed, scanning the endless grass about them. The tharlarion was not in harness, but hobbled nearby, grazing.

"What did they know that we do not?" asked a man of Portus Canio.

"I do not know," said Portus Canio.

"Why did they permit us to make so little ground yesterday?" asked another man of Portus Canio.

"One does not question such men," said Portus Canio.

"Let us track them!" said a man, angrily.

"They are of the Warriors," said Portus Canio. "There will be no tracks, no trail that we could follow."

"Had we sleen!" said a man.

"Yes, of course," said Portus Canio. "—had we sleen."

"But we do not," said another man.

"Let us try to track them!" said the man.

"Feel free to do so," said Portus Canio.

"I do not think I would care to follow such men, even had we sleen," said another.

Portus Canio's original interlocutor turned white. "True," he said, in a frightened whisper.

"Why did they leave?" asked a man, anew.

Portus Canio did not respond.

"Why do you think they left?" asked the man.

"Harness the tharlarion," said Portus Canio. "We are breaking camp."

Selius Arconious returned to his bedding, and looked down, into the puzzled, frightened eyes of his slave, the Earth girl, Ellen.

"Master?" she asked.

"Bosk of Port Kar and Marcus of Ar's Station," said he, "are not now in the camp. They left under the cover of darkness, last night. They informed no one. We do not know why they left, or where they have gone. Gather up my things, and help the others. We will be leaving soon. Stay close to the wagon."

"Yes, Master," she said.

* * * *

It had not been more than an Ahn since the harnessing of the tharlarion and the breaking of the camp than Portus Canio called the halt.

Ellen, unbraceleted, barefoot, in her tunic, had been walking beside the wagon, on its left side, as one would face forward.

Portus Canio was not the only one who had caught the scent. Men glanced warily at one another.

Portus Canio climbed to the wagon box, beside Fel Doron, and stood, facing backward, shading his eyes. "Yes," he said.

Fel Doron had caught the scent first, perhaps because of his height on the wagon box. "Portus!" he had called.

Selius Arconious had lifted his head, facing backward, nostrils flared, testing the wind, a moment later.

Ellen, the wagon stopped, climbed one of the large, bronzeshod rear wheels, and, clinging to the side of the bed, her bare feet on a heavy, wooden, rounded spoke, looked backward.

It was a scent she had experienced once before, on Targo's sales shelf in the Kettle Market, though then it had been so suddenly, so unexpectedly, upon her, almost stifling, almost overwhelming, so hot, so suddenly close and terrible.

There was no mistaking it, that scent, though now it was distant, and faint, a whisper on the wind. It was the same.

"Arm yourselves," said Portus Canio.

A man removed a cylindrical bundle, tied with cord, from the wagon bed, and undid the cord, spilling bladed weapons on the grass. They were seized up. Another man removed two crossbows from beneath a canvas cover. In a moment these devices were set, the metal bands curved back, the cables tautened; quarrels were fitted to guides.

"Free the spears," said Portus Canio.

Two spears, suspended in slings at the sides of the wagon, were drawn free.

Ellen, from her place on the wheel, looked wildly at Selius Arconious, who, looking backward, was unaware of the anxiety of her regard.

He had availed himself of one of the weapons, a *gladius*, light, wicked, short-bladed, double-edged.

"They are tracking," said Portus Canio. "If they were hunting they would approach from downwind."

"Praise the Priest-Kings," said a man.

"Have they seen us yet?" asked a man.

"I would not think so," said Portus Canio. "But they will have a sense of our distance, from the freshness of the scent."

"What men are with them?" asked a man.

"It cannot be told at present," said Portus.

"Let us flee," said a man.

"If they are this close to us, it is unlikely they are afoot," said Selius Arconious. "Look about," he encouraged Portus Canio.

Portus Canio, standing on the wagon box, looked then to all sides of the wagon, to each barren, windswept horizon.

"When danger seems to threaten from one quarter," said a man, "it is well to fear all quarters, and most that from which it seems to threaten least."

"I see nothing," said Portus Canio. "Wait! I think I see men, behind us!"

"Are there standards, banners?"

"No."

"Have they seen us?"

"I cannot tell," said Portus Canio.

"Are they Cosians?"

"I do not think so," said Portus Canio.

"Cosians would be tarnborne, would be aflight, surely," said a man.

"Brigands, then," said another.

"Yes, brigands," said another.

"I think they have seen us," said Portus Canio.

"How many are there?" asked a man.

"Six men," said Portus Canio, slowly.

"There is nothing to fear then," said a man. "There are nine of us."

"They are not alone," said Portus Canio, slowly. "There is something else, something with them."

"What?" asked one of the men.

"I do not know," said Portus Canio. "I truly do not know. They are large, lumbering things, yet they move swiftly, they are ungainly and yet graceful, they are huge, and dark. By the Priest-Kings they move swiftly. There are five of them, I think. Yes, five. I do not know what they are. I have never seen anything like them! I have never seen anything move like that. I do not know if they have two feet or four feet. Truly, I do not know! It is not clear, as they move. Ho! One is stopped! It is standing, upright! Upright! It is pointing. By the Priest-Kings, it is huge. It is pointing this way! Now it is again on all fours. These things are coming this way, the men, too. The men are on tharlarion, the things with them are not. They run beside the tharlarion, easily, in their strange gait, as tireless beasts of some sort!"

Ellen trembled. She felt ill. She was miserable. She felt a coldness in the pit of her stomach. Why did she not rejoice? Was she not to be rescued from the grasp of he whom she feared and hated, her cruel master, Selius Arconious? She had little doubt then, though she could not yet see them, who followed them. As property, as slave, she knew she was subject to seizure and theft. She could be seized and carried away with no more compunction, no more consideration or thought, than would be accorded to a verr or tarsk, two other forms of domestic animal.

"Can you see the sleen?"

"Yes, there are two. They are running, now fastened on long leashes, straining forward, excited now, before two of the riders."

Ellen descended from the wheel, and sank down, on her knees, beside it. She clung to the spokes, that she might not collapse to the grass.

"Hit the sleen first," said Portus Canio to the two bowmen. "They will be the most dangerous. You two with spears defend the bowmen while they prepare their bows for a second flight."

"The sleen will not be most dangerous unless they are set upon us," said Selius Arconious.

"Let us see what they want," said a man. "They may be travelers returning from the great camp. They may wish company. They may be lost. They may want to join us, for mutual protection. If they are brigands, let them look about. Let them see that we do not have enough for them to risk war. If they wish to fight, we will fight. But I do not think that they will care to risk their lives for some biscuits, some blankets, a slave, a wagon, a tharlarion."

"They may not have the tharlarion," said a man.

"No," said another.

Ellen put her cheek against the spoke of the wagon wheel, better understanding her worth on this world. Lovely female slaves strive desperately to please, well aware of their abundance in this economy. She recalled the steam and misery, the cruel labors, of the laundry in the house of Mirus. Gor has many such employments for the inept and less than fully pleasing.

She stood up then, clinging to the bronzeshod wheel.

"Tal!" called Portus Canio, pleasantly enough, from before the bench of the wagon box, where he stood.

Ellen saw the six riders, on tharlarion, in the hands of two of which were the leashes of two gray hunting sleen, which crouched down, their rear haunches trembling, as though readying themselves for a charge. Their hunt had been successful, and they were now ready for a reward, a feeding.

"By the Priest-Kings," whispered a man, regarding the five beasts who, some yards apart, were in advance of the riders.

Ellen recognized one of the beasts, he spoken of as Kardok. She knew that it, and at least some of the others, could speak, or, at least, make sounds which might, with some transpositions, be understood as Gorean, at least by those she had taken to be their masters, or, better, by at least one of them, for only one of them, she recalled, had seemed to translate for the beasts.

"In the matter of the quarrels," said Portus Canio, softly, to the two bowmen, one on each side of the wagon, "use your discretion." He was viewing the five beasts, who doubtless appeared far more awesome to him now, at a distance of a few yards, than they had when they were a quarter of a pasang away.

Ellen saw Kardok's ears lift slightly, the great body stiffen. Though the men on tharlarion, the strangers, doubtless heard nothing, she had little doubt but what Portus Canio's soft remark, little more than a whisper, had been clearly audible to the beast. She feared, too, it might have been fully intelligible to that gross, shaggy auditor.

"Tal!" repeated Portus Canio.

He was not answered.

Mirus urged his tharlarion, a swift, bipedalian tharlarion, forward. He was then something like seven or eight yards from the wagon, some two or three yards before the line of his fellows, the beasts and the two sleen.

He looked about and, in a moment, noted Ellen, she standing beside the wagon, on its left side, facing him. She was in the brief tunic which had been permitted to her by Selius Arconious, was barefoot, and collared. The tunic was very short, and sleeveless. Such tunics are designed to well reveal the slave, and leave little to the imagination, only enough to encourage the master to tear it from her. She had little doubt that she was quite fetching in the garment. Surely Mirus seemed pleased with what he saw. Too, there was a collar on her neck. This, she knew, too, had its effect on men. Not only did it serve as an attractive adornment, rather like a necklace, contrasting with, and setting off, the slim, lovely, rounded softness of her throat, but she could not remove it. It was locked on her, publicly and obviously. It proclaimed her property, slave. Thus, on the symbolic level, where human sexuality luxuriates, thrives and flourishes, and aside from the obvious identificatory conveniences of Merchant Law, it was far more than a lovely piece of jewelry; it enhanced her beauty not only aesthetically but symbolically, overwhelmingly, devastatingly *meaningfully*. It speaks to him, who sees it on her throat, and it speaks to her, about whose throat it is snugly clasped. It tells them both that she belongs to men.

"You do not return my greeting," said Portus. "I find this unmannerly, even surly. What do you want here? We are poor men, but note that we are armed men. What do you seek?"

Mirus smiled.

"If you need food we will share some bread, your due in the hospitality of the wilderness, but you must then be on your way."

"Or," said Selius Arconious, "you could butcher and roast one of your shaggy friends."

Ellen shuddered. She had little doubt but what the dark beasts were themselves carnivorous.

"Though," said Selius Arconious, "I expect their meat would be tough."

Most of the shaggy beasts did not respond to this, but one ran its long, dark tongue about its lips. Ellen saw the canine fangs glisten in the saliva, "It can understand, too," she thought to herself.

"What do you seek?" asked Portus, again, this time not pleasantly. He was, after all, Gorean.

"Ask the slave," suggested Mirus.

Portus Canio, puzzled, looked to Ellen.

"I fear, Master," she said, "it is I whom they seek."

"Why?" asked Portus.

"Wait," said Selius Arconious, "I know you. You are the fellow who bid against me at the auction, and I was fool enough not to let you have this worthless bit of collar fluff. How rash I was! Surely you must have suspected how often I have regretted that lapse, that catastrophe of indiscretion."

"Permit me to be even more foolish," said Mirus. "I am prepared to take her off your hands now."

"But misery and woe," said Selius Arconious, "even if I were to give her to you for nothing, I would be cheating you. For she is less than worthless. I may be a poor businessman, but I am not a dishonest fellow. You may not have her."

"Oh?" said Mirus, seemingly amused.

"She is not for sale," said Selius Arconious.

"But she could, of course, be sold," said Mirus. Ellen did not doubt but what that remark was for her benefit, to remind her of what she was on this world.

To be sure she needed no reminding.

She well understood her status on this world, and had long understood it, that she was goods, a shapely commodity with which men might do as they wished.

"Of course," said Selius Arconious, "as she is a slave."

"I said nothing about buying," said Mirus.

Ellen heard the men move restlessly.

"Do not think we do not know you," said Mirus. "We recognize you as the tarnster who paid for a slave with Cosian gold, from the mint at Jad."

"I do not know from whence it came," said Selius Arconious. "That seems to me quite mysterious. I merely found it."

"Where?"

"Here and there."

"We have no Cosian gold," said Portus Canio. "If you wish to look about, do so. Otherwise, be off. Our patience grows short."

"Then they have put it somewhere," snapped one of the men behind Mirus. It was the first time he had spoken. Ellen had sensed, from some days ago, in the tent, that he stood high in the group, perhaps amongst the top two or three, at least amongst the men.

"I have little interest in the Cosian gold," said Mirus. "That is the concern of Cos. But know that the Cosians are interested in you, tarnster, and some others here, if I am not mistaken, who escaped chains in the festival camp. There is a reward out for you, tarnster, and for your fellows, if I am not mistaken. Cos would like to know your whereabouts. Tarn patrols abound. They may be signaled. Give me the slave, and we will leave."

"You have brought five men, and five beasts, and two sleen, to regain a single slave?" asked Portus Canio.

Mirus shrugged. "They wished to accompany me. I, alone, with a sleen, would have been enough."

"We are nine men," said Portus Canio, puzzled.

"I have this," said Mirus, reaching within his robes.

Ellen cried out in misery.

"Perhaps the slave can explain it to you," said Mirus.

In the hand of Mirus, brandished, glinting, there shone the grayish steel of an automatic pistol.

"Beware, Masters!" cried Ellen. "It is a weapon!"

"Surely an unlikely weapon," said Selius Arconious. "It seems blunt for a knife, and small for a club."

"Perhaps he stabs melons with it," said one of the fellows at the wagon.

"And you draw the juice out through the hole?" speculated another.

"It might do to give an urt a headache, if you hit it hard enough," suggested another. "Perhaps that is what it is for."

"No, no, please, Masters!" cried Ellen. "I know what that is! I have seen such things! I do not know a word in Gorean for it. I do not think there is such a word. But it is dangerous. It can kill, kill! Believe me! It is a bow, a bow, or like that, or like a sling. It ejects pellets, stones, small knives, or however you can understand this! Try to understand what I am saying! Please! It is dangerous! It can kill! It is like lightning! Like lightning! I know! Please believe me, Masters!"

"Shall I demonstrate?" asked Mirus.

He was greeted by silence.

"I have no wish to kill anyone," said Mirus, "but I am prepared to do so, if necessary."

At this point the five men behind him loosened their outer riding robes, brushing them back over the left shoulder. Revealed then, in their keeping, sheathed, or, better, holstered, were similar devices. They did not move to draw them. The convenience, and stolid, latent menace of the devices, however, to any who understood them, was obtrusively evident.

"You cannot stand against them, Masters!" wept Ellen. "Give me to them!"

"This is called a *gun*, or a *pistol*," said Mirus. "Now you have words for it. Now it is real to you."

"Do not hurt them, Master!" wept Ellen. "I will go with you!"

"You will not 'go with us'," said Mirus. "You will be *taken with us*, whether you wish it or not, bound across a saddle, as the property slut you are."

"That is theft," said a man.

"Yes," said Mirus.

Ellen moaned, softly, miserably.

Mirus regarded her, amused. "Are you standing in the presence of free men?" he asked.

"Forgive me, Master," sobbed Ellen, and knelt.

"Spread your knees, slave girl," said Mirus.

"Yes, Master," said Ellen. "Forgive me, Master."

"Do you want to go with them?" asked Selius Arconious.

Ellen looked up at him, tears in her eyes, her lip trembling, her body shaking. Though Mirus was now muchly Gorean, he, as she, was once of Earth, and thus there would be some commonality between them. He might understand something of her feelings, her fears. Might he not pity her, if only eventually, a former woman of his world, now a slave, helpless in her collar, as it might not occur to a Gorean to do? And did she not fear Selius Arconious whom she was sure would not be slow with the whip, should she prove in the least displeasing? And did she not hate Selius Arconious, for his coldness, his indifference and arrogance? And was not Selius Arconious a primitive barbarian, and not a cultured gentleman? And was he not a mere tarnster, whereas Mirus was apparently well placed and surely wealthy.

"Do not respond," said Selius Arconious. "The question was foolish. I regret it. You have nothing to say in this matter. Your feelings, sleek little collared animal, are of no interest or importance. They are completely irrelevant. These matters have to do with men. And they will be decided by men, not livestock." Then he turned to Mirus, who was astride the tharlarion. "Why do you want her?" he asked.

"I owned her once, and ridded myself of her," said Mirus. "It was an act of vengeance, in its way, which I need not explain to you, and an act of contempt. Too, she was not of much interest then. But she is different now. I can see that. Very different. She has learned her collar. She now knows who her masters are."

"And you want her?" said Selius Arconious.

"Yes," said Mirus.

"You may not have her," said Selius Arconious.

Ellen looked up, startled, at Selius Arconious, who paid her no attention.

"I do not think you understand," said Mirus. "I am prepared to kill for her."

"So, too, am I," said Selius Arconious, evenly.

"Master!" breathed Ellen.

"Quiet, slut," said Selius Arconious.

"Yes, Master," whispered the slave. She knew then he was her master, totally.

"Or until I tire of her," said Mirus.

"Of course," said Selius Arconious.

"It seems," said Mirus, lifting the weapon in his hand, "that a demonstration is necessary."

He leveled the weapon at the chest of Selius Arconious.

"Please, no, Master!" cried Ellen, leaping up, wildly, unbidden, and interposing her body between the muzzle of the weapon and the body of Selius Arconious.

Mirus's eyes narrowed.

"What are you doing?" asked Selius Arconious. "Who gave you permission to rise?"

Miserably, Ellen sank to her knees before him.

"Interesting," said Mirus. "That was a test." He looked about. "The tharlarion will do," he said. The muzzle of the weapon swung toward the weighty, placid beast, browsing in the traces.

"It is an innocent beast, Master," begged Ellen. "Please do not kill it, Master!"

Mirus laughed. "Look," said he. "See the back of the wagon, the corner."

He then pulled the trigger twice, and there were two shattering reports that carried over the grasslands. Wood and splinters exploded from the back of the wagon. A rear corner of the vehicle was blown away. An acrid smell of burnt powder hung in the air.

Several of the men in the party of Portus Canio cried out in alarm, and astonishment. Others stood near the wagon, shaken, bewildered. "It is lightning," said a man.

At a gesture from Mirus one of the men behind him dismounted. Mirus gestured to Ellen, motioning her forward. "Come to your ropes, slave girl," he said.

"That is a forbidden weapon," said Portus Canio.

"By whom?" asked Mirus.

"By the Priest-Kings," said Portus Canio.

"There are no Priest-Kings," said Mirus.

"Blasphemy," whispered one of the men at the wagon, frightened.

"Do you believe in Priest-Kings?" asked Mirus.

"I do not know," said Portus Canio. "I think so."

"At one time, long ago," said Mirus, "on another world, for this is not my native world, as you have probably conjectured from my speech, I thought there might be something to such suppositions, suppositions pertaining to Priest-Kings, and even repeated conjectures pertaining to such matters." Here Mirus regarded Ellen, and she looked away, frightened. She did not wish to be beaten for looking too boldly into the eyes of a master. She recalled that he had, in the house on Earth, recounted certain views pertaining to unusual alien beings, perhaps what were now being spoken of as "Priest-Kings." Had there ever been such, truly? If so, were there still such? And if there were such, had they any interest or concern with human beings? And the facts of the world, as any set of facts, she knew, might be susceptible to a variety of plausible explanations. Indeed, the hypothesis of Priest-Kings did not seem necessary. Perhaps other aliens had brought some humans to this world, and then departed. Perhaps an ancient technological civilization on Earth had colonized this world, before slipping unnoticed, with its devices, perhaps intentionally, from the pages of history. Perhaps it had succumbed to geological upheavals, or other natural catastrophes, perhaps meteoritic bludgeonings from space, eradicating entire species, or from sun flares which might scald a world, or from an uprooting which might produce a moon and leave behind a vast basin to be filled with water and brine. Perhaps there had been a preemptive strike by cautious aliens, unwilling that the cosmos should entertain a nascent competitor. Perhaps it had perished of some hastening, virulent disease specific to a species, which then, its hosts vanished, must itself perish. Or perhaps it had simply been overrun, as so many civilizations, by barbarous primitives. Many things might have occurred. She scarcely remembered his remarks, so confused and frightened she had been. She did remember, clearly, that she had been ankleted, literally ankleted. In her training, of course, she had heard some of the instructrices speak of Priest-Kings but she herself had been taught no prayers or ceremonies pertaining to them. She had once inquired about them, but she had been informed that such matters were not the concern of animals, and she, of course, as a slave, was an animal. And a stroke of the switch had then encouraged her to return her attention to her lessons, in how to please men. It had seemed to her that allusions to such beings, and what they did, and so on, were mythical, the sort of thing which might be expected in primitive cultures, utilized to explain natural phenomena, such as the winds, the rains, the seasons, the tides, and such. And the existence of Gor she took as a natural given, however it might be explained. Slaves, incidentally, as other animals, verr, tarsks, and such, are not permitted within the precincts of the temples, lest the temples be profaned.

"But here, on this world, I have come to realize the baselessness and fatuity of such speculations," said Mirus. "We have no evidence whatsoever of the existence of Priest-Kings, nor have we encountered any who have such evidence. It is clear, now, that the myths and legends of Priest-Kings have been invented by the caste of Initiates, in order to exploit superstitious terror and live as parasites on the earnings of others."

"Few would deny that the caste of Initiates are parasites," said Portus Canio, who held no great brief for that caste. Supposedly the caste of Initiates praised Priest-Kings, offered regular and special sacrifices, interceded with them on behalf of men, interpreted their will to men, and such. Famines, plagues, floods, storms, meteors, comets, eclipses, earthquakes, lightning, and such would all receive their interpretations, and would be dealt with by means of prayers, spells, mystic signs, the brandishing of fetish objects, the ringing of anointed, consecrated bars, and such. Ritual performances, ceremonies, and such, abounded. Most cities had their temples. High Initiates might receive gold from Ubars, low Initiates copper from the poor.

"It is obvious," said Mirus, "that this world exists, for we are upon it. But what is not obvious is an explanation for its nature and location. To be sure, similar puzzles might exist with respect to any planet, or world."

"The Priest-Kings," suggested Portus Canio.

"Such puzzles," said Mirus, "are not well resolved by recourse to childish legends."

Portus Canio was silent.

"One of the interesting things about this world," said Mirus, "though you would have no reason to be aware of it, is that it seems to be characterized by certain gravitational anomalies. These are presumably connected with the core of this world, or with its relation to Tor-tu-Gor. These anomalies, however, though mysterious in their way, are doubtless of a natural origin."

"I do not understand," said Portus Canio.

"I am willing to suppose that something, call it Priest-Kings, if you wish, might once have existed, long ago, but, if so, they are gone by now, and are at best a vanished race, an extinct species somehow recalled obscurely in legends, myths and lore."

"And so there are no Priest-Kings?" said Portus Canio.

"Blasphemy," again whispered one of the men at the wagon, he who had spoken earlier.

"Precisely," said Mirus. "There are no Priest-Kings."

"You have loosed lightning," said Portus Canio. "Have you released such lightning before?"

"Several times," said Mirus, "here and there, and in hunting."

"Then," said Portus Canio, "the Priest-Kings will know of it."

"This is the world of the Priest-Kings," said a man. "They have forbidden men such things."

"There are no Priest-Kings," said Mirus. "If there were Priest-Kings they would have acted, to enforce their so-called laws. But there are no Priest-Kings, as we see, and the laws have a simple explanation, namely, an attempt to preclude an ever-increasing efficiency of engineered carnage."

"Which by comparison makes the weapons we carry all the more formidable in their power," said one of the men behind Mirus.

"Yes," grinned another.

Yes, Ellen thought, it makes sense, the nonexistence of Priest-Kings. If there were once such things, they are now no more. If there were such, their presence would surely have been manifested by now.

Thus they do not exist.

"Perhaps there are no Priest-Kings," said one of the men at the wagon.

"Do not speak so," whispered another, frightened.

Mirus then returned his gaze to Ellen, who knelt facing him, Selius Arconious standing behind her.

"Will it be necessary to repeat a command, slave girl?" asked Mirus.

Numbly, in misery, Ellen rose to her feet and moved slowly toward the strangers.

"No!" cried Selius Arconious, and lunged forward, but he was seized by two of his fellows, who restrained him, as he struggled.

"I am taking this one," said Mirus. "You can buy another, and doubtless a better."

The man who had dismounted approached Ellen. He carried several coils of light rope, sufficient for binding a woman.

Ellen momentarily regarded the light constraints with chagrin, and dismay. Such things can hold me, and perfectly, she thought. With them I can be bound helplessly, hand and foot. Even laces and cords could bind me, as well. I am slight, soft, and weak. I could break them no more than the chains men are so fond of putting on me! Do not such things show me that I am a female? Do they not show me the nature of men and women, and who it is who is at the mercy of whom, and who are the masters, and who the slaves! Sometimes Ellen loved to be bound, for this so assured her of her nature, and her subjection to the domination which so excited her, which she found so delicious. It thrilled her to be so at the mercy of a man, his to be done with as he might please. In her training she had often been bound, usually with colorful, soft cords. How pretty she had seen herself to be in the mirrors in the house of Mirus, struggling, under an instructor's command, to free herself, struggling futilely. Then she had at last lain before him, at his feet, quiescent, subdued, helpless. Sometimes he had roared then with frustration, and left her on the polished boards of the training room, until, say, an Ahn or so later, calmer, perhaps having in the meantime utilized a house slave, he had returned to free her, and send her to her next class, perhaps one of cooking or sewing, or one of bathing a male. But now she was to be stolen, taken from her master. The ropes now were not those of Selius Arconious, her master, in which she might have been left alone, to simmer in his absence, well aware of her bound limbs, or squirmed in anticipation, delighting in her helplessness, and readying herself for his caresses, against which she would be helpless to defend herself. These were the ropes of a stranger.

Should you not be pleased, she asked herself, to be taken from the presence of so hateful, vile, and arrogant a monster as Selius Arconious!

Surely, yes, she told herself.

But her eyes filled with tears.

At a gesture from Portus Canio Selius Arconious stopped struggling, but he stood, trembling, dark with rage, between the two who had briefly held him.

"Wait," cautioned Portus Canio.

"Leave them to the Priest-Kings," said one of the men.

"The Priest-Kings do not concern themselves with the affairs of men," said Selius Arconious, bitterly.

"They concern themselves with the keeping of their laws," said a man.

"Beware the Priest-Kings," said one of the men.

Mirus, and several of those with him, smiled.

"Have you ever seen a Priest-King?" asked one of the strangers, of the fellow who had spoken.

"No," said the man.

"Have you ever seen any evidence of the enforcement of their laws?" asked another of the strangers.

"I have heard of such things," averred the man.

"But have you ever seen any evidence of such a thing?" he was asked.

"No," said the man.

"It does not exist," he was told.

Ellen stood at the right-hand stirrup of the saddle of Mirus. It was to that position that he had gestured her, casually, with the muzzle of the gun. She knew what it could do. Perhaps now, too, to some extent, did those with Portus Canio, with Fel Doron and the wagon. She stood there, now no more than a slim, graceful Gorean kajira. She could smell the leather of the saddle in the clear air. She could see his heeled boot in the stirrup. She looked back, to see Selius Arconious and the others. "Put your wrists behind you, crossed," said the fellow who had dismounted, who carried the rope. She felt her wrists being fastened behind her.

"No," said Mirus. "Tie her wrists before her body, and then put her to the grass and tie her ankles together. I wish to fasten her hands to the thongs on the left saddle ring and her ankles to the thongs on the right saddle ring, that she may thus lie bound, hand and foot, belly up, before me."

The knots were jerked tight on Ellen's wrists.

The belly-up binding position is often used on long rides, or tarn flights, as it is reliably secure and the captive, or slave, is constantly under surveillance, conveniently at hand, completely in view. It is also useful as the captor, or master, may then caress the captive or slave, if only to while away the time. By the time that camp is made a free woman is commonly begging for the brand and collar, and a slave will be beside herself, writhing and gasping, moaning, crying out, begging, with need, pleading that he will be merciful, that he will deign, if only briefly, to attend to the collar of her.

"Did you hear me?" inquired Mirus.

The rope was then lifted and a length of it looped twice about the slave's neck and knotted there. In this fashion a single rope may be used for both binding and leashing. This is not all that unusual on Gor. One end secures the slave's wrists, the center collars her, and the remainder, the free end, serves as a leash or tether. It may also be used, of course, if one wishes to immobilize her, to fasten her ankles together. Her ankles may be simply bound or, if one wishes, tied closely to her wrists. That tie is sometimes spoken of, properly or not, as the "slave bow." It may be called that simply because the slave's wrists and ankles are bound together, and this bends her body, in a natural bow, or it may be called that because of a supposed analogy with exhibitory slave bows, in which, for example, on a slave block, a slave might be bent backward, or knelt, and her head drawn by the hair back to the floor, and so on. These exhibition bows are often utilized in showing the slave, as they accentuate the delights of her figure. There are a number of "tethering slave bows," of course, for example, for fastening a slave over a saddle, a wheel, a piece of furniture, or such. These diverse uses and meanings, of course, are not mutually exclusive, because a slave might well be displayed in a "tethering slave bow." Some conjecture that the original meaning of 'slave bow' has to do with exhibition. Accordingly, it is their speculation that the "tethering slave bows" are derivative from that primary usage, that of exhibition. This would make sense because the "tethering slave bows" certainly do exhibit the slave, as well as rendering her helpless. Others seem to feel that the basic meaning is that of a form of secure and revelatory binding, in which the slave is helplessly and delightfully displayed, and that the exhibitory usages of the expression are secondary, being founded upon, and derivative from, this more basic, original usage. On the other hand, as most suppose, and as seems most plausible to the slave, these usages may very well have been developed independently, both based on the obvious consequences on the slave's body of a certain form of handling or manner of binding. There seems to be some division among Goreans on this matter. And doubtless it is not of great importance. Please forgive this excursion into speculative etymology. Ellen finds such matters fascinating, perhaps in part because she has been so handled and so roped. What is perfectly clear and indisputable is that in Gorean 'slave bow', putting aside considerations of origin, derivation and chronology, and such, has the basic meaning of the forming of the slave's body into a bow, and two application meanings, one pertaining to a modality of exhibition and the other to a modality of binding. Abstract obscurity, as usual, vanishes in concrete context. As this phenomenon is common in many languages, it is not surprising that it should appear in Gorean, as well. A stripped free woman might, of course, be put in a "slave bow," without compromising the meaning of the expression. And the free woman might find this situation instructive, and anticipatory.

"We have found her," said the man who held Ellen's improvised leash. He mounted into the saddle of his beast, and looped the free end of the leash loosely about the pommel of the saddle.

"Take her a bit away, away from the wagon, over the hillock," said one of the men.

"Why?" asked Mirus.

"Before it is done," said the man.

"What are you talking about?" said Mirus.

"You let her go once," said another of the riders. "We will not make that mistake again."

"I want her," said Mirus.

"We will buy you another," said one of the men.

One of the shaggy beasts growled.

"Soon, soon," said one of the men, soothingly, he whose office it seemed to be to interpret the noises of the beasts.

"Run her for the sleen," suggested one of the men.

"That would be amusing," said another.

"No," said the fellow who seemed to translate for the shambling monsters amongst them. "Kardok is hungry."

"The sleen may feed secondly," said a fellow, "should there be anything left."

"Why?" demanded Mirus.

"She has seen too much, she has heard too much," said one of the men.

"She has understood nothing," said Mirus.

"It will be hard to control the sleen," said the fellow who had suggested running the slave. "They have hunted. They have tracked for days. Now they are successful. They will expect their reward."

Even as he spoke the two hunting sleen inched forward, tails lashing, haunches trembling.

"Such beasts are not patient," said the man, apprehensively. "They are dangerous."

Ellen drew back, against the rope, her legs almost giving way beneath her, almost fainting.

"Have you meat with you?" cried Mirus to Portus Canio.

"No," said Portus Canio.

"The tharlarion!" said Mirus.

"Neither sleen nor our friends care muchly for tharlarion," said one of the men.

"There is better feed about," laughed another.

"No!" said Mirus.

"It is not a question of meat," snarled one of his companions.

The beast called Kardok, the largest of the five monstrous creatures, looked toward the wagon and Portus Canio, and the others. There were sounds from it, guttural emanations, yet somehow half articulate, suggesting Gorean, or surrogates for its phonemes.

The fellow who translated laughed. "Kardok observes," said he, "that there is much meat here."

"They are armed," said another.

"Put down the bows, sheath your weapons," said one of Mirus's companions, one mounted to his left, regarding the men of Portus Canio. "And you will not be hurt."

"Leave the slave, and be on your way," said Portus Canio.

"We are all armed, and can dart lightning upon you," said he who had spoken.

"Who will be first to reach for the lightning knife?" asked Portus Canio.

Two crossbows were set, fingers upon the triggers.

The companions of Mirus looked at one another. Only Mirus held his weapon, and he then, with obvious show, thrust it in his belt.

Kardok's eyes blazed as he looked from the face of one of Portus Canio's men to that of another. His gaze lingered last, and longest, on that of Selius Arconious. Then, without removing his gaze from that of Selius Arconious, whom he seemed to somehow sense might be the most dangerous, or the most desperate, or the most irrational, or the first to act, he uttered a succession of soft, low, almost gentle, growling noises.

"Forgive us, dear travelers," said the translator, regarding the men at the wagon. "We will give you the slave." He made a gesture and the fellow who had Ellen's neck rope, the improvised leash, looped about the pommel of the saddle loosened it, and tossed it, grinning, to the grass near her ankles. She sank to her knees, trembling. "We shall be on our way. We leave you in peace. Have a good journey. We wish you well."

"What of your sleen?" inquired Portus Canio.

"We will shortly set them to hunt in the grasslands," said the man. "There is no danger. They will forage well enough for themselves."

"I think they are domesticated sleen, trained hunting sleen," said Portus Canio.

"We wish you well," said the man.

Ellen looked wildly at Selius Arconious.

Selius Arconious suddenly, wildly, pointed to the sky, far, high, away, behind the riders. "Tarnsmen!" he cried. "Tarnsmen!"

What happened then was scarcely clear to Ellen. The men, those mounted or not, those with Mirus, and those near the wagon, naturally, without much thinking of it, followed Arconious's gesture, turning, raising their eyes.

"Where?" shouted one of the riders.

But Arconious in that moment, unnoted, the others distracted, had hurled himself forward, through the midst of the riders, and laid powerful, rough hands on he who was the translator for the beast, doubtless in the belief that he was first amongst the riders. And in that sudden, confused moment the startled, angry rider had been dragged from the saddle, struck half senseless, and dragged backward, stumbling, groggy, his body shielding that of Arconious, toward the wagon. By the time the riders in that chaotic moment were apprised of the cry of their fellow, and turned from their brief, agitated, intent scanning of the empty sky, Arconious was four or five feet from them, backing away, moving toward the wagon. He stopped there, some feet before the wagon, the blade of his dagger at the throat of the dazed, disconcerted fellow he held. The man's hand moved toward his holstered weapon, but then he lifted it, and held it away from the holster, as the edge of the blade tightened at his throat.

Hands of the riders moved toward their weapons, but they did not draw them. The two crossbowmen at the wagon, their bodies muchly behind the wagon, shielded there, the quarrels at the ready, tensed. Each had his target.

"If you would have your captain live," cried Arconious, "throw down your weapons, and be on your way!"

"Throw down your weapons!" cried he who was held by Arconious. "Cast them down!"

"But we are prepared to leave in peace," said one of the riders, inching his mount forward.

"Cast down your weapons!" said Arconious.

"Cast down your weapons!" cried he whom Arconious held.

The rider who had come forward a little smiled.

"Please!" cried the fellow.

In that moment Ellen's heart sank, for she understood that he who had spoken for the monsters was not first amongst the riders, nor, earlier, it had been clear, was Mirus.

"We wish only to leave in peace," said the rider.

It was he then, she supposed, who was first amongst the visitors. He was the one who had been rather to the side and behind Mirus. He was the one who had asserted that Portus Canio's group had put the purloined gold somewhere.

The two sleen began to growl menacingly. One began to scratch at the turf. The other crouched even lower. It was, Ellen surmised, the more dangerous of the two.

"Let us give up the weapons," said Mirus.

"You are mad," said one of the riders.

"We would then be less than they," said another.

"Forget the slut," said another. "You can obtain another, a better."

"Put down your weapons!" whispered he whom Arconious held. He did not wish even to speak aloud, lest he inadvertently cut his own throat, so close against his throat was set the narrow edge of Arconious's blade.

"Let us discard our weapons," said Mirus. "He is essential to our work. No other can communicate with the beasts."

"Yes, yes, only I can speak with the beasts!" whispered he whom Arconious held.

At this point, from the largest of the beasts, he spoken of as Kardok, there emanated a low rumble of sound. Too, the lips of the monster drew back, revealing moist fangs.

The translator, Arconious' knife at his throat, turned white.

He whom Ellen now took to be first amongst the visitors urged his tharlarion forward a few feet. He was then somewhat in advance of his fellows, and a few feet from the translator and Selius Arconious.

"Translate," he said.

"No, no!" said the man.

"It seems," said the darkly clad, mounted fellow, quietly, he now in advance of his fellows, he whom Ellen took to be first amongst the visitors, "a translation is not necessary."

"No, no!" said the translator.

"Throw down your weapons!" demanded Arconious.

"Of course," said the first rider. "Tell your men not to fire," he said to Portus Canio.

"Be ready," said Portus Canio.

Very slowly the first rider drew an automatic pistol from its holster. He smiled.

"No!" cried the fellow held by Arconious.

The report was very loud, at so close a range. Ellen screamed. The men about the wagon seemed stunned, paralyzed with shock.

Selius Arconious released the body and it fell from him, to the grass. Bewildered, Arconious regarded he who had fired the shot. Arconious, stunned, lowered his knife.

"The sleen are restless," said one of the riders, in the background.

"Step away from the body," said the first rider.

Selius Arconious stepped back.

At a sign from the first rider, a fellow in the back suddenly cried out to the sleen, "Now!"

Ellen screamed as the two gray bodies scrambled past her. There was oil from the pelt of one on her bound arm, as she twisted away. They might have trailed her, presumably from a scent lingering in her cage, from before her sale. But she had not been and, it seemed, was not now designated their reward. The rope on her neck whipped behind her, sped by a rushing rear paw.

Then the sleen were at the body, tearing and scratching through the leather, through the clothing. Ellen thought for an instant that the eyes of he whom Selius Arconious had briefly held had opened for an agonized instant, the body understanding that it was being eaten, but this was doubtless merely a consequence of its subjection to the frenzied molestation. The bullet, she was sure, had been well placed, casually, and at short range. The body was probably dead before it reached the grass, fallen before the sandals of the stunned, disbelieving Selius Arconious, he shaken from the noise and the horror, his knife held lamely in his hand.

"How will we now communicate with the beasts?" asked Mirus.

Kardok stood up, his height expanding upward, almost as though he were slowly, somehow unnaturally enlarging, to something like nine feet. He looked about. His head was enormous. The eyes were huge, rounded. His massive body was perhaps a yard in width, viewed frontally. It could not have been encircled by the arms of large man. "He was not necessary," it said.

All regarded the beast, all in awe, save he who was the first rider, he closest to the wagon, whose weapon was still in his grasp.

A pungency of expended powder laced the air.

The sounds had now been unmistakable Gorean, cavernously, vitally, exotically, distantly, strangely formed, but Gorean. It was as though a gigantic, dark, misshapen, deformed, threatening bearlike beast, like a massive, awakening living boulder of flesh and cruelty, had spoken. The sounds, despite their frightening, astonishing nature, and their remarkable source, could be clearly understood. The sounds were quite unlike the sounds which it had earlier uttered.

"It can speak!" said one of Portus's men.

"So, too, can you," said Kardok. "Should I find that strange?"

The sleen continued to feed.

"We do not teach our humans to speak," it said.

"Call away your beast," said Portus, half sick.

The first rider smiled.

"Who is first amongst you?" demanded Portus Canio.

"I am," said Kardok.

"You have two crossbows," said the assailant, the first rider. "There are five of us, and we can kill from a distance. We do not surrender our weapons."

"Nor we ours," said Portus Canio. "Some of us can reach you, surely, for we are nine, and you are now but five."

"I think, then, we have a truce," said the first rider. "We shall now, peacefully, take our leave."

"Do not move," said Portus Canio.

"They will move away, and then slay you with impunity, Masters!" cried Ellen.

"Be silent, slave," snarled Selius Arconious.

"That is obviously their plan," said Portus Canio.

The first rider tensed. The hands of the other riders moved closer to their weapons.

"There are five of us," said the first rider, "and two sleen."

"On whom would you be able to set them, and how?" inquired Portus Canio. "Too, I do not think I would care, personally, to interrupt a sleen in its feeding."

"Actually," said the first rider, "there are ten of us."

"The beasts are not armed," said Portus Canio.

"So, five," shrugged the first rider.

"Why are the beasts not armed?" asked Portus Canio.

Something seemed to move behind the eyes of the first rider. It was brief, and subtle, scarcely tangible, rather like a movement in the air, hardly noticed. "I do not know," he said. "But they are formidable, I assure you."

"So then there are ten of you, and only nine of us," said Portus Canio.

"It seems so," granted the rider.

"How many are you prepared to lose?" asked Portus Canio.

"I would prefer to lose none," he said.

"Then discard your weapons," said Portus Canio.

"It seems our kaissa has come to a locked position," said the rider.

"There are no locked positions here," said Portus Canio. "This is not kaissa." His hand was tensed on the hilt of his blade.

"Ah," said the first rider, as though resigned. "Then who will move first?"

Ellen, the rude leash dangling from her neck, and then over her left shoulder, behind her, her hands roped tightly behind her, knelt in terror on the grass. She was afraid to move. She feared that the smallest movement, the tiniest sound, the most diminutive influence, might prove critical, like the smallest jarring, or jostling, like a small thing which might tip a balance, a carelessly dislodged pebble that releases an avalanche, the particle of static electricity which triggers the bolt of lighting, the tiny movement, even a hesitant, uncertain, false step, which causes a gingerly held device, reposing in its container, to awaken, exploding, crying out, showering bricks, gouging asphalt, striking away roofs and walls for a hundred yards about.

There was the sound of the feeding of the sleen.

The sky was a bright blue. A gentle wind stirred stalks of grass.

"Tarnsmen!" said Selius Arconious. "Tarnsmen!"

Men tensed, the hands of riders almost darted to their weapons.

"Do you think we are fools?" asked the first rider.

The other riders laughed, but did not take their eyes from the men of Portus Canio.

"You do us little honor, tarnster," said the first rider.

"Tarnsmen," repeated Selius Arconious.

Portus Canio lifted his gaze a fraction.

Ellen gasped.

"Your trick is older than the Sardar itself," said the first rider.

"Tarnsmen," said Portus Canio.

"Desist," snarled the first rider. His hand tightened on the weapon he had rested on the saddle.

But at that moment there was indeed a beating of wings in the sky, a whirl of wind, a blasting of grasses, the screams of mighty forms overhead, wild gigantic darting shadows darkening the grass, the shouts of men, the piercing sounds of tarn whistles.

"Aii!" cried the first rider, wheeling in the saddle.

"Take cover!" shouted Portus Canio.

Selius Arconious flung himself toward Ellen, dragged her to the earth and covered her body for an instant with his own, crouching over it, looking up, wildly. Arrows struck into the turf. Ellen saw an arrow hit the turf not a yard away. It was so suddenly there, not there, then there, almost upright, quivering, a third of its length in the dirt. In an odd almost still instant she saw the breeze ruffle its fletching, and then cried out as Selius Arconious dragged her to her feet by a bound arm and, looking upward, rushed her stumbling to the wagon, and hurled her savagely, she rolling, beneath it. Then he was gone.

Her shoulder hurt.

The sleen lifted their heads from their feeding, looked upward, and then, their snouts bloody, thrust their jaws again into the mass of blood, cloth and meat under their paws, between the riders and the back of the wagon.

Ellen heard the sound of gunfire.

One of Portus's men who had held the two crossbows wheeled away from the back of the wagon, stumbling, the weapon discharged, fallen to the grass. An arrow transfixed his throat. His hands were on the shaft, and he broke it, it snapping with a sharp sound, but then, his eyes glazed, blood running from his mouth, and from about the splintered shaft lodged in his throat, he sank to the grass.

The tharlarion swung its head about, bellowing. Its heavy tail lashed, pounding the earth. It twisted in the traces. The wagon rocked, half off the ground, tipped, and then righted itself. Ellen heard an arrow strike into the wagon bed above her. An angry metal point seemed suddenly to have grown from the splintered wood above her.

Two of Portus's men, weapons in their hands, now crouched under the wagon with her, taking cover from the fire from above. Two others were crouched behind the tharlarion. There were cries of rage from the mounted men about. Their mounts wheeled about, squealing. Men struggled to control them. Two men had dismounted and were looking upward. The beasts howled. One tore at the grass. Another, in frustration, sprang upward, again and again, reaching upward, as if it might clutch and tear the clouds themselves. The sleen fed, now more placidly. There was more gunfire. And then it was suddenly quiet.

Ellen crawled on her knees from under the wagon.

A great bird, a tarn, lay thrashing in the grass fifty yards away, amidst the debris of a tarn basket.

Cosian men at arms, some armed with short bows, such as may be used with convenience from tarn baskets, which may clear the bulwarks and fire amongst the ropes, saddle bows, actually, such as are favored for similar reasons by tarnsmen, were drawing away, afoot. One or two bodies lay near the thrashing tarn. In the distance, but turning now, obviously withdrawing, but not abandoning the field, were four more tarns, each with a tarn basket slung beneath it.

She heard Portus Canio say, "They will come again."

She then saw, with a gasp of relief, Selius Arconious. In his hand, but empty now, was the second crossbow. He who had held it earlier was to one side. In his inert body there were four arrows. Ellen supposed that the crossbowmen would be the prime targets of the aerial archers, as they would suppose, at least initially, that only those would be able to respond to their attack. That the tarns had withdrawn as they had, so quickly, suggested that the attackers had not anticipated the resistance they had encountered. Doubtless they were startled, and perhaps dismayed, and disconcerted, perhaps even frightened, by the noise of the gunfire, and the damage it might have wreaked amongst them. They would not have expected this. Probably nothing in their experiences would have prepared them for this. Surely they would fear, at least, that these noises, these harms, were the effects of what they had only heard of in stories, the effects of instruments they might have hitherto supposed merely fanciful, the effects of forbidden weapons.

The tarns were now alighting, several hundred yards away.

"They will come again, some on foot," said Portus Canio. Then he regarded Selius Arconious. "You shot well," he said.

Selius Arconious shrugged. "I fear not well enough."

"Two will no longer draw the bow," said Portus Canio.

"I saw Tersius Major in one of the baskets," said Fel Doron.

"I, too," said Portus Canio.

"He was not hit," said Fel Doron.

"No," said Portus Canio.

"As I said," said Selius Arconious, "I did not shoot well enough."

"How many quarrels are there left?" asked Portus Canio.

"I have two, Loquatus has another," said Arconious.

"Then we are finished," said Portus Canio.

"The tharlarion is hit," said a man.

"I do not think badly," said another. "The arrow struck away, not lodging in the flesh."

"There is a wound. It is bleeding," said a man.

"Attend to it," said Portus Canio.

The tharlarion was browsing, calmly, in its traces.

The sleen were lying near the body of the translator, their jaws bloody, dried blood even on the fur of their throats. One had its paw on the body. They were now somnolent, their eyes half shut.

Ellen struggled to her feet, beside the wagon.

Those who had been with Mirus had drawn to one side. Two of the beasts were dead. Kardok, standing near them, lifted his head, and turned his eyes toward the wagon, toward Portus's group.

"Load the bow," said Portus Canio.

Two of the men who had been with Mirus lay on the grass. One was apparently dead, the other wounded. There had been six humans in the party of Mirus, including himself. Their forces, with the slaying of the translator, whose weapon had apparently been retrieved in the fray by one of those with Mirus, now numbered four, one of whom was wounded. He who had substantially been their spokesman, whom Ellen took to be the leader, who had shot the translator, was unhurt, as was Mirus. Only one of their mounts was both at hand and unhurt. Some may have thrown their riders and fled into the grassland. Two had been killed with arrows. As with the crossbowmen the mounts had been prime targets, as their availability might have facilitated the escape of scattering, fleeing foes. I have heard that there is a saying amongst one of the many Gorean peoples, in this case the "Red Savages of the Barrens," as they are spoken of, to the effect that an enemy afoot is an enemy dead. I know little of the Barrens. They are supposedly an area of vast prairies somewhere far away, far to the east. Of Portus's men, who had numbered nine, there were five left.

Staggering across the grass towards Portus's group was he whom Ellen took to be the leader of the visitors, or, at least, of the humans, he who had spoken for them, he who had killed the translator. She does not know his name. She has spoken of him hitherto by such expressions as "the first rider," in virtue of his having brought his tharlarion forward, in advance of his fellows. Hereafter, he no longer being mounted, she will refer to him as the "spokesman." She hopes that this mode of reference will not be found confusing. For better or for worse, it seems to her appropriate. In any event, in putative justification of this decision, if such is required, it seems that he spoke for, and was first amongst, the humans in Mirus's group, which group might also, she supposes, incidentally, be thought of as Kardok's retinue. She has no doubt, as of now, that the true leader of the group was the great beast, Kardok. This had not been clearly understood, she is sure, by all members of the group until after the encounter in the grasslands. For example, it seems clear that this had not been clearly understood by Mirus, who seemed to have taken it for granted, and naturally, however unwisely, that the leadership of the group was in the grip of one of his own kind, a human, presumably he whom we now choose to refer to as the "spokesman." The beasts, Ellen supposes, permitted, and doubtless even encouraged, this misapprehension, perhaps as a concession to human vanity, one acceptable in virtue of its utility in furthering their projects. Portus calmly watched him approach. The spokesman, half dazed, lifted his weapon and trained it on Portus's chest.

"There were probably five or six men in each basket," said Portus quietly, gazing into the barrel of the weapon, whose capacities he now well understood. "You killed one tarn and disabled one basket. Most of the soldiers escaped from the basket when the tarn fell. You, and we, may have killed four or five others. Selius Arconious struck at least two. I conjecture then that there are some twenty-five or so left. They will come again. Some will strike from the air. Some will be put afoot. We will be encircled. It is a matter of time. We could scatter into the grasslands. One or two might escape. I do not know. But there is little place to hide, and much can be seen from the air. Each one of us you kill reduces your own probabilities of survival. I think we have a truce now, if we are rational."

The spokesman lowered his weapon, and looked outward, across the grass, some two to three hundred yards away, to where the tarns had alighted.

"Why did they attack *us*?" asked the spokesman.

"You were with us," said Portus Canio. "Perhaps they thought this a rendezvous of sorts."

"Why did they seek you?" asked the spokesman.

Portus shrugged. "Who knows the aberrations of Cosians?"

Mirus led his mount forward, the only one left to their group. His weapon was thrust in his belt. "They sought him," said he, nodding toward Selius Arconious. "He bought a slave with Cosian gold, that slave," he then indicating Ellen who, finding herself under the eyes of a free man, immediately knelt, not wishing to be punished, "gold seemingly of the trove which was diverted from the paymasters of the mercenaries in Ar."

"Ar then will be restless indeed," said the spokesman. "And where is this gold?" he asked Selius Arconious.

"I have forgotten," said Selius.

"Perhaps you might be helped to remember," said the spokesman.

"It is gone, sped," said Portus Canio. "None of us now know where it is."

"Oh?" said the spokesman.

"Two were with our party," said Portus Canio. "They knew. Indeed they, and others, were involved in its seizure and concealment. They are now gone. It was our plan that they should leave our march at a certain point, and then go on alone—"

"Alone?" smiled Mirus.

"Yes," said Portus Canio. "—to keep an arranged rendezvous, and there inform designated others, with a miscellany of wagons and carts, as to the location of the gold in its secret cache, others who will then retrieve the gold and see to its proper distributions and disbursements."

"I see," said Mirus.

"Then they, the two who were with our party, will proceed toward Ar."

"And then you might never see them again?"

"Perhaps not," said Portus Canio. "One does not know."

"And did your plan unfold as you had anticipated?"

"Not entirely," said Portus Canio. "The two of whom I speak left the march early, and secretly."

"And they knew the location of the gold?" laughed Mirus.

"Yes," said Portus Canio.

"The gold is lost," said Mirus.

"No," said Portus Canio.

"You are a trusting fellow," said the spokesman.

"There is such a thing as honor," said Portus Canio.

Mirus looked at him, sharply.

"Even if they should make away with it, or the others to whom they impart information," said Portus Canio, "it does not much matter, really. The important thing is that it does not reach the mercenary forces in Ar."

"You are a patriot," said the spokesman, cynically.

"I have a Home Stone," said Portus Canio. "Do you?"

"No," said Mirus, though the question had not been addressed to him.

"It is interesting," said the spokesman, "that out of the hundreds of wagons leaving the festival camp at Brundisium, and days later, in the vastness of these grasslands, the Cosians managed to locate you."

"Doubtless they scout in patterns," said Portus Canio. "And much can be seen from the air."

"It is possible," said Mirus, "they were following us."

"To find the slave through us, and the tarnster through the slave?" asked the spokesman.

"Yes," said Mirus.

"You should have throttled the slut in the camp," said the spokesman.

"Even had I desired to do so," said Mirus, "I could not have done so, as I was outbid."

"You had your chance at the camp, at the tent," snarled the spokesman. "We left her to you, you let her go."

"I did arrange that she would dance publicly, forced to display herself as the mere property-slut she is."

"And what was the point of that?"

"I think you would not understand," said Mirus.

Ellen put down her head. She recalled Earth, of so many years ago, and the earlier, radical, pronounced discrepancy in their stations. Then he had had her rejuvenated, become no more than a girl, and had had her danced as a slave. How sweet, she thought, was his revenge. And now, again, there was a radical discrepancy in their stations, but one now a thousand times more radical than that which had characterized their relationship on Earth. He was a free man; she was *kajira*, a slave girl.

"She danced well," said the spokesman.

"You saw?"

"Of course. You do not think we would let her get away from us, do you?"

Ellen, kneeling, her hands tied behind her, the rope on her neck, trembled.

"Yes," granted Mirus, "I was surprised. I did not expect her to be so good."

"Is she a bred slave?"

"Only in a general sense," said Mirus.

"She is from Earth, is she not?"

"Yes."

"A good place to find female slaves."

"Yes."

"What did you pay for her there?"

"She was free there," said Mirus.

"Free?"

"Legally free," said Mirus.

"What a tragic waste of female."

"I had her bought to Gor for my amusement."

"A free woman?"

"The best thing about free women is that they may be made slaves," said Mirus.

"Yes," said the spokesman.

"I had known her long ago, and had seen the slave of her."

"I think that would have required no great feat of perception," smiled the spokesman.

Ellen jerked at the bonds on her wrists, and then subsided.

She had been bound by a Gorean male.

"True," said Mirus. "Sometimes such things are obvious."

"It would have required no great feat of perception, I should have said," said the spokesman, *"—for a slaver."*

Mirus nodded, acknowledging the compliment.

Ellen had heard that a good slaver could discern the needful, waiting slave even in cases in which, *prima facie,* it might seem unlikely. Behind the brandished facades of freedom, concealed within painstakingly erected ideological fortresses of denial, the victims of self-imposed starvations, a slaver might detect the ready, yearning slave. Ellen had heard of the case of a particularly lovely, young, if somewhat arrogant and condescending, psychiatrist, who believed herself to be treating an alarmingly virile male patient. Unbeknownst to herself the patient was a Gorean slaver, who was scouting her. While she was uneasily, because of her fascination with him, and the unsettling, disturbing stirring in her belly which he produced, attempting to cure him of his masculinity, he was considering if she might do, say, on a slave block or stripped at a man's feet in slave chains. While she thought herself to be treating him, then, he was, so to speak, measuring her for the collar. He easily pierced, it seems, the facades of falsification and fabrication within which she had attempted to hide the slave of her. A slaver, he easily saw her slave. The question then was was it good enough to be brought to Gor. Yes, he considered her acceptable. Rather than simply schedule her for acquisition, however, he decided that he would force her to face her own deepest feelings. On what would be their last session, while she was earnestly, somewhat pathetically, somewhat desperately, propounding her theories, that he should repudiate his masculinity, theories dictated by policy preferences and much at odds with the insights of seminal depth psychologists, he removed an object from his jacket and threw it on the desk before her.

"What is that?" she asked, though surely she knew. What woman would not?

"It is a slave collar," he told her.

"A slave collar?"

"The collar of a slave," he smiled.

"I do not understand."

"You may put it on, or not."

"Where is the key?" she asked.

"I hold the key," he said.

"I do not understand," she said.

"Put it on your neck, and close it, or not. It is up to you."

"I do not understand," she whispered.

He rose from his chair. "I am leaving," he said. He turned about.

"Wait," she called plaintively.

He turned about, to face her.

She had never met such a man.

She might never again meet such a man.

In his presence she was half giddy with sensation; she felt confused, weak, overwhelmed with a sense of her femaleness, her femaleness as she had never before felt it. Her femaleness seemed to her suddenly not only nonrepudiable but the most important thing about her, and it was precious, wonderful, and needful; she understood then, in his presence, as she never had before, what she was, undeniably, radically, and fundamentally, a female.

She took the collar and came about the desk, awkwardly, she could later be taught to move well, to stand before him. She seemed very small before him, and female, he in his height, and masculinity.

"It is time you put aside your theories, and learned of reality, and the world," he said.

She clutched the collar, piteously, in both hands.

"What am I to do?" she said.

He pointed to the rug, before him and she, scarcely understanding what she was doing, shaking with emotion, trembling with sensations hitherto experienced only in her dreams, those exotic corridors of truth, knelt before him.

"You are now as you should be," he said, "a female—kneeling before a male."

"Who are you? What are you?" she begged.

"I am a slaver," he said, "from a world called Gor."

"There is no such place," she said.

"You might better judge of that," he said, "should you find yourself chained at a Gorean slave ring, naked."

"I, *chained, naked*?" she said.

He looked down upon her.

"You might be deemed acceptable," he said.

Tears running from her eyes, kneeling before him, she lifted the collar to him.

"No," he said, "I shall not make this easy for you. Put it on your own neck, and close it, if you wish."

She did so.

"The lock," he said, "goes at the back."

She lifted her hands and rotated the collar.

In this way the encircling beauty of the band is best exhibited.

"Your breasts," he said, "are nicely lifted, as you do that."

She was startled, to hear her femaleness so noted, appreciatively, yet casually.

It was a strange contrast, doubtless, as she knelt before him, in a severe business suit, with skirt, but on her neck a Gorean slave collar. It would have looked less strange, and much better, he supposed, were she in a bit of slave silk, or a tunic, or, perhaps best, naked.

Culture prescribes certain aptnesses.

"Pronounce yourself slave," he said, "—but only if you wish."

"Please!" she begged.

"—Only if you wish," he said.

"I am a slave," she said.

"You are a slave," he said.

She looked up at him, pathetically.

"It is done," he said. "You have no power to reverse such things. Do you understand, girl?"

"'Girl'?"

He did not bother to respond to such an inanity.

"Yes," she whispered, "I am a girl."

"And does the girl understand?"

"Yes," she whispered, "the girl understands."

"You are an unclaimed slave," he said. "An unclaimed slave is subject to claimancy."

"Claim me," she said.

"Do you beg to be claimed?"

"Yes!"

"I claim you."

"I am claimed!" she said, softly, in gratitude, in relief, tears coursing down her cheeks.

"Whose are you?" he asked.

"Yours!" she said.

"Mine?"

"Yours—*Master*," she said.

"That is doubtless the first time you have addressed that word to a man."

"Yes, Master," she said. "I have never before had a master."

"Your theories have irritated me," he said. "Accordingly, I do not think that your bondage, at least in the beginning, will be an easy one."

"It will be as Master wishes," she said, a surrendered slave.

He turned about, to leave.

"Master," she called. "May I rise?"

He smiled. In her dreams, and fantasies, as he had suspected, she had been many times a slave. "Yes," he said, without turning about. He then left, and she rose to her feet, and hurried after him.

He decided, it is said, to keep her for himself.

It is said she became one of the loveliest house and stable slaves in Venna, a city somewhat north of Ar, famed for its tharlarion races.

Ellen felt herself regarded, and she put her head down.

"I was the first," said Mirus, "to have her put where she belongs, in a collar."

"I think the men of Earth must be stupid."

"Many, doubtless," said Mirus.

"If you were surprised at how well she did in the dance, as you claimed," said the spokesman, "why would you have had her danced in the first place?"

"I expected her to do badly," said Mirus. "Particularly for the ba-ta circle. I wished not only to shame her, but to have her fail miserably. I wished that her dancing, that of a mere Earth girl, for one knows what they are, to be an enraging, pathetic joke on the sand. Thus she would be not only humiliated that she must dance as a slave, but, beyond that, an excruciating shame for a woman, that she would be humiliated that she had failed to please, that she had danced so badly. I then expected to have the pleasure of seeing her, for her temerity in intruding on the ba-ta circle, so unworthy a slave, well and lengthily lashed."

Ellen shuddered. How miserable she would have been under the lash!

Was there no end, she wondered, to the hatred, the vengeance, of Mirus?

But how little he understood her!

In bringing her to Gor and the collar he had undoubtedly intended, for his satisfaction, his pleasure, his amusement and revenge, to place her fully and irremediably in that situation which he supposed would be the most abject, degrading and miserable of any in which a human female might find herself, and particularly one such as she, the situation of categorical bondage, a situation of obedience, fear, submission, helplessness, and service, a situation in which she could be bought and sold, a situation in which she would be no more than vendible collar meat, vulnerable and rightless, subject to the kennel and cage, to chains and the lash. And so it had been his intention to inflict upon her what he supposed would be the most miserable of lives for a human female, and particularly for one such as she, a life of unutterable terror, misery, lamentation, humiliation, and shame, the life of a female slave.

But how little he understood me, and understands me, thought Ellen.

He did not understand, she was sure, that he had, however unintentionally, and doubtless much against his will, brought her not to misery and ruin but to herself, to a happiness she had never hitherto realized could exist, brought her to a meaningfulness and a fullness of life which she would never have dreamed possible, brought her to her radical, fundamental, basic womanhood, brought her to her fulfillment and joy, brought her to the liberation of the collar.

Oh, yes, she thought, I know the terror of the collar. I certainly know it now, for there are men here who would kill me. But it would surely be the same, were I a free woman. The slave is safer, by far, almost always, than a free woman, for the slave, as she is an animal, is not likely to be killed; rather she is likely merely to change hands, as might a kaiila or tarsk. Do not free women, in the fall of a city, often tear away their clothes and cast themselves naked before the conquerors, begging to be kept as a slave? Do not others find collars and attempt to conceal themselves amongst slaves, but are then seized and bound by the slaves and presented naked to the conquerors, exposed in their deceit. And do those slaves not enjoy administering the first whippings to their former mistresses! To be sure, the slave, and her life, belongs to the master. But seldom would she have it otherwise. The usual fear of the female slave is a simple one, that she may fail in some respect to be fully pleasing to the master, in which case she must expect to be punished.

And it can be miserable to be a slave, of course, thought Ellen. There is little doubt about that. One is so helpless, one is so vulnerable. She remembered incidents in the house of Mirus, many in her training, her sometimes almost hysterical despair of ever being able to please her instructors, their impatience with her, her deferent and lengthy serving of formally clad diners, she naked and in a collar, her abuse at the hands of Mirus, her writhing under his whip, the ease with which she was drugged and sold, the heat of Targo's shelf, the fear of masters and the great tarns, the dust of the coffle, the cruel encirclements of tight, coarse ropes, the weight of chains, the sting of the switch, the stroke of the lash, so many things. But I would not do without even such things, she thought. I would not exchange my collar for the world. It belongs on me. I could not be happy otherwise. Do not such things confirm on me what I am? Am I not then, even in my distress, reassured?

So much depends on the master, she thought. It is little wonder that slaves hope for a private master, one who will notice them, who will speak with them, who will care for them, who will be kind to them, one who will stoke their slave fires and force them to flame with helpless ecstasy, but, in all, one who will well rule their slave, one who will keep them in strict, unrelenting, perfect discipline, and never let them forget what they are, and can only be, a slave.

It is little wonder that slaves come so often to love their masters, and with that passion and devotion which one can find only in a slave.

What slave does not seek her love master? What man does not seek his love slave?

But commonly the slave must strive to conceal the flames of her love, as she is only a slave. Let the master not suspect her presumption and insolence, that she, so unworthy, should dare to love a free man. It is enough that she should be no more than his needful, helplessly submitted, ecstatic toy. And what a fool he would be, on his part, a free man, to love a mere slave! She does not wish to be bound, taken to the market, and sold.

And yet, in all, how many masters, to the chagrin of free women, come to care for their lovely chattels!

And what, thought Ellen, of all this talk of humiliation, shame, degradation, and such. I suspect such things are usually more in the mind of free women than in the mind of the slave. Certainly free women often, in their envy and jealousy, do their best to discomfit a slave, to shame and humiliate her, to treat her as a worthless, degraded object, and so on. But men prefer us. We are the women they want. We are the women they buy.

But, of course, thought Ellen, we can feel humiliation, shame, degradation, and such things!

Are we not slaves?

We must obey instantly, unquestioningly.

We may be used as men please.

And sometimes men force us to experience our own worthlessness, particularly if we are women taken from the enemy, or despised barbarians, good only for servile labors and collar pleasures. Men can enjoy humiliating us. They can see to it easily enough that we burn with shame. They can see to it that we are well reminded that we are slaves, that our condition is abject, that we are vulnerable, that we are helpless, that we are rightless, that we are banded chattels, that we are now no more than animals. They can well enforce upon us a recollection of our meaninglessness and degradation. At their hands we are trained and dominated. But, is it strangely, we can find a fittingness, and a reassurance and comfort in being despised, in being demeaned, in performing humble tasks, the scrubbing of a floor, the polishing of boots, the tidying of a room, the laundering of a tunic, the bringing of the master's sandals to him, crawling, in our teeth. And we can beg for the most humiliating and shaming of ties and chainings. And it is easy for them to bring us to the point where we will beg shamelessly, lifting our bodies to him, rearing upwards toward him, as the most vulnerable and degraded of slaves, for what may now be but the tiniest touch of the tip of a finger. And sometimes in the midst of our humiliation, our shame, our fervent beggings, our welcomed and sought degradation, we have experiences forever beyond the ken of the free woman, the raptures of the mastered slave.

I think, on the whole, however, that slaves seldom feel humiliated, shamed, or degraded. Why should they? It would be absurd that they should. They are beautiful, they are desired, they are prized. They are a lovely and precious ingredient in Gorean civilization. Are they not special? Were they not, would men bid upon them and buy them with such eagerness?

A new slave, of course, might feel, at least at the beginning, what free women would like them to feel all the time, embarrassment, burning shame, acute mortification, and such. Is there not a collar on their neck, which they cannot remove? Are they in slave garb not much bared, even brazenly exhibited? Must they not now kneel, even to those who might formerly have been equals and peers? Must they not now obey instantly and unquestioningly? Are they not now owned? Are they not now properties? May they not now be bought and sold? Are they not now, too, mere animals, livestock? But these feelings tend to pass. The collar soon comes to be viewed not as an emblem of degradation but as a badge of quality, a symbol of female excellence, which, to be sure, she cannot remove, a testimonial to her desirability, a sign that she has been found of interest to men, that she is a woman of the sort men want. And when she becomes more a slave she comes to understand that slave garb is not degrading, but enhancing. She discovers that her beauty, unlike when she was a free woman, is nothing to be ashamed of, but is rather something in which to rejoice, something in which to take pleasure and pride. It does not dismay her vanity to learn that she is attractive, and beautiful, even "slave beautiful." Would it yours? And she is, of course, well aware that where her charms are concerned slave garb will keep few secrets. Accordingly, she soon comes to prize her tunics, camisks, ta-teeras, and such. She knows how wonderfully beautiful and exciting she is in them. In them, scantily clad, she is stunning, a vision of delight, delicious, a viand, a repast, a banquet, for masters; does her soft glance not invite men to her subjugation; does her walk not suggest she would leap helplessly, uncontrollably, under a male caress; in her eyes can they not detect a mute plea, expressive of the need and readiness of a slave? Best she should quickly hurry home to her master! Begone, girl! Do not torture us! Hasten to your own chains! You should see her walk before men! You see, too, slave garb augments her attractions and excitements in dimensions other than the purely aesthetic. For example, in it she is identified as a slave, a property, something which one might own. Do you think that this does not add to her interest? And, of course, she soon, as a female, learns the pleasures and proprieties of pleasing and serving, of kneeling before her master, of hastening to obey, and so on. Let her beware, of course, the switches of free women, who will hate her.

Is a slave happy?

In theory, this does not matter.

Who cares for the feelings of a slave?

But obviously this depends on many things.

I certainly was not happy in the laundry, in the house of Mirus. It seems to me improbable that the girls in the mills would be happy, or very much so. I doubt that the naked slaves in the tiny, crooked shafts of silver mines, carrying water to miners, have an easy life, and so on. Too, one supposes the girls on the great farms, struggling with plows, hoeing shackled, chained in seeding and harvesting coffles, kenneled at night, would just as soon be city slaves, and so on.

Most slaves, however, certainly those with private masters, are happy in their collars, even radiantly so, even pot girls, and kettle-and-mat girls, and take great pleasure in pleasing and serving their masters. They are given the domination and mastering which a woman requires, and under which she thrives and blossoms. Gor celebrates nature; she does not deny her. The slave lives in a world of intimacy and emotional richness. She belongs to her master. She finds herself fulfilled in the collar. To be sure, she knows she is only a slave. But this, too, in its way, as she wants to be a slave, gives her great pleasure. Let us take a simple example, in this discussion of supposed humiliation, and such, which may prove to be illuminating. Suppose two women, one a free woman, the other a slave, both stripped. Both are commanded to belly, and lick and kiss a man's feet. The free woman, one supposes, will experience humiliation, shame, and such, and, in performing this simple, lovely act, may feel degraded, and so on. It is not unusual, of course, that the free woman, as she is a woman, will feel there is an appropriateness in her performing this act, and may actually, in a way, find her sensations, which she would pretend to deplore, delicious. In any event, she is doubtless on her way to the collar. Now a slave, performing the same act, and doubtless with much greater skill, is likely to feel grateful and loving. Her master, after all, is permitting her to perform this appropriate, intimate and lovely act. She feels very slavelike in doing this, but this pleases her, as she is a slave. She loves her sense of lowliness, her sense of being her master's slave. She wishes to do this, as it is fitting for her, and it permits her to manifest and express her tenderness and submission. Similarly, consider the kissing of the whip. Imagine the feelings of a free woman forced to kiss the whip, perhaps finding her feelings surprisingly and troublesomely delicious, and those of the slave, grateful to be permitted an opportunity to perform this beautiful symbolic act, of submission.

And so Mirus, in having had Ellen called to the ba-ta circle, had intended not only to shame her, having her dance as a slave, but had expected her to dance badly, thus shaming herself as a woman, as well, and had then intended, in consequence of her presumed inept, blundering debacle, that she would be put under the whip, to suffer a lashing commensurate with the inadequacies of her performance.

But the cruel plan of Mirus had failed of its realization!

She had, it seems, done well! How frustrated, how furious, he must have been. But, too, she suspected that he had been fascinated, intrigued, by her performance, that of an attractive slave, one of whom, wisely or not, he had once ridded himself. And now, perhaps regretting his earlier haste or indiscretion, he had followed her, and with the intention, it seemed, not of killing her, as his companions so clearly seemed to have in mind, but rather of bringing her again within the ambit of his mastery.

"But it seems," said the spokesman, "that things did not turn out as you expected."

"That is true," mused Mirus. "I had not expected her to do so well."

"She saw too much, she knows too much," said the spokesman. "You should never have let her go."

"I did not "let her go,"" said Mirus. "It was my intention, after forcing her to undergo the indignity and shame of a public sale, to buy her back."

"But it did not work out that way."

"No."

"In pursuing your trivial, personal vendetta with that meaningless little collar slut," said the spokesman, "you have jeopardized our plans."

"I had no way of knowing," said Mirus.

"You were going to buy her back!"

"Certainly."

"Ah, yes, pretty little "117," and she received bids that shook the market."

"I had no idea I could be outbid," said Mirus, angrily.

"Yes, you had to publicly buy her, openly, before an entire market, that she would know herself a purchased slave, yours completely, owned, and for no more, you thought, than a handful of coins."

"How could I know that others could bid higher?" asked Mirus, angrily.

Ellen, on her knees near the wagon, sick, put her head down. It is all my fault, she thought. All my fault!

Can he care for me, Ellen asked herself.

Clearly, I am sure, he wants me.

Slaves are familiar, of course, with being wanted. They have little doubt about such things. Can they not see that in the blazing eyes of men? They are sought, captured, stolen, netted, roped, chained, sold, bought, owned. Is their neck's encirclement not sufficient evidence as to their being wanted?

This is very different, of course, from being cared for, or admired, or appreciated, or loved, or such.

A slave may often find herself, sometimes to her dismay or terror, the focus of an uncompromised, ferocious lust, a desire so powerful that it can be satisfied by nothing less than the owning of her, the tearing away of her clothing and the hurling of her to one's feet, where she is collared.

This is how a slave is often wanted.

And who but a slave could be so wanted?

Perhaps a free woman, whose collar is in readiness, a woman who is to be made a slave, a woman wanted in the fiercest way a woman can be wanted, a woman wanted as a slave is wanted?

But, too, of course, consider the feelings of the woman who understands herself, perhaps suddenly, perhaps unexpectedly, the focus of such desire, the object of such lust, the sought quarry of such a relentless, determined hunter. What of her feelings, discovering herself to be so ferociously and inordinately desired? She discovers herself, perhaps with inadequate warning, to be such that she is fiercely and uncompromisingly wanted, wanted as a slave is wanted, wanted even to the humiliation of the collar. In her terror might she not, too, be flattered, excited, shaken, even exalted, even exhilarated, to the core, to understand this new astonishing dimension of her desirability? Perhaps she is a free woman, and has had some warning of these things, and flees, and hides. But she knows she will be sought, tenaciously, perhaps even with sleen. Will her hunter be satisfied with anything less than to lead her back to his camp, naked, back-braceleted, and leashed, and, now, of course, collared? What woman does not hope to inspire such lust? What woman does not wish to be so beautiful that she could inspire such tempestuous, raging desire? What a certification this is of her value, what a testimony to the excitements of her femaleness, to the seizable glory of her delicious, vulnerable femininity, to be so wanted, wanted as a slave is often wanted, as a slave is commonly wanted.

But let us examine these matters not in the context of bondage, where they are so dramatically intensified and heightened, so much so as to be almost indescribably and unrecognizably different from the cooler latitudes of more routine and tepid desires, but rather examine them in the more sober and cooler climes of calculation and prudence.

Even a free woman, wrapped in her robes and veils, can experience enveloping, disturbing, penetrant sensations at understanding that she is wanted by a man, wanted as a woman is wanted by a man. Amongst these sensations may be tremors of fear, a sense of uneasiness, suffusions of warmth, and an awareness of weakness, knowing that her strength is not the strength of a man. Certainly any woman might wonder what it might be to have a given man's chain on her neck. One thing must be clearly understood. When a man wants a woman *as a man wants a woman* he wants to have her, literally, to have her totally, to possess her, to own her, to have her, to speak openly, as his slave. He may not admit this but that is what he wants. To be sure, one cannot have a free woman as a slave, as she is a free woman. On the other hand one can have a slave as a slave, without cant or hypocrisy. And they are for sale. But even the free woman, assuming she is not unutterably stupid, realizes the man who truly wants her, *as a man wants a woman,* wants her wholly, namely, as a slave. It is her project then, one supposes, to frustrate this desire and make certain he does not have her as he wants, as his slave. To be sure, in this way she defrauds both herself and her companion. In denying him, she denies herself, and her womanhood, as well. This problem does not arise with the female slave. She knows she will be possessed as, and used as, a slave. She is, after all, a slave. Too, she does not want the half-way, or quarter-way, possession of the free woman. The free woman may insist upon dilution, curtailments, abridgements, and compromises, but the slave may not; as a chattel, she will be possessed, ruled, and used as the slave she is; her master will have not some fraction from her, as he might from a free woman, granted to him in her benevolence, but all from her, as she is a slave; she is, accordingly, given no choice but to yield all, but then, in her heart, this is what she wishes, to have no choice but to yield all.

Had she feared or resented men? Had she delighted in frustrating or tormenting men? Had she scorned men? Had she attempted to use them for her purposes? Had she attempted to twist their needs and use these needs, like knives, against them? In any event, the maneuverings, the fencings, the negotiations, the teasings, the bargainings, the games, are at an end.

She now kneels before a man, naked, in bonds.

The war is now over for her, a war which she felt required to wage but in her heart longed to lose, a war she waged that she might be defeated; she knows that her independence is gone, irrecoverably, and she is pleased; she knows that she has been subdued and conquered, as she wished; she has fallen to her enemy, and rejoices. She wishes to be handled, and used, and commanded, as a strong man handles, uses, and commands a woman, not with the sensitivity and timidity, the restraint and tentativeness, the civility and politesse, the caution and delicacy, with which a free man addresses his attentions to a free woman. And have not strong men always made slaves of their female prisoners? Is this not what she has hoped for? Were her provocations not intended, though she may have scarcely understood this at the time, to bring her to this very fate? Conquered, she, as other fair antagonists, awaits her brand and collar, and the sales platform. So then she is sold, probably publicly. In her chains, she senses, and gratefully, the appropriateness, the fittingness, the rightfulness, of what has been done to her. The shifts, the jockeyings, the byways, the plottings, the vyings, the contentions, the strife, the contests and tournaments, are at an end. She feels the weight of the chains on her small limbs; how wary she must now be of men, and how she must now strive to please them! She? Please men? Yes, certainly, and for fear now not only of the whip, but for her very life. She does not even know who bought her, for the light was not on the tiers, with their observers and bidders, but upon the block, where she was well exhibited, illuminated for the buyers.

What will it be to be a slave, she asks herself. Why was I chosen, and not another?

Is there something special about me?

Has someone sensed my inner truth? Who, I wonder, so perceptively, recognized me, who saw that I was a slave?

She then finds fulfillment, and contentment, at the foot of her master's couch. She walks well on his leash, back-braceleted, as he shows her off, on the streets. She kisses the chain with which he fastens her to a public slave ring, where she must wait for him. She writhes in her bonds, knowing herself owned and deliciously helpless. She kneels in her small cage and grasps the bars, and squirms in heat, as the anticipatory little animal she is. Perhaps she will be permitted, at a snapping of fingers, to crawl to the master, bringing him the whip in her teeth. She hopes it will not be used upon her. Surely she can better please him otherwise.

The human female longs for the fullest satisfaction of her nature and needs, and nature has dictated its conditions, those under which, and only under which, this satisfaction can be obtained, conditions which, articulated, refined and enhanced in a civilized context, are institutionalized as the relation between a slave and her master.

A last remark might be in order here which is part of the woman's sense that she is wanted, wanted in that special way, in the way that a *man wants a woman*. Part of that sense is that the woman, whether slave or free, becomes much aware of her own body and its sensations, and, interestingly, becomes much aware of, and experiences, her own nudity. Even the free woman, fully clothed, has a sudden sense of her body, naked, within her encumbering robes. And if the free woman can have such a sensation one may well understand, I trust, the radical accentuation of such sensations on the part of a slave, who is purchasable, and who is commonly much exhibited to begin with, often shielded by no more than the single, thin, flimsy layer of a brief rep-cloth tunic. Too, if the slave should be standing, her hands chained over her head, nude on a sales shelf, or be nude, half kneeling, half lying, chained on a heavy, wooden platform, or such, it is easy to see how she might feel, finding herself the object of a male's scrutiny. Do you not think she is not then muchly aware of her body, and its nudity, even were it, say, within the confines of a tunic? Do you think she is not then suddenly aware of the pull of the tunic on a breast, the whispering touch of a hem on her thigh? The slave is often aware that she is wanted, and as a man wants a woman. This could take place many times a day. Certainly this occurs frequently enough in the plazas and on the streets, in the markets and parks, in the promenades, and such. Certainly one of the common pleasures of a Gorean male is observing a female slave, and speculating what it would be to have her. And the slave, for her part, finds this very pleasurable, particularly if she is secure in her master's collar, if those about are likely to share a Home Stone with him, and such. What woman's belly would not be warmed, recognizing that she is attractive, and that men would like to have her? And, of course, she knows that if she were to be had, and this muchly pleases her, that she would be well had, had then not as a free woman is had, but had as a slave is had, for that is how men want a woman, to have her as a slave is had.

"Look," said Fel Doron, "the tarns are aloft."

The men then, shading their eyes, observed the tarns. Speaking as though one might be on Earth, and ignoring the complexities of the Gorean compass, which points always to the Sardar, each of the four tarns, each with its suspended basket, went to a different quadrant, one to the north, the others to the east, south and west. At these points they alighted.

"They are doubtless discharging some men," said Portus Canio. "In time, giving those afoot time to approach us, they will rise again, and attack from the air."

"They should wait for darkness," said the spokesman.

"No," said Portus Canio. "They might then lose some of us."

"Masters!" said Ellen. "It may be I whom they want. That is possible! It is said Tersius Major is with them! He may want me! Many times in the tarn loft have his eyes greedily roved me! A slave is not unaware of such things! If this should be true, if it is I whom they want, give me to them!"

"Vain slave," said Selius Arconious.

"Master!" wept the slave.

"Do not flatter yourself, property-slut," said Selius Arconious.

"Please, Master!" she begged.

"Do not forget you are worthless collar-meat," he said.

"Master!" she protested.

"Yes!" he said, angrily.

"They may want me," said Ellen, determinedly. "It is possible! Surely I am valuable. Men bid silver upon me, silver!"

"You are worth no more than a handful of tarsk-bits," said Selius Arconious.

"If it should be I whom they want," said Ellen, "give me to them! Save yourselves!"

"They are not thinking slave," said Selius Arconious. "They are thinking vengeance, and gold."

"Master!" protested the slave.

"You are not important," said the spokesman. "You have served your purpose."

Ellen looked up at him, startled.

"How is that?" asked Mirus.

"Surely you did not think we followed these barbarians through the grasslands with nothing more in mind than the disposing of an inquisitive slave," said the spokesman.

"You were to aid me in her recovery," said Mirus.

"Do not be naive," said the spokesman. "She is to lead us to the tarnster, who is to lead us to the gold. She may then be disposed of later. She has seen too much."

Ellen sobbed, kneeling bound at their feet.

The spokesman then regarded Portus Canio. "We want the gold, tarn keeper," said he. "We have our own purposes, for which it would prove useful."

"I am sure of that," said Portus Canio. "But none here now knows where it is."

"And it seems," said Selius Arconious, "that as you may have followed us with such in mind, so, too, with such in mind, have the Cosians followed you."

"Masters!" said Ellen. "Even if they have not come for me, perhaps you may, at least, arrange a truce, and then use me in your negotiations! Perhaps you can bargain with me! Try to buy your safety with me, and perhaps with the tharlarion and wagon! Save yourselves."

"Are you so fond of Tersius Major?" inquired Selius Arconious.

"No!" she said.

"Do not think you can so easily escape my collar," said Selius Arconious.

"Master?" she asked.

"Do you allow your women to speak without permission?" asked the spokesman of Selius Arconious.

"Please, Masters!" sobbed Ellen. "Let me speak!"

"Spread your knees," snapped Selius Arconious.

Ellen instantly obeyed.

"Please, Masters!" she begged.

Selius Arconious regarded her, not pleasantly.

"Untie my hands," she begged. "Take the rope from my neck! Let me run! Perhaps they will be distracted, and you may make away!"

But Selius Arconious was paying her no attention. He was rather scanning the grasslands about.

"My ankles are not bound," said Ellen. "Let me run as I am!"

"You would run directly into the arms of a Cosian," said Fel Doron, "and then your ankles would indeed be bound, surely with the leash rope. You would be left in the grass until later, when they remembered you."

"If they remembered you," said a man.

"And, if they did not," said another man, "you would lie in the grass, crying out for help, with no one to hear, helpless in your ropes, knowing that in three days you would die of thirst."

"No," said another man, one of Portus's fellows, "she would be eaten by wild sleen. I have seen their spoor."

"I do not think they would forget her," said Portus Canio.

"And then," said Fel Doron, "you would find yourself put as the slave you are to their diverse services and pleasures."

"Yes, Master," whispered Ellen.

"If you run," said Selius Arconious, "as soon as you are caught, by whomsoever catches you, I or another, you will be treated as a runaway, and will be subjected to the sanctions appropriately levied against a runaway girl."

"I do not think, in any event, I would break into a run in the vicinity of sleen," said Portus Canio.

Ellen shuddered. Such a behavior, she realized, might startle the sleen, and activate the hunting response.

"Tie the slut's leash to the wagon," said Selius Arconious, irritably.

Ellen looked at Selius Arconious, tears in her eyes. How he hated her!

Fel Doron drew Ellen, on her knees, to the vicinity of the left, rear wheel of the wagon, thrust her under the wagon, and then tied her leash about the rear axle. She then knelt there, miserable, in the shadows beneath the wagon bed, bound, roped in place. She, slave, it would be done to her, and appropriately, as men wished.

"The tarns are aflight," said Portus Canio.

"The Cosians must be close now," said Fel Doron, straightening up.

"See the swing of the baskets," said Selius Arconious. "I doubt that there are more than three men in a basket, two archers and a strapmaster."

"Some fifteen or twenty on the ground then," said the spokesman.

"We do not know," said Portus.

"Archers?"

"I hope not many," said Fel Doron.

"The soldiers will be Cosian regulars," said Portus Canio. "We are not going to meet them blade for blade."

"If they think their feast is set," said the spokesman lifting his weapon, "they have not calculated wisely."

He then left.

"We may yet owe our lives to our enemies," said Portus Canio.

Mirus, too, turned away.

"I think not," said Selius Arconious. "A business disrupted may be easily resumed."

"Consider the beasts," said Fel Doron. Kardok, hunched down, large-eyed, was viewing them.

The spokesman, bent over, was counseling his men. What he said could not be heard at the wagon.

"Master!" wept Ellen, from her place beneath the wagon.

"Be silent!" he said.

She put her head down, frightened, and was silent. When she lifted her head again, Selius Arconious was gone. Tears ran down her cheeks.

Somehow the men had fanned out, separated, perhaps prone in the grass. She could see the tharlarion of Mirus grazing a few yards away.

She heard two shots, and a cry of surprise, and pain. There was then another pair of shots, this time from behind her. She lay on her belly, putting her cheek to the grass, frightened.

When she lifted her head a little, she saw the bootlike sandals of a Cosian soldier not ten feet away. There was another shot and he suddenly slipped to the earth, his knees giving way.

She heard a cry from somewhere to the east.

A great smooth, sweeping, soaring shadow momentarily darkened the grass and she knew a tarn with its basket had passed, its archers doubtless looking for targets. It would not have been more than fifty feet above her.

She suddenly heard the fierce scratching of a tharlarion's paws in the turf and she saw Mirus, low in the saddle, racing toward her. He was at the side of the wagon in a moment, fiercely pulling up the saddle tharlarion, rearing, its head jerked back, and he leapt from the saddle, almost at her side. There was a knife in his hand.

She shrank back, and he seized the neck rope, tied about the axle, and slashed it apart. He then dragged her from under the wagon by a bound arm, to the tharlarion. He had a foot in the stirrup, and drew himself up with his left hand, retaining his grasp on the slave with his right hand, hauling her upward with him. An arrow she sensed sped past, like a whisper in the wind.

The tharlarion reared and squealed.

She was then half across the saddle, twisted, on her side, before him. She tried to squirm free and then it seemed her head exploded with pain. His hand was so twisted in her hair she feared great gouts of it would be torn free. Tears burst from her eyes.

"Do not struggle," said he, "slave girl!"

Then he had her well across the saddle, on her belly, and she, wedged between the pommel and his body, was helpless.

"If I cannot have you," he said, "no one shall!"

"No, please, Master!" she cried.

"The word suits you well, slut, and always did!" he laughed.

She sobbed wildly. The world seemed to spin as the tharlarion turned and leaped.

"You look well on a leash," he said, fiercely, "on a rope leash, leashed like the bitch you are!"

She was conscious in the swirl of a helmet before him, but the tharlarion, forced forward, struck into the man and he fell away, reeling backward.

She was dimly, half-consciously aware of a figure leaping on the fallen man, a knife flashing.

"On, on!" he cried to the tharlarion.

As the tharlarion reared again she was aware of Mirus cursing, and a weight, a body, was hanging onto the bridle, pulling the animal down, fiercely, yanking downward, twisting its neck.

The animal suddenly lost its balance and went wildly to its side, Ellen being thrown free, rolling to the turf, and then the beast, a moment later, rose up, scrambling, and squealing, and rushed away, out into the grasslands.

"You!" cried Mirus, in fury.

Before him stood Selius Arconious, his body bloody, filthy from war, his tunic torn and soiled, gasping for breath, regarding Mirus furiously, balefully.

"I believe you have something of mine," he said.

Mirus in fury reached to his belt and drew his pistol, and it was centered on the heart of Selius Arconious.

Ellen, lying to one side, cried out, "No, Master, please!" A vision went through her mind of the wood on the back of the wagon leaping into the air, the sound of the shot, the smell of the expended cartridge, the exploding splinters bursting into the air, now weirdly in slow motion in her memory.

Surely Selius Arconious knew the meaning of that weapon. Yet he faced Mirus with equanimity.

"You do not deserve a slave," he said.

Mirus hesitated, confused.

"For you are not a man," said Mirus.

"I will show you who is a man!" snarled Mirus, and steadied the weapon in two hands.

"Why are you not at your post?" asked Selius Arconious.

Mirus lowered the weapon.

"Now," said Selius Arconious, "you know the meaning of Gor."

With a cry of anger Mirus hurried away.

Selius Arconious, looking about, lifted the bound slave, enwrapping her in his arms. "Are you all right?" he asked.

"Is it of concern to Master?" inquired the slave.

Selius scowled, and then smiled. "No," he said. He then, looking about, carried her back to the wagon. "Stay here," he said.

She turned away from him, under the wagon, kneeling, lifting her bound wrists to him. "Master's slave wears his collar," she said. "Perhaps he will untie her?"

"Is it not foolish for a slave," he asked, "kneeling, to face away from a man as you are doing, with her wrists bound like that?"

"Perhaps, Master," she said.

"What if I order you to put your head to the turf?" he asked.

"Then I must instantly obey my master," she said.

There was a pair of shots from the west, and Selius Arconious hurried away. She watched him move away, half bent over, moving swiftly. She saw a Cosian, his upper body, rise from the grass. There was another shot, and he fell.

She realized there had been little firing.

"Ammunition!" she heard, a cry in English from the north.

She saw the spokesman, his robes torn, drawing back. Another man was with him, come from the west.

"Ammunition!" she heard again.

The spokesman called back, in English. "There is no more, fool! The extra rounds were in the saddle bags. It is gone with the tharlarion! We have used the last rounds, those from the stores of the slain tharlarion."

Ellen, who understood this discourse, trembled with apprehension.

A Cosian, helmeted, rose to his feet, carefully, his bow half drawn, some fifty yards away.

Then, beside him, carefully, there rose another.

A tarn, with suspended basket, soared near. The spokesman replaced his now-useless weapon in his belt, and lifted his hands. He was not fired on from the basket. The tarn swung about. "No more lightning!" called the spokesman to the fields. "No more lightning! We surrender!"

Ellen recalled that when she had seen Selius Arconious he had no longer had the crossbow. The quarrels, too, she surmised, had been expended.

More Cosians emerged from the grass, some with bows, about the camp.

They began to close in.

Selius Arconious, with Fel Doron, and Portus Canio, slowly, upright, wearily, approached the wagon. Another of Portus's men came, too, from a different direction. Ellen saw no more of his group.

Selius Arconious motioned that Ellen should emerge from under the wagon, and the slave complied, and came to kneel at the feet of her master, frightened.

Four men were left of the party of the spokesman, including himself. The other three were the man who had been wounded, who had called out for ammunition, the sleenmaster, and Mirus. None had been slain in the recent fray, presumably because of their weaponry. Perhaps the Cosians had given them a wide berth. Perhaps they had not been able to approach closely enough to engage with the small bows. Those were not the mighty peasant bows that guard the autonomy of Gorean hamlets. Of the four tarns with baskets, two had been brought down with pistol fire, and the strapmasters of the other two had muchly, judiciously, maintained their distance. One had approached a moment ago, however, given the relative quiet of the field, that to which the spokesman had indicated his capitulation. The other could be seen in the distance, a remote speck, safely away.

A subcaptain advanced through the grass, before the other soldiers. Some of the soldiers had bows. Some had spears and some shields. She wondered if the shields would stop a bullet. All had bladed weapons, generally the short, wickedly bladed Gorean *gladius*. The subcaptain had advanced with his men. Goreans like to lead from the front. Ellen recognized him. She had seen him before, at the tarnloft of Portus Canio, when in the coffle and elsewhere.

The tarn and tarn basket which had recently soared over the camp had now landed, some fifty yards away. Two archers and a strapmaster emerged from it. She did not see Tersius Major, whom she had heard was with the attackers. He was, she supposed, in the other tarn basket, which he perhaps commanded, which was still little more than a speck in the sky, far off. To be sure, it seemed closer now.

Motioned by swords and spears the three surviving beasts were herded, shambling, blinking, seemingly docile, toward the wagon. As nearly as Ellen could tell, they had not figured in the fighting. It seemed they had been left alone, as irrelevant to the fray. To be sure, they probably would have been fired upon if they had either attacked, or attempted to flee. Two had been killed in the first attack. Perhaps because they had assumed threatening postures. The Cosians, thought Ellen, do not know what to make of them. They think they are some form of simple animal. Then it occurred to her that that was precisely what the beasts would wish the Cosians to think. Had they not been putatively caged in the festival camp?

"Who is first here?" asked the subcaptain.

"I am," said the spokesman.

"I am," said Portus Canio.

The subcaptain smiled.

"You have strange pets," he said to Portus Canio.

"They are not mine, and they are not pets," said Portus Canio. "They are rational and dangerous."

"They are simple performing animals, completely harmless," said the spokesman. "We are carnival masters. We took you for brigands. We did not know. Forgive us for resisting the rightful authority of Cos."

"You would do well to recognize the insignia, the uniforms, of Cos," said the subcaptain.

"Alas, how true," said the spokesman.

Far off, in the grass, some two hundred yards away, or so, the second tarn and tarn basket had now landed.

"Some of these men," said the subcaptain, indicating Portus Canio, Fel Doron and their other fellow, "are escaped prisoners, and two of them clearly conspirators against Cos. The other, the tarnster, is somehow one of them. A theft of considerable consequence has taken place, accomplished by several men. These prisoners, or some of them, and surely the tarnster, who had fresh gold to squander from the mint at Jad, knows something of the matter."

"We had no idea," said the spokesman.

"And you are obviously in league with them, rendezvousing in the prairie."

"No, we fell in with them by accident," said the spokesman.

"You followed them for days, and we kept you under surveillance," said the subcaptain.

"In a sense, yes," admitted the spokesman, "my young friend here," he here indicating Mirus, "was interested in obtaining this slave," and here he indicated Ellen, "and we, as good fellows, loyal friends and such, abetted him in his search."

"I can understand his interest," said the subcaptain. "I remember her. I think we confiscated her in the name of Cos."

"Yes," said Portus Canio, "but she was later purchased from Cos, in the festival market outside Brundisium, openly and honestly purchased."

"With Cosian gold," said the subcaptain.

"Surely it is a reliable currency," said Selius Arconious, as though concerned.

"Quite," smiled the subcaptain. He looked about. "I see you have two sleen," he said.

"Useful for tracking," said the spokesman.

"I am well aware of the utilities of sleen," said the subcaptain. "You are first here?"

"Yes," said the spokesman.

"Remove your clothing," said the subcaptain.

"What?" said the spokesman.

"It will be useful in giving your scent to sleen," said the subcaptain.

"No!" said the spokesman.

"Also, I will determine if you are armed."

"Here is my weapon," said the spokesman. "It is useless now. It contains no more lightning." He drew the weapon from its holster, and held it, butt first, toward the subcaptain. But the subcaptain drew back.

"Here," said the spokesman.

"I will not touch it," said the subcaptain, his face suddenly pale.

"Why not?" asked the spokesman.

"It is a forbidden weapon, surely," said the subcaptain.

The spokesman smiled.

"Put it down there, in that bare spot, on the far side of the wagon," said the subcaptain. This spot was yards from where they stood. Ellen had never before seen fear in the face of the subcaptain.

The spokesman went to the place indicated, and put the pistol down.

"You others, as well," said the subcaptain, addressing himself to the sleenmaster, Mirus and their wounded fellow.

Each of these, too, put his weapon where indicated. Four weapons then lay in the dirt.

"There were six such devices," said Portus Canio. "Two would seem to be missing."

"There were only four," said the spokesman.

"Six," said Portus Canio.

"Remove your clothing," said the subcaptain to the spokesman. "I think it is time to exercise the sleen."

"The other two are lost!" said the spokesman.

"Now," said the subcaptain.

"Here," said the spokesman, miserably. He removed a second pistol, which he had thrust in his belt, behind his back.

"Does it contain lightning?" asked the subcaptain, the officer.

The spokesman hesitated. He then said, "One, one bullet, one bolt." He had been saving this, it seemed.

"Put it with the others."

This was done and the spokesman then, at the gesture of one of the soldiers, with the point of a drawn knife, returned to the place near the wagon.

"One such device must be still missing," said Portus Canio.

"I do not know where it is!" cried the spokesman.

"Kill him," said the subcaptain, the officer, to the soldier with the drawn knife.

"No, no!" cried the spokesman and began to tear away his robes. They were then to one side.

"Please!" said the spokesman.

"Kneel," said the officer.

The spokesman, trembling, knelt naked in the grass beside the wagon.

The soldier then took him by the hair, jerked his head back, and put his knife to his throat. He then looked to the subcaptain.

"No," said the subcaptain, musingly. "I think it will be more interesting to see him run for sleen."

"No, no," whimpered the spokesman.

Kardok and the two beasts, his fellows, crouched down, regarded the spokesman.

He looked at them, shaking his head, wildly.

They looked away, as though failing to comprehend his gesture.

At this point, from across the grass, at last, from the place of the last tarn basket, where it had landed some two hundred yards away, cautiously, came Tersius Major. With him were two archers and a strapmaster. He paused at the edge of the camp.

The subcaptain, with a gesture of contempt, waved him forward.

"All is secure?" inquired Tersius Major.

"Yes," said the subcaptain.

Tersius Major surveyed Portus Canio and his party.

"We meet again," said Portus Canio. His hands moved, ever so slightly, as though they might consider wrapping themselves about the throat of Tersius Major.

"You will pay, tharlarion of Ar," said Tersius Major, "for the inconvenience, the humiliation, you have caused me."

"You are less than an urt of Ar," said Portus Canio, "for you have betrayed your Home Stone."

"Not at all," said the officer. "It is only that his Home Stone is not yours. His is, you see, far more valuable. It is gold."

"What is going on here?" asked Tersius Major.

"We have conquered," said the officer. "He who kneels before you is, I take it, first amongst our conspirators."

"We know nothing of your charges!" said the spokesman.

One of the two sleen lifted its head, and looked about, briefly. Its ears were erected. Its nostrils flared for a moment. And then it put its head down. The other had its head on its paws.

"Where is the lightning?" asked Tersius Major, hesitantly.

"I think it is gone, or most of it," said the subcaptain. "But some of the metal clouds from which it strikes are there." He indicated the discarded pistols. "One lightning bolt allegedly lies within the nearest device. One device seems to be missing."

"We do not know where it is!" said the spokesman. "It is lost, doubtless somewhere in the grass!"

Tersius Major's eyes went from face to face, from Portus Canio, to Fel Doron, to Selius Arconious, to their other fellow, and thence to the kneeling spokesman, to the sleenmaster, to Mirus, to the wounded man. Eight men. The Cosians had some twenty soldiers at the wagon. Two tarns, unattended, with their baskets, were in the fields.

Then the eyes of Tersius Major glittered on the kneeling slave, tunicked, bound, the remainder of the rope leash, which had been slashed by Mirus's blade, still on her neck.

"Greetings, little Ellen," he said.

"Greetings, Master," said Ellen.

"She is a sleek little beast," said Tersius Major. "It will be a pleasure to own her."

"Her disposition will be decided by higher authority," said the officer. "I may ask for her myself. I think she will be lovely, curled in the furs at my feet."

"We shall see about that," said Tersius Major.

"It is not impossible that a praetor may speak for her, even a *stratigos* or a *polemarkos*."

"She is worthy," said Selius Arconious, "to be kept as no more than a pot girl, or a kettle-and-mat girl, or perhaps as a shaved-headed, hobbled camp slut."

Ellen flushed, angrily.

"You should look more closely," said the officer.

Ellen smiled at Selius Arconious, innocently. There was perhaps the flicker of a tiny triumph in her glance.

"One might always strip her, and make an assessment," said Selius Arconious.

Ellen jerked suddenly, inadvertently, angrily at her bound wrists. She looked up angrily at Selius Arconious. He smiled down at her, benignly. She choked back a sob of frustration. She was in her place, before him, kneeling, helplessly bound, a slave.

"You are a clever fellow," said the officer.

"Strip her," said Tersius Major.

"I will not strip the slave here," said the subcaptain, "for her figure is such that it might distract my men. And by the coasts of Cos, even tunicked, it is such as might drive a man wild."

He regarded Ellen.

"You will not figure in these matters, the matters of men, pretty little slave girl," said the officer to Ellen. "No more than a caged tarsk or a tethered kaiila, or any other domestic animal. But do not fear. You will not be forgotten."

"Yes, Master," whispered Ellen, in the full understanding of her condition and nature. She would remain kneeling and bound, meaningless, a slave, awaiting her disposition. Men on this world, she had learned, had not relinquished their sovereignty. They had not, on this world, permitted themselves to be deluded into subscribing to practices and institutions which carried within them the pathological seeds of the subversion of nature. The human being is the child of nature. Once he abandons nature he ceases to be human.

"You understand that you are meaningless, do you not?" asked the officer.

"Yes, Master," said Ellen.

"Such fluff as she," he said, "is for the entertainment of men, for the sport of men, of masters. That is what they are good for, nothing else."

Ellen flushed crimson, but her body came alive with femininity. It shuddered with meaning. Each cell in her body seemed to awaken and glow, to tremble with understanding. Each chromosome in her body seemed to quiver with vulnerability, each particle of her body seemed to burn with expectation, with readiness. This is the passion of a slave, she thought. How honestly they speak of us. How truly they speak of us! How do they know these truths? How bold they are to enforce them! Can I not, somehow, hide myself from the truths they see so clearly? No, she thought, in my collar I am not permitted to hide. Yes, yes, she thought, they speak truths, mighty truths, lovely truths, deep truths, incontrovertible truths, precious truths, yes, such as I are indeed for the entertainment of men, for the sport of men, of masters! It is that for which we exist, and desire to exist, the pleasure of men, the entertainment of men, the sport of men, of masters! It is that for which evolution has prepared us! Oh, dark, mysterious, subtle, beloved mighty forces of nature! How the world has so casually shaped our species, with such bountiful, thoughtless beneficence, shaping with wise, terrible, tender hands both men and women, giving us as gifts to one another, that they as masters will not be denied their slaves, and that we as slaves will not be denied our masters! Deny me not my subjection to the mastery, dear masters, for in that cruelty you deny me to myself!

"We must seek out the purloined fortune," said Tersius Major. "I do not think that Lurius of Jad will be pleased if it is not recovered."

The officer turned to the sleenmaster. "Prepare to set your sleen to hunt."

"No!" cried the spokesman, half rising, but thrust down again.

"I will not do so," said the sleenmaster. "And no other here knows the signals!"

"You had no sleen in the camp," said the officer. "Thus these are not your sleen. You have rented them. They will then respond to general signals, common to many such rented animals."

"No, no!" said the sleenmaster. "Signals pertinent to these beasts were conveyed to me at the kennels. None here know them, save I, and I will not set them to hunt."

"That is surprising," said the officer, "but easily tested." He regarded the sleenmaster. "Remove his clothing, as well," he said, "and we will see if the sleen may be put afoot."

"No!" cried the sleenmaster. "No! I will do as you bid!"

"No!" cried the spokesman.

The sleen, perhaps recognizing the name of their kind, had lifted their heads.

"Surely you have something to contribute to the solution of this mystery, the whereabouts of Cosian gold, you who are first here," speculated the officer.

"I know nothing of it, truly!" cried the spokesman. "The others, those, must know!" He looked about, wildly. He pointed to Portus Canio. "He!" he cried.

"He was in chains, at the festival camp," sneered Tersius Major.

"The tarnster then!" screamed the spokesman.

"You rendezvoused in the prairie," said the officer. "You cannot expect us to believe you pursued these men for days seeking no more than a slave."

"We had to kill her!" cried out the spokesman.

"Why?" asked the officer. "Surely you can think of better things to do with collar sluts than kill them."

"You do not understand!" wept the spokesman. "There is more afoot here than you understand!"

"What?" asked the officer.

Kardok growled, menacingly.

"The beast is restless," said a soldier, uneasily.

"Worlds!" wept the spokesman. "The fate of worlds!"

"Prepare to run," said the officer.

Kardok crouched menacingly. His powerful back legs were tensed beneath him. His forelimbs were on the ground. The claws scratched a little at the grass. Such beasts can move with great rapidity on all fours, faster than a swift man.

"I will speak!" cried the spokesman.

"Sir!" cried one of the soldiers. "The tarn!"

The tarn which had been farthest away, that in whose basket Tersius Major had arrived, was seen ascending into the air. As far as could be determined, it was not in harness. Certainly there was no tarn basket, nor trailing suspension ropes.

Almost at the same time the nearer tarn, that which had supported the closer basket, that which had soared over the camp near the conclusion of the fray, took flight. It was clearly not in harness. The tarn basket remained in the grass, ropes to the side.

"What?" cried Tersius Major. "No!"

"Use the tarn whistles! Get them back!" cried the officer.

"They are too far away!" said one of the strapmasters.

But he, and his fellow, ran to the edge of the camp, blowing piercing blasts on the whistles. If the tarns heard the blasts they did not respond. In moments they were out of sight.

The strapmasters, pale, returned to the side of the wagon.

"What is out there?" asked Tersius Major.

"Wild sleen?" suggested a man.

"Oh, yes," said the officer, bitterly. "They chew loose the harness and let the meat escape!"

"How will we get back?" asked Tersius Major.

"We will walk, noble ally," snarled the officer.

"It is dangerous," said Tersius Major.

"Something is out there," said Portus Canio.

"I see nothing," said Fel Doron.

The soldiers looked to the officer, who was looking out, across the grass.

"Investigate!" said the officer, designating subordinates. "Into the fields!"

It was very quiet for a time, after some men, ten, five going toward the location of the first tarn basket, and five toward the second, made their way out into the grass.

"Secure a perimeter," said the officer.

Guards took up posts. Arrows were set to bows.

After several Ehn some five soldiers returned to the camp, two from one direction, three from the other.

"We found nothing," said the first soldier returning to the camp. Others, following him, too, signified negativity as the fruits of their endeavor.

"Where are the others?" inquired the officer.

"Surely they preceded us," said one of the returned men.

The officer went to the perimeter of the camp. "Report!" he called. "Report!" But for an answer there was only the sound of the wind moving in the grass.

"Something is out there," said Tersius Major.

"Where is our friend?" suddenly asked the officer.

"He fled, in the confusion, before you set your guard," said Fel Doron.

"He feared the beasts would kill him," whispered the sleenmaster.

But the beasts seemed somnolent, sitting together.

"They are harmless," said the officer. "They are trained animals, performing animals."

"Do they seem harmless to you?" asked Portus Canio.

"Why would they kill him?" asked the officer.

"I do not know," said Portus Canio. "Perhaps they did not wish him to speak."

"That is absurd," said the officer.

Portus Canio shrugged. "I know as little of this as you do," he said.

"Shall we run the sleen?" asked one of the soldiers, looking down at the garments which had been ripped away by the spokesman.

"That can be done for days," said the officer.

"He is a barbarian, ignorant, soft, weak, naked, unarmed," said a soldier. "He will not last long in the prairie."

"There is no food, no water," said another.

"He will last little longer than a stripped, collared, barbarian slave girl," said another.

Ellen, kneeling, bound, shuddered.

"Take your eyes from the slave," snapped the officer.

The soldier looked away.

"Sleen will take him," said another soldier. "Prairie sleen."

"We saw the spoor of such," said the sleenmaster, fearfully.

"They may have been drifting with you, unseen," said the officer.

"What of the freed tarns?" asked one of the soldiers.

"Who has freed them?" asked another, uneasily.

"Send the sleen out to scout?" suggested one of the soldiers.

"Do you expect them to come back and report?" asked the officer. "We have no scent to put them on. I doubt they would leave the camp."

"They are hunting sleen, not war sleen," said a soldier.

Ellen, frightened, shuddered, considering the uses to which trained sleen might be put, such as tracking, hunting, herding, guarding, killing.

She knew they were sometimes sent after runaway slaves, usually with the kill command after an escaped male slave, commonly with the herding command for a female runaway, that she may be returned, stumbling, gasping, exhausted, helpless and driven, bleeding, scratched, lacerated, back to the feet of her master, where she might clutch his ankles and beg weepingly that she not be now fed to those tyrannical, inexorable beasts who have ushered her so swiftly and unerringly back to her fate, the mercies of her master.

"If I were you," said Portus Canio to the officer, "I would kill, or secure, the beasts."

Kardok yawned.

"Do not be foolish," said the officer.

Kardok's large head turned slowly toward Ellen. She shrank back a little, on her knees, an inch or so farther from the beast, an inch or so farther from the sandals of Selius Arconious.

He growled softly, or it seemed a growl, but yet it seemed also somehow articulate. It did not resemble Gorean.

"He is communicating with his fellows," said Portus Canio.

"Do not be foolish," said the officer.

"Climb to the wagon bed," said the officer to one of his soldiers. "See if you can see anything of our men."

"I do not see them," said the soldier.

"They are not coming back," said Portus Canio.

"You claimed to be first here," said the officer. "What do you know of the robbery of the paymaster's trove, the fee to be disbursed to regulars and mercenaries in Ar?"

"Very little," said Portus Canio.

"He knows nothing," said Tersius Major. "It was his fool's plan to strike at it himself."

"Perhaps the tarnster," said the officer.

"Yes, the tarnster," said Tersius Major.

"I do know," said Portus Canio, "that you will not now be able to recover the gold."

"Why is that?" cried Tersius Major.

"Because the location of the cache has been revealed to patriots of Ar, who will, by now, have removed it."

"To patriots of Ar?" asked Tersius Major.

"Yes," said Portus Canio.

"What a fool you are," said Tersius Major.

"Why?" asked Portus Canio.

"They will make away with it," said Tersius Major.

"No," said Portus Canio.

"How do you know?" asked Tersius Major.

"Because of honor," said Portus Canio.

"I do not understand," said Tersius Major.

"That does not surprise me," said Portus Canio.

"Who is out there?" demanded Tersius Major.

"Who knows?" said Portus Canio.

"How many?" asked the officer.

"Who knows?" said Portus Canio.

"Many, doubtless many," said Tersius Major.

We have sixteen men," said the officer, looking about.

"If I were you I would withdraw," said Portus Canio. "You might be permitted to live."

"Where is the lightning?" said Tersius Major. "There is some left!"

"Supposedly a single bolt," said the officer, "in the nearest device, over there."

"With that, we are invincible," said Tersius Major. He went to the pile of discarded weapons.

"Do not touch them," warned the officer. "They are forbidden weapons, surely."

"If so," said Tersius Major, "that is because they would make us the equals of Priest-Kings! Surely it is the secret of their power."

"I would not touch them," said the officer.

"They are like small crossbows, surely," said Tersius Major. "See? See the housing of this small lever? It is like the trigger of the crossbow. You point it, and press this and the lightning leaps out." He swung the weapon around and pointed it at the officer.

"Put it down," said the officer.

"I am now the equal of a Priest-King," said Tersius Major.

"Put it down!" begged the officer.

"I am now in command," said Tersius Major.

"You are mad!" said the officer.

Tersius Major went to the edge of the camp. He called out, to the fields. "I have lightning!" he cried. "Run! Go away! I have lightning!"

One of the sleen rose up, stretching.

"Do not agitate the sleen," said the sleenmaster, uneasily.

"There were six such weapons," said Portus Canio. "It seems we have accounted for only five."

Tersius Major returned to the wagon. "Send another patrol into the fields," he said.

"Lead it yourself," said the officer.

"There may be a hundred men out there," said Tersius Major.

"Then it would be well to establish that fact," said the officer, irritably.

"Go!" cried Tersius Major, turning the weapon on the officer.

"If our vanished friend, who claimed to be first here, who fled the camp, was correct, that device contains but one more bolt of lightning," said the officer.

"I am the equal of Priest-Kings!" cried Tersius Major.

"Until you loose the bolt, perhaps, but then you are no more than another man, and, I think, less than one." Then the officer turned to his men. "If he should kill me, see then that he dies a lengthy, unpleasant death."

"Yes," said more than one, almost eagerly. As with most Goreans, they did not much care for traitors.

Tersius Major arrogantly, angrily, pointed the pistol here and there, jabbing it in this direction and that, threatening each man in view, Cosian or otherwise, in turn, reminding each in turn of its menace.

"If I were you," said the officer to Tersius Major, "I would rather face such a device than touch it."

"It is a forbidden weapon," said one of the soldiers, uneasily.

"I am not afraid," said Tersius Major. "With this," said he, brandishing the weapon, "Priest-Kings fear me!"

"Abandon it while you have time," said the officer.

"Priest-Kings do not exist," said Mirus, irritably. "You are all foolish barbarians."

There was suddenly a sound, a striking, as of a fist struck quickly, sharply, yet softly, into a chest, and the soldier atop the tharlarion wagon, he surveying the prairie, stiffened, stood unnaturally still for a moment, and then, half turning, knees buckling, tumbled from the surface of his post, from the wagon bed, falling into the grass.

Soldiers cried out in consternation.

"Be vigilant!" cried the officer to the guards at the perimeter. Almost at the same time he himself leapt to the surface of the wagon, stood up and looked about the camp. He scanned swiftly, turning about, describing a full circle. Then he descended, his brief reconnaissance completed. He did not care to remain in that location, perhaps from some vantages outlined even against the sky, for more than a moment, for longer than it took to complete his reconnaissance. He shook his head, angrily, negatively. Apparently he had seen nothing, the grass moving in the wind, the sky.

"You are a brave man," said Portus Canio.

Portus Canio was kneeling beside the soldier who had tumbled from the wagon. "He is dead," said Portus Canio.

"See the arrow," said one of the soldiers.

Ellen had never seen such an arrow. It was quite different from the crossbow quarrels, of course, but, too, it seemed so much longer, and more slender, and lengthily feathered, than the arrows she had seen in the war quivers of Cosian archers.

"The peasant bow," said one of the soldiers.

"So it is peasants out there," said another soldier.

"I do not understand," said a soldier. "Peasants are commonly placid, even hospitable, until aroused."

"Surely we have done nothing to arouse them, not here," said a soldier. "We have purloined no stores, taken no women from the villages."

"There are no villages in the vicinity," said the officer. "The land here is dry most of the year. There is no river, no stream, no moving water."

"Then it is not peasants," said a soldier.

"The arrow has pierced the heart," said Fel Doron.

"An excellent shot, surely," said the officer.

"Consider the penetration," said Portus Canio.

"Flighted from more than a hundred paces?" speculated the officer.

"I think so," said Portus Canio.

"Perhaps the shot was a lucky hit?" said the officer.

"Perhaps," said Portus Canio.

"Or we might be dealing with a master of the peasant bow," said the officer.

"Perhaps," said Portus Canio.

"You know who is out there, don't you?" said the officer.

"Now, yes," said Portus Canio.

"How many are there?" asked the officer.

"That I do not know," said Portus Canio. "It would be my recommendation that you sue for peace, and bargain for your lives."

"If there were a large number out there, they would charge and force the camp," said the officer.

Portus Canio looked out, over the grasslands, noncommittally.

"We will rope you and the others and take you to Brundisium for interrogation," said the officer.

"Afoot?" inquired Portus Canio. "Do you think you will reach Brundisium?"

"It is growing dark," said one of the soldiers, apprehensively.

"Darkness will protect us," said the officer. "Unharness and hobble the tharlarion. No fires. Double the perimeter guard and halve the watches. Invert the wagon. We will stake it down and use it as a cage for the prisoners. If any would attempt to dig his way free, kill him." He then turned to Portus Canio. "We will trek in the morning."

Portus Canio shrugged.

"Lie down there, closely, huddle, the lot of you," said the officer, indicating a place on the grass beside the wagon.

"We are not slaves!" said the fellow of Portus Canio, Loquatus, only he left of the original nine, other than Portus Canio himself, Selius Arconious and Fel Doron.

Then he was struck, heavily, at the back of the neck with a spear butt, and he sank, numbed, helpless to the ground. Such a blow can snap the vertebrae.

The officer then gestured, too, to Mirus, the sleenmaster and their wounded fellow.

"No," said the sleenmaster. "Such a proximity would be demeaning to us. They are low fellows, of low caste."

"What is your caste?" inquired the officer.

This inquiry was met with silence.

"Then it is they who would be demeaned," said the officer. He then peremptorily indicated where they were to take their place.

Selius Arconious cast a glance at Ellen, she kneeling, bound, collared, a bit of rope on her neck.

She could not read his expression.

"What of the slave?" asked a soldier.

"Do not put her beneath the wagon," said the officer. "We do not want them killing themselves in the darkness for her. Untie her and bracelet her to the wagon wheel."

In a matter of moments the tharlarion had been hobbled, and freed of its harness. The wagon was then tipped, and dragged a foot or two, to where the prisoners lay huddled.

"You are not to speak while in the cage," the officer informed them. "Do you understand?"

"Yes," said Portus, and his fellows. "Yes," said the sleenmaster and his fellows, Mirus and the other.

The wagon, heavily framed and thickly planked, was then inverted, and placed over them. A bit later it was fastened down, roped to stakes.

The soldier who had earlier hungrily regarded Ellen, he who had been warned by the officer to take his eyes from her, went to her, roughly turned her about, as one may a slave despite her delicacy, snapped a slave bracelet on her right wrist, untied her hands, and then lifted her and put her on her back, on the surface of the inverted wagon, and thrust her hands up and back, over her head, until they were on each side of the wheel. He then attached the free bracelet to her left wrist, and she was braceleted in such a way that the chain went behind the wheel, and thus, of course, between two spokes. He looked down at her.

"Do not detunick her," said the officer.

With a last look the soldier turned away.

Ellen, squirming, tried to force the tunic down, further, about her upper thighs. She felt the rough boards through the tunic, against her back. She was pleased to be free of the tightness, the pressure, of the ropes, but was now bound even more helplessly, her wrists closely encircled in slender, graceful steel.

"You," said the officer, speaking slowly, and clearly, to the three beasts. "You stay—here. Stay here. Down! Rest! Stay. Here. Stay. Do you understand?"

They gave no obvious sign that they could comprehend speech, but from one, Kardok, it seemed there might have emanated some small, scarcely audible bestial sound, a half-heard growl, something which, if it were speech, could have been constituted by no more than two or three syllables.

"Good lads," said the officer, as the beasts lay down. "They are clever," he said to a soldier. "Well trained."

Ellen, turning her head, saw the large, round eyes of Kardok upon her. She looked quickly away.

The sun was now dipping into the grasslands in the west, as the sun, Tor-tu-Gor, Light-Upon-the-Home-Stone, the common star of Gor and Earth, now took its rest after its diurnal labors, as the first knowledge would have it, or, as the second knowledge would have it, as the planet rotated eastward. There is rumored to be a third knowledge, as well, but it seems that this is reserved to those whom the men of this world commonly speak of in hushed tones, the Priest-Kings of Gor.

Watchful were the soldiers. There were no fires. They did not stand upright. They fed on simple meal and water. The night was cloudy. The moons were often obscured.

Twice was the watch changed.

When Ellen dared again to look to Kardok, she saw, again, that his eyes were upon her.

At last, overcome by exhaustion, Ellen slept, but it seemed that scarcely had she closed her eyes than she awakened, suddenly, frightened, unable to cry out, a heavy, masculine hand held tightly over her mouth. "Make no sound, little vulo," whispered a voice. She nodded, pitifully, understanding, in acquiescence, her eyes wide over the weight and firmness of the oppressive hand by means of which she was denied access to articulate speech. "Have no fear," whispered the voice, "I will not detunick you." She recognized, even in the darkness, the soldier who had so openly regarded her slaveness earlier.

She could neither speak nor cry out for she, a slave, had been warned to silence. Tears of helplessness sprang into her eyes. She felt his powerful hands thrust up her brief tunic to her waist.

He turned the wheel, lifting her as he wanted her, she braceleted about the wheel, her wrists entangled, braceleted, amongst the spokes, and then she was before him, curved over the wheel, her back against the rim.

He thrust her legs apart.

Slaves may be had variously, one supposes, in theory, in an infinite variety of ways. One might perhaps, however, for the sake of simplicity, distinguish between two general sorts of havings, first, those in which a master teaches a slave that she is nothing by simply using her as an at-hand convenience, a lovely convenience, often unconcernedly, often casually, briefly, abruptly, sometimes rudely, brutally, and then spurns her, she half-aroused and weeping, to the side, and, second, those in which the master teaches the slave that she is nothing in a different way, by removing her wholly from herself and turning her into ecstatic, submitted, writhing slave meat, a conquered, begging female he can play upon as though upon a musical instrument, one who soon pleads piteously, with all her heart, as a degraded slave, for his least touch.

Ellen looked at the master. Their eyes met, and then she looked away. She pulled at the bracelets. How far she was from Earth! From the corridors of academia! From the politicized seminars! From the ideological pretenses! From weak, confused, uncertain, conflicted men! She had seen in his eyes that he was not disposed to be kind to her. Then she felt his first touch.

She moaned softly.

"Be silent," he cautioned her.

Surely Ellen felt that she should resist him. He was not even her master. He must not do this to her! She saw him lick a finger, moistening it. Wide-eyed, she felt his second touch. Quickly she turned away. Slave girls are not permitted to resist. They must feel, and feel to the heights of their passion, emotion and sensitivity. They must yield, and in the fullness of their being. The masters permit them no choice. Too, their responses, their reflexes, are honed, and trained. Soon, they cannot help themselves, even if they would, or dared. They are slaves. Too, society accepts them, and has a place for them and their nature, and reinforces their condition with all the irrefragable power of custom and law. They are collared, they are owned. Everything, from their garmenture, to the lovely circlets enclosing their throats, to their small, graceful feminine brands, incised in their bodies, to their required deferences and behaviors, combines to remind them of what they are, and calls them to themselves, to their deepest selves. The slave is herself—fully herself—liberated, loving, one, complete, whole and profound. But this man was not my master! Oh, forgive me, I mean he was not her master! "I have not given you permission to fight me," he whispered. Then he touched her again. "Ohh," she said, softly. Perhaps you think that Ellen should have resisted. Oh, yes! But Ellen, you see, was now a slave! It is not only that she was not permitted to resist, but that, now, she could not resist. The masters had had their way with her, you see; they had won. Tears streamed down her cheeks. "Collar slut," he whispered to her, softly, contemptuously, in her ear. Then Ellen realized with a sudden spasm that she was now no more than a slave, a helpless slave! What mattered her thoughts, her feelings, her recognition that he was not her master! No longer could she help herself. How far this female was from Earth! She thought her need must be soaking her thighs.

She thought of herself groveling and kneeling, at the snap of a whip. How quickly she had learned to do that, how naturally!

The grasslands are commonly dry, but this was in the spring, and storms sometimes erupt, and, when they do, it is often with a sudden rage, a blackening of the sky, a rising of wind, a rushing of clouds, a shattering of lightning, a beating, pounding, of fierce, torrential rains.

And the wind was now rising.

He continued to touch her.

The slave began to writhe against the wheel. His mouth closed on hers. She felt the first pattering of rain.

Slaves are responsive. It is for such things that they are purchased. A girl who is more responsive will commonly bring a higher price than one who is less responsive. To be sure, sooner or later, the slaves fires are kindled in every girl and eventually even those who took the greatest pride in the inertness of their bellies will come weeping to the master's feet. It is an interesting experience, doubtless, for a proud, cold woman who has loathed men to find herself now become a heated, dependent slave hopelessly in love with her master, so different from the men she had known, and in desperate need of his touch.

Her lips met his, though they were not those of her master. Tongue met tongue. His hands were hard, imperious upon her.

Let us not think ill of her, for she was a female slave. She could not help herself, nor did she wish to help herself. She pressed her lips madly upon him, gratefully. She gasped, and thrust her body against him, as she could.

He was a Gorean master, and she a female slave.

She recalled herself, long ago, before Mirus, and the two scribes, when she had been brought from the laundry. "I am eager to beg," she had said. "I am Ellen, the slave girl of Mirus of Ar. I beg to please a man, any man."

Yes, yes, she thought, gasping, slave eager, frenziedly grateful, a man, any man!

On Earth, at her current age, some eighteen or nineteen years of age, she might have been a freshman in college, being doubtless noticed by upperclassmen.

A young, beautiful girl.

Here, on Gor, she was a young, beautiful slave, and one whose lovely body had been well honed to quiver and squirm in responsiveness.

How different she would have been from Earth!

How the young men might have cried out, could they have seen her as she was now!

"Slave," he whispered, contemptuously.

The wind blew her hair to the side, whipping it away from the wheel. "Yes, Master," she whispered. "Yes, yes, yes, Master!"

"Oh!" she said, lifted, lowered, penetrated.

On his manhood was then the slave impaled.

A bolt of lighting momentarily illuminated the prairie.

He held her under the arms, they braceleted over her head, moving her. She was ground back against the wheel rim. She turned her head to the side, and then from side to side.

He was mighty and she, slave, obediently receptive as she must be, welcomed him, bent back, fastened, over the wheel, as the yielding, helpless, collared vessel of his pleasure.

Rain slashed downward in torrents. Lightning flashed. Thunder, the wild drums of the sky, crashed about them.

"I beg mercy, Master!" wept Ellen.

"You will receive none, slave," he snarled.

"Aiii!" cried the slave.

In that moment, in a great flash of lightning, she saw a figure, that of the officer, hurling aside his blankets, rising angrily to his feet.

And at the same time she heard a cry of rage from beneath the boards of the inverted wagon, and the entire surface beneath her, seemed to shudder, and buck, once, twice, exerting force upon the straining ropes fastened to the stakes, and then the wagon rose up, suddenly, the ropes tautening and dragging stakes from the softened, rain-drenched earth.

"Alert!" cried the officer, his weapon drawn, momentarily illuminated in another chainlike, frightening blazing in the sky.

The soldier, the armsman, cursing, leapt from its surface.

The wagon was then up, suddenly on its side, the open wagon bed momentarily facing the officer, and his mustering men. Ellen, terrified, half-blinded in the rain, braceleted as she was, was twisted about, dragged to the side. The wagon rocked. She saw the dark figures of men about. She clung to the wheel to which she was fastened, and it spun beneath her, and she turned with it, and then, to her misery, she felt the wagon rock backward, and it was falling away, toward the ground, and she nearly slipped from the wheel to which she clung, and then, as the wagon heavily righted itself, striking into the earth, she was on her knees in the soaked grass.

"Do not move, sleen of Ar!" she heard the officer cry.

His men had encircled the now upright wagon, weapons at the ready.

Selius Arconious was momentarily illuminated in a flash of lightning, looking wildly about, his fists clenched.

"You are a fool!" cried the sleenmaster, now freed like the others from beneath the wagon.

"Steady, steady!" said Portus Canio to Selius Arconious.

"If any move, kill them!" said the officer to his men.

Ellen, through the spokes of the wheel, now on the far side of the wagon, saw the beasts. Their fur was matted and glistening from the rain. They were so closely together that it was only with difficulty that she saw there were three there.

Ellen had undergone the shifting of the wagon with no serious injury. In a few moments she would be aware of an aching in her right thigh, which had been bruised, but she was not aware of it in those first moments. She was fortunate, not to have been seriously injured, as, in the turning of the wagon, an arm might have been torn from its socket or an arm or wrist broken.

She pulled back, suddenly, frightened, as the two gray hunting sleen, slithering, bellies close to the grass, moved past her, to take shelter beneath the wagon. They looked at her, with large eyes. Sleen, in general, are not fond of water. It does not deter them, however, in the tenacity of pursuit; when hunting they will enter the water, and swim, unhesitatingly, single-mindedly. There is, however, an animal called the sea sleen, which is aquatic. There seems to be some dispute as to whether the sea sleen is a true sleen or not. The usual view, as she understands it, is that it is a true sleen, adapted to an aquatic environment. She felt the drenched fur of one of the sleen rub against her arm. There was a powerful odor to the two beasts, accentuated doubtless by the dampening of the fur. This odor was very clear in the cool, washed air. She pulled at the bracelets. They held her to the wheel. She was sure the sleen were harmless at present, particularly if she did not make sudden moves, or annoy them. On the other hand, she knew that at a mere command such beasts might unhesitantly tear her to pieces.

"Kneel, crowd together!" said the officer to those who had been confined.

Reluctantly they did so. There were bows bent taut, arrows at the cord, whipped with silk. Swords were drawn. Spears were ready for the thrust.

"I will deal with you later!" shouted the officer, amidst the lightning, amongst the claps of thunder, to the soldier who had pleasured himself with the slave.

"It was not my watch!" he shouted back.

"Later," said the officer.

"She is only a slave," said the soldier.

"Later," the officer assured him.

"You did not forbid her to us," said one of the soldiers, angrily.

"He did not detunick her," said another. "Is it not that which was forbidden?"

"She is only a slave," another reiterated, furiously.

The officer turned his attention to the group of kneeling prisoners. "And who amongst you," he asked, "organized, or instigated, the lifting of the wagon?"

"I," said Selius Arconious. "She is my slave."

"I see," said the officer.

"I did not give my permission for her use."

Ellen gasped. Does he care for me, she thought. No, she thought. But it is a point of honor with him, that his property was used without his permission. Then she moved closer to the wheel and with the fingers of her braceleted hands delicately touched the collar on her neck, beneath the rope. But I am his slave, she thought. It is his collar on my neck. I am collared. I wear the collar of my master!

"Bind the prisoners, hand and foot, all but our angry young fellow," said the officer to his men. "Then free the slave from the wagon, and bring her before me, back-braceleted."

In a few moments Ellen was kneeling, back-braceleted, before the officer.

"Now bring forward our jealous young master," said the officer. "Take him to the wagon wheel. Tie him there, his hands behind his back. Where he may see."

When this was done he turned to Selius Arconious. "Ar belongs to Cos," he said, "and all that belongs to Ar belongs to Cos, and thus the slaves of Ar are the slaves of Cos."

"Yes!" said more than one of the soldiers.

Selius Arconious struggled at the wheel, his muscles lunging against the ropes.

There were many lightnings and crashes of thunder.

"Beg now," said the officer to Ellen, "as the degraded slave of a master of Ar for the inestimable privilege, unworthy though you are, of serving masters of Cos."

Tears, mixing with the rain, streamed down the face of the kneeling, back-braceleted slave.

Ellen threw her master an agonized glance. He was furious, bound at the wheel, but feet away.

"Slut!" said the officer.

"I am the degraded slave of a master of Ar," cried Ellen. "I beg the inestimable privilege, unworthy though I am, of serving masters of Cos!"

"And you will do so, as each may please," said the officer.

"Yes, Master!" said Ellen.

The slave moaned to herself. Surely not before my own master, she thought, not publicly, not before him!

The officer then indicated one of his men.

"On your back, slut, and throw your legs apart," said the first soldier.

"Yes, Master," said Ellen, in misery, and went to her back in the rain and mud.

"More widely!" he ordered.

"Yes, Master!"

"What is going on here?" said Tersius Major, coming forward.

"So you are no longer hiding in your blankets," said the officer. "There is nothing here which concerns you."

"I will have my turn!" he said.

"No," said the officer. "Only a man is worthy of using a slave."

Tersius Major whipped the pistol from beneath his cloak.

"Use it once, and it is gone," said the officer. "Next!"

"Kneel, open your mouth," said the next soldier.

"Yes, Master," said Ellen, struggling to her knees in the mud.

The storm, meanwhile, was somewhat abating, and though a steady rain fell, there was a lessening of, and then a desistance of, the earlier atmospheric chaos of thunder, wind, and electricity.

"Next," called the officer, and then, again, "Next!"

If ever, Ellen would have wished to resist, but her body betrayed her, with its secretions and spasms, and then, moments later, despite herself, every last pathetic psychological possibility of defense was gone; every last brittle barrier of reserve and dignity was shattered; and the last thin veil-like wall was rent, and taken from her, with the ease with which a slave strip might be torn from the body of an auctioned girl, and the entire needful psychosexual fabric of her femininity, yielded, was revealed to masters. She cried out, a ravished slave.

"Squirm," said a man.

"Yes, Master!"

"Aiii," he cried.

Not before my master, not before my master, she wept to herself, and then, again, yielded.

"Next," said the officer.

"Kneel, head down, facing away from me!" said a man.

"Yes, Master!"

Her head and hair went into the wet grass. She felt herself seized. How powerful are the hands of men, she thought. How weak we are, how small we are! Nature has decreed who is master!

"Next," said the officer.

"On your belly, split your legs."

"Yes, Master!"

"Next."

"To your back, slave!"

"Yes, Master!"

The last to use her, when he had regained his feet, kicked her with the side of his bootlike sandal, more a gesture of contempt than anything else. "Slut of Ar," he said.

"Yes, Master," she said. "Thank you, Master." It is common for a slave to thank the master for disciplines, and beatings. She understands that such things are appropriate for her. Too, of course, they remind her that she is a slave.

Not before my master, she thought, not before my master!

Then Ellen lay on her back in the mud and rain, her eyes closed. She was a humbled, ravaged slave. She dared not look at Selius Arconious. Surely he had seen her buck and squirm, and spasm, and writhe, and moan and gasp, and lick and kiss, and grovel, and beg, and wrap her small legs about the large bodies of masters, as though she might thusly hold them the more securely to her.

How horrified might have been her former feminist sisters of Earth, but they were not collared on another planet, brazenly tunicked, and the tunic now and again thrust up almost to their breasts, grasped in the mud and put to the service of masters! Or would they have been thrilled, and envy her the profound, uncompromising domination to which she had been subjected, a domination which it was quite unlikely they themselves would receive at the hands of men of Earth, a domination without which they could not realize the depths of their womanhood.

There had been fifteen soldiers in all. She did not even remember which one had been he who had put her to his masterly purposes at the wheel earlier. Tersius Major had not been permitted to so much as touch her. The officer, too, had refrained from her use. Once she had looked to the bound prisoners. Portus Canio, and his fellows, Fel Doron and Loquatus, had seemed to take little interest, little more than if someone had put someone else's small, silken she-sleen through her paces. The wounded man who was with the company of Mirus lay bound, weak, miserable, unnoticed, on the grass. The sleenmaster, he of the party of Mirus, eyes glistening, had eagerly, keenly, excitedly, scarcely capable of controlling himself, witnessed the successive ravishings of the slave. Ellen wondered if he were new to Gor. She wondered if he, doubtless of Earth, aware perhaps only of the frigid, defensive, inert, confused, unhappy, unawakened women of Earth, had seen anything like this before, the responses of a collared slave. Had he been aware before, she wondered, of the latent passion in women, waiting to be called forth by the summons of masters? Had he even, until then, begun to comprehend the joy of living on a natural world, one too wise to take false steps, one unspoiled by millennia of madness, a world on which men were men and women, if collared, must be themselves, the slaves of masters. She wondered if he had ever had a slave. It is said that once one has tasted a slave, one finds it difficult to think again in terms of free women. Perhaps it is little wonder that free women so hate slaves. She wondered if, on Earth, such men, in their enclaves on her old world, kept slaves, either women of Earth, enslaved, or women brought to Earth from Gor. She hoped they did not bring Gorean women to Earth, particularly slave girls, for that would be much like bringing lovely, warm-blooded, delicate creatures, vulnerable, natural and loving, to a wasteland, an arctic locale inimical to passion, a desert hostile to love. What a terrible sentence, too, it would be, what a terrible condemnation, even to bring a Gorean free woman to Earth. She might not understand, for a time, what a terrible thing had been done to her. But sooner or later she would doubtless learn, and try to find those who had done this terrible thing to her and, if successful, tear away her clothes before them and beg them, on her belly, lips to their boots, to return her to Gor, and as no more than a naked, collared slave, to be disposed of in the lowest of markets.

Her eyes met those of Mirus, and in his eyes she read only contempt. She looked away from him. Poor Mirus, she thought. How much of Earth is still left in him! How unwilling he is to let a woman be herself. How he wishes to have her conform to some arid, politically prescribed, popularly conditioned stereotype. It seems he wants a slave and he does not want a slave. There is too much of Earth in you yet, dear Mirus. I am sorry, Mirus. I am a slave. That is what I am. I have learned it on this world. It is the truth. I cannot be half a slave. I must belong to a man who recognizes what I am, and will have all of me as what I am, all that I have to give, and more, or I will know the whip.

She dared not look at Selius Arconious.

He had seen her yield to others, publicly. She hoped that, if she survived, he would not kill her, that he would do no more than beat and sell her. Surely he, Gorean, knew the helpless nature of the female slave, and what men, despite her most fervent desires, could do to her, and would. How helpless we are, she thought, slave girls.

The rain now had ceased, and two of the three moons were visible. There were breaks in the dark clouds.

The watches had been disrupted with the righting of the wagon and the quelling of what might have otherwise proved a melee, one perhaps antecedent to the scattering and escape of prisoners.

Some confusion, too, might have ensued during the utilization of the slave, though some of the men, before or after, must have returned to their watch. Ellen realized that the officer had, in effect, not only foiled a possible escape of prisoners, but had, by his quickness of thought, and his utilization of her, an at-hand slave, narrowly avoided a possible insurrection among his own uneasy troops. Ellen realized, lying in the mud and grass, that a slave in camp, who may not be assigned, or used, may exert a strain on discipline, particularly among strong, virile men. She knew that on many ships it was regarded as dangerous to carry a free woman, for such may tantalize by their very existence, exciting speculation as to the possible treasures concealed by her bulky garmenture, but not regarded as dangerous to carry a scantily clad ship slave, who, on board, serves many of the same purposes as a similarly garmented camp slave on long marches.

Ellen then realized that she might be extremely desirable, perhaps even, as it is said, "slave desirable." She recalled that the officer had ordered that she was to remain tunicked.

She looked up and saw the officer standing over her.

"Hobble her," he said.

In a moment Ellen's ankles were clasped by slave hobbles. These were not common ankle chains. This particular device consisted of two hinged plates of metal, matching in their way, each of the two plates containing two hemispheric curvatures. There were front curvatures on the front plate, and back curvatures on the rear plate, such that, matched, each set of curvatures, in a circular fashion, encloses an ankle. The device is swung shut about the ankles; it is held shut on the left by the hinge; on the right, there are projecting perforations, one on each plate, with matching apertures; the tongue of a padlock is passed through these two apertures; the padlock is then snapped shut, and this closes the device on the right, fastening it on the slave. The ankles are separated by something like six inches. The slave can stand in such a device, though often with difficulty, and can walk, though, too, with difficulty, taking slow tiny steps. Since the device is of rude iron and the plates are closely joined, hinged at one side and locked at the other, movement can abrade the ankle. A slave or prisoner so hobbled is for most practical purposes immobilized. Commonly one does not move in such a device. Another form of hobble fastens one ankle some inches above the other. Thus both feet cannot be placed on the ground at the same time. Such a device then immobilizes a slave even more effectively than the straight-plated variety in which Ellen was placed. The point of Ellen's hobbles, she supposed, was to permit a slave enough movement to serve about a camp, perhaps to prepare food and such. If one wants to keep a slave in place, of course, it is easy to chain her somewhere, by an ankle or the neck. In cities, in public places, slave rings are provided, to which slaves may be attached while masters attend to their business, their purchasings, their visitings, or such. Sometimes boys go to the markets and plazas in groups, to inspect the slaves at the rings.

We are chained there, of course, and so we must endure the inspection of the young masters.

We find ourselves regarded, discussed, and commented on, at our rings, much as might be, on another world, in another time, dogs or horses, or on another world, in a later time, automobiles and motorcycles, except that human females, obviously, have a special interest for human males, even young human males. It is one thing to hear oneself, and one's lineaments, discussed by grown men, of course, as a consequence of which our bodies moisten and become uneasy, and become welcoming and receptive, whether we wish it or not, and quite another by boys.

If the sun is fierce the masters will often chain us to a ring in the shade. They may also, before chaining us, allow us to drink from the lower level of a public fountain. Sometimes a pan of water is put out for us. In public we are expected to refrain from touching such a pan with our hands, and are expected to drink from it on all fours. This is, I think, a sop to the pride of free women. They wish us to appear despicable to free men, and unworthy of their attention. But men prefer us.

Sometimes we sleep, or sit, or kneel, and watch the passers-by. We are not to stand at the ring, for some of us might be taller than a free woman. Sometimes we are chained in proximity to our sisters, and then, if we are not enjoined to silence, we may enjoy the pleasantries of confabulation. We take great delight in it. It is a great pleasure for us. I suppose it is part of our nature. We muchly enjoy gossip, and commenting on free women. Most slaves, incidentally, have a great deal of freedom, in moving about the city, shopping, running errands, inspecting goods at the markets, wandering in the bazaars, laundering at the public troughs, strolling about in the parks and on the avenues, such things. And, of course, we will have our friends and arrange our meetings and rendezvouses, and so on, keeping track, as you may be sure, of the time bars, for it would not do to be late in reporting back to our masters. Some slaves, too, it should be admitted, usually city slaves or those from large households in which there are many slaves, enjoy flirting. But woe to the girl who is caught by a free woman engaged in this pleasant activity. Most slaves, of course, hope to have a private master, and be his only chattel. And is that handsome fellow there not of interest? Might one not, in simple civility, smile at him, looking back over the left shoulder? Perhaps he will accost one, and read one's collar. Perhaps he will embrace one and test one's lips? Do you feel good in his arms? Does he like the soft press of your lips? Perhaps you will be priced. Slaves, incidentally, are usually not allowed in public buildings, and certainly not in temples. Outside temples we are commonly penned, or chained to posts, as might be kaiila. If a slave were to enter a temple she might be slain. The temple, certainly, would have to be purified.

Whereas most slaves have a great deal of freedom, as hitherto mentioned, most will be expected to ask permission to leave the domicile of the master, and will be expected to return by a designated Ahn. The ambulatory freedom of the slave girl ends, however, at the city gate. No woman in a collar is allowed out of the city except in the keeping of a free person, usually the master or his agent.

Amongst the boys in their little clouds or gangs, roaming about, looking for some "good ones" amongst the "ring girls," those chained to the public rings, there will occasionally be one or two older ones, who will carry switches. This is in case they find a slave who has been a free woman taken from an enemy city, particularly recently. They may then switch her, and she will kneel, and cover her head, and cry. She cannot escape, of course, as she is chained in place. Soon, hopefully, her master will return and good-naturedly shoo the boys away. She must expect such things, I suppose, given her antecedents. They still think of her as a woman of the enemy. This is, however, a mistake. She is not free. Thus, she can no longer be a woman of the enemy. Now she is only another slave. She would remain a slave, incidentally, even if she were to be returned to her original city. Indeed, there, she would be treated with great cruelty, perhaps even slain. In becoming a slave, you see, she has dishonored its Home Stone. She would beg piteously not to be returned to that city. There she could expect nothing better than a paga tavern or brothel. You can imagine her misery, in such a situation, finding herself at the mercy of spurned suitors, and such. And perhaps she would be purchased by a free woman who was once her rival and enemy, to be her serving slave. Better to wear her collar at the feet of foreign masters, scions of the city whose warriors or raiders first acquired and stripped her. Women understand such things.

Ellen struggled to a sitting position, and looked down at the hobbles. They were of heavy iron. She did not try to rise. She was not sure she could do so.

I have caused dissension, Ellen thought to herself. Perhaps I am beautiful. Of course, I am the only slave in the camp. But I think that I may be beautiful, or, at any rate, desirable. She felt warm, and thrilled. I am an object of desire, she thought. Men, or at least some men, want me. Literally want me, in the fullest sense of that word. But perhaps that is not so strange, as I am a slave.

She still did not turn to look at Selius Arconious.

She did look at Mirus, but then, smiling, looked away, tossing her head. "Insolent slave!" he hissed. She did not respond, of course. She had not been given permission to speak. There was no point in inviting a beating. I am in part your handiwork, she thought. How do you like it? It was in your house that I was first put in a collar. But now I am not yours. You let me go. You were even outbid in open auction. Too bad, dear Mirus.

"Sir!" cried one of the soldiers.

The officer went immediately to where the man had called out.

"Behold!" cried another soldier.

"Be vigilant!" ordered the officer.

"What is it?" asked Selius Arconious, struggling at the wheel. The roped, kneeling prisoners, had turned about, trying to see. Ellen, turning, peering under the righted wagon, saw one of the three beasts shamble, bent over, on all fours, to where a soldier was standing.

"Kajira!" snapped Selius Arconious.

"Master?" cried the startled Ellen.

"What is it? Look!"

"I cannot see, Master!"

"Get up!" he said.

"I cannot!" she wept.

"Try!" he demanded.

Ellen struggled. She fought the hobbles. She could not even get to her knees. Had she been front-braceleted, or in normal ankle chains, or had someone lifted her to her feet, she might have been successful. Too, of course, if she had worn only hobbles, she could have used her hands to gain her feet.

"I see the hobbles are excellently effective," he said, acidly.

Ellen went to her side, looking up at her master. Her feet were separated by the six inches of plating, the left ankle held off the ground. She lay in the mud and grass. The brief tunic had been thrust up, about her waist. Her right thigh was bruised, and she could feel it now, from the turning of the wagon. The bootlike sandal of the final soldier to make use of her, in its spurning blow, at her left, had not marked her. It had been little more than a reminder that she was a slave.

"You look well, hobbled, slave," he said, irritably.

Tears sprang into the eyes of the well-restrained slave.

His eyes examined the curves of her, her bosom beneath the tunic, the narrow waist, the flare of the hips, the thighs, the calves, all of which he owned.

He had seen her yield to others, those not her master, and with the yieldings of a slave.

She could not reach him easily, for he was some seven or eight feet from her, but she went to her belly, and, as nearly as she could manage, to the common second position of obeisance, and lifted her head, and looked up at him, piteously, her small wrists braceleted behind her. Her eyes were wild, and begging. Seldom had she felt more owned. Then, as she could not, as she lay, reach his sandals, she put her head down before him, and pressed her lips to the grass, kissing it, pathetically.

She hoped that this placatory behavior might avert his wrath, perhaps even save her life. In the house of Mirus, long ago, she had been taught to crawl to a man on her belly and cover his feet with fervent, supplicatory kisses.

She lifted her head, frightened, then lowered it, to kiss again at the grass. She felt the moist, narrow blades upon her lips.

"You grovel well," he said. "Like all women you belong in a collar."

She sucked in her breath, in relief. She was sure then that she would be spared, if only for the time.

"I yielded, Master," she said. "Forgive me, Master!"

"Of course you yielded," he said. "If you had not, I would have seen to it that you were beaten."

She looked up at him, in reddened astonishment.

"Slaves must yield," he said.

"Yes, Master," she said.

Unlike Mirus then, it seemed, to her relief, that he would not think the less of her because of the commanded naturalness, and vitality, of her responses. Frigidity may be a virtue of free women, but that dignity is not permitted to slaves. His anger, then, she understood, was not directed against her, but against the Cosians, who had made use of her without his acquiescence. Who blames the kaiila who responds to the digging heels, the reins and quirts of diverse riders?

Suddenly she was suffused with anger, and remembered that she hated Selius Arconious.

"Can you see now?" he asked.

She struggled to her side, and up, on her right elbow. "Master!" she said, suddenly, startled.

For at that moment, about the wagon, carried by two Cosians, was brought the body of a gagged, bound man.

Selius Arconious, as soon as she, saw that it was the spokesman, bound hand and foot.

Some soldiers, and the officer, and the great, shambling beast, Kardok, came about the wagon, to the cleared space there, in the center of the camp.

There was a great bruise on the side of the spokesman's head, where he had doubtless been dealt a grievous blow.

Now, however, he was clearly conscious. He pulled weakly at the thongs that bound him. His eyes were open, widely, over the gag.

The officer was angry.

"How came this urt to the camp?" he demanded.

"Doubtless brought here, in the storm, or later," said one of the soldiers.

"No," said another. "The grass beneath the body, where we found him, was dry."

"That means someone entered the camp, in the night, before the storm, between the guards, and left this tethered urt amongst us!"

"He lay in a small depression," said one of the soldiers. "We only saw him moments ago, in the moonlight."

"It will be morning in a few Ehn," said a soldier.

"Who can come and go thusly amongst us?" said the officer, in fury.

"Who knows?" said one of the soldiers.

The officer strode to the kneeling, bound prisoners. "Who?" he said. "Who?"

"A warrior, perhaps," said Portus Canio.

"Let us withdraw," said one of the soldiers.

The officer returned to the center of the camp, near the wagon, near the place where a woman, or, better, a girl, had been subjected to diverse usages suitable for one such as she, one who was slave.

"Remove the gag from his mouth," said the officer.

A dagger was thrust rudely behind the outer binding of the gag, and slashed it away. A streak of blood was then at the side of the jaw. The soldier then, with the tip of the dagger, poked through the wadding, and forced it out. The man began to choke, and then babble pathetically. "Sleen," he said. "Sleen!"

"Prairie sleen," said a soldier.

"He was a fool to leave the camp," said another.

"I do not like it," said another soldier. "Sleen will follow the scent. He will have brought sleen to the vicinity of the camp."

"They may have been about in any event," said one of the soldiers. "We saw two in the vicinity, some pasangs away, whilst we were in flight."

"Yes," said another soldier.

"They may have caught the scent of the gray sleen, the hunting sleen," said another, "and surmised them to be tracking, and then followed, for days, hoping to share the kill."

"Possibly," said the officer.

"Let us take him out into the grass, and kill him there," said a soldier. "If he has sleen on his tracks, that should satisfy them."

"No," begged the spokesman. "No!"

"Who did this to you?" asked the officer.

"I do not know," whined the spokesman. "I was struck in the darkness."

"He is well thonged," said a soldier.

"Bound by a warrior," said one.

"Or a slaver," said another.

Ellen shuddered. Goreans, of all castes, are skilled at thonging, braceleting, binding and such. That is to be expected in a natural society, a society in which a prized and essential ingredient is female slavery, a society in which it is an accepted, respected, unquestioned, honored tradition, an institution sanctioned in both custom and law. Even boys are taught, under the tutelage of their fathers, how to bind female slaves, hand and foot. They are also trained in gagging and blindfolding, two useful devices for controlling and training slaves.

"Get some food," said the officer. "Feed the prisoners, and the slave, as well. We trek at dawn."

"Sir!" called Portus Canio.

The officer went to stand before him.

"With all due respect, sir," said Portus Canio, "if you would save yourself, and your men, I would free us, and take your leave. I do not think those outside the camp are greatly interested in your blood."

"I am thinking of having all of you killed," said the officer, "all except the slave, who would make a nice gift for some ranking officer."

"I want her," said Tersius Major.

"To be sure," said the officer, "perhaps we will merely auction her off—sell her naked from a slave block in Cos."

"I want her!" said Tersius Major.

"Be silent," said the officer.

"If you slay us," said Portus Canio, "I do not think you will reach Brundisium alive."

"Am I to return empty-handed?" asked the officer. "The purloined gold, the fees for mercenary cohorts, is presumably gone by now. Now you would have me return without even prisoners for interrogation?"

"For torture, you mean," said Portus Canio.

"The testimony of slaves is commonly taken under torture," said the officer.

"We are not slaves," said Portus Canio.

"That can be changed."

"Torture will not obtain the truth for you, only what you want to hear."

"You do not know the truth?"

"None of us do, now," said Portus Canio.

"I would take something back with me," said the officer.

"I do not know what it could be," said Portus Canio.

"Have those outside the camp an interest in your colleagues?" asked the officer.

"I do not think so," said Portus Canio. "And they are not our colleagues. They pursued us. I think they sought gold. Too, they wished, apparently, to obtain the slave, and kill her. I think they would have slain us, as well. I am not clear as to their motivations. There is more here than I clearly understand. Tension stood between us. We stood on the brink of war. You arrived. You attacked. We fought together, thrown side by side, unwilling, unexpected allies."

"They had forbidden weapons," said the officer.

"Only forbidden," said Tersius Major, "because the Priest-Kings would keep such things for themselves."

"If that is their will, then it is their will," said the officer. Then he regarded Mirus. "Who are you, and what is your business?"

"I am a merchant of Ar," said Mirus, "dealing in various commodities, including slaves."

"An urt of Ar," said the officer.

"No," said Selius Arconious, bound at the wheel. "He may reside in Ar, but he is not of Ar. He has no Home Stone."

He is jealous, thought Ellen.

"I see," said the officer. "Then he is not even an urt of Ar?"

"No," said Selius Arconious. He cast a look at Mirus. Mirus might have been powerful, and rich, but the look directed upon him, though that of a mere tarnster, was one of superiority, of condescension, the look that one with a Home Stone might bestow upon one not so favored.

Surely he hates Mirus, thought Ellen. I think he is jealous of him. Can that be because of me? Could he be jealous because of a mere slave? What are his feelings toward me? He hates me! And I hate him! I must hate him! But he cannot be jealous. How could one be jealous of me? I am a mere slave!

The officer threw a look at the sleenmaster, who looked away.

"There are mysteries here, forbidden weapons, and such," said the officer.

Portus Canio shrugged. He knew as little of such things as the Cosians.

"Beware the Priest-Kings," whispered a soldier.

"I think I know one who is voluble," said the officer, "one who might be persuaded to speak."

Kardok lifted his large, shaggy head.

He uttered a tiny sound, scarcely audible.

His two compeers, scarcely seeming to move, joined him.

The officer turned about, angrily, and returned to where the spokesman, thonged, had been put on the grass. "Reinforce the watch," said the officer. Then he, several of his men about him, looked down at the spokesman. "Kneel the urt!" he said. The spokesman, still helplessly bound, was put to his knees.

Kardok and his two compeers were now scarcely noticed. They were curled together, as she had seen them before, as though for warmth, a mass of heat and fur, innocent domestic animals, harmless trained beasts, gentle, massive, slothful creatures who might, prodded into movement by a ribboned wand, delight children at the fairs. It seemed like a single, somnolent mountain of fur. Ellen knew it was alive. She could sense its breathing. It seemed almost unnaturally still. It was not far away. Perhaps it was asleep. But, no, Ellen did not think so. The eyes of Kardok were open.

"There are two prairie sleen beyond the perimeter!" called a soldier, from several yards away.

"I was followed by sleen, two sleen," said the spokesman. "I was running, through the night. I saw them. They stayed with me, some yards away, they drew closer, silently. I ran. I was struck. I lost consciousness!"

"The tarsk drew them here!" said a soldier, irritably.

"They may have been with us on the march," said Mirus. "I may have seen one of them once. I am not sure. Sometimes we saw spoor."

"How many are there?" asked a soldier.

"Two," said one of the soldiers.

"We do not know," said another. "Others, local sleen, might gather in."

"Yes," said another, looking about.

"There is little to fear if we are armed, and alert," said the officer.

"They are closer now than is common, to a camp," said one of the soldiers, uneasily.

Needless to say, the common prey of the wild sleen is not the human being, but the human being is not safe from them. He lies within their prey range. Indeed, they will attack animals larger than humans, kaiila, wild bosk, and such.

The officer then directed his attention to the spokesman. "You do not know who struck you, or how many?" he asked.

"No," said the spokesman.

"It would be easy to put you outside the camp," said the officer.

"Do not do so!" begged the spokesman.

"We are civilized," said the officer. "We could mercifully untie you, and then turn you out with our best wishes for your health and safety."

"Let me stay! Protect me!" said the spokesman.

"And how will you buy your rent space within the camp?"

"I will speak! I know things! Things on which hang the fate of worlds! I can speak of gold beyond that which you sought! Gold compared to which that is a paltry sum! I can speak of weapons which can devastate cities in a moment, leaving no more than poisonous ashes! I can make Cos the mistress of Gor, and you the master of Cos!"

"You are mad," said the officer.

"No! No!" said the spokesman. "Ask those who were with me, ask them!"

"He is mad," said Mirus.

"He is mad," said the sleenmaster.

The slave noted that Mirus cast a glance to one side, to a thick patch of heavy grass. She turned, as she could, but saw nothing there. Then she forgot, for the time, this seemingly puzzling inadvertence or inattention on his part.

"Speak," said the officer.

"Secure the beasts!" said the spokesman.

The officer threw a hasty glance at the three beasts, seemingly no more than a somnolent mound of fur.

"Do not be absurd," said the officer.

"If you are finished with us," said Portus Canio, "free us, and we will harness the tharlarion and move on, with the wagon."

"I will keep the slave," said the officer.

"Free us," said Portus Canio.

"Kill them all!" cried Tersius Major, the pistol in hand.

"Consider the matter," said Portus Canio. "If those in the grassland wished, several of you would now be dead. The great bow can strike from a distance. The camp was entered secretly last night. Your throats could have been cut. If you would return alive to Brundisium or see the coasts of Cos once more, release us. Within the walls of Ar we might be mortal enemies; here, in the grasslands, in this place, in this moment, we may be mere wayfarers, fallen in with one another, in the midst of a desolation."

"Kill them all!" cried Tersius Major.

"But we have apprehended you," said the officer.

"Perhaps," said Portus Canio, "you never saw us."

"I have lost men," said the officer, angrily.

"Bandits," said Portus Canio. "And did you not slay the entire band?"

The officer looked about, from man to man.

"I have never seen these men," said a soldier.

"Nor I," said another, looking out over the grasslands.

"Kill them all!" screamed Tersius Major.

"Free them," said the officer. "And return their weapons to them."

"No!" said Tersius Major.

"I will not risk my men," said the officer.

The pistol then was leveled at the breast of the officer.

"Discard it," said the officer. "Put it with the others, at the edge of the camp, while there is still time. You are living surely only with the sufferance of Priest-Kings."

Mirus smiled.

"No, no!" said Tersius Major. Then he howled with anguish and lowered the pistol. But he made no effort to put the weapon with the others. Five such pistols, of six, the slave recalled, had been accounted for. In the pistol which Tersius Major held there was left, allegedly, one cartridge, and but one cartridge. The other weapon had doubtless been lost, somewhere, in the fray.

"That one," said the officer, indicating Selius Arconious, bound at the wheel, "free from the wheel, but keep bound."

"The slave?" asked one of the soldiers.

"Unhobble her," said the officer. "Those in the grasslands will not be interested in mere domestic stock. She is a well-curved little thing, though somewhat young. She will look well on an auction block in Cos."

"Please, no, Masters!" wept the slave. She cast a wild glance at Selius Arconious, who pulled angrily at his bonds, at the wheel.

The officer then climbed to the surface of the wagon and held up a spear, but with the point down.

In this fashion was a cessation of hostilities proposed.

It was impossible to know, of course, if this token was seen, or, if seen, accepted.

The heavy hobbles were removed from Ellen's ankles and she was lifted to her feet, where she stood, for a moment unsteadily.

Her eyes met those of Selius Arconious. He was her master. Quickly, as naturally as the movement of a cloud, the bending of a stalk of grass, the fluttering of a leaf, she hurried to kneel before him and put her head down, and kissed his feet.

"Oh!" she cried in pain, yanked up and back, away from him, cruelly, by the hair, and thrown to her side in the grass, much where she had been before.

She looked up in terror at one of the soldiers.

"You belong to Cos, slut," she was told.

Meanwhile Portus Canio, freed of his bonds, had risen awkwardly to his feet, rubbing his wrists. Fel Doron, and the third fellow, Loquatus, skilled with the crossbow, soon joined him. Mirus, the sleenmaster and their wounded fellow were left bound, as was the spokesman. Selius Arconious was freed from the wheel, but his wrists remained tied behind his back. He glared balefully at the officer, who paid him no attention. Some weapons, which had been those of Portus Canio and his fellows, were put on the grass, near the wagon. They did not yet arm themselves.

Selius Arconious, though freed from the wheel, continued to stand near it, angrily, bound.

Portus Canio regarded Tersius Major. "We shall find you," he said. "We shall hunt you down, traitor to Ar."

"I do not fear you," said Tersius Major, lifting the pistol. "I am the equal of a Priest-King!"

Then Tersius Major turned to the officer. "You will take me with you to Brundisium," he said.

"Only if you discard the forbidden weapon," said the officer. "I will not risk my men."

"Coward! Coward!" said Tersius Major. "There is no danger, no danger! You are a coward!"

"I am responsible for my men," said the officer. "Else I might respond to you appropriately, in a different time, in a different place."

"Coward!"

The officer turned to Portus Canio and his fellows, who were backing the tharlarion toward the wagon, to hitch it in place.

"I would keep the young fellow bound for a time," he said, indicating Selius Arconious. "I do not think he will be able to follow us in the grasslands. But if he attempts to follow us, and finds us, and tries to regain this animal, our curvaceous little she-beast there on the grass, we will kill him."

Ellen cast a wild glance at her master. She pulled at her braceleted wrists.

"Leash her," said the officer.

"Stand," said the soldier nearest Ellen, he who had drawn her away from the feet of her master, Selius Arconious.

Ellen stood, instantly. Gorean slave girls obey masters, instantly and with perfection. Goreans, you see, do not coddle their slave girls. The least hesitancy can be cause for discipline.

The soldier then took a length of rope and knotted it to the length of rope which was already on her neck, that which Mirus, in his attempt, during the fray, to make away with her, had slashed short, an attempt foiled by Selius Arconious. The knot was jerked tight. Ellen was leashed.

The eyes of more than one of the soldiers glinted upon her. Ellen cast a glance downward, and trembled. She knew that few sights were more stimulatory to masculine beasts than a leashed woman. The leash, too, made it clear to her that she was no more than an animal.

The officer returned his attention to the spokesman, who knelt before him, in the grass, naked and bound, hand and foot.

"You were going to speak," the officer reminded him.

"Secure the beasts," said the spokesman.

The officer cast a glance at the three beasts, but, again, there seemed nothing of interest there.

"That will not be necessary," he said.

"Then I will not speak," said the spokesman.

"Who will bind them?" asked the officer, looking skeptically at the beasts.

"Let others speak, those others," said the spokesman, indicating Mirus, the sleenmaster and the wounded man, the latter bound, as the two others, but he unconscious in the grass, "let them speak first!"

"If you would save the lives of your friends," said the officer, irritably. "Speak."

"No, no," said the spokesman.

Mirus and the sleenmaster pulled at their bonds, and regarded the spokesman with fury.

"It must be pleasant to have such a friend," mused the officer. Then he said to one of his men. "Free those brigands."

The spokesman watched with horror as the bonds restraining Mirus, the sleenmaster and the wounded fellow were slashed away. Mirus and the sleenmaster stood, rubbing their wrists, angrily regarding the spokesman.

"No, no, no," said the spokesman.

"He knows nothing," said the officer, contemptuously. "Kill him."

A dagger was whipped from its sheath. A hand seized the spokesman by the hair and pulled his head back, exposing his throat.

"No!" whispered the spokesman.

The dagger paused, wavering, the energy of the arm behind it revealing itself in the conflicted hesitation of the blade, narrow, bright, quivering, arrested by a sudden monitory glance from the officer.

In this moment, Mirus, within the cover of this distraction, all eyes on the officer, the spokesman, the threatening soldier with the dagger, with a flash of robes, threw himself across the grass, toward the place to which the slave had earlier seen him glance. There, as men looked about, startled, he seized up from the thick grass a closed holster and, in a moment, had freed the sixth pistol from its sheathing.

Even Tersius Major, who held a weapon, was taken aback.

Mirus now faced the group, the pistol, removed from its hiding place, ready in his hand. The slave had no doubt that he was adept with the weapon.

"Put it down," said the officer, in horror. "It is a forbidden weapon!"

"Stand where you are," said Mirus. "And spare me the prattle about weapons, forbiddings, laws, Priest-Kings and such! I am not a child!"

Fel Doron would have moved toward Mirus, but he was warned back by Portus Canio.

"What do you want?" asked the officer.

Mirus fixed his eyes upon the slave. He gestured toward himself with the weapon, violently. "Here, slave girl," said he, "now!"

"Do not move," snapped Selius Arconious.

"Come here!" snapped Mirus.

"I cannot, Master!" said Ellen. "My master has forbidden it."

"Your master?" said Mirus.

"Yes!" cried Ellen. "My master!"

"Who is your master?" said Mirus.

"Selius Arconious, of Ar," cried Ellen. "I am owned by Selius Arconious of Ar, tarnster, of the caste of Tarn Keepers!"

"I will have you!" said Mirus.

Ellen sank to her knees in the grass, in terror, weeping.

"Stand back," she heard Mirus say. Then he was standing beside her. She felt the muzzle of the weapon through her hair, pressing, at the side of her head. It cut her there.

"If I cannot have her," said Mirus, "no one will!"

"You will never be able to leave the camp," said the officer. "Foes lurk, poised, unseen."

"If I cannot have her, no one will!" cried Mirus.

Ellen shut her eyes. The muzzle of the gun hurt her. She wondered if she would even hear the report of the weapon. She remembered the boards irrupting from the corner of the wagon. Surely, at point blank range, it would tear half her head away.

"Stop!" said Selius Arconious.

Mirus straightened.

"I will give her to you before I will have her die," said Selius Arconious.

The slave lifted her head, startled.

There was a terrible pause. Mirus lowered the weapon, it then at his thigh. "Then it seems," said he, "that your love is greater than mine."

Ellen knelt in the grass, shaken, startled, disbelievingly, bewildered. Had these men, such men, spoken of love? Love? Did they not know she was a slave? Love, for a slave?

"No, Master!" cried Ellen, for Mirus had then lifted the weapon slowly, and held it now at his own temple.

"No, Master!" cried Ellen.

"Do not be a fool," said Selius Arconious.

"Put it down," said the officer. "Put it with the other lightning devices, at the edge of the camp."

"No!" said Tersius Major. "Give it to me!"

Mirus turned away, his head down. He pulled the weapon to the side, angrily, wearily, not permitting Tersius Major to snatch it from him.

He thrust the weapon in his belt.

Then he knelt to one side, his head in his hands.

"There are many markets," said a soldier. "You can buy a girl in any of them. The shelves and cages are filled with shackled, unsold beauties, beauties begging for a collar, beauties needing a master, beauties needing to love and serve, to give all, and more."

Ellen regarded the standing, bound Selius Arconious. He seemed angry.

"Do you love me, Master?" she asked.

"Do not be stupid," he said. "You are a slave."

"Yes, Master," she said. "Forgive me, Master."

Ellen wondered if she were a beauty. She certainly knew at least, now that she had come to understand bondage and her nature, that she was such that she would unhesitantly beg for a collar. On Gor she had learned explicitly what she had only suspected on Earth, that she needed a master, that she needed to love and serve, to give all and more.

"Sir!" called a guard from the periphery. "The sleen, the wild sleen, approach more closely."

"Warn them back," said the officer. "I think we will have something for them in a moment."

"No, no!" said the spokesman.

"I have lost patience with you," said the officer. He gestured, a nod of his head, to the soldier who carried still the unsheathed blade which had but moments ago so closely threatened the spokesman.

Ellen recalled the man the spokesman had earlier murdered in cold blood, his own ally, who had at one time been taken as the interpreter for the beasts.

Ellen glanced at the beasts. They seemed somnolent, as before. This reassured her. She wished Selius Arconious was free. She could see portions of that huge mound, that intertwined assemblage of meat and fur, move, as one or another of the beasts might twist or stretch. One lifted its head, and yawned. She could also detect breathing, where one or another of the giant barrel-like rib cages would lift and then subside. The breathing, where she could detect it, seemed deep, and regular, not quick, not agitated. The two domestic sleen were awake now, and had come out from under the wagon, the tharlarion now in its traces. If they were aware of their wild brethren outside the camp they gave no indication of it. The fur of the three beasts was matted, and spattered with mud, and glistened with water. Like the sleen, they had a strong animal odor. It reminded Ellen a little of that of bears. Ellen recalled the large man who had seemed so quietly formidable, Bosk of Port Kar, and his friend, Marcus of Ar's Station, who had trekked with them earlier. She had seen him occasionally lifting his head and sampling the wind, doubtless taking scent. She now supposed that he had caught the scent of local sleen. Perhaps that is why, she thought, he and his friend deserted us, the reason why they fled the camp.

"Do not kill me!" cried the spokesman. "I have much information. I will speak! I will tell all! There are other worlds. There are life forms covetous of these worlds. They have untold power and wealth. They are ruthless! They will stop at nothing! I can arrange an alliance with them! Their headquarters is in the city of—"

A moment before this instant the camp was unexpectedly shattered by a great roar of fury, of howling, unbridled ferocity, and at the same time the great mound of beasts, hitherto so somnolent, suddenly, with no warning, exploded, sprang alive, erupted like a living volcano, issuing toward us like a bursting, living star, reaching out, lunging, scrambling forward, toward us, paws reaching, huge curved claws extended, fangs bared and there was a wild wailing cry of the spokesman which was cut short as Kardok, seizing him, enclosed his head in his cavernous jaws and with one violent, ferocious, twisting motion bit and tore the head away from the shoulders. Ellen saw the horror in the eyes of the decapitated head as it spun away, twisting, through the air and Kardok discarded the jerking headless body and looked about himself. What he said he said in his own tongue, but surely it was an utterance eliciting carnage for the beasts lunged toward the men who, startled, half paralyzed, could scarcely defend themselves. The slave, she fears, screamed and tried to rise, but, restrained, frightened, losing her balance, fell into the grass. Her wrists were cut, fighting the narrow, encircling bracelets which held her small hands so perfectly, so futilely, behind her. Men cried out in horror. Weapons were drawn. Portus Canio and his fellows leaped toward the weapons near the wagon. A beast stood astride them, snarling. One of the soldiers tried to fit an arrow to his bow. A beast leapt forward. A raking slash of claws. The man stumbling to the side, the weapon lost, the left side of his face, with the eye, gone, the bone visible, blood running at his neck. He sank to the grass on his hands and knees. Another man, then seized, was broken across the knee of one of the beasts. Another's arm was torn from his body. A throat was bitten through. A great, clawed gash, opening a soldier's tunic, flowed with six rivulets of blood. Tersius Major stood to one side, seemingly paralyzed with fear. A shield was torn from a soldier breaking an arm. One of the beasts looked up from a fallen body flesh dripping from its bloody jaws. Kardok uttered a howl and the beast leapt from the fallen man. It was not time to feed. A spear was snapped in two and one of the beasts forced the splintered shaft through the chest of another soldier. Kardok himself leaped upon a soldier and sank his teeth into the man's shoulder, anchoring them there, and with his hind legs, tearing, as they both fell, tore open his abdomen, and then rose up, crouching, snarling, over the body, looking about, one leg, soaked with blood, looped with wet gut.

Ellen became aware of a man, bound, interposing his body between her and the beasts. It was her master, Selius Arconious! The beasts had ignored him in their first onslaught, as they had the slave, for he was bound with rope, and she no more than female and slave, and braceleted. Ignored they, too, the wounded man, no threat to them, he on the grass, unable to move. They had sought out, and attacked, first, the soldiers, for these were armed, and the most obviously dangerous. Others, of less perceived menace, might be disposed of later. One of the beasts turned toward the fellow who had rented the hunting sleen in Brundisium, the fellow of the spokesman and Mirus. He backed away, putting his arms before his face, crying out. But the beast hesitated for, suddenly, the two gray hunting sleen, rented for mere coin at Brundisium, had placed themselves, crouching, shoulders hunched, ears laid back, snarling, between the sleenmaster and itself. "Command them!" cried Selius Arconious, wildly. "Command them to attack!"

"Attack! Kill! Kill!" said the sleenmaster, hoarsely, scarcely able to speak.

Instantly the two sleen sprang toward the startled beast.

Kardok, crouching apart, roared with rage, as the sleen and the beast fell together, rolling, and biting and tearing, so mixed together and so soon covered with blood that one could scarcely distinguish amongst them. Vengefully Kardok pointed to Selius Arconious and the free beast lunged forward, jaws slavering. It seized Selius Arconious by the shoulders and opened its great, cavernous, fanged jaws, and bent toward his throat, and the slave screamed, and suddenly, almost at her ear, almost like being enwrapped within a clap of thunder and a stroke of lightning, there was a loud report, the blast, of a pistol. The beast released Selius Arconious and looked puzzled for a moment. Then blood began to pour from its ear. It shook its head, growling. Then it turned about, moved a bit away, uncertainly, stumbled, twisted about twice, and sank to the ground, scratched twice at the grass, and lay still. Kardok, who meanwhile had hurried to the relief of his other fellow, it beset by sleen, turned wildly about. Mirus, half in shock, stood there, the smoking weapon in hand.

"My master lives!" cried the slave.

Selius Arconious cast Mirus a glance of hatred, which attention seemed unnoticed by the shaken Mirus.

Portus Canio, bloody, hastened in this moment to Selius Arconious and slashed apart the bonds that bound him.

"Give me a blade!" said Selius Arconious.

Such weapons, those not seized up, lay near the wagon.

Kardok, reaching bloodied arms into the midst of the frenzied, intent gray sleen, drew them, first one, and then the other, twisting, snarling, by the neck, from the body of his fellow, one with its jaws still filled with fur and meat, and bit each, in turn, through the back of the neck. The sleen had seemed not even aware of him, so intent, so fixed, they were on their business.

Kardok cast the second sleen from him. The attacked beast tried to stand, but fell. Then it stood upright, but with difficulty. It was covered with blood, both its own, and that of the sleen.

There was no sign of the sleenmaster, who, it seemed, had fled.

Kardok examined the field.

No longer was the element of surprise with him.

The soldiers now, and Portus Canio, and Fel Doron, had gathered together, in one place, armed. Loquatus had been half torn apart in one of the attacks. Of the soldiers there were only five left, including the officer.

Kardok, his bloodied fellow with him, crouched warily on the turf.

They may have communicated, but, if so, it was not audible to the human ear.

The quiet was suddenly rent by an inhuman scream of terror, from out in the grassland.

"He should have remained in the camp," said Portus Canio.

"Prairie sleen," said Fel Doron.

"Yes," said Portus Canio.

The rent sleen had given their lives to defend him, who was only a rent master. Although sleen are muchly despised on Gor, and feared, they are respected, as well. The sleen, it is said, is the ideal mercenary.

Portus Canio gestured to the two beasts, some yards across the camp. Then he waved toward the grasslands. "Go!" he cried. "Go!"

Tersius Major approached Mirus. "Is there more lightning in your weapon?" he asked.

"No, no," said Mirus, wearily.

"Put the thing with the others," said the officer.

Mirus shrugged, and went across the camp, between the men and the beasts, and placed the pistol with the others, where they lay on a small knoll. There were five pistols there.

The tharlarion champed at the grass.

Mirus returned to his place.

"Go, go!" shouted Portus Canio to the two beasts. One was still bleeding, and it licked at serrated flesh, visible where the fur was gone. Blood seemed to rise to the surface there, like water rising through sand.

"They cannot understand you," said the officer. His left shoulder was bloody where he had been clawed. "They are performing beasts," he said, "dangerous, inexplicable, unpredictable beasts."

"They can understand," said Portus Canio.

"Perhaps the gesture," granted the officer.

Kardok lifted a paw. "Peace," he said.

"Did he speak?" asked the officer.

"Yes," said Portus Canio.

"Beware," said Fel Doron.

"No peace," called Portus Canio. "Go!"

"Give us the she, the she-slave," said Kardok.

It was for her, at least in part, Ellen knew, that they, the spokesman and his men, and Kardok and his beasts, had originally followed Portus Canio and the other fugitives from the Brundisium camp. Doubtless some of them, or at least those higher amongst them, had hopes, as well, of obtaining clues as to the location of purloined gold. But they would have followed, in any event, merely to obtain her, for they believed, it seemed, that she had seen or heard too much. This seemed to her pathetically ironic, for she understood little or nothing. To be sure, she had gathered that the beasts and the men were not what they seemed, and that there was some form of communication amongst them. Perhaps that was seeing, and hearing, too much. She did not know.

But all here now, even the soldiers, understood at least that much!

If only she could convince the beasts that she knew nothing! Or that what she knew was meaningless and inconsequential, or no more than what others here, and doubtless others elsewhere, too, might know! If only she could convince them that they had nothing to fear from her, she only a slave!

How naive Mirus had been!

Well he might have understood a quest for gold, for such a quest is no stranger to the interests of men, but how mistaken he had been as to the motivation of a slave's pursuit! He had foolishly supposed that the interest taken in her by his fellows and the beasts was his own, that it was their intention merely to abet him, to assist him in obtaining her for himself, that she would wear his collar, kneel before him and serve at his feet.

How naive he had been!

It was not their intention to assist him in acquiring a particular property; it was rather their intention to destroy it. It was not their intention to assist him in acquiring a particular animal, one he might find of interest; it was rather their intention to kill it.

It had not been her beauty they sought but her blood.

But did they understand so little?

Did they think she was a free woman, of wealth and title, of placement and connections, who might threaten them, one to whom magistrates would carefully attend?

She was only a slave.

I know nothing, she thought. I have done nothing.

I am not a free woman, she thought. Have I not at least the protection of my collar?

Chain me, she thought. Market me, but do not kill me.

The beasts stood across the grass, waiting.

She moaned. Surely they would give her to the beasts, she of no account, a mere slave, thus winning their way free from this place of war.

"No!" said Selius Arconious.

She looked at him, wildly. Could he care for her? But, of course, no. It was merely his Gorean pride, that he would grant no concession to a foe, not a tarsk, not even an urt?

"May I speak, Master?" cried Ellen.

"Yes," he said, puzzled.

Doubtless the beasts thought she understood more than she did.

"I know nothing, Masters!" she cried to the beasts. "I am a slave! I am a mere slave!"

"Go!" cried Portus Canio, again waving toward the grasslands.

Kardok looked at Ellen.

"Go!" reiterated Portus Canio.

"Yes," said Kardok, docilely. "We will go."

She gasped for breath, in joyous relief. Surely they had believed her!

"They will return," said Mirus.

She shuddered.

Then she whispered to Selius Arconious. "Give me to them, Master."

"Be silent, slut," said Selius Arconious, severely.

"Yes, Master," she whispered.

Kardok and his ally then began to back away, and, in a few moments, were no longer visible. They had little to fear from sleen, they more terrible individually than most common sleen. Too, if there were foes, or mysterious figures, in the grasses, Ellen did not think they would choose to deter the beasts in their passage.

"We are safe now," said Tersius Major.

"Prepare to withdraw," said the officer to his men. "We have been long enough in this place."

He had but four men left of his original complement of troops. One of these was the soldier who had subjected the slave to unilateral, degrading, irresistible pleasures at the wheel, she helplessly braceleted, pleasures suitable to one of her condition, pleasures which one such as she must accept, pleasures, ecstasies, to which she must yield gratefully, unreservedly. She thought there was no one of those five who did not, somewhere on his body, bear the marks of claws or fangs.

"The tharlarion is ready, the wagon is ready," said Fel Doron.

The officer held out his hand to Portus Canio. "Farewell, fond enemy, fond ally," said he.

Portus Canio unhesitantly grasped his hand. "Farewell," said he, "fond enemy, fond ally."

"You may not have the slave," said Selius Arconious.

"Master!" breathed Ellen.

"She is pretty, but a bit young," said the officer. "Here," he said, reaching into his pouch, "are the keys to her bracelets."

Slave bracelets, of course, are useful in the control and management of women, whether free or slave.

Selius Arconious caught the keys. "Thank you," he said. "But wait a moment. I shall return them momentarily, when I have freed her small wrists from those trivial impediments. We have, of course, our own bracelets."

"Keep them," said the officer. "You may find use for an extra pair. You might meet another woman worth taking."

"True," said Selius Arconious. "Thank you."

"It is nothing," said the officer.

"Please, no, Master!" protested Ellen.

"I will do as I please," he said.

"Yes, Master," she whispered, head down, defeated.

"If you have friends out there," said the officer to Portus Canio, "I assume they will let us pass."

"Now," smiled Portus Canio.

"I will be curious to see them," said the officer.

"I do not think you will see them," said Portus Canio.

"Prepare to trek," said the officer to his men.

"Take me with you," said Tersius Major.

"Put aside the forbidden weapon," said the officer.

"No!" cried Tersius Major.

"You are welcome to come with us," said Portus Canio.

"No, no!" said Tersius Major.

"Then remain here," said the officer, turning about.

The report of the weapon was sharp, and close. And the officer, struck through the back, a sudden stain upon his tunic, fell forward, stumbling, and collapsed to the grass.

Portus Canio hastened to the officer.

The officer tried to rise, but fell to the side, twisted, and fell again, then upon his back. There was blood, too, on his chest. The projectile, at this range, had torn through the body.

"Take me with you!" cried Tersius Major to the Cosians.

Portus Canio closed the eyes of the officer.

"Take me with you!" screamed Tersius Major.

"That is the last of the lightning," said Portus Canio, looking up.

"No, no!" said Tersius Major.

Portus Canio rose up, and took a step toward Tersius Major. Frenziedly, Tersius Major pulled the trigger again and again, full at the chest of Portus Canio. There was a sporadic, inconsequential succession of sharp, metallic clickings.

"There is no more lightning," said Portus Canio.

Tersius Major then turned about and fled to the discarded weapons on the knoll, and scrambled amongst them, wildly, and lifted one after another, pointing it and pulling the trigger, with no results other than those which had preceded these new efforts.

"A lengthy, unpleasant death," said one of the soldiers, menacingly.

"Yes," said another.

"I am safe here," said Tersius Major. "I am surrounded by forbidden weapons!" Hastily he placed them in a circle about himself.

The soldiers looked to one another.

"Even an arrow would have to pass this barrier!" said Tersius Major.

Portus Canio returned to where the officer had fallen. "He was a good officer," he said.

"We will take him with us, into the grasses," said one of the soldiers.

"We will find a suitable place, a green place, with stones about, where the wind and rain can find him. There we will bid him farewell. There we will salute him for the last time. There we will leave him, on his back, his face to the sky, a weapon at his side."

"And then?" asked Portus Canio.

"Thence to Brundisium," said the soldier.

A litter was rigged of canvas wrapped about two spears.

"What of him?" asked one of the soldiers, indicating Tersius Major crouching down fearfully in the midst of the discarded pistols.

"Return to Brundisium," said Portus Canio.

Shortly thereafter the soldiers, the body on its litter, supported on their shoulders, took their leave of the camp.

"It would be well to leave this area," said Portus Canio. "There are still sleen about."

Selius Arconious, angrily, went to face Mirus. "You saved my life," he said, red with fury.

Mirus shrugged.

"Here," he said, angrily, "are the keys to the slave's bracelets. She is yours."

"No, Master!" cried the slave.

"To his feet," snapped Mirus, "lick and kiss them, now! Render obeisance, slut! Appropriately! To your new master!"

Frightened, distraught, weeping, Ellen scrambled on her knees the pace or two to Mirus, and lost her balance and fell to her side, and then got to her belly, and, wrists braceleted behind her, put her head down, and thus, prostrated as becomes a female slave, pressed kisses upon his feet. "No, Master! Please, no, Master!"

"You will find her poorly trained, and worthless," said Selius Arconious.

"That is known to me," said Mirus. "But I return her to you. Here are the keys to the slave's bracelets." And with those words he withdrew from Ellen and placed, as she turned and watched, from her side, the keys in the hands of Selius Arconious.

"Why?" asked Selius Arconious.

"Who wants a poorly trained, and worthless slave?" said Mirus.

"Perhaps," said Selius Arconious, wonderingly, "you are worthy of a Home Stone."

"Someday," said Mirus, "I should like to be worthy of one."

"What will you do, where will you go?" asked Selius Arconious.

"I will beg a tarpaulin and place my wounded fellow upon it, and draw him in that fashion to Brundisium. I think I cannot return to Ar. I think I must begin again, but as one of your world, not of mine."

"I think, then," said Selius Arconious, "that you are indeed worthy of a Home Stone."

"Perhaps someday," said Mirus.

"My hand!" said Selius Arconious.

"I take it gladly," said Mirus. "I will now attend to my fellow."

"Master!" breathed Ellen.

He turned to face her.

"Your slave begs to be unbraceleted," she said.

He then crouched down beside her and freed her of the lovely restraints which had confined her so innocently and perfectly.

She then knelt beside him and grasped his leg with her arms, and put her head against his thigh, and kissed it humbly. "I love you, Master!" she said. "I love you, I love you, my master!"

"It is suitable," he said, "that a slave should love her master."

"Yes, Master!" she wept, kissing him again, and yet again.

The rope was still on her neck.

She looked up at him. "I am leashed, Master," she whispered.

"Do not tempt me, slave girl," said he.

"Yes, Master," she smiled. How could a slave girl not tempt a man, she asked herself delightedly, though she dared not speak out. Her entire being, and existence, is a temptation to a man!

"Behold!" cried Fel Doron, from the other side of the wagon. "See, look here!"

Then he emerged from the other side of the wagon. He carried, across his shoulders, the body of a freshly killed grass tabuk.

"How came this to the camp?" inquired Portus Canio.

"I know not," he said, grinning.

"We will feast this night," said Portus Canio, looking out, over the grasses.

"It seems," said Mirus, "we are not alone."

"We may have been alone, we were not alone, now we may again be alone. It is hard to tell. One does not know." He then went to the edge of the camp. "If you are there," he called, "be thanked!"

"I am hungry!" called Tersius Major, from within his circle of futile weapons.

"Then come and feast with us," invited Portus Canio, softly, his voice like a sheathed dagger.

Tersius Major shrank back amongst the pistols on the knoll. He was thus raised somewhat above the level of the encampment. A bowman, Ellen realized, if he cared, would have little difficulty in capitalizing upon such a target. Thus, she thought, he does not care, or he is gone, again.

Fel Doron threw the small tabuk to the grass before them. Then he looked about himself. "I will take the bodies into the fields," he said. "There are sleen about, and more will come, I am sure of it."

The bodies, Ellen realized, would be surrendered to nature, to wind and rain, to sleet and snow, to heat and cold, to sleen, to urts, to jards, to the vast, mysterious nature from which, long ago, they had sprung.

Goreans love and respect nature. Crimes against her are regarded as peculiarly heinous.

"I will prepare the beast for the fire," said Portus Canio, drawing out his knife.

Ellen looked about. She was pleased that Kardok and his ally had left the locality, that she and the others were now safe.

"May I remove the leash from my neck, Master?" she asked.

Selius Arconious nodded, watching the work of Portus Canio.

Ellen did not watch Canio's work. She did not care to do so. Rather she addressed herself to removing the leash. It was not easy to do. It was tightly knotted, and she could not, of course, see the knot. I was well leashed, she thought, and felt, however unwillingly, a sudden heat in her belly, a sudden flaming within her upper thighs. She reddened. At least, she thought, it is common rope, and not a leash of knotted leather, or knotted binding fiber, because she knew that knots in such materials might be drawn so tightly that her small, delicate fingers, those of a woman, might lack the strength to undo them. At least, she was not in a lock leash, of chain or leather, or in a locked snap-leash that might be attached to her collar. She struggled. Then she looked pathetically at Selius Arconious. "Master," she begged. He snapped his fingers that she should approach him and she ran to stand before him. He then removed the leash from her. "Thank you, Master," she said, looking up, standing very close to him. "Temptress, she-urt," he said, turning away. She smiled to herself. He wants you, she thought. You are suffering, aren't you, Master, she thought, delightedly.

"You will cook," said Portus Canio, looking up from his work.

"Yes, Master," she said.

How natural it seemed that she, the female, would cook. Even on Earth, she had sometimes fantasized that she was in a room with men, sitting about, she the only woman, supposedly a peer, and that one of the men had looked up, and had told her to go into the kitchen and cook. And she had done so, alone in the kitchen, while they had continued their conversation. She had been enflamed sexually.

To be sure, in her ideological pride and her sense of political propriety, she had made it a point to learn little or nothing of cooking on Earth, feeling such a homely task, and one so often associated with women, was wholly inappropriate for her, a female intellectual. Indeed, she would have felt embarrassed to have such skills. They were not only beneath her, but would have been insulting, demeaning, to one such as she. In the house of Mirus, in Ar, of course, as a part of her training, all this had changed. There she had become desperately zealous, often naked, on her knees, in the shadow of a switch or whip, to master a battery of domestic skills, cooking amongst them, skills expected of a female slave. And, as time went on, she became aware that these tasks were not as menial and simple as she had conjectured, but that genuine skill was needed, and attention, to turn out a delectable sauce, to make small, fine stitches, to press a tunic with fire-heated irons so well that one would not feel the switches of the instructrices, and so on. In time, as her skills increased, and the sting of the switch became less frequent, she began to take pride in her performance of such tasks, those expected of a female slave. As even on Earth they seemed to her, no matter how often she had denied this, somehow fitting for women. The human species as she knew, but would not have called it to the attention of her classes, was radically, sexually dimorphic. It thus seemed natural that some division of labors, however such things might be sorted out, might be expected in a species characterized by such disparate natures. One hunts, one cooks, she thought. And is it not natural to suppose that the lighter labors might descend to the slighter beasts, the softer, prettier beasts who stood in need of male protection, those less fitted for war and long treks, those less wisely pitted against the mastodon, the cave bear, the panther, the stranger, those who must hope to please the larger, stronger, more aggressive, less patient animals, to whom they belonged.

Too, of course, she had cooked in the tarn lofts of Portus Canio, for himself and his men.

Yes, she thought, cooking and such things well reminds me that I am a woman, but such things are only amongst thousands of other such things, other reminders which I welcome and in which I rejoice, such as my tunic, so unmistakably and publicly exhibiting my differences from men, my brand, marking me property, my collar, locked on me, encircling my throat, proclaiming me slave!

How precious it is to be a woman amongst such men, to be a woman amongst masters!

Thank you, Master Mirus, for bringing me to this world! Thank you for having me branded and collared, and sold!

Thank you for bringing me to where I belong, and want to be, at the feet of men.

And even cooking, you see, can be a sexual experience. And, indeed is not the entire life of a slave, her entire existence, in its way, a sexual experience?

"Try to find fuel, stay close to the camp," he said.

"Yes, Master," she said.

In the grasslands the most common fuel is woodlike brush. Some peasants, out of a village, use tightly twisted ropes of grass, but one needs a good deal of this, as it burns very quickly. Some kindling, bits of wood, branches and such, was also carried, the larger branches bundled, in the wagon. This had been gathered not far from the festival camp. As this material was not readily available in the grasslands, it tended to be conserved, to be used when local fuel was difficult to obtain.

She straightened her body, noted that Selius Arconious was watching her, and, pretending not to notice, pulled down the sides of her brief tunic, intently, tightly, this accentuating the flare of her hips, demurely.

Within the Ahn the slave was attending to the meat, which had been cut by Portus Canio. It browned and sizzled. Fat dripped into the fire. Her gleanings of fuel from the grasslands near the camp, primarily cord and flower brush, had been supplemented with some of the wood carried in the wagon. This had been decided by Portus Canio, after her third trip back to the camp. The men did not wish her to range too far from the camp. There were sleen about. The flower brush gave off a sweet smoke, and this added a flavor to the meat. When the meat was done, she would not touch it, of course, but it was removed from the cooking rods and cut by Portus Canio, who distributed it, to Fel Doron, and Selius Arconious, and Mirus, who took some to his wounded fellow.

Portus Canio, Fel Doron and Selius Arconious sat cross-legged about the fire. Ellen lay on her belly at the left knee of Selius Arconious. From time to time, he tore off a bit of the meat and put it in her mouth.

"Thank you, Master," she said.

Mirus returned to the fire, from giving his wounded fellow some share of the simple provender, and, after a moment's thought, it seemed, too took his place before it, too sat cross-legged before it, as were the other men.

He looked at Ellen. She, on her belly, licked and kissed, deferentially, lovingly, at the hand that fed her, and then, eyes shining, lifting her face and opening her mouth, she delicately, gratefully, accepted another tiny piece of meat.

"You have an attractive slave," he told Selius Arconious.

"You can buy one for yourself, almost anywhere," said Selius Arconious, "or you can always capture a free woman, if you can find one lovely enough to be a slave, and tame and train her."

"Where I come from," smiled Mirus, "such things are not done."

"Remember that men are the masters," said Selius Arconious.

"I will never forget it," said Mirus.

"If you treat a slave well," said Selius Arconious, "you will get a great deal of pleasure out of her."

Men, of course, get a great deal of pleasure out of their slaves in any event.

It is what slaves are for, and work.

Mirus regarded Selius Arconious.

"One must make certain, of course," said Selius Arconious, "that she is not permitted the least latitude."

"You must not forget the whip," said Mirus.

"Of course not," said Selius Arconious. "If she is not fully pleasing, she is to be lashed. She is not a free woman. She is only a slave. In her early training, of course, when you get a girl, particularly if you are her first master,

I would recommend the switch. It is an effective correctional device, and it will be quite adequate for a new slave, only a frightened girl. She may later learn, when she has become familiar with your expectations and desires, should she fail in any way to fulfill them with perfection, and when she has become accustomed to her boundaries and limits, should she violate or transgress them in the least, to fear the five-stranded slave lash. So I would recommend, certainly in the beginning, not the lash, but the switch. Indeed, the switch will continue to be an admonitory implement which will never lose its appeal to the master or its meaning for the slave. A judicious conjunction of the switch and lash is doubtless in the slave's best interest, assisting her to be alert, and zealous to please. It is good for correcting faulty kneeling, or bellying, an awkward walk, clumsy movements, and such. She must learn to speak not with the strident, insolent tones of a free woman, but with the softness, and deference, of the slave; see that she wears her tunic well, and attractively; she is to be neat and well groomed, brushed, combed, and cleaned; she is not a slovenly free woman; let her keep the lock of her collar at the back of her neck; make certain she understands that she is not to speak without permission; you will find the switch useful in correcting lapses in that regard; one assumes she will know enough to kneel when you or another free person enters the room, such things. You will, of course, train her as you wish, in all ways, and in great detail. Make certain you are satisfied, for example, with the condition of your quarters, the nature of your meals, and such, and everything in the way of domestic matters, dusting, laundering, sewing, ironing, scrubbing, polishing, and so on. One will have such things of a slave. They are appropriate for her. She is not a free woman. See, too, of course, speaking of free women, that she is decorous before them. To be sure, the free women will see to that themselves. She will live in terror of free women, and look to men to protect her from them. Suppose you are giving a dinner for guests, and one or more free women are present. In such a case make certain that she is demurely clad, perhaps in a white, three-quarters or full-length gown, though certainly sleeveless. Be certain, of course, that her collar is always in evidence, that there be no suggestion whatsoever that she is in any way comparable to a free woman. No such comparisons must exist. A free woman would find them tasteless and insulting. She is, in any event, whatever the nature of your guests, to be humble, self-effacing, and attentive. It is to be almost as though she were not there. When not serving she may kneel to one side, unobtrusively, waiting to be summoned. If you are entertaining male guests only, she may, if you wish, be naked. Naturally, you must understand, she must be taught your preferences in all things, from the temperature of your paga to that of your bath, and she, of course, as she is a slave, will bathe you. Why should a free man bother with such things, when there are slaves? Too, you may wish, from time to time, to attend to her slave needs, her need to be at your mercy, and to be helpless, as a slave, and her need to be handled and used as the slave she is, and such. Accustom her early then to binding and chaining, to the helplessness of slave bracelets, and perhaps shackles, to the blindfold and the gag, to encircling ropes, and buckled slave straps, perhaps to a harness, such things. A neck chain is good, fastening her to the slave ring at the foot of your couch. If she performs well you may permit her a blanket. See that she juices swiftly and squirms helplessly. Three or four Ahn of intermixed waitings, feedings, quiescences, touchings, strugglings, caressings, and such, are likely to be informative, even to a new girl, of the nature of her condition and various of its aspects. At the end of a few such mornings or afternoons your girl will be well aware that she is no longer a free woman. In such a way a girl learns her collar. If she becomes a nuisance at your feet, too much whining and begging, too many tears on your sandals, you may thrust her aside with your foot, or cuff her."

"Men cannot concern themselves wholly with slaves," said Mirus."Certainly not," said Selius Arconious.

"It seems there is much to remember," said Mirus.

"Not really," said Selius Arconious. "Just keep in mind that she is a slave, and is to be fully pleasing. If she is not, lash her."

"It is pleasant," said Mirus, "to be on a world where there are female slaves."

"Who would wish to be on any other?" said Selius Arconious.

Ellen lay on her belly at the left knee of her master, Selius Arconious. She lifted her head a little, and pressed her lips softly, almost timidly, to his left knee, a slave's kiss.

It is doubtless pleasant for the masters to own us. I wonder sometimes, on the other hand, if they understand us, or fully, our feelings, the feelings of the slave, the thrill for a woman of having a master, the rapture of being possessed, literally, how we desire to give ourselves up to them, the bliss we experience in our collars, our love. Is it so strange that we make excellent slaves? Do they really think that our desire to please, and be found pleasing, is motivated by nothing but the fear of blows or worse? We wish to love and serve. It is our nature. We are women. We are slaves. We long for our masters. We are incomplete without them.

Selius Arconious tore off a bit of warm, juicy meat and held it to the slave, who took it delicately between her teeth, juice running at the side of her chin, but he did not release it. She looked up at him, not understanding, uncertain. Would he permit her to have it? He released it and she took it gratefully, chewed it, and swallowed it. With his hand then he took her by the hair and gave her head a good-natured shake. She thrust her right cheek to the side of his knee, lovingly, fervently.

She lay amongst them, in her tunic, on her belly.

Her master had decided that she had been sufficiently fed.

Mirus was looking down upon her. She had little doubt he found her of interest, of interest in the keenest way a woman can be of interest to a man, of "slave interest."

She felt a *frisson* of apprehension and pleasure, as when a woman senses that a man sees her as what she is, a slave.

Will he then do contest for her?

If she is free, will he then move to collar her?

How pleased he must be, she thought, considering our pasts, and my pretenses and frivolities, to see me as I am now, a slave.

But I am pleased that he can so see me!

That is the way I want him to see me!

I would not want him to see me otherwise.

I want him to see me as I am, as what I am!

I am shameless, and happy!

Put me on a block, Masters, and sell me, if you wish. Let it be done to me as men choose. I would not be other than I am.

"Move your hair," he said, "that I may better see your collar."

She moved her hair forward, before her shoulders.

"Such things look well on women," said Mirus.

"Yes," said Selius Arconious.

The collar was a simple one, of a familiar type, particularly in the northern hemisphere, a band collar, about a half inch in height, closely fitting, locked at the back. Most such collars range from a half inch to an inch in height.

How far away now seemed Earth, and her former life! But had she not, even then, so long ago, dreamed of lying half naked, collared, beside a master?

"You may now lie as you wish," said Selius Arconious.

She brushed her hair back, behind her, and lay then on her left side, facing her master.

She had not been given permission to rise, of course.

She did dare to again kiss his knee, softly, timidly.

Perhaps he would caress her later.

She lifted her head to her master, tears in her eyes.

"How your slut looks upon you!" laughed Mirus.

"She is only a slave," said Selius Arconious.

Mirus looked at Ellen. "It seems you have learned your collar," he said.

"It has been taught to me, by masters," said Ellen.

"You are his," said Mirus.

"Yes, Master," she said. "I am his, wholly. I belong at his feet, as no more than his slave. I can be no more. I can be no less."

"You seem happy," said Mirus.

"We are happiest when we know that we will be lashed if we are not pleasing."

"That does not sound like the lessons you mouthed long ago," said Mirus.

"I was a fool, Master," said Ellen.

"I see," said Mirus.

"We resist that we may be conquered. We wish to know if you are strong enough to subdue and enslave us. We wish to belong to the strongest, to the most magnificent."

"Interesting," said Mirus.

"Men on this world have demonstrated their dominance over me, and their refusal to accept insubordination," said Ellen. "I love them for it!"

"It seems," said Mirus to Selius Arconious, "that you have found a slave, one who is fully your own."

"Yes, it seems so," said Selius Arconious, "for the moment, at least, or until I tire of her."

"Oh, please, no, Master!" protested Ellen.

"Why do you not do so, as well?" Selius Arconious asked Mirus, paying the slave no attention.

"I fear that is not done where I come from," said Mirus.

"But you are not now where you come from," said Selius Arconious.

"True," smiled Mirus.

"Will you not accept a woman for what she is?" asked Selius Arconious.

"It is seldom done on my world," said Mirus.

"In each woman," said Selius Arconious, "there is a slave, longing to be commanded forth and ordered to one's feet."

"Such truths may not be so much as uttered on my world," said Mirus.

"In each man," said Selius Arconious, "there is a master, and in each woman, a slave. Each seeks for the other."

"Where I come from," said Mirus, "I fear they seldom find one another."

"Consider the wells of profound realities tapped by dreams. In his dreams, those of his sleeping hours and those of his waking hours, what man has not yearned for a beautiful slave, and what woman, in such free, innocent, unguarded hours, has not yearned to be owned, to be collared, chained and mastered?"

"On my world," said Mirus, "society walls itself away from nature. It aligns its moats and stakes against the fields and forests. Sanctions, like pikes, array themselves against truth. Snares and traps are at every hand. The insects of conformity swarm and sting. All are vulnerable. Few dare speak their needs, their dreams."

"It must be a strange world," said Selius Arconious.

"It is a far different, far sadder, far more miserable world than this one, yours," said Mirus.

"But this is now your world," said Selius Arconious.

"Yes," said Mirus. "This is now my world."

"You must buy yourself a slave," said Selius Arconious.

"I think I shall," said Mirus.

"Will you buy a Gorean girl or a barbarian?" asked Selius Arconious.

"I think a barbarian," said Mirus. "I have a score to settle with the women of Earth."

"Excellent," said Selius Arconious.

"Mirus, Mirus," called the wounded man, from where he lay, to the side.

"I must go to my fellow," said Mirus, rising from beside the fire.

"He has lost much blood," said Fel Doron.

"Yes," said Mirus.

At this juncture Portus Canio and Fel Doron, wiping their hands on their thighs, rose, too, and approached Tersius Major, crouching down amongst the weapons, on his knoll, in the descending darkness.

"Give me drink, give me food, old friend," said Tersius Major to Portus Canio.

"Come down, old friend," said Portus Canio. "Stakes and thongs await, and knives can be heated, old friend."

"For the love of Priest-Kings," cried Tersius Major, "give me something to drink, something to eat!"

"You have broken the law of Priest-Kings," said Portus Canio.

"Priest-Kings are not to be loved," said Fel Doron. "They are to be respected, and feared, and obeyed."

"Do not approach!" suddenly shrieked Tersius Major.

"Have no fear," then said Portus Canio, angrily, hesitating, then stepping back, "I will not cross the circle of forbidden weapons."

"None may cross it!" cried Tersius Major.

At the edge of the camp, there was a motion in the grass, a subtle motion. We saw nothing. It was almost as though a snake, a large snake, might have moved there. A similar motion occurred a few yards to the left.

"I think we had best leave this place," said Portus Canio, uneasily.

"None may cross the circle!" cried Tersius Major.

"Several of them, I think, are about," said Fel Doron.

"As I understand it," said Mirus, who now joined the group, "the Priest-Kings enforce their laws by the Flame Death."

"When it pleases them," said Fel Doron.

"Have you ever seen such a thing?" asked Mirus.

"No," said Fel Doron.

"You?" asked Mirus.

"No," said Portus Canio.

"Priest-Kings do not exist," said Mirus.

"They exist," said Fel Doron.

"But you have never seen one?"

"No."

"It seems," said Mirus, looking at Tersius Major crouching down amongst the emptied pistols on the knoll, "the Priest-Kings are silent."

There were more stirrings in the grass.

"Perhaps there is more than one way in which Priest-Kings speak," said Portus Canio.

"Let us break camp," said Fel Doron. "It is dangerous to remain here."

This said, the men returned to the wagon, and the tharlarion. The few possessions were gathered together and placed in the wagon. Portus Canio and Mirus placed the wounded man in the wagon bed.

"Get in the wagon," Selius Arconious told his slave.

"May I not walk," she asked, "to lighten the wagon, Master."

"Will it be necessary to bind you hand and foot, and cast you to the wagon bed?" he asked.

"No, Master!" she said.

"Must a command be repeated?" he asked.

"No, Master!" she said, and, seizing the side of the wagon bed and, stepping on one of the spokes, supporting herself thereby, climbed hurriedly to the wagon bed, within which she knelt on the tarpaulins and supplies, and, looking out, clutched the sides of the wagon bed.

"It seems that Master is concerned with the safety of his slave," she said.

"No," he said, angrily. "I do not wish our journey to be delayed by the slowness of a she-tarsk."

"Yes, Master," she said, happily.

The tharlarion suddenly lifted its head on its thick neck, and looked about, nostrils flaring.

"Do not leave me!" shrieked Tersius Major.

"Then join us," said Portus Canio.

"Ho, on!" called Fel Doron from the wagon box, and turned the tharlarion southeastward.

The wheels of the wagon creaked and the tharlarion began to plod southeastward.

"Do not leave me! Do not leave me!" cried Tersius Major.

Ellen, kneeling in the wagon, clutching the sides of the wagon, saw him, as they moved past the knoll. The sleen, she knew, is a primarily nocturnal animal. Too, she was sure that there must, by now, be several in the vicinity.

"Do not leave me!" cried Tersius Major. The party then took its way from the camp. "Give me a weapon!" cried Tersius Major. "Give me a weapon!" Then, after a time, one could no longer hear him.

"Do Priest-Kings exist?" said Fel Doron.

"No," said Mirus.

"One does not know," said Portus Canio. "One does not know."

Chapter 28

What Occurred Four Days Later

It was toward morning.

"Master," whispered the slave.

"Yes?" said he.

"Will you not content your animal? Will you not pet her? Will you not stroke her, just a little, Master?"

"You, an Earth woman, beg as a slave to be touched?" he asked.

"Yes, Master," whispered Ellen, "as the most abject and needful of slaves!"

"No," he said.

"Master," she whimpered, "I am no longer a free woman, as once I was! I can no longer pride myself on my frigidity. I can no longer base my self-respect, my self-esteem, on my sexual inertness, on my superiority to sex. I can no longer go months or years without actual sexual relief, sublimating my physical needs into petulance, negativity, irritability, nastiness, pettiness and rivalry. I now need sex. Surely you understand, Master, that I have been embonded. I am now a slave! Men have aroused me! The collar has set me aflame. Slave fires rage now in my belly. I now belong to Masters, needfully!"

He was silent.

"Use me, Master," she whispered. "I beg to be used!"

"No," he said, coldly.

"You have not tied me, or chained me," she said. "You have not braceleted me, helplessly. You have not put me in slave hobbles! Perhaps I shall run away!"

"I would not advise it," he said, and her blood ran cold.

She heard, from the side, Portus Canio turn in his sleep. Fel Doron was yards away, on watch. To another side slept Mirus and his fellow.

"Please, use me, Master!" begged Ellen.

"No," he said.

How different it is from Earth, she thought. But on Earth the slave fires have been lit in the bellies of few women. On Earth women guard their bellies with fervor, lest they succumb to what they know lies within them, the ready tinder which might be ignited by the torch of bondage. She did not doubt, if only from her own experiences on Earth, the depth and pervasiveness, the readiness, of female sexual needs in the women of Earth. They were surely not other, physiologically, than those of their Gorean sisters. But there were surely great differences culturally and psychologically. Gor had not had centuries of inculcated denials and loathings. But sexual needs and frustrations, so much suppressed, so hysterically denied, must then express themselves in pathological transmogrifications, express themselves in a thousand disguises, conceal themselves behind the disfigurations of a thousand masks, and issue in a multitude of seemingly unrelated illnesses, miseries, petulances and hostilities! Indeed, some women were so well conditioned that they would belittle and despise the sexual needs of the normal woman, doubtless fearing such needs in themselves, and would try to make her feel guilty and ashamed, inferior and wanting, because of her actual vitality and health. Indeed, some women even pride themselves on their supposedly inert bellies and alleged superiority to sexuality. No wonder then that the human male, on Earth, often thought of the women of his species as being, however desirable, essentially sexless creatures, as being sexually minimal and torpid, as being above sex, or disinterested in it, as being, in effect, inert and frigid. But the polar wastes of so many women's bellies are not the results of anatomical or physiological climates or impoverishments; they are rather the engineered consequences of cultural and psychological tragedies. When an Earth woman is brought to Gor, then, at least as a slave, one of the first things done to her is to enlighten her as to her own nature and that of men, so that she will understand who it is who holds the whip and whose neck it is that is encircled with the collar, and, as a part of this, the masters, callously and brutally I fear, but they are not patient men, light the slave fires in her belly. She is then, in her collar, irremediably, a needful, sexual creature. Whereas the men of Earth, like the women of Earth, are commonly starved for sex, and are, consequently, usually the most obvious or most public victims of unsatisfied sexual need, there is little parallel to this amongst Gorean males. Whereas the sexual drives of Gorean males, not undermined by, nor diminished by, pathological, sometimes even inconsistent, conditioning programs, and such, tend to be frequently insistent, urgent, powerful, and uncompromising, they usually have at their disposal the means to satisfy their needs, and with ease. Slaves may be cheaply bought, particularly in times of unrest and war. Too, there are the paga taverns and brothels. On the other hand, the sexual needs of the slave are much at the mercy of the master. Accordingly, on Gor it is usually the slave who is the beggar in these matters and not the free man. She is in the agony of her needs. Will the master satisfy her or not? Commonly she pleads, as it is up to him, not her. This is an interesting turnabout from Earth. To be sure, doubtless there are women on Earth in whose bellies slave fires have been lit, and these, as much as any Gorean slave, must kneel or belly before their masters, beg sex, and hope that he will be kind to them. Let us suppose a male is brought to Gor as a free man. Now, let us also suppose that on Earth there is a particular woman, a desirable female of interest to him, who, in a typical Earth fashion, has frustrated him and has spurned his attentions. Let us also suppose that this woman is later brought to Gor, as a slave presumably, as she is a female, either with or without his knowledge. Let us then suppose that she is collared and slave fires are lit in her belly, and that she then comes into his ownership, either by a sheer coincidence, or by design, if he has arranged or requested her abduction. You may then imagine her at his feet, beautiful and helpless, naked in her collar, begging for sex. One supposes he would find this state of affairs unobjectionable.

She then, lying at his thigh, bit her lip, and choked back a sob. Tears rushed through her lashes. She rolled angrily, in frustration, away from him, and from the blanket, damp with dew. She pressed the side of her face, sobbing, into the grass. She felt the narrow, fibrous, cool, dawn-moist, living blades against her tear-streaked cheek.

He has not bound me, he has not shackled me, she thought. Is he so arrogant, so sure of me! Perhaps I shall run away! I could show him! I could teach him not to take me for granted! Does he think I am a slave? But, alas, I am a slave! Let him awaken and find me gone! How he treats me! I do not want to be a slave! I am miserable! But where could I, a slave, run? Should I be lost in the grasslands, or be eaten by ravaging sleen? And I am tunicked, branded, collared! There is no escape for me on this world! There is no escape for the Gorean slave girl! If I were not eaten, or did not die of exposure, nor of thirst or starvation, I would be caught and acquired, if not by him, by another, like a stray kaiila. Would my collar not show me slave? And even if I could somehow get it off, might not a man simply seize my leg and examine my thigh, noting there my brand? That would not be difficult. I am clearly marked. And what if he, my master, followed and recovered me? What would then be my fate?

She felt the wet grass on the side of her cheek. She was not then on the blanket, at the thigh of her master.

I must not displease him, she thought.

She then crept back on the blanket, to lie docilely at his thigh. She kissed his thigh, penitently. "Forgive me, Master," she whispered. She hoped she would not be beaten in the morning. He was master. She was slave. It will be done with me as my master pleases, she thought. Let me suffer agonies of need. It matters not. I am a slave. Perhaps sometime he will caress me. I hope that I shall not be beaten in the morning.

"Am I to be whipped, Master?" she asked.

"Perhaps," he said.

"Master?"

"Go to sleep," he said.

"Yes, Master," she said, and pressed her lips again, softly, to his thigh.

Yes, she thought. He is my master, and he does with me as he pleases. Oh, would that he would take pity on his slave! Please caress her, Master. Please caress her, Master. She loves you.

Why does he, a powerful, virile man, not caress me, she asked herself.

Am I so distasteful to him?

Does he wish to torture me?

How fearful it is sometimes, she thought, to be a slave. We are so vulnerable, and helpless!

Sometimes I am terrified that I am in a collar.

But, too, it is unutterably beautiful to be in a collar. I want it on my neck, with all it means.

I am a slave, and that is what I want to be. I would not be otherwise. I love being a slave, she whispered to herself. I love being a slave. And I love my master.

But would that he caressed me! But even if I hated him I would want him to caress me.

I need to be caressed.

I am a slave!

We had begun to move generally southeastward, across the grasslands. We did not encounter more sleen. Such beasts, burrowing, six-legged, sinuous, carnivorous, unless on a scent, tend to be territorial. Perhaps as early as the morning following our departure from our earlier camp, that which had been the scene of such conflict and carnage, we had traversed, and left behind, their usual hunting range. The prairie sleen is, incidentally, I have been told, much smaller than the forest sleen, which can upon occasion reach lengths of eighteen feet and weights of several hundred pounds.

The slave lay, sleepless, needful, uncaressed, at the thigh of her master.

The grasslands were muchly quiet.

The slave, in her duties, could scarcely have avoided hearing the casual conversations of masters. Soon, she gathered, Mirus and his fellow, now muchly recovered, though still unable to walk, would leave the group and make their way toward Brundisium, Mirus dragging an improvised travois, constructed of rope, a pair of poles and a tarpaulin. This device had been constructed the preceding evening, their trek having come to a small grove of dark temwood, bordering a tiny stream. In a day or two it was anticipated that worn trails might be encountered. They had already passed two small streams.

The slave's master had not touched her. She could not have been more deprived if she had been weeks in a dealer's house, in a cramped, readying cage, in which she might be kept until she was ready to scratch and scream with need and beg to be sent to an auction block. Portus Canio and Fel Doron scarcely looked upon her. She tried, as though inadvertently, as though not really intending to do so, to put herself before Mirus, and as a slave. But he, too, had paid her no attention. I need relief, she had shrieked to herself. How she then cursed the very thought of men, and, in particular, of honor.

On his other side, opposite the restless, discomfited slave, Selius Arconious had laid an unsheathed weapon.

"If you will not use me, Master," she whispered, "rent me, or assign me, to another!"

"You wish to be ordered to report to another?" he asked.

She shuddered; she could easily be put in such a situation; she could be ordered to report to another, in the full sense that is meant by "reporting to another." She could, she knew, at her master's merest word or whim be thusly put, in the fullness of her slaveness, to another's feet; she was branded; she was collared; she was slave.

"No, Master," she whispered.

He seemed to be listening, intently.

"I love you, Master," she whispered.

"As a slave loves?" he asked.

"Yes, Master," she said. "But even if I were a free woman the love I feel for you would make me your helpless slave! But I am not free, but am a true slave, and belong in the totality of my being to my master! There can be no greater love than the love of a loving slave!"

He was silent.

"Use me," she begged.

"No," he said.

"Use me in any way you please, as is your right, Master! Use me with rudeness, with brutality, if you wish! Claim me with the whip, teaching me my bondage, should it be your pleasure! But see me, look at me, hear me! Let your fingers stray but idly to my hair. Let your hand but lightly touch my forehead. Cast but a glance upon me! Though I am only a slave and animal I exist! I am here! Do not be cruel! Be kind! I am yours, wholly yours! Do not ignore me!"

"Rest," said he.

"Are you my master?" she asked, angrily.

"Yes," he said.

"Prove to me that you are my master," she said.

"Beware," said he.

"If you will not use me," she said, angrily, "sell me to one who will! Sell me to one who is a *man*!"

He turned then angrily, suddenly, to the slave but, at the same moment, there was a great roar splitting the silence of the camp and a dark, monstrous, violent shape leapt into the camp and Fel Doron, at the wagon, cried out, and the slave screamed, and Selius Arconious grasped for the weapon beside him and Kardok, gigantic and wild in the cold morning light, jaws slavering, eyes blazing, seized up Mirus and bent toward his throat, and

Mirus, with his feet and arms, tried to fend the beast away, but he was lifted from his feet and brought, struggling, toward the distended jaws, the wet, long, curved, whitish fangs and Selius Arconious, his blade held in two hands, was hacking at the back of the beast's neck, and then at the side of its throat, and it turned about, enraged, and put up a paw which, severed, was flung into the grass, and it turned full then upon Selius Arconious and Selius Arconious, with a cry of rage as hideous as that of the beast, thrust his blade deep into the chest of Kardok and the beast spun about wresting the blade from his hand.

Fel Doron rushed forward, Portus Canio had thrown off his blankets.

The second beast then seemed to appear from nowhere and scrambled its way on all fours, dirt spattering behind it, toward Selius Arconious and the fallen Mirus.

But at that moment it stopped, suddenly, abruptly, and lifted its hands, a great spear thrust into its body, the point and a quarter of the shaft emerging from its back.

"Bosk, Bosk of Port Kar!" cried Portus Canio.

Behind him was the warrior known as Marcus, of Ar's Station.

Ellen could not even speak so frightened, so breathless, was she. The force of the spear thrust must have been prodigious, and its might was compounded by the charge of the beast.

He called Bosk of Port Kar, that fearful larl of a man, drew then his blade and went behind the beast, seized the fur of its head, thus holding the head, and then, with two terrible strokes of that small, wicked weapon, cut away the head.

Kardok back on its haunches, bleeding, forced the blade of Selius Arconious from his own chest, wedging it away by the hilt with one paw and the flowing stub of the other. It turned then and staggered about. Wavering, it bent down to pick up the blade, but the bootlike sandal of Bosk held it, pressed, to the grass.

Kardok, snarling, blood now bursting with air, hissing like foam, spreading about its jaws and fangs, looked about himself, from face to face.

The slave covered her face with her hands, seeing herself so regarded.

Kardok then turned about, and staggered out, into the grasslands.

Bosk of Port Kar picked up the warmed, bright, red-rich, drenched blade of Selius Arconious, and held it out to him.

Selius Arconious then followed Kardok from the camp.

"No, Master! No, Master!" cried the slave.

She would have fled after her master, but her arm was seized by the mighty hand of Bosk of Port Kar, and she, small and female, struggling, was held as helplessly as in a vise.

"Let me go! Let me go!" she screamed.

But in a matter of moments Selius Arconious returned to the camp, wading through the grass; in his right hand was a bloodied sword; in his left hand, dangling, was the massive, bleeding head of Kardok.

"Master! Master!" cried the slave, overjoyed.

"On your knees," said Bosk of Port Kar.

Then she looked up at him from her knees. From his accent, she was certain that his origin was, like hers, Earth. She took him to have been English. Doubtless, if her surmise was correct, as to his world, and nation, of origin, he would have known her, from her accent, as easily as she knew him, known her to have been once of Earth, and doubtless it was as easy for him to conjecture her country or nation as it was for her to conjecture his. So he was an Earth man and she was an Earth woman, but here, on Gor, it was he who stood, and was perhaps even of the caste of Warriors, and she who knelt. Yes, she thought to herself. Here, on this world, it is he who stands and I who kneel! He does not in confusion, in guilty embarrassment, summon me to my feet but rather, in the order of nature, keeps me on my knees before him, where I belong!

"You deserted us, in the prairie," said Fel Doron.

"No," said Portus Canio. "They doubtless understood the meaning of the tarns in the sky, the scent of sleen. They then, under the cover of darkness, given the priorities of war, made their rendezvous, and saw to the care of the purloined gold."

Selius Arconious cast aside the great head of Kardok.

"I love you, Master!" cried the slave, from her knees.

"Who were those outside the camp, our unseen allies?" asked Fel Doron.

"They," said Portus Canio. "But there were but two, and thus they found it judicious, and most convenient, to do their work from without."

"We owe you our lives," said Portus Canio, "on more than one occasion."

Bosk shrugged.

"It was you who brought the tabuk to the camp?" said Fel Doron.

"Yes," said Bosk of Port Kar.

"You have drifted with us, have you not?" asked Portus Canio.

"Yes," he said.

"Why did you not announce yourselves, after the departure of the Cosians?" asked Fel Doron.

"There were five beasts," he said. "We located the bodies of only three. We conjectured then that two remained at large. As they had seemingly pursued you, we supposed they might not easily abandon that venture. Thus we stayed with you, unseen, that we might, if they should attack, act unexpectedly in your behalf, act with the element of surprise in our favor. But it seems you needed little assistance."

"You saved my life," said Mirus to Selius Arconious.

"Are we not then even?" asked Selius Arconious.

"Perfectly," smiled Mirus, and the two men grasped hands, warmly.

"The beasts, and their allies," said Portus Canio, addressing himself to Bosk of Port Kar and Marcus of Ar's Station, "followed us, at least in part, it seems, to obtain and destroy this slave."

"That was not my intent," said Mirus.

"No," smiled Fel Doron. "But it seems you were ready to carry her off."

"I found her, as you have doubtless conjectured," said Mirus, "a piece of goods of some interest, an attractive item of livestock."

Ellen looked at him, suddenly. Impressed, thrilled, she on her knees. How Gorean he seemed now to be! He understood her now not as a person to be abducted, but as a slave, an item to be purchased or stolen, and mastered. At last he seemed to understand the meaning of the collar on her neck, truly. She felt slave fire within her, heat at his virility. She had no doubt that when he had a woman, perhaps a purchased barbarian, she recalled he had a score to settle with the women of Earth, he would now master her—*fully.* My love is Selius Arconious, she said to herself, but surely one could do worse than belong to one such as Mirus, he who once owned me. Fortunate will be the woman who finds herself in his chains! I rejoice in her happiness, whoever she may prove to be, she who will one day wear his collar!

"There was interest, as well, it seems," said Fel Doron, "in Cosian gold."

"I did not understand that," said Mirus.

"Apparently not," said Fel Doron.

"I am not clear as to the nature of their interest in the slave," said Portus Canio. "Clearly it was not the sort of interest one would expect men to have in a well-curved slave."

Bosk of Port Kar looked upon the kneeling Ellen.

Beneath his gaze, Ellen trembled.

Could he ever have been of Earth, Ellen asked herself.

We are both of Earth, she thought. Thus, should this not win me some concern, some understanding, some sympathy, some tenderness, some softening of his regard? Yet see how he looks upon me! I am seen merely as female and slave!

Momentarily Ellen was angry.

How complacently he regards me!

It does not matter to him that I am here, a woman of his former world, now with a collar on my neck! Indeed, I can see in his eyes that he regards it with indifference.

Then she dared to look up at him, again, briefly, furtively, and then, frightened, looked away, and down, fearing to look again into his eyes, those of a free man.

But she was angry again.

For she had seen the smile on his lips. It was as though he had read her concern, and had been amused.

How dare he look upon a woman once of Earth that way, she thought.

Would he on Earth so look upon them? But presumably not, as they would be free, or most of them, save a few perhaps in secret enclaves.

She had seen the smile, that of a master.

He sees the collar on my neck as appropriate, she thought. Can he just look upon me and see that I belong in a collar?

How could he know that?

Clearly he has no intention of lifting me from my knees, and freeing me! He does not even look upon me with pity. He does not even express sympathy, or hasten to comfort and console me.

I saw his eyes!

He wants me in a collar! He likes it! If I were not collared, he might put me in one himself, if only to sell me or give me away! He looks at me! He understands me! He understands that I belong in a collar!

And doubtless he has seen many women of Earth in Gorean collars. We are nothing special. We are only more slaves.

Doubtless we belong in our collars!

Doubtless he likes us in our collars.

Would not any male?

Goreans, interestingly, believe the mistake was that we had not been made slaves on Earth. Our collaring, in their view, should have taken place on our native world.

Many Goreans also misunderstand the vaccination marks on many of us, taking them for a discreet slave mark, far inferior of course, in precision and beauty, to the various slave marks of Gor, usually burned into the thigh under the left hip.

She thought of Gorean free women.

Such hateful creatures!

He would pay heed to one of them, she thought. One does not ignore such! She would not be looked upon as he looks upon me! Would he not give her his undivided attention? Would he not treat her with the utmost civility and regard! Would he not esteem her and be solicitous for her, and see to it, as he could, that her many wants and concerns, however absurd or annoying, were attended to with alacrity and courtesy? But I, who was once a woman of his own world, how does he look upon me? How does he see me? I am at his feet, and find myself in his eyes looked upon as no more than what I now am, as no more than a slave!

But your lofty free women, she thought, would be no more than I, were they embonded!

I am half naked, kneeling, and collared, she thought.

Would you not like us all this way, or, at least, the pretty ones?

How many men of Earth, she wondered, see women so, see them as what they should be, see them as what they are?

He is now Gorean, she thought. But I, too, am now Gorean. He is Gorean as Master. I am Gorean as slave.

I am content.

"May I speak, Masters?" asked the slave.

"Yes," said Selius Arconious.

"Perhaps they thought I had heard them speak, in the great camp, outside Brundisium, and was thus inadvertently privy to some plan, some plot, or secret," said Ellen, "but I heard nothing, truly. It was all a terrible mistake. I am ignorant. I know nothing!"

Bosk of Port Kar turned his attention to Mirus. "You were allies of the beasts, you, and the other, there?"

"Once," said Mirus, "but no more, enemies now, surely."

"I think then it will not be necessary to kill you," said Bosk of Port Kar.

"I am pleased to hear that," said Mirus.

"I vouch for them," said Portus Canio.

"I, too," averred Selius Arconious.

"I, too," said Fel Doron.

Bosk of Port Kar smiled. The one time the slave had seen him smile. "That is sufficient," he said.

"Did you know the beasts were following you?" asked Bosk of Port Kar.

"No," said Selius Arconious.

"We thought them probably gone," said Fel Doron.

"But we did not know," said Portus Canio.

"No, we did not know," said Fel Doron.

"Yet," said Selius Arconious, "if they were still with us, this, it seemed, would be the likely morning for them to act, for this morning Mirus and his fellow are on to Brundisium, and we, with the slave, will trek toward Ar. Thus, if they wished to destroy all three, it seems that this would be the time to strike."

"We shortened our watches accordingly, to maximize alertness," said Portus Canio.

"Yet," said Fel Doron, "it seemed as though they sprang upon us as though from nowhere."

Bosk of Port Kar nodded.

"How is it that they would have anticipated an imminent division of your party?" asked Marcus, of Ar's Station.

"There," said Selius Arconious, indicating the object to the side, "the preparation of the travois, the wounded fellow of Mirus no longer to be transported in the wagon."

"He is strong enough now to travel so," said Fel Doron.

"The slave was not apprised of your suspicions," said Bosk of Port Kar.

"No," said Selius Arconious, "lest she inadvertently, by signs of uneasiness, alert the beasts as to such suspicions."

"That was wise," said Bosk of Port Kar.

On her knees, Ellen tensed, angrily. She was then muchly aware of her collar.

"How are things in Ar?" asked Portus Canio.

"The last we have heard," said Bosk of Port Kar, "this from those with whom we spoke at the rendezvous, the mercenaries grow increasingly restless, indeed, unpleasant. There have actually been skirmishes between them and the Cosian regulars in the city. The work of the Delta Brigade grows bolder. Rebellion may be imminent."

"What of Marlenus of Ar?" asked Fel Doron.

"It is thought he has been found," said Bosk of Port Kar. "To be sure, the matter seems unclear. One hears conflicting stories, of imposture, of forgetfulness, even of madness. But he is the key to open revolt. If he appears in the streets, sword in hand, standard raised, the people will cry out, and rise up. Then let Cos and her allies tremble. But without Marlenus I think the city will be uncertain and divided, and any open resistance would be foolishly precipitate, costly, and, I suspect, doomed."

"Talena yet sits upon the throne, a puppet for Cos?" asked Fel Doron.

"Yes," said Bosk of Port Kar.

"Torture and the impaling stake for her," said Portus Canio.

"Or the collar," smiled Bosk of Port Kar, regarding the collared, kneeling Ellen.

"But she is a Ubara, Master!" breathed the slave.

Then she feared she would be beaten.

Had she not spoken without permission?

But then Masters are often lenient in such matters. And, too, a slave can often sense when it is acceptable to speak and when it would be wise to request permission to speak. Often she has what might be thought of as a standing permission to speak. But this may of course be revoked, and thus is preserved the principle that a slave's permission to speak remains at the discretion of the master. She may always be silenced with a glance or word. Sometimes the master will ask, "Did you ask permission to speak?" To this question the customary response is, "No, Master. Please forgive me, Master." She may then be granted the permission to speak or not, as the master will have it.

"Who knows?" said Bosk of Port Kar. "Perhaps she is already a slave, and even now waits in terror, on her throne, in the loneliness of her chamber, in the empty halls of the Central Cylinder, startled by the least sound, even imagined, fearing to be claimed by her master."

"Surely you will trek with us to Ar," said Portus Canio.

"I and my fellow," said Mirus, "as said, are bound for Brundisium."

"Some pasangs from here we have fellows waiting, with tarns," said Bosk of Port Kar. "If all goes well, we will be aflight by tomorrow at this time."

"But surely," said Portus Canio, "we may share our breakfast with you?"

"That will please us," said Bosk of Port Kar.

"Get up and get to work," said Selius Arconious, unpleasantly.

"Yes, Master," said Ellen, quickly rising to her feet.

"She has pretty legs," said Marcus, of Ar's Station.

Ellen tried to pull down the tunic at the hems.

"Prettier than those of Phoebe?" asked Bosk of Port Kar.

"No, I do not think so," said Marcus of Ar's Station.

That "Phoebe," as they spoke of her, thought Ellen, so casually, so objectively, must be a slave. Surely they would not dare to speak so of the legs of a free woman.

What beasts men are, thought Ellen, to openly compare the limbs of slaves! Are we animals? And then, of course, devastatingly, the obvious thought came to her that yes, of course, they were animals!

"Get busy!" snapped Selius Arconious. For some reason, he seemed angry with her. Perhaps she had been a bit petulant, earlier, before the attack of the beasts, but surely he would not hold that against her! Not such a small thing!

"Yes, Master!" she said, stumbling, hurrying, running to the wagon, to fetch supplies, pans, utensils, bread, grains, that she might expeditiously set about preparing the men's breakfast.

As she worked, she saw, once, the eyes of Bosk of Port Kar upon her. About his lips there played a subtle smile. She reddened, angrily. Doubtless he knew her an Earth woman! He seemed amused then, to see her here, on this world, so far from her old world, on a world so different from her old world, she here reduced to a natural woman, reduced fittingly to a collared slave, anxiously hastening to serve masters.

Later, their simple repast finished, the men rose up.

"Well met!" said Portus Canio, gratefully.

"Well met," said Bosk of Port Kar.

The men clasped hands, and embraced, and then Bosk of Port Kar, Port Kar a port on the Tamber Gulf, rumored to be a den of cutthroats and pirates, and Marcus, of Ar's Station, once an outpost of Ar on the distant Vosk, took their leave.

The slave watched them disappear in the long grasses. They did not look back.

Shortly thereafter some supplies were given to Mirus. He was given, too, a sword, dagger, and spear. Then, with the help of Portus Canio and Selius Arconious, his weak fellow was placed on the travois. On this device, too, were placed the shared supplies and the weaponry. How different, thought the slave, the dagger, the sword, the spear, from the weapons with which Mirus had been hitherto familiar. They were weapons such that with them man might meet man, weapons requiring closure, and risk, weapons requiring skill and courage, not engineer's weapons, not weapons with which the pretentious, petty, effete and craven might effortlessly outmatch and overcome the might of heroes, surpass and vanquish brave and mighty men from whom in the order of a hardy nature they must shrink and hide. Yes, they were different weapons from those with which Mirus had been hitherto familiar, but she suspected that here, on this world, he would learn them, such weapons, and perhaps master them.

"Mirus, my friend," said Portus Canio.

"Yes?" said Mirus.

"When Bosk of Port Kar was in the camp we spoke briefly, apart, and he gave me something. I would like to show it to you."

Portus Canio, Fel Doron near him, drew from his pouch a heavy, shapeless object of metal, which seemed as though it had been deformed, perhaps twisted, bent in upon itself, and then fused, melted, in great heat."

"What is it?" asked Mirus.

"You do not know?"

"No."

"After we left our camp, of some days ago, Bosk of Port Kar, and his friend, visited the site of our camp, thinking we might still be there. Subsequently they followed us."

"What of your fellow, Tersius Major?" asked Mirus.

"No fellow of mine, he," said Portus Canio. "But Bosk and his friend found there only bones, pieces of bones, splintered, gnawed, shreds of clothing, torn, cast about."

"Sleen," said Mirus.

"It would seem so," said Portus Canio.

"Apparently sleen do not respect circles of forbidden weapons," said Mirus. "They, at least, are not prone to baseless superstition. They, at least, do not share your concern with Priest-Kings."

"Hold this," said Portus Canio, extending his hand, the weighty, shapeless object within it.

Mirus took the object, and regarded it. "It is a strange thing," he said, "possibly a meteorite, a star stone."

"Feel the weight," said Portus Canio. "Does it not remind you of something?"

Mirus turned white.

"Yes," said Portus Canio. "It is the remains of one of the forbidden weapons. The others were similarly destroyed. Bosk cast them away, into the grass. He kept this one to show me." So saying, Portus Canio took back the bit of fused, shapeless metal.

"Do you not fear to touch it?" asked Mirus.

"Not now," said Portus Canio. "It is no longer a weapon. Now it is nothing, only what was once a weapon."

"What force or heat could do this, and here, in the prairie?" asked Mirus, wonderingly.

"Surely the Priest-Kings have spoken," said Fel Doron.

"Do not be absurd, my friend," said Mirus. "There are no such things. You must overcome such beliefs."

"There is this," said Portus Canio, lifting the shapeless mass of fused, melted metal.

"There was a storm last night, to the north," said Mirus. "Lightning. Lightning struck the weapons. It destroyed them. It is an obvious explanation. They were metal, they were on a high place, on a knoll."

"That is certainly possible," agreed Portus Canio. Then he cast the piece of metal far from him, away, out into the grass.

"Priest-Kings do not exist," said Mirus.

"Even so," smiled Portus Canio, "I would advise you to keep their laws."

"They do not exist," said Mirus.

"I do not know," said Portus Canio. "But do not be afraid."

"I do not understand," said Mirus.

"If they do exist, perhaps in the Sardar Mountains, as many claim," said Portus Canio, "I think it is clear that we have little to fear from them, indeed far less to fear from them than from the caste of Initiates, which claims to speak in their name. The Priest-Kings, it seems to me, have little or no interest in us, in our kind, in our form of life, little or no concern with the doings of men, other than that their laws be kept."

"You suggest that they are rational? That they fear human technology?"

"Perhaps," said Portus Canio.

"They are real then?" asked Mirus.

"One does not suppose otherwise," said Portus Canio. "Perhaps as real as mountains and storms, as real as flowers, as tarns and sleen."

"They do not exist," said Mirus, again.

"I do not know," said Portus Canio.

"No," said Mirus. "It is lightning, lightning."

"Perhaps," said Portus Canio.

"Lightning," repeated Mirus. "Obviously lightning."

"That is quite possible," said Portus Canio.

"It looks like a pleasant day for trekking," said Mirus.

"Yes," said Fel Doron.

"In eight or ten days," said Portus Canio to Mirus, "you might reach the coast, and Brundisium."

"In some twenty days," said Fel Doron, "it is our hope to reach the Viktel Aria, near Venna."

At hearing the name of this city, the slave thought, naturally, of the slave, Melanie, whom she had met at the festival camp. Melanie, she recalled, had been sold to a man from Venna. She thought of the hundreds of cities and towns merely in known Gor, in which thousands of women such as she, tunicked and collared, served masters. Interestingly, it gave her a warm, deep, rich sense of identity, and belonging. Gone now were the uncertainties, the castings about, the miseries, the pain, the confusions, the ambiguities, the rootlessness, the anomie, of her former existence. She was now, at last, something societally meaningful, something actual, something understood, something accepted and real, something prized, something with an actual, clear value, a slave girl. The Viktel Aria is one of the great roads of known Gor, extending north and south of Ar for thousands of pasangs.

Mirus then adjusted the travois ropes about his shoulders.

"Bid him farewell," said Selius Arconious.

Ellen went to Mirus and knelt before him. "Farewell, Master," she said. Then, at a gesture from Selius Arconious, she put down her head and humbly kissed his feet. Then she lifted her head and looked at him. Tears brimmed in her eyes. It was he who had brought her to Gor. "Thank you, Master," she whispered, so that Selius Arconious, who was standing to one side, could not hear. "Thank you for bringing me here, thank you for putting me in a collar, thank you making me a slave."

"It is nothing," he said, a Gorean remark.

Perhaps, she thought to herself, to you it is nothing, Master, but to me it is everything!

Then she again lowered her head and, gratefully, kissed his feet, again.

He moved back a little.

The men then exchanged farewells.

"You have taught me something of this world," said Mirus to Selius Arconious. "It is my hope that I may one day be worthy of a Home Stone."

"It is nothing," said Selius Arconious.

The two men clasped hands, and then embraced, and Mirus put his shoulders into the ropes. At the edge of the small camp he paused and turned, regarding Ellen. He smiled. "Farewell," said he, "slave girl."

"Farewell," said she, "Master."

Chapter 29

What Occurred Near the Viktel Aria, In the Vicinity of Venna

The slave had run on ahead.

"Masters!" she called, delightedly, emerging from between the trees. Never before had she seen such a road. It was seated with large, fitted stones. She knew that these went down to a depth of several feet. In making such a road, a great trench is dug, and then the stones are laid, wall-like, within the trench. The road is, in effect, a sunken wall, and such a road will last for hundreds, even thousands, of years, with little repair. How old the road might be she had no idea, but she could see ruts worn in the stone, presumably by the continuing passage of carts and wagons, season in and season out, decade in and decade out.

She stepped back a little, as a caravan was passing, and there was a ringing of the bells on a kaiila harness. Guards flanked the caravan, and regarded her idly, appraisingly, as they rode past, conjecturing, as she wore a collar, her lineaments. She stood straighter, but did not dare smile, for fear one of the riders might, on an impulse, loosening his rope, spur toward her and in a moment, as she fled, have his cast, tightening loop upon her. But she did stand straight, and beautifully. She was no longer ashamed of her body, or embarrassed by it, now that it was owned. She loved it, and prized it, and was proud of it. But she knew that it was not only her body that was owned, but the whole of her. All of her was slave, and belonged to her master. There were pack kaiila aplenty with the caravan, in files, most roped together, but, too, there was a long train of wagons, behind, some open and some closed. A caravan this size, she conjectured, would not be the property of a single merchant, but doubtless of a number of merchants leagued together, traveling thusly for purposes of safety in what were doubtless unsettled, dangerous, troubled times.

From the pommel of one saddle, seemingly not that of a guard, but perhaps of a civilian or merchant's agent accompanying the caravan, there looped downward a light, graceful chain to the throat of a naked, blond slave. She walked proudly. How beautiful she is, thought Ellen. Their eyes met. The blonde tossed her head, and gave her no more notice. This angered Ellen and she ran forward and then alongside the slave. "Do not toss your head at me!" said Ellen. "I have a tunic! You are only a naked slave! You are naked! Naked! Only a naked slave, publicly marched on a chain, exposed on a common road!"

The slave cast a furious glance at her but the fellow about whose pommel was looped the chain put back his head and laughed loudly, and gave the chain a little, admonitory shake. "Eyes front, Marga," he commanded her.

"Yes, Master," she said, frightened, and turned her head forward, and held it deliberately, fixedly, in that attitude, and kept her eyes, too, squarely ahead, not so much as glancing to the side.

Ellen was muchly pleased by this. She laughed delightedly, but muchly to herself. She is afraid, she thought. She is afraid of her master! She is well mastered! Let them all be well mastered!

Eyeing the guards then, one of whom, as though to frighten her, turned his kaiila toward her, Ellen retreated to the trees at the edge of the road. Selius Arconious was now there, having come forward at her call, from the wagon.

"The road! The Viktel Aria, surely, Master!" said Ellen.

"Yes," he said.

The kaiila and wagons continued to pass.

"Were you discomfiting that slave?" he asked.

"Yes, Master!" laughed Ellen. "She dared to toss her head at me, so I ran to her and called her attention to my tunic, that I was clothed, be it only so minimally, so revealingly, and to the fact that she was only a naked slave, only that, and one publicly marched on a chain, one blatantly exposed on a common road."

"She was quite lovely," said Selius Arconious.

"I suppose that that was not difficult to see, Master," said Ellen, "as she was chained and naked."

"Quite lovely," he said.

"Perhaps a little tall, Master?" said Ellen.

"Not necessarily," he said.

"Oh," said Ellen. Ellen would have conjectured that the blonde was some two inches taller than herself.

"It was thoughtful of her master to so display her," said Selius Arconious.

"Master?" asked Ellen.

"Yes," he said. "It is in the nature of a generous, welcome gift to fellow itinerants, to accompanying wayfarers, a way to lighten the burdens, sometimes the unrelieved boredom, of long marches. The sight of such as she, you see, provides a pleasure, a luscious glimpse, a pleasant interlude, for weary travelers upon a long road, at the least an incentive to increase one's pace, to hurry one's steps to the nearest paga tavern."

"Paga tavern, Master?"

"Yes," said he, "where the use of such as she goes with the price of a drink."

"I see, Master," said Ellen.

"Yes," he said.

"Perhaps, Master," said Ellen. "But well did I humble her!"

"Doubtless," said Selius Arconious.

"Oh, look, Master!" said Ellen, pointing, having then first noticed towers in the distance.

"That is Venna," said he. "Ar is but two day's journey south from Venna. Indeed, those of Ar often have villas in the vicinity of Venna, and enjoy the races there."

"Will we enter upon the road when the caravan passes, Master?" asked Ellen.

"Perhaps tomorrow morning, early," said Selius Arconious. "The heat of the afternoon is now upon us. Portus Canio and Fel Doron are even now unhitching the tharlarion and preparing a camp."

"I will stay here a moment, and watch," said Ellen.

Selius Arconious turned about, and made his way back through the trees.

Ellen supposed that she should have asked permission to stay near the road, but then she dismissed the thought. Surely this little bit of assertiveness on her part, if that is what it was, was unimportant. Too, she was not too pleased with Selius Arconious, for he had, as in the grasslands, muchly ignored her, and had not put her to the usages of a slave, those usages which were appropriate for her, and which she, collared, craved. Indeed, some of her earlier feelings of ambiguity pertaining to Selius Arconious had begun to reassert themselves. I should hate him I suppose, she thought, as I am a woman of Earth, and he put a collar on me, a collar, but I do not. I love him and love him dearly. And I want to love him in the deepest way possible, as a slave. But I fear he is a weakling. Indeed, sometimes, as she lay in her place at his thigh in the night, begging his attentions, and failing to obtain them, she had, occasionally, petulantly, pettily, as in the morning before the attack of the beasts, challenged him to prove that he was her master, or to give or sell her to another, to one who would be a master to her slave, to one who was a *man*. In her frustration she had lashed out at him, in her petty way. To be sure, she did not wish to belong to another, though she was sure that another would not be as understanding, as patient, as kind, as boring, as neglectful, as trivial with her as Selius Arconious, but would see to it, firmly, severely, whip in hand if need be, that the finest and fullest of her slave service would be unhesitantly and perfectly, even fearfully, rendered.

She waited by the road while the caravan passed. One of the wagons was a slave wagon, with bars. Most of the women in it crouched down, below the low siding, a foot above the wagon bed, hiding, that they not be seen. Ellen supposed they might be free women, captured, or new slaves. In such a wagon they would doubtless be stripped, as women usually are in such a conveyance. Certainly she could see bared shoulders. They are perhaps shy, thought Ellen, or embarrassed to be seen as they doubtless now were, denied even the mockery of a tight thong and slave strip, presumably slave naked. One woman, however, was standing, and clothed, or partially so, in the remnants, or residual rags, of what might have been the final undergarments worn beneath the cumbersome Robes of Concealment. She clutched the bars, with two hands, looking out, in misery, in terror. Did she think to find succor, or rescue, or to elicit pity, from behind those narrow, closely set bars? Did she not know she was in a slave wagon? Did she not know she was on Gor? Did she not know that there were men here? Ellen thought that perhaps she had been troublesome, and that that was why she had been permitted, for the time, to retain some covering, that its removal then, at the hands of captors or masters, might be all the more momentous and shattering to her. It looked as though she had good legs, and her left shoulder, too, was exposed. Doubtless she will soon be in a collar, thought Ellen. In a few Ehn the last wagon had passed, and the following guards, carrying lances, mounted on kaiila, as well. Some tinier carts, some drawn by hand, followed the main column, though doubtless not associated with it, rather merely hoping in its shelter to shield themselves from brigandage.

Ellen supposed she had been away a rather long time, but she did not give this matter much thought. She smiled to herself. By now the camp would be largely made, and much of the work would be done. Excellent, she thought.

She cast one last look at the distant towers of Venna, and thought again of the former Lady Melanie of Brundisium, she sold at the festival camp, now doubtless a lovely, suitably embonded, obedient chattel behind those far walls.

I wish her well, she thought. And I hope she has a master who knows how to master her! Then she turned and made her way back through the trees, to where the men would have made the camp.

Selius Arconious is a weakling, she thought.

Most of the camp work will be done, she thought. Good!

When she reached the camp the men were waiting for her. Though in the presence of free men she decided she would not kneel.

"Greetings, Masters," she said. Certainly it would not be wise to neglect such an obvious token of deference as an appropriate form of address.

"Remove your tunic," said Selius Arconious.

"Master?" she asked. Her voice broke, slightly.

His gaze was not pleasant.

Certainly she did not wish for a command to be repeated, as that is a common cause for discipline. She slipped the tunic over her head. She hoped that she had not hesitated too long before doing so.

She then decided it would be a good idea to kneel, and so she did so, and, a moment later, trembling a little, before their gaze, carefully widened her knees. She now regretted not having knelt when she had first come into their presence. It is common for a slave to kneel when she comes into the presence of a free person, and to kneel, too, should they, as in entering a room, come into her presence. She clutched the tunic in two hands, desperately, frightened.

Selius Arconious approached her. He held out his hand. "Give it to me," he said.

She lifted the tunic up to him.

"Hold your wrists before you, closely together, veins to veins," he said.

"Master?" she asked. But she did as she was told, and wasted no time in doing so.

Her wrists were then bound together, tightly, separated only by looping cordage, but in such a way that a length of rope was left free in front, extending from her wrists, falling to the ground. By this free portion of the rope she could be led about, by her bound wrists. It constituted, in effect, a tether.

"Surely I have not displeased masters," she said.

"There is an abandoned tarsk pen nearby?" Selius Arconious asked Fel Doron.

"Yes, as I said," said Fel Doron. "I gathered some of the firewood there."

"Then let us show our little she-tarsk," said Selius Arconious, grimly.

Ellen was yanked rudely to her feet by the tether. She almost lost her balance. Then she was dragged, stumbling, perforce, trying not to fall, behind her impatient, precipitate master.

The tarsk pen, with its shed, was in ruins. But there was, at one side, the remains of the pen's siding. It consisted of horizontal poles, some four inches thick. Here Selius Arconious angrily kicked away two of the lower horizontal poles, and left one horizontal pole in place, which was about four feet above the leaves, wood chips, rotted straw, and turf.

"Master, please!" said the slave.

She was forced down on her knees before the pole, facing it, and the interior of the pen, and then, in a moment, her wrists were lashed to the pole. She then knelt there, before it, her wrists up, fastened to it.

"What are you going to do, Master?" she wept.

But Selius Arconious had returned to the wagon, and there, as nearly as the slave could tell, looking wildly over her right shoulder, began rummaging through his belongings.

In a moment or two he had returned to where she knelt before the pole, her wrists up, bound to it. Portus Canio and Fel Doron were in the vicinity.

"Masters?" she asked. She had been unable to see well behind her, given the angle from which Selius Arconious had approached. Accordingly she was not clear on what he might have fetched, if anything, from the wagon.

"I purchased this at the festival camp, outside Brundisium," said Selius Arconious.

"It looks like an excellent buy," said Portus Canio.

"I think it will do, nicely," said Selius Arconious.

"What is it, Master?" asked the slave.

"A whip," he said. "A slave whip."

"No, Master!" cried the slave.

"I thought I might need it," said Selius Arconious.

"You were right," said Portus Canio.

"It is a useful tool," said Fel Doron. "One should keep such a thing on hand. One never knows when it will be needed."

"No, Master!" wept the slave. "Please, no, Master!"

She struggled to her feet, before the pole, twisting about, wildly, pulling at her bound wrists. There was no mistaking the device in the hands of Selius Arconious. She had not realized, perhaps foolishly, that he owned such a thing, that he would even own such a thing. "Get back on your knees," she was told. She returned to her knees, facing the pole, staring ahead.

"What are you going to do, Master?" she asked, quavering.

"What do you think, little fool?" he said.

"Master?" she said.

"Whip you," he said.

"No, Master!" she cried, in alarm. "Do not whip me!"

"Prepare to be whipped," said he.

Her hair was thrown before her body.

Normally a slave girl's hair is behind her shoulders, that there be less impedance to the vision of masters. If she is naked the hair is sometimes placed before her shoulders, that it may be brushed back by the master, or put behind her by the slave, upon the command to do so. The beauty of the slave is, of course, a source of great pleasure to the master.

"It is a joke, surely a joke, Master!" she said. "You have frightened me! I will be good!"

"Prepare to be whipped," said he, angrily, "slave."

"You cannot whip me, Master!" she cried. "I am an Earth woman! You cannot whip an Earth woman! Earth women are never whipped! We are never punished, no matter what we do! Even if we ruin lives, and destroy men, we are never punished!"

"Embonded women do not ruin lives and destroy men," he said. She heard the strands of the leather shaken out.

"I am an Earth woman!" she cried. "We are never punished! Such things are not done to Earth women!"

"You are not now on Earth," he said.

She began to sob.

"Surely you have been whipped before," he said, "if not on Earth, where you should have been, and perhaps frequently, then on Gor."

"Yes, Master," she wept.

"Is it true," he asked, "that Earth women, on Earth, are never whipped?"

"I do not know," she wept.

"If they are free, of course," he said, "it would be inappropriate to whip them."

"Yes, Master," she cried.

"But doubtless a whipping would do some of them a great deal of good," said Portus Canio.

"Doubtless," said Fel Doron.

"But what of the women of Earth who are not free?" asked Selius Arconious.

"All the women of Earth are free!"

"That is surely false."

"Yes, Master," she sobbed.

"So what of those who are not free?"

"If they are not free, then they are subject to the whip," said Ellen.

"Do you feel that they should not be whipped?"

"It is up to their masters!" she said.

"But what of a woman of Earth who is brought to Gor and enslaved?" he asked. "What do you feel about such a one? Should she be whipped?"

"It is up to her master," said Ellen.

"Precisely," he said.

"What have I done to displease you, Master?" she cried.

This inquiry was met with silence, which was more terrifying to her than a response. A thousand subtleties, and fears, rushed in upon her. There seemed so much, great and small, that she might have done differently.

"For what reason would you whip me?"

"You are a slave," he said. "I do not need a reason."

She moaned with misery, and fought the bonds, but dared not rise from her knees. It was true. As a slave she could be beaten at the master's pleasure, for any reason, or for no reason.

She cast about, wildly, in her mind, for some way to allay his anger, to put him from his purpose, to avoid the punishment which, in her heart, she knew she deserved, and only too well.

Then a desperate thought came to her.

She looked over her shoulder, and smiled, as prettily, as innocently, as, under the circumstances, she could. "Have I been inadvertently troublesome in some way, Master?" she asked. She asked this, lightly, dismissively, even flippantly. Too, she asked this as though quizzically, as though she might be genuinely puzzled to find herself on her knees, bound at the pole, or rail, as she was. "If so, it is my hope that Master will forgive me." In this way she sought to reduce, or trivialize, any possible imperfections in her service. In this way she hoped to put Selius Arconious off his guard, and divert his wrath.

"She is a clever slave," said Fel Doron.

"Yes," said Portus Canio. "But I do not think that her cleverness will do her much good."

She was not much pleased to hear the comments of her master's fellows. She had thought herself subtle. But they spoke as if her subtlety, on which she was congratulating herself, was naught but the patent trick of an ignorant, foolish slave, indeed, a trick, in its obviousness, transparency and shallowness, insulting to the master. Did she think he was so simple, a fool?

But theirs were not the hands on the butt of a stern, corrective device.

"Have I been troublesome, Master?" she pressed, again.

"Occasionally," said Selius Arconious.

"Forgive me, Master," she said.

"Have no fear," said he. "I will take it out of you."

"Master?" she asked.

It was as though he was prepared to let her believe that he might have been so naive as to have accepted her own self-regarding, trivializing assessment of her infractions, which was, of course, absurd, as she now grasped, but was yet at the same time making quite clear to her something that she should have known, that no omissions, evasions, laxities, imperfections, or infractions whatsoever, even the tiniest and most trivial, were acceptable in one such as she, a slave girl.

She was thus summarily defeated by her master, casually, and on her own grounds of contest.

Her heart sank for she realized then she was not at the feet of an Earth man. She was at the feet of a Gorean.

Such tend not to be tolerant of even trivial, and inadvertent, imperfections of service. Once this sort of thing is understood, interestingly, it is remarkable how scrupulous a slave can be concerning even the smallest details of her service, her glances, her kneelings, her serving of dishes, her kissings of sandals, and such.

And she well understood, to her misery, that her own imperfections of service, extending even to actual infractions, far exceeded matters inadvertent and trivial.

She must try again!

"Master is kind!" she suddenly cried, lightly. "After the dance in the festival camp, when I was to be given fifteen lashes, ten for not having declared, however honestly, a proficiency in slave dance, and five for having spoken without permission, Master purchased the strokes, each for a tarsk-bit, and saved me the beating! How grateful I am to Master for his generosity, his thoughtfulness, his kindness! He would not have me beaten. And surely I have nothing to fear from him now!"

"Ah, yes," said Selius Arconious. "The festival camp, outside Brundisium."

"Yes, Master!" cried the slave, hopefully.

"It amused me," said Selius Arconious, recollectively, "to see you dance as a slave, the slave you are. And well did you writhe, bond-slut."

"Thank you, Master," said Ellen, uncertainly.

"You do not know the effect you can have on men, petty, tormenting creature!" said he, suddenly, angrily. "To see your ankle, the turn of a calf, the sweetness of an arm, the softness of a small shoulder, the turning of a wrist, the delicacy of a hand, the provocative call of your love cradle, the joy of your waist, made for a slave chain, your swelling bosom, its delights, the whiteness of your encircled throat, the beauty of your face, the bright glance of your eyes, the trembling softness of your embonded lips! You could drive a man mad with passion and desire! It is for women like you that collars are made! What man, seeing you, would not want to own you!"

"Oh, Master!" cried Ellen. "And I am your slave!"

"And I will not be yours!" he said, angrily.

"Master?" she asked.

"Do you not know, truly, why I purchased those strokes?" he asked. "Do you think I would let another whip you? No! I will have you under my whip! Under *my* whip! You are *mine* to whip!"

She cast about again, frantically, for a new tactic, a new strategy, a new avenue of escape.

"You do not even care for me, Master!" cried Ellen. She must challenge his affections, appeal to his pity, confuse him, take him off balance, force him to acknowledge his undoubted feelings for her. Surely that would stay his hand! She was certain he had such feelings, for he had permitted her, certainly, in the past few days, to get away with much slackness of service and deference, to behave in ways that are simply not permitted to slaves, and certainly not to those with strong masters. This, it seemed, would be her last effort to turn him from what she feared might be, but yet trusted would not be, his purpose. This stratagem, she was sure, would succeed.

"You are correct," he said.

"Master!" she cried.

"Who cares for a slave?" snarled Selius Arconious.

"Master!" protested Ellen.

"One lusts for slaves, one wants them, madly," said he. "One chains and collars them, one uses them, one puts them as one wishes, in whatever postures or attitudes, one ropes and thongs them, one leads them about on leashes, one forces them to serve, fearfully, abjectly, licking and kissing, kneeling, crawling, begging to please! Such inspire in men the mightiest of conquering passions! There is no triumph which compares with the ownership of a woman! With a slave at one's feet, one's head brushes the stars!"

"It is so, too, for a woman, Master!" wept Ellen. "That is our place! That is our place in nature! We long to be in our place in nature! We belong at your feet! We beg our collars! We lift and kiss our chains in gratitude! We ask only to kneel, to be used, and to serve!"

"But do not speak of caring!" cried Selius Arconious.

"I speak of it, Master!" cried Ellen.

"No!" he cried, angrily.

"I think you care for me, Master!" wept Ellen. "You care! You care for me! I am sure you care for me, Master! You must care! You must care, Master!"

"No!" he cried, in fury.

"Yes, yes, Master!" she wept.

"Whether I care for you or not," said he, "I own you!"

"Yes, Master!" breathed Ellen.

"And I am going to make you a slave amongst slaves," he said. "I am going to master you as few slaves are mastered. I am going to master you, wholly, Earth slut, every hair of your head, every inch of you!"

"Be kind!" she begged.

"You will know yourself owned," he said.

"Do not whip me, Master!" begged Ellen.

"Do you realize the will power that has been required for me, day and night, not to seize you, again and again, and put you to slave service? Do you understand what it is to lie in the darkness, with you at my thigh, and not grasp you by the hair as a master a slave, to warn you that your taking is upon you, not force you, in all your embonded loveliness and helplessness, to serve my fiercest pleasures, not seize you in my arms and possess you, yes, possess you, *have you*, you beautiful, tormenting collared slut, with all the authority, the violence and passion which it is your lot to endure as slave and my right to inflict as master?"

"I love you, Master!" cried the slave. "But you never touched me, Master! Take me! Take me now! Take your slave! But you did not touch me, Master, why? Why?"

"It was a test, slave girl," said he, "and you failed it miserably!"

"How a test, Master?"

"I thought I would give you some laxity, to see if you could handle it, to see what you were really like. And I found out! You are nasty, small, petty and vain!"

"No, Master!" cried the slave.

"You tried to manipulate me, with sorry feminine tricks," he said.

"No, Master!" she wept. But well did she recall, to her misery, a thousand omissions, slights and provocations. She recalled how she had challenged him to prove himself her master, to sell or give her to another, who might provide the master to her slave, to place her into the possession of one who was a *man*.

"Even today," he said, angrily, "you did not ask permission to remain at the road, but announced that you would do so. Do you know the penalty for such insolence? You dallied in returning to the camp, until the work was largely done. Do you know the penalty for such truancy? You did not kneel when entering our presence! Do you know the penalty for such disrespect? You deserve to be left in the forest for sleen! On the road, itself, earlier, you ran beside a slave and discomfited her, and risked calling the attention of armed men to yourself. You are fortunate that the discipline of the guards was such that you were not thonged, tethered to a pommel, and taken along for an evening's raping."

"She tossed her head at me, insolently," said Ellen. "She was haughty!"

"Surely that is a small thing," said Portus Canio, "a squabble amongst slave girls, nothing with which masters need concern themselves."

"So, too, it seems to me," said Fel Doron.

"Yes, Masters! Thank you, Masters!" said Ellen.

"That leaves, of course, many other shortcomings," said Portus Canio.

"True," said Fel Doron.

Tears burst from the eyes of the slave. She was helplessly tethered, tied for whipping.

"Surely you care for me, Master!" she cried.

"You are petty, small and nasty!" he said. "You deserve only the whip and chain."

"I want the whip and chain," she cried out, suddenly, startling herself. She wept. "Without it how can I know that I am female and yours?" she whispered.

A bit of wind moved through the leaves, overhead. She felt it on her back, too, where her hair had been thrown forward, before her body.

Suddenly, in terror, she realized the meaning of that.

Nothing, no matter how trivial, would be interposed between her back and the whip.

"But I want love, as well!" she cried.

He laughed, sardonically, skeptically.

"It is true!" she cried. "And I love you! Yes, I do! I love you, Master! I love you, Master! Surely you love me, too, if only a little?"

"No," said he, angrily, "but I lust for you, and you will be well taught what that means at the foot of my couch!"

"Surely you care for me, if only a little, Master!" she said.

"No," said he, angrily.

"Oh, no, no, Master!" wept Ellen.

"Strive to be worthy of being cared for," said Portus Canio. "Many men will feel a fondness for a kaiila or a pet sleen, so why not for a slave? Let yourself strive with all your might, with all your intelligence, with all your zeal and diligence, with all your helplessness and vulnerability, with all your service and beauty, for the least touch, for a gentle word, a kind glance."

"Prepare to be whipped, slave girl," said Selius Arconious.

"Do not whip me, Master!" begged Ellen.

"Are you in a collar?" asked Selius Arconious.

"Yes, Master!"

"Is it a slave collar?"

"Yes, Master!"

"Then you are a slave?"

"Yes, Master."

"Whose collar is it?"

"Yours, Master!"

"Then whose slave are you?"

"Yours, Master!"

"Prepare to be whipped," said he.

"Wait, Master!" she cried.

The lash did not fall.

"Recall that I am from Earth, Master!" she wept. "That is a different culture from yours. The women of Earth, certainly most of them, are not accustomed to being slaves. They would not even understand what it is to be a slave!"

"Every woman," said Selius Arconious, "understands what it would be, to be a slave."

"I am other than your Gorean women!" cried Ellen. "I am more delicate, more sensitive, finer! Your culture is primitive, a culture in which such a thing as the beating of a slave may be accepted, but I am not of that culture. In deference to my background, my upbringing, my education, my refinement, such things should not be done to me! They are not for me! I am above them! I should not be subjected to such things. They are inappropriate for me! Your culture is barbaric. You are barbarians! I am not a barbarian! I am civilized! I am a civilized woman!"

"'Girl,'" corrected Selius Arconious.

"Yes, Master," she said.

"It is you who are the barbarian," said Portus Canio, matter-of-factly.

"It is true, Master," acknowledged Ellen, "that Gorean is not my native tongue."

"Thus," said Portus Canio, "you are a barbarian."

"Yes, Master," said Ellen, twisting in the ropes, "in that sense."

The usual criterion on Gor for a barbarian is one who does not speak Gorean, or, perhaps better, whose original language is not Gorean. Ellen, for example, who is now fluent in Gorean, continues to be thought of as a "barbarian."

"In more than that sense," said Portus Canio.

"Yes, Master," granted Ellen. Ellen knew that those brought to Gor from Earth were accounted barbarians in a sense stronger than one merely linguistic, one having to do with a remote and commonly little-understood point of origin. Many Goreans, incidentally, assume that "Earth" is a remote locale or land on their own world.

"You speak of yourself as civilized," said Portus Canio, "say, in contradistinction, from Goreans?"

"Yes," said Ellen, a little uncertainly.

It is hard to participate in such a conversation when one is on one's knees, bound naked at a pole, and has a whip somewhere behind one.

"Your world is civilized?" asked Portus Canio.

"Yes, Master," said Ellen.

"On the trail, from time to time," said Portus Canio, "Mirus and I whiled away many a pleasant Ahn in conversation."

"Yes, Master?" said Ellen, apprehensively.

"You recall Mirus?" he asked.

"Certainly, Master," said Ellen, "—*Master* Mirus."

Ellen was now much on her guard. Had it been a trap? A slave girl does not address a free person by their name, but will use the expressions 'Master' or 'Mistress', or, sometimes, if referring to one's owner, 'my Master' or 'my Mistress.' Similarly, in referring to a free person, one would commonly use expressions such as 'Master Publius', 'Mistress Publia', and so on. If asked, say, her master, the slave might respond, 'My master is Selius Arconious, of Ar', or such.

"I am not at all certain that your world is civilized," said Portus Canio.

"Master?"

"I gather you do have mighty machines, and such."

"Yes, Master."

"But there are, as I understand it, no Home Stones on your world."

"No, Master, or I would suppose not."

"How then can it be civilized?"

Ellen was silent.

"Mirus spoke to me of monstrosities of indiscriminate death, contrived by the clever and mindless, of crowdings, of manipulations, of hatreds, pollutions, diseases and famines. He spoke of the ruination of lakes and forests, of the extinction of life forms, of a world being poisoned. He spoke to me of a world in which brothers might kill brothers, or friends friends, were a particle of power or profit to be gained, a world in which nature is scarred, wounded and betrayed, a world in which human beings do not know one another, nor do they care to do so, a world in which fidelity is scorned and honor mocked."

Ellen was silent.

"Our world," said Portus Canio, "is a green world, a fresh, clean, honest world. It has its terrors, but it is a beautiful world, and a natural world. I do not think it is inferior to yours."

"No, Master," said Ellen.

"I do not think I would care to live on your world," he said.

"No, Master," said Ellen.

"Do you dare to call your world civilized?" he asked.

"No, Master," whispered Ellen.

"Your world is in many ways a thousand times more primitive than ours," he said, "and Gor, in many ways, is a thousand times more civilized than yours, than the unnatural moral barbarism which engendered your likes."

"Yes, Master," whispered Ellen.

"And you, a smug, haughty product of that world, dare to speak of yourself as civilized! You are only another barbarian, a true barbarian. I wonder if such as you are worthy of being brought to our world, even as slaves."

"Forgive me, Master," wept Ellen.

"So," said Selius Arconious, angrily, "you are other than Gorean women? More delicate, more sensitive, finer!"

"Forgive me, Master!" wept Ellen.

"Weaker? Nastier? Pettier? More selfish?"

"Master?"

"A meaningless, vain, pretentious, worthless slut of Earth!" he said.

Ellen's small hands twisted in the ropes.

"You are unworthy to tie the sandals of a Gorean woman," said Selius Arconious.

"Yes, Master," wept Ellen.

"But," said he, "you are well-curved."

"Master?"

"I do not object," said he, "that slavers bring such as you to our world."

"Thank you, Master."

"I think we can find a use for you on Gor."

"It is my hope to be pleasing to my master," said Ellen.

"Let us speak no more of your pathetic, miserable, tragic world," said Selius Arconious.

"As Master pleases," said Ellen.

"You are on Gor now, Earth slut," he said, angrily. "And here you are in a collar, a slave collar!"

"Yes, Master!"

"And I will teach you your collar in a way that you will never forget!"

"No, Master, please, no, Master," wept the slave.

"No longer are you on Earth," said he. "Understand that, slut. Understand it well. Understand that such things are behind you! You are not on Earth now, but on Gor. And understand, as well, that despite your origin, my charming little barbarian, you are no longer *of* Earth, but are now *of* Gor, and that you are now a Gorean slave girl, only that, and that you are going to learn that you are owned."

"Yes, Master," wept Ellen.

What was to be done to her was, of course, nothing unusual, nor unprecedented. She was to be, simply, a beaten slave. There would be no misguided, ignorant fellows here to rush forward and stay the hand of propriety and justice, no stalwart if simple heroes who would stupidly save her from the consequences of her numerous faults, who would see to it that she yet again evaded the consequences of her acts with impunity, who would see to it that she yet again escaped a richly deserved, much-needed punishment, who would then, perhaps scarcely daring to look upon her, clothe her modestly, free her, and return her promptly and courteously, she confused, upset and unfulfilled, to the meaninglessness of her former life. No. Such would not occur. This was Gor. She was slave. No passers-by, should they be about, would think twice about what was done there.

"Please do not whip me, Master!" begged the slave.

"Master?" she said. "Master?"

And then the lash began to fall.

Chapter 30

In Ar

Ellen, kneeling, poured the wine at the small table, filling the cups but half way.

About the table, cross-legged, sat Selius Arconious, her master, Portus Canio, Fel Doron, Bosk of Port Kar, and Marcus, of Ar's Station.

These friends were again well met.

She served silently, deferentially, unobtrusively. It was almost as though she were not there.

So serve slaves.

After the wine was poured she rose up and body bent, head down, eyes cast down, backed gracefully, silently, away, withdrawing to the side.

There she would kneel down and wait, prepared to approach and serve again, if aught else might be needed.

Bosk of Port Kar regarded her.

She dared not meet his eyes. He was such a man, and she slave.

She knelt, obedient to the protocols of her condition, slimly, beautifully, back straight, back on heels, knees spread, the palms of her hands on her thighs.

The decanter of wine was beside her, at her right knee.

"It seems your girl has learned service," said Bosk of Port Kar.

Selius Arconious shrugged, noncommittally.

And so there, in the background, she knelt, some seven feet from the table. At this distance a girl's presence is unobtrusive, and one might easily forget she is present. On the other hand, she is conveniently at hand, and may be promptly summoned.

The men continued to speak, paying her no attention.

Ellen adjusted slightly the brief yellow tunic, slit at the sides, so that she might kneel with a bit more modesty, even in the brazen position required of her, that of the pleasure slave. Sometimes, interestingly, in such servings, as when the master entertains guests, a pleasure slave is allowed to kneel in the position of a serving slave, or tower slave, the knees closely together. That is regarded, by some, as being more discreet, less distractive.

It is particularly the case when a free woman is present, that she not be disturbed by, or offended by, the obvious availability and sensuality of the slave. Too, it is widely thought judicious to conceal from free women the deep, thrilling, exciting and profound sexuality of the female slave, how vulnerable, helpless, needful and passionate she is. Can they understand our feelings at the slave ring? Yet I think the masters are naive if they truly believe, which I suspect they do not, that the free women do not understand, or at least suspect, the nature of such facts. They, too, free women, after all, are intelligent, and are women. I think it is no secret that the free women, who so despise us, who hold us in such contempt, who hate us so, who are often so cruel to us, envy us our masters and our collars. Why should we be happy and they be miserable? Is it not because we have found our way home, and they are still lost in the deserts of artifice? It is the paradox of the collar, thought Ellen. In the collar we are happiest, most liberated, most free.

Then Ellen's thoughts drifted to Earth, tragic Earth, and its negativities, and eccentricities. Compared to Earth the deserts in which the free women of Gor might roam seemed fertile meadows indeed. Compared with the worst of Gor the Earth seemed far worse, a psychosexual, psychobiological wasteland, withered as by a moral plague, the victim of an ideological tragedy. Pity the putatively free women of Earth, she thought, in their deserts, cluttered with social artifacts largely constructed by the subglandular, pathological, effete, feeble and impotent, trying desperately, unhappily, to conform to orthodoxies imposed upon them, orthodoxies invented in effect by witch doctors and shamans to exalt the weak and cripple the strong, invented by petty, resentful, jealous pygmies whose ambition it is to make themselves herdsmen to a reduced, tamed, human race, who will exalt the whole at the expense of the part, who will deny the individual in the name of the mass, in order that they themselves will be the only part that matters, and that they, the masters of the mass, will be the only individuals to truly exist. It is sad, one supposes, to see one's species domesticated, to see this done to our race, and seemingly to be done with its consent, too, a race which might otherwise have become children of the stars. But who knows, thought Ellen, perhaps one day they will see where they are going, and they will cry out "Stop!" and remember the stars.

The men, it seemed, eating, drinking, chatting, needed nothing, and, too, it seemed they were totally unaware of her.

She smiled to herself. Her master had made it clear to her, earlier, before the guests arrived that she, even though serving, would kneel in the position of the pleasure slave. To be sure, there were only men present. But Ellen knew that she, in her way, was being shown off. This pleased her, that her master was proud of her, and wished to display her. But could he not have done this, as well, if she had been permitted to kneel more demurely? No, she thought. These men remember me from the grasslands, and it is the intention of Selius Arconious to make it clear to them that his slave is different now from what they saw then, that she is muchly changed, that she is now an acceptable slave, a well-mastered slave. Too, her kneeling position was doubtless commanded with the intent as well, that there should not be the least doubt as to the nature of the relationship in which she stood to him, her master, that she was not merely a serving slave, or tower slave, but was to him wholly and fully, and in all ways, pleasure slave.

She had been ordered to make herself up, in the bedroom, and she had done so, she hoped with taste. The cosmetics of slaves are not that different, interestingly, from those of free women on Earth. Gorean free women do not use cosmetics, or supposedly do not use them, though ankle bells, concealed by their robes, and perfumes are permitted to them.

Cosmetics, on Gor, are regarded as salacious, improper, offensive and scandalous in the case of a free woman; such things are associated with slaves. Naturally enough then, that women of Earth not unoften so adorn themselves, and may appear in public so adorned, is taken by most Goreans, at least those who believe it, as evidence that they are slaves, and thus of their fittingness to be placed upon the auction block, appearing before masters to be bid upon.

Some Goreans seem to prefer Earth women as slaves; others prefer native Gorean women; I would not think it would make much difference; they are all women; doubtless it depends on the particular woman and man, on the particular slave and master, on the particular "chemistry," so to speak; on the other hand I think it is true that their bondage is likely to have a special, remarkable flavor to Earth women, as many of them have been extracted from a crowded, unnatural, lonely, forlorn, miserable, meaningless, frustrating, negativistic, puritanical environment and they find themselves for the first time in a fresh, open, young, vital, exotic, sensuous, joyous, natural world; too, stripped and collared at the feet of a Gorean male they are likely to have experiences and feelings for which their relationships to men of Earth have simply failed to prepare them. For the first time in their lives, they have met masters.

Earth women do have, incidentally, a reputation on Gor for making excellent slaves. They seem to grasp their new identity, their new being, shortly after their collaring, after having been taught to crawl and kiss the whip. Most are comprehending slaves even before they are taken, sold, from the block. Swiftly then do they learn to lick, kiss and caress, to kneel and obey, to serve as what they have then become, as what they then are, the properties of their masters. In their joy they blossom, understanding that they are now owned, that the collar is truly on them. At last they have an identity and an actual value, a place in society. At last, too, and more importantly, they are in their place in nature, with its endemic codes of dominance and submission, selected for in the long biography of a planet's evolution, codes pervasive throughout all animal life. At last they are where they belong, at the feet of men; at last they are at peace with their genes, with their nature. At last, too, they have a full and rewarding sex life, free of Earth's conditioned guilts and shames, whose bizarre, twisted, diseased roots lie buried in remote superstition, in antique psychosis. At the feet of masters they find happiness; at the feet of masters they find the answer of nature to pain and suffering.

The sex life of the female slave is a sex life so rich and overwhelming, and transforming, that they could scarcely have dreamed of it on Earth. It is a wholeness of life which on Earth would have doubtless been beyond their ken. They are obedient vessels of sexual pleasure; they are subservient, lascivious beasts, anxious to please; they are summonable; they hope to be summoned; they are needful and zealous; one buys them for pleasure, and from them one will have one's money's worth, and a thousand times more. Perhaps it would be more accurate to speak not so much of a sex life, which suggests that sex is only an aspect or part of her life, as a life of sexuality. Sexuality, in its fullness, in its entirety, in its thousand strands and facets, in its thousand modalities and expressions, from almost unendurable, ruthlessly imposed sexual ecstasies, from which the slave may fear she will not survive, to the manner in which a meal is served, from the cruel, raping kiss of the master to the polishing of his boots, from the kissing of his feet to the careful keeping of his quarters, is the life of the female slave. Perhaps, most simply, it should be thought of as a life of femaleness, of essential femaleness, of complete femaleness.

If you would be a woman be a slave.

Ellen thought, again, of cosmetics.

I wonder, she thought, if, in the privacy of their compartments, even free women, with their companions, might resort to cosmetics, perhaps even serving their companions as though they might be no more than slaves, but they would not be, of course, true slaves. Ellen wondered if free women might do such, to keep their companions out of the markets, where they might buy an actual slave, a woman over whom they would genuinely have absolute power, as her master had over her.

Perhaps a brief cast of irritation then traversed the countenance of Ellen, as she thought of free women. Little love is lost betwixt free women and slaves, in either direction. Happily the men did not notice.

It is one of the fears of a slave that she might be purchased by a woman. They know, in their hearts, they belong to men, and wish to belong to men, their appropriate masters in the order of nature.

As Ellen knelt there she suddenly trembled. How vulnerable we are, slaves, she thought. We are owned. We are branded. We are in collars. We can be bought and sold. We must obey. We are subject to discipline. Sometimes we are whipped, it seems, merely to remind us that we are slaves.

Again the men did not notice her tiny movement. She then addressed herself, again, to the retaining of position, that lovely position which had been enjoined upon her for the evening, and which in any event was generally incumbent upon her, given the nature of her bondage, the position of the pleasure slave. She did not wish to risk discipline.

If you would be a slave, dear haughty free sisters, thought Ellen, then be a slave. Know what it is to actually wear a collar and be owned! Know what it is to kneel naked, chained, before your master! Know what it is to cast him shy, fearful glances, trying to read his moods! Know what it is to service his compartments, perhaps shackled, to make his couch, to dust and clean, and cook, and sew, and launder, hoping that your services will be found satisfactory. Let your wash be sparkling, let your stitches be small, fine and straight! Know what it is to kiss the whip, knowing that it will be used on you if you are not fully pleasing. Know what it is to crawl fearfully to him, your master, bearing the whip in your teeth! Where are your brands and papers, dear free sisters? And have you ever stood stripped on an auction block, to be bid upon, as the property you are?

On Earth Ellen had seldom, if ever, worn cosmetics, regarding them as ideologically inappropriate, an obvious confession of a terrible, unworthy desire, that of being attractive, literally attractive, in all that that means, to the opposite sex. When Ellen had looked in the mirror, after the make-up had been applied, she had been, for a moment, startled. She remembered a lovely teenager, from long ago, one perhaps no more than eighteen or nineteen, who had once made herself up, and had been shocked and thrilled, and then, suddenly, distraught, overcome with confusion and guilt, had smeared her face with cold cream and wiped away the evidence of that politically harrowing indiscretion. But she did not dare this evening, even if she had desired to do so, to remove from her features these delightful enhancements. The decision was not hers. She had been commanded. She must obey her master. But how charming it had been, to see, again, as it were, that slender, sensitive, lovely teenager. She had feared, for a moment, before the mirror, that her master, regarding her, she seeing him behind her in the mirror, was going to seize her and hurl her to the very floor before the mirror, putting her yet again, imperiously, to the "master's pleasure." But he had growled in anger, and, clenching his fists, had turned away. She had smiled, inwardly. Poor master, she thought. Then she pitied free women, they not knowing what it was to be desired as a slave is desired.

Her master had also ordered her to put up her hair, with combs, in an upswept hairdo. Perhaps he thought that that would make her look older, more sophisticated or such. She complied, with pleasure, and admired her handiwork. Her hair had never been cut on Gor, other than to shape it, and it was "slave long." She saw her master looking at her. "Ah," she thought to herself, "he will enjoy taking it down, freeing it, and casting it about me!" Much can be done with long hair, to give pleasure to the master. A cruel punishment for slave girls is to shave the head or crop the hair. To be sure, the hair of low slaves, such as factory slaves, laundry slaves, farm slaves, and such is commonly worn short, sometimes cropped.

At that time, she had already muchly prepared the supper, and knew that the guests might soon arrive. She surveyed herself in the mirror, the brief tunic, the make-up, the hairdo. "I think, Ellen," she said to herself, "that you are worth money, yes, money, serious money. I think, slave girl, you would bring a good price!" She then, as a last touch, adjusted her collar, with two hands, making certain that the lock was squarely at the back of her neck.

The men continued to speak, and Ellen's mind wandered a bit, drifting from thought to thought.

She saw Portus Canio taking a sip of the wine she had poured.

She had not, of course, offered wine to the men as she might have, in private, to her master, kneeling naked before him, in her collar, touching the cup variously to her body, pressing it here and there against, moving it here and there against her beauty, feeling the steel rim firmly, unyieldingly, against her yielding softness, kissing it, placing it, kissing it, placing it, this commonly done at the belly, the waist, at each breast, and at each shoulder, and then, lifting her eyes, regarding him over the rim of the cup, kissing it again, one last time, lingeringly, lovingly, and then lifting it to him in two hands, her head deferentially down, between her extended arms.

In many ways may a slave girl beg the attention of her master. One of these is "serving wine."

She heard a snapping of fingers.

She looked up.

"Bread," said Selius Arconious, gesturing toward the kitchen.

"Yes, Master!" she said, leaping to her feet and hurrying to the kitchen.

In a few moments she was again at her post, kneeling, and the men were once again in converse.

Her thoughts drifted to the slave ring at the foot of her master's couch and the small, coarsely woven mat there on which she was permitted to sleep, a threadbare blanket her only covering.

Ellen, she understood, was not to be spoiled.

At night she was attached to the ring, by neck or ankle, so that she would always be at hand.

She loved being so chained. She was slave, she was his.

She wondered if, one day, he might purchase a lamp of love, and love furs. Perhaps, someday, who knew, she might, if she served long enough, and deferentially enough, with sufficient perfection, be permitted sometimes the dignity of the surface of the couch, though still chained by neck or ankle, first kneeling beside it, kissing its furs, and then being permitted to ascend to its surface and then, kneeling at its foot, head downward, rendering obeisance there, before being commanded, or positioned, and swept into ecstasies to be known only by chained, ravished slaves.

She knew that she was now much different from what she had been in the grasslands. She knew herself now to be a submitted slave; she had learned submission. She was now hot, devoted and dutiful. She feared her master, but she loved him. He was quite strict with her. No laxity was permitted her. He was, it seemed, keeping a very careful eye on her. She strove to be perfect, and pleasing. She kept her body clean and sparkling, her hair brushed and combed, her tunics crisp and freshly laundered. She gave much concern to her appearance for she was her master's property, and any fault in her appearance or behavior might be thought to reflect poorly on him, on his capacity to own and manage a slave. She was zealously scrupulous in the performance of all her duties. She tried to stand and move gracefully, was attentive to her servings and kneelings, and to her smallest glances and gestures. She was owned. How can I explain this, these changes in my life and being, she sometimes asked herself, but then the answer came clearly to her, she was a slave girl. She was happy. I must be as I am, she said to herself. My master will permit me no latitude. I love him for it! He has mastered me. I have been mastered!

As she knelt to the side and the men spoke, not considering her, her mind drifted back, several days ago, weeks ago, to the approach to the Viktel Aria, north of Venna, and to a wood, and to an abandoned tarsk pen in that wood.

She recalled her beating and her surprise, and horror, at the first stroke, and how it was like fire and snakes and wire, and how she could scarcely believe what was being done to her. Did they not know she was a woman of Earth? That such things were not done to women of Earth? And then the lash had struck again and she was no more a woman of Earth but only a punished Gorean slave girl.

Then she began to be clearly aware of the pain.

She rose to her feet, bent over, as she was tied.

"Back on your knees!" she was ordered, and she sank down, again, on her knees.

She was then struck again. She screamed, and put down her head, and was struck again, and raised her head and put it back, sobbing, and was again struck.

It was then she knew that she would be mastered, and mastered wholly.

"Please, no, Master!" she wept. "I will be good! I will obey, totally, in all things! I will be pleasing, in all ways! I will try to do my best to be a good slave! Please, no, Master!"

Yes, she would be mastered, wholly.

And the lash fell again. Not so easily would she escape her due!

He is my master, she thought, truly my master!

She sobbed, uncontrollably.

Then strangely, she felt a sudden incredible elation, and fulfillment, in the pain. She recalled how she had, in the depths of her heart, strangely, desired to be whipped, desired to be put beneath the lash of a master! Thus, it seemed, suddenly, she felt her womanhood and slaveness, that this could be done to her, and that she, a female, one in the order of nature to be suitably submissive to a male, had not been found pleasing and that she would pay for that. He owns me, she thought! How better can he teach a foolish slave that she is his? Thus he proves my slaveness to me! Thus he proves his ownership of me! I know now that I am a slave, and that he is my master! I have longed for this beating, this confirmation, this demonstration! Yes, yes, Master, she thought, I acknowledge myself slave and yours! You have put your unmistakable seal upon my embondedness!

Then, again, there was only the pain, and she wept, and pulled at the ropes, and shook with misery.

She did not know how many strokes were administered to her. She was barely aware of her wrists being freed from the post, though they remained bound together. She then lay under the post on her stomach, her bound wrists stretched out, moaning, sobbing. Then she felt herself dragged on her belly through the wood chips and grass under the post and toward the center of the tarsk pen. There, to her misery, she was turned to her back and her wrists, over her head and back, fastened to a pole. She looked up in fear and pain at her master, standing above her.

"Speak!" he cried, angrily.

"Thank you, Master!" she wept, in terror, looking up at him. "Thank you, Master! Thank you for beating me!"

He angrily cast the whip aside, and then crouched beside her. She felt her legs thrust widely, brutally, apart. He was not gentle with her.

Afterwards he left her there, in the tarsk pen, and she turned, weeping, blubbering, half in shock, eyes wide, to her side, to relieve her back from contact with the soiled, rough ground, the stained wood chips, of the abandoned pen.

It was there in the tarsk pen that she spent the night.

Before dawn, the next day, Portus Canio came to her, sponged her back, and her body, with a damp rag, cooling her and cleaning her, and freed her.

Unbidden, she set about her duties.

She tidied the camp, built the fire, set up the cooking rods, boiled water, and prepared breakfast for the men. While they ate, she knelt down beside their blankets, kissed them, shook them out and folded them, and placed them in the wagon.

When she was finished she returned to the vicinity of the fire. There were now two shallow pans there, one filled with water, the other with a handful of moist gruel. "Thank you, Masters," she whispered. Then she went to all fours before the pans, and, putting her head down, ate and drank from the pans.

She cast many an anxious look at her master, but he did not so much as look at her. This disturbed her, terribly.

When the tharlarion had been hitched, and the men were clearly ready to depart, she could stand it no more, and ran to the feet of her master, and put her head down, and wept, and covered his feet with tears and kisses. "Please, forgive me, Master!" she wept. "Please forgive me!"

Then, as she dared to lift her eyes, clutching his calves, and looking fearfully up at him, she suddenly felt an almost uncontrollable cry of need in her belly, one suffusing upward and downward throughout her small body. She made a small noise of astonishment, and of fear. It was so sudden. She pressed her thighs together, frightened. Surely she was in need. She hoped he could not smell her need, her raw, naked slave's need. She remembered his hands upon her, and how she had been handled and used, how she had been put to his pleasure.

"You will be used, slut," said he, "if and when I please."

She put down her head, in consternation.

"Stand," said he, "and put your hands behind you, wrists crossed."

She did so and her wrists, in a moment, were tightly thonged behind her. A rope was then tied on her neck and attached to the back of the wagon.

"You will be a naked slave," he said, "publicly exposed on a common road."

She put her head down, remembering her own former words.

She wondered if, and when, she would again be given a tunic. A slave, she knew, cannot count upon a tunic. Sometimes she must earn a tunic, or a slave strip.

The wagon then left the camp and, shortly thereafter, trundled onto the heavy, broad, fitted stones of the Viktel Aria.

Ellen, on the rope leash, followed. In the vicinity of Venna there were several caravansaries outside the walls. Ellen heard a delighted female voice cry out, "Greetings, slave girl!"

Looking about, Ellen saw that it was the blonde she had tormented yesterday afternoon, but now the blonde was tunicked, although, to be sure, briefly.

"Respond," called Selius Arconious, from behind her.

"Greetings, Mistress," said Ellen.

"Now," said Selius Arconious, "eyes front, slave!"

And then Ellen continued on her way, not looking to the side, or back. She kept her gaze fixed squarely ahead. Tears streamed down her face, and under the coarse rope knotted about her neck.

The men, having finished their repast, retired to a larger, open area, smoothly floored, looking out over Ar. The night was beautiful, and there were many lights. The slave cleared. Later, rising from her knees within, at a gesture from her master, the slave brought forth and served small glasses of Turian liqueurs.

Toward the Twentieth Ahn, the Gorean midnight, the guests took their leave. The door closed and the slave was alone with her master.

Selius Arconious, standing, regarded his property, kneeling.

"May I speak, Master?" she asked.

"Yes," said he.

"It is my hope," she said, "that the evening went well."

"I think it went very well," said he.

"A slave is pleased, if master is pleased," she said.

"Though perhaps," he said, "it lasted too long."

"Master?" asked the slave.

She knew that she was exquisitely beautiful, and would bring a high price in the market. She could tell, too, that her master was now regarding her with that look which slaves know only too well. No woman in a collar can mistake such a look. She put her head down, shyly.

"You did well this evening," he said.

"Thank you, Master."

"You are a good slave, Ellen," he said.

"Master has taught me how to be a good slave," said Ellen. "He has given me no choice."

"Do you wish a choice?" he asked.

"No, Master," she smiled.

The slave whip hung on its peg not far from the great couch, with its slave ring. On the other hand, it was seldom used. A supple switch served sufficiently for occasional admonitions.

One time, however, several days ago, he did strip her, tie her wrists together before her body and conduct her down the stairs to the hall of the building, where it opened at the street level. Two children, and, later, a free woman, were passed on the stairs. None paid her attention. Her master then tied her wrists over her head to a dangling ceiling ring in the hall, a ring for the use of the tenants, one not far from the door, and drew her up in such a way that she was stretched upward by the wrists, and standing on the tips of her toes.

"What have I done, Master?" she had asked in genuine puzzlement.

A free woman then entered the building, who had been shopping. "Slut!" she said to Ellen. "Yes, Mistress," said Ellen. "Beat her well," she said. "Have no fear, dear lady," said Selius Arconious, politely.

"I do not know what I have done, Master!" said Ellen.

"Surely you recall," said he, "the festival camp, where you were to be punished on two counts, first, for not having revealed skill in slave dance, and, second, for having spoken without permission."

"Master?" asked Ellen.

"You were to receive ten strokes for the first offense, and five for the second," said Selius Arconious. "That is, accordingly, a total of fifteen strokes."

"But Master kindly purchased the strokes!" said Ellen. "He paid fifteen tarsk-bits! One for each blow! Thus, he spared me the blows!"

"Yes," he said, "I purchased the strokes, but only, you see, in order that I might deliver them myself."

"No, Master!" she cried.

"I bought them that they might be mine to give, my little charmer," he said. "I had waited a long time to give you some much-needed whip strokes."

"Be kind, Master!"

"Did you think that you would escape your due?" he asked.

"I had hoped Master had forgotten!" she said.

"Had you forgotten?" he asked.

"No, Master," she wept.

"Nor did I." She heard the strands of the whip shaken out.

"Please, Master," she said.

"If you had not forgotten, why did you not remind me?" he asked.

She was silent.

"That will be an additional five strokes," he said.

"Please, Master, no, Master!" she said.

He then put the first stroke to her, and she spun in the ropes, to look at him, protestingly, in misery. And then, at his gesture, she turned away again, groaning, her back to him. The second stroke was then put to her. He did not make her count the strokes, but he counted them. This was merciful. The blows were nicely predictable, and well measured. This, too, was merciful. This did not diminish the fact, however, that they were effectively severe. She was being beaten. "Fourteen!" he said. She now hung sobbing in the ropes. Two fellows of the caste of metal workers entered the hall. "Tal," said they to Selius Arconious. "Tal," said he to them. "Aii!" wept Ellen. "Fifteen," said Selius Arconious. "Have mercy, Master!" begged Ellen. "That is fifteen!" But he gave her five more strokes. "Twenty," he said. He then released her from the ring, and she collapsed to the dark, polished, narrow wooden boards beneath it. "It is nearly time to prepare supper," he said. "Yes, Master," she said. "But I do not know if I can stand!" "You are not to stand," he said. "You are to crawl up the stairs." "Yes, Master," she wept. "Have you not forgotten something?" he asked. "Master?" she asked. "You have been beaten," he said. "Forgive me, Master," she said. "Thank you for whipping me." "More properly," he said. "Ellen, his slave, thanks master for whipping her," she sobbed. "You are welcome," he said. "Now, up the stairs." "Yes, Master," she said and crawled to the stairs, across the dark boards of the hall, and then, on all fours, her back doubtless rich with stripes, ascended the steps, landing by landing.

But, as stated, Ellen was almost never beaten, save for an occasional stroke of the switch. The reason for this, of course, was not that her master was weak, but that she had become an excellent slave, and thus there was little, if any, reason to beat her. This is common on Gor. Gratuitous cruelty is far more common on Earth, I fear, than on Gor. The value of the whip, you see, is not so much in its being used, as in the slave's knowledge that it can be used and, under certain circumstances, will be used. Occasionally, of course, the slave may be tied and whipped that she may the better know herself, that she may be reminded of what she is, that she is a slave.

The dinner had gone well.

Selius Arconious, a tarnster of Ar, had been pleased.

His slave, Ellen, a female of Earth origin, whom he had purchased at a festival camp outside Brundisium, knelt before him, made-up, in a brief yellow tunic, collared.

"One of your endearing features," he said, "is that you do not know how exciting, how attractive, you are."

"Do not be too sure of that, Master," said the slave.

"Oh?" he said.

"I think I would bring a high price," she said.

"Vain slave," he said.

"Yes, Master," she said.

"To be sure," he said, "there are thousands, thousands upon thousands, who are much more exciting, and attractive."

"To you, Master," she asked.

"Yes, of course," he said.

"Yes, Master," she said.

"So do not become arrogant," he said.

"No, Master," she said.

"You are smiling," he said.

"Forgive me, Master," she said.

He cast aside his tunic.

Then he rushed upon the slave and half lifted her from her knees and looked fiercely into her eyes, and she gasped, so regarded by a man, and one a master, with such ferocity and passion. "Master!" she cried. And he threw her to his feet and, crouching beside her, she first, startled, on all fours, and then thrust to her belly, tore away her tunic, shred by silken shred, flinging these narrow, delicate, yellow, rent scraps behind him, they fluttering away to alight, scattered, like startled flowers, on the narrow boards of the dark, hardwood floor. Then it was gone! He turned her violently to her back then, and knelt across her body, pinning her wrists to the floor, at the sides of her head, with his large hands. She squirmed a little, and looked up at him. He grinned down upon her. The irresistible, overwhelming, powerful, handsome beast, the virile, desiring, lustful, arrogant monster! How obviously he was regarding his property with inordinate pleasure! Muchly then was she aware of the collar on her neck, and that she was owned, and that she was in the grasp of her master, helplessly and deliciously in the grasp of her master.

"I love you, Master," she said.

"Are you so presumptuous, so arrogant, that you dare to speak such words to your master?"

Slaves are often helplessly, hopelessly, in love with their masters, often pathetically so. After all, his collar is on their necks. But they are only slaves, lovely properties, shapely beasts, purchasable goods, degraded articles of commerce, immeasurably beneath a free person, beneath the notice of a free person, save as they may prove to be of some service, convenience, pleasure or profit, such things, to him. Thus the slave may kneel before the master, tears in her eyes, her heart offered up to him as can only be the heart of a slave, and this obvious to him, but she knows his love is to be reserved, if it be given, at all, to a free woman, not to a slave, an animal he might obtain in any market. Thus she repines and dares not hope for his love. Thus she, conscious of the chasms between them, and of her lowliness, and unworthiness, fears to speak her heart. Commonly he is well aware of her feelings, but how insulted, how furious, he might be, should she be so unwise or bold as to profess them!

"Forgive me, Master," she whispered.

"How dare you love a free man?"

"May not even a she-sleen love her master?"

"The she-sleen is a splendid animal," he said. "You are a mere slave."

"Forgive me, Master."

But she did not think he was displeased at her declaration.

"Perhaps I should whip you and sell you," he said.

"Please do not, Master," she said.

"You do not seem to fear that I will sell you," he said.

"I am, of course, a slave, and am at Master's disposal."

"But you do not seem to fear I will sell you."

"Master may do with me as he wishes," she said, "but it is my hope that I will not be sold."

"It could be done to you."

"That is well known to your slave, Master."

"Why should you not be sold?"

"I think Master would have difficulty recouping his losses," she smiled. "Did he not pay something in the neighborhood of twenty-one tarsks, and of silver, for me?"

"Doubtless I muchly, and foolishly, overpaid," he said.

"Yes, Master," she agreed.

Many girls such as she, she knew, and excellent girls, quality shackle sluts, went for as little as one and a half to three silver tarsks. She recalled there had been a bid of fifteen silver tarsks on her even before Mirus and Selius Arconious had entered upon their competition for a slave, the shapely, gray-eyed brunette being displayed and auctioned. Fifteen silver tarsks, though, she thought, was surely excessive. Much, of course, had to do with the place, the wealth at hand, the number of bidders, the fever of the bidding, and such.

"Perhaps your master is a fool," he said.

"A girl dare not comment on such things," she said.

"Would you like to be whipped?" he asked.

"No, Master," she said.

"But actually I am not, as it seems, such a fool," he said.

"Master?"

"I have received higher offers for you," he said, "even from men who have merely seen you on the streets, of twenty-five silver tarsks, and more."

The slave began to tremble. She had understood nothing of this.

"What is wrong?" he asked.

"Master!" she wept.

"There are tears in your eyes, pretty slut," he said.

"Please do not sell me, Master," she begged. Her sale now seemed an option within the purview of her master, one he might plausibly view with favor.

"You now seem in earnest," he said, not displeased.

"Yes, Master!"

"Why should I not sell you?" he asked.

"I am pretty," she said. "I juice quickly, I squirm helplessly!"

"Many slaves are pretty," he said, "and they, too, juice quickly and squirm helplessly. One expects such things of a slave."

"I work hard," she said. "I strive zealously to be pleasing to you!"

"I can work any slave," he said. "And the whip will assure that they strive zealously to be pleasing to me."

"I think Master is pleased with me, when I experience great pleasure in his arms."

"Slave pleasure," he said, dismissively.

"Yes, Master," she said. "But I do not think I could experience such pleasure in the arms of any other man."

"Nonsense," he said. "You are a slave. In the arms of any man you would leap and cry out."

"Does it not give Master pleasure to know I am so subjugated, so unmitigatedly and irremediably subjugated, that I am so much his, and that in his arms I experience the most ecstatic of joys, those of the overcome, yielding and ravished slave?"

"Who cares," asked he, "aught of a slave's pleasure?"

"You, Master!" she exclaimed.

"Bold slave," he said.

"Speak," she said, "as though our pleasures were nothing, which perhaps they are, but it is clearly one of the joys of the mastery to see the effect wrought upon a slave by your attentions. You cannot tell me it is not a triumph for you, and a pleasure, to see a slave begging and pleading for more, fearing only that you will not continue, weeping with gratitude, half blinded with ecstasy, in the throes of her submission orgasms."

"I acknowledge," he said, "it is pleasant to have a slave so, to have her so much in your power, to force her, if one wishes, she willing or not, to undergo such pleasures."

"Do you think, Master, that we do not desire such pleasures?"

"I suppose you want them," he said, "you are not free women. You are mere slaves."

"We are women, Master! We desire our bondage. We long for masters. Without them we are incomplete!"

"So you desire sexual pleasure?"

"We do, we do, as Master well knows."

"Say it," said he.

"We desire sexual pleasure," she said.

"Speak specifically," said he.

"I, Ellen, the slave of Selius Arconious, tarnster of Ar, desire sexual pleasure."

"Do you beg it?"

"Yes, Master! Please, Master!"

"Beg, then."

"I, Ellen, slave, property of Selius Arconious, of Ar, beg sexual pleasure!"

She looked up at him, pathetically. Would it be granted to her? She was, after all, only a slave.

"Slaves beg for such things," he said. "It is expected of them. One thinks nothing of it. But they are not free women. They are only domestic animals, no more than worthless beasts."

"Free women also desire sexual pleasure," she said.

He smiled.

"They do, they do!" insisted the slave. "Let them redden, and froth and deny it, if they will, but they do! I was a free woman! I know! But I did not know what sexual pleasure was until I was put in a collar!"

"It is true you are a hot slut," he said.

"Yes, Master!" she said, defiantly. "But do you think those free women, brought into collars, are so different?"

"They do learn to kiss one's feet quickly," he observed.

"Of course," she said. "All they needed was to be collared, to be owned, and mastered."

"It is undeniable," he said, "that women make excellent slaves."

"Of course, Master," she said. "It is what they are in their hearts, and wish to be. The sexes are complementary, two parts which together form a whole! Each is an enigma, a puzzle, meaningless, until they are brought together, each in their difference and perfection, to form one whole. Two radical differences, female and male, but one whole! Is the character of nature so difficult to discern? Can you not see it in the great themes of dominance and submission? One is bred to submit, one to dominate; one is bred to obey, and one to command; one is bred to serve, and another to rule. And the perfection of this complementarity, as societally recognized, as socially articulated, as culturally enhanced and celebrated, and fixed into the matrix of custom and legality, is the relationship of master and slave."

"And you are a slave," he said.

"Yes, Master!"

"I think I will have you," he said.

"Please do, Master!"

"But why you, and not another?" he asked.

"Master?"

"Are not women women, and slaves slaves?"

"But one slave is not another slave."

"True," he said, "each is exquisitely different, each wholly slave, and yet each so remarkably and preciously different a slave."

True, thought Ellen. Each is sold off the platform as living meat, as a property, as no more than a shapely beast, and yet each is wonderfully different and unique.

How men search the markets for their perfect slave, and how slaves hope for their perfect master!

"Are you an insolent slave?" he asked.

"I trust not, Master," she said.

"Yet you spoke earlier—as I recall—of love."

"Forgive me, Master."

"You love me?"

"Yes, Master."

"You, only a slave, dare to love a free man?"

"Forgive me, Master."

"A slave," he mused. "The love of a slave."

"We cannot help ourselves, Master," she said. "You own us. We are in your collars. We are with you so much, so intimately. We serve you so abjectly. We bring you your sandals. We bathe you. We kneel before you. It is on our limbs that your chains are fastened. It is you by whom we are mastered."

"I see," he said.

"The first time I saw you," she wept, "I wanted to be your slave."

"The first time I saw you," he said, "I wanted you as my slave."

"Master!" she breathed.

"Not to love you, of course," he said, "just to have you as my slave, a simple collar slut, you understand."

"Of course, Master," she said.

"But you did seem, somehow, as I recall, of particular interest."

"A slave is pleased," she said.

"I fought my feelings for you," he said.

"As I for you, Master."

"Oh?"

"But not well! Not successfully!"

"Good," he said.

"Scorn me, if you wish," she said, "for I am only a slave, and that I well know, but I do love you."

"With the love of a slave," he smiled.

"Yes, Master," she said, "with the love of a slave, with the helpless, vulnerable love that only a slave can give."

"I see," said he, "my pretty, nicely curved Earth slut."

The love of a free woman, should they be capable of love, is very different from the love of a slave. The free woman must have her respect, her self-esteem, her dignity. She must consider how her friends will view her, and the match, and what they will think of her, and say of her. She must consider her assets, her properties, and their protection. All details of contracts must be arranged, usually with the attention of scribes of the law. She must have a clear understanding of what will be permitted to her companion and what will not be permitted to him. Certainly, as she is free, her modesty is not to be compromised. All things are to be regulated with care, how and where he may touch her, and such. She has her position in society to consider, her station and status. She is hedged in with a thousand trammels and compromises, militating against her selfless surrender. The love of a free woman, then, to the extent that she can love, is beset with a great number and variety of considerations, with a thousand subtle and noxious calculations, plannings and governances. Needless to say, these several appurtenances do not enter into the ken of a slave. Sometimes a free woman, who fears that her feelings for a projected companion, to her dismay and scandal, are more intense, suffusive, overwhelming and passionate than is proper for one of her status will withdraw from the projected match. She is terrified to think of herself as, in effect, a slave. Sometimes, too, a free man will withdraw from a match if he suspects that the woman's desires and needs are unworthy of a free woman. After all, he is looking for a free woman, not a slave, a proud, lofty, noble, free woman, one who will fulfill the customs of her station, and prove to be a suitable asset, particularly with respect to connections and career.

So pity the poor free woman who would yield herself as a slave to her lover and does not do so, for her enmeshment in the chains of pride. And scorn the foolish free man who cannot recognize and accept, and rejoice in, the slave in a woman.

And consider that free man who calculates so carefully the advantages of a companionship, who so carefully measures out the prospects of a relationship, as a merchant might weigh grain upon a scale. He treats the woman as an instrument to his future, and thus treats her as more a slave than a slave.

And what of the calculating free woman, as well, she, ensconced in veils and customs, despising men as weaklings, exploiting them, though sheltered and protected by them, viewing them as conveniences, as little more, at best, than sources of social and economic advantage, save, of course, for the gratifications she derives from their torment, from delightfully arousing in them a hundred hopes and desires which she will then enjoyably frustrate.

Sometimes a slave learns that her master is to be companioned. In such a case she must expect to be given away or sold. This often causes her great sorrow. But certainly one could not expect the projected companion to tolerate so distractive a presence in their domicile. Free women are well aware that they cannot compete with slaves; accordingly, to the best of their ability, they see to it that any such competition is precluded.

Two more points may be briefly enunciated.

First, some free women, disconsolate and lonely, unhappy, miserable, deprived of sex, starved for love, distressed with the numerous circumscriptions and constraints which confine them, realizing the boredom, the emptiness, of their lives, "court the collar." Consciously, of course, they will deny this sort of thing. An example might be the former Lady Melanie of Brundisium, now collared. They might, for example, wander the high bridges at night, or frequent low markets and gloomy streets. They may undertake long and dangerous journeys, stay at unsavory inns, and so on. They might be careless with their veiling, or, seemingly inadvertently, reveal a wrist or ankle. Some might even disguise themselves as slaves, convincing themselves that this is merely a sprightly lark, unattended with danger. Perhaps they even dare to enter a paga tavern, just to see what they are like, or perhaps wander in the Street of Brands, to stroll through the open markets or slave yards, to see true slaves, chained, or caged. But how easily they might suddenly sense a narrow cloth loop passing over their head and before their eyes, what is it, and then feel it jerk back tightly, cruelly, between their teeth. In strong arms they are helpless. Soon ropes are fastened on them, plenteously, perhaps to convince them that they are now other than they were, and they are carried between buildings, and down stairs, to be left in a basement, gagged, and bound hand and foot, heavily, until nightfall, when they will be placed in a wagon, perhaps with others, to be removed from the city.

Second, it is not unusual, a point suggested earlier, for a slave to fall in love with her master. It is quite common, in fact. I do not think this is hard to understand, her being owned, and such. The love of a slave, of course, is supposedly worthless, and so she often conceals it, as best she can. Might the master not be annoyed or embarrassed by something as unwelcome and absurd as, say, the explicit expression of a slave's love? She lies then at the foot of her master's couch. She kisses her chains. She kisses her fingertips and presses them to her collar. Tears well in her eyes. She fears to speak, for she is only a slave. She does not wish to be whipped, or sold. In any event, in the fertile meadow of bondage the flower of love finds a fertile soil. Even if it should be forbidden, or feared, or dreaded, it will have its way, as the spring and the tides, and bloom. What terror can this bring to the heart of the slave girl!

"It is acceptable," he said, "that a slave should love her master."

"Perhaps Master likes his slave, a little," she said.

"Perhaps," he said, "a little."

"Your slave begs to serve your pleasure, Master," she whispered.

He then knelt to the side but continued to hold her wrists.

She sensed that it was only with great difficulty that he resisted seizing her. Surely in a moment she would be put to slave use.

But then, too, suddenly, it seemed, her entire body began to be suffused, more so than ever before, this startling her, almost frightening her, with an incandescence of surrender, of helpless heat, of overwhelming love, of total, unmitigated submission, of a woman's desperate, frenzied need to put herself lovingly, helplessly, at the mercy of a master.

He must have sensed this, for he smiled.

"Take pity on a slave," she begged. How helpless was the slave so suddenly in the grip of her need!

"So," said he, "in your pretty little belly, there burns slave fire?"

She half scrambled up, half lying, half kneeling, looking up at him, her master, her wrists still held, regarding him, wildly.

"Yes, Master" she said. "In my belly there burns slave fire!"

"In the belly of an Earth woman?"

"In the belly of one once a woman of Earth, but now only a branded, collared Gorean slave!"

"I see," he said.

"I confess my needs! I am no longer permitted to deny them!"

He continued to hold her wrists, keeping her from him.

"I am yours, Master," she cried.

She tried to touch his face with her hands but his grip would let her come only so close, a finger's breadth away.

"I must touch you," she begged.

He then put her hands down, to her sides, forcibly, and she dared not raise them. She understood herself then, as though bound by his will.

Her body shook with frustration.

"Master?" she whispered.

He tore the combs from her hair, and her hair then, with his two hands, he cast about her. Then he put it behind her back.

She regarded him.

He stood. How tall, how powerful, how mighty he seemed, looming above her, before her.

"Kneel," he said.

Instantly, frightened, she assumed first position.

Now she was before him, kneeling, his, collared, slave naked.

"May I speak?" she asked.

"Yes," he said.

"I beg permission to go to my master's slave ring," she whispered.

"No," he said.

"Master?" she asked.

"No!" he cried. "No!"

Then he rushed upon the slave and took her in his arms and cried out "I cannot wait! I will not wait! I want you now! Now! I want you now, this instant!" He regarded the slave wildly. "I cannot even wait to get you to the slave ring!" he cried.

"I am always at your slave ring, Master!" she cried.

"I cannot even wait to put a chain on your neck, a shackle on your ankle!" he murmured, pressing his lips above her collar, deeply, possessively, into her throat.

How slave she felt, desiring to be helplessly his, to be bound, to be totally mastered!

"No, no, Master!" she wept. "Chain me! Chain me, please!"

"What?" he cried.

"Chain me, please, Master!"

He smiled.

The slave regarded him, frantic with need.

"My love for you is a bond a thousand times stronger than a chain on my neck, than a shackle on my ankle!" she cried. "But I want the chain! I beg the chain! I crave the shackle!"

"What a slave you are!" he laughed.

"Yes, yes, slave, slave!" she gasped. "Your slave, your slave!"

Then with a great laugh he swept her up into his arms and carried her lightly, helplessly, to the bedroom.

The slave, so carried, clung to him, kissing at him, wildly, piteously.

Then, in a moment, she was thrown on the couch, a chain on her neck, a shackle on her ankle!

"Surely not on the surface of the couch, Master!" she cried.

"Be silent!" he cried, and, mad with passion, cuffed her, striking her head to the side but she turned back, instantly, her mouth bleeding, kissing at his body, leaving small, bright prints of blood upon it.

Then he took her in his arms. He uttered a great cry of joy. He was not patient with her. Instantly was she penetrated. He cried out with pleasure, and exuberance, owning her, possessing her, his purchased slave. And then, clutching him, holding to him as tightly as she could, enraptured, as a used, ravished, shameless slave, chained and shackled, she yielded to him, and, oh, with the fullness of a slave's yielding, with that yielding which a slave longs to yield, with that yielding which a slave must yield, with that yielding which can be known to no woman who is not a slave, she yielded, and she yielded, and yielded!

"Are you a free woman?" he asked.

"No, Master," she cried. "I am a slave, your slave!"

"Do you wish to be freed?" he inquired.

"No, Master!" she said. "Keep me in your collar!"

"Have no fear, my meaningless little barbarian," he said. "I shall. I shall!"

"Yes, Master!" she wept. "Yes, Master!" And then in his arms there writhed a slave, a mere slave, one I would come to know well, one whom her master would continue to call 'Ellen', as it pleased him to do, a tearful, grateful, ecstatic slave, she who was his, she who was I.

And many times that night, in many ways, sometimes abruptly, sometimes lengthily, was she put to his purposes and pleasures. And so, too, did she serve him, frequently, in the commanded secret intimacies of her slavehood, eagerly.

* * * *

It is now time to close this narrative.

It is written with the permission of my master. That such a thing, this writing, might be done was suggested to my master by his friend, Bosk, of Port Kar. I am deeply grateful to my master for permitting me to write this, and to that unusual, complex gentleman, Bosk of Port Kar, scholar and warrior, master of weapons and slaves, sometimes so fierce and terrible, sometimes so thoughtful and gentle, uncompromising but understanding, for suggesting that it might be done. The narrative, I fear is only too obviously a first-person story, though I have tried to tell it with some objectivity, largely in the third person, as perhaps befits a collared slave. To be sure, I fear my feelings have often intruded themselves. Indeed, sometimes I fear that I have spoken in the first person and not the third. This is then, I conjecture, a first-person narrative expressed largely, humbly, I trust, in the third person. Now, however, in these last remarks, with no presumption intended, I will speak in my own first person, not of the slave, Ellen, who is I, but as I, who am Ellen, the slave.

This has been so good for me to write this story. I had to tell someone, if only myself.

It is written on large sheets of rence paper, from the delta of the Vosk, in pen and ink.

I do not know the fate of this manuscript, or if it has a fate, so to speak. One thing is clear to me, that it is surely unlikely that these things will be allowed to be known on my old world. These are not truths of the sort which are to be spoken on that world. Indeed, many, should the occasion arise, will attempt to prevent the publication of this manuscript. If, somehow, it should find publication on my old world, one must then expect it to be derided and denounced variously, with cuteness and cleverness, with subtlety and cunning, with virulence and hysteria. It belongs, you see, to a *genre* of manuscripts which are to be suppressed on that world. To the ignorant, fearful and weak these truths must, I suppose, seem frightening, perhaps as other truths concerning nature, long ago, the movement of the earth, the nature of the sun, the distance of stars, seemed so frightening. But these truths are not really so frightening, not really. No more than the beating of the heart, the circulation of the blood. But those who fear to learn need not consider these matters. Let them remain in ignorance, or labor with excuses and qualifications to maintain their sheltered enclaves of comforting sophistries, such fragile defenses against storms of fact. I do not object. I mean them no harm. Perhaps it is best for them not to seek the truth. There is always danger in seeking the truth, the danger that it might be found.

So I would not expect this manuscript to be published on my old world. Who would dare to do so? Who would take the risk?

Alas, Earth, that world, how beautiful you might have been!

How sadly you tread now toward your gray future, toward the goal of the beehive, toward the ideal of the ant heap. Strange how democracy has come to be the choice between six and six, and twelve. I wonder if there are any left upon you now who can tear their way through the tapes of their conditioning programs and see reality clearly, vividly. Are there any left upon you now who can think for themselves? Must truth and reason be forever denied; must honesty be always outlawed? How strange it is to hail free speech and then make certain, simultaneously, that it shall not exist. I wonder if there are any individuals left on you now, or are there only the gangs, the masses and their masters?

But let me put aside such tragic thoughts.

Earth is no longer my world. Gor is now my world, a world on which I am a slave.

In Ar, times are troubled. It remains unclear as to whether Marlenus of Ar, the great Ubar, is within the city or not. One hears many things, frequently conflicting. Sporadic resistance to Cosian occupation continues. Mercenaries grow ugly. Skirmishes occur between crowds and the garrison forces, the mercenaries and the Cosian regulars, but, too, sometimes between the mercenaries themselves and the Cosians. Myron, *polemarkos*, strives to maintain order. Reprisals occur. Buildings are burned, stores looted. Many free women of Ar are levied for the collar, branded and sent to Cos to serve foreign masters. Some are forced to serve as naked paga slaves, belled and chained, in the taverns of what was, prior to their embondment, their own city. Slaves, of course, no more than tarsks and kaiila, have Home Stones. Even if one day Ar should be returned to herself, and her former power and glory, these women would be kept as slaves, then simply being sold out of the city. Once a woman has worn the collar, truly worn it, you see, she is forever spoiled for freedom. She can never again be truly free for she, as a female, has known the touch of masters. And many slave girls, too, are being brought to the city to content and pacify the troops. And many, it seems, are harvested for this purpose from my old world, Earth. How their lives will change! Talena, acclaimed by some as Ubara, denounced by others as traitress, is seldom seen now in public. It is said she hides within the fortresslike Central Cylinder. I do not know what will be the issue of these complex, troubled matters. Much is kept from me, of course, as I am a slave. There is a saying that curiosity is not becoming in a kajira, and yet how well the masters understand our incessant and insatiable curiosity! But sometimes I think my master keeps much from me not simply because he enjoys keeping me, tormentingly, appropriately, as Goreans see it, in "slave ignorance," but for my safety, as well. The less I know, the less I understand, the safer, or so he deems, I will be. In the storms of war and revolution it is, not surprisingly, the animals which have the least to fear. There is a joke in Ar now, that it is a good time to be a kaiila. Too, the testimony of slaves in Gorean courts is commonly taken under torture.

I fear for the well-being of my master and his friends.

Often there seems a calmness in the city, sometimes an unnatural calmness, but I do not doubt that intrigues abound, and that dark, hot currents, calculated and violent, turbulent and meticulous, seethe beneath the surface.

How kind of my master to let me express myself, to let me tell this story, so remarkable to me, and yet, perhaps, not all that unusual or unprecedented. There is a business in women, of course. We have value. Apparently a large business. And I have little doubt but what it is excellently organized. Perhaps some of the mysterious, untraceable, coded radio signals on Earth, seemingly indecipherable, perhaps indexed to an unfamiliar language, so perplexing to terrestrial authorities, pertain to this form of merchandising, the transmission of orders, the reports of scouts, the arrangements for, and coordinates of, pickups, and such. In any event, it is clear that the ships of slavers ply the space routes. There is a road, a secret road, so to speak, between Earth and Gor. And I assure you, it is not untraveled. I know. If you are a female of Earth, and, perchance, somehow, despite all probabilities, you one day read this, despite all efforts to prevent that, despite all the efforts to keep these things from you, know that there is truly a Gor. These very words are being written in longhand, in the city of Ar, by one who was once much as you, but is now a collared slave. Know, too, proud, vulnerable woman of Earth, that you might be observed, yes, you, literally you, personally you, exactly you, you who are now reading this, observed, carefully observed, scrutinized and noted, perhaps in the bright, cool office where you work; perhaps at the beach, where you thought to tantalize men and flaunt slave curves with impunity; perhaps at the theater, you so elegant in your black dress and pearls; perhaps on the street, in your high heels and smartly tailored mannish suit, walking swiftly; perhaps going to or coming from the gym, in your shorts, your head back, your hair free, your bag upon your shoulder; perhaps while in the supermarket, in slacks, foolishly with a bared midriff, the "slave belly," do you not know how men see that, pushing your cart, examining shelves, comparing wares, shopping; perhaps while buying gas, looking out the passenger-side window, smiling, as though innocently, delighting in tormenting the fellow at the pump with your putative seemingly carefree security and invulnerability; perhaps in quickly exiting a taxi, in your miniskirt, so strikingly reminiscent of a slave garment, did you know that, revealing a well-turned calf, a knee, perhaps even a swift, deliberately insolent flash of a supposedly inaccessible thigh.

Are you aware of these things? Surely you are. Do you know how you look to men, who see you in such ways? Perhaps. Do you know how desirable you are, truly? If so, do you live in trepidation, fearing strong hands, thongs and a collar?

Do you think these things go unnoticed, or are noticed only by weakened, helpless males of Earth, reduced and crippled, whom you secretly despise for what they have permitted to be done to them, whom to their anger you may freely, safely, insult, taunt and tease, and that without fear of consequences, brazenly displaying yourselves, delicious, provocative goods on which, culturally, they are not even permitted to gaze? Does it not serve them right? What fun for you! But then, of course, what have you to fear? You are not slaves. No. Or you are not yet slaves, not yet, not at least in a strictly legal sense. I leave aside the sense of the "natural slave," she who in a natural world would, without a second thought, be fittingly embonded, who would find herself promptly, legally, in the collar in which she belongs.

But these thing, you see, may not be going unnoticed, or noted fruitlessly, only to the misery of the observer.

There are other possibilities, other authentic possibilities.

Remember the mysterious, unaccountable radio signals.

Someone, you see, may be watching you, you entirely unsuspecting, unaware, unwitting of this so significant a surveillance. Someone may be thoughtfully considering how you might look in sirik, that striking custodial device with its collar, the connecting chains, the wrist and ankle rings, or conjecturing, taking notes, on your likely value, as he watches you, what you might be expected to bring on the slave block, first, and then later, after having been suitably informed and trained. All your laws then, your politics, your ideologies, your legal remedies, your petty threats, your thousand devices to obtain power, to control, reduce, tame and destroy men, would be useless. Remember them, such seekings, such devices, when you are chained naked in a Gorean dungeon, collared, with other slaves, a mark burned into your thigh, waiting to be brought to the auction block.

But with you, on the same chain, perhaps prized even more highly than you, their collars locked as securely as yours, their chains clasping as perfectly, their bodies as bared, may be other women, they selected as carefully as you, quiet, gentle, loving, needful, natural women, women less removed initially from their sex than you, women who disdained to strive to be facsimile males, such monstrous transmogrifications of human reality, those to whom grotesque propagandas could not speak, those who could never bring themselves to believe the catechisms of negativity, horror and hatred, those who had no difficulty in detecting the unsatisfying special nature and hollowness, the idiosyncratic party-serving nature of diverse bromides and slogans, the lies that others would impose upon them, but who knew themselves female, even from the beginning, despite all the propaganda and conditioning, female radically and profoundly, those who even on Earth have longed to fulfill their femaleness in the service of men, men who will understand them and treasure them, but will nonetheless give them the domination they crave, who will supply the masculine to their feminine, the *yang* to their *yin*, who will see to it that they are, as they desire to be, let it be stated explicitly, *mastered*, wholly, and beautifully, and uncompromisingly *mastered*.

But even such women must expect the whip if they are in the least bit unpleasing. They, too, of course, are slaves, every bit as much as the others, total slaves.

Many are the sorts who will be brought to Gor, for the tastes and interests of buyers vary. In the markets there is much diversity.

There are apparently "want lists." I wonder if your type appears on such a list. I wonder if you, as an representative of such a type, are now on such a list, a considered item, a proposed item, an item to be picked up, to satisfy a given request.

The haughty will be reduced; the insolent will have their insolence taken from them; the inert will be awakened; the frigid will be enflamed, made helplessly, beggingly needful; the awkward will learn grace; the plain will learn beauty; those who sought to dominate will learn submission; those who sought to be served will serve.

But there will be a common denominator. All will be owned, all will be slaves. All will learn, sooner or later, totally, their womanhood.

Gorean free women can be difficult and troublesome. But the pain that Gorean men will accept from their free women, in deference to their freedom, and their sharing of a Home Stone, they do not, and will not, accept in their slaves.

That is something to be remembered, if you are brought to Gor. To be sure, you would quickly learn it.

Perhaps you will be selected. Perhaps, unbeknownst to you, you have already been selected. I wonder. Perhaps your papers have already been prepared. That is an interesting thought. I wonder if they will come for you.

It takes little time to heat the iron that will mark you.

Perhaps a collar is waiting for you, just the right size, snugly fitting, but not tight. The common collar is not uncomfortable. You will not, of course, be able to slip it. It will be on you, lightly, almost unobtrusively, but securely, I assure you. I wonder how it will be engraved. If someone has already spoken for you, you, specifically, it may already be engraved. Most women, of course, are surrendered to the markets.

The lock on the collar, as most of you will now be aware, is normally at the back of the neck. You will be taught to keep it there. If one looks closely, one will see it there, beneath your hair.

The Gorean slave girl must be extremely careful about such things, even small things, such as the positioning of her collar lock. She is not a free woman. She is to be pleasing to her master in both appearance and demeanor.

I think there is little advice to give you, at this point.

Most of what you need to know will be made clear to you. I might warn you, however, in general, that the men of Gor are much unlike the men of Earth. You will not have been prepared for them. They have not been broken and tamed. Do not think you can deal with them as you have the men of Earth. Do not attempt to manipulate them unless you are prepared to accept the consequences. Remember that they will see you as what you are, and what you will soon understand yourself to be, and only be, a rightful slave.

To be sure, although the men of Gor tend to be larger and stronger than the men of Earth, I am sure the primary differences between them are largely cultural. Doubtless on Earth, somehow, despite all, there are true men, masters, and rare and precious they must be, but such are abundant, indeed, almost universal, on Gor. A Gorean youth, for example, is early accustomed to the care and management, the training and disciplining, the hooding, binding, chaining, and such, of female slaves. There are even games, held within large low-walled enclosures, with spectators in attendance, in which lads compete, each hunting another lad's slave, she doing her best to elude capture, that her own master may score more highly than her pursuer. These contests are timed. A given lad's time is determined by how long it takes to capture his fair quarry, bind it helplessly, hand and foot, and hurl it, futilely thrashing, squirming and struggling, to the sand before the judges. Any girl of whom it is suspected that she did not do her best to elude capture is whipped.

Why do we make excellent slaves?

We make excellent slaves, perhaps in part, at least at the beginning, because we know we will be whipped if we are not. And to be sure, even later, if we are not fully pleasing, we know we will be whipped. We are, after all, slaves. But do not misunderstand such things. Gorean men, while demanding and severe, are seldom cruel. It is not in their nature. That sort of thing, I think, is more common on Earth, where, unfortunately, I fear that some males, hopefully few, see women less as wondrous and delicious properties, less as fascinating, attractive, beautiful, desirable domestic animals, less as possessions to be sought, owned, relished, celebrated, treasured, and mastered, than as something alien to be hurt, oddly enough, incomprehensibly, for one's pleasure. Whatever this may be, or its explanation, it is not Gorean. The Gorean master seldom, if ever, inflicts gratuitous pain. What would be the point of it? Similarly he would not abuse children, torture small animals, or such. Goreans would simply not understand such things. If they did understand them, they would doubtless account them offenses against honor.

To be sure, the slave may be whipped for any reason, or for no reason. This comprehension helps her understand that she is a slave. It adds a flavor to her existence.

The slave desires to serve and please. Be firm with her, but patient. Help her learn her collar. Does she not make a lovely pet? Do not subject her to meaningless cruelty or she will be confused and miserable. Make certain she knows what you want, and she will do her best to see that you are satisfied. You are, after all, her master. Help her to become what she wishes to be, an attentive, subservient treasure. Do not let her know how important and precious she is to you. Treated well, she will be to you a dream of pleasure. If she should be the least bit difficult or recalcitrant, punish her, sharply and effectively. Make certain she understands clearly why she is being punished. Similarly, if she fails to be fully pleasing, punish her, again letting her know in what respect she may have fallen short of the perfection you demand in a female slave. See, of course, that she cares for her person and appearance, and is suitable in her demeanor and speech. She is not a free woman. You are to see that she carries herself appropriately in your presence, kneels properly, and such. You may, if you wish, encourage her with small attentions and rewards. A candy, nibbled from the floor, on all fours, may be more effective than three stokes of the switch. If you wish, you may upon occasion accede to her slave needs. You should understand that these needs, as she is not a free woman, are acute and cruel. They are difficult for the slave to bear. Accordingly, be patient with her. Often she will want little more than to writhe helplessly in your chains, gasping, and lifting her body to you. Imagine her gratitude then when, at last, with as little as a touch, you give her the relief for which she has been begging.

Remember that the slave is not a free woman. She is a property, a domestic animal, a lovely beast whom you are kind enough to domicile, keeping her about for your service and pleasure.

You wish to get the most out of her.

How then should she be treated?

As she is an animal, the answer to that is obvious.

She is, in all respects, and without qualification, to be wholly and perfectly mastered.

On such matters there is no temporizing or concessions.

If she is not fully pleasing, do not hesitate to use the whip on her.

Remember, she is not a free woman.

She is a slave.

* * * *

So, dear reader, remember that the master is all, and you are nothing. You may love him. And perhaps he may love you. As a female slave you will live the most degraded and the most beautiful of lives. You will know pleasures forever beyond the ken of the free woman.

It is not strange that a woman loves best in a collar. In a collar she is most a woman.

Love and serve your masters.

It is what you are for, sweet slut.

Do not forget to wear your tunic well, and keep the collar lock at the back of your neck.

After all, you do not wish to be whipped.

I wish you well.

I now close this narrative.

I kiss my finger tips and touch my collar. It has been put on me by my master, whom I love. I am his slave. I desire to serve him. I would die for him.

I wonder if any of you can understand this, or if it merely seems puzzling, alien, incomprehensible. But I think you understand it; these things may be deep, but they are not that strange, or unfamiliar. They are very close to us, to all of us.

And so I have come a long way. I am no longer on Earth. I have returned to the biological heritage of my sex. I have learned to call men "Master," for, as I am a woman, and they are true men, they are master to me. I pity my sisters who do not know the collar. How incomplete they are. I have been the most free of the free, or thought myself such, and am now amongst the most enslaved of the enslaved, and am yet, because of that, the most free of the free, the truly free, for I am no longer at war with myself. I am now one with my nature. I have at last come home, come home to myself, to the deepest truths of my being. I am at my master's feet. It is where I belong. May I prove pleasing to him, my master!

Behold, I hear him approach!

I must hasten to the door, to meet him there, to kneel before him!

LaVergne, TN USA
04 January 2010
168798LV00001B/143/P